The Johnson Sisters

The Johnson Sisters

Tresser Henderson

www.urbanbooks.net

Urban Books, LLC
97 N 18th Street
Wyandanch, NY 11798

ISBN 13: 978-1-62286-704-2
ISBN 10: 1-62286-704-1

First Trade Paperback Printing June 2015
Printed in the United States of America

10 9 8 7 6 5 4 3 2 1

This is a work of fiction. Any references or similarities to actual events, real people, living or dead, or to real locales are intended to give the novel a sense of reality. Any similarity in other names, characters, places, and incidents is entirely coincidental.

Distributed by Kensington Publishing Corp.
Submit Orders to:
Customer Service
400 Hahn Road
Westminster, MD 21157-4627
Phone: 1-800-733-3000
Fax: 1-800-659-2436

Acknowledgments

As always, I'm going to start out by thanking God for all of His many blessings. Without Him, nothing would be possible. God is the head of my life, and I thank Him for what He has done, what He is doing, and what He will do in my life.

Five years ago I dreamed of getting one book published, and here I am coming out with my fourth. All I can say is God is good. Never give up on any dreams you have, because they can come true. All you have to do is have faith. Please trust, even now my faith waivers. I doubt this gift that has been granted to me, and I still question if I should be doing this. Don't you know God has sent individuals my way to let me know not to give up? As soon as you are ready to throw the towel in on something, God shows you to keep striving because He has a plan and a purpose for our life. I know writing is my love, but even the things we love don't always turn out quite the way we want them to go, you know. My mother tells me all the time, "In God's time, not your time."

I want to thank my husband, Wil, for standing by my side and being my motivator. He is the man God has connected me to, my companion, my high school sweetheart, my lover, and my partner through thick and thin. Babe, I'm so blessed to have you in my life. I love you. I appreciate you. You are a wonderful man, and I can't say this enough.

To my children, who are growing up so fast: I love you. The older you get, the more you are interested in what I do, and it's funny because I find you guys are sometimes my motivational speakers during this journey. It's in those moments when I know I have to be doing something right with you. I see your personalities shine and wisdom being spoken, which makes me so proud of you. "Out of the mouths of babes."

To my parents, Clarence and Rebecca Atkinson, what can I say but thank you? Thank you for always being here for me no matter what. Anything, and I mean anything I need, you are always there for me, and I never take for granted the gift of having you as my parents. I can never repay you enough for what you have done for me. I love you so much, and I'm blessed to have you as my parents.

To my sister, Sabrina Atkinson, who always gives it to me straight, no chaser: you could be a character all by yourself (LOL), and sometimes you have inspired some of the characters I write about. You are hilarious and a joy to be around because you keep me in stitches from laughing so much. I love you, and I'm proud of you.

To my brother, Clarence Atkinson, A.K.A. Duddy. (That's right, Duddy): you are six foot four and my baby brother who I have to look up to. You are so sweet and kind. Please don't let anybody change that about you. You are going to make some woman a wonderful husband one day, but don't rush it.

I want to acknowledge some ladies who've played a major role in my life, who have picked up a phone, texted me, come by my house, took me to the side to talk to me, given me an uplifting card, or just said "I'm here." These ladies have done that for me, and maybe I shouldn't be writing this when I'm so emotional about this, but I'm going to do it anyway. As women we have to uplift one another, and I'm so thankful to God that he saw fit to place me in the position to receive blessings from these ladies. I don't like to list names because I feel like I always forget somebody, but I'm going to try.

To Rochelle Cicero, Crystal Townes, and Tina Walker: you ladies are the best friends ever, my ride or die as they say, and I love you very much for always being here for me. Not once have I doubted your friendship, which I don't take for granted. You are who I turn to and also the ones who are first to see what's up with me. I love you ladies.

To my wonderful aunties, Patricia, Thelma, and Rosaline: I love you for always supporting me for my entire life. You ladies are so fun to be around. I look forward to our family gatherings just so I can be around you. Although they are few and far between due to the distance, I still appreciate you. Thank you for always supporting me.

To Ms. Patricia Liggon, Ms. Wanda Hester, and Ms. Cheryl Boyd: you ladies exemplify grace with a smile and wisdom galore. I feel like I need popcorn and a soda when I talk with you because I learn so much from you. I love our talks, and I love you very much. Thank you for being here for me.

To Tracey Hodges: I love you. You are the epitome of greatness. You have had some challenges that would defeat the average person, but you have risen above it, and that was because of your faith. During your struggle, you still picked up the phone and checked on me. You don't know how much of an inspiration you are to me. I know we are cousins, but you are like my sister. Even miles apart I know you love me and I love you. Thank you for always being here for me.

To Angela Henderson, my sister from another mother: thank you for everything you do for me. You may not think it's much, but it's more than I can explain. You are such a strong woman. You bend but you don't ever break.

That's your faith in God, knowing He will always see you through. You are an amazing woman and I love you.

To authors Ni'chelle Genovese, Victoria Christopher Murray, and Ashley Antoinette: thank you for your patience when I have questions about a business I sometimes don't understand. Not only are you amazing authors whose work I love to read myself, but you are also humble enough to help me. A lot of authors don't do what you guys have done for me, and I thank you and appreciate your guidance.

To Sonia Gravely, Tammie Earick, Catherine Settles, Danielle Johns, Sha-Nae Mack, Rico Gill, and Shannon Brown: you all are wonderful individuals. You don't know how much you have touched my life. Who said work couldn't be fun? I think we spent more time together at work than we did with our families at times, but having you all around made work great. Thank you so much for being here for me.

To Ashley Kasey, who said she wanted her own paragraph because she crazy like that. She stood and watched me type this, and if you knew her, you know she meant it. (LMAO) Thanks for being here for me, keeping me laughing and in trouble at times at work because you know we can never be together because you know they think the two of us are troublemakers. I'm not. I can't speak for you. (LOL) Thanks for keeping a smile on my face and for being a great friend.

All of you at some point during this challenging time in my life have been there, said something, allowed me to vent and even cry without question. You pushed me when I didn't think I had the strength to continue trying. Sometimes somebody can say the right thing that's like a bell going off in your spirit, and I know God sent you and continues to send some of you my way as confirmation for me. You have helped me in ways you can't imagine. I'm so blessed to be surrounded by greatness. They say watch the company you keep, and I can say the company God has positioned around me are definitely some prayer warriors. If I forgot anyone, please don't think I did it on purpose. As they say, blame it on my mind and not my heart.

Special thanks to Carl Weber and Natalie Weber. Carl, thank you for this opportunity. I told you I was going to continue to bring it, and I'm doing that. Without you, I wouldn't have had my start. And Natalie, thank you for continuing to put up with all my e-mails. I feel like a pest sometimes, but you always respond to me and help me when I need it, and I thank you for that.

A special thanks to the editing staff and graphic designer, Lonnie Baskerville, on this book. You are amazing, and I appreciate what you have done. Thank you.

I want to thank Randi Jo Wines and everyone with the Gainesboro library in my area for always supporting me. You all are amazing.

And last but certainly not least, I want to thank all my family members who have supported me and encouraged me. A special thanks to my fans, who have supported me since book one. You all are awesome. Thanks for your feedback and support. To all the readers who took a chance on Tresser Henderson books, to the booksellers who carry my books, to the book clubs who have chosen my books, to all the other libraries who include my books in their establishment and to the online Web sites who've supported me, thank you.

Chapter 1

Vivian

I was sitting behind my mahogany desk when an administrator walked in, handing me a folder on a case I needed to call on and resolve. Being the director of underwriting for a major insurance company was daunting. I loved my job, but like anything, at times it really became too much for me to handle. Today was that day. I hadn't had a chance to breathe since I walked into this place. One issue after another walked in or called needing a resolution.

I knew I needed to hire a new manager to handle things ASAP. It had been a week since my manager quit on me. I mean, she just walked into my office, placed her badge down on my desk, and walked out. I ran after her, wondering what was going on. This was so sudden and done in such an abrupt fashion that it caught me off-guard. I needed to understand why she was choosing to make this decision.

"What's going on, Samantha? Why did you put your badge on my desk?" I had asked, stepping outside my office, looking at her saunter away.

"I'm quitting," she said, stopping and turning to look at me with frustration written all over her face. As nicely dressed as she was in her deep coral short-sleeved sateen jacket with matching straight-leg pants with black pumps, Samantha looked vibrant. Her outfit brought happiness to the space, but her demeanor was one of being overwhelmed.

"Why?" I asked.

"Vivian, I appreciate you taking a chance with me and offering me this position but I can't do this anymore. I'm not cut out for this."

"But you are doing so well," I said. And she was. Samantha had managed to move from mail clerk to manger in three years. Anything she worked on was done with flawless determination. I mean, she did make some mistakes, as most of us did, but she would correct them with no problems and keep on with her day. Sometimes when you gave feedback to someone on what they did wrong, they took it badly. Some believed they never made mistakes. Some blamed someone else for their mistakes, but Samantha took hers in stride. She was harder on herself than I ever had to be on her. So, for her to give up like this was surprising to me.

"I thought I could handle this job, but I can't. I've never been this stressed out in my life. Then I hear they are going to give me another team to manage," she said, putting her finger on her temple.

"I've heard the same thing, but nothing has been set in stone yet," I said.

"I already have forty-seven people under me, Vivian. I don't think I can handle another twenty-four. All of this downsizing and putting more work on the ones who are here just to save more money for the bigwig's pockets is bull."

"I know this job is stressful," I agreed. Everything she was saying were exact things I had thought about and argued to the higher-ups about myself, but in a business like this, you had to take one on the chin, do your job, or you could be without one.

"I don't want you to leave. Let me see what I can do. Give me two weeks. This way you can put in your notice and exit the right way. If I can't change things within that time, I will not stand in your way of leaving if you still choose to do so," I offered.

Samantha stood looking down at the gray carpet tiles , pondering what I was saying.

"Two weeks. That's all I ask. This will also give you time to find something else if you still feel like you need to leave."

She nodded, saying, "Okay. I'll do that."

Two weeks came, and as much as I had hoped I could change things, I couldn't. My power was useless when it came to downsizing and the overworking of individuals. Samantha never changed her mind, and she did leave the company. I can't say I blame her. Her last few days here, she seemed relieved with her decision, and a part of me envied her. She left despite the great money she was making, but this goes to show money isn't everything. Happiness most of the time outweighed finances, especially when it came with the cost of losing yourself.

Right now I didn't mind the stressful distraction. It wasn't like I had someone to go home to. This lifestyle afforded me the life I always wanted for myself. I grew up in the small town of Chase City, Virginia, a town known for having only two street lights. I grew up on five acres of land in a three-bedroom, one-bath house in which my five sisters, my mom, and dad lived.

Three girls slept in one bedroom and two in the other. So, needless to say, we had an argument about something every day. The one bathroom situation was enough to cause World War III because we would battle to be the first one in. Most times we had to do our hair sitting on the edge of our bed, holding a mirror between our knees in order to get ready and be out the door on time.

Bathroom time had to be timed. We only had twenty minutes each to do what we had to do in the bathroom, and that time flew. You were always reminded your time was up when you heard a tap at the door letting you know it was time to get out.

We didn't have running water for seven years of my life. I can still recall having to go to my aunt's house, who lived down the road, to get water in as many jugs as we could. Water needed to be heated on the stove in order for you to take a bath. There was no central air, so when it was hot as hell, we had to fight over who was going to sit directly in front of the fan to cool off. We heated the house in the winter with a wood-burning stove, which still to this day I consider to be the best source of heat. My dad would get it so hot in the house we had to open windows to cool off.; but when morning came and no one got up during the night to refill the stove, it felt as if we were lying outside in the snow, and it was then we wished we had that heat we let escape once we opened the windows to get some reprieve from the heat.

Back then, I didn't think we were poor. My parents never let me feel as though we were. We always had a roof over our heads, clothes on our backs, and food. Most of the vegetables were grown in the very large garden my parents planted every spring. You name it, we grew it. My mom cooked every night, and most times there were no leftovers. As many mouths as she had to feed, you can see why.

I am the oldest of our clan. Then comes Renee, Shauna, Dawn, Serena, and Phoenix, who was the spoiled baby of the bunch. I have to say we were all close. Unfortunately, about seventeen years ago Renee was killed. Her death was so devastating to our family. She was only sixteen and the one I was closest to growing up, since we were only a year apart. I miss her so much. There isn't a day that goes by that I don't think of her beautiful spirit.

We, as sisters, vowed on the day of her funeral to always remain close, no matter how hard it got at times. All we had was each other. To keep the closeness we even moved to the same city of Roanoke, Virginia. I was surprised by that. I thought Phoenix would be down in Atlanta, or somewhere trying to act in California. I'm still waiting on the day when she was going to break the news to us that she was moving away. You never know what to expect with the Johnson sisters.

Chapter 2

Phoenix

I was so excited about tonight. Two of my favorite things were about to come together as one: a party and sex. Now, I know what you're thinking. You think I was having some type of swinger party, but I was not. I was having a sex toy party. This was the first one I was hosting, but I had been to a few before. I think I was invited because most of my friends and some of my family members considered me to be one of the biggest freaks they knew, and they knew I would buy the products, which got them closer to getting as much free merchandise as possible. Now tonight was my turn to see how much free stuff I was going to get.

I looked at the table I positioned in my living room against the wall. It looked great covered with a black cotton tablecloth and red napkins. I thought about breaking out my dishes, but I didn't want these heifers tearing up my stuff, so I opted to use red square plastic plates for them to eat off of. I picked up one of the plates and loved the look and feel of them. I purchased the plates online and thought they looked terrific. They were disposable, but these bad boys might be washed and saved to use for other occasions. I might as well get my money's worth.

I stood back and was happy with the way everything looked. A cheese, fruit, and veggie tray, along with finger sandwiches surrounded by a chocolate fountain raining down luscious goodness adorned the table. A few bottles of Moscato were also chilling on ice. This was just for starters.

I picked up a strawberry and held it under the drizzling chocolate and let it cover half of the fruit. Holding the berry over a napkin, not wanting to drip anything on my outfit, I brought it to my mouth and took a bite. Oh, my goodness, it was so good. I closed my eyes, savoring the flavor. Strawberries are my favorite fruit, and to combine that with this russet liquid almost made me have an orgasm.

I finished the fruit, walking away so I wouldn't stand there and eat the entire tray by myself. I had to leave some for the guests, who should be arriving in about thirty minutes. Thinking about that, I thought the girl showing the products tonight should have been here. I hoped she hadn't forgotten.

I went into my dining room and looked at the meal I'd had catered. I decided to go with filet mignon with bacon-wrapped asparagus and seasoned, grilled potatoes served with brioche. For dessert we were having mini cheesecake bites. You thought I was excited about the strawberries and chocolate? The several different arrays of cheesecake excited me the most. The flavors consisted of plain, key lime, amaretto, chocolate, marble, and strawberry cheesecake, of course. I know all of this sounds extravagant, but I liked to go all out like this when it came to any event I threw. I was a diva for real. Nothing but the best, depending on the crowd. And I know what you're thinking: filet mignon served on plastic plates is going all out? Hell yeah, for me it is. Again, I didn't like people who tore up my things. Just because I had it didn't mean I had to show it off all the time. I worked hard to get everything I had, even if I did get men to supply most of my needs.

I went to my bedroom and looked at myself one last time in the mirror. Damn, I looked good. I snapped my fingers at myself as I twirled to make sure I looked good at all angles. "In the words of Kenya Moore, I'm *Gone with the Wind* fabulous," I said to myself, twirling.

With my long hair sophisticatedly curled and makeup done to perfection, I knew I looked hot. This was a casual event, but I couldn't help but put on my black-and-white form-fitting mini with one shoulder exposed and a cutout at the waist making it super sexy. Hell, I was sexy. I am five feet four inches, weighing 130 pounds, with measurements equaling 34-26-36, and yes, my butt is my main attraction. I'm talking about fastening your seat belt and enjoying the ride type of attraction. I am a walking rollercoaster of thrills and spills, if you get my drift. Being as beautiful as I am comes with a lot of advantages. One of them is the lifestyle I lead now.

I stood in the mirror thinking, *Damn, look how far I have come.*

I can remember when I was in high school, I was considered a rail. I was a stick figure. The boys used to hold up a pencil to me and compare me to it, laughing like it was so funny; but I didn't find a thing to laugh about. It hurt my feelings. Now those same boys were men who salivated over me. Most of them I dissed, but some I had to have just because I'd had a crush on them in high school.

One in particular scratched my itch on a regular. His name was Von. In school he was the quiet athlete who hung with the popular kids but still didn't want to be seen with the unpopular. Now he was an NFL football player with all the right moves. He still wasn't much of a talker, but that was fine with me, since all I wanted was his money and his dick, which both suited me very well.

The doorbell rang, snapping me out of admiring myself. I pulled my dress down a bit and went to the door, opening it. The consultant who would be showing us the products tonight was standing in front of me.

"I'm so sorry I'm late. I had a flat tire," she said, panting like she had run all the way here.

"Oh, you are fine. No one has arrived yet. Come on in," I said, watching as she pulled in two large suitcases.

"Good. I hate to be late. It takes me a little time to set this merchandise up."

"Do you have anything else to bring in?" I asked.

"I do, but I'll get it," she said.

"Okay. If you insist," I said, not really wanting to help her in the first place. I was trying to be nice.

She went back outside and proceeded to bring in a table for setting everything on and a briefcase, which held the order forms along with the pamphlets of products.

I picked up one and scanned through it, thinking I needed 85 percent of what she had in this booklet. New products came out so often that it made the old merchandise you previously purchased look prehistoric. These companies were on top of their game when it came to finding the many different ways to sexually please someone.

As she took each tool out of her suitcase piece by piece, I was getting eager. I looked at the clock to see that as usual, all these tricks were late. I'd said arrive at seven. I should have said six. That way they would have been on time.

It wasn't long before the representative had everything arranged on the tables. After she did that, she placed a folder in each space I had available, which consisted of my sofa, loveseat, and twenty chairs I had in my spacious living room. Then she turned her attention to me.

"So, I'm ready."

"I am too. I don't know why my guests are late. Forgive them," I said.

"No problem. It actually worked in my favor today," she said, breathing a sigh of relief. "Now, you know the more you sell, the more free products you get. You get ten percent of total sales."

"I know, and I hope these women buy, buy, buy."

When I said that, the doorbell rang. The first to arrive was my oldest sister, Vivian, and middle sister, Serena.

"Hey, you guys," I said with glee, giving them both a hug as they walked in.

"Sorry we're late," Vivian said. "Multiple outfits here delayed us," she said, pointing at Serena.

"I didn't know what I wanted to wear. I still got this baby belly," she said, grabbing her gut.

"It's almost gone," I said, rubbing her almost flat stomach. She only had a little pudge, and I believed if she took a dump, it would go down.

"I still need to lose another fifteen pounds, and then I'm good," Serena said.

"That will make you smaller than you were before you got pregnant," I said.

"Exactly. I'll feel better about myself. Looking at you in that dress is not helping either. I thought this was a casual event. Where the hell do you think you are going?" Serena asked.

"Girl, this old thing?" I joked.

"Please, Phoenix. Every time I see you, you got something on I haven't seen you wear before. Where the hell are you getting the money to afford so many clothes?"

"Serena, don't worry about my finances," I said, giggling. "It's none of your business."

"Y'all make me sick," Vivian interrupted.

"Why?" I asked.

"Y'all know why. Look at me. I'm the plus-size sister."

"And you look good every time I see you, too, Vivian."

"You do look good, sis," Serena cosigned.

"I know, but y'all skinny bitches always find a way to make me feel bad standing here with your perfect shapes. Serena is talking about losing more weight. Any more weight loss and you are going to disappear on us."

"Whatever, Viv. I'm doing this for me. This kangaroo pouch ain't cutting it," Serena said, jiggling her belly.

"That ain't a kangaroo pouch. This is a kangaroo pouch," Vivian said, lifting her shirt to reveal the Spanx she had on pulling everything in. Vivian rolled the garment down and let her belly expand outward. Serena and I giggled. "You see. So can y'all shut up about weight?" Vivian said, pulling the Spanx back up and fixing her clothes.

"You did not have to go that far," I said.

"Yes, I did, so y'all could shut up," Vivian said.

"Okay, you guys. Enough about our bodies. Where is everybody?" Serena asked.

"You two are first to arrive," I said.

"We can see that," Vivian said.

"Wasn't this supposed to start at seven?" Serena asked, picking up an appetizer off the table and putting it in her mouth.

"Yep. You know how black folks are," I said.

"Don't put this on black people. Kimara is Puerto Rican. Mayumi is Japanese. Bella is Italian, and Hanna, Mackenzie, and Paige are white. You should say this is a woman thing, or mother thing, or even diva thing, but not a black thing," Vivian corrected, walking over to claim the space she wanted for the party. She sat down on the sofa.

"Well, I didn't mean to offend black women," I said jokingly, checking out what Vivian was wearing. Even though she was considered plus-size, she could dress her behind off. She looked good in her red skinny-leg jeans with black dolman top and black stilettos. You would think that red would make her look bigger, but it didn't. It flattered her body nicely. With Vivian's thickness, she carried it in her hips, butt, and breasts, so I didn't really see what the issue was.

"Is that an apology coming from Phoenix? Because I need to voice record this on my phone," Vivian said, pulling out her cell and typing something. "You never apologize about nothing, and that's as close to one as I've ever heard you come to."

"Shut up," I said, playfully hitting her.

"I'm just saying."

Serena went over and sat on the sofa next to Vivian, yawning, leaving a space to her left for someone else to sit.

"All right, sleepy head. We can't have that. You got to get ready to have some fun tonight," I said.

"Phoenix, I'm tired. Nevaeh still isn't sleeping through the night. I know I get up every two to three hours. But when the sun rises, that girl sleeps for hours. Why do babies do that?"

"I don't know, and I don't want to know," I said seriously. "I don't want kids. Hell, I don't really like them. All that crying and throwing up and changing Pampers and always needing someone to care for them. Naw. Y'all can have that, because I don't want it."

"You just don't want anybody stealing your spotlight," Vivian chimed in. "Selfish is what you are."

"True," I agreed with her.

"At least she owns it," Serena defended.

"All I know is this party better be good. I worked ten hours today, and it was taxing. A guy got fired today and lost his damn mind. Security had to come and get this fool. They literally dragged him off our floor and out the building. He was screaming many threats of what he was going to do when he came back."

"When he came back?" Serena questioned. "I hope they called the police on his behind. Disgruntled employees go on shooting rampages all the time. I hope the company is taking his threats seriously."

"I hope so too. The only positive thing on my end was I tried to fight for him to keep his job. Hopefully he remembers that if he decides to come back and go crazy. Still, I hope human resources was smart enough to disarm his badge so he can't get back in the building, because he looks like the type who would come shoot up the place," Vivian said.

"I bet you he was white," I said.

Vivian sighed, saying, "There you go again with that race crap."

"Well, am I right?"

Vivian didn't say anything.

"See, I knew it. Only white people snap and want to shoot everybody and then turn around and shoot themselves. Why not just shoot yourself when you get home and eliminate all the tragedy?"

"You know what? I'm done with this conversation. I'm going to the bathroom before you find something else crazy to say," Vivian said, getting up and leaving the room.

It was around eight when most of my guests arrived, including my other sisters, Shauna and Dawn. Shauna was feeling good when she walked through the door. Probably that joint and beer she had in the place of bacon and eggs with some orange juice this morning. I wished she would calm down on her drinking and smoking, but I had to say she was fun to be around when she was tipsy. When that heifer was sober, she was hell to be around.

The only people who hadn't arrived were my best friends, Kimara and Mayumi. I texted them and they said they were pulling up. As soon as they arrived, my posse was complete and it was time to have fun.

It was good to see everybody mingling with each other. Drinks were being poured and appetizers were being eaten. Everybody knew each other already, which made things easier. The only two who might've had an issue with one another were my sister Dawn and my guest Paige. I could see the two of them giving each other the evil eye every now and then. They had a history and it wasn't a good one. I hoped this evening would go on without any hiccups.

"Ladies, have a seat. It's time to get started," I said as the women shuffled to their seats. "I want to first thank y'all for coming to my sex toy party, even though all y'all bitches was late."

The ladies laughed along with whooping and hollering with excitement.

"I'm going to introduce you to the woman of the evening. This is Ashley, and she is our consultant and educator for the next hour, so pay attention, get involved, and let your inner freak be your guide to purchase some sex goodies," I said, clapping and giving Ashley the floor. I sat next to Serena on my sofa.

"Hi, ladies," Ashley said and everyone greeted her back. "It's so good to see so many of you. I'm excited to be here tonight. I can't wait to show you all my merchandise. I made sure to place a folder in each of your seats. The folder contains a booklet, an order form, my business card for future parties, and also a sheet on how I did my showing. On that sheet, it also has a box to check yes or no if you would consider being a consultant like me. The job is very fun. I get to travel, make good money, and make women happy all while selling them products that bring them joy.

"I have a few items with me—not all, because we would be here all night. If you see something you like, put a checkmark beside it. If you decide to make a purchase, some of the merchandise can be taken home tonight, but it is first come, first served. I have a limited amount. The rest of your orders should be back in a week. Most of the things I'm going to show you are our bestsellers, so sit back, enjoy, and please know no question is wrong to ask."

Chapter 3

Phoenix

Ashley started out by showing us creams and lotions. Some were used for moisturizing and massaging, and some were used for licking. We tasted nipple drops and warming oils that tasted like candy. There was chocolate for the body, and primer to suck off the man's penis. There was not a woman in there who didn't get her savor on. I have to say I thoroughly enjoyed the tasting too. I could have sucked down a bottle of that apple-flavored warming oil. It tasted like a Jolly Rancher.

Ashley proceeded to show us a bottle of spray to numb the back of your throat for oral sex. She introduced this product along with giving each of us a flavored condom. Along with the condom, I stood to hand out bananas.

"What are we supposed to do with this?" Dawn asked.

For somebody who thought they knew everything, my sister was sitting here acting like she didn't know a damn thing. Common sense should come into play sometimes. If you are holding a condom and a damn banana, what do you think you are supposed to do with it? But maybe I shouldn't think that way. Maybe she's never used a condom before. Yeah, that's it.

"You supposed to take the condom you have and roll it down the banana."

"Oh, I can do that," Dawn said.

"But the catch is you have to use your mouth to put it on, and then you have to suck it," I explained.

"I'll be damned," Dawn said, causing everybody to laugh. "I'm going to put this condom on with my hands."

"That's fine too," Ashley said.

"If y'all would like to see if the spray works, try it," I said, squirting the elixir into my mouth. "Who in here likes giving head?"

"You," most of the women said, causing laughter to permeate the room.

"Like I'm the only one. Please. All y'all give head, so don't play innocent," I countered.

"I don't," Serena said, smiling devilishly, knowing damn well she was lying. She and Tyree had been together for a minute, and I knew that man looked like he wouldn't have stayed with Serena if she weren't giving him some head. My sister must have been thinking the same thing, because she called Serena out on her bull.

"That's a damn lie. You don't have that baby for nothing," Vivian joked.

"That's right. All of y'all are freaks to the tenth power. I know this because none of you ladies would be here if you didn't have some inner slut buried inside you," I joked.

"And you are the biggest slut of us all," my sister Shauna said, sipping on her glass of wine.

It was funny watching these women take these bananas into their mouths like it was their man. I was no exception. I joined in with them. Why perpetrate? I gave head and, honestly, I liked it. Throwing a flavored condom in only made the act tastier.

I looked over at my good friend Paige taking the entire banana down her throat. I mean, she made it disappear. She only had the tip of the banana's stem showing, and these weren't tiny bananas. I purposely picked the longest ones I could find, just so I could see how much these tricks could take.

Paige held her hands out by her side like she had performed the circus act of swallowing a sword instead of a banana. I was astonished. Homegirl didn't even bother to use the spray to eliminate the gag reflex. She wasn't choking. There weren't tears running down her face. She looked totally unfazed. Then Paige reached in and pulled the banana from her throat with no problem. There wasn't one blemish to the banana. None of her teeth had clipped it, and it didn't break during its journey down her throat.

"Damn, girl. Remind me to keep you away from my man," one of my guests said.

"I know, right? They do say white girls give the best head," another said. Paige didn't mind the joke. She knew it just like we did. She just made it factual by her demonstration.

I saw Dawn watching her and knew she was getting heated. How ironic it was for Dawn to watch this woman down this banana like a damn champ, knowing this same woman slept with her man and probably did this exact thing to his dick. Talk about adding insult to injury. After seeing what Paige did, I would be intimidated too. If swallowing that banana was any sign of how good she could suck a dick, Dawn's man still might be seeing her. I knew if I was a man, I would be.

After the room calmed down from the banana tricks, Ashley went on to show us some sexual position books and massage books. She passed them around for us to get a better idea of what the books entailed.

"I think I have done all these positions," Kimara said, taking a sip of her wine.

Scanning through the book, Vivian said, "If you did all of these positions, then you are truly the master at this craft, because I don't see some of these positions as humanly possible. Who thinks of this stuff?"

"Like we aren't already performing acrobatic moves in the bedrooms," Shauna said, looking in another book alongside Dawn. "Spin around on the dick. Put your legs behind your head and finger your ass. Now finger my ass. Lick your nipple while you squeeze my butt at the same time. Do a handstand while I eat you out. Twist your head this way so you can touch your toes with your tongue. And my favorite, can you Luke dance on my face?" Shauna joked.

Everybody burst into laughter. Tears were streaming down many faces as they laughed at the truth. Men did think we were gymnasts.

"You crazy, girl," I said, dabbing at the tears so as not to mess up my makeup.

"No, these men are crazy. If we could suck them, fuck them, and fix a sandwich at the same time while watching a ballgame, men would think we were goddesses, or should I say magicians," Shauna kidded. "How about they reach down and suck their own dicks? Show me that so I can be amazed for once," she said.

"You know they had a man from Africa whose dick was so long he could do that," Kimara said.

"I heard about him. They said his dick went to his knees," Bella agreed.

"See. They trying to outdo us again," Shauna said. "They are sucking their own dicks now. We have to perform our due diligence before all men figure out it's best to do one another," she said.

Everyone laughed at my crazy sister. One thing about the Johnson women, we damn sure speak our minds. Shauna and I are the two who are so much alike when it comes to our mouths. I am the diva version of Shauna, where she comes off more hood. I have to also admit she is as pretty and shapely as me. Out of all my sisters, we look the most alike. Sometimes people think we are twins, which makes me mad sometimes, since Shauna is four years older than me. Either they think I am old as hell, or she looks young. I'm going with Shauna looking young.

The party that was supposed to last one hour turned into two hours. Everybody had something to say about most of the merchandise and was having a ball. Where the excitement hit the fan was when we got into the toys. I have to say I could hardly contain my anticipation either.

"This is the bullet," Ashley said, holding up the rubber-covered bullet, which was black and had a remote control hooked to it for speeds specific to your pleasure.

"I've heard of this thing, and if it does what I heard it do, I want you to ring me up now," Bella said.

"It does work, girl. I have one, and it's the best investment ever," Kimara said. "I haven't hit high yet. I'm scared if I do, I'm going to blast off into orbit."

Everybody chuckled. Several "I'm getting that's" rang out, and all I could do was think about all the free merchandise I was going to be getting for myself.

"Do you have something like this that will benefit both the man and woman at the same time?" Mayumi asked.

"We sure do," Ashley said, turning to her table and picking up two toys. "This toy here is like a condom with benefits. You slide this down on your man's member."

"What's that big thing on the tip, where the man's head is?" someone asked.

"These little fringes are meant to massage and tantalize your insides when he goes in and out of you," Ashley explained. "This is the least expensive of our partnering toys."

"Will that thing come off, though?" my sister Serena asked.

"I'm pretty sure it will if the man has a little dick," Kimara said. "Ain't nothing worse than getting a condom stuck up in you."

Laughter erupted again.

"Most times it stays on, but there's always a chance it can come off," Ashley said. "I am going to show you another partnering toy. This one is our highest in price, but also one of our top sellers."

"Are those bunny ears?" Vivian asked.

"Yes. This is like a cock ring, which goes around the base of the man's member. The bullet comes with it and vibrates the both of you. The ears are meant to tickle your happy spot, and this part vibrates his ball region," Ashley explained.

"To get the best bang for your buck, ladies, you need to ride him. Get on top and ride until you can't ride no more. I have that, too," Kimara said.

"You're just filled with spiciness, aren't you, Kimara? Is there anything you don't have?" Vivian asked.

"I'd rather not go into my repertoire of freak-nasty toys," she joked, causing more giggles.

Finally we were getting to the nitty-gritty of the toys—the vibrators. Ashley picked up this chocolate dildo that looked so much like a black man's dick I had to wonder if she was into black men. From the way she was holding that seven-inch dildo, homegirl looked like she was. Regardless, I was in heaven.

"This is the part I've been waiting for," someone said.

"Me too. I need something that's going to satisfy me when a man ain't around," another said.

"Well, ladies, if I don't have it here, then shame on our company, because we usually have the best of the best," Ashley said. "Our rotating vibrators seem to be the bestsellers. With any of these, you can't go wrong. But in our traditional, this seven-inch is very popular," Ashley said, holding up the chocolate brown vibrator.

"Y'all skimping on some inches when it comes to this one, aren't you?" Shauna asked. "I've seen some chocolate ones at least nine inches or more."

"Me too," I concurred.

"Most women might not want something so big up in them," Dawn said, and the room erupted into mayhem. Most of the women were disagreeing with Dawn. I thought they were about to jump her.

"Girl, the bigger the dick, the better," I said.

"Hell, pain is pleasure," Shauna said, taking another sip of her wine.

"There's not a woman I know who wants a little-dick man. We need something to fill us up," Paige said. I had to wonder if this was said for vindictiveness. Regardless, Dawn didn't take her remark too well.

"We know how you like to get filled up. It's with dicks that already have girlfriends," Dawn said angrily.

"Well, if the dick was satisfied at home, then the dick wouldn't have to fill me up in the first place," Paige retorted, flicking her long, golden hair over her shoulders, causing a hush to go over the room.

Even though Paige is white, she's no pushover. A lot of black women think they can jump at a white woman and expect to win, but in this case, they might catch a beat down. Paige is a beast when it comes to fighting. She had to learn how to defend herself because she was always getting jumped on by somebody who hated the fact that she dated black men. Black women despised her. I saw it as more of a jealousy thing, and they had every right to be jealous due to Paige's beauty. It doesn't help that she also has nice boobs, a big behind, and long, blond hair that makes her blue eyes pop. She is my version of an urban Barbie. Paige doesn't care who she sleeps with. Dick is dick to her, regardless of where it had to go once it was done pleasing her. Too bad one of those dicks happened to be engaged to my sister.

"I punched you in your face one time, trick," Dawn said, standing to her feet. "I don't have a problem doing it again."

Also standing, Paige snapped back with, "It was a sucker punch, and your ass got punched right the hell back, didn't you? As I recall it, I punched you multiple times. I'm not scared of you, Dawn. Bring your ass over here if you want to; you will catch a beat down identical to the one I gave you before."

"Ladies, calm down. You are not doing this here, and definitely not in my house," I said, getting up and standing between the two of them.

"I don't know why you invited her in the first place," Dawn said with an attitude.

"Because I'm her friend, that's why," Paige yelled.

"Y'all sit down and be quiet. Ashley doesn't need to see this side of us, okay? Let her finish her showing so we can place our orders, eat, and go home," I said with a raised voice so they knew I meant business.

Paige sat back down with the help of Kimara. Vivian pulled Dawn back over to her seat. Even though neither wanted to back down, they kept their cool. It still didn't stop either of them from giving each other evil glares. That was fine, as long as they didn't tear up my place.

Serena changed the tension in the room by asking, "Do you have something for men? You know, something they can stick their dicks in besides us."

"Yes," Ashley said, giggling as she turned to the table and picked up this ivory concoction. "This is a masturbation sleeve, but I would like to call it a pocket coochie. It resembles the lips of the woman. He would be amazed at how real it feels. It should be used with our lubricant, of course, for easy penetration. I'm going to squeeze some lube inside and pass this around for each of you to stick your finger inside to see how realistic it feels. And the lube is warmed for more appeal."

"This toy hasn't been used, has it?" Shauna asked, frowning up her face.

"All of my products are not used," Ashley said with a smile.

"Some of us might not know what it's supposed to feel like, because we've never stuck our fingers inside ourselves," a guest said. All heads turned to her in shock.

"You haven't fingered yourself?" Shauna asked bluntly.

"No," my guest said.

"I have heard it all," Vivian said. "One doesn't like big dicks, and now we have one who doesn't know what her own coochie feels like. I'm done," my sis said, throwing her hands up.

"Imagine this would be how you feel," Ashley urged. "If you don't want to do it, then you don't have to."

Each woman, including my guest who said she never felt herself, slid her finger inside the sleeve, frowning her face in disgust.

"Damn, this feels real. I'm sold," Serena said. "I might get two, in case Tyree wears one out."

Everybody laughed.

Vivian looked at Kimara and asked, "Does your man have this?"

"Of course he does. Once I slid that thing up and down his dick, that fool went crazy. And to enhance his pleasure, I stuck the bullet in the other end of it to make it vibrate his head when he went deep into it," Kimara explained.

"You know, you would be a great consultant," Ashley suggested.

"Damn right she would. She's a walking billboard on these products," Vivian agreed.

The last product Ashley ended up talking about was the swing, and of course it was brought up by freak-nasty herself, Kimara.

"Yes, we do have the swing, but I don't carry it with me due to the fact that I can't assemble it in someone's home.

Once it's up, it's up. But, I do have the box, which has a picture of it and the different positions that can be done with it," Ashley said.

Ashley passed the box around the room, and most of the women didn't want to let the box go. They were impressed with the many positions that were possible.

Once Kimara got the box, she asked Ashley, "So, have you tried it?"

"I haven't, but I have associates who have, and they loved it," Ashley said, giggling.

"Forget swinging from the chandelier. We need this," Shauna said.

"How much is it?" a guest asked.

"It's two hundred dollars," Ashley answered.

"Damn. That's a lot of money to figure out what else we can do when it comes to sex," Vivian said.

"This coming from the one who would like to put a stripper pole in her house," I said.

"Okay, you got me," Vivian said. "Great point. Maybe I should invest in one of these bad boys, too."

"First you got to get a man," I joked.

"Who says I don't have one?" Vivian countered.

This got me to thinking. Did Vivian have a man we didn't know about? She was private like that.

Finally it was the end of Ashley's showing. Now it was time for her to go into a separate room to take us one by one to place our orders. This way no one knew what the other ordered. Privacy first and foremost, but most of them told what they were buying, especially my friend Kimara.

"I need some nipple drops and some more of that edible oil that heats up when you put it on your skin. I need another pocket coochie. I want some anal beads, and some of that lubricant for the anus. And I'm getting that fishnet garter set. I've wanted that thing for a minute. And you know what? I think I'm going to get that swing, too. That position with her in the swing and the man eating her out . . . hell, I'm getting the swing for that position alone. He can do the front and twirl me around and lick the back," Kimara said.

"You are so nasty. You let a man lick your anal region?" Dawn asked her.

"Damn right. I'd rather have that licked than my poon poon. You never had that done before?" Kimara asked.

"Hell no," Dawn blurted.

"Girl, you don't know what you missing. It's a different type of climax. It tickles at first, but once you get used to it, it's amazing."

I told the ladies to help themselves to the food I had catered. While they were getting their eat on, I was going to go pick out what merchandise I wanted. I went back last, because Ashley had to total up the amount of sales in order to figure out what my percentage of free merchandise would come to.

"So, how did we do?" I asked Ashley with enthusiasm.

"We did very well. The total came to $3,378," Ashley said, and I almost fell to the floor.

"Wow. I knew my friends and family were freaks, but not this freaky," I said happily.

"So you get to order $377 worth of merchandise for free."

There was nothing better than hearing the word "free" come out of her mouth. That's how I liked my life: receiving things that didn't cost me nothing but some fun and a nice reward in the end.

"You can give me your first item, and we can write up your order," Ashley said.

I made sure to start with the bullet.

Chapter 4

Vivian

I had to admit tonight was a lot of fun. I was glad Phoenix talked me into attending because I told her I wasn't coming at first. I didn't feel like being around a bunch of people, particularly my sisters. I loved each and every one of them, but I couldn't seem to get away from them. We would be together every day if we could, but I didn't. Our once a week dinner get-together was starting to get a bit much for me. I don't know why I was feeling this way, since after the death of Renee we promised each other we would at least be with each other once each week, even if it was to have coffee together.

After ordering my merchandise, I quickly left the party. Phoenix didn't want me to leave, but she didn't push it too much since I did show up. Since Serena rode there with me, she had to leave when I did, and she wasn't ready. She ended up asking Dawn to give her a ride home. Dawn didn't want to, but gave in, telling her she would. I was tired and was ready to get in my bed, the faster the better, so I said my good-byes to everybody and jetted home.

I don't know if I kicked off my shoes first to relieve my feet, or unsnapped my bra to take that restraint off. All I know is I wanted to get into a comfortable state. It didn't matter, because once those items came off, I was free. My Spanx was my next constriction to be removed before taking my shower. My bed was calling me, and I was answering it by saying, "I'll be right there."

No sooner than I put my legs under the cover and turned the television on, my doorbell rang. It could only be one person, and I wondered why he didn't use the key I gave him.

"What the hell do you think you are doing?" were the first words that fell out of my mouth as I looked into the face of my ex-boyfriend, Eric, standing on the other side of my door. I had thought it was my best friend, Sheldon, but I was wrong this night.

With his manhood hanging out, Eric had each hand propped up on the base of the door, with this smirk on this face, trying to lick his lips like LL. He looked down at his growing extension and looked back up at me.

"You are going to get arrested for indecent exposure," I said, giggling.

"Then you better let me in before I get in trouble."

I crossed my arms, asking, "What do you want?"

"It's not obvious?" he asked cockily, looking down at his manhood still hanging to the left.

"And what makes you think I want you or your dick?"

He looked down at his pride and joy and said, "Oh, you want this. I bet your thighs are wet with envy now."

I didn't say anything. I looked down at his manhood, which was beginning to become erect. I didn't get sex often because I didn't believe in sleeping around, but tonight I needed to get my coochie worked. After that sex party showed me all the different things that could be used to enhance my sex life, I was raring to go. And I didn't want to use a vibrator, even though I had just purchased a new one to use on myself tonight. Now I had the real deal and could use a hot, throbbing dick inside me.

I stepped to the side, giving Eric the signal to come in. He walked past me, and I shut the door. When I turned around, Eric was stroking his manhood like he was priming it for me. I didn't feel like doing much talking, so I jumped right on him. I don't know how we managed it, but in a matter of minutes we were in my bedroom, butt-ass naked.

Eric was hitting me from the back like he hadn't had pussy in quite a while. He gripped my hips, pulling my substantial buttocks into his adequate plumpness. I didn't know why I allowed myself to get screwed by this man since he dumped me months ago for being too fat. It wasn't like I had lost much weight. I wasn't skinny enough to be on his arm, yet my pussy was good enough for him to dip his manhood inside me. Damn hypocrite. And yes, I must be a hypocrite too. I didn't have to allow myself to be used like this.

I thought about this after I climaxed, which didn't take long, since Eric knew my body and how to please it. I'd climaxed three times already, while he kept trying to reach his pinnacle. After six months of batteries buzzing between my thighs, I needed to nut from the real thing. But now that I had, I didn't think it was even worth it. I actually pitied myself.

As Eric pounded and grunted, I tried to hold back tears for a minute. He might have thought he was bringing water to my eyes because he was that good, but feeling unworthy was the reason for my sorrow. Where in the hell was my self-esteem right now? As soon as I saw this man on my stoop, I should have slammed the door in his face and told him to never bother me again, but here I was playing booty call and being used yet again by a man who didn't respect me.

I dropped my head into the sheets as I went on an emotional rollercoaster. One minute I was confident and the next I hated myself. I let the tears soak deep into the fabric of my sheets as Eric continued to pound, probably thinking he was doing me a favor.

"You like that, baby?" he asked.

I didn't respond. How could I when I felt the way I did? His pounding increased like he was trying to get a reaction out of me. I pulled my head up from the sheets and frowned a bit, and he took this as me enjoying it.

"Oh, you like it, don't you. I can tell."

I couldn't take it anymore. I turned, pushing Eric off of me.

"You want it a different way?" he asked. "You want to get on top," he said, positioning himself on his back like I was going to climb on top of him. Eric was fine as hell and his body was worthy of the ride, but I couldn't bring myself to continue.

"No. I want you to leave," I told him, pulling the crinkled sheet around my body.

"Leave?" he asked, surprised, as his manhood glistened with my juices.

"Yes, leave," I said, getting up from the bed and putting on my pink silk robe.

"What the hell is wrong with you? Do you see this dick? I haven't cum yet," he replied, pointing to his extension.

"And you won't with me," I said, tying my robe closed.

"Come on, Vivian."

"You can beg all you want to, Eric, but I'm not finishing this."

He climbed from the bed angrily. He snatched his boxers off the floor and attempted to put them on, losing his balance and falling to the floor. I smirked a bit. He didn't find this funny as he got up from the floor.

"I can't believe you. You asked me to come over."

I frowned as I shook my head in disbelief before replying to his statement. "Don't get it twisted, Eric. You were standing on my stoop. Don't try to make it look like I begged your ass to come over, because I didn't. You were the one who just showed up unannounced," I said, pulling my long hair back in a ponytail.

"You knew what it was going to be when you saw me standing outside your door," he argued.

"I did, and I got mine, so we are done."

Eric picked up his blue jeans and shirt from my maple hardwood floors. Each movement was done with irritation.

"I knew it was a mistake messing with you, but I was doing you a favor," he said.

"Me!"

"Yes, you. I mean, look at you. Who wants to sleep with somebody who looks like you?" he said rudely, scowling at me.

"You, that's who! How many times have you begged to get all up in this?" I retorted, pointing between my legs. "I know this is good for you to keep coming back for more," I fired back.

"Please. I didn't have another honey to get with tonight, so I decided to slum with you," he dissed.

"This coming from the man who is the biggest whore around. You sleeping with sluts was the demise of our relationship, but I'm the one slumming. If I am, it's because I'm dealing with your trifling ass."

"Your weight was the reason I went out and got other pussy. I got tired of you squishing me when you got on top," Eric said.

"As hard as you're trying to make this out to be about my weight, I know it's about you being a damn dog. I let you mentally abuse me for months, but now I know better," I lied. His words did cut me to the core, but I wouldn't let him get the satisfaction of knowing it. I told him, "You miss me."

"Like hell I do."

"Then why be mad at all? If I were nothing to you, then you wouldn't be mad. You could leave here and get a nut elsewhere."

"And I am," he said, sitting on the side of my bed after searching on his hands and knees for his shoes. He looked up at me.

I knew I touched a nerve. Little did he know he had touched several in me months ago, making me second-guess the person I thought I was; and here he was trying to do it to me again.

"You know what, Eric? This is the last time I submit myself to you. As much as I loved you, having you come in and out of my life isn't worth it, so hurry up, get your shit, and get the hell out my damn house." I pointed to my bedroom door.

He stood, straightening his jeans. He reached down in his pockets and felt for his keys, but they weren't there. He patted both front and back pockets, and still there were no keys. I pointed at my dresser where they sat. He glared at me before walking over and snatching them off.

"Good luck with your weight," he snarled.

"And good luck with your blue balls," I retorted, watching Eric walk out of my life again.

The confidence I tried to maintain while he was there instantly diminished like someone letting air out of a balloon. His words had deflated me yet again.

Yes, I'm what you would call voluptuous, or at least that's what I call myself instead of fat, obese, or just plain huge. Voluptuous sounds so much better, and I see that word as sexy. I'm that, too. I feel that most days, and today was one of them. Skinny skanks might not think so, but that's okay. They ain't supposed to think it, because I don't like holes. I like my poles. They're jealous of me anyway. They wouldn't worry about me if they didn't see me as a threat. I may be five feet five inches, 223 pounds, but I carry it very well. A hundred pounds of that weight is in my breasts, thighs, and behind. My stomach isn't as flat as I would like, but a few sit-ups would help that.

For the most part of my life, I considered myself to be a confident woman. I didn't care what people thought of me. I was skinny, about fifteen years ago, weighing 124 pounds; and no, I'm not carrying baby weight. This is the weight of life's stress, which ended up being diagnosed as depression. Food became my peace, and that peace accumulated onto my body.

It has taken me a long while to accept I have depression. I thought any medication being taken for something mental made you crazy, especially in my family. They drown their issues in food, alcohol, weed, and sex. I have members in my family whose medicine are all four of those things. Yet, when I say I take medication for depression, they look at me like I'm getting ready to pull out a gun and go postal.

Actually, that is a plus for real. The more they think I am crazy, the more they know not to mess with me. Still, I don't want to be the one they think should be admitted into a rubber room. I'm not crazy. Life made me this way, and I have to wonder at what point things changed for me. I used to be my biggest cheerleader. Now, I am all cheered out. I needed to find that spirit to celebrate myself, but after Eric's visit, I would find it more difficult to look at myself as valuable at all.

Chapter 5

Phoenix

My house was finally empty, with a few stragglers. I had put up everything that wasn't toted up out my house from the dinner. These hungry heifers made sure to take plates, but I couldn't blame them, because I did have an amazing spread. With her attitude still evident, Dawn questioned me on where I was getting my money to be able to afford all this food.

"None-yah," I told her. First it was Serena, and now her.

"Filet mignon. Cheesecake bites. What you do, rob an upscale restaurant?" Dawn asked.

"No, I paid for it with my money," I stressed, cutting off the chocolate fountain and toting it to my kitchen with Dawn following me.

"You can't have money and no job, Phoenix," Dawn said.

"Again, you're all up in my business. Go home to your man. Use some of those products you purchased on him," I urged, hoping she would leave me alone. For a split second, I almost called Paige to come into the kitchen, knowing this would irritate the hell out of Dawn and shut her conversation down. As fate would have it, Paige showed up like a champ without me having to call her.

"Girl, you need some help?" she asked, looking at Dawn and rolling her eyes. Here she was, asking to help me when my very own sister didn't offer to lift a finger. All she was interested in was where my money was coming from. I couldn't lie; I was happy to see Paige, and the look of disgust on Dawn's face was enough to make me smirk a little bit. She was busy worried about my money. She needed to be worried about where her future husband was laying his pipe.

"You can if you want. I'm not going to turn it down," I said, looking at Dawn, who seemed noticeably pissed.

"I'll help some, but I have to get home and get me a piece. This poon poon ain't had a dick in me in a week," Paige boasted.

"Who's your conquest tonight?" I asked, not thinking as I poured the chocolate out of the fountain into a large container.

"I can't say," she said sarcastically.

"You see. That's the shit I'm talking about," Dawn blurted, pointing her finger at Paige.

"You talking to me?" Paige asked, putting her hand on her chest.

"Yeah, I'm talking to you. You've been saying slick shit all night."

"Girl, this is a fight you don't want," Paige warned.

"Oh, really?" Dawn asked.

"Really! Why you mad?" Paige asked.

"I'm mad because you a whore," Dawn said, walking closer to Paige.

"If you keep stepping to me like you want some, I'm going to give it to you again," Paige cautioned.

I thought my sister would heed the warning, but I guess the bad blood between them two was worse than I imagined.

"Bitch, I will whoop your. . ." Dawn said, not finishing her sentence as she went over to Paige and swung on her. Paige retaliated by punching her back, and before I could get to them good, they were fighting. I dropped the fountain, spilling some of the chocolate all over my counter. Trying to break them up, I ended up between them. Paige was reaching over me and punching Dawn in the back of the head as she held a handful of her long hair.

"Let her go, Paige," I yelled.

"Bitch, I told you not to mess with me," Paige screamed, steady landing punches to my sister's head.

Shauna and Serena ran into the kitchen and grabbed Paige, who wouldn't let go of Dawn's hair. I turned and grabbed Paige's hand to pry her fingers from my sister's hair. One by one I struggled to lift her fingers as she jerked with all her might to rip Dawn's hair from her skull. Once her grip was released, Dawn stood pushing her hair away from her face. I jumped in front of Dawn, pushing her away from Paige, because she looked like she was going to go in for some more.

"Stop it," Shauna yelled.

"She shouldn't have put her hands on me," Paige said, panting.

"And you shouldn't have slept with my man," Dawn shrieked.

"Check your man, not me. If you had any type of common sense you would see that, but nooooo, you want to play dumb wifey, thinking you can punk me. But you wrong, trick. Your ass got played. Jump again and I will whoop that ass again," Paige threatened.

Dawn breathed heavily as she defiantly scowled at Paige with so much rage. My sister knew Paige was right, but she would never admit it. Corey was the one who needed to be checked for real. Paige wasn't the only woman he had slept with during their relationship together. Her man was a dog, and I knew he would sleep around on her again. Why wouldn't he? Dawn always took him back. You teach a man how to treat you, and

Corey knew he could treat Dawn like crap and she would be dumb enough to deal with it.

"I'm leaving," Dawn said, pulling her mangled hair back in a ponytail. "Come on, Shauna and Serena," she yelled.

Both my sisters looked at me. Shauna shook her head.

"She's yelling at me like I slept with her man. I don't want him," Serena quipped.

"I'm getting pissed off now. They done made me lose my buzz," Shauna said, walking out of the kitchen behind Dawn with Serena following her.

I couldn't help but laugh at them.

"I'm sorry, Phoenix. I didn't mean to be fighting up in your house like this, but you know me. I don't care where I am; if someone wants to check me, then we going to handle the damn thing wherever," Paige said, fixing her clothes, which were hardly messed up since she was in control of the fight.

"I understand. And I'm sorry for my sister's behavior."

"You can't help who your blood is. I'm glad you are not like her. Talk about total opposites," Paige said. She ain't never lied.

Dawn was somewhat quiet, so to see her get bold and jump knowing she couldn't fight, from what I could see, was another side of her I hadn't seen before. It was almost like she was homie.

She isn't into clothes like me or trying to look her best at all times. For goodness' sake, she came over here in a jogging suit tonight. Don't get me wrong; a jogging suit is great for leisure around the house or running to the store or gym type thing, but not for gatherings. If she was going to wear a jogging suit, she could have at least put on a cute one. The one she was wearing was too oversized for her body and didn't hug her nice body at all, and it was an ugly pea green color that made me think of throwup for some reason.

As gloomy as she looked, I was waiting for her to pull that hood over her head and call it a night. She should fix herself up sometimes. She used to dress. I didn't know what had happened. Well, I did know. Corey happened. Ever since she'd been with him, Dawn had lost her own identity. She had been too busy playing private eye investigating what the hell Corey was doing. I used to feel sorry for her, but now I didn't. You make your bed, you lie in it, and she was lying beside a cheating dog. She was way too pretty for him. She could get any man she wanted, yet she chose this punk.

There was no excuse why Dawn should settle for the life she had. Dawn has a shape with just a tad bit more weight than me, but it is in the right places. Her skin tone is like mine, caramel but lighter. She has the best hair out of all of us, taking it from our great-grandmother. It is long and silky.

I love my sister dearly, but we don't get along that well. We tolerate each other because we're siblings. I always wished our relationship would get better, but as long as she was in denial about herself and her relationship, our relationship would remain like it was: tolerable. I knew after this episode with Paige, any type of rapport we had may be severed, just for the simple fact I was friends with the enemy.

Chapter 6

Dawn

Two things went wrong tonight. One was going to the sex party at all, and two was the fact that I trusted my sister, who knew my situation but still was selfish enough to invite the enemy. How shocked was I to see my nemesis, Paige, already there laughing with the woman next to her? My blood instantly began to boil.

How could Phoenix do me like this? She should have known only one of us should be there, and that one should've been me. When I found my seat with a tipsy Shauna behind me, Vivian spoke, giving me the look like, "Are you okay?" I stretched my eyes, letting her know I wasn't. My night went from sugar to shit real quick. I'm not sure everyone in the room knew the beef Paige and I had, but I didn't like being there with the ones who did know. Some women were giving me the eye, looking back and forth between me and Paige. I almost told them, "Either say something or get out my face."

Then when Paige and I made eye contact, she gave me this smirk like, "Yeah, I slept with your man. What are you going to do about it?" I wanted to run across that room and snatch that blond hair out of her head. I glanced over at Vivian, who sensed my anger. She held her hand out flat and lowered it to let me know to calm down. That was easier said than done.

That lady showing us toys reminded me of the sex Paige had with my man. Oh, and the damn banana down the throat thing was icing on top of an already rotten cake. Paige made sure to demonstrate in great detail how to force a banana down her throat. I wished she would have choked on it.

The entire night my irritation was building, until I lost it on Paige. I would do it again if she thought every time I saw her she could drop little innuendos about my man. I was surprised Phoenix intervened, but the worst part of the whole situation was my sister seemed to be on Paige's side and not mine.

Still steaming at the altercation between me and Paige, I roared into the garage of my two-story colonial, hitting the button to let the garage doors down. I sat in my car for a minute trying to gather myself. The harder I tried to calm down, the angrier I got. Picking up my purse from the passenger seat, I got out and stormed into the house, slamming the door closed.

Corey walked into the kitchen as I was taking off the jacket to my jogging suit. "How was the party?" he asked.

I thought that was stupid, because Corey should have recognized I was distraught. The slamming of the door should have clued him in along with the frown lines in my forehead. I guessed he was too busy trying to be cute dressed in black slacks and a black striped collared shirt.

"The party was terrible," I belted.

"Why? I thought all sex toy parties were supposed to be exciting," Corey said.

"It was humiliating, especially since my sister decided to invite Paige."

The smile on Corey's face dissipated. He asked, "She was there?"

"Hell yeah, and it felt like that bitch was taunting me all evening."

"What did she say to you?"

"What didn't she say? All night she kept saying things and doing things that were pissing me off, Corey. I knew she was doing this on purpose. Finally I confronted her, and from then we started fighting."

"Fighting. Dawn, you too old to be doing that."

"I was tired of her. I lost it."

Corey walked up to me and hugged me, saying, "Well, try to forget about her. We have plans. Let's go out and have some fun, just me and you."

"I don't know if I feel like going anywhere," I said, trying to push myself back out of his arms.

"But you said we were going. Are you telling me you don't want to do this now?" Corey asked.

I wanted to say yes, but I knew the reason why I didn't want to go was because Paige and Phoenix messed up my evening. All I wanted to do was crawl up on my couch and relax. I'd had enough excitement for the night, and I really wasn't in the mood to do anything else. As much as I didn't want to get dressed to go out, I had to. Me and my husband-to-be had been planning this for over two weeks now, and I couldn't allow the madness that happened earlier to interfere with a wonderful evening with Corey.

"Give me a few minutes and I will be ready," I told Corey, whose smile returned.

He kissed me on the lips and said, "Hurry up," smacking me on my butt as I walked past him.

After showering, I put on a sexy black strapless dress and my five-inch black heels. When I went to brush my hair, I got upset again when pieces of my hair came out in clumps from Paige jerking on it earlier. I pulled the clumps of hair out of the brush and took in a deep breath, trying to calm myself. I was not going to let that trick mess up my night. I brushed my hair down, letting it sweep my shoulders, and tucked my hair behind my ears.

Despite the hair she succeeded in pulling from my scalp, I still had plenty. I was ready to go.

When I walked into the living area, I saw Corey had put on the jacket to the black slacks he was wearing. He was standing at the door looking at his watch. When he saw me, his smile returned to his lips.

"Honey, you look good enough to eat," he said, walking over to me and embracing me. He nibbled on my neck.

I had to smile at my fiancé. As many issues as we had in the past, I knew I was the woman he wanted to be with. "Maybe you can do that later," I teased.

"Maybe I will," he retorted with a smirk.

"So, you ready?" he asked.

"I am if you are."

I still wasn't in the mood, but I was going to push through my frustration and try to enjoy a memorable evening with my man.

Chapter 7

Phoenix

Finally I was getting me a piece, and it was so damn good. Von pounded into me, giving me exactly what my body craved: an orgasm. I bucked and I yelled. I screeched with satisfaction, enjoying the weight of him on top of me. This man was nothing but the truth. I didn't need him in me to get off, because I would just look at this luscious man and get quivers throughout my body.

All was going great, until Tobias walked in. I saw him enter out of the corner of my eye, but I didn't bother to stop, and neither did Von, who was so wrapped up in my good pussy that he didn't notice Tobias come in the room.

Tobias stood there gawking. Nothing was falling out of his mouth. Not a "stop it" or "what the hell is going on?" He stood there like a knot on a log and watched as I got pounded by a man who wasn't him. My plan went down exactly like I wanted it to, with the exception of him not going off about the situation.

I arched my back and dug my nails deeper into Von's back, yelling louder with pleasure, hoping this surge of my desire would ignite a rage in Tobias. Von buried his face in the crook of my neck as he gripped my butt and lifted it to his manhood to enter me deeper and deeper. There were no sheets covering us, just our arms and legs intertwined for Tobias to see. I moaned and wailed, getting annoyed because Tobias still wasn't saying anything. I threw some words in to make matters worse.

"That it right there, baby. Pound this pussy. That's right. Like that," I urged as Von obeyed my orders and deepened his penetration, pleasing my center.

Now is when Tobias made himself known by clearing his throat. Von was so deep in me he didn't hear him. Tobias cleared his throat louder, and this time Von heard him. He looked around to see Tobias standing in the room, and then he looked down at me.

"What are you doing here?" I asked Tobias.

"You told me to come by."

"No, I didn't," I lied.

"Yes, you did," he said slowly.

"Well, I don't remember," I said as Von got off of me and sat on the side of the bed saying nothing. He was good. Even though Tobias interrupted, we both had reached our peak. I reached mine several times. Tobias had just walked into the second go-round.

Boldly, Von stood and pulled his boxers up on his magnificent frame. When he did this, he made sure to turn around so Tobias could get a good look at what he was working with. There was no smirk or frown on Von's face when he did this. He was straight-faced as he took his time getting himself together.

Tobias stood there looking like a damn punk. If he was supposed to be my man, then why wasn't he flipping out right now? There is not a man I know who would be calm about what Tobias just walked in on. I was confused and in utter shock at his reaction, which was none.

Once Von was completely dressed, he leaned down and kissed me on the cheek. "I'll holla at you later," he said to me as he stood back up and glanced at Tobias. Von casually breezed past Tobias, who still stood watching.

Maybe that was his thing. Maybe he liked voyeurism and this scene turned him on. Well, it wasn't turning me on. If anything, it was weirding me out even more and further let me know this was why I didn't want to be around this man anymore.

"So you're just going to stand there?" I asked sardonically.

"How could you do this to me?"

Now I was getting a reaction, even though it was still a composed one.

"What are you talking about?" I asked, playing stupid, pulling the sheets around me and leaning back on the headboard like I didn't have a care in the world.

"This. You and this man."

"Tobias, we are not together," I said loudly, trying to get this through his thick skull.

"Yes, we are," he argued.

"No, we are not. I broke up with you three months ago, but you keep coming back. You keep showing up thinking I still want you."

"You do. You want me enough to screw me," he said.

"And? I like to have sex. That doesn't mean I want to be in a relationship with you. If that was the case, I would be with Von. Did you see what that man was working with?" I asked.

He rubbed his head, saying, "I can't believe this. You have really hurt me."

Now, mind you, when he was talking, it was not done in an angry tone. He was standing there looking like a wimp. If this were me and I caught the person I wanted to be with fucking somebody else, I would be going the hell off. But not Tobias. He was cool as a cucumber, which made no sense to me. Who would be calm at a moment like this? I swear I didn't understand this man, but I really didn't care to.

"I wish I could say I'm sorry, but I'm not, Tobias. You needed to see this in order to know whatever you thought we had we don't have anymore. No matter how many times I tell you this, you don't believe me. I'm hoping this incident will convince you I've moved on to bigger and better."

"It has opened my eyes up a bit about you," Tobias said, looking like he was getting ready to cry.

"Good. Now maybe you can give me back my key and get rid of the copies you have made."

"Phoenix," he said, pausing.

This punk was really getting choked up by what I was saying. I rolled my eyes. I mean, what the hell? *Get a damn backbone already and handle your business. Leave me alone,* I thought.

"What, Tobias?" I asked in frustration since it was taking him so long to speak.

"I'm willing to forgive you for this," he said.

What he said almost made me fall out my damn bed and hit my head on the corner of my nightstand to knock myself out. Was he kidding me? "You are going to forgive me?" I asked in shock.

He walked over to the bed and sat down on the side Von just had me sprawled out on. I knew he had to be sitting on our wet spot. He went to reach for my hand, but I moved it before he could touch me.

"I forgive you. You needed to get this out of your system, and now that you have, we can start fresh in our relationship."

"What relationship? I don't want you!" I yelled.

This frustrated me, because even after catching me with another man, Tobias still couldn't see how bad I wanted him out of my life. I knew I was good, but damn. This man had lost his ever-loving mind over me.

"Actions speak louder than words, Phoenix, and our actions the other night were pure love and ecstasy."

"It was only sex," I shrieked.

"Which I love more than life. Phoenix, I love you so much, and I want to show you how much you mean to me."

Tobias reached down in his pocket and pulled out a black velvet box. He then got down at the side of my bed on one knee. Opening the box, he asked, "Phoenix, will you marry me?"

Was he kidding? I mean really. He caught me screwing another man, and now he was asking me to be his wife minutes after Von extracted his dick out of me. Was he serious right now?

I looked down at the ring, curious to see how much Tobias claimed to love me, and for a moment the diva in me almost said yes as a two-carat princess-cut diamond was sparkling back at me. He had excellent taste, but he was not my cup of tea.

"Phoenix, did you hear me? Will you be my wife?" Tobias asked again, begging me with his eyes to say yes.

I got out of the bed on the other side, away from him. I couldn't take it anymore. I grabbed my robe and put it on, wrapping it tightly around my naked body. "Look, Tobias, I don't want to marry you. I don't want to be your wife. I don't even want to be your girlfriend or your friend at this point. You need to leave," I told him. I didn't bother to hear what he had to say because I walked out of my bedroom and headed downstairs with him following me.

"You have to say yes," he begged.

"No, I don't. I want you to get out of my house and never come back. If you try to use your key, you will find my locks will be changed again," I said.

I began to remember how he got the key to my new locks. He removed my key when I was asleep and made a copy before I had a chance to realize it was missing. I was getting my locks changed again, even though this would be the third time.

"You can't do this to us."

"Like hell I can't. Get out, Tobias."

"But, Phoenix—"

"Now, before I call the cops on you," I threatened.

"You wouldn't do that to me," he said ignorantly.

I sighed and walked over to the phone, dialing 911. "Yes, I need the police. I have an intruder in my house who refuses to leave."

Chapter 8

Serena

I had to think of other ways to please my man, and I used to let my lips do the talking, but after that party tonight, the first purchase I made was that pocket pussy thingy. As much as Tyree wanted to get deep inside me, I couldn't let him, because I had to wait at least six weeks before we did anything, since I had just given birth to our daughter, Nevaeh. My scared behind was paranoid, because I didn't want to get pregnant again. I had a couple of friends who let their men sweet talk them into doing it, and when they went for their six-week checkups, their behinds were pregnant. So I wasn't going to be doing anything. I was going to wait. This toy would have to suffice.

Tyree was against it at first, but when he stuck his finger into that toy, his eyes lit up with curiosity. I laid that man back and slid that rubbery toy onto his manhood and watched as my man climaxed with pleasure minutes later. Before this, I was licking this man into a deep coma, but my jaw muscles could relax for a change. Nothing worse than giving and not being able to receive. My monthly was still present, so I had to suffer until I had the go-ahead.

The banging at my door woke me up out of my sleep. I had just dozed off good and was not happy my slumber had been disturbed. Unlike me, Tyree didn't budge. He was dead to the world.

The person banged again, and I hoped the loud knocking wouldn't wake Nevaeh up like it did me. I nudged Tyree to get up, but he moaned, never waking from his sleep.

Pushing him again, I said, "Tyree, get up. Somebody is at the door."

He never budged. He just moaned again, but never awoke from his sleep. I didn't understand how he couldn't hear this loud knocking. Whoever it was really wanted to get in, but I didn't want them on this side of my door. It was after two in the morning. I didn't feel like leaving the comfort of my bed. It was a cool night, and I was snuggled beneath my warm covers with the ceiling fan above giving me the light breeze I needed to sleep even harder.

The banging on the door persisted. I sighed as I slowly willed myself out of my comfort zone and to this door to see who in the hell had the audacity to wake me up this time of the morning. I prayed it wasn't Tyree's baby mama, Juanita. I swore if it was her, we were going to have a problem. She would do something like this. The last time she showed her face on our doorstep, it was after two in the morning, and the trick came over because Zamir, Tyree's son, was running a temperature of 99.7. She wanted Tyree to go with her to the hospital to have him checked out. At the time I didn't have Nevaeh, but even I knew a 99.7 temperature didn't warrant an emergency room visit. All it was was she was jealous Tyree didn't want her trifling behind anymore, and she was doing any- and everything to make our lives miserable and using their child to do it.

The knocks became more tenacious, and I prayed this crazy woman wasn't on the other side of my door. When I swung the door open, my sister Shauna ran in my house. She pushed me out of the way and slammed the door to my place like some maniac was chasing her.

"What the hell is wrong with you?" I asked, looking at a hysterical Shauna. For a minute I didn't care about the state of mind she was in. I was pissed that she pushed me back, almost causing me to fall, and slammed my damn door.

"Are you going to answer me or not? What the hell is going on, Shauna?"

She still didn't answer. She put her face against my door, hugging it like it was her lifeline. I could see she was trembling. Then I could hear her crying uncontrollably. This stunned me to the point of fear, because Shauna didn't cry. She was so hardcore it wasn't funny. This was the same sister who fought guys in the street and didn't give a damn about nobody, so to see her like this frightened me.

I placed my hands on her shoulders, and Shauna jumped, causing me to back away. Once I paid full attention to how she was looking, I noticed she looked a hot mess. Her face looked like she rubbed Vaseline all over it. It was so shiny. I think it was actual tears that had encased her face as water poured from her eyes. Shauna was always the talker of our family. There was never a time she had nothing to say, so for her to stand there and not say anything caused my panic level to increase an octave.

"Is it Mama? Is she okay? Shauna, tell me what's wrong," I said as my sister came over to me. She dropped to her knees, wrapping her arms around my waist, and she sobbed loudly.

"Shauna, you can tell me anything," I encouraged as water filled my own eyes to see my sister like this.

Shauna continued to weep hysterically. I tried to bring her to her feet and managed to do so as I walked us over to my sofa. Sitting her down, I sat beside her. She pushed her long, untamed hair out of her face, asking, "You don't see it?"

"See what?" I asked.

She kept pushing her hair back from her face, saying over and over again, "Look at me, Serena. Look at me."

I did as she asked, but I couldn't see anything. Really I was still trying to wake up, so I didn't have my wits about myself to focus clearly on what was going on.

"How can you not see this?" she asked desperately.

"See what?" I questioned, feeling like maybe Shauna was losing it. She was not the emotional sister. Well, let me take that back. She was, but most of the time her emotion was anger, not hysteria.

"Look at me. Look at me," she yelled repeatedly, looking at her body, and it was then I noticed she was in my living room in a T-shirt and socks. I couldn't tell if she had on underwear because the shirt was long.

"Why are you over here like this?"

Shauna didn't answer as she broke down in tears again. She dropped her head, causing her hair to fall down around her face. I tried to push her long hair from her face, but when I attempted to do so, she began to shriek.

"Ooooouuuuuch." She winced. She smacked my hand away as she tucked her hair behind her ear.

That's when I saw it; a huge knot was near her temple. It came into view because she turned her head, giving me a better visual as the knot protruded from her head. I reached out and touched it, not thinking, causing Shauna to recoil in pain.

"What happened to you?" I asked worriedly, feeling the tears she had shed start to dwell within me.

"Cal tried to kill me tonight."

"He did what?" I asked as rage entered me. And then my thoughts immediately went into beat down mode.

"I told him I was tired of his crap and if he didn't like what was going on with us, he could leave. Evidently he didn't like me telling him to get out my house, since he doesn't have a pot to piss in. Yet, I guess he expected me to kiss his ass and beg him to stay or something, but you know me, Serena. I don't beg no man to stay with me. Hell, I prefer to be by myself. Next thing I know he just snapped."

"What did he do to you?" I asked, trying to listen calmly, all the while thinking how I was going to get at dude. He put his hands on a Johnson sister and Cal had to pay.

"I was sitting there smoking my cigarette, and all of a sudden he punched me in my face."

"He did what?" I belted, not believing, or maybe it was the fact that I didn't want to believe this man had the nerve to do this.

"Look at my lip," she said, but nothing was showing. It was then Shauna pulled her lip out. I could see where her tooth cut into her inner bottom lip.

"What did you do?"

"I couldn't do anything because he jumped on me. He picked me up off the bed and slung me across the room. The way I fell, I hit my head on the corner of my dresser," she said, reaching for the area where she'd hit her head.

"I hit the floor, and Cal jumped on me again. He straddled me and punched me in my face I think three times; I can't remember. It could have been more because I was still stunned after hitting my head on the dresser. He was yelling he was going to kill me. I tried to scratch at his hands, chest, and face to get him off of me, but it was like he didn't feel anything. Then he tried to choke me," she said, touching her neck.

"He choked you?" I yelled, moving her hand out of the way. I saw some cuts, like his nails dug into her skin. There was some slight swelling and some discoloration to her skin. Fury began to grow within me.

"He kept squeezing and squeezing, still telling me he was going to kill me. I tried to beg him to let me go, but he wouldn't. I guess when I didn't pass out or die, he began to bang my head into the floor over and over again."

I sat there listening intently, already getting in my head the cousins I was going to call to go beat this punk down. First I was going to call our cousin Big Ray. Then I was going to call Gerald and Pookie. All I needed was them three and I knew the job would be done. Pookie was going to come strapped. He stayed strapped and had no qualms about putting a bullet in anybody. At this point, I didn't care. He could shoot Cal and I wouldn't care. Cal had hurt my sister and tried to kill her tonight, and I wanted the punk to get dealt with.

"Serena, I must have passed out, because the next thing I remember is waking up on the floor and seeing Cal stepping over me with his packed bags. I just lay there like I was still passed out until I heard him go out the front door. As soon as I realized he was outside, I got up and ran to the front door, closing it and locking it."

"He has a key, don't he?" I asked.

"He does, but he doesn't have it to the deadbolt."

"How did he leave? He doesn't have a car," I said.

"He didn't. He was still there when I left."

I shook my head at this story, not knowing what else to say. Shauna continued, "He tried to come back in the house but realized he couldn't get in. I sat in my room, trying to wrap my mind around what had just happened. I could hear him outside screaming at me to let him in so he could apologize."

"Apologize. It's too late for a damn apology. And he's screaming at you to let him come in so he could do this. That sounds really sincere," I said sarcastically.

"He kept tapping at my bedroom window for me to open the door so he could come in, but I wouldn't. I just wanted him gone. After I didn't hear him anymore after a while, I figured he had left."

"How did you get away?"

"I ran to my car thinking he was gone. Once I got in I locked the doors, and that's when I saw him sitting in the yard chair outside my house."

"Did he say anything?" I asked.

"He came over to the car and started banging on the window, saying he was sorry and to open the door. I ignored him and pulled off."

My sister began to cry again. My anger hadn't diminished. I really wanted to get this man, or shall I say coward, who thought he could put his hands on a woman.

Shauna gathered herself enough to say, "I wonder if he planned to do this."

"Why do you say that?" I asked.

"You know the bat I keep beside my bed?"

"Yes."

"It was gone. I think he moved it knowing that would be the first thing I would go for. My blade was in my purse, but I wasn't able to get to that. I guess that's a good thing, because I could be sitting here telling you how I murdered this fool."

"He would deserve it. It would have been self-defense. But you don't have to worry about revenge, because I'm calling Big Ray," I said, getting up off the sofa. Shauna grabbed me by the wrist, stopping me.

"Don't," she belted.

"Don't what? This man tried to kill you tonight. He needs to get the same beat down he put on you tonight so he will know how it feels," I said assertively.

"But Big Ray and them will kill him."

"And?"

"And I don't want him to die," Shauna said.

"You just sat here and said if you could have got to your blade you would have stabbed dude to death, so why you worried about his livelihood now?" I asked irritably.

"It's different, Serena."

"How? Dead is dead regardless of how it's done," I argued.

"Why should Big Ray and them get in trouble for somebody like Cal? You know Big Ray probably already on parole," she said convincingly.

"If Big Ray is involved, no one is going to know about it. You know that. He's been around way too long to not know how to get away with beating this punk down."

"Please, Serena. Don't call him. Then he's going to get Gerald and Pookie, and you know any one of them will shoot Cal."

I had to laugh at her saying it, since I had just thought it.

"Please sit down with me for a minute," Shauna begged, still holding my wrist so I wouldn't dial up the entourage.

"Shauna, don't you know you could be dead now?" I said, causing tears to cascade down her face again.

"I know," she said, dropping her head in shame.

"The thought of that scares me, sis," I said with tears welling up in my eyes. "You are my sister and I couldn't stand losing you. Not after . . . Not after . . ." I got choked up and sat down beside my sister. We looked into each other's eyes and understood the pain the other felt.

She nodded and said, "I have done a lot of foul things in my life, but I've never had a man beat me like this. I still can't believe I allowed it to happen."

"You didn't allow this to happen. Now, if you stay with him after this, then yes, you are allowing it, but now, it's not your fault, Shauna."

"I can't believe this," she said, massaging her scalp through her hair. "My head hurts so bad."

"I think I need to take you to the emergency room to get checked out," I suggested.

"I'm not going. I don't feel like telling nobody else what happened, especially a damn doctor."

"Fool, what if you have a concussion?"

"My head is hard. I'll be all right," she said, grinning for the first time since she got there.

"I know that, but even hard heads can get damaged. The knot on your temple is enough for me to worry about the injuries you could have," I said.

"All I need is some ice and some sleep."

"You can't go to sleep. You have to stay up for at least a few hours to make sure you don't slip into a coma or something," I said.

"What are you, Dr. Serena?"

"Yes. I got my PhD from the school of common damn sense," I said jokingly.

"Funny."

"Sis, I think you really need to get checked out seriously," I said.

"Serena, I don't feel like dealing with any doctors, nurses, or cops for that matter. Besides, I've been drinking and smoking."

"And? What does that mean? You also been battered," I said.

"Just leave it alone. I'm not going and that's that."

"You have to do one or the other. Either go to the doctor or let me call Big Ray. You choose."

"You know what? I'm leaving," she said, standing to her feet but stumbling a bit with dizziness.

"You see? You can't even stand up without stumbling."

"I'll be all right," she said, walking to the door.

"And where are you going?" I asked.

"Home."

"You know what? Something is wrong with your head if you making all these crazy decisions. You are not going home. What if that fool is still there? Do you expect me to let you go back to that?"

"He won't be there," Shauna said confidently.

"And how do you know that?" I asked.

She said nothing. She gawked at me.

"Exactly. Look, you are staying here tonight. No ifs, ands, or buts about it." I held my hand out, saying, "Give me your keys."

"I'm not going anywhere."

"I know, but I'm making sure, so hand them over," I said, wiggling my fingers in the "come here" fashion.

Shauna put the keys in my hand even though she didn't want to give them up. I knew her. If I didn't take those keys away from her, when I woke up in the morning, Shauna would be gone.

"You can rest in the guest room next to Nevaeh's room. But don't go to sleep."

"Okay," she said dejectedly.

"And, Shauna, if you decide to be hardheaded and leave here without me knowing, I'm going to call Big Ray to handle things with Gerald and Pookie in tow."

Shauna didn't say anything. She walked out of the living room, heading for the bedroom. I knew I would be up for a while, because there was no way I was going to be able to sleep knowing there was a possibility my sister wouldn't wake up.

Chapter 9

Phoenix

Don't you know that fool thought I was playing a joke on him? He thought I was talking to a dial tone and hadn't called the police on him because my love for him wouldn't do that to him. Well, that punk realized I did call when he saw the cops pull up. He looked at me in disbelief.

"Maybe this will convince you I mean what I say. I don't want to be with you, Tobias."

"I still don't believe you. We are having a rift right now, but eventually it will get solved."

The cops walked up to my open door waiting on them. "Ma'am, did you call about an intruder?" the tall, well-built officer asked as he glanced at Tobias, who was acting like he lived there.

As striking as this cop was, I almost forgot Tobias was there. This cop was fine as hell.

"Ma'am," the handsome cop called out, snapping me back to why he was here in the first place.

"Yes, I'm sorry," I apologized, smiling at him like a shy schoolgirl. But there was nothing girly about me. I was all woman, and I was getting immediately turned on by the magnificence of the chocolate brother.

"Officer . . ." I paused, looking at him questionably as I searched for his name on his uniform.

"I'm Officer Winn. And this is my partner, Officer Taylor," he said, pointing to the dainty brunette woman standing behind him.

She was eying me in a way that made me want to check her. She was giving me a look like I shouldn't be ogling Officer Winn at all. Maybe she was jealous because she was trying to get it or had already gotten it, and that was the reason why she was giving me the stank eye.

"Ma'am," Officer Winn called out again, and when I made eye contact, his stern face changed into one of ease.

"Yes, Officer," I said sweetly.

"Why are we here again?" he asked.

"This man will not leave my house," I said, changing my tone to one of urgency.

"Did he touch you?" Officer Winn asked.

Instantly I wished Officer Winn would touch me. He could have his way with me any kind of position he wanted, because this man was so fine.

"Did he touch you?" Officer Winn asked again, snapping me back from daydreaming about his attractive behind.

"No, he wouldn't be dumb enough to do that. He just will not leave my house," I said, looking back at a pathetic Tobias.

"Is this true?" Officer Winn asked Tobias.

"Officer, this is a misunderstanding. My girlfriend is mad with me right now. I don't know why she called you all."

"First of all, I'm not your girlfriend. Second, I called because I want you out my house," I said, pointing to my door. My robe loosened a bit, almost causing one of my breasts to come tumbling free.

Officer Taylor frowned, but Officer Winn smirked, giving me the impression he didn't mind as his eyes looked as though he wished he got a free look. His partner eyed him and shifted uncomfortably.

Pulling my robe closed, I said, "Get out!"

"I live here too," Tobias said, surprising me with this bit of information.

"Is this true, ma'am? Does he live here?" Officer Taylor interjected.

"No!" I belted.

"Please calm down," the female officer warned.

"This is my house and my house only. I'm the only one who stays here," I asserted, ignoring this woman telling me to calm down. Just because she was behind that badge and police uniform didn't mean I had to respect her.

"Stop lying, Phoenix. My clothes are upstairs in your closet. My shaving kit is in your bathroom."

"No, it's not," I said.

"Ma'am, if he lives here—" the female officer attempted to say, but I cut her off in annoyance.

"But he doesn't! I pay this mortgage. I pay all the utilities."

"Well, that's a lie too, babe," he said softly, like this wasn't an issue. "I've been paying your mortgage, electric, and water. Officer, if you would allow me to show you, I have the receipts and my account information showing I paid it," Tobias said, going over to my console table and pulling out his checkbook and receipts.

When did he put his things there? And if he put that there, he probably was right about having some clothes and his shaving kit upstairs. Had this man slowly moved his things in my place without me even knowing?

"See? I made sure the clerk wrote down I paid and my information," he said, walking back over to the officers and pointing at the slips of paper.

"Ma'am, this does show he's been paying the bills at this address. If he didn't live here, why would he be paying your mortgage?" Officer Taylor asked, leering at me like she was happy I was caught in a lie.

I wanted to put my hands on this woman. She was getting a kick out of making me look stupid. The snide smirk on her face let me know that.

"He helped me out a few times. So what? That doesn't mean he lives here," I disputed.

"I can take you upstairs to show you my clothes and other items. I even bought the food for her dinner party she had tonight," he said, bringing out yet another receipt.

I wanted so bad to snatch all of those pieces of paper out of his hand and stuff them all in his damn mouth so he could choke on it. How dare he make me out to look like a liar? If I would've known he kept track of him helping me out, I wouldn't have had anything to do with this punk. To me, this was looking like a setup that I allowed to happen because I was too busy enjoying the fruits of his labor. But the cops couldn't believe this, could they?

"Ma'am, I'm sorry to tell you we can't make this man leave. It appears that he does reside here, and by law, regardless if his name is on your lease or not, he has tenant rights. All the evidence is here," Officer Taylor said, taking over this little interrogation.

"You got to be kidding me," I said, putting my hands on my hips in frustration. I peered at Officer Winn, who stood back watching as his partner did all the work. As good-looking as he was, he was there to do his job.

I asked him, cutting off his partner, "Is this true?"

Officer Winn nodded, saying, "If you want this man to leave, Ms. Johnson, you have to give him at least a thirty-day notice to leave your residence. If he doesn't leave within that time frame, then you will have to file an eviction notice with the court," Officer Winn explained.

"Eviction notice, on my own damn house?" I questioned.

"Yes, ma'am," he said.

"Even if he hit me?" I tried to lie.

"You said he never put his hands on you. Your exact words were . . ." Officer Taylor said, looking down at her notepad. She proceeded to read, "'He wouldn't be dumb enough to do that.'" She looked up at me, happy at my humiliation right now.

I was mad at myself at this point. Why did I say that? I could have said he hit me and he would be gone and I would be back in bed getting some sleep. As usual, my mouth worked faster than my brain. Now Tobias was the one who had rights over property that was mine. I was pissed.

"If there's another problem, please feel free to call us," Officer Taylor said to Tobias like she was on his side. I didn't bother to say anything else. I did get one last glance at Officer Winn as he proceeded to leave my stoop.

"Thank you, Officers," Tobias said in his chipper voice.

This just made me cringe with resentment.

"You all have a good night," Officer Taylor said, and I slammed the door in her face.

"Phoenix, you can get arrested," Tobias said.

"Why, for closing my own door? She lucky I didn't do more," I bellowed. "I can't believe you lied like that," I said through clenched teeth.

"Honey, I didn't lie. Everything I said was the truth."

"I'm going to get you out of here if it's the last thing I do," I said, stomping up my stairs and slamming my bedroom door closed, locking it.

Chapter 10

Shauna

Serena ended up staying up with me until she thought it was okay for me to fall asleep. I slept in the third bedroom they had. When I woke up, the first person I thought about was Cal and what he did to me. My second thought was how my head was killing me. I had a hangover without the drunkenness. I knew this pain came from Cal slamming my head into the floor. For a minute, I didn't want to move for fear the pain would increase. I lay there looking up at the speckled ceiling, wishing things were different. I never thought I would have anything like this happen to me.

I managed to sit up, making sure to move slowly, and was happy the pain didn't escalate. I was more sore than I thought. I threw my feet over the side of the bed and sat there for a bit. I still had on the T-shirt and panties I ran over here in. I looked at the side table next to the bed to see my sister put a change of clothes there for me to put on. I picked it up to see she put a pair of gray jogging pants and fitted white V-neck tee with a pair of socks and underwear. I ran my hand through my tangled hair, wincing a bit, and when I brought my hands back down, I saw clumps of my hair came out in my hand. Tears threatened to escape as I recapped the night and wondered how in the hell this had happened.

Here I was thinking I had to worry about my sister calling our cousins, and I never considered what Tyree would do once he found out. I knew I should have kept what happened to me to myself. Cal beating me was the least of my worries. Now that Tyree knew too, it was enough to stress me the hell out.

All because of the simple act of Tyree going to the restroom in the middle of the night, and that's when he realized Serena wasn't in the bed with him. He thought she was with Nevaeh but quickly found out she was with me, since the spare bedroom was right beside my niece's room. When Tyree saw me, he knew something was up. As much as I didn't want to tell him, I had to. Seeing him standing before me caused me to burst into tears again. Needless to say, Tyree was heated by what happened, and he immediately began calling his boys, letting them know to serve Cal with a pretty ass-whooping if they saw him.

I could stop Serena, but Tyree was another story. He was the brother I never had, and he acted the role of one, too. Tyree let me know way back he didn't like Cal. He only dealt with him because he loved me, so for this to happen, he was ready to stomp a hole in him.

Really Cal was hated by many men in the street. He always thought he was big and bad all the damn time, running his mouth like he couldn't be beat. All mouth and little action was what he was. "I'm from Jersey, yo," he would say all the time, like that was going to make somebody back down. I had family in Jersey, but none of them bragged like he did. I guess since Virginia was more down south than upstate, he thought everybody from here was supposed to be punks. Boy was he ever wrong.

He learned one lesson when his ass got stabbed in his back on the basketball court four months ago for running that mouth. It was through the grace of God that the blade missed his spinal cord and he lived. That alone should have been enough to clue him in on keeping his mouth shut, but if anything it made him cockier because he survived the stabbing. He walked with his chest stuck out more than ever now, with not one damn lesson learned. All he got out of it was he had street scars, and the fact that he survived proved his toughness. This punk really began to think his ass was invincible.

Like a dummy, I still stayed with him. Look where that got me. I could have lost my life at the hands of this fool. He couldn't beat a dude, so he thought it was fitting to make himself feel better by beating me. I was the only one he had in his corner. A lot of his own family didn't have his back, so now he was going to stand alone, and I knew this was the time he would run to them. The only one who seemed to have his back was his mother. She was a good woman. Out of this entire situation, she would be the one person I would miss.

The shower I took made me feel a hundred times better. The hot water helped ease my aching bruises, and I washed my hair, pulling it back in a ponytail. With clean clothes on and feeling refreshed, I felt good.

The aroma of sausage swarmed the air, and I knew Serena wasn't in the kitchen. Tyree was. He was the one who did the cooking most of the time between the two. I also smelled coffee, and for once I craved to have a cup with lots of sugar and cream.

When I got downstairs, to my dismay, my sister Phoenix was sitting at the island in the kitchen. I heard her say, "Cal needs to start counting his nine lives, because Big Ray and them getting ready to take what's left away from him. I promise you that."

She was always so damn loud and dramatic. And they said I was the crazy sister.

Serena was sitting beside Phoenix. Both were drinking the coffee I smelled earlier. I turned to see, like expected, Tyree at the stove preparing breakfast.

"Why did you call her?" I asked Serena as I walked into the kitchen painted a sunny yellow. It wasn't overpowering at all. It made you feel like happiness should always be within this space; but I wasn't feeling any type of happiness right now, not after seeing Phoenix here. If anything I was feeling dread at the days ahead, knowing I would be the brunt of conversation between my sisters and whatever other family they decided should be brought into my troubles.

"Phoenix called me this morning because we were supposed to go walking so I can start losing this baby weight," Serena said, grabbing her little pouch from having Nevaeh.

"And you couldn't wait to tell her what happened to me," I said, crossing my arms in frustration.

"She is our sister, Shauna. Don't you think she should know?" Serena asked.

"If I wanted her to know, I would have run to her house. I thought I could trust you, Serena," I said, walking around the island to retrieve a mug from the cabinet.

"Shauna, you can be mad all you want. Serena's right. I should know about this," Phoenix chimed in.

"Why? What business is this of yours?"

"We're sisters. How many times do we have to say this to you? Cal stepped way over the line when he thought it was okay to disrespect you like this. And with him disrespecting you, he has disrespected us. That's why I called Pookie and Gerald over."

"You did what?" I blurted in the middle of pouring the hot elixir into my mug. I halted my coffee-pouring midair, trying really hard not to drop the pot onto the granite countertop.

"You heard me," Phoenix said.

I looked at Serena, who stretched her eyes and picked up her own cup to take a sip. The mug was so big it looked like it was covering her entire face. Maybe she was trying to hide from me.

With Phoenix at the reins, I knew this situation was going to get worse, which was why I knew Serena told her instead of any of our other sisters. To be as pretty as she was, Phoenix was *boughetto*—bougie and ghetto. Yesterday she was high-class snooty; now she was ready to scream whooty-who. Just call my sister Phoenix the diva of the family. She was the type to start trouble and then finish it, even if it meant somebody else was fighting her battles. Don't get me wrong; Phoenix fought. She had to, as many times as she slept with somebody's husband.

My sister let her beauty work for the good of her pockets. Where she got that behavior from, I don't know. Her attractiveness managed to get her a house, a brand new Range Rover, and monthly installments of money given to her. Whoever her sugar daddy or daddies were this time, they were definitely taking good care of her. Still, I had to wonder at what cost.

"You see why you shouldn't have told Phoenix," I said to Serena, putting some sugar into my coffee.

"Don't be mad at her. Be mad at me," Phoenix said.

"Oh, I am. I wish y'all would let me handle this on my own," I said.

"Just like you handled him last night? From the looks of your damn eye, it looks like he handled you good," Phoenix responded, taking a sip of her coffee as she eyed the bruise on my eye.

"Phoenix," Serena called.

"What?" Phoenix asked, looking dumbfounded.

"Really? You had to talk about the bruises."

"I'm pretty sure she saw them when she looked into the mirror this morning. Maybe that will further help her decide not to go back to that punk."

I rolled my eyes, saying, "You see why I don't ever want to come to y'all with anything."

"Why you trippin'? You lucky to be alive from what I heard from Serena, and you complaining," Phoenix said with a sneer.

"Phoenix, don't start with me today. You know you don't want none. I might have got caught off-guard last night, but this morning I'm more than lucid enough to know how to whoop your ass."

"I'm trying to help," she blurted like she was doing me a favor.

"But I didn't ask you to, did I?" I said, leaning forward for her to read my lips and hear me good.

"Get your panties out your ass and be happy you got family willing to be there for you. All you have to say is thank you and leave it at that," Phoenix countered.

I sighed my frustration, asking Serena, "Did you call Dawn and Vivian, too?"

"No, I didn't. I figured we would see them later at our dinner."

"That's if I go," I murmured.

"Why aren't you going?" Phoenix asked, frowning.

"I don't need to hear why I let this happen. It's bad enough having to deal with you two."

"Are we that bad?" Phoenix asked.

"Hell yeah," I shouted.

"Shauna, I know I come off hard sometimes—" Phoenix began to say.

"You think?" I responded.

"And I acknowledge that, but I act crazy when it comes to the people I love."

"Not only with the people you love," Serena said under her breath.

Phoenix nudged her with her elbow, causing Serena to say, "Ouch."

"Like I was saying before I was rudely interrupted," Phoenix said, side-eyeing Serena, "I love you, Shauna. I hate this happened to you. Yes, I have overreacted, but I want Cal to get dealt with for what he's done to you."

"But why is this any of your business?" I asked.

"It's my business because you are my sister. Plus, this has struck a nerve in me because it's happened to me too," Phoenix confessed.

"Really?" Serena asked in shock.

"Yes," Phoenix said warily. "I went to this get-together with a guy I was seeing, and he thought he could smack me in front of a bunch of his people because I talked to him a certain type of way and came out my face wrong."

"He smacked you?" Serena asked.

"Yep," Phoenix said, nodding.

"What did you do?" I asked.

"I blacked the hell out."

Tyree giggled as he took the biscuits out of the oven.

"It took four of his family members to pull me off of him. By the time I was finished with him, it looked like a cat had attacked him. Plus, I gave him a black eye."

"Dammit," Tyree said.

"He was lucky I wasn't toting my pistol. I swear on my mama I would have shot him dead," Phoenix said, holding her right hand up like she was being sworn in by a court officer.

"You would have shot him?" Serena asked, giggling.

"You damn right I would have. A man putting his hand on this pretty face? Please. And to do it in front of people trying to prove he had some kind of control over me," she said with eyebrows raised. "I think what triggered my departure—"

"Departure?" Serena asked, frowning.

"My mind leaving the building," Phoenix said.

"Oh. Okay."

"I snapped because this jackass had the nerve to laugh after he slapped me. I think that's what made me lose all sense of reality."

As much as I loved my sisters and family members, we tended to be a little crazy. No. Let me scratch that. We were a lot crazy. I mean crazy in the sense of some members having papers showing they've been in a mental institute. I had to sometimes question our stability. None of us were quite right upstairs and I knew this.

Just when I didn't think my morning could get any worse, I saw Big Ray walk in the kitchen. He hugged Serena and Phoenix and then went over to Tyree, giving him the brotherly handshake. I was last on his journey of affection. After he hugged me, he pushed my hair back gently and took my face into his massive palms. He tenderly moved my head back and forth, looking at my developing bruises. When he let go of my face, I could see him clenching down on his teeth, causing his jawbone and temples to flex. I knew what this meant. It meant things were about to get real.

"Big Ray, you don't have to do this. I'm okay," I said, looking up at my six foot five inch cousin built like a brick building, weighing about 320 pounds. His size alone was intimidating, but when it came to the women of the family, he was a big teddy bear. Trying to convince him everything was okay, I said, "I think Cal knows not to let this happen again."

"I don't know about all that, cuz. He messed up when he touched one of ours," he said with his deep baritone voice.

"I know he's not crazy enough to try anything else with me," I said, changing my words.

"How do you know that, Shauna? He hasn't had to deal with any consequences behind this," Big Ray said, looking sincerely into my eyes.

I could see the pain and anger within him. I still tried to smooth things over so he could leave it alone. "Ray, by the time he hears about all y'all looking for him, he's going to be long gone. He ain't dumb enough to stick around for an ass-whoopin'," I said.

"He violated you. No man ever violates my peoples. Y'all are like my sisters. Your mama help raise me when my mama was cracked out in the street, so to see you hurt like this, it pains me, Shauna," he said, visibly upset.

I wanted to cry so bad, but I held back my tears. That would have only added to him wanting to hurt Cal. As bad as Cal deserve whatever he got, I didn't want Big Ray to risk himself for someone as sorry as Cal.

"So I can't change your mind?" I asked Big Ray.

"I'll tell you what; we won't go looking for him. The word will be put out in the street. But, Shauna, if we see him, he will get dealt with."

I nodded.

"I'm serious, Shauna. I can't lay eyes on this punk and not do what I say I'm going to do if I see him," Big Ray stressed.

"I understand, Ray," I said, smiling at him.

"I don't know what you saw in him anyway," Phoenix said, ruining the loving moment I was having with my cousin.

"For goodness' sake, sis," Serena said, but Phoenix kept talking.

"He ain't cute. His breath stank, and his grill is busted. I still can't believe that punk thought he was the prettiest thing walking."

"Well, I did care for him," I replied, wishing she would shut up.

But that would be too much to ask of Phoenix, so she replied back, "Love wouldn't have allowed him to kick your ass. I hope you are done with him. From the looks of that eye, you need to take a picture for it to be a constant reminder of what he did to you so you won't take him back."

"Taking pictures is a good idea, Shauna," Serena agreed. "I'm going to get my camera," she said, hopping down from the stool and jetting past us to go upstairs.

"Bump the camera," Phoenix said, taking out her cell phone. "I'm going to snap this right now," she said, taking numerous pictures of my bruises. "This is evidence."

"I better not see this on Facebook or any other Web site, Phoenix. I know you."

"Why not?"

I scowled at her, and she said, "Okay. I wasn't going to do that anyway."

It didn't matter how many pictures they took of me; the emotional toll of this situation was enough to wound me for life. I was done with Cal. As much as I hated agreeing with Phoenix, love wouldn't allow something like this to happen to me. I came to the realization that what he had for me wasn't love at all. It was straight-up abuse.

Chapter 11

Serena

My house was finally empty of my family. Shauna decided to go home, and Big Ray and Phoenix decided to follow her to make sure that fool Cal wasn't still waiting outside her house.

I expected to be exhausted from going on my walk with Phoenix this morning, but I was worn out mentally by the drama my family brought into my home. Don't get me wrong; I loved my family, and yes, I would have welcomed Shauna into my house anytime, but this was a bit much for me to deal with because I hated drama. I always tried to avoid it, but somehow drama was always brought to me.

Maybe it was because I was a nice person. Maybe it was because I was that person people loved to confide in. Either way, sometimes it was a bit much. Still, I've learned to deal with it because being a Johnson sister comes with its fair share of tumultuous situations.

The day went by so fast, and now it was time for me to go over my sister's house for our dinner we had together. Tyree walked into the bedroom soaking wet with his body dripping with sweat. He had just come from playing basketball with his friends. I was mad because he was supposed to be here thirty minutes ago to get Nevaeh while I went over my sister's house. He knew this before he left but, like Tyree, he did whatever he wanted, only thinking about himself.

"You're late," I said, sliding on my gold-and-orange bangle.

"The game ran long," he said.

"I don't care. You knew I had something to do. You should have cut your game short," I snapped.

"Serena, please don't start."

"Don't start? Don't start what?"

"This," he said, holding his hands out to me. "I'm not in the mood to deal with your attitude."

"Fine, Tyree. You won't have to deal with it once I leave. Hell, I'm thinking about leaving permanently. Then you wouldn't ever have to worry about my attitude again," I said angrily.

"Do what you got to do. I'm tired of you threatening to leave me. If you are going to go, then leave already," he said, peeling off his soggy shirt.

"Don't tempt me," I said, glaring at him.

"Do me the favor," he shot back, walking to the bathroom.

"Oh, so you want me to leave?" I asked, getting angrier by the minute.

Sometimes I wished he wouldn't be so damn nonchalant about us. Why didn't he ever fight for us? Like now, he could have apologized and left it at that, but no, he had to push me further away from him. This unnerved me and made me wonder why I was trying. If he could give up on what we had so easily, why shouldn't I leave? It was always the same thing with him. He came with the "whatever" attitude like he could be with or without, and that always hurt me.

"I wouldn't stop you if you did want to leave," he said.

"Why wouldn't you? I'm not worth fighting for?" I asked, rushing to the bathroom behind him and getting up in his face.

"Seriously, Serena. Why would I try to keep you somewhere you don't want to be?" he asked.

"At least show me you want me by fighting or begging me not to leave, or apologize to me sometimes when you do stupid things like this," I retorted.

"You are not making any sense. I'm not going to beg nobody to stay where they don't want to be. That's crazy. And can you say that if I didn't want to be here anymore, you would try to get me to stay?" he said, frowning.

I thought about what he said and instantly understood his thinking process. As much as I hated to agree with him, Tyree was right. If he wanted to leave, I wouldn't beg him to stay either, so how could I want him to do something I knew I wouldn't do myself? I dropped my head as I got caught up in my feelings. Tyree saw the sadness on my face and came closer to me.

"Babe, come on. You know I love you, but you are not going to keep threatening to leave me. You've done it way too many times, and now I'm numb to it," he explained gently.

"I get it," I said solemnly, trying to hold back my tears.

"Is this stemming from the fact that I won't marry you?" he asked, turning his back to me as he reached in the linen closet and pulled out a baby blue towel and washcloth.

"Maybe. I still don't understand why you won't marry me."

"You knew going into this relationship with me, Serena, that I never wanted to get married. I told you about my parents and how their divorce destroyed our family," Tyree explained.

"But your parents are not us," I tried to argue.

"Again, you knew going into this relationship what it was. I never hid that from you, so for you to try to get me to do what I told I would never do pisses me off," he said, reaching into the shower to turn on the water.

"And it pisses me off you can't get past a past that wasn't your fight in the first place. That was your parents' fight. I'm your right now, Tyree. You do love me, don't you?" I asked.

"Of course I do," he said, turning to look at me honestly.

"But not enough to put a ring on it," I said, holding up my left hand, pointing at my fourth finger.

"I'm sorry, Serena, but I can't."

"You know what? Maybe we do need to take a better look at our situation," I said seriously.

"Maybe we should. All I know is I'm tired of talking about this. Nothing is going to change," he said, sliding his shorts off. "You know as well as I do both of us have issues to work through with us and our past. Yours is checkered too, Serena. I think you want to break this curse you think has plagued the Johnson women for generations. I don't see it as a plague. I see it as women choosing their situation that dictates their destiny. I also believe women teach men how to treat them."

"So I taught you how to treat me?" I asked.

"Yes," he said convincingly.

"What? Did I teach you to make me feel unworthy, unloved, what?"

"The love is there and it's real. Your worth is something you have to find within yourself. I can't do that for you. Nor did I ask for that job. As for the lesson to be learned here, you chose to go down this road with me, and that road was clouded. I cheated. You cheated. We knew what it was. You know about my baby mama, my son, and other women I've been with. I know about you and the men you been with. It is what it is," he said, pulling the curtain back farther. He took off his boxer briefs and was standing in front of me naked before stepping into the shower and closing the shower curtain.

"So, just like that I'm supposed to accept this?"

"You don't have to accept anything, Serena," he answered. "I know I want you in my life."

"But only as your girlfriend, not your wife?" I asked.

"Exactly. Even though I love you, I haven't gotten over you cheating on me, and I'm pretty sure you haven't forgotten about me cheating on you. You want to take all of this baggage into vows said before God like it's going to make our situation better. I'm sorry, but I'm not about to do that."

"It would make me feel better. All I've asked for is the ring. We can wait a couple of years to get married to see where our relationship takes us."

"You say that now. As soon as I give you the ring, then you will be hounding me about when are we getting married."

Tyree might have had a point.

"I know you, Serena. As soon as you get what you want, you find something else that's wrong and beat me over the head with it until you get that, and then so on and so on. It never ends with you."

"You don't know that," I lied because everything he was saying was the truth still. For some reason I couldn't get out of my head that the ring would prove his love to me.

"Who are you trying to kid? I wasn't born yesterday. You and I have a dysfunctional relationship, and I refuse to commit to that for the rest of my life. I always knew if I ever got married, it would be 'til death do us part. I'm not ever going into it lightly. Babe, I don't want you to leave me, but you are not going to scare me into giving you a ring. I fear God more than I fear losing you, and I will not play around when it comes to marriage."

What could I say to that? Even I knew I could not compete with God. Not that I would ever try to, but what Tyree was saying made sense. It angered me that it did, because I wanted what I wanted and that was the ring and then us getting married to one another.

I don't know how long I stood there thinking about what he said, but I finally snapped out of my thoughts and spoke to him.

"I'm leaving, and I'm taking Nevaeh with me," I said, giving up on this conversation, knowing it wasn't going anywhere.

"I thought you said you wanted me to watch her," Tyree said, cutting off the water and opening the shower curtain. He reached for his bath towel and wrapped it around his waist. As mad as he made me, Tyree looked so sexy with the water trickling down his dark chocolate skin. His muscles rippled as the water made its way down his body.

"I changed my mind. My sisters would love to see her."

"Can I get a hug before you go?" he asked with outstretched arms and a smirk on his face.

"No."

"Come here, baby. You know I love you."

"But I'm not wifey material," I shot back.

"In my eyes you are my wifey."

"But not officially. It's only in your meek little imagination. Hug that imaginary wifey, because your girlfriend is leaving."

With that I left him standing with his arms still outstretched to embrace the fact that one day I might not be there for him to hug at all.

Chapter 12

Dawn

I could not wait until I got over to my sister Vivian's house for our weekly dinner. This time it was Vivian who would host the dinner, so I knew we were going to have something scrumptious to eat. Out of all four of my sisters, Vivian was the best cook. I didn't know if it was because she was the oldest or what, but homegirl could throw down.

The last time she made spice-rubbed barbecue ribs with homemade coleslaw, broccoli salad, cornbread, and sweet potato casserole. You're talking about good. Vivian slow-grilled those ribs so long the meat was falling off the bone.

We made pigs of ourselves as we chowed down with BBQ sauce all over our hands and faces, even though she provided kitchen towels for each of us to wipe our hands with. She had enough food to feed an army, so it wasn't a problem for any of us to leave there with Styrofoam plates filled with food to eat the next day.

When I got to Vivian's, I didn't bother knocking as I walked into her house.

"Knock knock. It's me, Viv," I yelled.

"I'm in the kitchen," she replied.

When I walked in, Vivian was standing at the stove, stirring something in a huge pot. "Hey, sis," she said.

"Hey. How it's going?"

"I can't complain, or rather, there's no need to."

"True. You look good," I complimented her, looking at Vivian wearing a pair of black jeggings with a red off-the-shoulder top and leopard-print wedges.

"Thank you."

"Where did you get those shoes, girl? They are so damn hot," I said, admiring the wedges.

"I ordered them off the Steve Madden Web site. Feel them," Viv said, walking over to me.

I bent over and rubbed the shoe. "Is that fur?"

"It feels like it. I love these shoes, and they are so comfortable."

"They don't look comfortable," I said, looking at the five-inch shoe.

"The platform helps. All I buy is shoes with platforms these days. It takes inches away from the actual heel height, but still makes it look like you are rocking high heels. You can try them on if you like," she said, stepping out of the shoes.

I giggled as her height shrank dramatically. I was curious and stepped into the shoes. "Wow. I like these. They are comfortable," I said, pleasantly surprised as I looked down at the fabulous shoe.

"Told you," she said.

"I'm going to have to get me a pair. How much were they?"

"Please don't ask," she said as I stepped back out of the shoes and watched as she walked over and put them back on.

"Seriously, how much?" I asked again.

"With shipping I think I paid close to one hundred and forty dollars."

"Vivian!" I yelled.

"I know, but they were cute and I love shoes, so here I stand," she rationalized. "But that's nothing compared to the price of other shoes I've purchased," she said.

Vivian never lied. She had a nice collection of shoes. My sister had shoes she hadn't worn yet. I would have expected this type of glam from Phoenix, but Vivian even beat her when it came to how many shoes she possessed. I know many may think $140 for shoes is not bad, but when you came from the humble, or should I say poor, beginning like we did, you would understand why I frowned at the mention of the price. We used to think paying fifty dollars for shoes was a lot.

But I couldn't be mad at Vivian. She'd worked hard to get to where she was and rightfully deserved to buy whatever she wanted. Next, I would expect her to be stepping around in Giuseppes and Christian Louboutin. That's if she didn't have any already. Knowing my sister, she did. "I wish I could buy expensive shoes like you."

"You can," she quipped.

"Girl, I'm comfortable in my sneakers. I'm not trying to break my neck in shoes like that."

"Beauty is painful sometimes. I twisted my ankle last year, and it killed me to let my heels go for two months. Don't get me wrong; I do enjoy my sneakers, but I like to dress up sometimes too, unlike yourself," Viv said.

"I dress up," I defended myself.

"When?"

"When I go to church," I retorted.

"And when was the last time you did that?" Vivian asked, reaching into her cabinet and pulling out a bottle of spice. She took the cap off and shook it into the pot.

"Okay, enough with the interrogation. What do you have in the pot?" I asked, trying to change the subject.

Vivian knew what I was doing, eyeing me skeptically, but she went along by answering, "I made some gumbo. This is my first time making this, so I hope it's going to be good." She picked up a spoon and dipped it into the liquid, brought it to her lips, blowing it slightly, and sampled it. “It tastes good, but I feel like it’s missing something. Come over here and taste it,” she said, putting the spoon she used to taste her food in the sink.

Vivian retrieved a fresh spoon out of the drawer and dipped it into the pot, lifting the mixture to my lips. I blew it, holding my hand under the spoon so none of it got on my clothes, and then I consumed it. “Mmmmm. Girl, that’s good. I should have known you couldn’t mess up anything.”

“But doesn’t it need something?” Vivian asked.

“Maybe a little bit more salt. Other than that, I think it’s great,” I said, taking the spoon out of her hand and licking it before putting it into the sink.

Vivian pinched some salt into the pot and stirred it some more. “This is going to be as good as it gets,” she said, turning off the eye under the pot and moving it to one that was cold.

“I see I’m the first one again,” I said.

“Yes. You know you are always the first one, unless Sheldon is here.”

“Is Sheldon coming tonight?” I asked, hoping he was, just so I could stare at his fine behind.

“No, not this time. He had plans,” Vivian said.

Sheldon was Vivian’s best friend, and damn, he was sexy as hell. Tall and dark like the deepest of chocolates, and built like a stallion. You could see his six pack through the fitted shirts he wore; his body was so chiseled. To top it off, he had dreads, which he kept looking and smelling nice all the time.

I thought I loved a man with a bald head, but damn, after seeing Sheldon with his locks, he made me take a second look at brothers with them. Every time I hugged Sheldon I dove my face into his tresses. He looked even sexier when he pulled them back off his gorgeous face. The man had a smile to die for, with the whitest teeth

I'd ever seen on a man and a dimple in his left cheek. I swear Sheldon was one man that could make me cheat on Corey.

I always wondered how Viv and Sheldon became such good friends, and most of all why my sister hadn't taken that fine specimen of a man as her own. For a minute I thought he was gay, but Sheldon let it be known real quick he was a ladies' man. I then had to wonder what the hell was wrong with my sister for not jumping that man's bones. I then questioned whether she was gay. One day I asked her, and she damn near had a heart attack.

"Hell no," she screamed. "I'm strictly dickly, sis."

"I had to ask, as fine as Sheldon is," I told her.

"We're just friends," Vivian would always say, but I still couldn't believe it. They acted like an old married couple but weren't getting the benefits of being one.

As I stopped daydreaming about Sheldon, Vivian said, "I swear we need to make our dinner time an hour earlier just so our sisters can get here on time."

"I know, right? And you know who's going to be last."

"Phoenix," we both said simultaneously.

"Speaking of Phoenix, did you hear about the fight I had with Paige at her house?" I revealed.

"Do you mean fighting as in arguing, or fighting as in coming to blows?" Viv asked for clarification as she leaned against the granite countertop to listen.

"Both, and you know I don't fight unless I have to."

"What happened?" Viv asked.

"I got tired of all the little jabs Paige kept saying the other night. I was standing in Phoenix's kitchen when Paige comes walking in talking about she was getting her some but didn't want to reveal who she was getting some from. That did it for me, Viv. I pushed her. From there we started fighting."

Vivian looked at me like I was crazy.

"What?"

"You know you were wrong, right?" she asked.

"How was I wrong?" I asked, surprised.

"Dawn, you started it by pushing that woman. What did you think was going to happen?" Vivian asked.

"I don't like her, and I wanted to hurt her."

"The one you should be hurting is Corey."

"I had it out with him, too, about Paige," I said unconvincingly.

"Yeah, but you took him back. You handled Paige like you should have handled Corey. Paige doesn't have love for you, but your man supposedly does."

"He does love me," I said.

"He's had a funny way of showing it since he's been with you. You're not with Paige, yet you treat her worse than the man who betrayed you. Yeah, that makes perfectly good sense to me," Vivian argued.

"So you want me to be her friend?" I asked with an attitude, getting heated that Viv didn't seem to be on my side.

"I'm not saying that. What I am saying is Corey is the one you should have been smacking. Paige didn't do anything that Corey didn't allow, is all I'm saying."

There was a knock at the door and I was glad. I was getting tired of discussing me tonight, even though this conversation was my own damn fault for bringing up; but I figured if I didn't bring it up, Phoenix would. I had to get my side out before Phoenix contorted it into something that didn't happen at all.

"Can you get that for me?" Viv asked, pulling out the bowls from the cabinet to set the table.

I went and answered the door. When I opened it, I saw my sisters Serena and Shauna standing there. "It's about time," I said jokingly.

"We ain't late," Serena said, holding the baby carrier with our newest member.

"Maybe you are on time by your clock, but you are late here. Y'all were supposed to have been here at five, and it's five thirty-seven. I almost started eating without y'all," I said, taking the carrier away from Serena and toting my niece into the kitchen.

"You could have eaten," Serena said, dropping her purse on the sofa as she followed me. "I bet you we beat Phoenix here."

All of us burst into laughter.

"What do we always say about Phoenix? She is going to be late for her own funeral," I said, putting the carrier on the countertop.

"And that's because she probably hired her own personal glam squad to make her over after death," Shauna said, causing us to laugh again.

"Let me hold my niece," I said, unbuckling the straps across her little chest.

"Y'all are not going to spoil her. She hardly sleeps at night now. She thinks somebody supposed to hold her all the time," Serena quipped.

"I wonder why?" Vivian asked, giving Serena a sideways glance.

"It's not me. It's her daddy. Tyree holds that girl all the time. I'm surprised he let her come over here with me today," Serena said, climbing onto the barstool at the island.

"Aw, daddy's little girl," Vivian said, speaking in a baby voice.

"I know, right? He even sleeps with her on his chest. I'm so scared he's going to turn over and squish her. He sleeps, and she lies there just as content. But when it comes to putting her in her bassinette, homegirl isn't having it. I'm surprised she's 'sleep now," Serena said. "That's why I don't want you bothering her, Dawn."

"Well, I'm her auntie, so I want to hold her. You are just going to have to get mad at me," I said, picking her up and placing her little frame up on my shoulder.

"I wasn't supposed to bring her," Serena admitted.

"Why?" Vivian asked.

"I was going to have some me time and leave her with her daddy, but we got into an argument, which is why I'm late."

"What are y'all arguing about this time?" I asked.

"What else? The ring he refuses to give to me."

"You need to leave that dead horse alone. That man is not going to marry you," Shauna said.

"I want to get married one day," Serena stated.

"Then you need to decide if the love you have for Tyree is worth losing to find a man who will marry you. And please know finding a good man who's going to take on you and your child, with a job, a car, his own place, not abusive, and loves you, and is not gay, is going to be a task in itself," Shauna explained.

Me and my sisters giggled.

"Why does it have to be so hard? Why don't men want to commit?" Serena asked no one in particular.

"Because that means giving up any other chance at random women," Shauna said.

"But he's supposed to be faithful to me anyway. He isn't supposed to be cheating. So if that's the case, why not make it legal?" Serena asked.

"It's something about that piece of paper men are afraid of. You see comedians joke about it all the time. It's the lockdown. The ball and chain for life, the clink clink," Viv said, holding her wrists together, causing us to chuckle.

"Well, Tyree needs to get over it and soon, or else I'm leaving," Serena declared.

"Yeah, right. You are not leaving that man. If you do, you're a fool. Especially if he is faithful and has a job," Shauna said.

"And good sex. You said his sex was amazing, so where you going again?" I joked.

My sisters laughed, and Serena found herself amused too.

"All we are saying, sis, is think about it good before you make an abrupt decision. Don't let love go over legalities," Viv cautioned.

By now I had checked out of the conversation as I snuggled my face against my little niece, saying, "I love the way babies smell. She makes me want to have one."

"Help yourself. She makes me not want anymore. I love her, but giving birth hurt like hell," Serena countered.

"I thought you got the epidural?" Shauna asked as she went over to the table to claim her spot.

"I did, but it wore off by the time it was time for me to push. I asked could they shoot me up again, but they said no because I was fully dilated. Girl, when her head started to come out, I thought the doctor was blowing flames down there. The nurse said something like it's the ring of fire. I started to tell her then cool it off with some cold water or ice cubes, anything that would reduce the burning I was feeling. That pain was excruciating," Serena stressed.

"But once you saw this little face, you had to forget about the pain," I said, rubbing my cheek against Nevaeh's curly black hair.

"That's true. You do forget about the pain you went through, but the fear is still there. And now I'm faced with a child who hates to sleep at night."

"But that's normal. Most infants do that. It will get easier," Vivian tried to convince her.

"Easy for you to say; you are the one getting six to eight hours of uninterrupted sleep," Serena said, crossing her arms with a frustrated look on her face. "I would kill for an eight-hour nap."

"I can watch her for you one night," I offered.

"Is Tyree going to stay with you too?" Serena asked, causing all of us to cackle. "That man ain't going to let her stay nowhere until she's thirty."

"Don't you mean forty?" Shauna joked.

"Exactly," Serena said, pointing to her as we giggled together.

"He can stay too," I said, rubbing her tiny little head.

"Good. Then maybe he won't try to ride me all night."

"You keep it up, you are going to have another little Nevaeh," I said.

"What's with the shades, Shauna?" Vivian asked, staring at Shauna, whose head leaned against her fist as she looked at us around the island.

And just like that, the mood shifted for some reason. I saw Serena give Shauna this look, but she didn't say anything.

"I'm just trying to style and profile," Shauna replied.

"You can take your shades off in here," Vivian suggested.

"I'd rather not," Shauna countered, as her chipper mood changed to a somber one. All of us looked at Shauna then Serena, who dropped her head.

"Uh-oh. What's going on?" Vivian asked as her eyes darted back and forth between the two.

I was lost also and wanted to know what was going on.

"You see. I knew I shouldn't have come over here," Shauna muttered, turning to face the window.

Vivian put down the spoon after she stirred the gumbo, and she went to Shauna. She pulled the shades from her face. When she did, we both gasped. "What the hell!" Vivian yelled.

"It's nothing," Shauna said, rubbing her bruised face.

"So a black eye is nothing these days," I said.

"Serena, explain please," our matriarch, Vivian, demanded as she walked back over to the stove.

"Her and Cal got to fighting, and he got the best of her. That's all," Serena explained like it was no big deal.

"That's all. You saying it like that's nothing," Viv said heatedly.

"Why are y'all just telling us?" I asked, trying my best not to raise my voice since I was holding the baby.

"We figured we would wait until today. It wasn't any need getting anybody else involved," Shauna said, looking at Serena, who turned her head like she didn't know anything.

"Anybody else. Wait." Vivian held her hand up. "Who else was involved?" Vivian asked.

"Big Ray, Pookie, Gerald, Tyree, and Phoenix," Shauna listed.

"Y'all can call them, but you can't call us. That's messed up," Vivian said furiously, walking over to the fridge to retrieve the lemonade she prepared.

"It wasn't like that, Viv. I wanted to handle this on my own, but some people thought it was in my best interest to call the cavalry," Shauna said, eyeballing Serena.

"I didn't do anything. It was Phoenix."

"But you called her."

"No, I didn't, Shauna. I told you she came over because we were supposed to go walking. She saw your car and knew you were there. Y'all know I'm not good at lying. She questioned me until I caved in, and things happened from there," Serena explained.

"All I have to say now is that y'all are lucky I'm even here. I didn't want to come. I heard it all before. I don't need it today, too. I know everything I need to know, and the main thing is I'm not taking him back before y'all come out your mouth with it," Shauna snapped. "So leave it alone."

All of us held our hands up like we were done with the subject. We knew when it came to Shauna's business, she never wanted anybody in it. This was why we only knew what she wanted us to know. Really she was much like Vivian in that way. They liked their privacy.

"Fine. I guess it's wrong for us to care," Vivian said, scooping ladles of gumbo into a large bowl she took out of her cabinet. While she did this, the room was quiet.

I kept my attention on my niece as we watched Viv scoop the liquid into the bowl. Once she was done, she picked up the steaming hot gumbo and carried it to the table. "Let's forget about this for now and eat," Viv suggested.

"What about Phoenix?" Serena asked.

"I'm not waiting on her anymore. She knew what time to be here. I'm tired of Phoenix thinking the world revolves around her. So if y'all ready, let's dig in," Viv said, and we all gathered around the table to get our grub on.

Chapter 13

Phoenix

I had a good reason why I was running late to Vivian's dinner. It was a man, of course. My sisters might not think it was a good enough reason to be late, but I thought it was, especially when it benefitted me. My extra, Eldon, was over, and I had to get me some of his yum-yum first. Lucky for me, Tobias wasn't home to mess up my flow. He went to play golf with some buddies of his, and while he was gone, I got my workout on with Eldon.

Eldon called me to see if he could drop by, and his timing couldn't have been more perfect. He was leaning against the doorframe trying to be cool, but it looked odd on him. Cool was the last thing Eldon was. He stood six feet one inch, 190 pounds, wearing a tight pair of jeans with a button-down blue-and-white striped shirt with a red bow tie and black slick bottoms. He wore his red-framed glasses today, I guessed to match his bow tie. Who wears a bow tie in the middle of the day, with denim jeans, no less? As hard as he tried to be cool was as hard as he was a royal failure at it.

I almost burst into laughter at his attempt, but I managed to hold back my hilarity. He was a little out of the ordinary from the men I was used to dealing with. The men I messed around with were damn near thugs or the business-corporate type. It was hard to place Eldon in either of these categories. Maybe *nerdy* was a better term, but this nerd had stacks of money and didn't mind hitting me off with some of his hard-earned cash every now and then.

Eldon not only had money, but the man knew how to eat some pussy. The man stayed hungry for it, and I really loved that he stayed hungry for me. As soon as we got to my bedroom, I couldn't get my panties off fast enough before he was laying me down on the bed. He dove between my thighs, feasting like it was Thanksgiving, I was the turkey, and my liquid pleasure was the gravy that saturated his face. He acted like he hadn't eaten in days and I was the meal that would conquer his hunger.

I sent up a big thank-you to the heavens as he salivated over my nucleus. He licked and sucked and plunged his tongue and fingers deep inside me. I was ready to hand this man an award for best pussy-eater ever, and I had quite a few who made attempts. Some failed miserably. Some could hold their own, but after having Eldon lay down his proficiency, it was hard to think of any man who could make me feel like this with his tongue.

I could feel my gravy running rapidly, yet he consumed it like he was drinking from a gravy boat.

"You taste so good," he muttered through licks.

I moaned my approval by saying, "Yes, baby, eat. Eat me good, baby."

I know I climaxed at least five times before he came up for air. Not only could he eat, but he would stay down there for a long period of time. When he came up, he wiped his face as I lay back, thinking I could go right to sleep now. His job was done to excellence. I could see his Johnson angling to get inside me, but this was the time I was ready to end this feast fest of ours and send him home. As much as I enjoyed Eldon eating me out, when it came down to the penetration, he really didn't do a good job with his stroking performance. One gift took away from the other. As good as he could eat me was as bad as he could screw me. He was really bad at it.

Honestly, there were very few men who held the title of total package in my book, and that's a man who can eat and fuck me like a champ. In Eldon's case, he could only eat. It wasn't like he had a very small penis. It was average, but he just didn't know what to do with it. That "motion in the ocean" crap was true, because when he tried to ride the waves of my ocean, his paddle got lost and the next thing I knew, Eldon was crashing to shore, releasing moments after he entered my sandy beach. I guess I shouldn't complain when it took him a minute or two to reach his orgasm. That was all of him I had to endure.

Yes, I hesitated, not wanting him to enter me, but since I knew it wouldn't take long, I let him inside. Like I thought, Eldon was crashing to the shore of my sandy beach, and all I had to do was gyrate my hips to pull his explosion from him quicker.

I was running late and needed to get cleaned up so I could leave. Unfortunately, this time I think I showed my disapproval for his motion in my ocean.

"What's wrong?" he asked after he bust his nut, panting like a dog needing water.

"Nothing," I said nonchalantly.

"It's something. You don't look pleased," he said, unclogging himself from me.

"I was pleased until you put your dick in me," I said, not thinking.

"What?" he asked, frowning.

I pushed Eldon off me and got up, saying, "Eldon, I enjoy what we do, but—"

"But what?" he asked, sitting there like a bump on a log.

"But you can't fuck. I'm sorry to be so blunt about it, but you can't."

"Yes the hell I can," he defended himself.

"No, you can't, sweetie," I said, scrunching my nose.

"Then why are you involved with me?"

"I'm with you because I like the way you eat my pussy. From what you lack in your strokes, you totally make up in your tongue. I swear if I could make your tongue platinum, I would certify it today, so you shouldn't get too upset, because at least you got that going for you," I tried to say convincingly.

Eldon got up off the bed and began gathering his clothes like a kid who was picked last on the playground. "I didn't come over here to be insulted."

"It's better you hear it from me than somebody else," I said, standing there buck-naked.

"I haven't had any other complaints from women," Eldon said.

"What woman do you know will complain? Most just lie there and deal with it. I did for a while, but I've gotten tired of pretending. I like to get into what I'm doing, and if you're not doing it for me dickwise, then I have to say something. Hell, life is too short to fake the funk."

"I guess you think you are the total package?" he asked angrily.

"You're here, aren't you? Not only do I taste good, but my cooch moved enough to make you cum in less than one minute flat, so yes, I think I'm the total package," I said, giggling. "You got a nice-sized Johnson, but you couldn't keep it wet inside me long before you were losing it."

Eldon was putting on his shirt when he caught on to me laughing at him. From the way he paused, his look went from one of anger to one of pure rage. Next thing I knew, he came over to me and grabbed me by the arm.

"What do you think you are doing? Let me go," I demanded.

"You want to get fucked, I'll fuck you," he said, pushing me back down on the bed. I wasn't scared. I was actually excited by his take-charge attitude. Now, this was what I was talking about. To urge him on, I started taunting him.

"What? You're going to fuck me now? Please don't if you aren't going to last but one minute again. I don't think you can handle my wetness for five minutes."

Eldon flipped me to my stomach, pulling my hips in the air.

"Don't let my fat ass cause you to shoot prematurely now," I teased.

Eldon pushed his Johnson inside me, causing me to take note this time. Not only did it feel bigger, but it felt like it was in control this time.

"Is this good enough for you?" Eldon shot back, plunging in and out of me. I didn't reply, because I didn't think he was going to last long again. Talk was cheap. Eldon had to show me what he was made of.

"If you last five minutes, I might scream your name," I coaxed.

Eldon pushed deep, hard, and with vigor. That nerdy man who showed up had disappeared, and now a champion had emerged. I turned my head to the right to look at my nightstand at the clock and realized he had lasted two minutes. I guessed he noticed what I was doing and plopped his body on top of mine to get me from looking. He came down and tongued me. I turned my head away as he continued to slide in and out of me. There was nothing gentle about this, and I liked it. I could feel my body coming to the point of heightened exhilaration. Eldon was doing his damn thing.

Making a mockery out of Eldon ended up being the best thing I could have done for him. This man put in work, causing me to reach my climax three more times, something I had never done from his manhood. When he finally finished, I turned to look at the clock to see he lasted forty-six minutes. I turned onto my back and clapped my gratification for a job well done. He was sweating profusely. His anger had turned into animal magnetism, and I loved every minute of it.

When Eldon left, I had an extra $2,000 in my purse after I told the sad story about falling behind on my mortgage. I guessed he wasn't mad at me anymore, and I damn sure had to pay respects to him for doing a damn good job at pleasing me.

When I arrived at Vivian's house, my sisters were already eating. They were damn near finished.

"So y'all are just going to start without me? Y'all never started without me before," I said, sitting at my place at the table.

"If you get any later, we might be washing dishes and putting the food up next time you come late," Vivian said.

"Probably was a man who made her late anyway," Shauna interjected, being right, but I wasn't going to admit it.

"I overslept," I said.

"Until six forty-five this afternoon?" Serena questioned.

"Y'all, I couldn't help if I had company," I said, picking up the ladle to scoop the mixture into my bowl.

"Like I said: a man," Shauna repeated.

"Shut up and go put some ice on that black eye," I joked, but I knew she wouldn't laugh. And she didn't.

"Phoenix, don't make me—" Shauna started before Vivian interrupted.

"Please don't do this today. Let's have a nice dinner without the arguing, okay?"

"On that note, I have something to tell y'all," Dawn said. "I was waiting for Phoenix to get here before I said anything."

"Let me eat some of this gumbo so I'll be able to stomach whatever you have to tell us," I said, picking up my spoon and putting the mixture into my mouth. I savored the food and thought, *Damn, this is good.*

"You ready now?" Dawn asked sarcastically.

"Hold up. Let me take another bite," I said, picking up the spoon two more times, putting some of the gumbo into my mouth. I held up my thumb, giving her the go-ahead, but I wished I would have waited to swallow before she belted the words:

"I'm getting married."

Chapter 14

Dawn

The room fell silent as Phoenix's spoon halted midair. She coughed and started choking on her food. Shauna reached over and hit Phoenix on the back until her coughing fit got under control. No one was saying anything. They were looking at me like I had something bizarre written across my forehead. Serena got up from the table looking like she was mad. She went over to the sink and rinsed her empty bowl out before putting it into the dishwasher.

"Let me be the first to break the ice. Who are you marrying?" Phoenix asked with a perplexed look on her face.

"I'm getting married to Corey, that's who. Stop acting like you don't know who I've been in a relationship with."

Phoenix shook her head. I heard Shauna sigh like she disapproved. My sisters were known for saying whatever came to their minds, and now none of them had anything to say. This caused me to get heated.

"No congratulations. Y'all not saying anything," I said.

"Congratulations," Vivian said.

I couldn't tell if she meant it. Their silence put me in a place of being uncomfortable. I was beginning to take their reaction the wrong way. I studied Vivian to see if she was sincere, but she was stone-faced. She didn't look happy, but she didn't look upset either.

"Thank you," I said apprehensively.

Another silence fell upon the table, and I blurted, "What's the problem, y'all? What the hell is with the silent treatment all of a sudden? Are y'all not happy for me?" I asked.

"We are," Vivian said.

"Stop lying, Vivian," Serena said, drying her hands off on the kitchen towel as she stood over the sink.

"I'm not lying," Vivian defended herself.

"Yes, you are," Serena argued.

"Y'all tell me the truth. You never hold back, so don't do it now," I said, looking around at each of them.

Vivian was eyeballing Serena. Phoenix was still eating on her gumbo, and Shauna was shielding her eyes with those sun shades so I couldn't see her eyes at all. From her index fingers massaging her temples, I felt like she didn't like the idea of me getting married either.

"Is anyone going to say anything?" I asked, glancing around at each of them.

"Okay, here it is. Who the hell are you fooling?" Serena asked, walking over to the table, but she didn't bother to take a seat.

"What is that supposed to mean?" I asked, looking up at her.

"I mean, why are you getting married to a man who can't keep his damn dick in his pants? How many times has he cheated on you? Seven?" Serena asked.

"More like seventy," Shauna chimed in.

"But he's changed," I reminded them.

"Since when?" Shauna asked, still rubbing her temples. "Did he get some type of counseling or sex therapy teaching him how to remain faithful? Hell, he just cheated on you two months ago, and now y'all getting married."

"Sounds like a guilty proposal to me," Phoenix said, dipping her bread into the bowl.

"A guilty proposal?" I asked.

"Yeah. He's trying to take the negative tension off of himself for being a damn dog and bringing something like marriage to the forefront to throw you off. As you can see, it worked," Phoenix said.

"Did it work? She acting like she can't recall the type of man she's marrying," Shauna cosigned. "He pulled a Kobe."

"A what?" I asked.

"A Kobe Bryant. You know, cheat on your girl only to buy her the ring to keep her from acting a damn fool until things die down," Phoenix explained.

"Please. He had this ring for a while," I explained.

"That's the lie he told you," Serena said, picking up Shauna's empty bowl off the table and walking it over to the sink to rinse out.

"Hell, you just got into a scuffle with Paige over them sleeping together the other day, so if it didn't bother you, then that incident shouldn't have happened," Shauna surmised.

"I'm not going into this marriage blind, you guys," I enlightened them.

"Then let's get your ass a seeing eye dog, because your ass is blind as hell if you can't see how wrong marrying Corey is," Shauna said.

This caused Phoenix to spit her gumbo across the table laughing.

"Eeeww," Shauna and Vivian blurted.

"I'm so sorry, y'all. That was a good one, Shauna. I almost choked on that one," Phoenix said, holding one of her hands over her mouth while using the other hand to wipe the spewed residue with a napkin.

"Make sure you wipe all that juice off my table. As a matter of fact, Serena, can you reach under the sink and pass me the Lysol disinfectant wipes?" Vivian asked.

Serena walked over to the table, handing her the container. Vivian opened it, pulling out a couple of sheets for Phoenix to clean up her germs.

"Why can't y'all be happy for me?" I asked.

"We are, but we also don't want to see you walk into something we know is not going to work," Serena said, taking her position back over at the sink.

"You sure you're not jealous because you been with Tyree longer than I've been with Corey and I'm the one getting married?"

"Oh, no she didn't," I heard Shauna mumbled under her breath.

I kept on talking. "Are you mad because Tyree isn't trying to make an honest woman out of you? I thought marriage was supposed to come before the baby carriage," I said defensively.

"Oh, no she didn't," Shauna said again, this time louder than before.

"Yes, the hell I did," I responded angrily. "Y'all are being so damn honest with me. I think I should tell some truth too," I said with major attitude.

Serena took in a deep breath before saying, "First of all, ain't nobody jealous over you and your dog of a man Corey. If I had a man like him . . . Let me rephrase that," she said, walking toward me with her finger in the air, pointing at me. "I'm not going to have a man like him, because I love myself enough to not want to put up with a man disrespecting me by sticking his dick in every woman willing to spread her legs for him. Second, what Tyree and I have going on will still be better than what you have, even without the papers, so get the shit right, Dawn. Ain't nobody jealous of you."

"Please, Serena. You acting like your relationship is first rate. How's his baby mama doing?" I asked with my head tilted to the side like I was pondering this but I couldn't care less.

Serena was really pissed now. She was so mad she couldn't think of anything to say as she practically stood over me with her chest heaving in and out.

Vivian stood to stop her from getting any closer, but I wasn't budging. I looked at her like, "Please try something." I'd got to fighting once in the past few days; I would do it again if I had to.

"You dead wrong for saying that, Dawn," Shauna retorted.

"Why? Y'all can beat up my happy occasion, but you don't expect me to say anything," I responded furiously.

"Everybody is wrong by how they are coming off, but, Dawn, we are also right about how Corey has been treating you," Vivian chimed in.

"Y'all don't have to live with him," I said.

"And we don't want to. Lying piece of crap," Serena uttered.

"Y'all are always against me. You think I'm stupid."

"No one has called you stupid, Dawn," Shauna said.

"Well, I think you stupid," Phoenix agreed.

"Ever since . . . Ever since . . ." I kept pausing.

"Leave it alone, Dawn. It's not that. Plus, this is not the time to bring up the past," Vivian said, figuring out what I was going to say.

"I think it is. I think none of you have ever forgiven me for what happened. That's why I'm treated the worst out of all of us."

"Hold up," Vivian said, standing to her feet with her hands up. "I never once treated you bad, so quit with the damn sob story. You are starting to piss me off now. Quit your damn temper tantrum. Either take what we are telling you as sisters caring about your well-being and happiness, or leave it alone. If anybody here should be mad at you, it's me," Vivian said angrily.

I knew Vivian was right, and I should have left well enough alone. I didn't know why I continued to live in the past, but it was hard not to. I couldn't help the way I felt. I wondered if the feelings inside me would ever get to a place where I would be settled with myself.

"I bet you I know what's going on. Dawn wants to be the first to break this family curse of the Johnson women," Phoenix said, finishing up the last of her gumbo.

"What curse?" Shauna asked.

"You know, the one where there hasn't been a woman in our family to get married for at least four generations. She wants to beat us to the altar," Phoenix said. "Not that I want to get married. I want to be single forever."

"I'm getting married because I love Corey, not because I'm trying to break some damn curse. Why can't y'all see that?"

"You can't sit here and tell me you don't love the fact that you are having a wedding. You've talked about this since you were a teen. Now your dream is coming true," Serena said. "And Corey knew this. He's playing with your emotions, which is the reason why he asked you to marry him in the first place. He was counting on your love for a wedding to shield his need for cheating."

"All I can say is I think you should wait," Shauna warned.

"This coming from you," I said.

"Damn right. I told y'all I'm never getting married either. I agree with Phoenix. I don't need a damn piece of paper confirming my love or commitment to a man. I do love the idea of a wedding, but all I want to do is walk down the aisle in my wedding dress to say I did it and walk the hell up out of there."

"Without saying vows?" Phoenix asked, giggling.

"Exactly. That's what most women want anyway: the actual wedding," Shauna explained.

"Would you have the reception, too?" Serena asked.

"Hell yeah. That's the best part. I would dance in my dress and kiss my man and be happy we are not legally bonded," Shauna said. "Dawn, maybe you should do the same thing. Corey is not the man you supposed to spend the rest of your life with. You know it. I know it. All of us know it. So stop fooling yourself, because you damn sure ain't fooling us."

"Amen," Serena agreed, her lips tight with aggravation.

"Y'all need to leave Dawn alone. Let her have her wedding with the man she loves," Phoenix said. "She's already following in the footsteps of her mother."

"Watch it," Vivian said.

"What? You don't remember when Daddy couldn't keep his dick in his pants?"

"Phoenix!" Vivian yelled.

"Well, it's true. What fantasy world are y'all living in to not remember that? Mama would've been a damn fool to marry our daddy too. As much as we love him, he is a male whore," Phoenix let slip.

"Our grandmother and great-grandmother had cheating men too, and you see they didn't bother to get married either," Serena cosigned.

"Here you are starting your marriage off with the same kind of man who has already slept with multiple women, and you want to make him legal," Phoenix said, chuckling.

"Cheaters learn how to get better at cheating. I mean, come on. Like he's going to come and say, 'Baby, I slept with another woman last night. Please forgive me,'" Shauna said, trying to mimic Corey's voice.

"The one thing y'all are forgetting is our daddy wasn't the only one who cheated," I said.

The room fell silent then.

"Mama cheated on him also."

"Can you blame her, Dawn? She got tired of him doing it, so she did it too," Phoenix responded. "I would have too."

"Two wrongs don't make a right," I countered.

"True, but in the end, both of them forgave one another and that's all that matters," Shauna said.

"Is it? Has Cal asked you to forgive him for whooping your ass?" I asked sternly.

Vivian and Serena shook their heads. I knew then what I said was a low blow, but hell, I was mad. I was tired of them beating up on me and the decision I was making to marry Corey. Yes, in my anger I may not have said things the right way, but I was mad.

"Aw, you have done it now," Phoenix said, picking up her bowl and going over to the stove to scoop her some more gumbo out of the pot, since the bowl on the table was empty.

Vivian and Serena snickered nervously, but Shauna wasn't laughing at all. All of our tempers were bad, but Shauna's was the worst. I watched as her jaws tightened and she gritted her teeth. I knew she was getting ready to let me have it, but I wasn't prepared for how far this disagreement would go.

Chapter 15

Shauna

Was this Beat Up On Shauna Week? I had had enough of people thinking they could come at me any type of way. First it was Cal thinking it was okay to put his hands on me. Then it was Phoenix and Serena wanting to handle things for me and Phoenix telling me I better not go back to him. Then it was Viv mad because I didn't say anything to her at all. Now I had Dawn casting out low blows because she was insecure in her relationship. She was upset because she, in actuality, wanted our blessing and we didn't give it to her.

Now because she felt bad about what we were saying, she wanted everybody to feel bad like she did. I had enough misery of my own without Dawn kicking me when I was down, and she should have known I was the wrong one to come for.

Taking my shades off, I looked around the kitchen and saw my sisters eyeballing me. My temples throbbed. My heart sped up its rhythm as my wrath began to ascend in my throat to the point of choking me. I began to tremble. I bounced my knee anxiously, knowing I was on the brink of snapping.

"I think we need to end this conversation before more feelings get hurt," Vivian suggested, trying to pacify the situation as she sat at the head of her kitchen table.

"I agree. We need to let this go and talk about something else," Serena agreed, looking at me. She shook her head at me, knowing what was coming, but I didn't think I could hold my temper back. Serena mouthed the words, "Leave it alone," shaking her head again.

I closed my eyes and dropped my head into my hands, trying to listen to what she was telling me, but I couldn't. The more I thought about what Dawn said, my throat closed up even more with the pressure of me trying to maintain what yearned to be released.

"All I wanted was a peaceful evening with my sisters, but I guess that was too much to ask," I said with my head down.

"You forgot who your sisters were," Phoenix joked.

"Evidently, but I thought today would be better. I mean, I knew you all would get on me about my eye," I said, pointing at my discolored bruise, "and what happened with Cal, but for it to be used in the way you used it . . ." I lifted my head to stare at Dawn. "This is why can't nobody say anything to you. You sitting here playing Ms. Self-righteous by dissing what happened to me, not wanting to look at this fake-ass relationship you have."

"Oooh. Shauna said fake," Phoenix said, giggling more as she spooned more gumbo into her mouth.

"You sitting here bragging about my fight when you just got your ass whooped by Paige, who screwed your soon-to-be husband. By the way, did you enjoy the banana show?"

Phoenix was steady cracking herself up over at the counter, leaning over her bowl and listening. Dawn shot her an evil glance, but Phoenix rolled her eyes and kept on eating.

"I didn't ask to get beat by Cal like you didn't ask to get crabs from Corey."

Phoenix spit her gumbo across the room again when I said that. This time she was coughing, choking, and laughing at the same time as she went over to the sink and coughed up the rest of gumbo that had lodged in her throat.

"What is it with you spitting your food across my kitchen?" Vivian asked. "In my sink, Phoenix? Why don't you stop eating?"

"Would you rather it had been on your floor?" Phoenix retorted once she gathered herself.

"The only difference with me, Dawn, is I'm not going to take Cal back. A man putting his hands on me is a lesson learned. You, on the other hand, didn't you have to go to the doctor to get treated several different times for STDs Corey brought back to you?" I asked cruelly.

Dawn scowled at me without saying anything as Phoenix stood holding her chest, still trying to recover from her choking a second time that night.

"I think I'm done. Damn, Shauna. I wish you would have warned me with that one. That was a good one. Who gets crabs these days? I thought the critters were extinct. Corey had to be digging into the dirtiest and oldest poon-poon to catch that," Phoenix said, still laughing.

This caused Vivian and Serena to giggle too.

"You might as well be talking to the wall, Phoenix, because Dawn ain't hearing you. She's not going to be satisfied until she catches a disease she can't get rid of. But I wish you the best of luck with that, sis," I said coldly, putting my hand on my forehead and saluting her. "Now, go on with your fake-ass wedding, but don't expect me to support you in ruining your life."

"So you saying you're not coming to my wedding?" Dawn asked.

"That's exactly what I'm saying," I answered, getting up from the table and walking over to the island, needing to get away from her.

"Do all y'all feel like that?" Dawn addressed our other sisters, looking at each of them.

Vivian was the only one at the table with Dawn, but the other two were standing at the stove and sink while I glared at her from the center island.

"I'm just saying Shauna has a point. No matter how you try to make shit smell like roses, it's still going to be shit," Phoenix said.

Dawn giggled agitatedly and said, "Y'all jealous."

"We jealous?" Phoenix asked.

Dawn held her hand up for her to shut up as she stood to her feet.

"You see. She hasn't heard anything we said. That's why I can't talk to her," I said, turning away.

Dawn looked at me first and said, "Shauna, you mad because you with a woman-beater who damn near killed your behind. But why should we be surprised when most of the times you pick men who don't do anything for you anyway? They have no job, no money, and not a pot to piss in, but you run to them like something stupid."

I turned to face her with my eyes stretched, but before I could say anything pertaining to what she said, Dawn turned her anger to Vivian.

"Vivian, you mad because you don't have a man. You have booty calls, or I should shorten it to *a* booty call. You think you are the rock of this family, but you really not. If you were so strong, you wouldn't let your ex-man use you when he's good and ready to. But keep doing what you doing, because you might get a man one day."

Dawn then turned her attention toward Serena and said, "You have a man, but you were dumb enough to have a child with him out of wedlock. Get used to playing wifeym because as long as you are with him, his son, and his baby mama, you and Nevaeh will always be second best."

"Dawn has lost her ever-lovin' mind," Serena replied.

"And now to my baby sister, Phoenix. You're nothing but a high-class whore. You walk around all the time dressed to kill, with money all in your pockets and living a lifestyle none of us understand, but we know you pimping yourself out. Ass for cash, right?" Dawn said, taking away that smirk Phoenix had had on her face most of the night. It was now replaced with a scowl.

Dawn continued to say to her, "No man wants to turn a whore into a housewife, so I understand why you have chosen to never marry. No man with common sense would want to marry a common whore."

"Okay, that's it. I'm going to kick her ass," I said, snapping as I dropped the towel I was wrapping around my hand to relieve the anger bursting to release, but that was it. I was so done with Dawn's mouth. I sprinted across the room so fast she didn't see me coming. Vivian jumped up and stepped in my path to stop me as Dawn stepped back, knowing I was about to snatch her up.

"You want to talk truth? Here's the truth," I yelled.

"No, Shauna, don't do this," Vivian urged, but I ignored her as she continued to hold me back from putting my hands on Dawn.

"You settling just like our dad did when he chose to sleep with your mother and leave our mom for her. You're calling Phoenix a whore. What was your mother?"

Silence fell upon the room as each of my sisters looked around at one another. Viv was the one breaking the awkward silence by yelling, "Shauna, that's enough!"

But I was ticked off. Dawn wanted to take it there and hurt people's feelings. She was about to get a dose of her own medicine.

"After all we have done for you. After our mom took you in as her own daughter when your mother committed suicide because she couldn't handle the fact that our daddy wanted to come back home to us. She was too weak to want to live for you. You want to throw around jealousy."

"Shauna, no!" Serena screamed with tears forming in her eyes.

"You are jealous of us. You can't accept the fact our dad chose our mother and tossed yours to the side. You can't turn a whore into a housewife; isn't that what you said? She was a side whore who settled and would rather die than live for you, and now you are doing the same thing: settling. I guess you are going to die for this punk, too."

"Stop it, Shauna," Viv said, trying to cover my mouth, but my rage was stronger as I removed her hand and kept spewing the anger that had built up for years.

"We always treated you like you came from our mother, but you have always thought you were better than us, somehow, which I can't understand, because you are the result of adultery. You sitting here talking about Serena's baby being born out of wedlock. What about you? At least we were created in love and not lust."

"Please, can somebody shut her up?" Serena begged.

Vivian tried to push me out of the room but couldn't. She then tried to put her hand over my mouth again, but I moved her hand and continued my rant.

"You thought we were the enemy, but it was our father," I said, moving my arms in a circular motion to include all of us, "and your mother," I said, pointing at Dawn, "who tore this family apart. And, who was the rock that held us together and looked beyond blood to be the bigger person? Our mom. Who took you in? Our mom," I said, beating my chest. "Who loved you regardless of how you were created? We have. And who has been there for you despite the bad circumstance? We have."

Tears began to stream down Dawn's face. I knew my words were cutting her deep as I hoped they would. The truth had been dormant for way too long. We all went on like things were great, never speaking of this, but today I was letting Dawn know how it really was. She needed to be reminded so she could get knocked down off that self-righteous pedestal of hers and see things the way they really were.

Serena, along with Vivian, was wiping tears now also.

"So that's how y'all have felt about me?" Dawn asked glumly.

"No, Dawn," Vivian answered.

Dawn was trying to hear what anybody had to say now. She reached down to pick up her purse, which was hanging off the back of the dining room chair she was sitting in. She wiped tears away as she pulled out her car keys, saying, "I don't need none of y'all to show up to my wedding. As far as I'm concerned, our sisterly bond has officially been severed," she said shamelessly as she exited the kitchen and stormed out of Vivian's home.

Chapter 16

Shauna

Once I calmed down, I immediately regretted what I had said to Dawn. My sisters were looking at me like I'd done the worst thing imaginable. Vivian was so livid she didn't say anything to me. She started clearing the table and putting things up like we weren't in her house. In our commotion, little Nevaeh had woken up, so Serena was tending to her. She was sitting at the island on the barstool feeding her, and Phoenix was leaned against the wall, gaping at me.

"Y'all, I'm sorry," I said sincerely.

"I can't believe you, Shauna," Vivian spat. "How could you do that to her?"

"She made me mad and I lost it."

"You more than lost it. You destroyed Dawn in the process, and possibly this entire family. You know we have promised ourselves we would never speak on those events, especially in anger," Phoenix reminded me.

"I know, and I can't enough that I'm sorry," I pleaded.

"The person you need to be saying sorry to is Dawn," Vivian urged.

"Do you think she's going to want to hear anything I have to say after what I just did?" I asked.

"Hell naw," Phoenix said. "But you are still going to have to apologize. Call her now and see if you can get her. You shouldn't go to sleep with this lingering in the air among us."

I took Phoenix's advice and pulled out my cell phone to call Dawn. Pulling her number up, I dialed it. The call was sent straight to voicemail. I tried again, only for the same thing to happen.

"She's not accepting my calls," I said dejectedly.

"Well, can you blame her?" Viv asked, putting the leftover pot of gumbo into the refrigerator and pulling out a bottle of Moscato. "Now she's thinking this is how all of us feel, and it's not that way at all."

"Honestly, I've thought about telling Dawn the exact thing Shauna did," Serena confessed, looking down at little Nevaeh drinking her bottle of milk.

"So you agree with how Shauna let Dawn know?" Vivian asked, looking in a drawer for the bottle opener.

"Yes," Serena said, looking up and speaking matter-of-factly. "Dawn hit below the belt first, and Shauna returned the blows."

"I can't believe what you are saying right now," Vivian retorted, finally finding the contraption that would get her closer to easing her stress with a glass of wine.

"For years I've had an issue with Dawn, but I embraced her because it wasn't her fault she was brought into a situation of adultery, just like it wasn't our fault our daddy created another sibling outside his relationship with our mother. It wasn't Dawn's fault her mom gave up on life. At the same time, we were supposed to go on like this happy little family, letting her come into the fold like everything was sunshine and rainbows. I've never understood that. Did anyone ever think how it would affect us?" Serena asked.

"Exactly," I agreed, nodding to what Serena just said.

"Mom wanted it that way," Phoenix reminded us.

"Did she, or did she feel sorry for a child who didn't deserve the hand that was dealt to her?" Serena asked.

“Mama was good for helping people,” I agreed. “So why not help the very child her man created? She had already taken him back. What was she supposed to do, tell him, ‘I don’t want that child in my house’ after hearing Dawn’s mother blew her brains out?”

“Regardless of how things played out in our past, what happened tonight never should have happened. We have all come a long way,” Vivian argued.

“Dawn always starts stuff by running that mouth of hers, and she can’t ever take it when she’s on the losing end of the situation. Case in point, Paige. And let us not forget what she did to our dad.”

The room fell silent then.

“Our dad is in jail because of her,” Serena said, picking up Nevaeh and laying her over her lap to burp her as she bounced her leg gently. “Have you all forgiven her for putting him there? Because I haven’t. I love Dawn, don’t get me wrong, but it’s been difficult for me to pretend I don’t have a problem with her.”

“You’ve done an awesome job hiding your feelings,” Phoenix said.

“I didn’t have a choice. I didn’t want to be the one rocking the boat on us getting along,” Serena revealed.

“Don’t put this on us. You could have said something or brought it up before now,” Phoenix said.

“And then what, have y’all mad at me and talking to me about how I need to forgive and forget? Y’all know y’all would have done that,” Serena replied.

“You’re right,” Vivian agreed.

“Look, I went ballistic tonight. It brought things out that should have been brought to the forefront years ago. Now it’s time to deal with them,” I said.

“I’m not ready to deal,” Vivian countered, surprising us all.

"Why? You are always the one who wants to work things out," I said.

"Things are not always what they appear to be," Vivian responded.

"What does that mean?" Serena asked.

"Look, I'm done talking about this tonight. I'm ready to go to bed," Vivian said, clicking off the light over the sink.

"I guess that's our cue to leave," Phoenix said, walking over to the table and grabbing her purse. "We Johnson sisters never fail to entertain, regardless of the outcome."

"You ain't never lied," Serena agreed, picking up a now sleeping Nevaeh and hopping down off the stool carefully. She walked over to the carrier and placed little Nevaeh in it, strapping her down for the trip home.

"One day these issues are going to have to be dealt with for us to move on. We can't keep pretending like they don't exist. That's all I'm saying," I said, looking at Vivian, who was still holding her unopened bottle of Moscato. I guessed she was waiting to open it after we left, probably fearing we would want some, which I would. I wasn't going to push it. She was ready for us to be gone, and I was ready to go home.

"Tonight doesn't have to be the night to resolve our issues, so let's sleep on it and figure out what to do later," Vivian said, practically pushing us out of the door.

Yes, I had opened a can of worms, which had been created a long time ago, and now I was the one who turned the can over, making a mess of things. This was our elephant in the room that we had been ignoring for quite some time. We didn't realize how the actions of our father would affect us in the long run. Tonight seemed to be filled with skeletons rolling out of the closet, and I couldn't help but wonder what other remains were going to appear before all of this was over.

Chapter 17

Vivian

As much as I loved these dinners with my sisters, I was always glad when they were over, especially tonight. Like always, there was an argument and disagreements. Who knew tonight Dawn's soon-to-be marriage would be the beginning of a squabble that caused issues from the past to spill out like red wine on white carpet? These issues were the tarnish we couldn't get rid of. For Dawn to go off on us like she did was so uncalled for, but the response Shauna delivered was way worse than anything Dawn said. I wondered if our relationship could withstand some of the things that came out of her mouth tonight. I didn't think so, and I wished things would have been left alone. As deep as the wounds were dug, I wasn't sure this time was the right time to heal them.

Even in all of that commotion, I'm not going to lie, a part of me was a bit jealous of Dawn announcing her soon-to-be wedding. I was the oldest, so I felt like I should have been the first to get married. At the same time, how could I be jealous when I didn't even have a man to tie the knot with? She was right about that. My career was my man. I was making money and buying my home and car and basically living a lucrative life, but all of this was done with no one to share it with.

As together as it seemed like I had it, no one knew the turmoil that brewed beneath my exterior. My hair stayed done, nails done, everything done. I sauntered like I owned the world. I looked like I had it together, but deep down inside I didn't. I think the toll of trying to be this perfectionist was finally catching up to me. Around people I could fake it better than anybody, but once I was alone, the reality of everything always hit me like a ton of bricks. My mind became the devil's playground, and some of the things he'd been telling me to do scared me.

After work, all I looked forward to was coming home, slipping out of my clothes, and crawling into bed. There had been days when I didn't get up until the next morning without so much as a morsel of food consumed. My bed was my haven. One of the things that seemed to take my mind off my own issues was watching other peoples' lives unfold on reality TV. I would watch it until sleep took over. This was when I was my happiest, in slumber land without having to do a thing but rest. It was the only time when my mind was in a state of peace.

Crawling into my refuge with my Tinker Bell sleepwear on, I turned on the TV, jumping quickly back into my routine. It was a little after 10:30 p.m. and I was surprised, after all the drama tonight, that I wasn't sleepy. I guessed Dawn's engagement and Shauna's mudslinging were more than I could handle. I wished I could be happy for Dawn, but I couldn't. How could I, when I felt like my life was somewhat over at the ripe age of thirty-four? I had become a hermit. The only drive I had was with my job. When it came to quality time with me, I shafted myself.

The bottle of wine I gripped earlier was sitting on my nightstand in a bucket of ice. I was waiting for my sisters to leave so I wouldn't have to share any of it with them. Tonight, the entire bottle was mine. I reached over and grabbed it, along with the corkscrew to open it. Twisting it into the cork, I had the bottle opened in seconds. The popping sound was like music to my ears as a small cloud escaped the bottle. I reached over and put the corkscrew down and grabbed my wine glass. I was almost tempted to drink out of the bottle but thought a glass would be better.

Filling the glass halfway, I gulped down the cold, delicious liquid. I moaned with delight as the cool liquid made its way down my esophagus. I poured another glass, filling it to the rim. This time I sipped. I put the bottle with the remaining Moscato back in the bucket of ice on my nightstand and got cozy. Leaning back on my pillows, I was going to sip until I felt the wine do its magic and relax me.

My cell phone rang, breaking my tranquil moment. I reached over to my nightstand and answered it. "Hello."

"Yo, open the door. I'm pulling up now."

"What happened to your key, Sheldon?"

"Oh, I forgot you gave me one. I can't get used to having it," he said, giggling with the music blaring in the background. I was surprised he could hear me at all with the way his music was blaring in my ear and I wasn't even in the car.

"Just come in. I'm in the bedroom."

"Are you watching TV or reading a book?" he asked.

"I'm watching TV. There's nothing else better to do."

"I'll be in there in a minute to perk you up."

"Okay, and make sure you lock the door back when you come in. You are good for leaving it unlocked," I told him.

"Like somebody is fool enough to come in there while I'm here."

"A gun doesn't know anybody, so lock it please. You can't play hero if you're dead."

Sheldon laughed and hung up.

All my sisters thought I was a fool to not be with Sheldon. He was fine as hell, but I loved the six-year friendship we had developed, and I didn't want to do anything to jeopardize it. We'd never had sex or even kissed one another. I mean, we kissed each other, but it was on the cheek with a hug. Nothing more than that. He was the fun part of my life, and a lot of times I lived through him. He did bring me joy. I honestly didn't know if I could make it without him.

About five minutes later, Sheldon was walking in my bedroom. "I swear you need to find something else to do other than cuddle in your bed all the time," Sheldon said, coming in. Then he saw me holding a glass. "And you are drinking. You didn't tell me that."

"I didn't think it was important."

"Of course it is when I might want some."

"Sorry. This bottle is all mine. If you want one of your own, you can get it out the fridge," I told him.

"Not even a sip?" Sheldon asked, walking over and picking up the bottle of wine from the bucket.

"Here, boy," I said, handing him my glass. "And only a sip. I know how you do. You will gulp that—"

Before I could get those words out of my mouth, Sheldon downed the wine, leaving my glass empty once again. I frowned at him like, "Really?"

"Sorry, Viv. I needed it after the night I've had," he said, handing me the empty glass.

"Trust me. I've had the same type of night," I retorted. "Well, you look nice," I complimented him, looking at him wearing a pair of dark denim jeans, a black shirt, a black leather jacket, and black Timberlands.

"Thank you," he said, kicking off his boots. He took his jacket off, tossing it on my bench at the foot of my bed. "You know I had to come over here and tell you about my date," Sheldon said, coming over to the bed and climbing in.

"Boy, are you clean? I don't want no other woman's remnants in my bed," I told him.

"Viv, I'm good. You know I know better than that," he said, crawling next to me.

"Okay. I'm just checking. You know you have before," I said, pouring me another glass of wine.

"That was so long ago," he said, smiling.

I looked at him like, "Boy, please."

"So why is your date over so soon?" I asked. "I thought you would be taking her home and hanging out like you do."

"Viv, it was the *Nightmare on Elm Street* reincarnated through this woman," he said jokingly. "I'm never going on a blind date again."

"What? Did she look like Freddie Krueger or something?"

"No, this woman wasn't bad looking at all."

"So what was the problem?" I asked.

He sighed, tilting his head like he didn't want to say, and just his hesitation made me burst into laughter. I said to him, "Sheldon, it couldn't have been that bad."

"Yes, it was. Like I said, this woman was cute and had a nice little shape on her, but her mouth . . ."

"What about her mouth?" I asked.

"I thought Phoenix and Shauna cursed a lot, but this chick had 'motherfuck this' and 'fuck that' flying out of her mouth to the point I was embarrassed to be around her. And I curse," Sheldon said.

I laughed.

"Not only did she curse a lot, Viv, but she revealed to me she had eight kids," he said, holding up eight fingers.

"Eight?" I asked, frowning.

"Yes, eight with seven different baby daddies."

"She told you this?"

"Yes," he yelled like he still couldn't believe it. "Who admits something like that on the first date?"

"Didn't she know that was a date killer?"

"Right," he agreed. "And, Viv, she was only twenty-nine. All night I kept thinking how in the hell do you have eight kids by thirty? You know I love kids, but eight?" Sheldon said, causing me to giggle. "I thought one of her kids was going to interrupt our dinner, singing the song, 'One, two, my daddy's coming for you. Three, four, gonna lock the door. Five, six, trying to get your chips.'"

I burst into laughter again, happy that Sheldon had taken me out of my dreadful mood. He always knew how to do this, even if it sometimes came at the expense of his horrible dates.

"I was looking for a little girl wearing that same dress that kid wore in *Nightmare on Elm Street* for real, Viv. I was scared."

"Boy, you weren't scared."

"Like hell I wasn't," he said seriously.

"Where did y'all go to eat?" I asked.

"Cheddars. You know I love their croissants."

"And you didn't bring me any?"

"Damn. I did. I brought nine. I left them in the car. I'll get them in a minute."

"I'm not going to eat nine croissants," I said.

"I got them for the both of us. Did you make that gumbo like you said you were?"

"Yes, it's some left. I made sure to save you some."

"That's what I'm talking about," he said, rubbing his hands together. "Thanks for looking out, because I know Phoenix would have taken all them leftovers home with her," Sheldon said.

"Oh, believe me, she tried, but I hid some before they all got here. It eliminates one less issue between us."

"So tonight was crazy?" he asked. "I can tell by your mood and your bottle of bubbly."

"Was it? Why did Dawn tell us she's getting married?"

"To who?" he asked in astonishment.

"Corey of all people," I revealed.

"Cheater cheater pussy-eater."

"Sheldon!"

"Well, that's what he's known for in the streets. Dude dives down more than a SCUBA instructor giving diving lessons. Why you think he gets so many women? They're trying to see what the tongue feels like."

"You didn't have to say it like that. You can't say coochie or poon-poon?" I joked.

"Viv, what I look like saying *coochie*? I'm a man for goodness' sake, and I say pussy," he retorted.

"I forgot who I was talking to," I replied, taking a sip of my wine.

"Evidently you did. Now, did you tell Dawn she lost her damn mind?" Sheldon asked, lying down on his left side to face me, propping himself up on the pillows.

"Of course. I think the only one who didn't really argue tonight was Phoenix."

"Tell me you're lying."

"I'm serious. She made her little comments, but me, Shauna, and Serena had it out with Dawn."

"Phoenix always got something smart to say," Sheldon said.

"I know, but tonight she was too busy spitting gumbo all over my kitchen."

"Okay. That explains it. She was busy laughing her ass off, huh?"

"Basically. Shauna was the one who lost it tonight. She got so mad at Dawn she told her she's not going to have anything to do with the wedding," I told him.

"Daaaaamn. Y'all really went at it."

"That wasn't even the half. Dawn decided to tell us about ourselves and ended up throwing all of us under the bus."

"How?" Sheldon asked.

"Well, I'm being used by men. Serena was stupid for having her baby by a man who already has a kid out of wedlock. Shauna's dumb enough to be with a woman-beater. And Phoenix is a whore who's never going to be good enough to be any man's wife," I recapped.

"Daaaamn. Dawn took it there for real. I wish I was here to play referee. It would have been better than my nightmare of a date."

"It gets worse," I said.

"Viv, I don't think it can get worse than that."

"Believe you me it did. Shauna lost it. I mean, she blacked the hell out. She brought back so much stuff I wanted buried from our past that I think only Jesus Himself needs to come down here and be the intermediary between them two now. I feel like this will cause a major rift between us sisters."

"Please tell me she didn't mention anything about Dawn's mother?" Sheldon asked.

I nodded, saying, "She took it there. And now I don't know how to fix it."

"First off, Viv, you can't fix it. It's not up to you to fix everything. All you can do is be the big sister you are. You are putting too much pressure on yourself. Pray about it and let God handle it."

Sheldon was right. I always wanted things perfect, even though I knew this wasn't a perfect world we lived in. It did feel good talking to him about it. Sheldon knew everything about how we grew up. I told him about Daddy cheating on Mom and having a child outside his relationship. I told Sheldon everything. Well, almost everything.

"Enough about my night. What did you do? Because I know you did something. Did you leave her sitting at the table? Because you're good for ditching a woman," I said, looking at *Family Guy* on Cartoon Network.

"I was a gentleman this time. I stayed as long as I could stand her, and then I was honest and told her I had somewhere else to be. She didn't seem happy and made it known."

"How?" I asked.

"Viv, she went off on me in the middle of this restaurant, talking about I was leaving her to go sleep with some other woman."

"Shut up," I said, putting my hand to my mouth.

"She said she felt disrespected because she was really feeling me and was hoping our relationship was going to go to another level."

"Damn, she was getting ready to make you baby daddy number eight," I said, laughing.

"I felt like that too. I only knew this chick for a couple of hours and she acted like we had been dating for years. You know I hate confrontation because of my temper, Viv. I told you on several occasions I need anger management."

"Boy, do I know," I said sarcastically. "So what did you do?"

"I tried to be nice," Sheldon explained.

"What did you do?" I asked again.

"I called her out her name and told her she didn't know me like that."

"And?" I said, knowing there was more.

"And I told her she was a whore and needed to learn how to keep her legs closed and I wouldn't sleep with her if her pussy spit out hundred-dollar bills."

"Sheldon!" I yelled, hitting him on the arm.

"She deserved it. She screamed on me until I exited the restaurant. I don't know if I can ever show my face there again."

"Take me next time," I said jokingly.

"They might turn me away at the door once they see me coming with another female," he said, causing me to laugh.

"Well, I'm glad you escaped without any charges being filed."

Sheldon was so nice and sweet, but don't let his laidback demeanor fool you. He really did need anger management. I think he liked confrontation. His frame alone was intimidating, since he lifted weights a few times a week. He wasn't real big, not like those weightlifters looked with veins popping out of their necks. Sheldon had a nice build, but his size was threatening to some people.

One time Sheldon and I went to the grocery store to get items to have a hot dog night, so we could chill and watch movies. While we were in the bread aisle looking for some hot dog buns, this middle-aged Caucasian man came walking up and stopped right in front of us, blocking our view. Sheldon looked at me, pointing at the dude like, "What the hell?"

"It's okay," I said, upset by this man's ill manners also, although I couldn't show this because I knew how Sheldon was. He wasn't racist, but as an African American man, he felt like he was always been targeted. I do believe this has been the case sometimes. So when it came to some races, he felt like he needed to be on guard, and for this man to blatantly stop dead in front of us like we were a nonfactor ticked both of us off. One disrespectful person doesn't define an entire race in my book, and Sheldon believed this too, but when things like this happened, his judgment sometimes got clouded.

"Yo, my man. You didn't see us standing here looking for bread too?"

The man turned and looked at Sheldon but didn't say a word. Then he turned back around like Sheldon didn't say anything. I knew it was going to be on now. Here was the nonfactor situation that this man put us in, and Sheldon was about to let him know the true facts about the type of man he was.

Sheldon stepped around the dude, getting all up in the man's face. "Did you hear me talking to you, man?" he asked furiously as the man backed up fearfully now. "Where are your damn manners?"

"Don't make me call the cops," the man said.

"You see, Viv, this is the type of shit I'm talking about. The man sees I'm black and immediately thinks the cops need to be involved," Sheldon addressed me.

"Sheldon, it's okay. Let him get his bread and go."

Sheldon turned his attention back to the middle-aged man and asked "How are you going to dial the cops with broken fingers and the ability to not say nothing once I knock all your damn teeth out your mouth?" Sheldon threatened.

"I just came here for some bread."

"So did we, before you rudely stood in front of us. Now, I would advise you to get the hell out of here, but not before apologizing to this young woman." Sheldon gestured toward me.

The man ended up saying he was sorry. He looked at me when he said it, because Sheldon was still up in his face. I nodded it was okay, but I did that because I wanted this to be over. I didn't want Sheldon to get in trouble.

"Sheldon, he said he was sorry. Step back and let the man get his bread," I told him.

Sheldon listened, and the man left without any bread. I was waiting for management or security to come and escort Sheldon out of the store, but no one ever came, thank goodness.

Then there was the night we went out to a bar for drinks and this dude wasted a drink on Sheldon's back. Instead of apologizing, the guy started laughing like it was funny. Sheldon punched the guy in the face, breaking his nose. Sheldon ended up with an assault charge, having to pay the man's medical bills. So yes, he did need to get some help for his anger.

"Viv, I'm going outside to get the bread. Can you heat up some gumbo and we can have a little pajama party?" he asked.

"You don't have any pajamas."

"I came prepared. I packed a bag just in case to come over here. So I brought some."

"Well, aren't you the one who plans ahead?" I said.

"I knew it in my gut that this date wasn't going to work, and I was right. I should have stayed here and ate dinner with y'all."

"We can eat now. Go get my bread and I'll heat us up some gumbo," I said, pulling the covers back to get up and go into the kitchen. I drank the last bit of wine that was in my glass.

Sheldon jumped up too, sliding on his boots to go get the bread. My night had turned around quickly, and I was happy for the diversion. Thanks to Sheldon, my evening was turning out to be a good one after all.

Chapter 18

Dawn

Just when I didn't think my night could get any worse, I was being pulled over by the police. I merged over to the shoulder of the road, with the police car doing the same. I did not need this right now. I wiped at the tears that were steadily falling from my eyes. More tears trickled down my face as I watched the officer walk up to my window and tap on it.

"Good evening, ma'am," the African American officer said, with his left hand holding a flashlight and the other hand on his gun.

"Yes," I said angrily, looking up at him. His skin was dark like chocolate. I scanned his body, which looked like he worked out. The uniform was tight across his chest, and the silver shield identified him as Officer Winn.

He shined the light around my car to see if anyone else was with me, which there wasn't. "Can I see your driver's license and registration please?" he asked.

I reached into my glove compartment, retrieving my registration. I then pulled my license out of my wallet and handed both to the officer.

He shined the light down on it and then asked, "Do you know why I pulled you over, ma'am?"

"No, sir, I don't." I shrugged, answering him through tears, which were still trickling from my eyes.

"Are you okay, ma'am?" he asked, bending down a bit to get a better look at me.

"No, not really. I've had a really bad night," I explained.

"I'm sorry to hear that. And I'm pretty sure this isn't making it any better," he said kindly.

"You would be correct."

"I'm just doing my job. I pulled you over because you were doing forty-two in a twenty-five mile an hour zone."

"Okay," was all I could say. I was so defeated at this point I didn't care. I was hurting. I was sad. I was angry. He stood there like he expected me to say something else or talk my way out of this, but I didn't have any fight left in me. I wasn't Phoenix, who would probably show some cleavage or pull out her breast to get a warning, or Shauna, who would probably cuss the officer out and get arrested. I was Dawn, the Dawn who had no fight left.

The officer must have caught the hint and said, "Ma'am, I'm going to run your information. I'll be right back." He walked to his car and got in.

I saw there was another officer with him and a camera on the dashboard, recording this violation. I lowered my head, willing the tears to stop falling, but they wouldn't. As hard as I tried, the stress of my evening won and broke me down. I didn't want to look up, because I didn't want the people riding by, as their speed slowed after seeing the flashing lights, to see who it was who got pulled over. Just like I had done in the past, they were probably counting their lucky stars it wasn't them.

Minutes later, the officer was back at my car with a slip of paper, letting me know he went through with giving me the ticket. *Great,* I thought. *Like I should expect anything less with the type of night I'm having. Let's just add more things to my already terrible evening.*

"Sign here, ma'am. This is stating I stopped you for doing forty-two in a twenty-five mile an hour zone. Your court date is here if you want to dispute this. And here is the address you can mail your money to if you decide not to dispute it. There is a number here if you have any questions. Do you understand what I have told you tonight?"

"Yes," I said dejectedly.

"Honestly, I would have let you off with a warning, but my superior officer is with me, and I had to do it," he said kindly.

I nodded as I agreed and signed the paper. I didn't care. I took the ticket, rolled my window up, and tried my best not to squeal tires as I pulled off.

When I walked into the house, I walked to the den to see Corey lying on the couch, watching a football game. I was so happy to see him.

"Hey, baby. How was dinner?" he asked.

"Horrible," I said, dropping everything in my hands to the floor.

"Baby, what's wrong?" he asked, sitting up. "Come over here," he said, patting the spot next to him.

I did what he asked and fell into his open arms.

"I guess you told them about us getting married."

"I thought regardless of how they felt about you, Corey, they would be happy for me, but they jumped on me, saying you are a dog and a cheater," I said through tears.

"Wow. Strong opinions coming from people who mean nothing to me in my life," he said.

"But they mean something to me. Rather, they did," I said glumly.

"You can't help who your siblings are, but you can control your own happiness. I hope being with me will make you happy," he said, kissing me on the cheek.

"You do make me happy, baby," I said, wrapping my arms around him.

"I know I've made mistakes, and I hoped they wouldn't hold those mistakes against me, but I guess I was wrong. I have changed. I hope you can see that. They haven't changed your mind about us getting married, have they?" he asked.

I looked up at him, saying, "No. I want to be your wife."

"Even if it costs you your sisters?" Corey asked.

I paused, thinking about it for a minute. I knew I hadn't told Corey the full story about what happened tonight, but he didn't know everything that pertained to my past either, and I wanted to keep it that way. I was pretty sure there were things I didn't know about his also, so why tell him how my life had turned out? All he knew was my real mother passed away. He didn't know which mother I was referring to, because as far as he knew, my sisters and I had the same mother and father. He knew my dad was in jail, but he didn't know the real reason why. I told him it was for embezzlement and fraud. Of course, that was a lie. I knew going into our marriage with a bunch of lies was wrong, but what else was I supposed to do? My business was my business, with the exception of my sisters knowing the huge aspects that made up my dysfunctional life.

Until tonight, I didn't know the things that happened had affected them like they did. Shauna's words hurt more than anything I'd felt in my life. It began to make me wonder how they all really felt about me. I felt like the black sheep, and in a way I was, due to the fact that our dad and my real mom caused all this drama in our lives. Why did we, as the children, have to pay for the sins of our parents? As mad as I was, I had to look at all sides, which was something I was not ready to do at this time. My antagonism prompted the floodgates to release devastation on us. I could have heard what each of them had to say and kept it moving, but I had to push back like I always did. This time it backfired, leaving me brokenhearted and my spirit destroyed. I had to figure out how I was going to put the pieces of this situation back together.

My sisters were my world, but Corey was going to be my husband and my life. He should come first before them. After what went down tonight, it made it that much easier choosing him over them.

I looked up at Corey and said, "Even if it costs me my relationship with my sisters, I'm going to be with you forever."

"I love you," he said, kissing me again and wiping away my tears. "I can't wait to make you my wife. I want a big wedding. I want everybody to know how much we love one another. So . . ."

"So, what?" I asked, smiling.

"You ready to make some money for this extravagant wedding we are going to have?" he asked devilishly.

"You want to do that tonight? We did it last night."

"I know. We said a couple of times a week, but the more money we can make, the better. Did you see the last amount of money we made?" Corey asked.

"Yes," I said, remembering my excitement when I had seen four figures.

"Then let's make this money, baby," he said, chuckling.

"Okay. Give me fifteen minutes to freshen up and get ready. You go set everything up," I told him, removing myself from his arms and rising from the sofa.

"It's already done. All I need is my leading lady," he said, causing me to blush.

Corey smacked my behind, causing me to giggle. Even though my night had turned out horrible, I was going to make sure the ending was fantastic.

Chapter 19

Serena

I got a crazy baby mama in my life. I'm not talking about her getting on my nerves every now and then. I'm saying she's literally crazy. The elevator don't go all the way to the top crazy. It gets stuck in the damn basement where darkness lies crazy. I'd never been a person who was scared of anybody, but this demented chick had me reconsidering.

"Is you and your baby dead yet?" she asked, calling my house for the seventeenth time that day. "Your baby too ugly to be living. Maybe you should drop her from the second floor of your house."

"Trick, I told you to stop calling my damn house," I yelled.

"Or what? What are you going to do?"

"Keep calling and you will find out."

"I been calling you, bitch, and you ain't done a damn thing. You ain't nobody, and neither is that ugly baby of yours," she yelled.

"Oh, okay. I know what this is about. You mad because Tyree is with me and I gave him the daughter he's always wanted and you couldn't," I taunted.

"I'm pregnant now with his child, bitch," she revealed.

"In your dreams," I tried to say back with confidence, hoping she didn't hear the uncertainty in my voice from her revelation. I can't lie; her saying that was like a gut punch, but then again, everything she said to me was gut punches. Still, a small part of me wondered, was she telling me the truth?

"No, bitch, in my reality. You think you have Tyree all to yourself. Please. He comes over here all the time, and it's not only to see his son. He keeps coming back to get some of my good pussy."

I didn't believe Juanita. After all the hell she took Tyree through, the sliced tires, the bleached clothes, getting him fired, and even cheating on him, he would be a damn fool to go back and screw her.

"If you call my house one more time, I'm going to call and have a restraining order put on you for harassment," I threatened.

"Well, get ready to dial, because I'm going to call as many times as I damn well—"

I hung up on her. I didn't have time to argue with this trick. As soon as I walked away from the phone, it rang again. I looked at the caller ID to see it was Juanita again. I clicked the line on, but immediately clicked it right back off, hanging up on her again.

Tyree walked into the kitchen, yawning and wiping the sleep out of his eyes, asking, "Who keeps calling?"

"Juanita, that's who," I said furiously. "You better check her, Tyree, or I'm going to hurt her, and I mean it," I warned.

"Baby, calm down," he said nonchalantly.

"Don't tell me to calm down. She calling here asking me if our baby is dead yet and how I should drop her from the second-floor window. I mean, who does that?"

"Juanita," Tyree said, walking over to the coffee pot on the counter and pouring himself a cup of coffee like this was a normal day for him.

"Tyree, I'm tired of this. It was bad enough she had the nerve to call me in the hospital while trying to deliver

Nevaeh, wishing we both died during childbirth. Now she's calling our home."

The phone rang again, and I picked up the receiver to see it was her again. I held the phone up to show Tyree, and he held his hand out to take the phone.

"Naw. Let the voicemail pick it up. The more threatening messages she leaves, the more evidence I'll have against her to file harassment charges and put a restraining order against her," I said, slamming the phone down on the counter.

"You don't have to do all that," he said, walking over to the kitchen table to sit down.

"You suggested I do that at the hospital. Then you talked me out of it for your son's sake. She's taking this thing too far. I listened to you and left it alone, but look where that has gotten me," I said with outstretched hands.

"She's not worth it. She's mad because I chose you, babe," Tyree said convincingly.

"Are you sure you chose me? Because she told me you two are still sleeping together and she's pregnant with your baby."

Tyree took a gulp, forgetting he was drinking hot coffee. He yelped as the hot liquid burned his mouth. He ran over to the sink and ran cold water into his hand, cupping it as he brought the liquid to his mouth to help cool it.

I stood there with my arms crossed. Was that a sign of guilt or what? He was that damn nervous to forget what he was drinking. "So you are sleeping with her," I said suspiciously, hoping his further behavior wouldn't make the hairs on the back of my neck stand up more than they already were.

"No," he said, standing and turning to me. "You know I don't want her."

"Then why burn yourself?"

"You caught me off-guard. There is no way in the world I would ever go back to her. I regret the day I ever met her."

I gave him a skeptical look.

"Come on, Serena. I wouldn't do that to you or my daughter. For goodness' sake, she's threatening my child. I couldn't be with anybody like that."

The phone rang again, and again it was Juanita. He dropped his head in defeat as I held the phone up again for him to see it was her. I waited for the phone to stop ringing and decided to listen to the voicemail messages to see what else this trick had to say. I put the phone on speaker so Tyree could hear what his baby mama was saying.

"You have five new messages. First message . . ."

"Bitch, I know you still at home. Don't make me come over there and check you and that ugly baby of yours. Will y'all please die already? It would make this world so much better. Two ugly bitches gone for good. So kill your baby first, and then kill yourself."

I saved that message and went to the next, looking at Tyree like, "You see what I'm saying?"

Second message: "Trick, pick up the phone. I need to speak to my man for a minute. His son would like to speak with him. Pick up, trick. I know you there."

I saved that message also, still looking at Tyree, fuming with each message that played.

Third message: "Say, 'Die, bitch,' . . . Die, bitch."

Tyree stood straight up then. Juanita had the nerve to have their son on the phone repeating what she was telling him to say.

I looked at him and tilted my head at him like, "Now what?"

"Say, 'Your baby ugly.' . . . Your baby ugly.

"Say, 'I hate you.' . . . I hate you.

"Say, 'bitch.' . . . Bitch.

"Say, 'bitch' again. . . . Bitch.

"Say, 'Kill yourself, bitch." . . . Kill self, bitch."

"That's enough!" Tyree yelled.

I saved that message too. I started to listen to the next one knowing it was from her, but I decided to click the phone off. I placed the phone down on the counter and looked at him. "But you don't want me to file charges."

"I can't believe she's got my three-year-old son saying that," Tyree said in disbelief.

"Believe it. If she can do that, Tyree, what else is she capable of? I'm trying to protect our daughter here. You might not take Juanita seriously, but I do. I remember the stories you told me she did to you when y'all were together, and it was enough to make me leave you; but I didn't because I loved you too much. I'm here now, with your daughter, in our house, trying to make this work, but, Tyree, I can't deal with Juanita. Something has to give," I pleaded.

Tyree walked up to me. He wrapped his arms around me and pulled me close to him. "Babe, I'm sorry. You are right. You don't deserve what she's doing. If you want to call the cops, I'm behind you."

Tyree backed away a bit to look down at me. I looked up and our eyes met.

"I love you, Serena. I love our daughter. Do whatever you got to do, okay?"

I nodded and leaned in to kiss him as the phone rang once again.

Chapter 20

Vivian

I didn't know who to talk to, but the first person who popped in my mind was Renee. Man, I missed her for times like this. I really needed her shoulder right now. Then I thought about Dawn, but she wasn't speaking to me, so she was not an option. Shauna was at work, and Phoenix didn't answer her phone, so that left Serena. I called her, and she told me to come right over, which I was happy about.

Serena and I didn't talk much without the others around. It wasn't like I didn't love her. I was used to turning to Renee before she passed. Now that she was gone, I turned to Dawn with my issues, and I saw where that had gotten me. She used my situation against me. I called Dawn to apologize about what happened, but she kept sending my calls to voicemail. She had yet to return my call. Why I was apologizing was beyond me, but I felt like somebody needed to step up and try to start mending things between us. I was willing to do that to get back our sisterly bond, but nothing was working. Dawn was stubborn, but I was persistent and wouldn't stop bugging her until she spoke to me. But today that wasn't going to happen. I was going over to Serena's home to talk to her about some things going on with me.

I walked into my niece's nursery to see Serena changing little Nevaeh's Pampers. My niece was not happy about it either. She was screaming at the top of her little lungs and had the nerve for some tears to run down the sides of her little face.

"Aw, what's wrong, sweetie?" I asked, leaning down and rubbing her head, but she kept squalling.

"She's mad because I'm changing her butt. Some days she's good, and other days she squeals like this. I think this time she's hungry, but I didn't want to feed her without getting that poop off her first," Serena said, snapping her pink onesie and then picking Nevaeh up. "You can stop crying now, Miss Thang. I'm going to feed you," Serena told her as Nevaeh whimpered. She even had the nerve to stick out her bottom lip before she burst into tears again.

"Can I feed her?" I asked, putting my purse on the first shelf of the changing table.

"Sure," Serena said, handing my niece to me.

She was still crying. I placed her on my shoulder and bounced with her for a bit, but it wasn't working. Serena picked up her bottle out of the warmer and put it to her cheek. She then squirted some of the milk on her wrist, checking the temperature, making sure it was perfect.

I sat down in the reddish brown swivel chair trimmed in pink contour lines and the matching ottoman, which was positioned next to the window. I didn't know the cushiony chair glided until I sat in it. "I like these chairs," I said, looking at an identical one on the other side of me. A pink table sat between the two chairs positioned right under the window.

"They were a gift from Tyree. He wanted us to have two so one of us wouldn't feel left out on nights we could sit in here together."

"Aw, that's sweet. Have you guys sat in here together yet?" I asked.

"We sit in here a lot. I think it's the tranquil innocence of the space. This room definitely calms me," Serena said, looking around the nursery.

I put Nevaeh in the crook of my left arm, covering her with her pink receiving blanket. Serena handed me the bottle, and I placed it in my niece's little mouth. As soon as she felt the nipple, she began sucking the warm liquid down.

"You see. She eats all the time," Serena said, gathering the dirty Pampers up and placing it into the Diaper Genie. "Would you like something to drink? I got water, juice, and soda."

"I'll take some water," I said, gliding back and forth.

Serena left the nursery. I looked around at how my sister had decorated the space. Light pink was on the walls. Nevaeh's name in white letters was over the espresso-colored crib. Pink-and-brown bedding adorned the crib with ruffles and soft blankets. The closet was open to reveal the tiniest of clothes hanging up. And it was full. This room was beautiful and serene. I leaned my head back, continuing to rock back and forth in the rocker. I looked down at my niece. She had her little fist balled up around her face as she looked up at me.

"You are so precious," I said to her. I knew she couldn't understand what I was saying, but she had to feel my words were said in love.

Serena came back into the room, putting the water down on a coaster she placed on the pink table. She then sat down in the glider across from me and began drinking the bottle of water she brought for herself.

"Serena, you have done a beautiful job in this nursery."

"Thank you," she said, looking around at her work.

"I know you were surprised to hear from me," I said.

"It has been a while since you wanted to talk to me. You usually talk to Dawn. I guess she's not an option now," Serena said.

"You're right. She's not speaking to me right now."

"Nevertheless, I know whatever you have to say has to be big for you to come over here and see me," she said, taking another sip of her water.

"I hope you don't mind me wanting to talk to you?" I asked, looking down at Nevaeh, who was still looking up at me.

"Girl, I don't mind. I'm here for you always. So what's going on?" Serena asked, getting more comfortable as she brought one of her knees to her chest, with the other tucked beneath her. My sister looked comfortable in a pair of gray drawstring pants and a white tee with a gray feather print on the front.

"Before we get started on me, what's wrong with you?" I asked.

"Nothing. Why are you asking?"

"Come on, Serena. I can tell something is going on with you. I know we don't talk often, one on one, but you are still my sister. I can tell when something is up with you."

She sighed and paused, taking another sip of her water. She looked at me and said, "You didn't come over here to hear my problems, Viv."

"Just like you just told me and, yes, I'm going to give your own words back to you. I'm here for you always."

Serena smiled and got up off the chair, walking out of the room. For a minute I thought I had offended her, but I couldn't see how. It wasn't long before Serena came back into the room. She plopped down in the chair with an envelope in her hand. When she held it up for me to read, my mouth fell open.

"What in the hell is that?" I asked.

"It's what it says it is," she explained.

"But medical facilities aren't supposed to print up envelopes like that. That's an invasion of someone's rights to privacy. Hell, I know about the HIPAA laws."

"This was in my mailbox today," she said glumly.

"Stop lying," I said.

"Vivian, I wish I were."

I was looking at a stamped envelope addressed to Tyree Coleman. In big, bold capital letters across the front for everybody handling this piece of mail to see, it said HERPES TEST RESULTS INSIDE.

"Did you open it?" I asked.

"You damn right I did. Sis, I was so mad I forgot about any federal offense laws and the possibility of me being arrested for opening his mail. I didn't care. I had to see what was inside."

"And?" I asked curiously.

Serena reached in the envelope, pulling out the piece of paper. She opened it and began reading it to me:

"Get checked, Tyree, because you may have herpes. And since you have been sleeping with me, I thought you should know you need to get checked. Sorry for any inconvenience, sweetie. Love, Juanita."

"You have got to be kidding me," I said in astonishment.

"This woman is certifiable. I mean, who does this? She sent this through the postal service on purpose, stamped, delivery confirmation and all. Look where it came from," Serena said, pointing to the postal stamp.

"New York," I said.

"Exactly. This bitch just left New York, taking her son to visit with some of her family. She sent the letter from there with this official-looking envelope," Serena explained.

"I'm sorry, sis. My problem is nothing compared to what you are dealing with right now. Does Tyree know?"

"Yeah, I showed it to him and he was pissed."

"I hope he hasn't left to go over and confront her," I said.

"He said he wasn't, but who knows. As mad as he was, he might have. Really, I don't care at this point. This is too much for me to deal with. I was so happy when you called me this morning wanting to come over."

"I feel bad now."

"Please don't. As you can see, I needed you as much as you need me. Now let's stop talking about me. What's your deal?" Serena asked.

"I did something that I think I might regret," I began to reveal.

"And what's that?" She looked at me suspiciously.

"I slept with Sheldon," I said, flinching like what I said hurt.

"For real?" she asked excitedly. "When?" Serena damn near jumped up and down on the chair.

"The night of our disaster dinner. He came over after his hell date, and we chilled out like we always do."

"I know it was good. He looks like he can lay some good pipe—and real long pipe," she said.

"Serena," I said, giggling.

"I'm sorry, but that man is fine, Viv. I know it was good, wasn't it? I want to know. Give me all the juicy details," she said eagerly as she propped her elbow on the arm of the glider and leaned in to listen.

I paused before saying, "It was real good. I mean, it was so good he had me *gon* good. G-o-n, gon. No man—and I mean no man—has ever made my body feel like Sheldon did."

"Damn, Viv. He put it down on you like that?"

"It was so good, Serena, that when we got up the next morning, we did it again, and it was just as good, if not better, than the hours before. I was sore as hell, but I didn't care. To have that man's body next to mine felt right," I said, looking down at little Nevaeh's eyes beginning to close.

"So, what now?"

"That's just it. I don't know. Sheldon and I are best friends."

"A fine best friend at that," Serena said.

"Now that we've crossed this line, I wonder how is this going to affect our friendship. This man knows more about me than y'all do. He knows my favorite ice cream and has seen me looking my worst without makeup. He knows my bad habits and deals with my attitudes no matter what. He knows about all the men I've slept with and vice versa. We are so close that if I get a pimple, this man will pop it. We pass gas around each other. As crazy as all this sounds, Serena, I love him for that. He is my comfort zone."

"Wow. He sounds like the perfect man for you, Viv," Serena said in a suggestive tone.

"But he's my perfect friend. I never thought of him as my man."

"Never?" she questioned.

"Never," I said.

"Y'all didn't talk about what happened that morning?"

"When we finished, we both fell back to sleep. When I woke up, he was gone."

"You haven't called him?" Serena asked.

"And say what? 'Hey, how's it going? By the way, let's talk about the sex we had the other night'?"

"Yes," Serena blurted, chuckling.

"I can't do that."

"Why are you scared?" my sister asked.

"I just am. I can't explain it."

"You have known Sheldon forever. Talk to him. You will be okay. Just like you said, this man knows everything about you, so regardless if you talk to him now or later, when you do see him, he's going to know something is up by your demeanor."

My sister was right. I never looked at it like that. This man could read me like a book.

"I don't want this to ruin our friendship. Sheldon is the best thing that's happened to me in a very long time. I could confide in him about anything, Serena. If sex changes this between us, I'm going to be devastated."

I removed the bottle from Nevaeh's mouth and picked her up, placing her on my shoulder, patting her back to burp her. She was sound asleep and looked so beautiful. I could feel her little breaths on my cheek, which caused me to smile.

Serena said, "Viv, you can't pretend like this never happened. You never know; you might get around him again and your hormones might start to rage. You know you are going to jump his bones again."

"It can't happen again," I disagreed.

"If you say so, but I know it is. If it's as good as you say it is, and for that man to come back for seconds the following morning, it's going to happen again. You two need to talk this over if you don't want it to ruin you all's friendship for real."

Serena was right. As much as I wanted to pretend like nothing happened, my body let me know it did. I could still feel the residual effects of what his manhood brought to my body. Thinking of Sheldon used to make me happy. Now the thought of him made me horny. I loved him as my friend, but I loved him even more as my lover. I didn't want to fall in love with him, but in a weird sort of way, I already had. The sex took it to the level I'd been fighting a long time. I didn't want to feel this way if he didn't feel the same about me. I knew that was what my hesitation in this entire situation was about: him not feeling anything for me after our night together.

I hoped Dawn wasn't right. I hoped Sheldon wouldn't be another man who would use me for what he could get out of me. But why should I think this way? This was my best friend. He would never use me. I did know him better than that. What I didn't know, and feared most, was if this would break our bond. The thought that I could lose him saddened me.

Chapter 21

Vivian

I took Serena's advice and decided to call Sheldon, who agreed to come by and see me that afternoon. I was so nervous. I had never been nervous about him coming over. This man could walk in my house without knocking and it hadn't bothered me one bit, but now I was pacing the floor like a stranger was about to walk through my door.

Every time I heard a car drive by my house, I peeped out the window to see if it was him. I was disappointed at least ten times, until I looked out and saw Sheldon's gray SUV pull up in my driveway. Just like Sheldon to have this music blasting when he arrived.

I wrung my hands together, hoping it would help decrease the uneasy energy rocketing throughout my body, but it wasn't working. I then went over to my loveseat to sit down like things were cool. I had to look normal. I had to act like what happened between us didn't affect me one bit.

My front door swung open and Sheldon walked in, saying, "What up, Viv?"

He was in a great mood, which helped a bit with my own anxious mood. I smiled and said, "Hey, Sheldon."

"I see you chilling. And you not in the bed," he said, tossing his keys on the coffee table. "That's good to see."

When he said I wasn't in the bed, I got more rigid, because I kept envisioning the two of us having sex.

Sheldon sat down beside me on the chair, and I pushed back a bit, sitting with my legs beneath me. As usual, this man looked sexy as ever. He smelled even better as I caught a whiff of his cologne. Black and gray were Sheldon's favorite colors, so it was surprising to see him in dark blue denim jeans and a bright green collared polo shirt and white sneakers. Of course, his clothes fit his body like a glove. Just looking at him brought out sensations in me that I knew I had to restrain, the main awareness being the sudden throbbing between my thighs.

"Man, I'm tired," he said, slouching down and leaning his head back on my sofa.

"You had a rough day?" I asked as casually as I possibly could.

"It was a'ight," he said, pushing his dreads from his face. He didn't have them tied back today. He was letting them hang freely around his chiseled face. He had a midnight shadow effect going on, as his beard had grown in slightly. It looked sexy on him. I liked when he let a little stubble grow.

Sheldon continued to say, "I washed my ride, did a little bit of grocery shopping, and then washed some of my clothes. You know, the small stuff you let go until you really need to do it."

"I know. I need to wash clothes myself," I admitted, trying to sound normal, but I guess I didn't.

Frowning, Sheldon tilted his head and asked, "Is everything okay with you?"

"Everything is good," I lied. "Why do you ask?"

"Are you sure? Because earlier you sounded like something was wrong. Now you're looking like you about to cry or something. Did something happen?"

"No," I said.

"Please tell me it's not Eric or your sisters again," he said, reaching over and putting his hand on my knee. Just that touch caused me to become tense, but the smell of him caused me to drip.

Trying to urge the sexy thoughts of Sheldon out of my head, I said, "I'm done with Eric. As for my sisters, nothing has changed really between us. The only one I've talked to since the altercation is Serena."

"Okay, so what's going on with you?" he asked, staring back at me as he got more comfortable with the cushions of my loveseat.

Sighing, I said, "I called you over here to talk about what happened between us the other night."

"Okay. I was wondering when we were going to get around to talking about that."

"So what happened, Sheldon?"

"You don't know?" he said jokingly with a smirk on his handsome face.

"Boy, I know, but you know what I'm saying. How did it happen? We are friends. Best friends at that," I said, sincerely happy that the conversation was underway.

"You talking like what happened between us was a bad thing," he said apprehensively.

"No. I'm not saying that. I don't want what happened to affect the friendship we have," I said.

"And how will it do that?" he questioned, clasping his fingers together as he positioned them across his broad chest. I felt like this was some type of defense mode, but I kept talking.

"You know once sex gets involved things change," I said.

"Nothing has changed for me. Are you trying to say it has for you?" he asked.

"I don't know," I said with uncertainty. "I don't want what happened to change our friendship, that's all. I love what we have."

Sheldon nodded as his full lips thinned from bringing them together. This let me know he really wasn't feeling what I was saying. Then he stood, saying, "Okay. I understand. Look, I got to go. I got some things to handle."

Standing, I said, "Sheldon, what's wrong?"

"Nothing's wrong, Viv. I got what you saying."

"So why do you seem upset?" I asked worriedly.

"I'm not. I just got things to handle," he said, opening the door. "I'll talk to you later." And out the door Sheldon went, leaving abruptly.

And there it was: the changing dynamic of our friendship that I feared would happen. I didn't know how to take his reaction. The awkwardness crept in. I was wondering, should I have said anything at all? He came in fine but left distressed. Maybe I should have kept my mouth shut and pretended like nothing happened; but something did happen, and no matter how many times I tried to erase the moment we had with one another, it crept back like raging waters during a flash flood. I'd thought about our moment at least a hundred times.

That night we had ended up falling asleep after eating in bed and watching a mini marathon of *Family Guy,* which was one of our favorite shows. The next thing I knew, Sheldon was cuddled up behind me, asleep. We were in the spooning position. His arm was around my waist. I had to admit I loved when he did this. We did this quite often, and at times I did wonder if that was what friends did. Nevertheless, I felt like this was how it was supposed to be.

I tried to fall back to sleep, but it was difficult with Sheldon's hardness against my behind. Feeling it up against me did cause emotions within me to stir, but I knew I couldn't react to them. I also couldn't figure out why, of all the times we'd done this, I was now turned on by this man's body being pressed up against me like this. Had he always been erect like this and I never paid attention? No, as big as he felt, I knew I would have remembered this feeling.

I closed my eyes and tried to fall back to sleep. Sheldon shifted a bit. It seemed like he moved closer to me, pushing his stiffness into me. I think I sucked in breath when he did this. I must have, because the next sound I heard was Sheldon asking me a question.

"You okay?" he muttered.

Hearing his voice startled me. I thought he was asleep. I replied by saying, "I'm good."

"Why you jump?" he asked in his deep baritone voice.

"I didn't."

"Yes, you did."

"Boy, go back to sleep. You talking crazy," I said, trying to play it off as his hardness continued to stimulate me.

"I know why you jumped, Viv," he said, moving his hand to my hips. He began rubbing me soothingly, sending tingles through me.

"Why?" I asked naively.

He pushed himself closer to me, causing me to feel his full erection even better, saying, "This is why."

I couldn't say one word. His manhood stole my voice. Sheldon continued to stroke my hips. With each stroke the heat between my thighs intensified. As much as I liked it, I didn't move. I didn't know what to do. He was my best friend, and things like this weren't supposed to happen.

He nestled closer to me, his chin resting in the crook of my neck. I could feel his warm breath on the nape of my neck. I knew my heart was pounding at this point, and I hoped he didn't hear it or feel it. Sheldon then kissed the nape of my neck gently. It was a seductive kiss, the kind of kiss where I felt the warmth from his mouth and the softness of his lips, which made my body quiver.

My mind was spinning and my womanhood was throbbing. The more he stroked and laid kisses on me, the more turned on I became.

Sheldon tugged on my shoulder, turning me to my back. He wanted to take this further, which made my heart thump even more. I didn't think it could pound any harder. I didn't want to push him away and say this couldn't happen, but I didn't know if I wanted this to stop. Was it the wine? Was it feeling his hardness against me, or was this inevitable? Either way, I was going to go with the flow.

Sheldon propped himself up on his elbow and gazed down at me. I wouldn't allow myself to look at him. Not yet. I peered up, looking at the ceiling. He gripped my chin, gently tugging for me to face him. Our eyes met. He didn't say anything, but the expression on his face told me everything I needed to know. He wanted me. Sheldon leaned in and kissed me tenderly. Just our lips converged, soft sensual pecks done leisurely and seductively. I didn't kiss him back. I closed my eyes, relishing the fact that this was happening but wondering what we were doing. It wasn't seconds before my lips perked up to gently kiss him back.

What started out as a sensual kiss soon became animalistic. Sheldon began to kiss me deeply. I recklessly responded as I threw myself into him. His hand roamed my body, becoming familiar with it for the first time ever in this erotic way. As much as I was enjoying this, I was still uncomfortable, because I wasn't happy with my body.

I released our kiss and tried to pull away from him, thinking this was going way further than I thought it should, but Sheldon wouldn't let me. He begged, "Please don't pull away from me."

The way he said this mesmerized me into a trance to obey. He kissed me again, this time letting his hand maneuver its way to my womanhood to explore regions that had been off-limits during the duration of our friendship. Sliding his hand beneath the material of my PJs, Sheldon found my opening. One of his fingers parted my lips as another made its way inside me. Gently plunging as far as he could push his fingers into me, he skillfully pleasured my womanhood, making it drip with bliss. I was in heaven.

Sheldon removed his hand from me after I reached an orgasm. He smirked at my quivering body and climbed out of the bed. He pulled the covers back and then proceeded to get on his knees. He began to remove my bottoms, exposing the body I was unhappy with. I wanted to pull the covers back over me to hide myself, but I got comfortable with the fact that the darkness helped in him not seeing me fully. Once my clothes were removed, I could hear him scuffling around. I knew Sheldon was removing his shorts also. My heart was thrashing so fast I thought it was going to come up through my throat and suffocate me. What in the hell were we doing?

Before my mind had a chance to register an answer, Sheldon climbed on top of me, pulling the cover around his waist. Like magic, my legs opened wide, welcoming him to cross into my threshold. On one elbow, he reached down and angled his manhood to my opening. The tip touched my lips, but he didn't push himself into me immediately. He brought his hand back up and began kissing me again. The tip teased but never entered me completely as his tongue engulfed me. Just the anticipation of him thrusting forward was enough to make me want to have a panic attack. It was the not knowing when he would enter me that was driving me crazy. Each time I thought this was the stroke as he continued to tease me with his head, he didn't thrust his way in. I wanted to lose it. I wanted to say, "Stick it in already," because I couldn't take his hesitancy.

I finally got my wish. Sheldon propelled forward with all of his depth, penetrating me like no man had ever done before. My nails dug into his masculine back as he submerged his girth in my wet walls. In and out of me, he plunged into shallow waters as the rock hardness of his manhood quickly took me to unfathomable depths. Everything about him felt good: the weight of his body, the muscles flexing in his arms with each stroke, his scent, his sweat, and his taste. I loved it all. It didn't take me long before I was erupting all over his manhood, raining down a tsunami of pleasurable waves. A slight smirk crept across his handsome face as he watched my seismic quake tentatively. With shortened breaths, I asked, "Why are you looking at me like that?"

With that same smirk, he said, "I love the reaction you are giving me."

I didn't know whether to smile or be embarrassed at him watching. I wasn't used to a man looking at me the way he was taking me in. It felt uncomfortable, but I had to quickly think that these were my own insecurities. So I smiled and decided to say, "I love the way you make me feel."

Before this interaction of sexual desire, I wanted to go to sleep, afraid of this very thing happening. Now I was going to sleep because the sex we had put me to sleep. And for us to wake the next morning doing it again hadn't bothered me. I was motivated by the sure excitement of what I knew his body could bring to mine. I wanted him so bad, and for once I didn't care if he saw me. The sex was better the second go-round. This time I was in the "ass up, face down" position, one of my favorites, I might add. Sheldon worked me over like a damn champion.

Back-to-back explosions ripped through me, which slipped me right back into slumber land.

It wasn't until I woke up to see him gone that I began to have regrets. And from the way things had gone down today, our relationship was heading down a road I never wanted to travel with him. I wanted him as my friend, but it felt even better to have him as my lover. One wasn't an option in my opinion, so now what? Where were we going to go from here?

Chapter 22

Shauna

I was at the end of my shift and was having a great day so far. I had made $247 in tips, which made this day even better. I was tired though. I worked hard for every dime of that money. I had a couple of large groups to serve, but it paid off. Twenty more minutes to go and I would be going home.

One of my coworkers came back saying someone was sitting in my section, and I thought, *Damn*. It would be my last table. Didn't it always happen like this? As soon as I was getting ready to leave, I had to start serving another table.

When I approached the customer I said, "Hi, my name is Shauna and I'm going to be your server today." I got tired of saying this sometimes. I hated being fake. It was too much like kissing ass to me; but this time I didn't know I would have an asshole sitting at the table.

As soon as I saw it was him, I turned to walk away, but he grabbed me by my arm to stop me. "Wait a minute, Shauna," Cal said.

"Let me go," I said, jerking away from him. This sudden movement caused a couple sitting behind me to glance in our direction to see what was going on. I turned to look at them and smiled even though I didn't feel like it.

I hadn't seen this man since the night he put his hands on me. My bruises were just starting to go away, and here he was sitting in my section like I was supposed to be cool talking with him.

"I'm going to get someone else to serve you," I said, still with this fake grin plastered on my face. I didn't want to cause a scene and give the patrons around me a reason to be worried; but when Cal grabbed my arm again it was hard not to have this look like some type of altercation was going to break out.

"Please wait. I need to talk to you," he said, gripping my wrist.

"I don't want to talk to you," I said, trying to pull away, but this time he had my wrist gripped extra tight so I couldn't jerk away. I didn't want to cause a scene on my job, but the way he was holding my wrist was pissing me off. I knew I was seconds away from going off on him.

"Look. Calm down, please, and I will let you go," he said, looking around nervously. He had a black-and-orange San Francisco Giants snapback on his head with a matching shirt. Cal had the snapback pulled down so far over his eyes that it looked like he was trying to hide. He probably was, since my cousin Big Ray and them was still looking for him. He must not have cared much if he showed his face here.

I told him again, "Let me go, Cal."

"I will when you calm down," he said through clenched teeth.

"Oh, you are going to let me go whether it's with a scream, with force, or with the cops coming to arrest you for assault," I said sternly.

"Okay, Shauna," he said, releasing my wrist, "but please give me two minutes. Can you please do that for me?"

"What would you like to drink?" I asked him, hoping this would clue him in that he had two minutes.

"I didn't mean to come by your job, but you wouldn't take any of my calls."

"Tick, tick, tick," I said, looking at my watch.

"I'm sorry for what happened. I didn't mean to hurt you. You know I love you."

"Love doesn't require you abusing me like you did. You damn near killed me," I snapped.

"I don't know what happened. I lost it."

"And your losing it caused me many bruises physically and psychologically, Cal. No man has ever put his hands on me, not even my father, and I'll be damned if I'll be with a man who thinks he can," I said angrily.

He dropped his head, clenching his hands in front of him on the table. When he looked up, he had tears streaming down his face.

Wow, he really wanted his apology to look genuine. What pathetic depths did he have to dig down and pull from in order to produce these fake-ass tears? They didn't mean a damn thing to me. This punk cried all the damn time anyway. I think if we watched the childhood movie *Charlotte's Web* this man would cry like a baby. I truly believed he could will his tears to come when he wanted them to. It was his "I'm a sensitive man" thing, where in the past women swooned over men like him. At one time, I was one of those women, but never again. I wasn't a fool who fell for the same trick twice, and no matter how many tears he shed, I was never going back to him again.

Isn't that like abusers? The first ones to smack you upside your head, and then they drop tears later, feeling sorry for what they did. This may work on the Lifetime Network, but here today it meant absolutely nothing to me.

"Babe, I'm really sorry," he said, getting choked up and grabbing his face like he was trying to hold his sobs back.

I looked at him like, "Whatever."

"For real I am. I love you too much to ever hurt you like that again. I want you to know that. I want you to give us another chance. We are great together," he begged.

"Apology noted. Now, what can I get you to drink? Your time is almost up," I said, holding the pad to take his order.

"Shauna, I love you, babe. Please give us another chance."

"I'm not ever getting back with you, Cal. You can cry buckets of tears and it still will never make me take you back. So if you didn't get it before, hear me now. We are done. Your time is up. I will send another waitress to serve you," I said, attempting to walk away, but this fool jumped up from his table.

I looked at him, wondering what his sudden movement was about. I knew he wasn't stupid enough to put his hands on me in here. If he did, I had plenty of eyewitnesses to help put his behind in jail.

"You can't do this, Shauna," he said loudly, causing others to look at us even more.

No, he wasn't doing this here and now. Not at my job. Not when I was fifteen minutes away from leaving for the day. Hell, I would have preferred he confront me in the parking lot. Yes, it was less safe, but at least it wasn't in front of a roomful of people where I made my money.

"You are causing a scene," I tried to mumble as I looked around to see who was watching.

"Is it someone else? Are you fucking another man?" he asked.

"What?" I questioned him like I didn't hear him the first time; and I wished I hadn't, because he repeated himself, but louder this time.

"Are you fucking another man? Is that why you are not taking me back?" Cal yelled.

"Please leave," I said, walking away. I didn't have to stand here and be the target of his craziness.

"All you had to do was tell me. You don't have to be a bitch about this, Shauna. Be a woman and tell me if you are fucking another man," he said, following me.

"Is everything okay?" my manager asked, coming up to me, placing a comforting hand on my shoulder. My manager looked around me to Cal and then back down at me. I knew Cal would take this wrong because that was the type of guy he was. It didn't help that my manager was very attractive. Standing six feet two inches, about 220 pounds, with a clean-shaven face, close-cut hair, and almond-shaped eyes, my manager, Grayson, was hot to trot.

"Oh, is this the guy you fucking?" Cal asked heatedly.

"No, everything is not okay," I answered my manager. "This is my ex, and I told him to leave, but he keeps harassing me," I explained.

"Sir, we are going to have to ask you to leave," my manager told Cal.

This infuriated him even more.

"Is this your loverboy?" Cal asked, ignoring Grayson. I refused to answer him.

"Leave," I told Cal.

Cal began to come toward me, but my manager stepped in front of me. "Sir, please leave," Grayson demanded.

"I'm not going no damn where," Cal said, stepping so close to Grayson that they were practically nose to nose.

Without flinching or stepping back, Grayson calmly replied, "Then we are going to call the police and have them remove you."

"Call them. I don't give a damn. By the time they get here, I will have beaten your ass anyway for sleeping with my woman," Cal threatened.

"We don't want any problems here," Grayson said, voice still as calm as could be.

I stood back watching, hoping Cal wouldn't be stupid enough to try to fight my manager; but this was Cal we were talking about. He was always trying to play the big man who didn't take any shit. I didn't know when he was going to learn there were plenty of people who could always teach him a lesson.

Cal said, "I have a problem with you butting your nose in me and my girl's relationship."

"There is no relationship," I said, stepping to the side so I could look Cal in his face.

"We are over when I say we are over," Cal retorted.

"Shauna said it's over, then it's over," Grayson responded.

"Move out of my way," Cal said, trying to push past Grayson.

Grayson held his hand up to stop him as I stepped back to get away from Cal, and that's when Cal swung on Grayson. I screamed when I saw this. I couldn't believe this was happening.

"Stop it, Cal!" I screamed.

Before I knew it, Cal was lying on the floor. Grayson blocked his punch and threw Cal down. Cal got up again to try to rush Grayson, but Grayson caught him again and threw him to the floor. It was as if Cal was a puppet to Grayson. He was hardly moving as he tossed Cal around like he was nothing.

When Cal got up again, he reached over to one of the tables and grabbed a steak knife, but before he had a chance to swing the blade, Grayson took it from him. He then grabbed Cal by the wrist and twisted his arm around, bending Cal's arm behind him, causing him to scream in pain. Grayson had him locked down. The more Cal tried to move, the more he screamed in pain.

"Let me go!" Cal yelled.

"Not until the police get here."

Chapter 23

Shauna

Cal was taken away in handcuffs by the police. My drama-filled love life had played out over baked potatoes and iced tea. My fifteen minutes of work turned into over an hour being here in this restaurant, and the sad part about it was this was not overtime.

After questioning me, the police were taking statements from several people about what happened, and I was embarrassed beyond belief. After everything calmed down, I had to meet with my manager in his office. I knew this would be my very last day working there. I couldn't blame him for firing me. What went on in my life outside of this place jeopardized the safety of the patrons who attended this establishment, and that wasn't cool.

"Come in," Grayson said as I tapped at the open door. "Can you shut the door behind you?" he asked, writing something down. I did as he asked. "Have a seat."

I did that, too. I was a person moving as if someone was sending signals of action. I kept quiet, waiting for him to ream me out about what happened between me and Cal. I looked around his office, and the tan walls were bare. There was nothing hanging up, not even a clock or painting. The room felt cold and intimidated the hell out of me. A window behind Grayson held miniblinds that were open. The sun beaming in was the only refreshing thing about the space.

Grayson wrote for a couple more minutes before he gave me his undivided attention. I had to wonder if this was another intimidating tactic he used to make people like me nervous.

"You do know why I called you into my office?" Grayson asked.

"Yes."

"We can't have what happened here today ever happen again, Shauna. This is a place of business."

"I know, and I'm sorry for everything that happened. I tried to make him leave, but he kept coming at me," I said sadly.

"I know. I watched the entire thing."

"You did?" I asked, surprised. His once-stern face softened, causing my shoulders to relax a bit.

"Shauna, as much as you think I don't pay attention, I do. Just like when you tried to cover up your bruises with makeup," he said, causing me to drop my head in shame. "I'm not saying this to embarrass you. I'm saying this because you could have come to me."

I looked up, taken aback by what he was saying.

"I know most people don't want other people in their business, and I get that, but I thought you felt comfortable enough to come and talk to me about what was going on," Grayson explained.

"I don't like telling anybody about my life. I told my sisters, and things escalated before I knew it. You are my boss. What do I look like coming to you saying my boyfriend tried to kill me?"

"It would look like you telling a friend. I know I'm your boss, but we were friends first, Shauna. I've known you since high school."

"But things change, and so do people."

"I haven't changed," he said sweetly. "I might have some authority here, but I'm still the same Grayson from back in the day. I got a bit bigger and matured a lot, but nothing else about me has changed. You could have come to me."

"This is embarrassing for me to talk about. I haven't been able to register what has happened myself. Nothing like this has ever happened to me before."

"I know that," he said.

"How?" I asked curiously.

"Because I know you. I remember you fighting in school and not taking junk from nobody. Not even a dude. You didn't play, nor did you back down from anything. So why would I think you allowed this to happen? No woman allows abuse to happen to her."

I nodded and said, "He caught me off-guard."

"Exactly. Even the best fall sometimes. As much as you think you can fight like a man, there is always a man stronger than you. That punk had no right to put his hands on you."

"Well, you made him fall pretty good," I said, smiling.

"I wanted to punch him in his nose and break both of his arms, but I couldn't," he said.

"I wish you would have."

"My hands are deadly weapons. One punch from me and I could have killed that dude," Grayson admitted.

"Your hands are deadly?" I asked, frowning a bit.

"I have a black belt in martial arts," he boasted. "Not many people know that. Only my mom and my two brothers know this."

"Impressive. No wonder you could throw him around like he was nothing," I retorted.

"So now you know why I didn't swing. It wasn't a fair fight."

"Still, you should have hurt him. He tried to stab you with a steak knife."

"As long as no one was hurt, I'm good. He's in a better place now."

"I plan on pressing charges and getting a restraining order against that fool," I said.

"I hope so. I hope you know after today you can come to me about anything," Grayson offered.

"So you are not firing me?" I asked.

"No," he said, frowning like he couldn't believe I'd said that. "You tried to resolve the issue. You couldn't help that it escalated like it did. Your ex has been banned from this establishment for good, but just in case he manages to get back in here and approaches you, come find me. Yell, even. You have to take care of yourself regardless of your setting, especially with someone as unstable as he is."

I smiled and told him, "Thank you, Grayson. I appreciate this."

"You are so welcome."

"I'm going to have to make you dinner or something as a thank-you, but you are my boss, so I'm not trying to overstep any boundaries between employee and employer," I joked.

"What people don't know won't hurt them," he said with a look that made me wonder if Grayson wanted more than friendship from me.

"So dinner tomorrow night at seven?" I asked, throwing the hook out to see if he would bite.

"Tomorrow at seven sounds great," he agreed, smiling, and just like that I went from sad to delighted.

Chapter 24

Shauna

Boy, was I tired. I thought the day would never end. It was so hard pretending like I loved my job when I hated dealing with people. Only my dumb self would get a job that required dealing with people all damn day. Still, the day ended well despite how Cal tried to ruin it. I was off for the next two days, so I was looking forward to relaxing a bit, and also my dinner with Grayson tomorrow.

I walked into my home and plopped down on my sofa, wishing my shower was already taken. I took one before I went to work, but I always needed to take another to wash off the stench of the restaurant, which to me smelled like grease and onions. I sat up and unbuttoned the burgundy collared shirt and took it off because I was tired of smelling it. I needed a few minutes before I willed myself to the bathroom to wash this aroma off of me.

Picking up the mail I'd just gotten out of my mailbox, I saw that all of the envelopes were bills. *Can once, just once, somebody send me a damn check? I'll even take a credit for overpayment on something; anything that would require money coming in instead of always going out.* I tossed the pile of envelopes back on my coffee table. When I did that, Dawn's invitation fell to the floor.

"If that ain't a damn sign," I mumbled to myself. I leaned down to pick it up. I read the black-and-white invitation again.

Dawn Cherie Johnson and Corey Raquon Lewis
Request the honor of your presence
at their wedding
On Saturday, the ninth of January two thousand and sixteen
At five o'clock in the evening
At the Mount Zion Baptist Church.

Who in the hell gets married two weeks after Christmas? They must call themselves starting the year off right. How wrong was she? She was marrying a man who was no damn good for her, and she was too stupid to see it, yet she was mad at us. *She puts us down for trying to help her stupid behind, but raises this punk up like he's a saint.*

Every time I read this and thought about Dawn and how she went off on us over a month ago, I got pissed off all over again. The nerve of her, taking my ordeal with Cal to make her own situation look better. It was so wrong to me. What happened to me was a one-time thing, like I told her. If a man puts his hands on me, it's a done deal. Hell, if he cheats on me, his behind could get to steppin' then, too. I was not going to put up with any type of bullshit from nobody, and that included my impolite sister.

I hadn't tried to call Dawn, and she hadn't bothered to call me either. I guessed she was busy planning her nuptials. I was surprised she sent me an invitation at all, but maybe she did this to rub her wedding in our faces, and maybe it was just to let us know she was still going through with it.

The only one who really knew what was going on was Vivian. Even after all the stuff Dawn said to her, Vivian took it upon herself to try to resolve things. It took her a while to get through to her, but at least now they were talking. I didn't know why Viv tried to resolve things with Dawn. We weren't wrong. How Dawn treated us was uncalled for, and she just got dealt some of her own medicine.

Vivian kept us in the loop on what was going on with our sister. Things got so good between them two that Vivian was now a bridesmaid in her wedding. The last I heard from her was that she was trying to get Serena and Phoenix to come around also, just like she tried to do with me, but I wasn't having it.

"Come on, Shauna. Dawn is our sister," Vivian said.

"And?"

"And we need to work this out. You have to be there. How can you not come?"

"It's easy, Viv. I don't agree with it, and I damn sure don't appreciate what she said to us," I argued.

"A lot of things were said that night that were wrong. Now we need to come back together and let all of that go. One day you don't want to look back and regret not being there for her."

"Then I'll deal with that day when it comes, but for now, I don't give a rat's ass about Dawn or her bogus wedding."

"If she apologizes, will you come to her wedding?" Vivian asked.

"Like she's going to do that. Dawn is more stubborn than I am. You know damn well she's not going to let the words 'I'm sorry' pass through her lips."

"But what if she does?" Vivian asked.

"I don't know, Viv."

"We are going to fix this. This has gone on for too long."

I hadn't heard anything from Dawn yet, but I didn't expect to hear from her. She was standing her ground and I was too. Dawn getting married to Corey was a big mistake. As her sister, I had a right to say so. You can't force anything in life to work, especially a relationship doomed for disaster.

Look at me. I didn't try to work it out with Cal after he beat me. Before our confrontation today, he was texting me over and over again, talking about how sorry he was and how he would never do it again if I gave him another chance.

Baby plse txt me bck.

I'm sorry baby. U no I luv u. It will never happen again.

What can I do 2 make us wrk?

I'm miserable w/o u.

U no u made me do it.

I'm sorry. I need you baby.

Nothing but a bunch of lies. I may not be the smartest person in the world, but I knew never to take an abusive man back for him to do it again. That next time could possibly kill me. I wasn't the one, and I wouldn't be the one for Cal. I thought the only reason he really wanted to come back to me was because he needed a place to stay. He didn't want to go back and live with his mother, her man, his sister, and her four kids in a three-bedroom apartment, which was exactly where he had to go unless he wanted to live in the park. As far as I was concerned, Cal could continue to kick rocks, because I was done with him. Hell, I was done with stupid people. If you didn't get it and didn't want help, you could get out my face. It was simple as that. I have this one life to live, and I wasn't about to waste my time on people who only cared about themselves.

I finally managed to get up to go take my shower when there was a knock at the door. Instantly I became panic-stricken. I wasn't expecting anyone, so who was knocking at my door? Was it Cal coming back to exact more revenge after what happened today? I tiptoed to the door to check the peephole first to see who was standing on the other side before I opened it. If it was Cal, he wasn't getting in here to try to hurt me again. I would immediately call the cops, because he would be violating the restraining order I filed against him before I got home.

Peeping through the hole, I saw it wasn't Cal, but the person standing there shocked me. Picking up my shirt, I put it back on, attempting to button it back up. I swung the door open.

"Hey, Grayson," I said, smiling sheepishly.

"I hope you don't mind me dropping by like this."

"No, not at all. Come in." I gestured, stepping back for him to walk in, and he did.

I shut the door, making sure to lock it just in case Cal managed to get out of jail and was somewhere scoping out my place. As crazy as he acted earlier, I wouldn't put it past him. I hoped he was still in jail, but I knew his mom had probably already bailed him out.

"I'm sorry to show up like this, but I'm here making sure you made it home okay," Grayson said with his hands in his pockets.

"Aw, that's sweet," I said. "You can sit down if you like," I suggested, and he did so nervously. "You know you could have called me to see if I made it okay, Grayson." I smirked.

"I know, but seeing you for myself is better than hearing it from your lips," he said.

I stretched my eyes at how he said that, and instantly got turned on. I guessed he noticed the surprised look on my face, because he backpedaled and tried to find a better way of saying it.

"I meant I wanted to see for myself," he corrected.

"Well, here I am, and as you can see, I'm okay."

"I'm glad, but I'm seeing more than you probably want me to," Grayson said, nodding toward me.

I looked down to see one of my buttons was undone, revealing my black lace bra.

"Oh, I'm sorry," I said, embarrassed as I buttoned my shirt. "I was getting ready to get out of these clothes and take my shower when you knocked."

He giggled, saying, "You know I didn't mind."

Again with his slick remarks, I thought. After making sure none of my body parts were showing, I looked back up at Grayson.

"You know, I don't think Cal would be dumb enough to try anything stupid." I lied because I didn't know what he was capable of, but the one thing I did know was I wasn't scared. Well, maybe a little bit, but I was prepared for him now. The gun I kept in my top drawer now made me feel more secure, and I wouldn't hesitate using it on him if need be.

"You can't put anything past someone like him," Grayson said.

"You are right, but I'm going to be okay," I said, feeling like I was trying to find something to talk about with him. I felt like there was something else he wanted to talk to me about, but I couldn't put my finger on it, so I asked.

"Did you come over for something else, Grayson?" I asked, not beating around the bush. I wasn't at work now, so I could talk like I wanted to.

He dropped his head as he smiled. "You got me," he said, clasping his hands together.

"So what's this visit really about?"

Chapter 25

Serena

It was not even seven in the morning when I heard a horn blaring outside. It woke me out of my sleep. At first I thought I was dreaming, but when I opened my eyes and still heard the high-pitched horn, I realized I wasn't. Whoever it was wasn't just beeping the horn. They were laying on the horn for a long time. I was so aggravated because Nevaeh had finally done well sleeping last night, and the one morning I was able to sleep in, a car blowing its horn wakes me up.

I sighed with much frustration and crawled out of bed to look out of the window to see who it was disturbing the entire neighborhood this early in the morning. To my dismay, it was Juanita. I recognized that bright red coupe anywhere. She was parked in front of our house in the wrong direction, making a spectacle of herself. Something was on the side of her car, but I couldn't quite make it out.

I snatched my robe off my chair and went over to Tyree's side of the bed, shaking him.

"Hum," he said, making me mad because he was able to sleep through all of this commotion. This man could sleep through a category-five hurricane, which could rip our house to shreds, and he would still be snoozing like nothing was happening.

I shook him again but made sure to do it harder this time. If I couldn't sleep, he wasn't going to sleep either.

"What?" he muttered.

"Get up, Tyree. Juanita is outside."

"What?" he asked again, disoriented.

"Get up!" I yelled. "Juanita is outside waking the neighborhood with her horn blowing. You need to get her out of here."

Tyree was lying on his stomach and positioned himself up on his elbows. His head was down in his hands, and then he rubbed his eyes. Juanita blew her horn again, and Tyree shook his head. I stood over him with my arms crossed, waiting for him to get up. He slowly rose. He sat up on the side of the bed, stretching and yawning; all the while Juanita was still blaring her horn like a maniac.

"Hurry up and come on. This is embarrassing, Tyree. Get her out of her," I said, pulling on him.

"I'm coming," he said, rising to his feet. His morning erection was saluting me. He reached down and grabbed it as he walked to our master bathroom.

We made our way downstairs. Tyree opened the front door to an even louder horn being blown, since we didn't have the walls of our home to block out some of the sound now. What I saw shocked the hell out of me. This woman had the nerve to have a banner with Tyree's picture on it plastered to the sides of her car, reading: TYREE WANTED FOR CHILD SUPPORT. HE IS A DEADBEAT DAD.

When Juanita saw us standing in our doorway, she laid on the horn even harder. By now some neighbors were coming outside or peeping out of their windows to see what was going on.

She rolled her window down and began yelling, "Deadbeat dad. Deadbeat dad," over and over again.

"Juanita, what in the hell do you think you are doing?" Tyree yelled, trying to scream over her blowing the horn.

"What does it look like I'm doing? I'm protesting your sorry ass because you a deadbeat father to our son," she screamed and then laid on the horn again.

Tyree ran over to the car. Juanita let the window up before he could get to her. He tried to open the door, but she had them locked. She was looking at him with evil intent, still blaring her horn like somebody crazy.

"You got my son with you," Tyree said, looking in the back seat to see Zamir. "Where's his car seat? Open the door, Juanita, and give me my son," Tyree yelled, banging on her window.

I could tell Tyree was getting mad. I ran over to him and grabbed him by the arm to stop him before he did something stupid. "Come on, Tyree. Let's call the cops. This is what she wants," I told him.

"But she has my son," he said, looking at Zamir, who was looking at us crying. Tears were streaming down his little cheeks. "Give me my son," Tyree demanded again, banging on the window, but Juanita ignored him, still pushing down on her horn.

I tugged at Tyree, but it was no use. He was not budging. He kept jerking his arm away from me, which was ticking me off. I finally gave up and ran into the house. Picking up the phone off the console table in our living room, I called the police. The dispatcher let me know a call had already been made about a disturbance in the neighborhood, and a unit was on its way. I was happy to hear that, but I needed them here now before Tyree did something that could land him in some trouble.

When I went outside, I saw it was too late. Tyree had put his fist through the driver's side window of Juanita's car. This was the only time she let go of that damn horn. She was screaming like somebody was trying to kill her. Tyree was reaching in, trying to unlock the door, and Juanita was fighting him and screaming for someone to help her.

He wasn't even touching her, but Juanita was screaming, "He's attacking me!"

"Tyree, stop!" I yelled to him, but he didn't.

He managed to get the door open. Juanita went wild, swinging and punching at him while he struggled to reach on the door to unlock all the doors, giving him access to open the back driver's side door. Once he did that, Tyree went to the back door to open it.

Juanita hopped out, punching him in the back. I had to hand it to Tyree; he didn't swing on her. As a man he knew he couldn't, but I could. I went over and jerked Juanita by her left arm, causing her to now turn her rage to me. I didn't care, because this allowed Tyree to reach into the back seat and retrieve his son.

Juanita swung on me and landed a nice right hook to my jaw, which caused me to stumble back. I lost my balance and fell to the ground. Juanita resumed inflicting her rage on Tyree. She didn't care that he was holding their son, who was screaming his little heart out.

Tyree held his arm out like he was trying to push her back from landing any blows to his son. The next thing I know, Juanita was throwing herself to the ground. I turned to see the cops arriving at the worst moment possible. I wasn't sure how much they'd witnessed, but as they came to a stop, the two officers jumped out of the squad car and drew their weapons on Tyree.

"Get down on the ground!" one of the officers demanded.

"He beat me," Juanita lied.

"Ain't nobody beat you," Tyree yelled, bouncing his son, who seemed to have calmed down.

The officer yelled his demand again. "Sir, get down on the ground now!"

Tyree stood there disobeying the officers. "Are you serious? You want me to get down on the ground holding my son?" he asked angrily.

"Tyree," I said, now on my feet. I began to approach him.

"Ma'am, get back," the other officer said, pointing his weapon at me to halt as I threw my hands in the air.

"Why?" I asked. "I'm just going to get Zamir from him. His son doesn't need to see your guns being drawn on his father," I said.

"Just do as we asked," the officer said.

I didn't move, but I said, "Tyree, listen to the officers. Please get down before they shoot you and your son."

Tyree gaped at me as I gave him an assuring look. He then dropped to his knees, still holding his son.

"Put your hands on your head," the officer demanded.

"Now you have gone too far. Explain to me how that is feasible," Tyree exclaimed, looking at his son. The officer caught the hint. He really did need to think before he spoke.

"Ma'am, you can get the little boy," he told me. I approached Tyree and took Zamir from his arms.

"Just do what they want, babe. This will be resolved, okay?" I said softly.

Tyree looked at me with skepticism, and I couldn't blame him. Two Caucasian officers had their weapons drawn on him when he didn't do anything wrong. We didn't need another black man getting slain because a police officer got trigger-happy.

"Now step away from him, ma'am," the officer yelled.

Tyree proceeded to put his hands behind his head like he was familiar with the procedure. The officer who told him to get down kept his weapon drawn on Tyree, while the other officer approached him from behind and began to handcuff his hands behind his back.

"You are under arrest," the officer who was putting his handcuffs on him told him.

"For what?" Tyree questioned.

"Assault and battery," the officer answered.

"Assault? I haven't assaulted anybody."

"He hurt me. He tried to kill me!" Juanita screamed, lying on the ground and holding her face like Tyree had hit her. "He broke my window and then hit me, Officers. I'm pregnant with his child," she yelled.

"Like hell you are. I didn't do anything to you," Tyree retorted, still on his knees as the officer holding the gun went over to check on Juanita like she was the victim here.

I ran over to the officer who was putting the handcuffs on Tyree to explain, but he got all nervous, putting one hand on his gun and holding the other hand up to stop me.

"Ma'am, get back. I'm not going to tell you again."

"But he didn't do anything. She's the one who's causing the disturbance. Just ask them," I said, pointing at the people who were watching this spectacle happen. "She's the one you need to be arresting. Plus, I have a restraining order against her. She's not even supposed to be here," I tried to explain.

"I was dropping off my son, Officer. It's Tyree's weekend to have his son, and out of nowhere he attacked me," she lied.

"No, he didn't," I yelled.

"Look at my car. Look at how he punched the window out, which our son was in. What kind of father does that?" Juanita was putting on the performance of her life. She then gripped her stomach, saying, "I'm hurting. I hoping I'm not miscarrying our child."

One of the officers spoke into his shoulder walkie-talkie, saying they needed an ambulance dispatched.

"But she's not pregnant," I yelled.

"Yes, I am. How many times do I need to tell you that? Here, if you don't believe me, look at this," Juanita said, reaching in her jacket pocket and pulling out a white stick. She threw it at me, and I jumped back so it wouldn't hit me.

Like it was meant to happen, the white stick she threw to me landed face up. I saw this stick was indeed a pregnancy test, which showed two pink lines. Juanita was pregnant.

I was dumbfounded. *Pregnant?* I looked at her as she acted like she was in pain, holding her stomach and everything. In my heart I still didn't believe her. She could have gotten somebody who was pregnant to pee on this stick for her, just so she could make me upset. Still, I wasn't sure. This crazy woman was about to get away with her lies. Or was she lying? Either way she had no business outside my house this early in the morning, making a scene like she was doing.

Snapping back to the reality Tyree was about to be arrested, I said, "Officer, please let him go. He didn't do anything."

"Ma'am, we saw him throw this woman to the ground."

"She threw herself to the ground. She was swinging on him while Tyree was holding their son. Why aren't you arresting her for assault and battery, trespassing, disturbing the peace, and driving without a license for that matter?" I said, looking at Juanita angrily.

The police officer's eyes fell on her too. She looked back and forth between the both of us like I had burst her little bubble.

"Why don't you check that? Run her name and you will see the suspended license and the restraining order I have against her," I said as little Zamir laid his head on my shoulder. I could tell Juanita didn't like this, but I didn't care. Her son probably knew his mother was crazy too.

"I was bringing my son to his father," Juanita repeated through clenched teeth.

"We're supposed to pick Zamir up at your mother's house, Juanita. That was what the court order said. You know you're not supposed to be over here. And still that had nothing to do with you blaring your horn so early in the morning, waking the neighborhood."

As if what I was saying was lies, Juanita said, "I knocked on the door and no one would answer. I called and you all ignored my call, so I blew my horn a couple of times."

"Officer, she laid on her horn for a good fifteen minutes. She woke me out my sleep. Ask the neighbors," I said, pointing again to the ones who were still standing on their lawns to witness this nonsense. "When I called the police, a call had already been made by one of my neighbors, complaining about her. She's lying to you. I will go get my and Tyree's phone to show you she didn't call," I said, peering at Juanita. "I got voicemail evidence of her continued harassment, but we were trying to be nice by not having her arrested for going against the order; but, as you can see, she does what she wants to do, regardless of what the law says," I said strongly. If she thought she was going to play us, she had another think coming. I would do everything in my power to have this trick get exactly what she deserved.

"Ma'am, we will take their statements and verify your information, but we still have to take this man downtown until we verify everything," the police officer said.

"I want to press charges. What do I have to do?" Juanita asked.

"Just lie here until the ambulance gets here, and someone will take your statement," the officer told her.

"I would like to press charges on her also. She hit me. Ask the neighbors, because some of them witnessed this," I said, glaring at Juanita.

I could tell by her expression she was surprised I'd said this. For too long I'd let things ride for the sake of Tyree and Zamir, but I was done giving in to this tramp. If she wanted to play games, then I was going to show her how the game was really played.

One of the officers lifted Tyree from the ground and escorted him to the police car. Juanita smirked at me as she looked at Tyree being put in the car. It wasn't long after that the ambulance arrived to take Juanita to the hospital. She was still lying on the ground, playing her poor, defenseless role, while I stood to the side, watching and holding their son. Juanita was placed into the ambulance, and I heard her call one of the officers over to her. He walked up to the ambulance where she was. I couldn't hear what she was saying, but when he looked at me, I knew whatever he was being told was not going to be good. He spoke something into his walkie-talkie on his shoulder as he stared at me.

I looked over to Tyree sitting in the patrol car. He was looking at me with so much anger on his face. I smiled and he tried to return it. I knew how hard this was on him, and I had to wonder, in moments like this, did he regret ever getting involved with someone like Juanita?

It wasn't long before I found out what Juanita was talking to the officer about. He approached me to inform me that social services was on their way to get little Zamir from me. When I questioned him about this, he informed me Zamir couldn't stay with me because I wasn't a family member. I asked him what that had to do with anything, since I was with Zamir's father. He went on to explain Juanita didn't want him around me because she felt I was mistreating her son. I told the officer this was another fabrication on the part of a crazy, jealous, spiteful woman, but he told me he still had to let Zamir go with this social worker until everything got resolved.

To see little Zamir grasping at my clothing as the social worker peeled him from my arms broke my heart. Tears streamed down my cheeks as I watched the woman walk a screaming Zamir to her car and strap him into the car seat she had centered in her back seat.

I was furious. Juanita was so hell bent on making me and Tyree pay that she couldn't see she was making her son pay in the process also. She would rather have him go into the system than see him safe with us, and that was trifling. Did she think about what could happen to her child once social services got involved? They could take him away from both of them and place that little boy into a foster home until they decided it was fit to put him back into either of our homes. Did she realize what people did to children once they got them? A lot of individuals taking in foster children weren't in it because they loved these children. Most of them were in it for their own selfish reasons, and the main one was money. It really sickened me when I considered what the next one was. Children were sexually abused all the time in the system; yet Juanita didn't care. She was willing to take that risk, which went to show what type of unfit mother she was. And she had the nerve to be having another one, so she said.

I stood in my yard a minute, watching as all the vehicles left the scene. I had not had a cup of coffee yet, and I had already dealt with guns drawn on us, the arrest of my man, a fight with Tyree's baby mama, a pregnancy test thrown at me, and social services taking Zamir away. This was too much to be dealing with this early in the morning. Now I had to get dressed, go downtown, and see what I needed to do in order to get Tyree released. But before all of that, I needed to go in the house and check on Nevaeh to make sure she was okay. I was worried about Zamir when I needed to be worried about my own daughter.

Chapter 26

Serena

Once the officers took statements from our neighbors and ran Juanita's name in their database to see the restraining order I had against her, they let Tyree go. There were too many witnesses who corroborated our story on what went down. As hard as Juanita had tried to press charges against Tyree, it didn't work. Now the so-called victim was found to be the perpetrator of this entire event, and the cops knew this. She was now facing multiple charges, including her assault on me. I would have given anything to see the look on her face once she found out Tyree was freed and she was the one who was having charges filed against her. That would teach her not to mess with us.

One thing Tyree was charged with was failure to pay child support. He had to go to court to appear in front of a judge in a month to handle the issues with that. Still, that was nothing to us, since the charges he would have been facing were more serious to the point he would have had to pull some jail time. I knew not paying child support also could land him in jail, but after Tyree showed the receipts and other documentation showing what he had contributed to Juanita, we were pretty sure the judge would throw the case out, finding that Juanita was a spiteful baby mama looking to cash in.

Needless to say, when we got home we were exhausted. Tyree was still in his basketball shorts, wife beater, and slides when we walked into the house. On our way home, I attempted to pick Nevaeh up from Vivian's home. I had asked Viv if she minded watching her while I went to get Tyree out of police custody. My sister jumped at the chance, excited that she could do this for me. She acted like she didn't want to give her up when I came by to pick her up. When she offered to keep Nevaeh while we rested, I didn't look that gift horse in the mouth. I took her up on her offer. Now it was just me and Tyree, alone in our home, and I couldn't wait to get back in my bed and take a nap.

"I'm so glad this is over," I said, plopping down on my sofa.

"Me too, and I'm glad I filed for custody of Zamir. He doesn't need to be with her."

"I'm happy you did, too, but you do know it's going to be hard for a judge to take a child away from his mother and give the child to the father. That rarely happens," I said.

"I know, but I have to try. We have—or rather, you have—collected evidence of how she's taunted us. The judge has to see it our way."

Tyree went to the fridge and pulled out some turkey, cheese, lettuce, and tomato to make himself a sandwich. "I'm so hungry. I haven't eaten anything all day."

"They didn't feed you there?" I asked.

"I didn't want that food," Tyree said, frowning.

"I bet you would have eaten it if they kept you for a few days," I said.

"Probably so, but lucky for me I didn't have to go through all of that."

"If you would have listened to me, Tyree, things might have turned out differently."

"I know. I should have. I was so mad though. Seeing my son crying like that pissed me off," Tyree said, taking out the bread and pulling out two slices and placing it on a plate.

"That's all Juanita wanted was for you to act a fool, and you fell right into her trap," I said, kicking off my shoes to bring my feet up on the couch.

"I know that now," he said, spreading mayonnaise and mustard onto his bread.

"Juanita is good at trapping you, Tyree."

He looked over at me, saying, "Why you say it like that?"

"She tossed me a pregnancy test showing me she was expecting."

There was a slight pause, which I didn't like at all. It was one of those moments when the hairs on the back of your neck stand up and you know things aren't right.

"And you believed it?" Tyree finally asked. "You know Juanita ain't right. She probably rummaged through somebody's garbage until she found it. Or maybe she got one of her chickenhead friends to pee on it for her."

"That may be true, but my gut is telling me she's not lying," I said, crossing my arms, waiting to see how Tyree would react. I watched him, paid attention to his mannerisms to see how he reacted to my line of questioning, and I didn't like what I was seeing. He kept looking down like he was concentrating that hard on making that damn sandwich. He would glance my way but never looked into my face fully, like he was trying to avoid eye contact. But I wasn't going to get mad. Not now anyway.

Tyree looked up to see me still staring at him. He paused long enough to say, "Honey, come on. It ain't true. You know you can't believe anything she has to say."

"Tyree, you know I love you, right?"

"I know this, babe. I love you too," he told me.

"If you slept with Juanita, I hope you would be man enough to tell me, because if I find out some other way, things aren't going to go well for us," I threatened.

He sliced the completed turkey sandwich in half and then grabbed the bag of sour cream and onion chips out of the cabinet.

"You did hear what I said, didn't you? Or are you trying to ignore me?" I asked.

Tyree paused, leaning against the counter like he wanted to say something.

"Tell me the truth," I told him.

He looked over at me, and it was an expression I hadn't seen from him before. The look was enough for me to feel an ache in the pit of my stomach. I crossed my arms tighter to squeeze the pain away as I stared him down. I was waiting for him to come clean. As much as I wanted to know the truth, I didn't really want to know, because that meant what we had had been a lie.

Tyree came over and sat next to me with his turkey sandwich, potato chips, and a glass of Kool-Aid in hand. He set his drink down on the coffee table along with the chips, but held on to his sandwich. He glared at me for a moment too long to deny his innocence, and I knew then that he had indeed slept with her.

I closed my eyes in anguish.

"Serena, it was one time," he said as his words cut me like a hot knife through butter.

"When?" I managed to mumble.

"A few months ago. I went to see my son, and things just happened," he said regretfully.

I nodded slowly, tongue to cheek. He placed his hand on my knee and said, "Baby, I'm sorry. I didn't mean for any of this to happen."

"This explains why Juanita has been acting nuttier than ever. She thinks you two still have a thing."

"But we don't."

"But you do. As soon as you slept with her, Tyree, you let her know she still has a chance. All that taunting she's been doing to me and our baby, yet I'm the one looking like the damn fool in the end."

"Baby."

"How do you think that makes me feel? I believed you, and you made me look stupid. I was giving birth to your daughter and this crazy bitch was wishing death upon us. Hell, she still is. Got your son calling us bitches. The phone calls, the herpes letter in the mail, and now this," I said, beginning to cry.

"Serena, please don't cry."

"All of this happening wasn't enough to make you not want to fall into her bed?" I asked.

Tyree set his sandwich down on the coffee table. He attempted to move closer to me on the sofa, but I held my hand up for him to remain where he was. He didn't know how hard I was trying to control my anger right now, because all I wanted to do was get up off this sofa and beat the living hell out of him.

Taking a deep breath, I managed to ask, "Do I need to get checked? Was the herpes test a lie, or was there some truth to it?"

"No, baby, it was fake."

"Juanita is crazy enough to spread disease, Tyree. Especially if she thinks it's going to affect us in any way. She'll do anything to get back at you and me."

"Serena, no. It was forged. I don't have anything," he said assuredly.

"How do you know?" I asked. "Did you get checked?"

Tyree couldn't answer.

"Exactly. You don't know for sure." I turned away from him and got up off the sofa, saying, "I need some time to think."

"Where are you going?" he asked.

"I don't know. Somewhere quiet. Somewhere away from you," I said, picking up my purse and keys from the counter, and then I was out the door.

Chapter 27

Vivian

I didn't know how I managed it, but I did it. I got my sisters together for dinner again. We hadn't eaten together since that night things exploded between us over five weeks ago. For us not to all be together for that amount of time didn't seem customary. We'd always been close. As crazy as we were, as much drama as had happened, we still never went more than a week without speaking to one another.

I made the decision to have dinner at a restaurant this time. I hoped this would alleviate some craziness with us being in public; but just in case, I asked to be seated in a room in the back. We were a boisterous bunch. We all spoke our minds, and I knew even this restaurant might not keep us from exploding on one another.

The waiter sat me down at a round table covered in white linen. "Can I get you something to drink?" the brunette man asked.

"Just water for everyone now, thanks," I said, and the guy left me to myself.

I was so happy tonight was not a busy night. The room we were seated in was empty. I had to wonder if that was a sign. Did something happen here and that was the reason the restaurant didn't have many patrons? I hadn't heard anything about it. At the same time, I didn't watch the news much or read the paper to find out. That's usually where you hear about places not being up to code. It wasn't like it was Friday or Saturday, which seemed to be the busiest for most places; still, I wondered if everything was okay here. I had had one too many bad experiences with restaurants. To this day the thought of this one place I used to eat at frequently made my stomach churn in disgust.

It was about two years ago. I used to order Chinese food from this place. I had to admit it was really good; that was, until I saw them on the six o'clock news. The crew was shooting footage of the back door of the kitchen open and the cooks having the meat sitting in a large metal bowl near the door on the floor. Like that wasn't bad enough, they showed a damn dog come up and start licking the meat in the pan. One of the workers tried to catch the dog, but the dog scampered away. The man then picked up the pan of tainted meat and took it back in the restaurant to cook. I mean really. He didn't rinse it or nothing, not that water running over the meat would have mattered much. He threw some of the meat on the grill like it was nothing. Who does that? That couldn't have been the first time they did that. Then it was suspected the meat they cooked was cats and dogs. That's why they had the pan of meat sitting by the open door to lure the animals so they could catch them, kill them, and serve them up like some General Tso's chicken. I was sick for days after that footage.

And don't you know they didn't shut this restaurant down. I mean, they did for a few days, until they got things up to code, but they were back open within a week, and people actually still showed up to eat. Don't get me wrong; I know different cultures eat different things, but let me be the chooser of what goes in my mouth.

More power to them. I knew I was a customer they lost for life. It's one thing to not know what they do to the food in the kitchen of these restaurants, but it was another to find out the meat you were eating could be someone's pet dog Rover. To this day I couldn't eat Chinese food for fear it was man's best friend.

I took a sip of the water the waiter put before me, wondering where my sisters were. I looked at my watch and realized I did arrive early. Twenty minutes early, to be exact. For some reason I was nervous. I didn't feel like any arguing tonight. I wasn't in the mood, but my love for my sisters pushed me to go through with this.

"Hey, sis," Serena said, walking in with Phoenix.

"What the . . . ?" I said in shock.

"I know. I'm on time," Phoenix said. "You can thank Serena here," she said, leaning down to give me a quick hug.

She looked cute in a pair of dark denim jeans, caramel-colored riding boots, a white tee, tan jacket, and orange scarf. Serena had on jeans also, with a white tank, gray jacket, with a pink scarf and gray boots.

"Don't y'all look cute," I complimented them.

"Thanks," Serena said. "I think Phoenix was looking through my window when I got dressed."

"Girl, please. You're biting my style. We all know I'm the fashionista of all of you guys, so don't act like you don't know," Phoenix retorted, looking Serena up and down.

"You wish," Serena joked, knowing if she kept pushing the issue, this would get Phoenix started.

"Boo boo, look at me. You better recognize. I know you biting. Just admit it and sit your little tail down," Phoenix countered.

"Please sit down," I said, giggling. "Phoenix is the cutest sister. You happy now?" I said, looking at her.

"I know that. I don't need you telling me that, but I appreciate the love." She grinned. "So who's sitting where?" Phoenix asked, looking at the four empty chairs.

"I think you should sit beside Vivian, and we will sit Shauna beside you. That way you and Shauna will not have to sit by Dawn," Serena suggested.

"I think that is a good idea," Phoenix said, pulling out the chair beside me and sitting down. "I'm going to tell y'all like this: I'm not in the mood for Dawn's BS this evening."

"Please don't start," Serena said, sitting down and leaving an empty chair between her and Phoenix.

"I'm just saying. Y'all know how I am. If she decides to diss us like she did the last time we were together, I'm going to shut her mouth with my fist," Phoenix said.

"There is not going to be any fighting here tonight," I said.

"That's why you had us meet here, isn't it?" Phoenix asked.

"Exactly. We all know if this had been at any of our houses, things would have turned left real quick. I'm hoping being in public will make us rethink our actions," I said.

"True," Phoenix agreed.

"We are sisters. We shouldn't be taking it to the point of hand-to-hand combat anyway," I said.

"I'm just saying if Dawn wants to bring it, then I'm going to get to swinging," Phoenix said, rolling her eyes as she picked up a straw the waiter placed on the table and put it into her water to take a sip.

"Dang, I don't know who's more upset, you or Shauna," Serena quipped.

"Does it matter?" Phoenix retorted, positioning her diva sunglasses on the top of her head. "I got a headache and I'm not for the bull tonight."

"Why didn't you take something for your headache?" I asked.

"I wanted to, but I'd be 'sleep right now," Phoenix said.

"What are you taking that's going to have you 'sleep?" Serena asked. "I know Motrin don't put you to sleep."

"My doctor prescribed me muscle relaxers because it helps with my tension headaches. I was this close to not coming," Phoenix said, holding her pointing finger and thumb an inch from each other. "Y'all better be glad I love y'all."

"We love you too. Hopefully this won't take long. Then you can go home and pop you a pill to go to sleep," I said.

As hard as Serena was trying to look happy, I could tell she wasn't. Something wasn't right with her either, and I had to wonder if it had to do with the crazy baby mama she talked to me about the other day. When she picked up Nevaeh, she was obviously upset, but she refused to talk about what was wrong, so I left the situation alone.

"Serena, are you okay?" I asked, looking at her sincerely.

"Yes, I'm okay."

"You see. Even Vivian noticed something is wrong." Phoenix turned to me and said, "I've been trying to get whatever is bothering her out. On our car ride here she was quiet as a church mouse, and when have you ever known Serena to be quiet?"

"Serena, come on, sis. You can talk to us. Remember, I'm here for you no matter what," I said, looking at her with a smile. "You were there for me, so let me return the favor and be here for you."

Serena managed to smile even though it was a bleak one. She put her elbows on the table, bringing her hands together and leaning her face against them. Water began to form in her eyes.

"Oh, hell no," Phoenix said. "Who do we got to beat down this time?" she asked indignantly. "Say the word and it's done."

"Phoenix, why does it always have to end in violence with you?" I asked.

"Because most times that's the way it is. Individuals never get it when you trying to be nice. You always have to act a damn fool in order for them to understand the picture. If someone is bringing my sister to tears, they need to get dealt with," Phoenix explained, getting as ghetto as she could.

"You guys, I'm okay," Serena struggled to say.

"No, you not," Phoenix yelled. "You're messing up your makeup and everything. You are not all right."

"Really, Phoenix. You had to go to her makeup?" I asked.

Phoenix pointed to Serena and said, "She's starting to look like a raccoon. Her eyeliner and mascara is running all over the place."

Serena giggled through her tears as she picked up a napkin, which surrounded the silverware, and unrolled the utensils from it. She placed the silverware down on the table and dabbed at her tearstained face.

"Make her feel better why don't you," I said.

"I'm just saying," Phoenix shot back.

"We can talk about this another time if you like," I told Serena.

"No, it's fine. We can discuss it now," she said, sniffling.

Both Phoenix and I looked at her while she got herself together enough to tell us what was wrong with her.

Our sister looked up at us dejectedly and said, "Tyree told me he cheated on me with Juanita a few months ago."

"What?" Phoenix said, hitting the table with her fist hard enough for the silverware Serena placed on the table to clank.

Serena nodded and continued to say, "And it gets worse."

"Worse?" Phoenix bellowed.

"She might be pregnant with his child."

"Hold up," Phoenix said, raising her right hand. "Tyree cheated with nutcase Juanita."

Serena nodded. "There was an altercation in front of our house. Tyree bust her window out. Me and Juanita got into a fight. The cops came. Social services came to take Zamir. Tyree went to jail, and—"

"Whoa, slow down, Serena," Phoenix said. "When did all of this happen?"

"A few days ago. To make a long story short, this trick had the nerve to toss a pregnancy test to me, showing me that she was knocked up supposedly with Tyree's child," Serena continued to explain.

"Wait, wait, wait, wait, wait," Phoenix repeated. "Let's back this thing up. How in the hell did she toss a test to you in the first place?"

Serena went on to explain about the incident. Here I was thinking today was going to be about resolving our sister-issues, and it looked like all of us had our own personal ones to deal with. So far this was not turning out like I expected; but at the same time, I should have expected this, because this was what always seemed to happen with us. The great thing was that Serena was getting it out and letting us know what had been going on instead of holding all of that in.

"I can't believe we are just hearing about this now."

"Phoenix, I haven't had time to register this information myself. This is hard for me," Serena said, starting to cry again. "I love him so much, and we've been through a lot with this crazy-ass woman. For him to do this after everything we've had to deal with regarding her, I don't know if staying with him is worth it at this point, especially when I can't trust that he won't do it again."

"Leave his ass. That's what you need to do," Phoenix blurted.

"Phoenix," I called out to calm her.

"What? You know I'm right. I'm so sick of all these dogs thinking it's okay to go from one bitch to another. He was dead wrong. What he needs to do is apologize and then pack his belongings and leave. You did kick him out, right?" Phoenix asked, looking at Serena like, "You better have." I could see her hesitating.

"No, I didn't kick him out yet," she said.

"Yet! Do you need me to help you dispose of his possessions?"

"No, Phoenix," Serena said, giggling.

"'Cause I can do that for you. Call me Sister Kick a Negro Out, 'cause I can make that happen."

I couldn't help but laugh at Phoenix's antics. My sister never held any punches. As many difficulties as Serena was having I did believe Phoenix's foolishness brought some happiness to her today. I hoped she would make the right decision for her and Nevaeh. Tyree was a good guy. He made a bad decision, but sometimes you have to make difficult decisions based on what is going to be in your best interest. I wished I could take my own advice.

Chapter 28

Vivian

"Where's the waiter? I need a drink," Phoenix said sardonically.

"You can't drink if you are going to take that medication when you get home. Are you trying to kill yourself?" Serena asked.

"Hell naw. I love myself too much to hurt me."

"Then it's either drinking or relaxers later. Pick one," Serena said, finally getting herself together.

"I choose drinks, please. I'm going to need it to get through this dinner," Phoenix admitted as she turned to find the waiter.

I wondered where he was also. It wasn't like this place was packed.

"Waiter," Phoenix yelled, holding her hand up for him to come over.

I hit Phoenix on her arm to stop her from yelling across the room, but she looked at me with a frown and kept waving her hand frantically until she got his attention to come over.

"Yes, ma'am. Can I help you?" the waiter asked.

"Yes. I would like a glass of Moscato, please. Better yet, if you have a bottle, I would prefer that in a bucket of ice. I'm going to need it," Phoenix told him.

"Yes, I can get that for you. Can I get you ladies anything else?" he asked. "Are you ready to order?"

"Yes, can we get the menus please?" I said.

"Yes, ma'am. I'm sorry about that. I will bring everything to you in a few minutes," he said, walking away.

"Hey," Shauna said, walking up to the table, surprising us.

We didn't see her approaching since we were too busy trying to get Phoenix's wine and our menus so we could order.

"It's about time, Ms. Thang," Phoenix said.

"Look who's talking, the one who's always late," Shauna said, giggling.

"I'm not late today. I beat you here."

"All because of me," Serena murmured.

Shauna walked around and gave each of us a hug, which was unusual for her, because Shauna didn't give hugs. "Sorry I'm late. I just got off of work and I had to run home and get those stinky clothes off of me."

"You're fine," I said. "Phoenix just ordered some wine and we are still waiting for Dawn to arrive."

"If she arrives," Shauna mumbled.

"She said she was coming," I countered.

"I'll believe it when I see it," Phoenix retorted.

The waiter brought over the menus and the wine Phoenix requested. She and Shauna didn't waste any time pouring themselves a glass and downing their Moscato like it was the last one they were ever going to have.

Serena and I eyed one another knowing this was not good. Yes, things were going okay for the moment, but once alcohol was introduced into any situation, especially ours, it tended to change the mood of things. I knew if my two sisters kept downing that wine like they were, their lips would become loose and things were going to come out in the crudest ways.

"Okay, y'all. We are going to get along tonight. This tiff we've had going on for the past few weeks has to end. We are sisters," Serena blurted. "I want to enjoy our evening. I need this."

"Me too. We might not always agree, but we still have to love one another," I said.

"Are y'all done with the 'can't we all just get along' speech? I'm hungry and I'm ready to order," Phoenix said.

"Don't you think we should wait until Dawn gets here?" I asked.

"No." She looked at me with a scowl. "Because I don't think she's going to show. She's already late."

"She's only twenty minutes late."

"Come on, Viv. We are talking about Dawn here. You know, the one who never likes to be late to anything. If she wanted to be here, she would have been here already," Phoenix countered.

She had a point. Punctuality should be Dawn's middle name.

"So I'm getting ready to order my food," Phoenix said, picking up her menu. "And if she does show up, then we can get down to business."

Just then my cell phone rang. My sisters looked at me. Shauna gave me the look like, "That's her." When I looked down at my cell, Dawn's face was on the screen and my stomach sank.

"Hello."

"Hey, Vivian," Dawn spoke.

"Hey, girl. Where are you? The gang's all here and we are waiting on you to show up."

"Aw. I'm sorry, Vivian, but I'm not going to be able to make it," Dawn said.

My sisters stared in my face, knowing exactly what she was telling me.

"Why?" I asked pitifully.

Phoenix threw her hands in the air like, "I told you so." I frowned for her to quit it.

"I forgot about a dinner date Corey set up for us tonight. If it weren't for that, I would be there," she said.

I felt like she was making excuses, but I continued to be as nice as I could. "Okay, I understand."

"But we will get up, I promise," she said cheerfully. "And I promise I will double check my schedule to make sure, okay," Dawn said.

"Okay."

We both hung up. My sisters were still staring at me.

Phoenix said, "Told you."

"But she told me she was coming," I said with disappointment. "I didn't want to believe she would bail on us."

"I can believe it. I mean, come on, Viv, the last time we got together, it was damn near a knockdown, drag-out fight. Dawn is not ready to face us after everything that went down," Serena said.

"What was her excuse?" Phoenix asked.

"She said she had a previous engagement with Corey," I revealed hesitantly, knowing what my sisters' reactions would be.

"You know that's a bunch of bull, right?" Phoenix asked. "She could have cancelled being with Corey to be with us. Dag, she's getting ready to spend the rest of her life with him. What's one night for a couple of hours with us?"

"I want this fixed. She's getting married soon. I think we should be there to support her marriage," I said.

"I told you how I felt about it," Shauna said.

"You can't swallow your pride and give in just this once? This is our sister's first marriage."

"I bet you it won't be her last," Phoenix joked.

"Regardless, we should support her," I urged.

"Okay, Viv. You have finally talked me into it. I will support Dawn and go to her wedding," Shauna said, shocking me.

I knew she was going to be the hardest one to convince about going, so it did stun me that she agreed so easily now. I thought I would be trying to convince her all the way up to the day of the wedding.

"You will?" I said, excited. "And what about you guys?" I asked.

"I'm willing to go," Serena said.

"Phoenix," I called her.

"I don't know."

"If Shauna can come, so can you," Serena said.

Phoenix looked at Shauna, who was staring her down. She said, "Okay, I will go."

I clapped my hands with excitement. "That's great. I'm so glad you guys are going to do this."

"I'm not going to be happy about it. I still don't like Corey," Shauna admitted.

"Can we not talk about them since they are not here? Can we talk about something I'm going through right now?" Phoenix asked.

"Sure, anything for the almighty Phoenix," Serena said teasingly.

"Thanks, sis. Let me tell y'all about what the hell is going on with me. I got a man living with me."

"You finally snagged Tyson Beckford?" Shauna said, causing laughter around the table.

Phoenix had always said there wasn't a man on earth who could ever move in with her, unless he was Tyson Beckford. I didn't think Phoenix met that hunk of a man yet. If she had, I was going home with her just to gawk at that delectable piece of chocolate.

"I wish. More like Tyson Weakford. I knew I shouldn't have slept with this man. My poon-poon was too good for him to handle, and now he's lost his damn mind in the wonders of me and won't leave my house."

"What do you mean he won't leave your house? It's your house, right?" Shauna asked.

"Hell yeah," Phoenix answered with an attitude, and I could tell the headache was subsiding and the Moscato was taking effect.

"Did you call the cops?" Shauna asked.

"I did. But don't you know they couldn't make him leave my house."

We all frowned. It was her house, so how could the cops not make this man leave? Things weren't making sense to me, but Phoenix went on explaining her dilemma.

"This man convinced them he had been living with me and they couldn't remove him because he had tenant rights."

"Now that's a hot mess," Serena said, taking a sip of her water.

"I know, right? I had to go down to the courthouse and file an eviction notice, which means this man can be in my house from three to six months until this thing is resolved."

"Wow!" Shauna said in amazement.

"I've done everything possible to get him to leave. I've asked him nicely. I've cussed his ass out. I've ignored him. I've had other men over to flaunt in his face. I've even slept with other men, screaming like it's so good to me just so he can hear me, and he still hasn't budged," Phoenix explained with frustration. She picked up her glass and took another sip of her wine.

"What did he say about your passionate screams?" I asked, smirking.

"He told me he wanted to be next."

We burst into laughter, and for once it felt like old times.

"Hearing me moaning and groaning only made him horny for me. He had the audacity to tell me he has jerked off a couple of times listening to me having sex."

"What did you say to that?" Shauna asked.

"I cussed him out. He just stood there grinning and had the nerve to get a hard on right there in front of me while I was screaming on his ass."

"Did you give him some?" Shauna asked teasingly.

Laughter exuded from the table again.

"Hell naw," Phoenix said loudly. "Something is wrong with him. I ignore him and the man makes me a five-course dinner. I scream louder and the man buys me gifts, along with jerking off in my spare bedroom. The more I do to him, the more he seems to want me."

"Well, have you thought about giving in?" I asked, knowing the answer. "Maybe he's the one for you."

"What's wrong with you, Vivian? I mean really. Have I ever committed myself to one man?" she asked.

"It was—" Shauna started to say, but Phoenix held up one finger to shush her.

"We must never discuss him. He's my past, and I'm talking about my present life. Since the name that shall remain dead among us, have I committed to a relationship?"

"No," I said along with Shauna and Serena shaking their heads.

"Now then, y'all know me. He's going to know me too if he don't get the hell up out of my house."

"He sounds like somebody crazy," Shauna said.

"Damn right. What rock did you find him under?" Serena asked.

"No rocks. I don't deal with men coming from under rocks. He owns his own business," Phoenix explained.

"Was he at least good in bed when you slept with him?" Shauna asked noisily.

"I'm not going to lie," Phoenix said, holding up both her hands in the air. "He may be a dork and get on my nerves, but the man can lay some pipe. Looking at him you can't tell he has anything, but get him excited and that man has dick for days," Phoenix described.

"I don't see the problem. He lets you do what you want. He buys you what you want. The man is packing and he has money."

"Not the type of money I need to take care of me for life," I returned.

"He has money," Shauna repeated, "and his own businessm and he has good dick. Isn't that what you've always wanted in a man?"

"Shauna is right. No one has had those traits since . . ."

Phoenix glared at me with warning to not say her past lover's name.

"Why can't we say Noah? What's the big deal?" Shauna said, being defiant like I knew she would.

"Because," Phoenix finally spoke, but hearing his name caused her to get choked up.

"Because what?" Shauna asked.

"Look, y'all don't know what I've been through with that man," she said with hurt feelings.

"We know he hurt you," I said.

"No!" she said, pointing at me. "He did more than hurt me. Look, I told you all I don't want to hear his name, and I damn sure don't want to talk about my past."

Seeing Phoenix's mood change so drastically did make me wonder what else could have happened. I saw she was more like me than I thought. We were good at putting up a front, but beneath the surface lay a lot of pain. I knew Phoenix acted like she did to cover up something, but I never knew what that something was.

The skeletons beneath our surfaces were more than I could imagine, and I wondered, would I and my sisters ever get to a place of dealing with all of the demons that were slowly creeping their way into our lives?

Chapter 29

Phoenix

My head was still pounding when I got home. It was dark outside and I still wore my shades to shield my eyes from the light that intensified the hammering in my head. I thought the couple of bottles of Moscato I drank with Shauna would ease the throbbing at my temples, but it did nothing. The pain had moved down to between my eyes, which meant this was only going to get worse.

When I walked into the house, I heard Tobias in the kitchen doing something. At this point, I didn't care. I was going upstairs to my bedroom, closing my door, and getting in my bed to call it a night. I knew I promised my sisters I wouldn't take my muscle relaxers just so I could drink wine, but I had to. The pain was too much to bear right now.

The reason why I probably had this migraine at all was from the stress of dealing with Tobias in my house. I wanted him gone, and the more I thought about him walking around here like he owned the place, the more ticked off I got about it. Talk about making my life miserable. I knew as soon as he left my migraine would leave too. I hadn't had one of these headaches in over a year, and then it was when I was ending my relationship with Noah.

The thought of him made my temples throb even more. I stripped out of my clothes, dropping them to the floor until I had nothing on. My curtains were already pulled closed, and the only light I had on in the room was from the lamp on my nightstand. I couldn't wait to turn that off. I needed darkness as soon as possible, but I needed to take my pill first.

Reaching in the third drawer of my dresser, I pulled out the relaxers. Pouring two into my hand, I paused, thinking it may not be a good idea to take two since I was taking these after drinking. I put one back, put the top back on the bottle, and walked to my bathroom. I turned the light on without thinking, and the illumination caused pain to radiate through my head. I quickly turned it back off. Tossing the pill into my mouth, I turned the faucet on and cupped my hand under the cold water. I bent down and sucked the water into my mouth. I knew I should have used a cup, but I didn't have one in there and I wasn't about to go downstairs to my kitchen to get one. This would have to do. Swallowing the pill and water, I cut the water off. I dried my hands and made my way to my bed.

Clicking the light off, I climbed under my sheets and comforter, turning to my right side to lie down. It felt so good to be in the dark. I couldn't wait for the pill to take effect.

As soon as I could feel myself drift off, I heard a slight tap at my door. I ignored it. There was another knock, along with my door being opened. I knew this because my dark room was now lit by the light coming from the hallway.

"What!" I yelled, reaching for the pillow on the other side of my bed and putting it over my head for darkness to return.

"Are you okay, Phoenix?" Tobias asked.

"No!"

"Do you need me to do anything for you?"

"Yes. I need you to get out my house and stop stressing me out to the point of me getting migraines again," I told him through the pillow.

I heard the door shut and came from under the pillow, breathing a lot better. I never opened my eyes. I began to think about how my life had turned so drastically wrong. Then Noah came to my mind, and the thought of him caused water to well up in my eyes.

Noah was my fiancé, who I was with for six years. I knew this man was the one for me. I ate, drank, and slept me some Noah. I truly did love this man with everything in me and thought he loved me the same. That was until he came home one day to tell me he was moving to Italy.

Now, mind you, when he said he was moving, I was hearing *we* were moving to Italy. I was jumping up and down happy that my baby got another promotion that allowed him to move to a different location to work. He was one of the top marketing representatives in his firm, and his bank account proved it.

Please know that when I was with Noah, I wasn't this money-hungry woman I was today. I came from a background of humble beginnings. I knew I wanted better than how I came up, but I never imagined meeting someone like Noah and living the life his hard work provided.

We lived in this two-story brick colonial with five bedrooms, three-car garage, large kitchen with granite countertops and island. Our bedroom was huge, with a separate sitting area for reading and two walk-in closets and an immaculate master bath. He drove a Hummer and I drove a black Range Rover. When he asked me to marry him, he got down on one knee in front of all my family, sliding a four-carat diamond ring on my finger. I had the life and the perfect man, or so I thought. We were engaged for seven months with me planning this extravagant wedding. Even though Noah was the main breadwinner, I had a job, too, bringing in more money. My money wasn't what he was making, but I was a woman who liked to share in the finances also.

My imaginary world came crashing down when Noah revealed to me that we weren't moving. He was going to Italy without me.

"So you are going to go set up and send for me?" I had asked stupidly with his hands in mine.

"No, Phoenix. I mean, I'm going alone."

"You are coming back for the wedding, right?"

He paused, looking down.

"Right, Noah?" I asked with the smile on my face now disappearing.

"I'm not coming back at all, which means we are not having a wedding."

I let go of his hands like they were on fire, saying, "What do you mean there isn't going to be a wedding?"

"Phoenix, I've met someone else."

"What? What do you mean you met someone else?"

"I've fallen in love with someone else," he admitted to me boldly.

"How can you fall for someone else when you are with me? We are supposed to get married in a couple of months, Noah."

"I'm sorry you had to find out like this. No time would have been the right time to tell you. When I got this job offer, I knew this was the right time."

"So is she going with you?" I asked, distraught.

"Yes."

"Are you serious right now?" I yelled. "You are leaving me for someone else after you asked me to marry you, and you're moving her with you to Italy?"

"I'm so sorry about this."

"When are you leaving?" I asked him.

"I leave in two weeks."

"How can you leave me for her, first of all? And how are you going to leave me here to have to explain to everyone the wedding is off?"

"I've already told my family," he admitted. "My family knows exactly what's been going on and what my plans are."

"They know?" I asked vehemently.

"Yes. You were the only one left I needed to tell."

Putting my hands on my hips, I was in shock at his audacity. Not only was he standing here telling me he was moving to the other side of the world with another trick, but he'd already told his family our wedding was off. I was the last to know.

"I already have someone who's willing to buy this house and my car. You can keep yours," he told me.

"Oh. Is that my consolation prize for giving you over six years of my life?"

"If you want to look at it like that, then that's fine."

The look on his face was so callous, yet it still felt like he was not telling me something. I knew Noah like the back of my hand, but then I guess I didn't if I hadn't seen this coming. I thought he was happy with me. Maybe I was too caught up in planning our wedding to pay attention and see this man was cheating on me.

"What aren't you telling me?" I asked him through squinted eyes.

He sighed.

"Tell me, Noah."

"Emma is pregnant with my son."

I dropped to my knees right there where I stood. It felt like he had punched me in my stomach with that news. "A boy. Pregnant," I said, trying to process the information.

"Yes," he said softly.

"Emma. So that's her name. Forget that. It doesn't even matter. What matters is you're bringing her up like she's important."

"She is to me," he admitted.

"You say her name so freely, like that's supposed to sit well with me."

"What else am I supposed to call her?"

"How about bitch? Whore? Slut, even? She did break up this relationship."

"I broke this up. This was my choice, so don't blame her. If you want to blame anyone, blame me only, but leave her out of this."

I couldn't believe him. Now he was taking up for her. I shook my head in disgust. "How do you know it's a boy? How far along is she?"

"She's six and a half months."

I dropped my head in grief. Was he kidding me right now?

"Ever since I found out you couldn't have kids . . ."

I looked up at him and shot daggers his way, causing him to pause. "I can't have kids because you wanted me to get an abortion!" I screamed with tears running down my face. "You begged me to do that for you because you weren't ready for children. I told you we could make it work, but you kept on insisting we wait. So I listened and did what you asked."

"How was I supposed to know there were going to be complications from the procedure?"

"You never should have asked me to do something like that. I was killing my child for you," I yelled through tears. "Now you want to backpedal and leave me because of the complications, which ruined our chances of ever having children?" I spat.

"I eventually wanted kids, Phoenix. You knew this," he said coldly.

"And now that I can't give you what you want, you move on to the next trick," I said. "I guess the timing was perfect this time. You asked me to kill my child because it wasn't the right time, but Emma is getting ready to give birth, and now it's the right time."

"Phoenix, I told you I'm sorry."

"Do you really think an apology is going to lessen my ache and humiliation, Noah? You are standing here telling me you are leaving me for your pregnant girlfriend when just one year ago I got rid of our child for you. It's like you are punishing me because I did what you asked me to do and now I can't have kids."

"I'm sorry if it's coming off that way."

"Why did you ask me to marry you?" I asked angrily.

"Because at the time I did want to marry you. I wasn't planning on meeting Emma, but when I did and she got pregnant, I realized I had a second chance."

"A second chance. You had a second chance. What about my second chance, Noah? You took that away from me," I said, pointing at him.

"You made the final choice, Phoenix. I couldn't make you do anything you didn't want to do yourself," he retorted.

I jumped up from my knees and lunged for him. I punched, scratched, and even bit into Noah's flesh. I didn't know what else to do. Any way I could get this anger out of me, I was willing to do it. I knew if I had a gun in my hands, I would have shot him dead without even blinking an eye.

That man hurt me more than anyone knew. As far as my sisters knew, Noah called off the wedding and moved away for his job. They knew nothing about this other woman who was pregnant with his child, and they didn't know about me having an abortion and not being able to have children of my own. I played the role, acting like I never wanted kids, but if they only knew the truth. I did want children. I wanted at least three, and I thought those children would be by Noah. That's what I got for having faith in a man. I should have known from my own father's past that men couldn't be trusted.

Every day of my life I felt like I was being punished for taking a life. This was God's punishment for me not going with the order of things and interfering with what God set forth for me. But Noah got to go on with life, with a new woman and a baby who should have been ours. Was I bitter? Hell yes. Was I hurt? More than you could ever imagine.

So now I was the scornful Phoenix who used men like Noah used me. He left me with a vehicle and some money, but that was nothing compared to the scar he left on my heart and my womb. Ever since he did that to me, I promised myself I would never love another man again.

Chapter 30

Dawn

I wished I could say I regretted not going to the dinner tonight with my sisters, but I didn't. Not after how they treated me the last time we were together. Vivian had been the only one who reached out to me. In the beginning she was annoying the hell out of me, but the more she called and talked with me, the more I came around. I knew she loved me, but it was difficult to see this when I was still trying to get over how I ever came to exist.

I know that sounds crazy when they had nothing to do with our dad and my mom coming together to create me; still, I felt like our dad chose them over me. It took my mother taking her life for any of them to have anything to do with me. I knew I should be grateful, but at the same time, I felt like the charity case they were forced to take on, and hearing Shauna say I wasn't created in love hurt me to the core, because it was already a residual feeling I had about myself.

Shauna laying everything out on the table made me have to relive the moment I came home to find my mother dead. She decided to eat the end of a pistol. Just like any other day when I was eight years old, I got off the bus and let myself in the house with the key my mom put on a long necklace for me to keep around my neck. I always kept it hidden under my clothes so no one would see it. I let myself in the house like I always did. I knew when I got home, I was supposed to take my school clothes off first and change into my around-the-house clothes. Then I would go to the living room couch to do my homework. Mama told me to do it at the kitchen table, but I figured what she didn't know wouldn't hurt her, especially since I was getting my homework done anyway. Once my homework was done, I would get a snack, which usually consisted of some fruit and chips, and then I would relax back on the couch until Mama got home to fix dinner.

But this day was different. None of those things would happen, because on a Thursday afternoon twenty years ago, I found my mother's car still in the driveway. This time when I walked into the house, I called out to her, but she didn't answer. Entering the living room, I proceeded to go to the kitchen, thinking maybe she was there getting ready to prepare dinner. But she wasn't. I called out to her again, and still there was nothing.

I walked down the hallway to see Mama's bedroom door closed. Usually this meant she had somebody in there with her, but there was not another car outside indicating she had company. I knocked on the door gently. Nothing. I called out to her again and still nothing. I knocked harder the next time, hoping she would hear me this time, but still nothing. I was starting to get scared. This was not like my mother.

I remember putting my little hand on the knob and turning it. The door wasn't locked. What I saw next would change the person I was originally supposed to be. There, lying on her back, propped up on pillows, was my mother. It looked as though she was sleeping peacefully, but the blood spewing from her mouth and brain matter splattered on the wall behind her let me know my mother was not sleeping. She was gone.

I remember standing there staring at her for the longest. I don't know how long I stood there looking at my mother's lifeless body, the color red being singed into my consciousness to the point that for years the color made me cringe.

To this day I don't remember calling the paramedics. All I remember is the police arriving and trying to get me to leave the room where my mother's body was. They pronounced her dead at the scene. It didn't take a rocket scientist to see that. Even if my mother had been alive after such a wound, there was no way she would be normal, so death had to be the better of the two options. The option that should have been chosen was her wanting to live for me.

The social services worker showed up to take me into custody, and it was then when they asked me who my father was. I told them Edward Johnson. From the day he came to get me, things would always be weird and uncomfortable for me. In a matter of days, I went from having a mother who I thought loved me to living with my real father, a stepmother, and five half sisters. My dad and his wife welcomed me, along with Vivian and Renee, but it took Phoenix, Shauna, and Serena a bit longer to accept that I was going to be a part of their family. Eventually they did come around, or so I thought.

I thought they got past what happened, but I guessed if I couldn't, how could I expect them to? I knew they loved me, but I also knew I would never have a close sister-bond like the five of them had. And losing Renee like we did didn't help matters when it came to our relationship.

When I got home after running a quick errand, it was close to eight-thirty. I knew Corey wanted the lights, camera, action to go down around nine, so that only left me thirty minutes to get myself together.

"Honey, I'm home," I yelled.

"I'm in the kitchen getting a bottle of wine. Go get ready and I'll be right up," Corey yelled back.

When I walked in my bedroom, it was dimly lit with candles all around the room. Corey took it upon himself to change the black satin comforter to a champagne-colored one, which he must have purchased that day. I loved it.

I scurried into our master bathroom and took a quick shower. Once out, I dried off and wrapped the towel around me to get my hair looking good, which didn't take much since I had just had it done two days ago. I went into my walk-in closet and opened a drawer, pulling out a pink lingerie set. It was lace, and I liked the way you could see my nipples through the mesh material. Slipping it on, I oiled my body down and sprayed on some Victoria's Secret body spray to enhance the senses. Now I was ready.

Corey was lying down on top of the shimmery fabric with his hand behind his head, leaning against the headboard when I walked back into our bedroom. All he had on was a pair of red boxer briefs.

"Nice, baby. I like what you did," I told him, slowly making my way to him, trying my best to look sexy.

"I hoped you would," he said. "I figured our bodies would illuminate off this shiny material. You know, putting more of a spotlight on our love."

"Well, you did a good job picking it out. Too bad we are about to get it dirty," I said seductively.

"I'm ready to get it dirty," he said with his eyes stretched. The closer I got, the more I could see the hardness of his dick.

"Ready or not, here I come," I told him, crawling over to him and kissing him on the lips.

"Ummm. You are going to make me get all up in you without our viewing audience."

"It's not like we can't do a second take," I teased.

Corey kissed me again before sitting up to get off the bed. He went over to the camera and turned it on. Once the light was on, he came back over and resumed his position next to me.

"We are back, people, to give you what you love to watch, which is us," Corey said. "We appreciate your support and hope you enjoy the show."

If you haven't figured it out, Corey and I did amateur porn. Don't judge. It's a job, and one that paid well enough for me to quit my job. The more we performed, the more money we made. The kinkier we were, the more supporters paid to watch us. I had the looks, I had the body, and I was doing it with the man I loved in the confines of our bedroom. What could be better?

I have to admit at first I was against this. The day Corey came up with this idea made me furious. I wasn't a whore or a porn star. The thought of it made me feel grimy, but Corey convinced me to try it one time. With hesitation, I did it, and when I saw the money we made from that one act of love, I was sold.

Corey leaned over and began to kiss me deeply as his hands explored my body. "Damn, baby, you got me so hard," Corey said.

"You haven't seen anything yet," I told him, getting up from beside him and standing up on our bed. I began to dance seductively, swaying my hips and rubbing on my breasts as I looked at Corey lovingly.

"Do that shit," he said.

I smiled and began to slowly remove my lacey garment. I popped out one breast at a time, licking each nipple once it became exposed.

"Do you like this?" I asked him.

"Oh, yeah, baby, I like that," Corey moaned.

I caressed and squeezed my breast and slowly moved one of my hands downward until it was tucked between my thighs. I leaned my head back as I began to finger myself while Corey watched, slowly stroking himself.

"Yes, baby, plunge those fingers deep inside your sweetness," he said.

I enjoyed the pleasure I was giving myself. I dipped in and out of my hub until my hands were sopping wet with my juices. It wasn't long before I was exploding all over my fingers. My legs trembled as my body erupted into a bliss that made me drop to me knees on the bed before him. Corey was still stroking his erect dick but hadn't climaxed himself. I knew he wouldn't, because he always loved to climax on me.

"I want to blindfold you," Corey told me. As good as I was feeling right now, I didn't care. I nodded, easily submitting to whatever he wanted me to do. He laid me down on my back. He leaned over and placed the blindfold over my eyes.

"Can you see me?" he asked.

"No, I can't," I said, feeling the wind from Corey's hand moving back and forth to check, but I really couldn't see him.

"Get ready, baby," he told me.

I felt his warm hands touch my body. It sent immediate quivers all over me. His hands moved beneath the lace material to enter my folds, and he proceeded to please my center once more. His hands sent me to new levels of ecstasy. I bucked and grinded with each stroke of his large fingers. The closer I got to releasing, the more I bucked and grinded on his hand, until I released my warm juices all over him.

Corey lifted my legs. I tried to regain my composure, but he was eager to make me feel even better. He positioned himself between my thighs. I was on my back in the L position, legs straight up in the air, with Corey's manhood tapping at the outer core of my bull's-eye. With the beating of his manhood hitting my pleasure spot, I jumped with each knock of his hard wood. I wanted to remove my blindfold, but there was something more sensual about not being able to see what was going to happen next. My sense of touch was elevated by the loss of sight.

Corey's tip opened me slowly, and he pushed his way deep inside me. Like always, the first thrust was breathtaking. My feet curled around his neck as he penetrated me deeper than ever before. He held my legs and pounded his way to the finish line.

Moments later, a new position would happen as Corey turned me over and wanted to get deep inside me from the back. He gripped my hips and pulled me into his force as the finish line he was trying to get close to was fast approaching with each eager stroke of his manhood. This felt so good. My moans let him know I enjoyed what he was doing to my body. The closer he got, the harder he pounded and the more I screamed with delight. And the more I screamed, the more money was increasing in our account.

Corey whipped his manhood out of me and slid his thickness between the crevices of my butt cheeks, shooting his ooh-wee goodness all over my behind. I collapsed downward with my behind still in the air. Corey slowly removed himself off of me, and I fell down completely, waiting for him to bring me something to clean myself up with.

After he cleaned me up, I turned to my back. I had to take a minute before removing my blindfold, but once I did, I wished I had left it on.

Chapter 31

Dawn

I was in shock. Utter shock. With mouth open, I was looking at Corey sitting in the chair, which had been moved beside the bed. He was sitting in it, with some woman on her knees, butt-ass naked, giving him a blow job. Corey reached out, wanting me to hold his hand, but I couldn't take my eyes off this woman who was slurping on my soon-to-be husband's manhood like her life depended on it, while he was looking at me with a damn smile plastered on his face. What in the hell was there to smile about?

And then it hit me. If he was getting his manhood sucked by her, then who in the hell was fucking me? I looked around the room and didn't see anybody. Was there some invisible man? Or had Corey done me and then sat down quickly to finish getting his babies drunk by this nasty-ass heifer savoring his flavor? And that's when I heard the toilet flush. I looked toward the bathroom doorway and wondered who in the hell was in there. I knew we didn't have one of those toilets that flushed on their own, which meant someone else was here. As much as I wanted it to be this imaginary apparition, I knew it wasn't.

I watched the door intensely to see who would cross over into what used to be a love den meant for only me and Corey. I took a second to see the woman still lapping her way to pleasing Corey as his damn head leaned back like his ass was enjoying it.

This was in our home, where only the two of us were supposed to indulge in one another. This wasn't okay with me at all. Corey had brought up the idea of bringing other people into our bedroom, but I was against it. He'd already taken me out of my comfort zone by doing this Internet porn. Bringing others into our bedroom was a definite no, and I had told him this, but here he was choosing for me. I felt dirty, like someone had taken advantage of me. I had to wonder how I had not known it was someone else doing me. Or did I know and was too caught up in the moment to care?

A voice snapped me out of my thoughts, causing me to look in the direction the sound came from. Standing in the doorway of my bathroom was this Adonis of a man with dark chocolate skin and neatly trimmed goatee, which connected to a close cut faded to perfection. His muscles rippled from every part of his body, which had this sheen that made him glow. He was fine as hell. The brother walked closer to my bed. I didn't know whether to look at his gorgeous face or his massive manhood swinging and tapping his leg when he approached. *Is that what was inside me?* I thought. Corey's manhood—or what I had thought was Corey's manhood—felt bigger, but damn, this man right here was nothing but the truth. He had to be taking it easy on me from the looks of his extension.

I looked at Corey, who sat up to attention now. He was looking at me, still with that whack-ass grin on his face, all the while homegirl was still lapping him up. Damn, what type of jaw power did she have to be sucking on his manhood this damn long? I pulled the pillow around me as if to hide my nakedness from this stranger who had just rocked my world. He'd already seen what I had to offer and sampled it very well, but now that I knew it was someone else having sex with me, it was so different.

I was angry, and yet I was oddly attracted to the man who stood before me. I could not deny that he turned me on. He looked better than Corey hands down. And from the looks of his body, he took very good care of himself. Then my eyes fell to his inches again. He was lengthier and had more girth than Corey. The more I examined this stranger, the more I loved the idea that it was him I'd had inside me. But I couldn't let it go down like this, not after Corey tricked me into doing this.

I turned to say something, but homegirl finally came up for air. Corey gripped her by the arm to help her stand to her feet. She, too, was very attractive. I could see what Corey saw in her. Where my hair was long, hers was cut into a cool Mohawk, colored blond, and the style fit her face well. She smiled at me like we were friends, but I didn't return the gesture. I was too busy taking in how beautiful she was. The woman didn't have one blemish on her olive-tinted body. Looking at her did spark some jealously within me. She couldn't have been more than 130 pounds with her stomach flat, nice-sized breasts, a tight ass, and flawless appeal.

Corey mouthed, "The cameras are still rolling. Big money, honey."

I guessed he said this to keep me from going off in front of hundreds, or even thousands, who could be watching us right now. Honestly, I forgot we were taping when I realized two other individuals were in our bedroom.

This female leaned down, bending over to the camera and me, and began to tongue Corey down right there in front of me. It was then I noticed that she had her tongue pierced. I guessed that was something used to assist in pleasing men. He was stroking his dick while kissing her, like he needed any help at all getting up. She must have felt the movement of him doing this, because her hand joined his. I wanted to scream.

I wanted to jump off the bed, grab her by the hair and drag her out of my home, but I didn't. I watched as the two of them became more intimate with one another.

I looked over at the stallion who was still standing patiently by the bed, and he was staring me down with a smirk on his face. He, too, was watching along with me, and was stroking himself back to life. To see his manhood expand and grow to its maximum capacity made me sigh with amazement. My eyes went from his manhood back to his handsome face, and our eyes locked with one another. The way he looked at me was enough to make me cream right there in front of all of them.

Out of the corner of my eye, I saw the woman stand back up. Corey was still sitting in the chair and admiring this woman's body. Corey then scooted down a bit before reaching out to her. She took his hand, and he guided this woman to sit on his manhood backward. From the looks of it, she had done this plenty of times before. Once she was down on it completely, homegirl began to move her hips slowly back and forth. She leaned all the way back onto Corey's naked chest, and he wrapped his arms around her naked body. The two of them kissed again as he proceeded to grind into her.

And then it hit me. Was Corey slowly molding me to fit this woman he wanted me to be? You know, the woman who would be okay with my man—scratch that, my husband—sleeping with other women? Was this form of making money giving him the green light to do whatever he wanted, since he also allowed me to sleep with another man? Going into this amateur porn thing, I never thought other people would enter our bedroom.

I snapped out of my thoughts when the guy who just finished doing me walked over to this woman, who was now bouncing like a champ up and down on Corey's manhood. He gripped her hips with pleasure. The other guy stood in front of her and held out his manhood for her to take into her mouth. Without hesitation, she did just that. This Adonis's head fell back with pleasure as she bounced and slurped, showing she was very good at multitasking. I knew my juices were still on this man, but she clearly didn't care. As she sucked him, she was giving me a look like she wanted to come over and do me next. I'd never been with a woman and didn't know if I wanted to tonight. Corey had already taken this thing further than I ever anticipated.

This woman had both Corey's and this Adonis's minds blown so bad that neither of them noticed I was still in the room. I didn't know what to do. I didn't know how to feel. Should I be happy the two of them wanted her? I wasn't. I felt like the lonely, lost puppy who wanted attention also. Then I was mad at myself for feeling this way when the main feeling I should have been having was one of disrespect. I had no say-so in any of this. Corey decided all of this for me and didn't consider how I would feel.

The Adonis held his hand out to me, welcoming me in on the threesome they were having. The woman released her lips from his fully extended member long enough to hold her hand out to me also. I glanced at both of them. Then Corey leaned up to see what my next move was going to be. Both the woman and the Adonis had smiles on their faces like they were hoping I would take their hands. This was decision time. This was my chance to walk away; but instead, I reached out and grabbed their hands as I got off the bed.

Standing, the Adonis pulled me into him and kissed me deeply. The woman was still holding my hand but used her other to caress my hips. Next thing I knew, her fingers were inside me. I hate to admit it, but it felt good. She was pleasing me better than any man had. And just like that, Corey pulled me deeper into his uninhibited world as this sexual adventure swiftly turned into a foursome.

Chapter 32

Vivian

I did something I'd never done before. I went to a bar by myself to get some drinks and relax a bit. I'd always wanted to do this but felt like I should never come without a man on my arm or at least one of my sisters. Tonight I didn't care. I needed a drink or two, or five at this point. I wasn't happy with the way things had turned out with my sisters tonight. The fact that Dawn didn't show up only made things worse in my eyes and made it look like she wasn't interested in trying to work things out with us. After all I did to make this happen, she betrayed me by not showing up and made me look stupid in front of my sisters. I was offended.

"What can I get for you?" the blond, blue-eyed bartender asked, snapping me out of my thoughts.

"I would like a Painkiller, please."

The bartender's eyebrows rose and he said, "You don't look like you should have any pain to kill."

Was he flirting with me? The smirk on his face made me think so. *How flattering,* I thought. He was cute, too. Probably too young for me, but I could look at his nice physique

I smiled and responded by saying, "You would be surprised."

"Too bad. A woman as attractive as you shouldn't have any pain to kill," the cutie pie said.

"Thank you."

"I will get that to you in just a bit, okay?"

I smiled back at him and watched as the cutie pie walked away to take other drink orders. I looked around to see the place was crowded. Everybody was talking and smiling, and some men were watching the basketball game that was on the televisions above the bar. I looked up to see who was playing, but as I did that, I felt a hand on my shoulder. I turned and rolled my eyes when I saw him. As if my night could get any worse, I was staring into the eyes of Eric.

"What are you doing here?" he asked with a grin.

"Minding my own business," I said coldly, pushing his hand off of me.

"Aren't we in a bad mood?"

I ignored him and looked up at the television to see two college basketball teams playing.

He pulled out the chair next to me and sat down, saying, "I hope you don't mind if I join you."

My eyes were slits as I said, "Don't do me any favors. I don't want you slumming tonight."

"Okay, I deserve that, but come on, Vivian. You can't still be mad at me."

"Oh, I'm not mad," I said, sitting back on the tall stool and crossing my arms.

"You see. You got your guard up already."

"When it comes to you, Eric, I have to. You never do anything unless it's going to benefit you, so what is it tonight? Do you think I'm going to fall for your whack-ass charm and jump into bed with you again?" I asked heatedly.

"No, Vivian. Look, I'm sorry for saying the things I said to you the last time I saw you. I was having a bad night," he tried to explain.

"So you decided since your night was bad, you would make mine bad also, just like you are doing right now," I said, watching the bartender set my drink in front of me.

"Are you good?" cutie pie asked me, giving Eric a look that wasn't really nice.

I started to say, "Hell no, can you please ask security to remove this man from me?" Instead I said, "I'm okay."

Cutie pie winked his eye and walked away.

"Dude better watch himself," Eric said.

I ignored him, picked up my drink, and took a sip. The drink was really strong. I wasn't expecting it to be, but it was still good.

"I'm celebrating tonight," he said, waiting on a response from me, which I wasn't about to give him. I took another sip of my drink.

"You are not going to ask me what I'm celebrating?"

"Nope," I said curtly.

"I know you don't care, but I got a promotion today," he said excitedly.

"Great," I said uncaringly, hoping he would leave. Again he was making this about himself, and I didn't need this.

"Do you want me to leave you alone?" he asked.

"I sure do."

"So you are not going to give me any conversation. Just short answers?"

"I just agreed with you that I want you to leave," I said, glaring at him.

"Viv."

"Don't call me that. Only people who love me call me that," I snapped, instantly thinking about Sheldon.

He held his hands up, saying, "Okay, Vivian."

"You know what, Eric? I would appreciate if you would leave me alone. We have nothing more to say to each other. We said our hellos, so now can you excuse yourself so I can say good-bye?"

"You don't mean that. Not to the man you love."

"*Loved*. Get it right."

"I love you. You have to know you still have some feelings for me too," he said, fishing for compliments.

"Disgust comes to mind when I think about you. Regret, loathing, selfish, heartless, and even hate comes to mind when I think about you. Yeah, I think I may hate you, too. But the love is gone. Now, go celebrate your little promotion with someone who cares," I said, using my hand to shoo him away like an aggravating fly.

I went to pick up my drink again, but Eric grabbed my wrist. I looked at him like he was crazy, but he was giving me the same expression back. It was the same look he had on his face the night I kicked him out of my place.

"Who are you to ignore me?" he asked furiously.

"Here's the Eric I'm familiar with," I said, not being afraid of his reaction.

"I'm trying to be nice to you and you are dissing me?" he asked like he couldn't believe it.

"Dissed and dismissed, as a matter of fact, so let me go," I demanded.

"You should be happy I'm even talking to you. I mean, look at you. No one wants a woman like you," he told me.

"If that's the case, then why are you upset, yet again? Hear you tell it, I'm not worthy. So why you mad?" I asked him inquisitively.

"You will not get away with disrespecting me in front of all these people like you are somebody, because you are nothing."

"Eric, I'm not going to tell you again. Let me go before I have security drag your sorry ass out of here," I said, trying to pull away from him, but he had too tight a grip on my wrist.

"Oh, you don't need security."

I looked back to see Sheldon standing behind me.

"I would be happy to do the honors of kicking this fool out of here for you, Viv."

Sheldon gave Eric a look that told him if he didn't get his hands off of me immediately, he wouldn't have hands to enjoy the promotion he just got. Eric let go of me and adjusted his blazer as he sat back in his stool.

"Just like I thought," Sheldon said in a threatening tone. "You okay, Viv?"

"I am now," I said, rubbing my wrist. I could tell Eric caught that Sheldon called me Viv. As he glared at me, I said, "Only the people I love." Eric was ticked but didn't dare say anything with Sheldon standing here.

"Is this seat taken?" Sheldon asked, pointing at the seat Eric was sitting in.

"It's available. He was just about to leave," I said, glowering at Eric.

Eric hesitated for a moment. I think he wanted Sheldon to remove him from the seat, but I guess his better judgment kicked in knowing Sheldon was the type of guy who would do just that if need be. He stepped down from the stool without saying anything. He grimaced at me and then Sheldon before walking away. Sheldon took his place next to me, looking at Eric making his way to the other side of the bar.

"Thanks for that," I said.

"Anytime. You know I'm here for you."

His words touched me. And they were true. Sheldon was always here for me.

"What are you doing here?" he asked.

"I'm trying to relax."

"Oh, really, with dude here with you?"

"He just showed up. He was the last person I expected to see here," I said, picking up my drink and taking a sip.

"It's weird seeing you here, Viv. This isn't you. You don't do this," he said, looking at my drink and the bartender, who was waiting on two women sitting three stools down from me. When I looked their way, I saw them checking Sheldon out.

"You have admirers," I told him.

He looked at the women and smiled but turned his attention back to me, saying, "Those skeezers. They are here all the time. Probably thinking those eyes are going to make me send them a free drink. That's not going to happen."

I laughed louder than I expected to. I put my hand over my mouth to contain the giggles, but I couldn't stop.

"How many of these have you had?" he asked, picking up my drink.

"This is my first, Sheldon."

"And it's your last one for tonight."

"Dag. Can a girl unwind?" I asked, frowning at him and pulling my drink back to me to take another sip.

"Not here and not by yourself," he said.

"I'm a grown woman, boy. My daddy is . . ." I paused.

Sheldon must have seen my sadness creep in. He tossed a twenty on the bar and stood. He held his hand out to take mine.

"What?"

"I'm taking you home."

"But I'm not ready to go. I haven't finished my drink."

"Let's go, Viv."

I hesitated. I picked up my drink and finished what I could. Sheldon smirked but still had his hand out for me to take. I really wasn't ready to go, but I knew he would drag me out of there kicking and screaming, so I reached out, took his hand into mine, and got down from the stool. As soon as I stood, I felt my legs tingle from the drink I had just consumed.

"You good?" he asked, grinning.

"I'm fine," I said convincingly.

Once we were in the parking lot, Sheldon tried to get me to give him my keys. He wanted to drive me home, but I wouldn't let him. I wasn't drunk, so I could drive myself. After arguing in the parking lot for a bit, Sheldon finally conceded and told me he was going to follow me closely and to not speed. He knew I had a heavy foot, and tonight was not the night to get a speeding ticket along with a DUI.

I made it home without any mishaps. Sheldon pulled in to the driveway beside me. He got out of his ride and came around to my driver's side door and opened it.

"I think I got it from here," I told him.

"I'm making sure you get in the house first before I leave."

Getting out of my car, I said, "I haven't heard from you in days, and you show up treating me like a kid. Who do you think you are?"

"I'm your friend," he countered.

"Are you? My friend used to check in every day if it was just to say hey. My friend would drop in sometimes just to chill. I haven't heard or seen that friend in quite a while. Not since he fucked me."

Sheldon's jaws tightened at my words. He took two steps back, looking at me.

"What? You can't say anything."

"Look, you are tipsy."

"I'm not tipsy off of one damn drink, Sheldon," I lied.

"Let me take you in the house so I can go."

"You can go now. You don't have to wait until I'm safe. I can get myself in the house just fine, thank you," I said, slamming my car door shut and walking down my sidewalk. As I put my keys into the lock to open the door, I heard Sheldon cranking his ride to leave. I opened the door and looked back to see him backing out of my driveway.

Shaking my head, I went into my house slamming the door with tears in my eyes, wishing he would have stayed with me. I knew I pushed him away, but it was easier than accepting the fact that our relationship might never be the same again.

Chapter 33

Serena

I wasn't ready to go home yet. I didn't feel like dealing with the issue of Tyree's cheating ass sleeping with his crazy baby mama. We had yet to talk about it since I walked out that day. Each time we were around each other, there was silence. The only one in our home who was making any noise was Nevaeh.

I drove up to a stoplight wondering where in the hell I could go, because I really couldn't afford to ride around like this since gas was so high. Nowadays when you put gas in your car, you only drive it when you have a destination to go to. Riding around was not an option. While I was waiting on the light to change, my cell phone rang. I saw it was Tyree calling me. As much as I didn't want to answer, I did, just in case it had something to do with Nevaeh.

"Hello."

"Babe, where are you?"

"I'm out. Why?"

"I need you to come home. It's important," he said urgently.

"Is Nevaeh okay? Did something happen?" I asked nervously.

"Nevaeh is fine."

"So what's so important?" I asked.

"I'd rather not discuss this over the phone, so can you please come home? You know I wouldn't have called you if it wasn't important, Serena."

"I hope you are not going to tell me some more bad news about you and Juanita," I said, hoping this was not the case. I didn't think my heart could take another blow right now.

"No. This has nothing to do with her. Baby, please, come home," he begged.

"Okay. I'll be there in a bit."

When I walked through the door, I saw Tyree sitting on the sofa watching television. To me it didn't look like anything crucial as he screamed at the television about some basketball player missing a three-point shot. When he saw me, he instantly cut the television off and stood to greet me.

"Hey, babe," he spoke, looking uneasy.

"So what's so important that you needed me to come home?" I asked nonchalantly.

"It's about your sister."

"Which one?" I asked, thinking maybe this had something to do with Shauna or even Phoenix.

"Dawn."

"Did something happen to her?" I asked apprehensively.

"Nothing bad. Well, you might think it's bad."

"Tyree, spit it out already, because you are starting to scare me," I said with a raised voice.

"Come here," he said, taking my hand and pulling me into the bedroom.

"What?" I asked irritably, hoping this wasn't his way of getting me to sleep with him, because I wouldn't. Not after finding out his dick was in nasty-ass Juanita.

Tyree led me to our bedroom and over to the computer, which was in the corner by our window. We had to put it in here since we didn't have an office. It used to be in Nevaeh's room, but once she was born, we had to make the office into a nursery for her.

"Sit down," Tyree told me, and I did. Standing behind me, he leaned over and moved the mouse around. He began clicking on some things. He brought up the video player, and instantly the images of an African American woman popped up on the screen. She was lying on the bed, playing with herself.

"It's not bad enough you cheated on me. Now I find out you have a porn addiction too."

"Serena, I don't have a porn addiction," he countered.

"So what is this?" I said, pointing at the screen.

"Please watch."

"I don't feel like watching porn right now, Tyree."

"Serena, will you be quiet and watch this," he said, raising his voice. He clicked on the button, and all of a sudden a bedroom showed up on the screen. In this bedroom were the bodies and faces of Dawn and her soon-to-be husband, Corey.

"What is this?" I asked, trying to figure out what was going on.

"One of my boys called me and told me he had something for me to check out, that I wouldn't believe who was performing in this new video he just burned. He dropped it by today and told me to watch it. When I put the CD in, this is what came up," he said, pointing at the computer screen.

"This looks like their bedroom," I said, figuring out the space was my sister's private sanctum.

"I figured that."

"I can't believe this. Why would Dawn do something like this?"

"I don't know. And it gets worse," Tyree said.

As much as I wanted to turn away, my nosiness got the best of me. I had to see how far this would go, but I wasn't prepared for what happened next.

"What the . . . ?" I said in shock as my hand covered my mouth.

"I know. Can you believe it?"

"When did this happen?"

"My boy didn't go into details. He just recorded it to this disc and brought it to me," Tyree explained.

"Who else has seen this?" I asked angrily. "Has he been showing all your friends?"

"Serena, I don't know. I guess he brought me a copy to let us know what was going on, since he knew Dawn was basically like a sister-in-law to me."

"He could have just told you. He didn't have to record it," I yelled.

"Do you think you would have believed him, or me for that matter, if I told you without proof?" Tyree said.

He was right. I wouldn't have believed him. Not after he lied to me about sleeping with Juanita. Plus, it was something degrading regarding my sister. This couldn't be the Dawn who fell out with us over her no-good man. Not Ms. Goody Two-shoes. Seeing this made me question her sanity.

"I can't believe this," was all I kept saying. "She's having sex with someone else and posting it on the Internet."

"But that's not it," he said, reaching over me to eject the disc of my sister and her sexual escapades. He placed another one in, and I watched as the disc booted up. I wasn't sure if I wanted to see anything else, not after seeing my sister butt-ass naked getting screwed by some strange guy, while good-for-nothing Corey watched in the background with some floozy sucking on his manhood.

An image came up on the screen, and it appeared to be someone else's bedroom that I was not familiar with.

A woman walking backward to the bed came into view as she gave the come-here finger to someone else in the room. Then a man appeared, walking up to her and holding the woman in his arms. They kissed deeply.

"What is this, Tyree? This doesn't look like Dawn," I said.

"But pay attention to who the man is."

At first I didn't pay attention because the man's back was to the camera. The woman crawled up on the bed, again backward, scooting to the middle, and the man climbed on top of her. He kissed her again before making his way down her body until his face rested between her thighs. And then he looked at the camera with a smirk.

"You have got to be kidding me," I said.

"This CD has several different women on it, with Corey being the main actor on this disc."

"So Corey is a porn star. I don't even want to call him a star or actor, because this man isn't acting. He's doing what he loves."

"And it's one more thing, babe."

"You know I'm getting tired of you saying that," I said, not wanting to see another thing, but if Tyree was telling me this, then it had to be important.

He reached over me and clicked the mouse, going from chapter to chapter through the different women Corey was playing hide-the-salami with, until Tyree came to chapter eight.

"Prepare yourself," Tyree said, but what came up on the screen was nothing I could prepare myself for.

"What?" was all I could say as water filled my eyes. I turned to Tyree, who looked at me lovingly. "Is this real?"

"It has to be, babe," he said sincerely.

"Why would my sister do this?"

"I don't know."

"Turn it off," I spat. "Please turn it off," I said, getting up from the chair and walking to the other side of our bedroom to catch my breath. Tyree did as I asked, closing the video player down.

He then turned to me and asked, "Babe, are you okay?"

"No, I'm not okay. Would you be okay if you saw that?"

Tyree didn't say anything. He sat down in the office chair and ejected the disc from the computer tower. "I'm sorry, Serena," Tyree said genuinely. "I didn't want you to find out this way, but I felt like you needed to know."

"What is happening in my life?" I said, sitting down on the bed and beginning to cry. "What is she thinking?" I asked.

"I don't know, but you really need to talk to your sister. Something is definitely up with her."

"I appreciate you telling me this, or should I say showing me this," I said with a nervous giggle, even though nothing about this situation was funny.

"You know I love your sisters like they are my own. I have three sisters myself, and I hope if you heard or saw something like this you would tell me," he said honestly.

"You know I would," I said, loving this man even more, despite him betraying me.

Tyree put both discs in a plastic case and set them on the desk. He then came over to the bed and sat down beside me. "You sure you are okay?" he asked with concern, rubbing my back.

"It's too much going on. First it was Juanita threatening me and Nevaeh. Then it was my sisters falling out. Now you've told me you cheated on me and could have a child on the way, and now this. The problems keep stacking up."

"But our relationship does not have to be one of those problems."

"Your cheating on me is a problem," I yelled.

"I know I was wrong, but I swear I was only with her one time," he pleaded.

"How do I know that? Far as I knew, you weren't with her or anybody else. I trusted that you were faithful to me, and you broke that trust."

He nodded, saying, "Serena, on everything I love, my mother, my sisters, and my own daughter, I only cheated on you that one time. It was the biggest mistake I've ever made in my life."

"No, your biggest was ever getting involved with that woman."

"I can say that, but then I wouldn't have my son," he retorted, and I understood. "I hope this mistake doesn't cause me to lose you," he said compassionately. He got up and kneeled down in front of me, positioning himself between my thighs so we were face to face.

"Serena, I love you with everything in me. Baby, I don't want you to leave me. I promise as long as I live, I will never cheat on you again."

His words were gentle, loving, and felt genuine. Tears ran down my cheeks as I looked down, fiddling around with the hem of my orange sundress. As much as I wanted to believe him, I was afraid to. Tyree reached up and wiped my tears away, but more tears replaced them when he touched me. His hands were so warm.

"You really hurt me, Tyree," I said through tears.

"I know, baby, and I'm so sorry."

"I'm worried you will do this again."

"Look at me, Serena," he said with a comforting voice.

I looked into his sincere eyes.

"Don't leave me. Please don't leave me. Give us another chance. I'll do anything you want me to do to make this work."

"I wish you didn't have to deal with Juanita," I said. "But I know that will never happen since you two have a child together, and you may be having another one with her," I said overwhelmed by this realization.

Tyree dropped his head in defeat. He said, "I would never wish any ill will toward Juanita and this unborn child, but I do wish she weren't pregnant."

"Me too."

"This child didn't ask for the turmoil it will be born into. And you know if it is my child . . ."

"You have to take care of it," I said, finishing his sentence.

"And you best believe I'm going to find out whether this child is mine."

"Well, I hope it's not. It's bad enough you had one with that crazy woman," I said.

"True, but it did give me my beautiful son, who's my world along with Nevaeh."

"They are beautiful children, aren't they?" I said, smiling. "Despite the unstableness of Juanita, Zamir is a good boy."

Tyree nodded. There was a silence between us as we stared at one another.

I broke the silence by saying, "As much as I would love to leave you, I love you too much to do so."

Tyree leaned in and kissed me tenderly on the lips. Nothing lustful, just a kiss of admiration.

"Thank you," he said.

"Don't thank me yet, because I still haven't forgiven you."

"I understand."

"It's going to take some time for me to get over this, Tyree."

"I wouldn't expect any less," he said. "I'm glad we had this talk."

"And it was all due to my sister's sex acts," I said, giggling.

"Make sure you thank her for me," he said jokingly.

"I'm not sure I like the way you said that. I mean, you did just see my sister naked," I said, smiling.

"And it sickened me," he said, smirking.

"Sure," I said.

"I'm serious. I told you your sisters are my sisters. Who wants to see their sisters getting it on with any dude?"

"I get that," I said, looking down at my hands in his.

"I love you, Serena."

I looked into his loving eyes and leaned forward, wrapping my arms around Tyree, who returned the embrace. It felt good to have one problem resolved somewhat. Now I had to figure out how I was going to handle Dawn's situation. Would this be something else that would drive another wedge between us?

Chapter 34

Vivian

An emergency sister-meeting had been called by Serena, who rang my phone off the hook last night until I picked up to talk with her. She wanted to use my house as the location, but she wouldn't tell me what it was about. By the tone of her voice, I knew whatever she had to tell us couldn't have been good.

I really didn't need this right now after the night I had. I'd finished my bottle of wine after Sheldon dragged me from the bar and left me standing on my stoop to wallow in the grief of losing him. As soon as I entered my home, I called him, but he wouldn't answer his phone. He was sending me to his voicemail, which was something Sheldon never did. I was feeling so low about this situation.

The strength needed to maintain this demeanor of mine was wearing thin. And who could I tell, Dawn? No, because she was planning her wedding. Serena? She had her problems with Tyree cheating. Phoenix was dealing with a squatter, and then there was Shauna, who would probably tell me to get a drink and let things roll off my back. The only one who would have been here regardless of anything going on in my life was my sister Renee, and she was no longer among us. The thought of her caused water to well up in my eyes. A tear ran down my right cheek.

"I miss you so much," I whispered, hoping her spirit heard me. I wished she could answer me.

"Why did you have to die?" I questioned. "Why, God? Why did you have to take her from me?" I asked, knowing God wasn't going to answer me. I hadn't had that moment yet where God spoke to me. I didn't know what that felt like. I always wanted it to happen to me, but I'd never experienced it. I knew there was a higher power, but I wondered why He never talked to me. What was wrong with me? What was the reason God didn't answer?

I dropped my head in sorrow, sitting on the side of my bed. It was close to eleven. That was the time my sisters were supposed to get here, and here I was still in my pajamas. I wasn't going to change. For what? I was at home. It was Saturday, my day to concentrate on me. If it were really up to me, I wouldn't have any of them over here. I would close the blinds, unplug the phone, and watch TV in darkness.

I knew I had to get it together before any of them arrived, even if it was just washing my face. I willed myself to get up, and when I did, my cell phone rang. I looked over at my nightstand, watching my cell phone ringing and buzzing as it moved around the wooden top. To my surprise, it was Sheldon's face smiling back at me. I quickly picked it up.

"Hello," I said with eagerness.

"Viv."

"Yeah, Sheldon, it's me."

"You okay?" he asked questionably. "You sound funny."

"I'm okay," I lied.

"No, you are not," he said, causing more tears to form.

"Sheldon, I never could lie to you. I'm not okay. I got a lot going on right now."

"I know some of what you are going through has to do with me," he said.

I paused for a moment before saying, "Yes. I miss you."

"I miss you too."

"So what's going on with us? Things have been different ever since that night we . . . we . . . you know."

"Slept together," he finished.

"Yes."

"Look, Viv. This is not anything I want to talk to you about over the phone. Can I come over so we can talk?"

"Me and my sisters are having an emergency meeting this morning, and they should be arriving any minute, but you can come over after that."

"What's going on now?" he asked.

"I don't know. Serena called the meeting, so I will find out when she gets here."

"Okay. Hit me up when your sisters leave, and I will swing through then. Is that okay?"

"That sounds good. You never know; depending on what Serena has to tell me, I might need your shoulder. You know how things go once all of us get together."

"I know, right."

There was a slight pause before either of us spoke again.

"Sheldon, thank you," I told him.

"For what?" he asked.

"For not giving up on me. I know I've overreacted and treated you bad after our episode, but I didn't mean to."

"I know."

"I'm serious. You calling me today has made me so happy, and I can't wait to see you," I admitted.

"I can't wait to see you either. So don't forget; call me when they leave, a'ight?"

"I will."

I hung up the phone.

Hearing Sheldon's voice was the boost I needed to get ready for whatever my sister Serena had to reveal to us.

Now that I had a little bit of pep in my step, I went to my bathroom to at least wash my face. As I made my way, a small voice said, *I got you.* I halted and looked around to see who said it, and then this warm feeling came over me. I smiled, thinking God had heard me—and now He'd spoken to me.

Chapter 35

Shauna

With his black jacket tossed over his shoulder, Grayson caressed the side of my face as he kissed me. I hated to see this man go. Our night together was amazing, and I wished I could rewind time to do it all over again. I was still left pondering what it would be like to sleep with this man. Well, we slept together in the sense of lying beside one another all night long, but that was as far as things went with us. There was kissing. Boy, was there kissing. That man's tongue in my mouth only piqued my curiosity, wondering how it would be to have his manhood inside me. We touched and caressed and felt each other up through our clothes to the point that I wanted to rip his off and tell him to take me right then and there, but I didn't want to come off like a common whore. We'd gone out a few times, but not enough to warrant me giving up the goodies so quickly. That was a mistake I'd made with Cal.

I knew it was wrong to start any type of relationship with my boss, but I would quit my job to keep this man in my life. So far no one knew we had anything going on. We both kept the employer-employee relationship just that at work, not wanting to give anyone any reason to get all up in our business, which we'd done a great job at so far.

"I had a wonderful time with you, Grayson."

"I hope we can do this again real soon," he suggested.

"How about tonight?" I asked with a smile.

"Tonight sounds good to me," he said, smirking. He leaned in and kissed me again. "I'll see you later."

Grayson left my apartment and left me with a smile that would last until we saw each other again—that's if whatever Serena had to tell us didn't rip the smile off my face.

I started to go to my room to get ready to go to Vivian's house when there was a knock at the door.

I jogged over, opening it with a smile, saying, "Did you forget something?"

As those words slipped from my lips, my eyes landed on an angry Cal standing before me. I quickly tried to shut the door in his face, but he placed his foot in the door, prohibiting me from closing it. As hard as I struggled to shut the door, it was no use. Cal was too strong for me. Using his shoulder, he rammed the door, causing it to knock me backward, giving him just enough time to come into my home and slam the door shut. I quickly ran across the room to get away from him.

"Get out of my place, Cal," I told him, but the evil look in his eyes let me know he was not about to go anywhere. "Did you forget about the restraining order?"

Ignoring my question, he asked his own. "So you're cheating on me now?"

"How can I cheat on you when I'm not with you?" I asked sarcastically.

"You couldn't wait to get rid of me so you could sleep with someone else."

"You got rid of yourself when you put your hands on me," I told him.

"After all I've done for you. After everything I did to help you get where you are."

I looked at him with a scowl, puzzled because I didn't know what he was talking about. I asked, "What did you do for me?"

"I helped you get this place. I gave you money. I bought you things. I made a car payment for you."

"Ummmmm, Cal, you must be getting me mixed up with one of your other women, because you haven't done none of those things for me. If anything, I gave you money. I paid your mama rent where you were staying to help y'all, and I bought your non-dressing behind clothes. So before you come out your mouth all crazy, you better rethink the situation and the woman, because you got me mixed up with somebody else."

Cal looked off like he was pondering my statement. He knew he made a mistake just like I said he did. Now he stood there looking stupid. *He's going to come over here like he cares about me, but sticks his foot in his own mouth by getting me mixed up with his other women.* I had suspected he was doing a little something outside of me, but I could never prove it. Now he just did.

"It's all coming back to you now," I said, giggling. "That's what happens when you got too many women on your roster. But you know what? You can take me off permanently, because I'll be damned if I'm going to deal with any more of your bullshit."

"Are you sleeping with dude?" he asked, dismissing my statements.

"What do you think? I mean, he is leaving this morning, isn't he?" I said disdainfully. "That's the reason why you are asking, because you saw him leave, right?"

"I thought you loved me," he said pitifully.

"No. I never loved you. I had a strong like for you. Now Grayson, I could see myself loving that man."

"You just met him."

"But I've known him for quite some time. In just a few weeks, this man has shown me what it's supposed to feel like to have a good man next to me. I'm sad to say I never knew that until I met him."

"Well, you can end it because I want you back," Cal admitted.

"You can want me all you want. It's not going to happen, Cal. You think I'm supposed to fall into your arms after you bust your way into my place, coming up in here like you're Mr. Big Stuff. Like I'm supposed to be scared of you, but I'm not afraid."

"You should be," he threatened.

"Please, of what? What are you going to do, beat me again?"

"I told you I was sorry about that."

"And I'm supposed to forget the way you pounded my head into the floor screaming, 'I'm going to kill you, bitch'? I'm supposed to forget about all of that and say, 'Yes, Cal, I love you and I want you back'?"

"Yes," he said sternly.

"Then you're crazier than I thought. You need help. Go find some doctor to help you work on that mind of yours, because you have truly lost it," I said, crossing my arms across my chest.

"Shauna, you know you want me," he said, holding his hands out like he was some sort of male model. Little did he know he was far from it.

"Look at me and look at you. I don't need a lot of men to validate me. Ain't that why you got Laura and Janice and Cookie waiting for you to call them?"

Cal's arms fell dejectedly at the mention of their names. He rubbed his head as he pivoted from foot to foot. I knew he didn't like the way this conversation was going.

"That's right. I know about those women. Two of them called me, and another showed up at my job the other day, letting me know she's your woman and to stay away from you. Funny how things turn out, isn't it? All the while you trying to get me back, your women are going behind your back, letting me know they already have you. You better talk to them, because they blew up your spot. You are used to dealing with chickenheads who are willing to settle, but that's not me. You got the wrong one here if you think I'm going to take you back and deal with your cheating-ass, beating-on-women ways," I said coolly.

The more I talked, the madder he got. His rage seemed to increase when he realized I knew a lot more than he thought I did. He was probably cussing those women out in his mind.

"Get out of my place before I call the cops and have you locked up again, and this time it's going to be for violating your restraining order."

Cal didn't say anything. He stood scowling at me. I guessed he had a chance to think about what I was telling him.

I walked in his direction to the door to open it for him to leave. When I attempted to pass him, he grabbed me by the arm. "You really think it's going to be this easy to get rid of me?"

"Let me go, Cal," I warned.

"Or what? You don't have your little boss here to protect you now."

When Cal said that, he reared back and swung. His fist landed on my right cheek. The force from his punch caused me to fall back onto my sofa, releasing me from his grasp. Cal didn't halt one minute before he was on me, swinging and punching. I held my hands up to block his blows, but they were coming too fast. Too many were landing on my head. I think I was screaming. And then all of a sudden, he was off me.

I looked up to see Grayson throwing Cal to the floor. Cal quickly jumped up and swung at Grayson. He missed. Grayson retaliated by hitting him in his throat. That one move caused Cal to stumble back. He grabbed his neck, struggling to breathe. His eyes began to bulge like he couldn't catch his breath. Grayson grabbed him, wrapping his hand around Cal's throat.

"Don't do it, Grayson," I yelled to him.

The look he gave me asked, "Why not?"

I answered by saying, "He's not worth it. He's not worth you ruining your future."

I could see this registering within him. He looked back at Cal, who seemed like he didn't want any more. That one punch to his throat was enough to make Cal recoil like the coward he was. Grayson let go. Cal moaned while I ran and called the police.

The police arrived, taking Cal away in handcuffs. Once we told the police about the restraining order, Cal tried to say I called him over there. Then he tried his best to say Grayson was the one who attacked him, but it was two against one here. Plus, the bruises on my body were enough to let the police know Cal was the perpetrator.

Once the police were gone, Grayson came over to check on me again to see how I was doing. "Are you okay?" he asked for the twentieth time already.

"I'm fine, Grayson," I told him with a smile.

"I want to make sure. I wish I would have got here in time."

"How did you know to come when you did?" I asked curiously.

"I sat in the parking lot for a minute because the restaurant called me with an issue. After talking with my coworker for a bit, I pulled off and looked at my gas hand, seeing I needed to get some gas. Then it hit me. How could I pay for gas with no wallet?"

"You left your wallet on my dresser?" I asked in amazement.

"Yep. I turned around, and when I got to the door, I heard you screaming. That's when I burst in. I wish I would have shown up earlier than that."

"Grayson, it's okay. I'm glad you showed up when you did. You're my hero again," I said, reaching over and caressing his hand.

Grayson lifted his other hand to my bruised face. He gently rubbed it, saying, "We need to get some ice to put on that."

"I know it looks bad," I said.

"Can I ask you a question?" Grayson asked.

"You can ask me anything."

"Do you believe in love at first sight?"

"I do," I responded, grinning slyly. "So what are you telling me?"

"I'm saying I can see us going really far in this relationship. I know my timing may be terrible, but, Shauna, I've liked you for quite some time. I don't want to waste another minute."

"So are you saying you want to be in a relationship with me?" I asked.

"That's if you would have me," he said.

This man knew all the right things to say. I know this seemed like we were moving fast, but we were friends first, from back in the day. Why would I want to waste time when I could see if it could work with him?

"Do you think we are moving too fast?" I asked him.

"Not at all. No one knows when love will strike."

I smiled at Grayson and said, "I would love to have you in my life."

Grayson leaned toward me and planted his lips on mine. We kissed for what felt like forever. Grayson broke our connection to ask me, "Aren't you going to be late for your meeting with your sisters?"

"I sure am," I said, leaning forward to kiss him again.

Chapter 36

Serena

The gang was all here, aside from Dawn, who I didn't want to be here anyway for what I had to tell my sisters. It was still early in the day, so we were all dressed down in jogging pants and tees. Even Phoenix was dressed down in a pair of black-and-white geometric-print leggings and a long black top. She even had her hair still wrapped up. She was on Viv's sofa with her feet beneath her, lying down like she was getting ready to go back to sleep.

"Viv, you didn't cook breakfast for us?" Phoenix asked.

"No, I did not. Besides, it's close to lunchtime."

"Then you don't have any lunch made for us?" Phoenix griped sleepily.

"Again, no, I do not. How many fast food places did you pass on your way over here? You should have picked me up something to eat," Vivian retorted.

"I didn't stop and get anything because I figured you were going to cook."

"I've never cooked breakfast or lunch for you guys. You know we usually do dinners."

"You could have made an exception this time. Now what am I going to do? I'm starving," Phoenix said with her arms clamping down on her stomach like she had bad cramps.

"I got some leftover lasagna in there," Viv told her.

Phoenix jumped up with a quickness and ran to Viv's kitchen.

Viv looked at me as I shook my head and we both made our way to the kitchen. When we walked in, Phoenix was placing the lasagna on the counter. She also pulled out a bowl filled with tossed salad, along with taking out two different salad dressings.

"I guess you weren't lying when you said you were hungry," I said to Phoenix.

"Y'all know I'm not usually up this early on a Saturday. My body is not used to this," she said, taking the red plastic lid off the long glass dish. She retrieved a spatula and cut a nice-sized piece of lasagna, placing it on a clear glass plate. She then went over to the microwave above the stove, placed the food inside, and set the timer to heat for two minutes.

"Where's Shauna?" I asked, eager to get this little meeting started.

"Here I am," she said, walking into the kitchen. "I hope you don't mind I let myself in, Viv."

Shauna was the last to arrive and shocked the hell out of us when she came bopping her behind in there with a big bruise on the cheek. We all were ogling her, but she had the biggest smile on her face.

"I wouldn't be smiling if I had that bruise on my face," Phoenix blurted. "What happened to you?"

"It's a long story that I don't feel like discussing."

"You better tell us something," Viv retorted.

"Uhhh, you guys," Shauna said.

"Spill it," I said.

"Okay. Cal showed up at my place this morning and—"

"Please tell me that fool is locked up," Phoenix said, cutting Shauna off like she didn't want to hear any more details. "Because if he isn't, I'm going to call our cousins to handle this fool once and for all."

"Cal is locked up for violating his restraining order, and the man who came to my rescue is Grayson."

"Wait, wait, wait. Who in the hell is Grayson?" Phoenix asked with a frown on her hungry face.

"He's my boss and my new man," Shauna revealed, grinning from ear to ear.

The microwave beeped and Phoenix opened it to retrieve her heated pasta. The steam rose from it as she placed it down on the island. While Phoenix turned her attention to her food, me and Vivian went back to talking to Shauna.

"You can't be in a relationship with your boss," Viv said.

"Yes, I can," Shauna replied.

"Isn't that a violation of some code of ethics?" I asked.

"It might be, but we are keeping things cool until I find me another job."

"Shauna, did Cal hit you in the head too many times? Because you are talking crazy. One minute you down and depressed about this man beating your behind, and the next we know, you are in a new relationship with your boss," Phoenix said.

"Yes, pretty much, but Cal ain't beat me in the head too many times. Hell, maybe that needed to happen in order to find the man who is meant for me," Shauna explained.

All of us stood there looking at Shauna like she had lost her mind. I knew my mouth was open. She didn't pay any attention to me as her happy behind walked over to Phoenix.

"Ooohh, that smells good. Can I get some? I'm starving," Shauna said, reaching to take the fork out of Phoenix's hand to taste her heated food.

"Oh, no you are not. I don't know where your mouth has been," Phoenix said.

"It's been the same place yours has been," Shauna shot back.

"Which is the exact reason why you shouldn't be eating after me."

"Point taken. I'll fix my own," Shauna said, going over to the cabinet and retrieving a plate to fix her own lasagna to heat up in the microwave.

"Can we get this little meet and greet started before you heifers eat everything in my kitchen?" Viv joked.

We climbed up on the barstools at the island and watched Shauna fix her food and Phoenix eat.

"Okay. I called us together to tell you something I found out about our sister."

"What? She finally came to her senses and decided not to marry Corey?" Phoenix kidded.

"No. I haven't spoken to Dawn."

"Then what is this about?" Shauna asked.

"If you two motor mouths will shut up, I will tell you."

"Okay. Go ahead," Phoenix said with frustration as she squeezed ranch dressing on her salad.

"Our sister is a porn star," I blurted. I knew there was no other way to say it but to say it.

The room fell silent. I looked around at each of my sisters to see all eyes were on me. It was like someone had pushed a paused button on our life, and I was ready for the playback to continue.

"Did y'all hear me?" I asked.

"I think we heard you, but we are not sure if we heard you right," Viv said, looking baffled.

"Come into the living room. I have something to show you," I said, jumping down from my stool. Viv and Phoenix were right behind me, but Shauna was too busy fixing her food.

"Don't start without me," she yelled.

When I popped that disc into Viv's Blu-ray player and turned her television on, the same visual of our sister's room came on the screen. It wasn't long before my sisters were watching Dawn in action.

"You have got to be kidding me," Viv said in astonishment.

"I told you," I said, looking over at her stunned face.

"What does she think she's doing?" Viv asked.

"Well, it looks like she's getting hammered by some dude," Phoenix said with a mouthful of food.

"I can see that," Viv retorted. "But what is she thinking?"

"Evidently she's not," I said.

"And here we were thinking little miss innocent Dawn was a prude. She's the biggest freak of us all," Phoenix responded.

"Who knew she was a whore?" Shauna said, taking a sip of wine before putting a forkful of food into her mouth.

"How? What? Who gave you this disc?" Viv stammered.

"Tyree showed this to me. His boy brought it over to him after coming across it."

"So people have seen this?" Viv asked.

"Isn't that what porn is made for, for the enjoyment of others watching?" Phoenix said.

"I'm calling her," Viv said, getting up and going over to her phone.

"For what? She is on her way over here. Besides, what are you going to say to her?" I asked.

"I don't know," Vivian snapped.

"Don't get mad at me. I thought you guys should know," I said in my defense.

"What else is going to happen?" Viv asked no one in particular.

"Viv, you might want to sit back down before you make that call, because that's not all I have to show you."

The looks on their faces told me everything. They couldn't believe I had to reveal something else to them. Little did they know the next video I would be showing could permanently destroy the sisterly bond we were struggling so hard to maintain. For a moment I wondered if I should show it at all, but there were enough secrets among us. This needed to come out, although I hated to bring more damaging revelations to our slowly diminishing family.

Chapter 37

Shauna

All eyes were on me now. My fork was midair when all of a sudden I lost my appetite. A day that had started out great, turning ugly to end up amazing, had all of a sudden taken another dark turn down a road I was not ready to travel.

Vivian was standing across the room with her arms folded across her chest, watching with her mouth slightly open. Serena was sitting on the sofa, looking at me distrustfully, while Phoenix was still chomping on her food, glaring at me like she was waiting for an explanation. All of them were waiting on one, but I didn't have any words to say.

I reached over and put my plate down and replaced it with the glass of wine I had before me. I turned the glass up to my mouth and finished what was left in the glass. Lucky for me, I had brought the bottle into the living room with me. I quickly poured me another and took a large sip before the silence between us was broken.

"Seriously, Shauna," Viv said, being the first one to speak. "How could you?"

I looked at Serena, who dropped her head in disgust, I guessed. The shame and humiliation was taking over.

"Say something," Viv demanded.

"What is there to say?" I finally spoke.

Nervously pivoting from one foot to the other, Viv said, "Explain yourself."

"What can I say? I was wrong."

Serena rolled her eyes as she crossed her arms across her chest. Both she and Vivian were blocking me out, while Phoenix was finishing up the last bit of her food.

"And y'all thought I was the whore," Phoenix said.

I glared at her.

"Well, it's true. All y'all were worried about how I get my money, and we had two sisters bouncing their ass for the world to see."

"You guys. I'm not a whore," I told them.

"Then what does this make you look like? You were so quick to call Dawn one a few minutes ago, yet your ass is up on that screen doing the exact same thing," Vivian said, pointing to the fifty-inch flat panel hanging on her wall.

I was just as shocked as they were to see myself appear on the television, but what made this revelation even worse was the fact that my debut performance was being performed with Dawn's fiancé.

"You slept with Corey?" Vivian asked.

"It was a few times," I tried to explain.

"What's a few?" Viv asked.

"I don't know. Ten. Twenty."

"That's not a few. That's an affair," Phoenix interjected, putting her now empty plate down on the coffee table.

"That's our sister," Vivian stressed.

"She's our half sister, okay? And one I never asked for," I said angrily.

"You didn't ask for us either," Viv shot back.

"True, but at least we came from the same people. She was created through deceit and mistrust."

"So that gives you the right to betray her?" Serena finally butted in.

"I tried to tell her he was no good," I explained.

"Why? So you could have him all to yourself?" Serena snapped.

"I didn't want him. We just had a sexual thing. I didn't want to marry him."

"Just sex, huh? Isn't that what it was for our dad?" Viv asked coldly. "Didn't he sleep with Dawn's mother for just sex?"

I couldn't say anything. It's funny because I'd never looked at it like that. Talk about a smack in the face.

"How are you any different than Dawn's mother?"

Hearing Vivian say that stung more than I was prepared to receive. I dropped my head in disgrace and clasped my hands in front of me, wringing them nervously. Vivian's words did hurt, but that didn't stop me from coming back at her.

"Dawn and Corey are not married, so what's the problem?" I asked angrily.

"But you were going to let her marry him knowing what you two had done together?"

"Would it have made a difference? I tried to talk her out of it. I mean, look at how many women Corey has been with and she stayed by his side. She accepted his hand in marriage for goodness' sake, so why should I care?"

"You don't think that if she knew Corey stooped so low as to sleep with her very own sister it could have changed her mind?" Serena asked.

"I don't know, and to be honest, I don't care. I'm tired of pretending I have been cool with Dawn joining our family. Looking at her every day reminded me constantly of the betrayal Daddy did to our mom. She died with this burden on her heart. That could have been one less thing Mama had to deal with before she left this world."

"Mama was at peace about everything and you know it. If she weren't, she wouldn't have taken Dawn in as her own," Viv explained.

"How do you know? Mama could have died of a broken heart."

"Do you know our mother at all? That woman was so strong. She had the strength to forgive our father and raise the child he had with his mistress. You know Mama never faked anything for nobody, not even Daddy. When she kicked him out, she meant it; but when she took him back, she meant that, too. Mama left this world knowing she was going home to be with Jesus. Her main priority in life was to live the best life possible and treat people to the best of her ability. Mama was a great woman. She knew there was no need to hold grudges because that would hinder her from getting into God's Kingdom," Vivian explained.

I knew she was telling the truth. Mama's main purpose in life was to live right, because she wanted heaven to be her home once this earthly world was done for her.

"I think you can't forgive what happened, Shauna," Serena said. "You can't put this on Mama."

"Maybe you are right," I said.

"And that anger has allowed you to be another one of Corey's pawns," Phoenix said.

"I didn't know he was recording us," I said.

"If Dawn finds out about this . . ."

Chapter 38

Vivian

"Finds out about this . . ." was all I heard when I looked up to see my sister Dawn standing before us. In the midst of our squabble, none of us noticed her enter. And when she did, it was too late. The expressions on all of our faces were ones of shock. I didn't think my heart could take any more. Looking into my sister's eyes, seeing the pain radiating through her was enough to destroy me.

Dawn was glaring at the television as the visual of Shauna and Corey played on my flat screen. We all halted briefly when we saw her. Serena managed to gather her senses, picking up the remote to the television to cut it off.

"Wait! I want to see this," Dawn said coolly.

"Aw, hell," Phoenix replied.

Dawn walked deeper into the room as she watched Corey going in and out of Shauna. He was enjoying himself, and so was our sister. The way they looked at one another and kissed one another was enough to devastate me, and he wasn't even my man.

"Dawn, let me—" I started to say, but she held her hand up to stop me from talking.

"What should I do?" Serena asked. I hunched my shoulders.

"Well, you wanted everything out in the open," Phoenix said. "You got your wish."

"I didn't want it like this," I said.

"Sometimes the way we ask for something is not the way we get it," Phoenix countered.

I looked over at Phoenix, who was shaking her head, looking back and forth between Shauna and Dawn. I gave her a look to leave it alone, but I should have known better, because Phoenix began to speak.

"Y'all need to turn this off, because Dawn doesn't need to be viewing this. She's seen enough," Phoenix said.

Dawn snapped her head around and glared at Phoenix, asking, "Did you know?"

"Know what?"

"Know the two of them were sleeping together."

"No, I didn't know. We all found out about this today," Phoenix explained with a frown.

"Is this why you called me over here, Vivian, so you could humiliate me like this?" Dawn asked.

"You know I would never do anything as cruel as this," I explained.

"It's on the television. All y'all sitting in here watching it like it's some X-rated Lifetime movie," Dawn replied.

"You have to think very little of me to think I'm sick enough to gather our sisters together to watch Shauna in action. Heck, there's a disc on you too," I said, letting her know.

"What?" Dawn asked, confused.

"That's right. We know about your little extracurricular activities. When were you going to tell us?" I asked.

"What I do in the confines of my bedroom is my business," Dawn snapped, pointing at me for emphasis.

"Well, it looks like what's done in the confines of your bedroom is Corey's and Shauna's business too," Phoenix quipped.

"Shut up, Phoenix," Shauna told her.

Dawn dropped her head when Phoenix said this.

I stepped closer to Dawn, saying, "Look, sis. I called you over here to resolve what's been going on with us. I don't like this friction we all have had lately. This is not us. This is not the Johnson sisters."

"She's not a Johnson," Shauna countered. "She had to come from our mother for her to earn that name."

"Shauna, please," I urged.

"Y'all wanted things out in the open, so here it is. Yes, I've been sleeping with Corey. Now what, huh? He caught me out there and taped our little escapades, and I will handle him on that note later, but for now, let's get things resolved," Shauna said callously.

"How could you do this to me?" Dawn asked Shauna, who was sitting back like she didn't have a care in the world. She seemed unfazed by the fact that Dawn just walked in to see her on the big screen doing her fiancé.

"It just happened," Shauna said nonchalantly.

"I swear if I hear another person say, 'it just happened,' I'm going to scream," Serena interrupted, walking across the room with her hands on her hips.

"Well, it did."

"Sex doesn't just happen, Shauna. If it were that simple, then you wouldn't be mad at Daddy and Dawn's mother for having sex either," Serena said.

"That was different," Shauna argued.

"How's it different? Sex is sex," Serena countered.

"Dawn is not married to him," Shauna said.

"And our parents weren't married either. Regardless of the fact that we didn't come from the same mother, we carry the same blood because we all have the same father," Serena retorted. "Mama was Dawn's mother too, so don't sit there and act like Mama would have had it any other way. When you talk like that, you are disgracing the kind act our mother did, so you need to shut your damn mouth about that," Serena said angrily as water filled her eyes.

Dawn began to speak. "I always felt like you hated me, Shauna. I tried to look past it and be the best sister ever. I was grateful for what Mama, your mother, did for me. I couldn't have asked for a better upbringing. I didn't ask for this path in my life. Our dad and my mother chose that for me," Dawn said. "Just like we can't choose our siblings, I couldn't choose my parents either. You've taken your hate and frustration out on me, when the person you should have taken it out on was our dad."

Shauna clapped her hands. "Bravo, Dawn. That was an excellent performance."

"This is not a performance," Dawn said, frowning.

"Come on, Shauna. You are being insensitive here," I told her.

"Has everybody forgotten about what this so-called sister did?" Shauna asked as she scooted to the edge of the sofa.

"Oh, here we go," Phoenix said under her breath as Serena turned her back on what Shauna was saying.

"Don't do this, Shauna," I warned.

"Why not? Isn't this what you wanted, for us to get everything out in the open?"

"Not like this," I said.

"Did you think it was going to go down calmly, with voices composed and smiles on our faces? Please. You know us better than that."

"Okay, Shauna. Let me have it. Say it. Say what Vivian's trying to stop you from saying," Dawn demanded.

Everybody in the room looked around at one another. I hoped Shauna wouldn't say it, but my gut knew this was the moment she'd been waiting for all her life. It was probably why she drank as much as she did. She was trying to forget about the pain our father brought to our family and the end results, which led to us losing our sister.

Chapter 39

Dawn

The words spilled out of Shauna's mouth so easily, like she longed to say those words to me but she had been holding them in for years.

"You killed Renee."

And there it was. The big elephant in the room was even bigger than the revelation that our father was unfaithful. Hearing Shauna say it with such disgust and rage was gut-wrenchingly hurtful. I could feel my throat struggling to close, as the will of my body fought against the anxiety that was setting in.

I nodded and said, "Yes, Shauna. I killed Renee."

I looked into Serena's face, which had tears rolling down her cheeks. Phoenix was on the sofa, leaning on the armrest with her head propped against her open hand. Vivian was standing near me with her back to me and her hands on her head in disbelief. Shauna was giving me a look that could kill me where I stood.

"Finally you admit it," Shauna said.

"I never denied it," I told her.

"But you never admitted to killing her either," Shauna said heatedly. "You let our sister Viv take the fall for you."

"You are right again, Shauna, but while we are coming clean, let's be clear. Not only do you resent me for being the illegitimate child of our father, but you hate me because I took Renee away from you."

"You damn right," she spat. "My sisters have been able to walk around like things within our family are okay, but I've never been able to forgive you for what you did. I've tolerated you for years because of Mama, may she rest in peace.; and I even continued to try to deal with you after her passing, but every time I see your face, I see my sister lying on that floor, struggling to take her last breath," Shauna said, choking on her words as she struggled to resist the tears from falling.

"I didn't mean to—" I started to say, but Shauna cut me off.

"What? You didn't mean to pick up the gun? What? Did it fascinate you after you saw how it blew your mother's brains across the wall, so you needed to see how it worked?"

"Come on, Shauna, that's enough. You don't have to be this heartless," Phoenix said.

"If she knew what guns could do, then why would she ever pick one up?" Shauna asked no one in particular, though she was looking at Phoenix.

No one had anything to say.

"Exactly. She should have known better."

"It was an accident," I pleaded.

I was twelve years old when I accidently shot Renee. I was fooling around in Dad's den and decided to pick up one of the many guns he had in the house. This one was in the gun cabinet, which was usually locked, but this day, it was open for some reason. There was a slight crack in the cabinet door. Being nosy as I was, I went over and picked up one of the handguns.

Renee walked in, saying, "What are you doing?"

Startled, I turned and fired the gun at her by accident. It took me a moment to realize I had even pulled the trigger. I didn't know Daddy kept bullets in the gun. I remember Renee looking down in shock as her mint green T-shirt became crimson.

She dropped to her knees and fell to the floor. Vivian was the first one to enter the room. She ran over to me and took the gun from my shaking hands, asking me what I'd done. Moments later, Daddy and Mom came running in the room, along with Shauna, Serena, and Phoenix.

Daddy tried to save her life. He applied pressure, while Mama called 911. Unfortunately for our family, the wound was fatal and Renee died right there in the den from the negligence of me playing with my father's weapon, resulting in a tragic end for our family.

For years, Vivian took the fall for that incident, saying that she had dropped the gun and it went off. Why I let her do that, I don't know. Maybe it was because I felt like I wasn't supposed to be in their home, and there I was an outsider who had taken someone who was already there and who had welcomed me with open arms. I didn't want anyone to be mad at me, because they were already dealing with the situation of my father and mother, and me having to move in.

It wasn't until Mama was on her deathbed that the truth came out. Mama always knew the story Vivian told wasn't the truth, and she wanted the real story, which Vivian gave her. Mama understood Vivian had taken the blame so the family wouldn't spend my entire life blaming me. Just like Vivian, she felt I had already been through enough tragedy. It still hadn't stopped me from blaming myself. I'd always felt like if I had never moved into their home, Renee would still be here today.

I knew this day would come eventually and I'd figured that with me being an adult now, it would be easier to deal with. But it wasn't. It was as hard, if not harder, than I could ever imagine. The sheer fact that Shauna was bringing it up and had resented me all these years for it hurt me more than I could put into words. I suspected this was why she took it upon herself to sleep with Corey.

"How could you live with the fact that Viv covered for you?" Shauna asked. "Our father was so angry with Vivian about that, because he felt like she knew better than to touch his guns. And she did. It was you, but he didn't know it at the time. Your carelessness cost my sister precious time with our dad, all because of you."

"Shauna, me taking the blame was my decision," Vivian admitted in my defense.

"Did Daddy not treat you differently after that?" Shauna asked.

Vivian didn't say anything.

"She could have spoken up and said it was her," Shauna said.

"She was a child already dealing with drastic changes in her life," Vivian said.

"It was drastic for us too, Vivian, but she had to go and make it worse by killing Renee," Shauna yelled.

"You act like she did it on purpose," Vivian replied.

"I don't know. Did you?" she asked me.

"I loved Renee. I never meant to hurt her," I explained.

"Yeah, just like your mother never meant to break up our happy home," Shauna retorted, leaning back.

"You know what? That's enough, Shauna. I'm tired of this. You need to let this anger go before it ruins you," Serena interjected.

"I'm fine," Shauna said with a smirk.

"Yes. I can see how fine you are. Beat up weeks ago by your crazy boyfriend for him to beat you up again today. You are sleeping with your boss, and then we find out you were trifling enough to sleep with our sister's fiancé. Yeah, I see you are doing real well," Serena scolded her.

"Don't judge me, Serena."

"I'm not judging. I'm stating facts. And here's another one for you: what if I didn't forgive you for sleeping with my man?"

Everybody's eyes widened with the shock of what Serena revealed. Even Shauna looked surprised, like she couldn't believe Serena had brought this up.

"She did what?" Vivian asked, dumbfounded.

"That's right. She did the same thing to me; and I'm your real blood. We have the same mother and father, and you betrayed me first before moving on to Dawn's fiancé."

Shauna glared at Serena angrily, not saying anything.

"With Dawn, you may have done it for revenge, but with me, what was it? Can you tell me why you slept with my man back in the day?"

"I can't believe you brought this up. You told me things were squashed," Shauna said furiously.

"It is, but you need a reality check, because you sitting here beating up on Dawn, when you are the one who's dead set on destroying our family," Serena shot back.

"Me!" Shauna yelled. "Oh, so our family is ruined because of me now."

"Serena didn't mean it like that," Vivian said, trying to ease the tension.

"Then how did she mean it? I didn't cheat, and I damn sure didn't kill anybody," she said, looking at me.

"But you drink and you've crossed the boundaries that never should be crossed when dealing with your sisters' men," Vivian explained.

"Wow! I see how y'all want to do me," Shauna said, picking up her glass of wine and guzzling it. "Since when did this turn into Gang Up On Shauna Day?"

"Since you decided to stoop so low as to disrespect your sister and disrespect yourself, for that matter," Phoenix told her.

"You know what? I don't have to deal with this," Shauna said, getting up from the sofa.

"Oh, so you are going to run," Phoenix taunted.

"I never run," Shauna replied.

"Looks like it to me," Phoenix retorted.

"You guys need to remember I'm your blood. She's not," Shauna said, pointing at me.

"We are all sisters," Vivian said.

"Dawn will never be any sister of mine. I put that on everything, including my mother's Johnson name."

All eyes widened when Shauna said that. She picked up the wine bottle, turned it up to her mouth, and finished what was left in the bottle. All my sisters shook their heads at her.

She put the empty bottle down on Viv's coffee table and headed to the door. Shauna opened it, turned, and looked at all of us before slamming the door behind her.

Chapter 40

Phoenix

As bad as things had been with my sisters, I was in a great mood. I was ecstatic that Tobias had to leave my home that day. When that officer told me I had to file an eviction notice to get this man out of my house, I was down at the courthouse first thing that Monday morning doing just that. Today was the last day he could legally stay in my home. I was all smiles as he sulked and held his head low, like I was going to feel sorry for him. Believe you me, I didn't. He had to get the hell up out of here so I could resume a lifestyle I was so accustomed to—living alone.

Tobias thought living together would make me fall for him, but after today, he would see I hadn't. There had not been one time I hid the fact that I wanted him out of there. He should have taken heed when I told him, but then I poured gasoline on the fire by having my men come through to lay a little, or should I say a lot, of pipe. And still this man refused to leave. Well, now he didn't have a choice. It was adios, sayonara, vamoose, skedaddle, and peace out.

Tobias toted the last of his bags to his car as I sat on the sofa sipping a glass of wine. He stared me down as he stood near the front door. I rolled my eyes and turned from looking at him. I was hoping he wouldn't say anything and walk his ass out of my house so I could get on with my life.

Tobias came around and sat on the chair in the living room and said, "This is it."

"You sure? Because I don't want you to have any reason to come back up in my house."

"No, I got it all."

"Good. I wish I could say it was nice having you here, but I didn't want you here in the first place, so good riddance."

"That's cold, Phoenix."

"Too bad. That's me," I said, crossing my legs at my ankles. His eyes landed on my exposed legs, since I was wearing a pair of cutoff shorts and a T-shirt.

"Why couldn't you just love me? I love you," he proclaimed.

"Look at you, Tobias. You are weak. No woman wants a weak man. The only thing you have going for you is money, and you don't have a lot of that."

"That's why you dealt with me in the first place, isn't it? Because you thought I had more money than I do."

"Yep. Money makes Phoenix come around, but only for a brief moment. Your money was good, but it's not like Diddy money."

"So you looking for a man who can take care of you the rest of your life financially?" he asked, leaning forward with his elbows propped against his knees.

"Yes," I said, nodding.

"What if I told you I could give you that?"

"Tobias, stop playing games. Just get your little briefcase and leave. You know and I know you don't have Diddy money."

Tobias smiled slyly, and I didn't like the way he was looking at me.

"Who hurt you, Phoenix?" he asked coolly.

"What?"

"I said who hurt you?"

"You hurt me by telling lies to stay here," I told him.

"You still have not recognized me," he said, smirking.

I looked at him, wondering what in the world he was talking about.

He reached to the floor and picked up his briefcase. Placing it on my coffee table, he opened it. I didn't say anything, because I was wondering what he was doing. He reached in and pulled out a newspaper clipping and handed it to me.

At first I was hesitant about taking it, but I did anyway. Staring him down, I waited a few seconds before my eyes landed on the picture. It was a photo of Tobias standing beside my ex-fiancé, Noah.

I frowned when I looked at him and asked, "Is this some sort of joke?"

"Not at all," he said calmly.

"Who are you?" I asked frantically, sitting up and placing the glass of wine on the coffee table.

"My name is Tobias. I was partners with your ex, Noah, at the firm he worked at before he moved away."

"I don't remember you," I said, going through my memory bank of all the different individuals I'd met when I was with Noah. Tobias never came to my memory.

"I was more of a silent partner."

"Did Noah put you up to this as some sort of sick, twisted joke?" I asked, glaring at him.

"No. He doesn't know I'm here."

"So you still keep in touch with him?" I asked nervously.

"We talk all the time," he said, wringing his hands together.

"Does he know you are here with me?"

"No."

"So when you got with me, you knew who I was?" I asked him curiously.

"Yes."

"But you decided to keep this bit of information to yourself."

"Yes," he said again.

"You know what? I need you to leave," I said, standing to my feet. This was some weird shit, and I didn't understand anything that was going on right now.

Tobias stood and walked up to me.

"Don't come any closer," I said, causing him to halt.

"I need you to calm down," Tobias said calmly.

"How can I calm down when you're friends with my enemy?" I said furiously.

"Phoenix, let me explain."

I held my hands up and walked away from him, saying, "I don't know if I want to hear anything else you have to say. I think it's best if you leave," I told him.

"Please, Phoenix. Just hear me out."

I paced back and forth, wanting an explanation but fearful of what this man had to say. This was some twisted shit I didn't understand but wanted to understand. If I kicked him out, I may never know the full story of how this came about, which would drive me crazy; so maybe it was a good idea to let him say what he wanted to say.

"Okay, Tobias. Explain yourself."

"I know this may sound cliché, but the first time I ever laid eyes on you, I knew I wanted you to be mine. I knew you were Noah's fiancée at the time, so I knew I couldn't cross that friendship or partnership line with Noah and betray him. I stood back and watched as he destroyed the good thing he had when he had you."

I didn't respond as he continued.

"I know about Noah leaving you for Emma. I know about this baby the two of them had together. And I know about the baby he made you get rid of that caused you never to be able to have children."

"How do you know this?" I asked, frowning.

"Noah would talk to me. I was mad when he betrayed you like he did, but he didn't care, because he was moving on with his life in a new country. I actually hated him for a bit for what he did to you. I also worried about how you were doing during this time. I used to drive by your house to see if I could catch a glimpse of you. I wanted to knock on the door and check to see how you were doing, but I knew I would have looked crazy because you didn't know me."

"You sound crazy now, because it sounds like you were stalking me."

"Maybe."

"So you admit it?" I asked, shocked.

"Every time I saw you, I got excited. I'd seen you in coffee shops and grocery stores, and not once did you pay attention to me. You always paid attention to those business types who looked like male models. I know I'm not a bad-looking guy, but I also knew I really wasn't your type."

"Yet, we got together," I said.

"Buying you that drink that night in the bar was the best moment of my life, because you finally saw me. You might have been looking at my money or the expensive attire I wore, but I didn't care because I was next to you," he explained sincerely.

I walked over and plopped down on the sofa due to my knees wanting to buckle from beneath me. I trembled at the memory, which had taken way too long to forget. Every time I thought about it or heard Noah's name, all of my heartbreaking past came flooding back, making me grieve a life I knew I would never have again.

Tobias came and sat on the coffee table in front of me so he was facing me. He clasped his hands in front of him as he stared into my eyes.

"I know it's hard for you to believe, Phoenix, but I do love you. I know I may not be the best-looking guy out there or have Diddy money, but I can take care of you. I've tried to show you that ever since I've been here. You don't know how hard it was to see you degrade yourself by sleeping with these men who used you for what you could give them. Each time, I wanted to run into your bedroom and snatch them up, throwing them out of here. I hoped you would see how much I cared by not tripping about what you were doing."

"Real men don't allow their women to sleep with other men. And as for me degrading myself, as you say, I don't see it as that at all. I was having fun. I was doing what I wanted to do, and I don't give a damn what you or nobody else has to say about it," I said to him.

"Phoenix, you care."

"No, I don't."

"Why did you allow Noah to change the vibrant woman you were? This is not you. I know this isn't you. You are trying to mask the pain of what Noah did to you by using others to make you feel better about yourself, and this is not the way to go."

"It works for me," I said.

"Why couldn't I work for you?" he countered.

I couldn't say anything.

"I know you call me dorky and wimpy and maybe even a punk, but those are things I can change. I'm not the best-looking dude, but I know I'm not a bad-looking one either." He grinned.

"Who gave you the right to try to save me?" I asked him.

"No one. I wanted to because I wanted you."

"Why?" I asked.

"Again, because I love you."

"You don't know me."

"Do I have to know you to love you?"

"Yes," I blurted.

"I told you: when I saw you, I wanted you. Something happened within my heart that told me you were the woman I wanted to spend the rest of my life with. I know it sounds crazy. I know it doesn't seem real, but it's my truth."

"You know what? This is too much," I said, getting up and moving from in front of him and walking over to the door. "I need you to leave, Tobias."

He lowered his head in defeat. Pursing his lips together, he pushed himself up. Walking over to his briefcase, he reached in and pulled out a manila envelope and placed it on the table for me. Clicking his briefcase shut, he picked it up and walked over to me by the door. I turned the knob and opened it.

He paused in front of me and then leaned down, kissing me on the cheek. I didn't move out of his way. He brushed his thumb against my face and then left. I closed the door behind him, leaning against it, trying to figure out what had just happened.

Then my eyes fell on the envelope he had placed on the table. I walked over to it and picked it up. Hesitating, I wondered what else Tobias was trying to show me. Curious, I opened it. Pulling out the documents, I sat down and began to read.

Chapter 41

Vivian

I was damn near in my birthday suit, having on nothing but a towel wrapped around my body, when Sheldon came walking into my bedroom. I didn't hear him come in. Usually he would be screaming my name from the front door, but today he walked in without so much as a peep.

I stood there gripping the towel around me like it was my lifeline. I had my hair up in a clip so it wouldn't get wet from the shower. Sheldon stared at me with his hands in his pockets, rocking his all-black jeans, tee, and sneakers, with a silver link chain around his neck. He had his dreads down today, and it wasn't long before the scent of his cologne caressed me. He smelled so damn good and looked even better.

Nervously, I said, "I didn't hear you come in."

"Do you want me to leave?" he asked tenderly, like he didn't want to go. Just the tone of his voice was causing my center to tingle.

"No, you don't have to."

Sheldon looked at me from head to toe, taking all of me in. I felt insecure, because I knew I didn't have the best body. Loving myself for who I was and what I had was still a struggle for me, but the way he was looking at me made me feel like the most beautiful woman ever.

He started walking toward me. We were supposed to talk today, and I knew if he came any closer to me, things could end up back in my bed again, even though that wasn't a bad thing. Trust me, I wanted him, but I knew we needed to deal with what had already happened. I felt vulnerable in this moment but managed to stand still until he was standing inches in front of me.

Our eyes locked, and I knew I was in trouble. Sheldon leaned down and kissed me gently on my lips. His dreads fell down around my face, caressing me as his soft lips tantalized me. His hands were still in his pockets and I was still grasping to hold onto the towel, which shielded my nakedness.

The kiss was succulent. I craved to have more of him but pulled away, taking a couple of steps back.

"What are we doing?" I asked him, still tasting the minty freshness of his kiss.

"I thought we were kissing."

"Is this what you came over here for?"

"Yes and no," he said with a smirk.

I frowned, and he began to explain.

"I've thought about kissing you for a long time. When we decided to take things further, Viv, I was in heaven. All this time I've been looking for a woman to fill my day, but I knew all the time I had already found her. I found that woman in you," he said affectionately, causing my heart to melt.

"But . . ."

"I know. We are friends, and you are afraid this will mess up the friendship we have. This could be true, but I'm willing to take the chance and take this friendship thing further. You are worth the risk. I would love if you would allow me to be your man."

The way Sheldon said that made me want to run to my bathroom and find my vibrating friend and use it immediately on myself. I closed my eyes, loving what he was telling me, but doubt hindered me from responding. I was still afraid this would ruin the only good thing I felt like I had in my life—him. He must have seen the doubt on my face because he continued.

"I know you are afraid because you've been hurt, and I can't promise I won't hurt you, but, Viv, I love you with everything in me. I've loved you for a long time now and reveled in the fact that we were great friends, when all the time I was wishing our friendship would become more. Making love to you solidified my feelings for you."

I looked down at the floor, not being able to take in his words. Sheldon removed his hand from his right pocket and used it to lift my face to meet his.

"As your friend, I know most of your fears. As insecure as you think you are, I love everything about you, Viv. I love your smile. I love your laugh. I love your body. I love you," he confessed.

He stopped talking as he gazed at me. I wondered if he paused to hear what my response would be, but I couldn't say anything.

"I hope you don't reject me. That's why I left the other night like I did, because I could not stand you not wanting me."

"It wasn't that I didn't want you. I did," I finally managed to say.

"Then why didn't you say so?"

"Just like you, Sheldon, I don't like rejection either."

"I'm telling you now I want you, but you haven't reacted."

I smiled, saying, "It's kind of hard responding when I'm standing in front of you with nothing but a towel on."

He smirked and said, "I see this as a good thing."

"Oh, you do?"

"You can't tell?" he said, looking down. I could see him holding on to his extension in his pants from his pocket.

All this professing of his love didn't hinder his manhood from saluting me.

"I thought that was your hand."

"Do you want to shake it?" he said, removing his hand from his left pocket to reveal more of the stimulation that radiated throughout his body to create such a wonderful extension.

"I would love to," I said to him with a smile.

I stepped toward him and reached out to grip his manhood. Sheldon closed his eyes with my touch, and it felt like his length got even harder. When I let go, he opened his eyes to look into mine.

"I love you so much," he said to me.

"I love you too," I finally admitted.

Sheldon cupped my face with his massive hands and pulled me to his lips. He kissed me deeply this time. I let go of my towel to wrap my arms around his waist. I could feel the towel slip from my body and fall to the floor, leaving me exposed to whatever he was going to do. Never had I felt so comfortable with a man. This felt right with Sheldon. This was the feeling I'd been looking for all my life.

Once our lips disconnected, he looked down at my wonder. I didn't try to hide myself from him, and he smiled, I guess noticing the comfortable demeanor I had with him. He reached down and pulled at the hem of his shirt, pulling it over his head to reveal something I hadn't seen before.

"What did you do?" I said, looking at a tattoo on his chest.

"It's your name, Vivian."

"You did this for me?" I asked.

"I wanted you to see I'm not playing when it comes to my love for you. I know you are the woman meant for me, and I wanted to show you by placing your name near my heart. No woman has ever captured it like you have."

Tears welled up in my eyes as I reached out and ran my fingers over my name engraved in his chest.

"It's beautiful."

"Just like you," he said. "So would you do me the honor of being in a relationship with me?" he asked.

I smiled and said, "I would love to be in a relationship with you."

The biggest smile ever crept across his face, and he reached down and pulled me into his arms, hugging me tight. He rocked back and forth, holding me like he didn't want to let me go. This felt good. This felt right, and I'd never been happier in my life.

When he let me go, he said, "I want to make love to you."

Hearing him say "make love" made my heart pulsate with eagerness. I had a man who loved me for who I was and everything I was about.

He leaned down to kiss me again as he backed me up to my bed. This was the moment when I knew I was going to spend the rest of my life with this man.

But like most perfect moments, it was quickly shattered by a phone call that would leave me stunned.

Chapter 42

Dawn

I was devastated. I walked into my home like I was a zombie as I replayed the visual of Corey and my sister, Shauna, on the big screen together. In addition, finally dealing with accidently killing Renee was way too much for me to handle. I cried all the way home. Vivian, Serena, and even Phoenix tried really hard to make me feel better about what had happened. I appreciated them being there for me, but Shauna's words had mutilated me. She had said what I'd told myself all my life: I was not an official Johnson woman. I was one by default, created by the sins of my mother and my father.

I walked into my kitchen to see if Corey was in there, but he wasn't. Nor was he in the living room. The next place I headed was our bedroom. I needed to talk to him about what I had just found out, and I wanted answers from him. How could he want to marry me if he was doing my sister?

When I got to my door, it was closed. I turned the knob and opened it only to get one more devastating blow. Corey was in our bed with some light-skinned woman with long, bone-straight black hair. He was hitting her from the back, and across the room was the camera, taping their little sexual escapade.

When he turned to look at me, he had the audacity to smile and wave me over to join them. Was he serious right now? Could he not see my face and tell I had been crying my eyes out? If he was my man, then one, he wouldn't be doing this; and two, he would stop what he was doing to run over to me and find out why I was upset. I guessed he was so deeply enthralled with his manhood being buried in this chick's wetness that he didn't notice my mood. He never stopped his stride. Was this because the camera was on, or was this because this man was playing me and was having his cake and eating it too?

My body trembled from anger, rage, and hurt. My world was crashing down around me, and I wanted the pain to end. My mother's face popped into my mind, and in that moment, I could understand why she gave up on life. I knew why she pulled the trigger and ended it once and for all. Sometimes it was better to not deal than to struggle with things that seemed to be out of control in your life.

I walked to our master closet, dropping to my knees in front of our safe, which was on the floor in the back of the closet. Turning the dial, I put in the combination. After putting in the third number, I pulled on the handle and watched as the safe opened with ease. In there were stocks, bonds, government documents, and some cash. And also in this space was a gun.

I picked up the cold steel and lifted it out of the safe. Bringing it to my chest, I hugged it, wishing it could comfort me in my time of sorrow. Tears streamed down my cheeks as so much pent-up pain released from me. It came in tsunami waves, crashing to the core of my being. I rocked back and forth and prayed to God to instantly take this pain away from me, but He wasn't hearing me. The pain was still piercing my soul.

I struggled to stand to my feet, looking around at all the clothes and shoes in the small walk-in closet. Material things meant nothing if I wasn't happy with myself and my life. Then I looked at Corey's things and wondered how I could allow this man to degrade me like this. What was wrong with me, for me to think this was okay? I had agreed to marry him, and I couldn't figure out for the life of me why.

I swiped at my tears and looked up to the ceiling, still praying for something to happen. I needed immediate satisfaction. I turned and walked out of the closet and back into my bedroom. Corey was still going to town on the woman. He didn't notice me enter the room again. I stared at him one last time before lifting the gun.

"God forgive me."

I pulled the trigger.

Chapter 43

Serena

Aw, hell naw, was my first thought when I walked into my home and found Juanita sitting on my couch. And who was sitting on the couch with her? Tyree. I was standing in my door with my keys in my hand, gawking at the two of them talking like they were old friends. I slammed the door, and Tyree stood to his feet.

"Hey, baby," he said like he didn't have the enemy sitting on our sofa.

"What is she doing in our house?" I asked angrily, glaring past Tyree at Juanita, who had this same condescending smirk on her face.

"Serena, stop yelling. Nevaeh and Zamir are sleeping."

"I don't give a damn. Tell me what is she doing in our home, Tyree?" I demanded.

"It's cool. She came to reconcile things with us," Tyree said dumbly.

"What?"

"She came over to apologize."

"She could have called. She didn't have to come to our home to do that." I looked at Juanita, who stood to her feet. I said, "You do know there is still a restraining order on you, right? You don't like abiding by the law?"

"Look, Tyree, I didn't come over here for all this," she said with an attitude.

"Serena, come on. Hear her out," he said to me.

Was he kidding me right now? Was I his woman, or was Juanita? I put my hands on my hips and said, "Get that bitch out my house."

"Bitch," she said, frowning at me.

"That's right."

"Don't get it twisted, Serena. Just because I'm pregnant with our man's baby and in your home don't mean I won't stomp that ass," she said, bristling up.

"Juanita, cool it," Tyree told her.

"You better tell her, Tyree," Juanita threatened him.

Tyree looked at me like he wanted me to chill.

"You know what? Both of y'all can get the hell out my house," I said, waving my arms and pointing to the door.

"Calm down, Serena," Tyree urged.

"I can't believe you, Tyree. You got your baby mama up in our house after all she's done. She's threatened me and your daughter. She's had you locked up by lying, and now she wants to apologize. Well, I'm going to tell you and her, I don't accept her apology. Now get the hell out my damn house," I yelled.

"You see. You try to do right and your trick-ass girl going to trip on me," Juanita said to Tyree.

"Trick-ass! Let's wait to see who that baby's daddy is," I said, pointing at her belly, "and then we will see who's been tricking."

"Yeah, we will see. I can't wait to see your face when you find out it's Tyree's baby."

Her words upset me because I was still trying to get over the fact that he even slept with the bitch. I thought things between us were working themselves out, but to see he had the audacity to allow Juanita in our home made me look at Tyree differently and wonder if he was really in this relationship fully with just me.

"Juanita, can you please leave?" he asked her.

"Gladly, but this will be the last time I try to work things out, Tyree," she said, wobbling her behind to my door. "Kiss our son for me," she said, looking at me and smirking.

Tyree looked at me knowing damn well she was egging me on by saying that. That's what that bitch did: she pushed you until you were ready to catch a damn charge from beating her ass.

Once that door shut behind her, I turned all my rage to Tyree. "What were you thinking?" Holding up my hands, I said, "Wait. You weren't. You never think. That's why she might be pregnant with your second child—because you didn't think."

"I wanted all this tension to stop, Serena. It's been going on way too long."

"It's been going on because she started it. She can't get it through her thick skull you guys are over. Or maybe you are not done with her. Is that it?" I asked him.

"No. We are done."

"It doesn't seem that way to me. You seemed to be more up her ass than being on the side of the woman who just gave birth to your daughter. You live with me. You are in a relationship with me, so you should have confided in me before you allowed her to step foot in our home."

"I tried to do a good deed for our kids."

"That woman wanted your child dead. Does that sound like somebody I'm going to forgive anytime soon?" I asked him. "Why would I accept her apology after all she's done?" I asked him.

"I just thought—"

"Again, you weren't thinking. You could have called me to see if I even wanted to consider talking with her instead of bombarding me."

"I'm sorry," he apologized.

"You sure are," I retorted angrily.

"It will never happen again," he said.

"I know it won't, because you are getting out of here today."

"What?" He looked at me, dumbfounded.

"Get your shit and get the hell out my home," I said sternly.

"You joking right?" he said, laughing nervously.

"Does it look like I'm kidding?" I asked him, looking more serious than I had at Vivian's house earlier.

"So you breaking up with me?" he asked.

"Yes. I'm done with you, because I can't trust you."

"Wow! I can't believe you right now," he said, walking away as he started to catch an attitude himself.

"You can't believe it? I can't believe I wasted my time with you, trusting you, loving you, for you to still find another way to hurt me, Tyree."

He leaned on the arm of the sofa, looking straight ahead. I continued.

"Give me a reason to continue this relationship, especially when I know one day I want to be married. You gave me an ultimatum before, so you know what? I've decided I'm done. I don't want to be with you anymore."

Tyree nodded and didn't say anything. He stood and started walking to our bedroom. I followed him to see what he was doing, and sure enough, when I entered, he was pulling out his suitcase and loading clothes into it.

I chuckled, and he looked at me, asking, "What's so funny?"

"You're funny. You were fighting harder for Juanita to apologize than you are to make us work. It's bit of an eye opener for me."

"I told you, Serena, if you want me gone, I'm not going to fight."

"Maybe if you did, then that would show how much you want to be with me, but I guess I'm not worthy."

"You are. I do love you."

"You've had a funny way of showing it."

He sighed and turned back to pack more clothes in his suitcase. Then he asked, "What about Zamir?"

"He can stay; that's if you and Juanita don't mind. There's no need to wake him. You can come pick him up tomorrow," I told him, knowing Zamir and our daughter were the innocent ones in this mixed-up situation.

Once Tyree had the majority of his things packed, he walked to the door and placed them all there. I sat on the loveseat with my arms crossed, watching and thinking about everything that had transpired over the past few months.

"I got all my things," he said.

"Good."

He looked heartbroken, but I didn't care. As much as I looked like I was happy about our relationship ending, I was the heartbroken one here. I truly did love Tyree, but not enough to be used and abused by him or his baby mama.

"Are you sure about this, Serena?" he asked gloomily. "We can make this work. If you want me to marry you, I will."

My breath caught in my throat, and I got annoyed as I looked his way. "So you mean to tell me you want to marry me now?" I asked heatedly.

"That's what you want. Isn't this why you are doing this, to scare me into marrying you?" he asked.

"You're steady revealing yourself to me." I chuckled. "You think I'm doing this to make you marry me?"

He didn't respond.

"I'm doing this because I'm done. I am fed up with our bullshit; and for you to think I'm doing all of this so you can marry me further lets me know I'm making the right decision. Why would I want a man I had to force to be my husband? Think about what you are saying. I want a man who knows it's me he wants for the rest of his life with no doubt, and who doesn't base his future on the past of his parents," I said with certainty.

He dropped his head when I said this.

"So please trust, I don't want to marry you. I want you gone."

Tyree nodded as he picked up his duffle bag and slung it over his shoulder. Opening the door to leave, he picked up his suitcases.

Turning to look at me again, he said, "I love you, Serena."

"I love you too, Tyree."

And he was gone.

Chapter 44

Serena

One Year Later

Tyree kept his word when he said he was going to drop Nevaeh off early this morning, since our daughter and I had big plans today.

"Hi, honey," I said to my daughter, who grinned back at me. "What did Daddy get you?" I asked her, looking at her wearing a tiny gold necklace with matching bracelet and a new baby doll.

Tyree put Nevaeh down, and I watched as she took off running to her room. She looked so cute as her little head bobbed and her ponytails bounced. I smiled, amazed at how fast she was growing up.

"Thank you for dropping her off early. I know this is your weekend to have her, so if you want, you can spend some time with her tomorrow," I told him.

"It's okay. I will see her on Wednesday. I'm going to let her enjoy this happy occasion with you," he said coolly.

I thought after Tyree and I broke up that we were going to have issues with him wanting to see her and him not taking his responsibility seriously by paying me child support for Nevaeh. To my surprise, we'd worked things out between ourselves. Like adults, we talked and agreed that Tyree would get to spend time with his daughter every other weekend and every Wednesday. Concerning support, Tyree gave me $200 a month for her, and if I ever needed more from him, he didn't have any issue giving me what I needed. Plus, he brought her things all the time.

"You know she didn't need any jewelry, Tyree. She might break it."

"It's okay. I think it looks cute on her."

"It does," I said.

"You look beautiful," he complimented me.

"Thank you."

It was weird feeling awkward around the man I once loved and had a child with, but a lot had changed. When I kicked Tyree out of my place, I meant what I said by never allowing him back in my life. Concerning our daughter I had to deal with him, but pertaining to any intimate relationship between us, it never crossed that line after that day. Trust me; he wanted it to. Just the way he looked at me let me know he wanted me at times. Like now.

"Congratulations. I heard you and Juanita were getting married," I said.

Tyree dropped his head as he shifted uneasily. He couldn't marry me, but he proposed to the woman who made his life a living hell. I guess misery loves company. I was happy for them. I mean really, I was truly happy for him.

Tyree stuttered to say something, but I said, "It's okay, Tyree. I'm not mad," I told him.

"I knew you would find out eventually," he said. "I've been trying to figure out a way to tell you."

"You don't owe me an explanation."

"But I feel like I do," he said.

I giggled and said, "Tyree, it's okay. I'm happy for you. I know Juanita is happy too," I said.

"She is."

It was funny how Tyree went back to the very woman who caused so much turmoil in our relationship. Juanita got what she wanted, which was her children's father. Yes, the baby Juanita had did turn out to be Tyree's baby. She gave birth to another boy and they named him Shamar.

"Hey, baby, which tie do you think I should wear today?" my boyfriend said, walking into the living room holding up a red-and-black tie and a gray-and-blue tie.

"I like the gray-and-blue one. I think it's going to look better with your suit."

"What's up, Tyree?" my new man, Dorian, said.

Tyree nodded but didn't speak. I found this funny, because I could clearly see he had an issue with me moving on. I don't know why he had a problem. He made his choices and was with the person he wanted to be with. He had seven months to get used to seeing Dorian around. Dorian hadn't moved in with me, but he stayed over some nights. He had stayed over the night before because we had big plans, plus I didn't have Nevaeh, which gave us some time to spend alone with each other. We agreed to keep living separately to see how things went between us, and fortunately Dorian was a wonderful guy.

"I'm going to take my shower," Dorian said.

"Okay."

Dorian left the room. I turned to see Tyree clenching his jaw. He rubbed his head in annoyance and said, "I guess I should be going."

"Thank you again for switching weekends. I'll see you Wednesday," I said.

"Yes. I'll be here around six."

"Sounds great," I said, walking around him to open the door.

Tyree proceeded to walk out of the door but stopped directly in front of me, looking like he wanted to say something. When his face shifted, I knew he wasn't going to say whatever was on his mind.

"Good-bye, Tyree."

He pushed his full lips together before saying, "Good-bye, Serena."

Chapter 45

Phoenix

I'd never been so happy with my life. And you know why? I had gone on a man hiatus. That's right. I gave up men for a while. After Tobias put things in perspective for me, letting me know I needed to take a look at my life and how I was making detrimental decisions regarding myself, I had decided to cut all ties with the men I was dealing with. It took Tobias for me to realize I was putting myself out there like a paid whore.

I was celibate for five and a half months. Can you believe it? Me, Phoenix, didn't have dick for that period of time. It was like not having that animate object penetrating me allowed my mind to become clear as to where I wanted my life to go. That's when I decided to follow my dream and go to school to become a chef. I couldn't be happier with my decision. Becoming enthralled with something I loved, like taking different types of meat, vegetables, and spices and turning them into something magnificent, was enough to make me have an orgasm from the pure joy of it all.

Still, as fate would have it, I did end up with a guy in my life, and that guy ended up being Tobias. One day he just stopped by to check on me. I hadn't seen him in months. I guess instead of driving by my house, wondering how I was doing, he decided to park, get out, and knock on the door to see this time. I was surprised to see him, and I wasn't rude. I invited him in, and from there we'd been talking.

I realized there was more to being with someone than just money and nothing else to offer. I needed to be with a man who was willing to love me and give me the world. Lucky for me, Tobias was that man. The ironic thing was Tobias did have Diddy money. Those papers he gave me that night he had left revealed a lawsuit he'd filed against Noah, who had embezzled money from a company they were partners in. Tobias not only gained the joint venture company he and Noah acquired together, but he ended up winning a multimillion-dollar lawsuit against Noah, who was ordered to pay the money he stole back to Tobias.

Now, mind you, I had no clue about any of this. I had never been involved with how Noah made his money. Hell, I never cared how any man I dealt with made his money, just as long as he took care of me.

That was then; this was now, and I was a woman making her own money. Even though Tobias had Diddy money, I wasn't that same woman who felt privileged to this money. I liked that about myself now.

As irony would have it, Noah's baby mama left him for someone else when his money dwindled. I heard she took the baby and moved to France with her new man, and Noah was back in California living with his parents, so the child he yearned to have was still not in his life.

Don't you know he had the nerve to call me one day. He called to apologize and said he hoped we could be friends. I told him I didn't need any friends and to not get any ideas about trying to come back into my life, because I had moved on with Tobias. Needless to say, this was shocking to him, because he didn't have a clue I was with his once great friend. I can't lie; that shit felt good telling him that. I know it was wrong to feel great about him feeling bad, but I am human. I never thought the day would come when I felt like I got one up on Noah, but I did, and it helped me move on to develop a better relationship with Tobias.

"Phoenix, we need to go. You know we can't be late," Tobias said, looking handsome in his suit. That once-dorky man was looking way better than he used to, and that was due to me changing up his attire a bit. I think it was Dawn who told me you couldn't turn a whore into a housewife. I wasn't a housewife yet, but the fact that I could be with this man made me happy because now I knew that anybody could change.

Chapter 46

Vivian

I never thought I would see this day in my life. Looking into the long mirror, I stood in my wedding gown, getting ready to walk down the aisle to marry the man I loved. I had thirty minutes to be a free woman before I became Mrs. Sheldon Garrison. I smiled at my reflection, amazed at how far I'd come. Not only was I marrying the man I loved, but I'd learned to love myself more and be confident in the skin God had blessed me with.

Rubbing my hands down my waist, pushing out any imperfections, I turned right and then left to make sure everything was like it was supposed to be. My tiara on my head sparkled as ringlets of curls fell freely. My face was made up, nails were done, and the only thing left to do was slide on my five-inch heels and make my way to becoming a married woman.

"You look beautiful," Serena said, looking me over. She was holding Nevaeh's little hand, who looked cute with her white flower girl dress on and a ringlet of flowers around her little head. When I looked down at her, she smiled up at me with her little teeth and the dimple in her right cheek. She looked adorable.

"Hello, Nevaeh," I said in the baby voice I used with her, and she ran over to me and wrapped her little arms around me.

"No, Nevaeh. You are going to get Auntie dirty," Serena said, trying to stop her.

I said, "It's okay." I scooped my niece up in my arms and hugged her lovingly. Feeling her little arms around me felt wonderful.

"You better give her to me before she gets something on your dress," Serena said, reaching for her. Nevaeh went to Serena as she continued to speak. "You don't know how hard it is to keep this little one from getting anything on her. As much as this is your day, I can't wait until you walk down that aisle so I don't have to worry about her getting dirty."

I giggled.

"Are you ready?" she asked excitedly.

"I am. I'm so happy," I said joyfully.

"Here we were thinking Dawn was going to break the curse of the Johnson women, and now you are the first in four generations to get married."

"You know I never fed into that curse on the Johnson women thing," I told her.

"I know, but I did."

Phoenix burst into the room, saying, "You have ten minutes, Vivian."

I giggled and said, "I'm ready."

"I still can't believe you are getting married," Phoenix said.

"Me either, but I am happy I am, because I really do love Sheldon," I proclaimed.

Both of my sisters were wearing lavender-colored bridesmaid dresses with matching heels. It was so good having them both by my side today. Mama and Daddy crossed my mind, along with Renee, who I wished was there with me. I knew they were there in spirit, but it still made this moment bittersweet.

Shauna came walking into the room with her bridesmaid dress on, saying, "You should see all the people out there."

"Is it a lot?" Phoenix asked.

"You know it is. Sheldon has a huge family, and some of them brothers are fine as hell."

"We are in a church, fool," Serena said.

"Oh, my bad," Shauna said, covering her mouth.

If anyone had come a long way, it was Shauna. That night when my and Sheldon's moment was interrupted by a phone call, it was Shauna calling me from jail because she was arrested for reckless driving and DUI. That girl was a nervous wreck. I'd heard of karma, but she got it as soon as she left my home that day, and she had vowed she would never drink and drive again.

She didn't drink that much anymore. I think her being behind bars for that short stint was enough to scare the alcohol out of her. Here she was living in the past, not realizing she should have been working on how her future was going to be.

Another silver lining for Shauna was the fact that she was still with Grayson. Cal was finally out of the picture for good, since he received time for assaulting her and disobeying the restraining order. My sister couldn't be happier.

"Look, before we leave, I have something to show you guys," Shauna said, walking over to me. "I need you to sit down."

"Do you know how tight this dress is?" I said, laughing.

"Try anyway."

I did as she asked, and Shauna knelt down beside me as Serena and Phoenix stood behind me. Shauna took out her cell and pushed a few buttons until a video began to play. Dawn's face popped up on the screen, and my hand flew to my mouth with joy.

"Hi, you guys. Hey, Vivian, I heard you were getting married today. I wish I could be there, but you know I'm currently tied up right now," she joked. "I wanted you to know how happy I am for you. No one deserves this more than you. I'm there in spirit. You know I love you. I love all of you, and I can't wait until we have one of our sister-dinners again. It's going to be a while, but trust, it's going to happen. Congratulations, sis. You are marrying a wonderful man. Enjoy your day, and party enough for me. I love you," she said, putting her hand to her mouth and blowing me a kiss.

Tears streamed down my cheeks.

"How are you going to make her cry right before she walks down the aisle?" Phoenix asked, wiping tears from her own eyes.

I looked at all my sisters, and each one of them had tears falling.

The reason why my sister Dawn couldn't be here was because she was in jail for shooting Corey in the back. She had unloaded the gun completely before she walked back to her living room and sat waiting for the cops to arrive. This incident was made worse by the fact the camera was recording the entire incident. It quickly went viral all over the Internet.

She was arrested and charged with attempted murder. I say *attempted* because Corey ended up surviving. Unfortunately for him, he would be paralyzed from the waist down for the rest of his life. Again, there goes that karma. You can't do people any kind of way and not have to pay for what you've done. I don't agree his payment should have been him getting shot, but at the same time, you can't predict people a lot of times. I hated that it was at the cost of my sister's life, but she had to pay for what she did. She ended up getting a ten-year sentence, which was reduced due to the fact that she pled guilty due to being mentally unstable. She was getting the help she needed, despite the fact that she was behind bars. I missed her so much and tried to visit her as often as I could. Seeing her on the video made my day.

For Shauna being the one to show me the video, I knew this meant she had gone to visit her. She had blamed herself for Dawn snapping like she did, and she said she wished our last sister-gathering turned out better than it had. Shauna was dead wrong for what she did and realized her mistakes. I was glad she'd grown up to learn to be accountable for her actions. She finally made peace with everything. I think both Shauna and Dawn had. Sometimes it takes getting down to your lowest points to help you rise above and beyond even what you thought you could achieve. This couldn't be truer for them. As Mama always said, "As long as you learn and grow from your mistakes, I'm happy."

"It's time," Serena said, looking at me.

I stood and walked over to my white blinged-out shoes and stepped into them. Phoenix held her hand out for me to hold so I wouldn't fall.

"Let me look at myself one more time," I told Phoenix, who helped me over to the mirror again. She dabbed at my face again, making sure my makeup was on point.

"Can't have you looking like a raccoon out there," she said.

I gazed at my reflection, knowing this would be the last time I would see myself as a single woman. I smiled at myself and tried my best not to cry so I wouldn't ruin the fabulous makeup job Phoenix did for me.

"I'm ready," I said with a smile. "I can't believe this is happening."

"Believe it, sis. You are marrying the man of your dreams," Serena said, coming up behind me and placing her loving hand on my back.

All of my sisters stood around me, and I looked at how beautiful we all were. Despite our ups and downs, we were still here, standing as one.

The curse on the Johnson women was mentioned earlier, and I had to smile, thinking I didn't know if it was a curse at all. Maybe it was just about the choices we made, especially the ones who settled for less than they deserved.

I thanked God in this moment for bringing me such a long way. He had blessed me with the man of my dreams. He blessed me with the gift of loving myself; and most of all, He blessed me with wonderful sisters. Life sometimes deals you a bad hand, but it is up to you how to play it. Each Johnson sister went about playing the hand they were dealt differently, but the one thing I was happy about was that we still remained close in the end.

> over you, as I pray he will, and keep you from all dangers. Amen.

Other circumstances besides Gracián's absence increased Teresa's loneliness. She no longer felt sure of the loyalty, or even the affection, of the band of daughters whom she had chosen and trained with such loving care – her prioresses. Ana de Jesús, the most outstanding of them, the friend and spiritual peer of St John of the Cross, upset her by the way she mishandled the foundation at Granada which Teresa had been unable to undertake herself. Teresa thought it 'all wrong from beginning to end'. She sent Ana a sharp letter of reproof for failing to keep the Provincial and the Foundress fully informed, for treating her nuns inconsiderately and for favouring those most attached to her person and thus fostering the formation of cliques, for lavishing money on an expensive convent building, and for fussing about whether the Superior should be addressed as 'Prioress' or 'President', and for other frivolities. If a foundation were to flout the principles of humility and obedience enjoined by the Constitutions it would be better not to undertake it at all, Teresa concluded, since the aim of the Reform was to increase not the mere number of convents but the spirituality of those living in them. Either the hardships undergone by the nuns must have caused them to take leave of their senses, or else 'the Devil is introducing the principles of Hell into this Order'. Ana de Jesús took these strictures to heart and emerged after Teresa's death as her wise and worthy successor. Since few of Teresa's letters to her have survived, it would be rash to draw conclusions from one sharply worded reproof, but the Foundress would seem to have preferred María de San José to succeed her. Though Teresa had had brushes too with the Prioress of Seville, she felt deep affection for the younger woman's warm nature and ready wit.

> If my opinion were to be acted upon, they would elect you Foundress when I am dead; indeed, I should be delighted if they

> were to do so during my lifetime [Teresa wrote to her]. I am rather more experienced than you, but little notice will be taken of me now. You would be shocked to see how old I am and of how little use for anything.

In Valladolid one of the bitterest experiences of Teresa's last years awaited her. María Bautista had grown into a managing and opinionated woman who ruled her convent with a self-confidence which made her impatient, and at times resentful, of her aunt's prestige. Doña Beatriz de Castilla y Mendoza, who had come to Valladolid determined to confront the Foundress and prevent Teresa's dowry from being made over to St Joseph's, found a ready ally in the Prioress. Doña Beatriz threatened that, unless Teresita renounced her share of the inheritance, she would contest Lorenzo's will. Her lawyer made a scene in the convent parlour, taxing the Foundress with obstinacy and lack of charity. María Bautista sided with the attackers. Even Teresita, overawed by the violence of the onslaught and confused by appeals to her sisterly affection, began to think that her aunt was being unreasonable.

> I have had a terrible time here with Don Francisco's mother-in-law [the Foundress wrote to Gracián]. She is indeed a strange woman, and bent upon going to law to contest the validity of the will. Although the right is not on her side, she has influential connexions and some supporters who have advised me to come to an agreement to save Don Francisco from ruin and ourselves from having to bear the cost. This will mean a loss for St Joseph's, but I trust in God that, since its claim is sound, the convent will eventually get the inheritance. I am quite worn out with it all.

Though Teresa had to bow her head and admit defeat, her confidence was not misplaced. The feckless Francisco went off to Peru, squandered his wife's dowry and died childless, the remainder of his estate reverting in the end to St Joseph's.

Teresa makes no mention in her letter to Gracián of the shadow which had fallen between herself and María Bautista. According to Ana de San Bartolomé, they were sent on their way with the harsh words of the Prioress ringing in their ears: 'Begone! And mind you don't come back!' Another account, by Gracián's younger sister María, who had recently taken the veil in the convent, speaks of the affectionate farewell which the Foundress took of the other nuns, embracing each in turn and bidding them in moving terms to remain true to their vocation of obedience, humility and poverty. Teresa normally avoided emotional leave-takings; but this, as she and her daughters instinctively felt, was to be the last, and her words had the solemn ring of testament and benediction. Their sweetness dispelled the sour taste of María Bautista's dismissal.

In Medina, where the travellers spent the next night, the Foundress suffered the indignity of a further rejection. Alberta Bautista, the Prioress, was a woman of austere and unsmiling piety. When young, she had once been chided by Teresa for priggishly refusing to join in the nuns' recreation on the grounds that they should concern themselves only with contemplation, not with singing. When Teresa last visited Medina, Alberta had been ill in her cell, but at a word from the Foundress she had got out of bed apparently quite cured, so that the nuns accounted it a miracle. But now all was sadly changed. Teresa herself was sick, worn out with the fatigue of the journey. A remark made with her wonted frankness caused the Prioress to take offence and go abruptly to her room. Teresa retired to hers. Her distress was so acute that she would neither eat nor sleep.

Fifteen eventful years had passed since Teresa came to Medina to found her first reformed community outside Avila. There too she had chosen the two men who were to carry the Reform to the friars. John of the Cross was now absent in Andalusia, but not from her thoughts; her last letter to Gracián concludes with a message of warm remembrances for him. With Fray Antonio de Jesús her relations had also remained close but sometimes clouded. The one-time Prior of the Toledo Calced had never overcome his chagrin at being unable to claim undisputed priority as the first Discalced friar; that distinction was commonly accorded to John of the Cross. Nor could he reconcile himself to the bitter fact that, for all his seniority and good intentions, he had been forced to play second fiddle to the brilliant Gracián, and latterly to the thrusting Doria. The new Constitutions laid down that when the Provincial for the Discalced was in Castile he must appoint a Vicar for Andalusia, and when in Andalusia a Vicar for Castile. Since Gracián was at the time in Seville, Fray Antonio was vested with full powers for Castile, and he now appeared in Medina with a most unwelcome mandate. Instead of going straight to Avila, the Mother Foundress was to make a detour to Alba in order to attend the election of a new Prioress there and also to offer the consolation of her prayers and her presence to the Duchess of Alba's daughter-in-law in her approaching confinement. The Duchess had long been an influential supporter of the Reform and a good friend both of Teresa and Friar Antonio; her wishes had the force of a command, and the ducal carriage was already at the convent door.

Before she left Medina Teresa wrote her last letters. Only one of them has come down to us, and its text is defective. She seems to have begun it in Valladolid, but adds in a postscript: 'We are now at Medina, and I am so busy that I can only tell you we have arrived safely.' The letter is addressed to Catalina de Cristo, her Prioress at Soria, and it deals with usual convent matters – the profession of a young nun, the alterations to be done to the kitchen and refectory, the possibility of a new convent at Pamplona, her hopes of seeing one founded in Madrid and her plans to stay only a short time in Avila and then to visit Salamanca, where the Prioress was unwisely bent on buying a new house. It is an astonishingly normal and natural letter to come from a hand growing almost too weak to hold the pen, and from a heart wounded by rejection and anxiety. Not a word of the writer's failing strength, the ingratitude of her daughters or the ordeal of a journey wearily prolonged. It treats of the familiar affairs of this world with the serenity of one who is on the threshold of the next.

For the remaining days of Teresa's life we must turn to the accounts left by her companions. Ana and Teresita both describe the intensity of her distress on learning of Friar Antonio's order to defer her return to St Joseph's and take the road to Alba. 'Never have I seen her suffer from a command given by a superior so much as she did from this one', Ana recalls. Doña María de Mendoza and other friends urged her to excuse herself on the grounds of ill health. The Foundress would not hear of it. Unquestioning obedience had ever been her rule; 'Out of obedience I would go to the end of the world. . . . Obedience makes all things possible.' It was not for her to demur or to seek excuses. Old and infirm though she was, she would still obey.

The ducal carriage, despite its grand name and imposing appearance, was a cumbrous, ill-sprung conveyance which jolted every bone in the body as it rattled over the fifteen leagues of rough road towards Alba. Teresa was weak for lack of food and sleep, and the offended Prioress made no provision to lighten her sufferings. Ana records the agony of that last journey:

> We set out without taking anything with us for the road, and the saint stricken with her last sickness. I could discover nothing on the way to give her; and at night when we came to a poor village near Peñaranda de Bracamonte, where we could get nothing to eat, she found herself exceedingly weak and said: 'Daughter, give me something, for I feel faint.' I had nothing but some dried figs, and she was suffering from fever. I gave the servants four reals to get some eggs for her, whatever they might cost. When I saw that nothing could be had for the money, which they gave back to me, I could not look at the saint without weeping, for her face seemed half dead. I can never describe the anguish I felt then. My very heart seemed to be

> breaking and I could only weep when I saw the plight she was in, for I saw her dying and could do nothing to help her.

Teresa noticed her companion's distress and made light of her own sufferings: 'Don't worry on my account, daughter. These figs are very good. There are many poor folk who don't get such a treat.'

They spent the night at a wretched inn and came next day to a hamlet where the only fare offered was a dish of onions cooked with herbs. Teresa forced herself to take a few mouthfuls. They were nearing Alba, and a message reached them that the Duke's daughter-in-law had given premature birth to a son. Throughout the jolting discomfort of her moving cell, the Foundress had been silently praying for the woman in travail. The Lord was pleased to grant her petition. 'God be praised!' she exclaimed with a flash of her wonted self-mockery. 'Now they will no longer have need of this old saint!'

On the evening of 20 September the carriage, escorted by Friar Antonio, who had been inquiring fussily why the Foundress was so uncommonly silent, lumbered into Alba de Tormes. 'I haven't a sound bone left in my body!' Teresa told the nuns with a wan smile as they helped her to her room. She blessed them and let them kiss her hand, no longer refusing them those marks of affectionate veneration which her humility customarily declined. They had prepared her bed with fresh, white linen – an attention reserved for those seriously ill, and one most pleasing to her taste for fastidious cleanliness. 'It is more than twenty years since I have gone so early to bed!' she exclaimed, recalling those long hours spent in prayer and vigil, the endless stream of letters read and answered by candlelight, the accounts of conscience, the books written at the command of confessors or the behest of daughters.

The next morning Teresa was somehow up and about again, leaning heavily upon her stick. She attended mass and went round the convent inspecting every detail with her accustomed thoroughness and interesting herself in the coming elections when

Juana del Espíritu Santo, an old friend who had left the Incarnation to join the Discalced, was due to hand over her office of Prioress. The convent had been going through difficult days. Its benefactress, Doña Teresa de Laíz, who had once seen in a vision the family of holy virgins whom God was to give her instead of children, had been presuming too much on a parent's right to regulate their affairs. Her interference had become so intolerable that it was difficult to find anyone willing to serve as prioress. Teresa reasoned with her and all difficulties seemed to be smoothed out. But the nun elected Prioress was a partisan of the benefactress and treated Teresa with marked coolness. There were long and tiring negotiations too with the Rector of Salamanca, who had come over to persuade Teresa to withdraw her objections to the purchase of a new house in that city. The matter was anyway already settled, and the deal virtually concluded, he declared, when he found his arguments failed to move her. 'Settled?' replied Teresa with spirit. 'It is anything but settled, and never will be. The nuns will not move into the house on which their Prioress has so mistakenly set her heart. It is quite unsuited to their needs and not what God wishes for them.' The Rector had left the contract ready for signature, but on his return to Salamanca he found that the owners had unaccountably withdrawn their offer.

Thoughts of St Joseph's still obsessed her. Would hunger again distract her nuns from their devotions, now that she was not there to care for them? Would Teresita make her profession amongst them? 'As soon as you see me a little better, do something to please me, daughter!' she begged Ana. 'Find some carriage or other and take me back with you to Avila!' She had transacted her last business for the Alba convent, and her strength was failing so fast that she had to be carried to the grille to take leave of her sister Juana. The little girl whom she had brought up in her own cell in the Incarnation was now herself prematurely aged. Her life with Juan de Ovalle had not been easy, and she had continued to lean heavily on her sister for practical and spiritual support. Their leave-taking was tender and painful.

The last ties were being severed one by one. The new Prioress, on the pretext of preserving her guest's health, imposed a seclusion bordering on ostracism. Only the Duchess, with the privilege of rank, disregarded all restrictions and came repeatedly to sit at Teresa's bedside. The Duke her husband was in Lisbon, his former disgrace eclipsed by his latest triumphs in the sovereign's service. Teresa spoke of him, asking her visitor several times whether she loved him very much, as if foreseeing that the conqueror of Portugal too had only a short time to live. Once, just before the Duchess came to visit her, one of the evil-smelling medicines uselessly prescribed by the doctors was spilt over the sheets, to Teresa's vexation. The Duchess replied to her apologies with surprise: 'But what unpleasant smell do you mean? It is as if angel-water had been sprinkled over the bed!' All those present agreed; the whole sick-room was redolent with a delicious fragrance.

At Michaelmas, nine days after reaching Alba, Teresa suffered a severe haemorrhage. They carried her to an infirmary which had a grille looking out onto the chapel below so that she could watch mass being celebrated. For a whole day she lay there absorbed in prayer. Friar Antonio was summoned. When the old man knelt beside her bed to hear her confession, he exclaimed helplessly: 'Mother! Pray God not to take you now; do not leave us so soon!' 'Hush, Father', she murmured. 'How can you say this? I am no longer needed in this world.'

On 2 October Teresa knew that she had only a few more hours to live. She had neither the time nor the strength for homilies beyond a few simple words for her nuns:

> My daughters and ladies: For the love of God I beg you to observe most carefully the Rule and the Constitutions. If you keep them as faithfully as you should, you will need no further miracle for your canonization. Do not imitate the poor example set you by this bad nun, but forgive me.

When the Blessed Sacrament was brought, Teresa struggled to

her knees and would have prostrated herself before it if they had not held her back. Her face was transfigured with love and adoration. A torrent of exclamations poured from her lips: 'My Lord and my Bridegroom! The longed-for hour has come! Now is the time for us to meet, my Lord and my Beloved! Now is the time to set forth!' After receiving the Host, she returned thanks to God for letting her die in the bosom of the Catholic Church. She kept repeating with joy and fervour: 'Lord, I am a daughter of the Church!'

Friar Antonio, well-meaning but clumsy as ever, asked what wishes she had for her burial: should it be there in Alba or in Avila? 'Jesus! Why do you need to ask, Father? Have I anything at all of my own?' She turned to Juana del Espíritu Santo, who was holding her in her arms. 'Won't they have a little earth to spare for me here?' she asked. 'You are Prioress at Avila, Mother, and it is good that we should go back there', put in Ana, remembering Teresa's earlier injunctions. Could they already be disputing the possession of her worthless body? Teresa showed no interest; her thoughts were still for others. 'Go and get some rest, Father', she said to the friar. 'The nurse will fetch you when it is time.'

The last night was one of great pain. When it slackened she would repeat passages from the psalms, lingering with particular unction over the verse, 'The sacrifices of God are a broken spirit. A humble and contrite heart, O Lord, thou wilt not despise.' Then she would break off to beg her nuns once more to be sure to observe the Rule and the Constitutions.

The next day was the feast of St Francis. Dawn found her lying on her side, her face towards the nuns. It was clear and radiant, as if the hand of an angel had passed over it, smoothing away the wrinkles and leaving the skin fresh and translucent as a young girl's. She lay there silent and serene, united in ecstatic prayer with her Lord.

Only once did a troubled expression come into her eyes. Friar Antonio had sent Ana away to snatch a little food and rest. The dying woman noticed her absence at once and Teresita, perceiving her distress, hurried from the room to fetch the little lay sister back. Teresa smiled as she took her hand. Then she lay still again, her head cradled in Ana's arms, until she expired peacefully at nine o'clock the same evening.

The cell was bathed once more in that mysterious fragrance, now so irresistible that it penetrated corridors, rooms and chapel. The mourners declared that it was stronger and more pervasive than the incense offered the following day at the saint's obsequies.

The human record of Teresa's life ends on this evening of 4 October 1582. But, for the saint, death means entering into that fuller life which lasts 'for ever and ever and ever', as she and her small brother had loved to repeat in childish wonder at their first glimmering awareness of the mystery. So, to those striving to follow in her footsteps, Teresa's death brought enrichment as well as deprivation. In Beas, the visionary Catalina de Jesús declared that the Holy Mother had appeared to her and bade the nuns cease from mourning, for she would now be interceding for them on high. 'Her daughters experienced a great renewal of spiritual ardour', observed Gracián's young sister María in Valladolid. 'They saw that she was helping them from heaven.'

The fame of the departed Foundress continued to attract many recruits to the ranks of the Discalced. Sixteen convents and fourteen priories were in existence at the time of her death. Within the next five years six more houses for women and fifteen for men had been established. Their numbers entitled the Discalced to the quasi-autonomous status of a separate 'Congregation', linked to the Calced only in the person of a common Father General. Six years later a papal bull made them into a fully independent Order with a General of their own. They had founded many houses outside Spain and carried the Reform to Portugal, Italy, France, Belgium, America and other parts.

The price of this rapid expansion was a sharpening of personal rivalries and a widening divergence of views. Teresa had believed at first that the two outstanding figures amongst the friars, Gracián and Doria, would co-operate and complement one another, the charm, eloquence and idealism of the former combining with the Italian's tenacity, administrative flair and worldly wisdom to form an incomparable partnership. The methods and personalities of the two men proved in fact incompatible and the resulting clash between them almost fatal. Doria, sure of official backing in Italy and cunningly exploiting the jealousies aroused in Spain by the younger man's rapid rise, moved skilfully to isolate him and to centralize power in his own hands. Gracián was eased out of office and, ingenuous as ever, even proposed Doria as his successor, causing St John of the Cross to warn that he was voting for the man who would one day strip him of his habit. The ex-Provincial was then relegated to Portugal, and there was talk of packing him off to the Indies. But once assured of the support of the Crown and the Pope, Doria preferred to inflict the ultimate indignity of expelling him from the Order. It was only after the death of the Genoese, who did not live long to enjoy his triumph, and after a spell of heroically borne slavery at the hands of Moslem pirates, that Teresa's dear 'Paul' was rehabilitated and able to resume work for the Reform.

Others who had been closely associated with the Foundress also suffered from Doria's despotism. Of the friars, only Antonio de Jesús, nursing his grievances against Gracián, lived on undisturbed into his nineties. St John of the Cross was persecuted and died in disgrace. Teresa's favourite daughters suffered equally. María de San José, transferred from Seville to found a convent in Lisbon, was defamed and imprisoned. Ana de Jesús, who had so pained Teresa by her errors over the foundation in Granada, made ample amends by her courageous championship of the principles of the Reform. Whilst insisting on strict obedience to superiors, Teresa had stood for the nuns' democratic right to elect their own prioress and choose their own confessors; Doria strove to bring them all under his personal and centralized control. Ana resolutely appealed to the Pope to uphold the Constitutions. She enlisted the help of the now venerable Báñez, other old friends of the Foundress, and new allies like the fiery controversialist and famous scholar-poet Luis de León, who set about editing the saint's works. Rewarded by Doria with three years' penal detention, she emerged to carry the Carmelite Reform to France, Belgium and the Low Countries and to crown her devotion by publishing, with Gracián, Teresa's *Book of the Foundations*.

The dissemination of Teresa's writings deepened the veneration felt for their author and strengthened demands for her canonization. But some dissentient voices were also raised. Dr Francisco de Pisa, a learned historian and Professor of Scripture, urged that her writings should at least be banned; their author, whom Rome was later to declare a Doctor of the Church, he described as an unlettered albeit virtuous woman whom ignorance had led into error. A handful of fanatical friars went so far as to brand her a heretic. The most vehement was Friar Alonso de la Fuente, who had hounded the *alumbrados* of Estremadura and professed to find their contagion in her books, which he delated no fewer than five times to the Inquisition. Another Friar, Juan de Orellana, demanded that 'the Holy Office ban the book on account of its false doctrine, burn the heretic, and pay no heed to any alleged miracles'. Finding the Spanish Inquisition unresponsive, his colleague Juan de Lorenzana carried the charges to Rome, where they were pressed for a dozen years until silenced by the chorus of voices testifying to the Spanish nun's orthodoxy and personal sanctity.

In 1614 Rome decreed Teresa's beatification and eight years later her canonization. Her devotees pressed for even more. As Spain's military and political fortunes declined, it looked as if Santiago Matamoros, St James the Moor-slayer, was no longer dispensing the protection expected of a warrior-saint. Demands were raised that he should be given the new saint as co-patron. The Cortes approved the proposal and the King gave it his assent. Controversy at once broke out, the Moor-slayer's partisans finding an eloquent spokesman in the famous satirist Quevedo, himself a Knight of Santiago. Finally the Pope pronounced a compromise: St Teresa should be considered a patron only in those places, such as Avila and Alba de Tormes, which wished to accord her such an honour.

Those two cities, which had respectively witnessed the birth and the death of the saint, disputed the possession of her mortal remains with a passionate and macabre zeal. The cult of relics was still as fervent in sixteenth-century Spain as ever it had been in the Middle Ages. Teresa, as a true daughter of the Church, would never have dreamed of questioning it, though it seems to have played little part in her own devotional life and hardly figures at all in her writings. Nor could she ever have imagined that her own remains would be added to the sacred stock, to be avidly fought over, ghoulishly examined, discussed, subdivided, and ultimately distributed throughout Christendom.

The Foundress was buried in the convent chapel at Alba fifteen hours after her death. The mourners, led by the Bishop of Salamanca and the Duke of Alba's eldest son, filed past the bier where the body lay swathed in rich brocade and reverently kissed the saint's alabaster foot. The masons had hastily dug a deep grave beneath an archway in the wall just below the choir. Loads of stone, rubble and moist earth were tipped in on top of the coffin and pressed down so firmly that, as one of the nuns observed, it looked as if they were laying the foundations for some great building. Doña Teresa the benefactress was determined to make the most of the unexpected good fortune which had brought her celebrated namesake to die in the convent, and she feared that St Joseph's, and perhaps other claimants too, might claim her treasure. Friar Antonio, self-important in his office of Vicar Provincial, was whole-heartedly on her side and determined to disregard what he knew Gracián's wishes would be. 'Here she is, and here I mean her to stay for all eternity!' he was heard to declare in altercation with an angry Juan de Ovalle, who although living near Alba himself believed his sister-in-law should lie at rest in her native Avila.

Gracián's chance came nine months later, when he arrived in Alba on an official visitation. The nuns willingly offered their help in exhuming the saint's body. The tomb had continued to emit its mysterious fragrance and several miracles had been reported, to say nothing of the visionary appearances vouchsafed by the saint to Ana de Jesús in Granada and a number of other nuns and friars elsewhere. The whole community was consumed with a pious urge to look once more on the face of their holy Foundress. After four days of hard and furtive work – for no inkling of what was afoot must reach the ducal palace – the coffin was reached and the lid, which had been staved in by the weight above it, removed. The damp earth had rotted the habit, but the body itself was intact and uncorrupt. 'My companion and I retired whilst they undressed her', Gracián records. 'They called me back again when they had placed a sheet over her. Uncovering her breasts, I was surprised to see how full and firm they were.' The Provincial then cut off her left hand with a knife and deposited it in a sealed casket in Avila, after removing the little finger, which he kept about his person as a talisman. The body was replaced in the mouldering coffin and the tomb resealed.

But the possession of a mere hand only whetted appetites in Avila. Gracián was determined to follow up his success with a decisive victory. He felt under an obligation too to Don Alvaro de Mendoza, who was resolved that he would leave his own bones in the sumptuous tomb already prepared for them in St Joseph's, and that those of the great Foundress he had befriended should rest on the other side of the altar. Though no longer Provincial, Gracián persuaded the Chapter of the Discalced, when it met for its second official session in Pastrana three years after Teresa's death, to authorize a further exhumation of her body and its secret transfer to Avila. It was agreed that one arm of the sacred body might be left with the nuns of Alba to console them for their loss. Dr Juan Carrillo, the Bishop of Avila's former secretary, was nominated a member of the Commission appointed to carry out this delicate task and has left us a detailed account of its proceedings. His colleagues were Gracián, Julián de Avila, and Father Gregorio Nacianceno, who had accompanied Teresa on her arduous journey to Seville.

When the Commission arrived in Alba, they confided the real reason for their coming only to the Prioress, sub-Prioress, and Teresa's old friend, Juana del Espíritu Santo, who were overcome with consternation but could do nothing in the face of their superiors' categorical commands. The rest of the nuns were sent to sing Matins in the choir as usual so that their suspicions should not be aroused as the Commission set about its gruesome work. The old Duchess and her son the present Duke were fortunately away, but speed and secrecy were still essential. The body was found to be in much the same excellent state of preservation as before, only slightly shrivelled, though the sheet and the new habit with which it had been reclothed two years earlier were already rotted. Inside the coffin they also discovered a piece of linen which had been used to staunch the 'flux of blood' – the result of a broken blood-vessel – which was said to have been the immediate cause of the saint's death. It was still bright red and was found to possess the marvellous property of communicating the blood-stains to any piece of cloth placed in contact with it. The body continued to exhale an odour of sanctity so powerful that it dispelled the mustiness of the open grave and penetrated to the choir, alarming the nuns, who broke off their singing and hurried back in dismay to discover their loss.

Friar Gregorio drew a knife from his belt and

> with extreme repugnance – he has since told me it was the costliest sacrifice he ever made for Our Lord – and in fulfilment of his vow of obedience [Teresa's biographer Ribera records] he

> inserted it under the left arm . . . and with no more effort than it needs to cut a melon or a little fresh cheese, he severed the arm at the joints.

Disregarding the tearful protests of the nuns, the friars quickly removed the body to a room opposite the convent where they could inspect it at leisure. They found the face somewhat flattened but clearly recognizable, the body 'the colour of the bladder-skins into which beef-fat is put . . . well covered with flesh from head to foot, the stomach and breasts as if they were made of a corruptible substance', firm yet pliant, and the whole body weighing no more than a baby's. When they had gazed their fill, the friars wrapped the body in a sheet and a covering of frieze, sewed it well up, and carried it over to the inn, where Gregorio and Julián guarded it until the following morning. It was then carefully packed between bundles of straw and taken on mule-back to Avila. 'The precious relic was handed over to the sisters at St Joseph's', Carrillo concludes his narrative, 'who were as overjoyed at receiving it as the nuns of Alba were grieved at its loss.'

For a time the nuns of St Joseph's were left in proud possession of their treasure. They kept it in a coffin-shaped casket lined with black taffeta trimmed with silk, silver and gold, and adorned on the outside with gilt studs and two gold and silver shields inscribed with the name of Jesus and the Order's coat-of-arms. On New Year's Day the Bishop of Avila, attended by some twenty dignitaries, crowded into the convent porch, where the body was brought out and laid before them on a carpet. They 'gazed upon it with reverent awe and many tears'. The doctors pronounced that, since it had not been embalmed in any way, its preservation in such a perfect state was clearly supernatural. The bishop, fearing the wrath of the great house of Alba should the pious theft be discovered, forbade those present to divulge what they had been privileged to see under pain of excommunication. But such a miraculous event could not be hushed up; piety and local patriotism exultantly proclaimed that Avila now had a new saint, and the Bishop was obliged to lift his ineffective ban. The news quickly reached Alba, infuriating the Duke and sending the dowager Duchess into a paroxysm of rage and grief. Tradition has it that one of the nuns communicated the secret by slipping a note into a pie destined for the ducal table, and that on learning its contents the old lady rushed out into the street screaming: 'They have taken St Teresa from me! They have taken away my saint!' The Duke calmed her by declaring that he would get the Pope to order the body to be returned. The Pope complied; Father Doria, now Provincial of the Discalced, was commanded to make the necessary arrangements. He was forced to obey, though he tried to save face by declaring that the body was only being sent back 'on loan'. Once more, the precious burden was strapped onto a mule and escorted by two friars back to Alba. They broke their journey at Mancera, where a friar keeping vigil over it at night was rewarded by being cured of his chronic ague.

On 23 August 1586 the friars completed their thankless mission. The bundle was once more uncovered before the gaze of the assembled nuns, whilst a notary duly recorded their jubilant and unanimous assurance that this was indeed the body of their beloved Foundress, Mother Teresa de Jesús. Armed guards were posted at the church door, for who could tell what new tricks the defrauded friars might try to play? A stout iron grille kept the body, which now lay exposed to public veneration, from the prying hands of relic-hunters. Father Ribera was amongst the eager crowds, and nearly two years later he returned for an opportunity of examining it more closely. By that time he found the body

> straight, though rather bent forward, as is the way with old people . . . It can be lifted up and held in place with one hand, and dressed and undressed as if alive. The whole body is the colour of dates . . . The head is as thickly covered by hair as when they buried her, the eyes are dry but whole . . . even the

> hairs on the moles of her face are still there. The mouth is tightly closed. . . . So greatly was I consoled by the sight of this hidden treasure [the good Father concludes] that I think it was the happiest day I have ever spent in my life, and I could not gaze at her enough. My one anxiety is that the body will some day be dismembered at the request of great personages or the importunity of her convents.

Ribera's forebodings proved to be gruesomely justified. Five times, beginning with the Provincial's pious spoliation, the body was disinterred, displayed, mutilated and replaced. Even within the lifetime of Teresa's family and friends treasured pieces of her anatomy found their way to distant parts. Gracián, the first to appropriate his share, had the finger confiscated by Barbary corsairs but bought it back from them for twenty reals and some gold rings. Agustín, the youngest and most restless of her brothers, somehow procured a 'piece of flesh, white as milk, and about a finger's length and thickness', which comforted him on his deathbed in America. By the time the mortal remains were publicly exhibited in the middle of the eighteenth century they had been pitifully mauled, although the individual members remained uncorrupt. Not only the arm removed by Friar Gregorio but the right foot, the left eye, part of the upper jaw and much of the neck had gone. The head had been severed and several of the ribs and other bones and pieces of flesh had been ripped out, and the heart also. The latter became the object of particular veneration, for it was found to be seared as if by a knife thrust, about an inch and a half in width, the edges of the wound appearing charred – clear evidence, her votaries claimed, of its transverberation by the Seraph's flame-tipped spear. Rome secured the right foot, Madrid a portion of the saint's cheek, Paris and Brussels a finger each, Mexico a fragment of flesh.

Most remarkable of all have been the posthumous adventures of the saint's left hand, which found its way into the possession of the

Carmelites of Ronda. Stolen from its shrine there in the opening turmoil of the Civil War, it was later recovered in Málaga, in its heavily bejewelled reliquary, from a suitcase containing the personal effects of a Republican officer. It was then presented to General Franco, who kept it by him for four decades. Teresa's hand accompanied the dictator wherever he went and was at his bedside when he died. Now it is back in Ronda and the Carmelites are happy again. Need we envy them their treasure? We have her own writings, with their record of a unique personality and an extraordinary spiritual odyssey; and (if we share her faith) the most human of saints as intercessor in the heavens above Mount Carmel.

Notes

CHAPTER 1

Evidence for the Jewish ancestry of Juan Sánchez and his family is given in the depositions of witnesses cited in a law-suit of 1519; Narciso Alonso Cortés, *Pleitos de la Cepeda*, in the *Boletín de la Real Academia Española*, XXV, pp. 85–110, and Homero Serís, *Nueva geneología de Santa Teresa* in *Nueva Revista de Filología Hispánica*, Mexico 1956, X, pp. 365–84. Orozco's eye-witness account of the Toledan *autos de fe* has been published by Fidel Fita in the *Boletín de la Real Academia de Historia*, 1887, XI, pp. 291 *et seq*. For a general discussion of St Teresa's ancestry and *converso* associations, Francisco Márquez Villanueva, *Espiritualidad y Literatura en el Siglo XVI* (Madrid 1968), pp. 141–205. For Toledo in the sixteenth century, Francisco de Pisa, *Descripción de Toledo*, Madrid 1605; republished 1974.

CHAPTER 2

The chief source for Teresa's early life is the account given in the first four chapters of her own autobiography, of which numerous English versions exist. A good modern translation is that by J. M. Cohen, *The Life of Saint Teresa*, Penguin Books, London 1957. The Spanish text will be found in the convenient one-volume edition of the saint's collected works in the *Biblioteca de Autores Cristianos*, Madrid 1967, edited by Efrén de la Madre de Dios and Otger Steggink. The same authors have collaborated in the invaluable *Tiempo y Vida de Santa Teresa* (Madrid 1968), pp. 3–60. The fullest annotated biography is Silverio de Santa Teresa, *Vida de Santa Teresa*, Burgos 1935–7, 3 vols. Of the earliest biographies the most interesting are: Francisco de Ribera, *Vida de la Santa Madre Teresa de Jesús*, Salamanca 1590, reprinted, with notes, Barcelona 1908; Julián de Avila, *Vida de Santa Teresa*, edited by Vicente de la Fuente, Madrid 1881; Diego de Yepes, *Vida de Teresa de Jesús*, Madrid 1587, Buenos Aires 1946.

CHAPTER 3

Life, chs. 4–6; Efrén and Steggink, pp. 59–88; Francisco de Osuna, *Tercera Parte del Abecedario Espiritual*, Toledo 1527, Madrid 1911. On Teresa's illnesses: M.

Izquierdo Hernández, *Santa Teresa – Enfermedades y Muerte*, Madrid 1963, and Pablo Bilbao Arístegui, *Santa Teresa de Jesús, enfermera*, Vitoria 1952.

CHAPTER 4

Life, chs. 5–9; Efrén and Steggink, pp. 88–101.

CHAPTER 5

Life, chs. 10–29; *Mansions*, chs. 3, 6, 7; *Account of Conscience*, October–December 1560; Efrén and Steggink, pp. 102–27. Bernardino de Laredo, *Subida del Monte Sión*, Seville 1532; Eng. trans. by E. Allison Peers, *The Ascent of Mount Sion*, London 1952. Teresa's locutions and visions, E. Allison Peers, *Studies of the Spanish Mystics*, vol. 1 (London 1951), pp. 153–7.

CHAPTER 6

Life, chs. 20–1; *Account of Conscience*, 1960; *Mansions*, iv, ch. 3; vi, chs. 4–6. Herbert Thurston, *The Physical Phenomena of Mysticism*, London 1952.

CHAPTER 7

Life, chs. 32–4; *Letter* to Lorenzo de Cepeda, 23 December 1561; Efrén and Steggink, pp. 128–50; Ribera, chs. 13–16; A. Barrado, *San Pedro de Alcántara*, Madrid 1965; Silverio de Santa Teresa, *Historia del Carmen Descalzo*, Burgos 1935–49, vols. 3 and 4.

CHAPTER 8

Life, chs. 34–5; *Letter* of June 1562 to García de Toledo; Pedro de Alcántara's letter of 4 April 1562; Efrén and Steggink, pp. 150–60.

CHAPTER 9

Life, ch. 36; Efrén and Steggink, pp. 161–82; Jerónimo de San José, *Historia del Carmen Descalzo*, Madrid 1637; Julián de Avila, *op. cit.*

CHAPTER 10

Life, chs. 37–40; *The Way of Perfection*; *Meditations on the Song of Songs (Conceptions of the Love of God)*; *Constitutions of the Discalced*; *Letters*, December 1576–June 1578; Efrén and Steggink, pp. 183–215; Ribera, Julián de Avila, *op. cit.*; Emilio Orozco, *La Poesía de Santa Teresa; el canto en la vida conventual* in *Poesía y Mística*, Madrid 1959.

CHAPTER 11

Book of the Foundations, chs. 1–20; *Accounts of Conscience*, 1570; *Letters*, 1568–71; Julián de Avila, Ribera, Yepes, J. de San José, *op. cit.*; Efrén and Steggink, pp.

262–458; E. Allison Peers, 'The History of the Discalced Carmelite Reform' in *Handbook to the Life and Times of St Teresa and St John of the Cross*, London 1953; María de San José (Salazar), *Libro de Recreaciones*, Burgos 1913; F. Márquez Villanueva, *Santa Teresa y el Linaje* in *Espiritualidad y Literatura en el siglo XVI*, Madrid 1968; Gaspar Muro, *Vida de la Princesa de Eboli*, Madrid 1877.

CHAPTER 12

Foundations, chs. 13–21; *Accounts of Conscience*, 1571–5; *Letters*, 1572–5; Julián de Avila, Ribera, Yepes, J. de San José, *op. cit.*; Efrén and Steggink, pp. 286–93, 324–9, 342–6, 367–72, 395–412, 459–71, 495–504, 520–43; Allison Peers, 'History of the Discalced'; Crisógono de Jesús, *Life of St John of the Cross*, London 1958; Francisco de Santa María, *Reforma de los Descalzos*, Madrid 1644–55.

CHAPTER 13

Foundations, chs. 22–6; *Letters*, 1575–6; *Accounts of Conscience* 1575–6; Jerónimo de Gracián, *Obras*, Burgos 1932, 3 vols.; E. Llamas Martínez, *Santa Teresa de Jesús y la Inquisición Española*, Madrid 1972.

CHAPTER 14

Letters, June 1576–June 1579; *Life*, ch. 24; *Foundations* (Epilogue); *Mansions*; Efrén and Steggink, pp. 595–605; Allison Peers, *op. cit.*

CHAPTER 15

Letters, June 1579–February 1582; *Foundations*, chs. 28–31; *Accounts of Conscience*, May 1581; Efrén and Steggink, pp. 605–742; Ana de San Bartolomé, *Autobiographie*, Paris 1869; Gracián, Ribera, *op. cit.*

CHAPTER 16

Letters, March–September 1592; Efrén and Steggink, pp. 742–72; A. de San Bartolomé, Gracián, Ribera, Allison Peers, *op. cit.* For posthumous events – Silverio de Santa Teresa, *Procesos de Beatificación y Canonización de Santa Teresa de Jesús*, Burgos 1934–5, 3 vols., and 'La Mano de Santa Teresa redimida de la esclavitud bolchevique' in *Monte Carmelo*, XLI, Burgos 1937, pp. 147–56 and 195–201; L. Carbonero y Sol, 'Catálogo de las reliquias de Santa Teresa' in *La Cruz* II, Madrid 1882, pp. 563–71.

Index

Index

The Adventures of Sherlock Holmes

Sir Arthur Conan Doyle

Word Cloud Classics
San Diego

Canterbury Classics
An imprint of Printers Row Publishing Group
10350 Barnes Canyon Road, Suite 100, San Diego, CA 92121
www.thunderbaybooks.com

Printers Row Publishing Group is a division of Readerlink Distribution Services, LLC. The Canterbury Classics and Word Cloud Classics names and logos are trademarks of Readerlink Distribution Services, LLC.

All correspondence concerning the content of this book should be addressed to Canterbury Classics, Editorial Department, at the above address.

Publisher: Peter Norton
Publishing Team: Lori Asbury, Ana Parker
Editorial Team: JoAnn Padgett, Melinda Allman
Production Team: Blake Mitchum, Rusty von Dyl

Library of Congress Cataloging-in-Publication Data

Doyle, Arthur Conan, Sir, 1859-1930.
The adventures of Sherlock Holmes / Sir Arthur Conan Doyle.
p. cm. -- (Canterbury classics)
ISBN-13: 978-1-60710-556-5
ISBN-10: 1-60710-556-X
1. Holmes, Sherlock (Fictitious character)--Fiction. 2. Private investigators--England--Fiction. 3. Detective and mystery stories, English. I. Doyle, Arthur Conan, Sir, 1859-1930. Adventures of Sherlock Holmes. II. Title.

PR4621.S52 2012
823'.8--dc23

2011049594

PRINTED IN CHINA

20 19 18 17 16 9 10 11 12 13

CONTENTS

A SCANDAL IN BOHEMIA

To Sherlock Holmes she is always *the* woman. I have seldom heard him mention her under any other name. In his eyes she eclipses and predominates the whole of her sex. It was not that he felt any emotion akin to love for Irene Adler. All emotions, and that one particularly, were abhorrent to his cold, precise but admirably balanced mind. He was, I take it, the most perfect reasoning and observing machine that the world has seen, but as a lover he would have placed himself in a false position. He never spoke of the softer passions, save with a gibe and a sneer. They were admirable things for the observer—excellent for drawing the veil from men's motives and actions. But for the trained reasoner to admit such intrusions into his own delicate and finely adjusted temperament was to introduce a distracting factor which might throw a doubt upon all his mental results. Grit in a sensitive instrument, or a crack in one of his own high-power lenses, would not be more disturbing than a strong emotion in a nature such as his. And yet there was but one woman to him, and that woman was the late Irene Adler, of dubious and questionable memory.

I had seen little of Holmes since the singular chain of events which I have already narrated in a bold fashion under the heading *The Sign of the Four*. My marriage had, as he foretold, drifted us away from each other. My own complete happiness, and the home-centred interests which rise up around the man who first finds himself master of his own establishment, were sufficient to absorb all my attention, while Holmes, who loathed every form of society with his whole Bohemian soul, remained in our lodgings in Baker Street, buried among his old books, and alternating from week to week between cocaine and ambition, the drowsiness of the drug, and the fierce energy of his own keen nature. He was still, as ever, deeply attracted by the study of crime, and occupied his immense faculties and extraordinary powers of observation in following out those clues, and clearing up those mysteries which had been abandoned as hopeless by the official police. From time to time I heard some vague account of his doings: of his summons to Odessa in the case of the Trepoff murder, of his clearing up of the singular tragedy of the Atkinson brothers at Trincomalee, and finally of the mission which he had accomplished so delicately and successfully for the reigning family of Holland. Beyond these signs of his activity, however, which I merely shared with all the readers of the daily press, I knew little of my former friend and companion.

One night—it was on the twentieth of March, 1888—I was returning from a journey to a patient (for I had now returned to civil practice), when my way led me through Baker Street. As I passed the well-remembered door, which must always be associated in my mind with my wooing, and with the dark incidents of the Study in Scarlet, I was seized with a keen desire to see Holmes again, and to know how he was employing his extraordinary powers. His rooms were brilliantly lit, and, even as I looked up, I saw his tall, spare figure pass twice in a dark silhouette against the blind. He was pacing the room swiftly, eagerly, with his head sunk upon his chest and his hands clasped behind him. To me, who knew his every mood and habit, his attitude and manner told their own story. He was at work again. He had risen out of his drug-created dreams and was hot upon the scent of some new problem. I rang the bell and was shown up to the chamber which had formerly been in part my own.

His manner was not effusive. It seldom was; but he was glad, I think, to see me. With hardly a word spoken, but with a kindly eye, he waved me to an armchair, threw across his case of cigars, and indicated a spirit case and a gasogene in the corner. Then he stood before the fire and looked me over in his singular introspective fashion.

"Wedlock suits you," he remarked."I think, Watson, that you have put on seven and a half pounds since I saw you."

"Seven!" I answered.

"Indeed, I should have thought a little more. Just a trifle more, I fancy, Watson. And in practice again, I observe. You did not tell me that you intended to go into harness."

"Then, how do you know?"

"I see it, I deduce it. How do I know that you have been getting yourself very wet lately, and that you have a most clumsy and careless servant girl?"

"My dear Holmes," said I, "this is too much. You would certainly have been burned, had you lived a few centuries ago. It is true that I had a country walk on Thursday and came home in a dreadful mess, but as I have changed my clothes I can't imagine how you deduce it. As to Mary

Jane, she is incorrigible, and my wife has given her notice, but there, again, I fail to see how you work it out."

He chuckled to himself and rubbed his long, nervous hands together.

"It is simplicity itself," said he; "my eyes tell me that on the inside of your left shoe, just where the firelight strikes it, the leather is scored by six almost parallel cuts. Obviously they have been caused by someone who has very carelessly scraped round the edges of the sole in order to remove crusted mud from it. Hence, you see, my double deduction that you had been out in vile weather, and that you had a particularly malignant boot-slitting specimen of the London slavey. As to your practice, if a gentleman walks into my rooms smelling of iodoform, with a black mark of nitrate of silver upon his right forefinger, and a bulge on the right side of his top-hat to show where he has secreted his stethoscope, I must be dull, indeed, if I do not pronounce him to be an active member of the medical profession."

I could not help laughing at the ease with which he explained his process of deduction. "When I hear you give your reasons," I remarked, "the thing always appears to me to be so ridiculously simple that I could easily do it myself, though at each successive instance of your reasoning I am baffled until you explain your process. And yet I believe that my eyes are as good as yours."

"Quite so," he answered, lighting a cigarette, and throwing himself down into an armchair. "You see, but you do not observe. The distinction is clear. For example, you have frequently seen the steps which lead up from the hall to this room."

"Frequently."

"How often?"

"Well, some hundreds of times."

"Then how many are there?"

"How many? I don't know."

"Quite so! You have not observed. And yet you have seen. That is just my point. Now, I know that there are seventeen steps, because I have both seen and observed. By the way, since you are interested in these little problems, and since you are good enough to chronicle one or two of my trifling experiences, you may be interested in this." He threw over a sheet of thick, pink-tinted notepaper which had been lying open upon the table. "It came by the last post," said he. "Read it aloud."

The note was undated, and without either signature or address.

"There will call upon you tonight, at a quarter to eight o'clock," it said, "a gentleman who desires to consult you upon a matter of the very deepest moment. Your recent services to one of the royal houses of Europe have shown that you are one who may safely be trusted with matters which are of an importance which can hardly be exaggerated. This account of you we have from all quarters received. Be in your chamber then at that hour, and do not take it amiss if your visitor wear a mask."

"This is indeed a mystery," I remarked. "What do you imagine that it means?"

"I have no data yet. It is a capital mistake to theorize before one has data. Insensibly one begins to twist facts to suit theories, instead of theories to suit facts. But the note itself. What do you deduce from it?"

I carefully examined the writing, and the paper upon which it was written.

"The man who wrote it was presumably well to do," I remarked, endeavouring to imitate my companion's processes. "Such paper could not be bought under half a crown a packet. It is peculiarly strong and stiff."

"Peculiar—that is the very word," said Holmes. "It is not an English paper at all. Hold it up to the light."

I did so, and saw a large "*E*" with a small "*g*," a "*P*," and a large "*G*" with a small "*t*" woven into the texture of the paper.

"What do you make of that?" asked Holmes.

"The name of the maker, no doubt; or his monogram, rather."

"Not at all. The '*G*' with the small '*t*' stands for 'Gesellschaft,' which is the German for 'Company.' It is a customary contraction like our 'Co.' '*P*,' of course, stands for 'Papier.' Now for the '*Eg*.' Let us glance at our Continental Gazetteer." He took down a heavy brown volume from his shelves. "Eglow, Eglonitz—here we are, Egria. It is in a German-speaking country—in Bohemia, not far from Carlsbad. 'Remarkable as being the scene of the death of Wallenstein, and for its numerous glass-factories and paper-mills.' Ha, ha, my boy, what do you make of that?" His eyes sparkled, and he sent up a great blue triumphant cloud from his cigarette.

"The paper was made in Bohemia," I said.

"Precisely. And the man who wrote the note is a German. Do you note the peculiar construction of the sentence—'This account of you

we have from all quarters received.' A Frenchman or Russian could not have written that. It is the German who is so uncourteous to his verbs. It only remains, therefore, to discover what is wanted by this German who writes upon Bohemian paper and prefers wearing a mask to showing his face. And here he comes, if I am not mistaken, to resolve all our doubts."

As he spoke there was the sharp sound of horses' hoofs and grating wheels against the curb, followed by a sharp pull at the bell. Holmes whistled.

"A pair, by the sound," said he. "Yes," he continued, glancing out of the window. "A nice little brougham and a pair of beauties. A hundred and fifty guineas apiece. There's money in this case, Watson, if there is nothing else."

"I think that I had better go, Holmes."

"Not a bit, Doctor. Stay where you are. I am lost without my Boswell. And this promises to be interesting. It would be a pity to miss it."

"But your client—"

"Never mind him. I may want your help, and so may he. Here he comes. Sit down in that armchair, Doctor, and give us your best attention."

A slow and heavy step, which had been heard upon the stairs and in the passage, paused immediately outside the door. Then there was a loud and authoritative tap.

"Come in!" said Holmes.

A man entered who could hardly have been less than six feet six inches in height, with the chest and limbs of a Hercules. His dress was rich with a richness which would, in England, be looked upon as akin to bad taste. Heavy bands of astrakhan were slashed across the sleeves and fronts of his double-breasted coat, while the deep blue cloak which was thrown over his shoulders was lined with flame-coloured silk and secured at the neck with a brooch which consisted of a single flaming beryl. Boots which extended halfway up his calves, and which were trimmed at the tops with rich brown fur, completed the impression of barbaric opulence which was suggested by his whole appearance. He carried a broad-brimmed hat in his hand, while he wore across the upper part of his face, extending down past the cheekbones, a black vizard mask, which he had apparently adjusted that very moment, for his hand was still raised to it as he entered. From the lower part of the face he appeared to be a man of strong character, with a thick, hanging lip, and a long, straight chin suggestive of resolution pushed to the length of obstinacy.

"You had my note?" he asked with a deep harsh voice and a strongly marked German accent. "I told you that I would call." He looked from one to the other of us, as if uncertain which to address.

"Pray take a seat," said Holmes. "This is my friend and colleague, Dr. Watson, who is occasionally good enough to help me in my cases. Whom have I the honour to address?"

"You may address me as the Count Von Kramm, a Bohemian nobleman. I understand that this gentleman, your friend, is a man of honour and discretion, whom I may trust with a matter of the most extreme importance. If not, I should much prefer to communicate with you alone."

I rose to go, but Holmes caught me by the wrist and pushed me back into my chair. "It is both, or none," said he. "You may say before this gentleman anything which you may say to me."

The Count shrugged his broad shoulders. "Then I must begin," said he, "by binding you both to absolute secrecy for two years; at the end of that time the matter will be of no importance. At present it is not too much to say that it is of such weight it may have an influence upon European history."

"I promise," said Holmes.

"And I."

"You will excuse this mask," continued our strange visitor. "The august person who employs me wishes his agent to be unknown to you, and I may confess at once that the title by which I have just called myself is not exactly my own."

"I was aware of it," said Holmes dryly.

"The circumstances are of great delicacy, and every precaution has to be taken to quench what might grow to be an immense scandal and seriously compromise one of the reigning families of Europe. To speak plainly, the matter implicates the great House of Ormstein, hereditary kings of Bohemia."

"I was also aware of that," murmured Holmes, settling himself down in his armchair and closing his eyes.

Our visitor glanced with some apparent surprise at the languid, lounging figure of the man who had been no doubt depicted to him as

the most incisive reasoner and most energetic agent in Europe. Holmes slowly reopened his eyes and looked impatiently at his gigantic client.

"If your Majesty would condescend to state your case," he remarked, "I should be better able to advise you."

The man sprang from his chair and paced up and down the room in uncontrollable agitation. Then, with a gesture of desperation, he tore the mask from his face and hurled it upon the ground. "You are right," he cried; "I am the King. Why should I attempt to conceal it?"

"Why, indeed?" murmured Holmes. "Your Majesty had not spoken before I was aware that I was addressing Wilhelm Gottsreich Sigismond von Ormstein, Grand Duke of Cassel-Felstein, and hereditary King of Bohemia."

"But you can understand," said our strange visitor, sitting down once more and passing his hand over his high white forehead, "you can understand that I am not accustomed to doing such business in my own person. Yet the matter was so delicate that I could not confide it to an agent without putting myself in his power. I have come incognito from Prague for the purpose of consulting you."

"Then, pray consult," said Holmes, shutting his eyes once more.

"The facts are briefly these: Some five years ago, during a lengthy visit to Warsaw, I made the acquaintance of the well-known adventuress, Irene Adler. The name is no doubt familiar to you."

"Kindly look her up in my index, Doctor," murmured Holmes without opening his eyes. For many years he had adopted a system of docketing all paragraphs concerning men and things, so that it was difficult to name a subject or a person on which he could not at once furnish information. In this case I found her biography sandwiched in between that of a Hebrew rabbi and that of a staff-commander who had written a monograph upon the deep-sea fishes.

"Let me see!" said Holmes. "Hum! Born in New Jersey in the year 1858. Contralto—hum! La Scala, hum! Prima donna Imperial Opera of Warsaw—yes! Retired from operatic stage—ha! Living in London—quite so! Your Majesty, as I understand, became entangled with this young person, wrote her some compromising letters, and is now desirous of getting those letters back."

"Precisely so. But how—"

"Was there a secret marriage?"

"None."

"No legal papers or certificates?"

"None."

"Then I fail to follow your Majesty. If this young person should produce her letters for blackmailing or other purposes, how is she to prove their authenticity?"

"There is the writing."

"Pooh, pooh! Forgery."

"My private notepaper."

"Stolen."

"My own seal."

"Imitated."

"My photograph."

"Bought."

"We were both in the photograph."

"Oh, dear! That is very bad! Your Majesty has indeed committed an indiscretion."

"I was mad—insane."

"You have compromised yourself seriously."

"I was only Crown Prince then. I was young. I am but thirty now."

"It must be recovered."

"We have tried and failed."

"Your Majesty must pay. It must be bought."

"She will not sell."

"Stolen, then."

"Five attempts have been made. Twice burglars in my pay ransacked her house. Once we diverted her luggage when she travelled. Twice she has been waylaid. There has been no result."

"No sign of it?"

"Absolutely none."

Holmes laughed. "It is quite a pretty little problem," said he.

"But a very serious one to me," returned the King reproachfully.

"Very, indeed. And what does she propose to do with the photograph?"

"To ruin me."

"But how?"

"I am about to be married."

"So I have heard."

"To Clotilde Lothman von Saxe-Meningen, second daughter of the King of Scandinavia. You may know the strict principles of her family.

She is herself the very soul of delicacy. A shadow of a doubt as to my conduct would bring the matter to an end."

"And Irene Adler?"

"Threatens to send them the photograph. And she will do it. I know that she will do it. You do not know her, but she has a soul of steel. She has the face of the most beautiful of women, and the mind of the most resolute of men. Rather than I should marry another woman, there are no lengths to which she would not go—none."

"You are sure that she has not sent it yet?"

"I am sure."

"And why?"

"Because she has said that she would send it on the day when the betrothal was publicly proclaimed. That will be next Monday."

"Oh, then we have three days yet," said Holmes with a yawn. "That is very fortunate, as I have one or two matters of importance to look into just at present. Your Majesty will, of course, stay in London for the present?"

"Certainly. You will find me at the Langham under the name of the Count Von Kramm."

"Then I shall drop you a line to let you know how we progress."

"Pray do so. I shall be all anxiety."

"Then, as to money?"

"You have *carte blanche*."

"Absolutely?"

"I tell you that I would give one of the provinces of my kingdom to have that photograph."

"And for present expenses?"

The King took a heavy chamois leather bag from under his cloak and laid it on the table.

"There are three hundred pounds in gold and seven hundred in notes," he said.

Holmes scribbled a receipt upon a sheet of his notebook and handed it to him.

"And Mademoiselle's address?" he asked.

"Is Briony Lodge, Serpentine Avenue, St. John's Wood."

Holmes took a note of it. "One other question," said he. "Was the photograph a cabinet?"

"It was."

"Then, good-night, your Majesty, and I trust that we shall soon have some good news for you. And good-night, Watson," he added, as the wheels of the royal brougham rolled down the street. "If you will be good enough to call tomorrow afternoon at three o'clock I should like to chat this little matter over with you."

*****

At three o'clock precisely I was at Baker Street, but Holmes had not yet returned. The landlady informed me that he had left the house shortly after eight o'clock in the morning. I sat down beside the fire, however, with the intention of awaiting him, however long he might be. I was already deeply interested in his inquiry, for, though it was surrounded by none of the grim and strange features which were associated with the two crimes which I have already recorded, still, the nature of the case and the exalted station of his client gave it a character of its own. Indeed, apart from the nature of the investigation which my friend had on hand, there was something in his masterly grasp of a situation, and his keen, incisive reasoning, which made it a pleasure to me to study his system of work, and to follow the quick, subtle methods by which he disentangled the most inextricable mysteries. So accustomed was I to his invariable success that the very possibility of his failing had ceased to enter into my head.

It was close upon four before the door opened, and a drunken-looking groom, ill-kempt and side-whiskered, with an inflamed face and disreputable clothes, walked into the room. Accustomed as I was to my friend's amazing powers in the use of disguises, I had to look three times before I was certain that it was indeed he. With a nod he vanished into the bedroom, whence he emerged in five minutes tweed-suited and respectable, as of old. Putting his hands into his pockets, he stretched out his legs in front of the fire and laughed heartily for some minutes.

"Well, really!" he cried, and then he choked and laughed again until he was obliged to lie back, limp and helpless, in the chair.

"What is it?"

"It's quite too funny. I am sure you could never guess how I employed my morning, or what I ended by doing."

"I can't imagine. I suppose that you have been watching the habits, and perhaps the house, of Miss Irene Adler."

"Quite so; but the sequel was rather unusual. I will tell you, however. I left the house a little after eight o'clock this morning in the character of a groom out of work. There is a wonderful sympathy and freemasonry among horsey men. Be one of them, and you will know all that there is to know. I soon found Briony Lodge. It is a bijou villa, with a garden at the back, but built out in front right up to the road, two stories. Chubb lock to the door. Large sitting-room on the right side, well furnished, with long windows almost to the floor, and those preposterous English window fasteners which a child could open. Behind there was nothing remarkable, save that the passage window could be reached from the top of the coach-house. I walked round it and examined it closely from every point of view, but without noting anything else of interest.

"I then lounged down the street and found, as I expected, that there was a mews in a lane which runs down by one wall of the garden. I lent the ostlers a hand in rubbing down their horses, and received in exchange twopence, a glass of half and half, two fills of shag tobacco, and as much information as I could desire about Miss Adler, to say nothing of half a dozen other people in the neighbourhood in whom I was not in the least interested, but whose biographies I was compelled to listen to."

"And what of Irene Adler?" I asked.

"Oh, she has turned all the men's heads down in that part. She is the daintiest thing under a bonnet on this planet. So say the Serpentine Mews, to a man. She lives quietly, sings at concerts, drives out at five every day, and returns at seven sharp for dinner. Seldom goes out at other times, except when she sings. Has only one male visitor, but a good deal of him. He is dark, handsome, and dashing, never calls less than once a day, and often twice. He is a Mr. Godfrey Norton, of the Inner Temple. See the advantages of a cabman as a confidant. They had driven him home a dozen times from Serpentine Mews, and knew all about him. When I had listened to all they had to tell, I began to walk up and down near Briony Lodge once more, and to think over my plan of campaign.

"This Godfrey Norton was evidently an important factor in the matter. He was a lawyer. That sounded ominous. What was the relation between them, and what the object of his repeated visits? Was she his client, his friend, or his mistress? If the former, she had probably transferred the photograph to his keeping. If the latter, it was less likely.

On the issue of this question depended whether I should continue my work at Briony Lodge, or turn my attention to the gentleman's chambers in the Temple. It was a delicate point, and it widened the field of my inquiry. I fear that I bore you with these details, but I have to let you see my little difficulties, if you are to understand the situation."

"I am following you closely," I answered.

"I was still balancing the matter in my mind when a hansom cab drove up to Briony Lodge, and a gentleman sprang out. He was a remarkably handsome man, dark, aquiline, and moustached— evidently the man of whom I had heard. He appeared to be in a great hurry, shouted to the cabman to wait, and brushed past the maid who opened the door with the air of a man who was thoroughly at home.

"He was in the house about half an hour, and I could catch glimpses of him in the windows of the sitting-room, pacing up and down, talking excitedly, and waving his arms. Of her I could see nothing. Presently he emerged, looking even more flurried than before. As he stepped up to the cab, he pulled a gold watch from his pocket and looked at it earnestly, 'Drive like the devil,' he shouted, 'first to Gross & Hankey's in Regent Street, and then to the Church of St. Monica in the Edgeware Road. Half a guinea if you do it in twenty minutes!'

"Away they went, and I was just wondering whether I should not do well to follow them when up the lane came a neat little landau, the coachman with his coat only half-buttoned, and his tie under his ear, while all the tags of his harness were sticking out of the buckles. It hadn't pulled up before she shot out of the hall door and into it. I only caught a glimpse of her at the moment, but she was a lovely woman, with a face that a man might die for.

" 'The Church of St. Monica, John,' she cried, 'and half a sovereign if you reach it in twenty minutes.'

"This was quite too good to lose, Watson. I was just balancing whether I should run for it, or whether I should perch behind her landau when a cab came through the street. The driver looked twice at such a shabby fare, but I jumped in before he could object. 'The Church of St. Monica,' said I, 'and half a sovereign if you reach it in twenty minutes.' It was twenty-five minutes to twelve, and of course it was clear enough what was in the wind.

"My cabby drove fast. I don't think I ever drove faster, but the others were there before us. The cab and the landau with their steaming horses

were in front of the door when I arrived. I paid the man and hurried into the church. There was not a soul there save the two whom I had followed and a surpliced clergyman, who seemed to be expostulating with them. They were all three standing in a knot in front of the altar. I lounged up the side aisle like any other idler who has dropped into a church. Suddenly, to my surprise, the three at the altar faced round to me, and Godfrey Norton came running as hard as he could towards me.

"'Thank God,' he cried. 'You'll do. Come! Come!'

"'What then?' I asked.

"'Come, man, come, only three minutes, or it won't be legal.'

"I was half-dragged up to the altar, and before I knew where I was I found myself mumbling responses which were whispered in my ear, and vouching for things of which I knew nothing, and generally assisting in the secure tying up of Irene Adler, spinster, to Godfrey Norton, bachelor. It was all done in an instant, and there was the gentleman thanking me on the one side and the lady on the other, while the clergyman beamed on me in front. It was the most preposterous position in which I ever found myself in my life, and it was the thought of it that started me laughing just now. It seems that there had been some informality about their license, that the clergyman absolutely refused to marry them without a witness of some sort, and that my lucky appearance saved the bridegroom from having to sally out into the streets in search of a best man. The bride gave me a sovereign, and I mean to wear it on my watch-chain in memory of the occasion."

"This is a very unexpected turn of affairs," said I; "and what then?"

"Well, I found my plans very seriously menaced. It looked as if the pair might take an immediate departure, and so necessitate very prompt and energetic measures on my part. At the church door, however, they separated, he driving back to the Temple, and she to her own house. 'I shall drive out in the park at five as usual,' she said as she left him. I heard no more. They drove away in different directions, and I went off to make my own arrangements."

"Which are?"

"Some cold beef and a glass of beer," he answered, ringing the bell. "I have been too busy to think of food, and I am likely to be busier still this evening. By the way, Doctor, I shall want your co-operation."

"I shall be delighted."

"You don't mind breaking the law?"

"Not in the least."

"Nor running a chance of arrest?"

"Not in a good cause."

"Oh, the cause is excellent!"

"Then I am your man."

"I was sure that I might rely on you."

"But what is it you wish?"

"When Mrs. Turner has brought in the tray I will make it clear to you. Now," he said as he turned hungrily on the simple fare that our landlady had provided, "I must discuss it while I eat, for I have not much time. It is nearly five now. In two hours we must be on the scene of action. Miss Irene, or Madame, rather, returns from her drive at seven. We must be at Briony Lodge to meet her."

"And what then?"

"You must leave that to me. I have already arranged what is to occur. There is only one point on which I must insist. You must not interfere, come what may. You understand?"

"I am to be neutral?"

"To do nothing whatever. There will probably be some small unpleasantness. Do not join in it. It will end in my being conveyed into the house. Four or five minutes afterwards the sitting-room window will open. You are to station yourself close to that open window."

"Yes."

"You are to watch me, for I will be visible to you."

"Yes."

"And when I raise my hand—so—you will throw into the room what I give you to throw, and will, at the same time, raise the cry of fire. You quite follow me?"

"Entirely."

"It is nothing very formidable," he said, taking a long cigar-shaped roll from his pocket. "It is an ordinary plumber's smoke-rocket, fitted with a cap at either end to make it self-lighting. Your task is confined to that. When you raise your cry of fire, it will be taken up by quite a number of people. You may then walk to the end of the street, and I will rejoin you in ten minutes. I hope that I have made myself clear?"

"I am to remain neutral, to get near the window, to watch you, and at the signal to throw in this object, then to raise the cry of fire, and to wait you at the corner of the street."

"Precisely."

"Then you may entirely rely on me."

"That is excellent. I think, perhaps, it is almost time that I prepare for the new role I have to play."

He disappeared into his bedroom and returned in a few minutes in the character of an amiable and simple-minded Nonconformist clergyman. His broad black hat, his baggy trousers, his white tie, his sympathetic smile, and general look of peering and benevolent curiosity were such as Mr. John Hare alone could have equalled. It was not merely that Holmes changed his costume. His expression, his manner, his very soul seemed to vary with every fresh part that he assumed. The stage lost a fine actor, even as science lost an acute reasoner, when he became a specialist in crime.

It was a quarter past six when we left Baker Street, and it still wanted ten minutes to the hour when we found ourselves in Serpentine Avenue. It was already dusk, and the lamps were just being lighted as we paced up and down in front of Briony Lodge, waiting for the coming of its occupant. The house was just such as I had pictured it from Sherlock Holmes' succinct description, but the locality appeared to be less private than I expected. On the contrary, for a small street in a quiet neighbourhood, it was remarkably animated. There was a group of shabbily dressed men smoking and laughing in a corner, a scissors-grinder with his wheel, two guardsmen who were flirting with a nurse-girl, and several well-dressed young men who were lounging up and down with cigars in their mouths.

"You see," remarked Holmes, as we paced to and fro in front of the house, "this marriage rather simplifies matters. The photograph becomes a double-edged weapon now. The chances are that she would be as averse to its being seen by Mr. Godfrey Norton, as our client is to its coming to the eyes of his princess. Now the question is, Where are we to find the photograph?"

"Where, indeed?"

"It is most unlikely that she carries it about with her. It is cabinet size. Too large for easy concealment about a woman's dress. She knows that the King is capable of having her waylaid and searched. Two attempts of the sort have already been made. We may take it, then, that she does not carry it about with her."

"Where, then?"

"Her banker or her lawyer. There is that double possibility. But I am inclined to think neither. Women are naturally secretive, and they like to do their own secreting. Why should she hand it over to anyone else? She could trust her own guardianship, but she could not tell what indirect or political influence might be brought to bear upon a business man. Besides, remember that she had resolved to use it within a few days. It must be where she can lay her hands upon it. It must be in her own house."

"But it has twice been burgled."

"Pshaw! They did not know how to look."

"But how will you look?"

"I will not look."

"What then?"

"I will get her to show me."

"But she will refuse."

"She will not be able to. But I hear the rumble of wheels. It is her carriage. Now carry out my orders to the letter."

As he spoke the gleam of the side-lights of a carriage came round the curve of the avenue. It was a smart little landau which rattled up to the door of Briony Lodge. As it pulled up, one of the loafing men at the corner dashed forward to open the door in the hope of earning a copper, but was elbowed away by another loafer, who had rushed up with the same intention. A fierce quarrel broke out, which was increased by the two guardsmen, who took sides with one of the loungers, and by the scissors-grinder, who was equally hot upon the other side. A blow was struck, and in an instant the lady, who had stepped from her carriage, was the centre of a little knot of flushed and struggling men, who struck savagely at each other with their fists and sticks. Holmes dashed into the crowd to protect the lady; but just as he reached her he gave a cry and dropped to the ground, with the blood running freely down his face. At his fall the guardsmen took to their heels in one direction and the loungers in the other, while a number of better-dressed people, who had watched the scuffle without taking part in it, crowded in to help the lady and to attend to the injured man. Irene Adler, as I will still call her, had hurried up the steps; but she stood at the top with her superb figure outlined against the lights of the hall, looking back into the street.

"Is the poor gentleman much hurt?" she asked.

"He is dead," cried several voices.

"No, no, there's life in him!" shouted another. "But he'll be gone before you can get him to hospital."

"He's a brave fellow," said a woman. "They would have had the lady's purse and watch if it hadn't been for him. They were a gang, and a rough one, too. Ah, he's breathing now."

"He can't lie in the street. May we bring him in, marm?"

"Surely. Bring him into the sitting-room. There is a comfortable sofa. This way, please!"

Slowly and solemnly he was borne into Briony Lodge and laid out in the principal room, while I still observed the proceedings from my post by the window. The lamps had been lit, but the blinds had not been drawn, so that I could see Holmes as he lay upon the couch. I do not know whether he was seized with compunction at that moment for the part he was playing, but I know that I never felt more heartily ashamed of myself in my life than when I saw the beautiful creature against whom I was conspiring, or the grace and kindliness with which she waited upon the injured man. And yet it would be the blackest treachery to Holmes to draw back now from the part which he had intrusted to me. I hardened my heart, and took the smoke-rocket from under my ulster. After all, I thought, we are not injuring her. We are but preventing her from injuring another.

Holmes had sat up upon the couch, and I saw him motion like a man who is in need of air. A maid rushed across and threw open the window. At the same instant I saw him raise his hand and at the signal I tossed my rocket into the room with a cry of "Fire!" The word was no sooner out of my mouth than the whole crowd of spectators, well dressed and ill—gentlemen, ostlers, and servant-maids—joined in a general shriek of "Fire!" Thick clouds of smoke curled through the room and out at the open window. I caught a glimpse of rushing figures, and a moment later the voice of Holmes from within assuring them that it was a false alarm. Slipping through the shouting crowd I made my way to the corner of the street, and in ten minutes was rejoiced to find my friend's arm in mine, and to get away from the scene of uproar. He walked swiftly and in silence for some few minutes until we had turned down one of the quiet streets which lead towards the Edgeware Road.

"You did it very nicely, Doctor," he remarked. "Nothing could have been better. It is all right."

"You have the photograph?"

"I know where it is."

"And how did you find out?"

"She showed me, as I told you she would."

"I am still in the dark."

"I do not wish to make a mystery," said he, laughing. "The matter was perfectly simple. You, of course, saw that everyone in the street was an accomplice. They were all engaged for the evening."

"I guessed as much."

"Then, when the row broke out, I had a little moist red paint in the palm of my hand. I rushed forward, fell down, clapped my hand to my face, and became a piteous spectacle. It is an old trick."

"That also I could fathom."

"Then they carried me in. She was bound to have me in. What else could she do? And into her sitting-room, which was the very room which I suspected. It lay between that and her bedroom, and I was determined to see which. They laid me on a couch, I motioned for air, they were compelled to open the window, and you had your chance."

"How did that help you?"

"It was all-important. When a woman thinks that her house is on fire, her instinct is at once to rush to the thing which she values most. It is a perfectly overpowering impulse, and I have more than once taken advantage of it. In the case of the Darlington substitution scandal it was of use to me, and also in the Arnsworth Castle business. A married woman grabs at her baby; an unmarried one reaches for her jewel-box. Now it was clear to me that our lady of today had nothing in the house more precious to her than what we are in quest of. She would rush to secure it. The alarm of fire was admirably done. The smoke and shouting were enough to shake nerves of steel. She responded beautifully. The photograph is in a recess behind a sliding panel just above the right bell-pull. She was there in an instant, and I caught a glimpse of it as she half-drew it out. When I cried out that it was a false alarm, she replaced it, glanced at the rocket, rushed from the room, and I have not seen her since. I rose, and, making my excuses, escaped from the house. I hesitated whether to attempt to secure the photograph at once; but the coachman had come in, and as he was watching me narrowly it seemed safer to wait. A little over-precipitance may ruin all."

"And now?" I asked.

"Our quest is practically finished. I shall call with the King tomorrow, and with you, if you care to come with us. We will be shown into the sitting-room to wait for the lady, but it is probable that when she comes she may find neither us nor the photograph. It might be a satisfaction to his Majesty to regain it with his own hands."

"And when will you call?"

"At eight in the morning. She will not be up, so that we shall have a clear field. Besides, we must be prompt, for this marriage may mean a complete change in her life and habits. I must wire to the King without delay."

We had reached Baker Street and had stopped at the door. He was searching his pockets for the key when someone passing said:

"Good-night, Mister Sherlock Holmes."

There were several people on the pavement at the time, but the greeting appeared to come from a slim youth in an ulster who had hurried by.

"I've heard that voice before," said Holmes, staring down the dimly lit street. "Now, I wonder who the deuce that could have been."

I slept at Baker Street that night, and we were engaged upon our toast and coffee in the morning when the King of Bohemia rushed into the room.

"You have really got it!" he cried, grasping Sherlock Holmes by either shoulder and looking eagerly into his face.

"Not yet."

"But you have hopes?"

"I have hopes."

"Then, come. I am all impatience to be gone."

"We must have a cab."

"No, my brougham is waiting."

"Then that will simplify matters." We descended and started off once more for Briony Lodge.

"Irene Adler is married," remarked Holmes.

"Married! When?"

"Yesterday."

"But to whom?"

"To an English lawyer named Norton."

"But she could not love him."

"I am in hopes that she does."

"And why in hopes?"

"Because it would spare your Majesty all fear of future annoyance. If the lady loves her husband, she does not love your Majesty. If she does not love your Majesty, there is no reason why she should interfere with your Majesty's plan."

"It is true. And yet—Well! I wish she had been of my own station! What a queen she would have made!" He relapsed into a moody silence, which was not broken until we drew up in Serpentine Avenue.

The door of Briony Lodge was open, and an elderly woman stood upon the steps. She watched us with a sardonic eye as we stepped from the brougham.

"Mr. Sherlock Holmes, I believe?" said she.

"I am Mr. Holmes," answered my companion, looking at her with a questioning and rather startled gaze.

"Indeed! My mistress told me that you were likely to call. She left this morning with her husband by the 5:15 train from Charing Cross for the Continent."

"What!" Sherlock Holmes staggered back, white with chagrin and surprise. "Do you mean that she has left England?"

"Never to return."

"And the papers?" asked the King hoarsely. "All is lost."

"We shall see." He pushed past the servant and rushed into the drawing-room, followed by the King and myself. The furniture was scattered about in every direction, with dismantled shelves and open drawers, as if the lady had hurriedly ransacked them before her flight. Holmes rushed at the bell-pull, tore back a small sliding shutter, and, plunging in his hand, pulled out a photograph and a letter. The photograph was of Irene Adler herself in evening dress, the letter was superscribed to "Sherlock Holmes, Esq. To be left till called for." My friend tore it open and we all three read it together. It was dated at midnight of the preceding night and ran in this way:

> My Dear Mr. Sherlock Holmes,
>
> You really did it very well. You took me in completely. Until after the alarm of fire, I had not a suspicion. But then, when I found how I had betrayed myself, I began to think. I had been warned against you months ago. I had been told that if the King employed an agent it would certainly be you. And your address had been given me. Yet, with all this,

you made me reveal what you wanted to know. Even after I became suspicious, I found it hard to think evil of such a dear, kind old clergyman. But, you know, I have been trained as an actress myself. Male costume is nothing new to me. I often take advantage of the freedom which it gives. I sent John, the coachman, to watch you, ran up stairs, got into my walking-clothes, as I call them, and came down just as you departed.

Well, I followed you to your door, and so made sure that I was really an object of interest to the celebrated Mr. Sherlock Holmes. Then I, rather imprudently, wished you good-night, and started for the Temple to see my husband.

We both thought the best resource was flight, when pursued by so formidable an antagonist; so you will find the nest empty when you call tomorrow. As to the photograph, your client may rest in peace. I love and am loved by a better man than he. The King may do what he will without hindrance from one whom he has cruelly wronged. I keep it only to safeguard myself, and to preserve a weapon which will always secure me from any steps which he might take in the future. I leave a photograph which he might care to possess; and I remain, dear Mr. Sherlock Holmes,

Very truly yours,

IRENE NORTON, NÉE ADLER

"What a woman—oh, what a woman!" cried the King of Bohemia, when we had all three read this epistle. "Did I not tell you how quick and resolute she was? Would she not have made an admirable queen? Is it not a pity that she was not on my level?"

"From what I have seen of the lady she seems indeed to be on a very different level to your Majesty," said Holmes coldly. "I am sorry that I have not been able to bring your Majesty's business to a more successful conclusion."

"On the contrary, my dear sir," cried the King; "nothing could be more successful. I know that her word is inviolate. The photograph is now as safe as if it were in the fire."

"I am glad to hear your Majesty say so."

"I am immensely indebted to you. Pray tell me in what way I can reward you. This ring—" He slipped an emerald snake ring from his finger and held it out upon the palm of his hand.

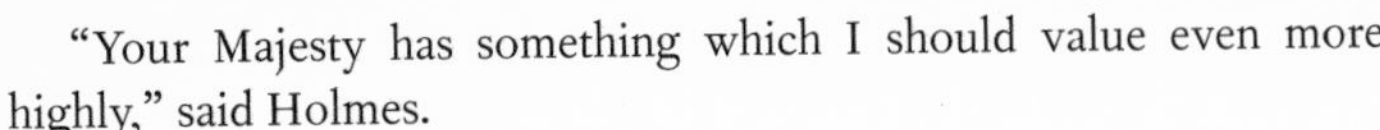

"Your Majesty has something which I should value even more highly," said Holmes.

"You have but to name it."

"This photograph!"

The King stared at him in amazement.

"Irene's photograph!" he cried. "Certainly, if you wish it."

"I thank your Majesty. Then there is no more to be done in the matter. I have the honour to wish you a very good-morning." He bowed, and, turning away without observing the hand which the King had stretched out to him, he set off in my company for his chambers.

And that was how a great scandal threatened to affect the kingdom of Bohemia, and how the best plans of Mr. Sherlock Holmes were beaten by a woman's wit. He used to make merry over the cleverness of women, but I have not heard him do it of late. And when he speaks of Irene Adler, or when he refers to her photograph, it is always under the honourable title of *the* woman.

THE RED-HEADED LEAGUE

I had called upon my friend, Mr. Sherlock Holmes, one day in the autumn of last year and found him in deep conversation with a very stout, florid-faced, elderly gentleman with fiery red hair. With an apology for my intrusion, I was about to withdraw when Holmes pulled me abruptly into the room and closed the door behind me.

"You could not possibly have come at a better time, my dear Watson," he said cordially.

"I was afraid that you were engaged."

"So I am. Very much so."

"Then I can wait in the next room."

"Not at all. This gentleman, Mr. Wilson, has been my partner and helper in many of my most successful cases, and I have no doubt that he will be of the utmost use to me in yours also."

The stout gentleman half rose from his chair and gave a bob of greeting, with a quick little questioning glance from his small fat-encircled eyes.

"Try the settee," said Holmes, relapsing into his armchair and putting his fingertips together, as was his custom when in judicial moods. "I know, my dear Watson, that you share my love of all that is bizarre and outside the conventions and humdrum routine of everyday life. You have shown your relish for it by the enthusiasm which has prompted you to chronicle, and, if you will excuse my saying so, somewhat to embellish so many of my own little adventures."

"Your cases have indeed been of the greatest interest to me," I observed.

"You will remember that I remarked the other day, just before we went into the very simple problem presented by Miss Mary Sutherland, that for strange effects and extraordinary combinations we must go to life itself, which is always far more daring than any effort of the imagination."

"A proposition which I took the liberty of doubting."

"You did, Doctor, but none the less you must come round to my view, for otherwise I shall keep on piling fact upon fact on you until your reason breaks down under them and acknowledges me to be right. Now, Mr. Jabez Wilson here has been good enough to call upon me this morning, and to begin a narrative which promises to be one of the most singular which I have listened to for some time. You have heard me remark that the strangest and most unique things are very often connected not with the larger but with the smaller crimes, and occasionally, indeed, where there is room for doubt whether any positive crime has been committed. As far as I have heard it is impossible for me to say whether the present case is an instance of crime or not, but the course of events is certainly among the most singular that I have ever listened to. Perhaps, Mr. Wilson, you would have the great kindness to recommence your narrative. I ask you not merely because my friend Dr. Watson has not heard the opening part but also because the peculiar nature of the story makes me anxious to have every possible detail from your lips. As a rule, when I have heard some slight indication of the course of events, I am able to guide myself by the thousands of other similar cases which occur to my memory. In the present instance I am forced to admit that the facts are, to the best of my belief, unique."

The portly client puffed out his chest with an appearance of some little pride and pulled a dirty and wrinkled newspaper from the inside pocket of his greatcoat. As he glanced down the advertisement column, with his head thrust forward and the paper flattened out upon his knee, I took a good look at the man and endeavoured, after the fashion of my companion, to read the indications which might be presented by his dress or appearance.

I did not gain very much, however, by my inspection. Our visitor bore every mark of being an average commonplace British tradesman, obese, pompous, and slow. He wore rather baggy grey shepherd's check trousers, a not over-clean black frock-coat, unbuttoned in the front, and a drab waistcoat with a heavy brassy Albert chain, and a square pierced bit of metal dangling down as an ornament. A frayed top-hat and a faded brown overcoat with a wrinkled velvet collar lay upon a chair beside him. Altogether, look as I would, there was nothing remarkable about the man save his blazing red head, and the expression of extreme chagrin and discontent upon his features.

Sherlock Holmes' quick eye took in my occupation, and he shook his head with a smile as he noticed my questioning glances. "Beyond the obvious facts that he has at some time done manual labour, that

he takes snuff, that he is a Freemason, that he has been in China, and that he has done a considerable amount of writing lately, I can deduce nothing else."

Mr. Jabez Wilson started up in his chair, with his forefinger upon the paper, but his eyes upon my companion.

"How, in the name of good fortune, did you know all that, Mr. Holmes?" he asked. "How did you know, for example, that I did manual labour. It's as true as gospel, for I began as a ship's carpenter."

"Your hands, my dear sir. Your right hand is quite a size larger than your left. You have worked with it, and the muscles are more developed."

"Well, the snuff, then, and the Freemasonry?"

"I won't insult your intelligence by telling you how I read that, especially as, rather against the strict rules of your order, you use an arc-and-compass breastpin."

"Ah, of course, I forgot that. But the writing?"

"What else can be indicated by that right cuff so very shiny for five inches, and the left one with the smooth patch near the elbow where you rest it upon the desk?"

"Well, but China?"

"The fish that you have tattooed immediately above your right wrist could only have been done in China. I have made a small study of tattoo marks and have even contributed to the literature of the subject. That trick of staining the fishes' scales of a delicate pink is quite peculiar to China. When, in addition, I see a Chinese coin hanging from your watch-chain, the matter becomes even more simple."

Mr. Jabez Wilson laughed heavily. "Well, I never!" said he. "I thought at first that you had done something clever, but I see that there was nothing in it, after all."

"I begin to think, Watson," said Holmes, "that I make a mistake in explaining. '*Omne ignotum pro magnifico*,' you know, and my poor little reputation, such as it is, will suffer shipwreck if I am so candid. Can you not find the advertisement, Mr. Wilson?"

"Yes, I have got it now," he answered with his thick red finger planted halfway down the column. "Here it is. This is what began it all. You just read it for yourself, sir."

I took the paper from him and read as follows:

> To The Red-Headed League—On account of the bequest of the late Ezekiah Hopkins, of Lebanon, Pennsylvania, U. S. A., there is now another vacancy open which entitles a member of the League to a salary of 4 pounds a week for purely nominal services. All red-headed men who are sound in body and mind and above the age of twenty-one years, are eligible. Apply in person on Monday, at eleven o'clock, to Duncan Ross, at the offices of the League, 7 Pope's Court, Fleet Street.

"What on earth does this mean?" I ejaculated after I had twice read over the extraordinary announcement.

Holmes chuckled and wriggled in his chair, as was his habit when in high spirits. "It is a little off the beaten track, isn't it?" said he. "And now, Mr. Wilson, off you go at scratch and tell us all about yourself, your household, and the effect which this advertisement had upon your fortunes. You will first make a note, Doctor, of the paper and the date."

"It is *The Morning Chronicle* of April 27, 1890. Just two months ago."

"Very good. Now, Mr. Wilson?"

"Well, it is just as I have been telling you, Mr. Sherlock Holmes," said Jabez Wilson, mopping his forehead; "I have a small pawnbroker's business at Coburg Square, near the City. It's not a very large affair, and of late years it has not done more than just give me a living. I used to be able to keep two assistants, but now I only keep one; and I would have a job to pay him but that he is willing to come for half wages so as to learn the business."

"What is the name of this obliging youth?" asked Sherlock Holmes.

"His name is Vincent Spaulding, and he's not such a youth, either. It's hard to say his age. I should not wish a smarter assistant, Mr. Holmes; and I know very well that he could better himself and earn twice what I am able to give him. But, after all, if he is satisfied, why should I put ideas in his head?"

"Why, indeed? You seem most fortunate in having an employee who comes under the full market price. It is not a common experience among employers in this age. I don't know that your assistant is not as remarkable as your advertisement."

"Oh, he has his faults, too," said Mr. Wilson. "Never was such a fellow for photography. Snapping away with a camera when he ought to be improving his mind, and then diving down into the cellar like a

rabbit into its hole to develop his pictures. That is his main fault, but on the whole he's a good worker. There's no vice in him."

"He is still with you, I presume?"

"Yes, sir. He and a girl of fourteen, who does a bit of simple cooking and keeps the place clean—that's all I have in the house, for I am a widower and never had any family. We live very quietly, sir, the three of us; and we keep a roof over our heads and pay our debts, if we do nothing more.

"The first thing that put us out was that advertisement. Spaulding, he came down into the office just this day eight weeks, with this very paper in his hand, and he says:

"'I wish to the Lord, Mr. Wilson, that I was a red-headed man.'

"'Why that?' I asks.

"'Why,' says he, 'here's another vacancy on the League of the Red-Headed Men. It's worth quite a little fortune to any man who gets it, and I understand that there are more vacancies than there are men, so that the trustees are at their wits' end what to do with the money. If my hair would only change colour, here's a nice little crib all ready for me to step into.'

"'Why, what is it, then?' I asked. You see, Mr. Holmes, I am a very stay-at-home man, and as my business came to me instead of my having to go to it, I was often weeks on end without putting my foot over the door-mat. In that way I didn't know much of what was going on outside, and I was always glad of a bit of news.

"'Have you never heard of the League of the Red-Headed Men?' he asked with his eyes open.

"'Never.'

"'Why, I wonder at that, for you are eligible yourself for one of the vacancies.'

"'And what are they worth?' I asked.

"'Oh, merely a couple of hundred a year, but the work is slight, and it need not interfere very much with one's other occupations.'

"Well, you can easily think that that made me prick up my ears, for the business has not been over-good for some years, and an extra couple of hundred would have been very handy.

"'Tell me all about it,' said I.

"'Well,' said he, showing me the advertisement, 'you can see for yourself that the League has a vacancy, and there is the address where you should apply for particulars. As far as I can make out, the League was founded by an American millionaire, Ezekiah Hopkins, who was very peculiar in his ways. He was himself red-headed, and he had a great sympathy for all red-headed men; so when he died it was found that he had left his enormous fortune in the hands of trustees, with instructions to apply the interest to the providing of easy berths to men whose hair is of that colour. From all I hear it is splendid pay and very little to do.'

"'But,' said I, 'there would be millions of red-headed men who would apply.'

"'Not so many as you might think,' he answered. 'You see it is really confined to Londoners, and to grown men. This American had started from London when he was young, and he wanted to do the old town a good turn. Then, again, I have heard it is no use your applying if your hair is light red, or dark red, or anything but real bright, blazing, fiery red. Now, if you cared to apply, Mr. Wilson, you would just walk in; but perhaps it would hardly be worth your while to put yourself out of the way for the sake of a few hundred pounds.'

"Now, it is a fact, gentlemen, as you may see for yourselves, that my hair is of a very full and rich tint, so that it seemed to me that if there was to be any competition in the matter I stood as good a chance as any man that I had ever met. Vincent Spaulding seemed to know so much about it that I thought he might prove useful, so I just ordered him to put up the shutters for the day and to come right away with me. He was very willing to have a holiday, so we shut the business up and started off for the address that was given us in the advertisement.

"I never hope to see such a sight as that again, Mr. Holmes. From north, south, east, and west every man who had a shade of red in his hair had tramped into the city to answer the advertisement. Fleet Street was choked with red-headed folk, and Pope's Court looked like a coster's orange barrow. I should not have thought there were so many in the whole country as were brought together by that single advertisement. Every shade of colour they were—straw, lemon, orange, brick, Irish-setter, liver, clay; but, as Spaulding said, there were not many who had the real vivid flame-coloured tint. When I saw how many were waiting, I would have given it up in despair; but Spaulding would not hear of it. How he did it I could not imagine, but he pushed and pulled and butted until he got me through the crowd, and right up to the steps which led

to the office. There was a double stream upon the stair, some going up in hope, and some coming back dejected; but we wedged in as well as we could and soon found ourselves in the office."

"Your experience has been a most entertaining one," remarked Holmes as his client paused and refreshed his memory with a huge pinch of snuff. "Pray continue your very interesting statement."

"There was nothing in the office but a couple of wooden chairs and a deal table, behind which sat a small man with a head that was even redder than mine. He said a few words to each candidate as he came up, and then he always managed to find some fault in them which would disqualify them. Getting a vacancy did not seem to be such a very easy matter, after all. However, when our turn came the little man was much more favourable to me than to any of the others, and he closed the door as we entered, so that he might have a private word with us.

"'This is Mr. Jabez Wilson,' said my assistant, 'and he is willing to fill a vacancy in the League.'

"'And he is admirably suited for it,' the other answered. 'He has every requirement. I cannot recall when I have seen anything so fine.' He took a step backward, cocked his head on one side, and gazed at my hair until I felt quite bashful. Then suddenly he plunged forward, wrung my hand, and congratulated me warmly on my success.

"'It would be injustice to hesitate,' said he. 'You will, however, I am sure, excuse me for taking an obvious precaution.' With that he seized my hair in both his hands, and tugged until I yelled with the pain. 'There is water in your eyes,' said he as he released me. 'I perceive that all is as it should be. But we have to be careful, for we have twice been deceived by wigs and once by paint. I could tell you tales of cobbler's wax which would disgust you with human nature.' He stepped over to the window and shouted through it at the top of his voice that the vacancy was filled. A groan of disappointment came up from below, and the folk all trooped away in different directions until there was not a red-head to be seen except my own and that of the manager.

"'My name,' said he, 'is Mr. Duncan Ross, and I am myself one of the pensioners upon the fund left by our noble benefactor. Are you a married man, Mr. Wilson? Have you a family?'

"I answered that I had not.

"His face fell immediately.

"'Dear me!' he said gravely, 'that is very serious indeed! I am sorry to hear you say that. The fund was, of course, for the propagation and spread of the red-heads as well as for their maintenance. It is exceedingly unfortunate that you should be a bachelor.'

"My face lengthened at this, Mr. Holmes, for I thought that I was not to have the vacancy after all; but after thinking it over for a few minutes he said that it would be all right.

" 'In the case of another,' said he, 'the objection might be fatal, but we must stretch a point in favour of a man with such a head of hair as yours. When shall you be able to enter upon your new duties?'

" 'Well, it is a little awkward, for I have a business already,' said I.

" 'Oh, never mind about that, Mr. Wilson!' said Vincent Spaulding. 'I should be able to look after that for you.'

" 'What would be the hours?' I asked.

" 'Ten to two.'

"Now a pawnbroker's business is mostly done of an evening, Mr. Holmes, especially Thursday and Friday evening, which is just before pay-day; so it would suit me very well to earn a little in the mornings. Besides, I knew that my assistant was a good man, and that he would see to anything that turned up.

" 'That would suit me very well,' said I. 'And the pay?'

" 'Is 4 pounds a week.'

" 'And the work?'

" 'Is purely nominal.'

" 'What do you call purely nominal?'

" 'Well, you have to be in the office, or at least in the building, the whole time. If you leave, you forfeit your whole position forever. The will is very clear upon that point. You don't comply with the conditions if you budge from the office during that time.'

" 'It's only four hours a day, and I should not think of leaving,' said I.

" 'No excuse will avail,' said Mr. Duncan Ross; 'neither sickness nor business nor anything else. There you must stay, or you lose your billet.'

" 'And the work?'

" 'Is to copy out the *Encyclopaedia Britannica*. There is the first volume of it in that press. You must find your own ink, pens, and blotting-paper, but we provide this table and chair. Will you be ready tomorrow?'

"'Certainly,' I answered.

"'Then, good-bye, Mr. Jabez Wilson, and let me congratulate you once more on the important position which you have been fortunate enough to gain.' He bowed me out of the room and I went home with my assistant, hardly knowing what to say or do, I was so pleased at my own good fortune.

"Well, I thought over the matter all day, and by evening I was in low spirits again; for I had quite persuaded myself that the whole affair must be some great hoax or fraud, though what its object might be I could not imagine. It seemed altogether past belief that anyone could make such a will, or that they would pay such a sum for doing anything so simple as copying out the *Encyclopaedia Britannica*. Vincent Spaulding did what he could to cheer me up, but by bedtime I had reasoned myself out of the whole thing. However, in the morning I determined to have a look at it anyhow, so I bought a penny bottle of ink, and with a quill-pen, and seven sheets of foolscap paper, I started off for Pope's Court.

"Well, to my surprise and delight, everything was as right as possible. The table was set out ready for me, and Mr. Duncan Ross was there to see that I got fairly to work. He started me off upon the letter A, and then he left me; but he would drop in from time to time to see that all was right with me. At two o'clock he bade me good-day, complimented me upon the amount that I had written, and locked the door of the office after me.

"This went on day after day, Mr. Holmes, and on Saturday the manager came in and planked down four golden sovereigns for my week's work. It was the same next week, and the same the week after. Every morning I was there at ten, and every afternoon I left at two. By degrees Mr. Duncan Ross took to coming in only once of a morning, and then, after a time, he did not come in at all. Still, of course, I never dared to leave the room for an instant, for I was not sure when he might come, and the billet was such a good one, and suited me so well, that I would not risk the loss of it.

"Eight weeks passed away like this, and I had written about Abbots and Archery and Armour and Architecture and Attica, and hoped with diligence that I might get on to the B's before very long. It cost me something in foolscap, and I had pretty nearly filled a shelf with my writings. And then suddenly the whole business came to an end."

"To an end?"

"Yes, sir. And no later than this morning. I went to my work as usual at ten o'clock, but the door was shut and locked, with a little square of cardboard hammered on to the middle of the panel with a tack. Here it is, and you can read for yourself."

He held up a piece of white cardboard about the size of a sheet of notepaper. It read in this fashion:

THE RED-HEADED LEAGUE IS DISSOLVED.
OCTOBER 9, 1890.

Sherlock Holmes and I surveyed this curt announcement and the rueful face behind it, until the comical side of the affair so completely overtopped every other consideration that we both burst out into a roar of laughter.

"I cannot see that there is anything very funny," cried our client, flushing up to the roots of his flaming head. "If you can do nothing better than laugh at me, I can go elsewhere."

"No, no," cried Holmes, shoving him back into the chair from which he had half risen. "I really wouldn't miss your case for the world. It is most refreshingly unusual. But there is, if you will excuse my saying so, something just a little funny about it. Pray what steps did you take when you found the card upon the door?"

"I was staggered, sir. I did not know what to do. Then I called at the offices round, but none of them seemed to know anything about it. Finally, I went to the landlord, who is an accountant living on the ground-floor, and I asked him if he could tell me what had become of the Red-Headed League. He said that he had never heard of any such body. Then I asked him who Mr. Duncan Ross was. He answered that the name was new to him.

"'Well,' said I, 'the gentleman at No. 4.'

"'What, the red-headed man?'

"'Yes.'

"'Oh,' said he, 'his name was William Morris. He was a solicitor and was using my room as a temporary convenience until his new premises were ready. He moved out yesterday.'

"'Where could I find him?'

"'Oh, at his new offices. He did tell me the address. Yes, 17 King Edward Street, near St. Paul's.'

"I started off, Mr. Holmes, but when I got to that address it was a manufactory of artificial kneecaps, and no one in it had ever heard of either Mr. William Morris or Mr. Duncan Ross."

"And what did you do then?" asked Holmes.

"I went home to Saxe-Coburg Square, and I took the advice of my assistant. But he could not help me in any way. He could only say that if I waited I should hear by post. But that was not quite good enough, Mr. Holmes. I did not wish to lose such a place without a struggle, so, as I had heard that you were good enough to give advice to poor folk who were in need of it, I came right away to you."

"And you did very wisely," said Holmes. "Your case is an exceedingly remarkable one, and I shall be happy to look into it. From what you have told me I think that it is possible that graver issues hang from it than might at first sight appear."

"Grave enough!" said Mr. Jabez Wilson. "Why, I have lost 4 pound a week."

"As far as you are personally concerned," remarked Holmes, "I do not see that you have any grievance against this extraordinary league. On the contrary, you are, as I understand, richer by some 30 pounds, to say nothing of the minute knowledge which you have gained on every subject which comes under the letter A. You have lost nothing by them."

"No, sir. But I want to find out about them, and who they are, and what their object was in playing this prank—if it was a prank—upon me. It was a pretty expensive joke for them, for it cost them two and thirty pounds."

"We shall endeavour to clear up these points for you. And, first, one or two questions, Mr. Wilson. This assistant of yours who first called your attention to the advertisement—how long had he been with you?"

"About a month then."

"How did he come?"

"In answer to an advertisement."

"Was he the only applicant?"

"No, I had a dozen."

"Why did you pick him?"

"Because he was handy and would come cheap."

"At half-wages, in fact."

"Yes."

"What is he like, this Vincent Spaulding?"

"Small, stout-built, very quick in his ways, no hair on his face, though he's not short of thirty. Has a white splash of acid upon his forehead."

Holmes sat up in his chair in considerable excitement. "I thought as much," said he. "Have you ever observed that his ears are pierced for earrings?"

"Yes, sir. He told me that a gipsy had done it for him when he was a lad."

"Hum!" said Holmes, sinking back in deep thought. "He is still with you?"

"Oh, yes, sir; I have only just left him."

"And has your business been attended to in your absence?"

"Nothing to complain of, sir. There's never very much to do of a morning."

"That will do, Mr. Wilson. I shall be happy to give you an opinion upon the subject in the course of a day or two. Today is Saturday, and I hope that by Monday we may come to a conclusion."

"Well, Watson," said Holmes when our visitor had left us, "what do you make of it all?"

"I make nothing of it," I answered frankly. "It is a most mysterious business."

"As a rule," said Holmes, "the more bizarre a thing is the less mysterious it proves to be. It is your commonplace, featureless crimes which are really puzzling, just as a commonplace face is the most difficult to identify. But I must be prompt over this matter."

"What are you going to do, then?" I asked.

"To smoke," he answered. "It is quite a three pipe problem, and I beg that you won't speak to me for fifty minutes." He curled himself up in his chair, with his thin knees drawn up to his hawk-like nose, and there he sat with his eyes closed and his black clay pipe thrusting out like the bill of some strange bird. I had come to the conclusion that he had dropped asleep, and indeed was nodding myself, when he suddenly sprang out of his chair with the gesture of a man who has made up his mind and put his pipe down upon the mantelpiece.

"Sarasate plays at the St. James's Hall this afternoon," he remarked. "What do you think, Watson? Could your patients spare you for a few hours?"

"I have nothing to do today. My practice is never very absorbing."

"Then put on your hat and come. I am going through the City first, and we can have some lunch on the way. I observe that there is a good deal of German music on the programme, which is rather more to my taste than Italian or French. It is introspective, and I want to introspect. Come along!"

We travelled by the Underground as far as Aldersgate; and a short walk took us to Saxe-Coburg Square, the scene of the singular story which we had listened to in the morning. It was a poky, little, shabby-genteel place, where four lines of dingy two-storied brick houses looked out into a small railed-in enclosure, where a lawn of weedy grass and a few clumps of faded laurel-bushes made a hard fight against a smoke-laden and uncongenial atmosphere. Three gilt balls and a brown board with "JABEZ WILSON" in white letters, upon a corner house, announced the place where our red-headed client carried on his business. Sherlock Holmes stopped in front of it with his head on one side and looked it all over, with his eyes shining brightly between puckered lids. Then he walked slowly up the street, and then down again to the corner, still looking keenly at the houses. Finally he returned to the pawnbroker's, and, having thumped vigorously upon the pavement with his stick two or three times, he went up to the door and knocked. It was instantly opened by a bright-looking, clean-shaven young fellow, who asked him to step in.

"Thank you," said Holmes, "I only wished to ask you how you would go from here to the Strand."

"Third right, fourth left," answered the assistant promptly, closing the door.

"Smart fellow, that," observed Holmes as we walked away. "He is, in my judgment, the fourth smartest man in London, and for daring I am not sure that he has not a claim to be third. I have known something of him before."

"Evidently," said I, "Mr. Wilson's assistant counts for a good deal in this mystery of the Red-Headed League. I am sure that you inquired your way merely in order that you might see him."

"Not him."

"What then?"

"The knees of his trousers."

"And what did you see?"

"What I expected to see."

"Why did you beat the pavement?"

"My dear doctor, this is a time for observation, not for talk. We are spies in an enemy's country. We know something of Saxe-Coburg Square. Let us now explore the parts which lie behind it."

The road in which we found ourselves as we turned round the corner from the retired Saxe-Coburg Square presented as great a contrast to it as the front of a picture does to the back. It was one of the main arteries which conveyed the traffic of the City to the north and west. The roadway was blocked with the immense stream of commerce flowing in a double tide inward and outward, while the footpaths were black with the hurrying swarm of pedestrians. It was difficult to realise as we looked at the line of fine shops and stately business premises that they really abutted on the other side upon the faded and stagnant square which we had just quitted.

"Let me see," said Holmes, standing at the corner and glancing along the line, "I should like just to remember the order of the houses here. It is a hobby of mine to have an exact knowledge of London. There is Mortimer's, the tobacconist, the little newspaper shop, the Coburg branch of the City and Suburban Bank, the Vegetarian Restaurant, and McFarlane's carriage-building depot. That carries us right on to the other block. And now, Doctor, we've done our work, so it's time we had some play. A sandwich and a cup of coffee, and then off to violin-land, where all is sweetness and delicacy and harmony, and there are no red-headed clients to vex us with their conundrums."

My friend was an enthusiastic musician, being himself not only a very capable performer but a composer of no ordinary merit. All the afternoon he sat in the stalls wrapped in the most perfect happiness, gently waving his long, thin fingers in time to the music, while his gently smiling face and his languid, dreamy eyes were as unlike those of Holmes the sleuth-hound, Holmes the relentless, keen-witted, ready-handed criminal agent, as it was possible to conceive. In his singular character the dual nature alternately asserted itself, and his extreme exactness and astuteness represented, as I have often thought, the reaction against the poetic and contemplative mood which occasionally predominated in him. The swing of his nature took him from extreme languor to devouring energy; and, as I knew well, he was never so truly formidable as when, for days on end, he had been lounging in his armchair amid his improvisations and his black-letter editions. Then it

was that the lust of the chase would suddenly come upon him, and that his brilliant reasoning power would rise to the level of intuition, until those who were unacquainted with his methods would look askance at him as on a man whose knowledge was not that of other mortals. When I saw him that afternoon so enwrapped in the music at St. James's Hall I felt that an evil time might be coming upon those whom he had set himself to hunt down.

"You want to go home, no doubt, Doctor," he remarked as we emerged.

"Yes, it would be as well."

"And I have some business to do which will take some hours. This business at Coburg Square is serious."

"Why serious?"

"A considerable crime is in contemplation. I have every reason to believe that we shall be in time to stop it. But today being Saturday rather complicates matters. I shall want your help tonight."

"At what time?"

"Ten will be early enough."

"I shall be at Baker Street at ten."

"Very well. And, I say, Doctor, there may be some little danger, so kindly put your army revolver in your pocket." He waved his hand, turned on his heel, and disappeared in an instant among the crowd.

I trust that I am not more dense than my neighbours, but I was always oppressed with a sense of my own stupidity in my dealings with Sherlock Holmes. Here I had heard what he had heard, I had seen what he had seen, and yet from his words it was evident that he saw clearly not only what had happened but what was about to happen, while to me the whole business was still confused and grotesque. As I drove home to my house in Kensington I thought over it all, from the extraordinary story of the red-headed copier of the *Encyclopaedia* down to the visit to Saxe-Coburg Square, and the ominous words with which he had parted from me. What was this nocturnal expedition, and why should I go armed? Where were we going, and what were we to do? I had the hint from Holmes that this smooth-faced pawnbroker's assistant was a formidable man—a man who might play a deep game. I tried to puzzle it out, but gave it up in despair and set the matter aside until night should bring an explanation.

It was a quarter-past nine when I started from home and made my way across the Park, and so through Oxford Street to Baker Street. Two hansoms were standing at the door, and as I entered the passage I heard the sound of voices from above. On entering his room I found Holmes in animated conversation with two men, one of whom I recognised as Peter Jones, the official police agent, while the other was a long, thin, sad-faced man, with a very shiny hat and oppressively respectable frock-coat.

"Ha! Our party is complete," said Holmes, buttoning up his pea-jacket and taking his heavy hunting crop from the rack. "Watson, I think you know Mr. Jones, of Scotland Yard? Let me introduce you to Mr. Merryweather, who is to be our companion in tonight's adventure."

"We're hunting in couples again, Doctor, you see," said Jones in his consequential way. "Our friend here is a wonderful man for starting a chase. All he wants is an old dog to help him to do the running down."

"I hope a wild goose may not prove to be the end of our chase," observed Mr. Merryweather gloomily.

"You may place considerable confidence in Mr. Holmes, sir," said the police agent loftily. "He has his own little methods, which are, if he won't mind my saying so, just a little too theoretical and fantastic, but he has the makings of a detective in him. It is not too much to say that once or twice, as in that business of the Sholto murder and the Agra treasure, he has been more nearly correct than the official force."

"Oh, if you say so, Mr. Jones, it is all right," said the stranger with deference. "Still, I confess that I miss my rubber. It is the first Saturday night for seven-and-twenty years that I have not had my rubber."

"I think you will find," said Sherlock Holmes, "that you will play for a higher stake tonight than you have ever done yet, and that the play will be more exciting. For you, Mr. Merryweather, the stake will be some 30,000 pounds; and for you, Jones, it will be the man upon whom you wish to lay your hands."

"John Clay, the murderer, thief, smasher, and forger. He's a young man, Mr. Merryweather, but he is at the head of his profession, and I would rather have my bracelets on him than on any criminal in London. He's a remarkable man, is young John Clay. His grandfather was a royal duke, and he himself has been to Eton and Oxford. His brain is as cunning as his fingers, and though we meet signs of him at every turn, we never know where to find the man himself. He'll crack a crib in Scotland one week, and be raising money to build an orphanage in

Cornwall the next. I've been on his track for years and have never set eyes on him yet."

"I hope that I may have the pleasure of introducing you tonight. I've had one or two little turns also with Mr. John Clay, and I agree with you that he is at the head of his profession. It is past ten, however, and quite time that we started. If you two will take the first hansom, Watson and I will follow in the second."

Sherlock Holmes was not very communicative during the long drive and lay back in the cab humming the tunes which he had heard in the afternoon. We rattled through an endless labyrinth of gas-lit streets until we emerged into Farrington Street.

"We are close there now," my friend remarked. "This fellow Merryweather is a bank director, and personally interested in the matter. I thought it as well to have Jones with us also. He is not a bad fellow, though an absolute imbecile in his profession. He has one positive virtue. He is as brave as a bulldog and as tenacious as a lobster if he gets his claws upon anyone. Here we are, and they are waiting for us."

We had reached the same crowded thoroughfare in which we had found ourselves in the morning. Our cabs were dismissed, and, following the guidance of Mr. Merryweather, we passed down a narrow passage and through a side door, which he opened for us. Within there was a small corridor, which ended in a very massive iron gate. This also was opened, and led down a flight of winding stone steps, which terminated at another formidable gate. Mr. Merryweather stopped to light a lantern, and then conducted us down a dark, earth-smelling passage, and so, after opening a third door, into a huge vault or cellar, which was piled all round with crates and massive boxes.

"You are not very vulnerable from above," Holmes remarked as he held up the lantern and gazed about him.

"Nor from below," said Mr. Merryweather, striking his stick upon the flags which lined the floor. "Why, dear me, it sounds quite hollow!" he remarked, looking up in surprise.

"I must really ask you to be a little more quiet!" said Holmes severely. "You have already imperilled the whole success of our expedition. Might I beg that you would have the goodness to sit down upon one of those boxes, and not to interfere?"

The solemn Mr. Merryweather perched himself upon a crate, with a very injured expression upon his face, while Holmes fell upon his knees upon the floor and, with the lantern and a magnifying lens, began to examine minutely the cracks between the stones. A few seconds sufficed to satisfy him, for he sprang to his feet again and put his glass in his pocket.

"We have at least an hour before us," he remarked, "for they can hardly take any steps until the good pawnbroker is safely in bed. Then they will not lose a minute, for the sooner they do their work the longer time they will have for their escape. We are at present, Doctor—as no doubt you have divined—in the cellar of the City branch of one of the principal London banks. Mr. Merryweather is the chairman of directors, and he will explain to you that there are reasons why the more daring criminals of London should take a considerable interest in this cellar at present."

"It is our French gold," whispered the director. "We have had several warnings that an attempt might be made upon it."

"Your French gold?"

"Yes. We had occasion some months ago to strengthen our resources and borrowed for that purpose 30,000 napoleons from the Bank of France. It has become known that we have never had occasion to unpack the money, and that it is still lying in our cellar. The crate upon which I sit contains 2,000 napoleons packed between layers of lead foil. Our reserve of bullion is much larger at present than is usually kept in a single branch office, and the directors have had misgivings upon the subject."

"Which were very well justified," observed Holmes. "And now it is time that we arranged our little plans. I expect that within an hour matters will come to a head. In the meantime Mr. Merryweather, we must put the screen over that dark lantern."

"And sit in the dark?"

"I am afraid so. I had brought a pack of cards in my pocket, and I thought that, as we were a *partie carrée*, you might have your rubber after all. But I see that the enemy's preparations have gone so far that we cannot risk the presence of a light. And, first of all, we must choose our positions. These are daring men, and though we shall take them at a disadvantage, they may do us some harm unless we are careful. I shall stand behind this crate, and do you conceal yourselves behind those. Then, when I flash a light upon them, close in swiftly. If they fire, Watson, have no compunction about shooting them down."

I placed my revolver, cocked, upon the top of the wooden case behind which I crouched. Holmes shot the slide across the front of his lantern and left us in pitch darkness—such an absolute darkness as I have never before experienced. The smell of hot metal remained to assure us that the light was still there, ready to flash out at a moment's notice. To me, with my nerves worked up to a pitch of expectancy, there was something depressing and subduing in the sudden gloom, and in the cold dank air of the vault.

"They have but one retreat," whispered Holmes. "That is back through the house into Saxe-Coburg Square. I hope that you have done what I asked you, Jones?"

"I have an inspector and two officers waiting at the front door."

"Then we have stopped all the holes. And now we must be silent and wait."

What a time it seemed! From comparing notes afterwards it was but an hour and a quarter, yet it appeared to me that the night must have almost gone and the dawn be breaking above us. My limbs were weary and stiff, for I feared to change my position; yet my nerves were worked up to the highest pitch of tension, and my hearing was so acute that I could not only hear the gentle breathing of my companions, but I could distinguish the deeper, heavier in-breath of the bulky Jones from the thin, sighing note of the bank director. From my position I could look over the case in the direction of the floor. Suddenly my eyes caught the glint of a light.

At first it was but a lurid spark upon the stone pavement. Then it lengthened out until it became a yellow line, and then, without any warning or sound, a gash seemed to open and a hand appeared, a white, almost womanly hand, which felt about in the centre of the little area of light. For a minute or more the hand, with its writhing fingers, protruded out of the floor. Then it was withdrawn as suddenly as it appeared, and all was dark again save the single lurid spark which marked a chink between the stones.

Its disappearance, however, was but momentary. With a rending, tearing sound, one of the broad, white stones turned over upon its side and left a square, gaping hole, through which streamed the light of a lantern. Over the edge there peeped a clean-cut, boyish face, which looked keenly about it, and then, with a hand on either side of the aperture, drew itself shoulder-high and waist-high, until one knee rested upon the edge. In another instant he stood at the side of the hole and was hauling after him a companion, lithe and small like himself, with a pale face and a shock of very red hair.

"It's all clear," he whispered. "Have you the chisel and the bags? Great Scott! Jump, Archie, jump, and I'll swing for it!"

Sherlock Holmes had sprung out and seized the intruder by the collar. The other dived down the hole, and I heard the sound of rending cloth as Jones clutched at his skirts. The light flashed upon the barrel of a revolver, but Holmes' hunting crop came down on the man's wrist, and the pistol clinked upon the stone floor.

"It's no use, John Clay," said Holmes blandly. "You have no chance at all."

"So I see," the other answered with the utmost coolness. "I fancy that my pal is all right, though I see you have got his coat-tails."

"There are three men waiting for him at the door," said Holmes.

"Oh, indeed! You seem to have done the thing very completely. I must compliment you."

"And I you," Holmes answered. "Your red-headed idea was very new and effective."

"You'll see your pal again presently," said Jones. "He's quicker at climbing down holes than I am. Just hold out while I fix the derbies."

"I beg that you will not touch me with your filthy hands," remarked our prisoner as the handcuffs clattered upon his wrists. "You may not be aware that I have royal blood in my veins. Have the goodness, also, when you address me always to say 'sir' and 'please.'"

"All right," said Jones with a stare and a snigger. "Well, would you please, sir, march upstairs, where we can get a cab to carry your Highness to the police-station?"

"That is better," said John Clay serenely. He made a sweeping bow to the three of us and walked quietly off in the custody of the detective.

"Really, Mr. Holmes," said Mr. Merryweather as we followed them from the cellar, "I do not know how the bank can thank you or repay you. There is no doubt that you have detected and defeated in the most complete manner one of the most determined attempts at bank robbery that have ever come within my experience."

"I have had one or two little scores of my own to settle with Mr. John Clay," said Holmes. "I have been at some small expense over this matter, which I shall expect the bank to refund, but beyond that I

am amply repaid by having had an experience which is in many ways unique, and by hearing the very remarkable narrative of the Red-Headed League."

* * * * *

"You see, Watson," he explained in the early hours of the morning as we sat over a glass of whisky and soda in Baker Street, "it was perfectly obvious from the first that the only possible object of this rather fantastic business of the advertisement of the League, and the copying of the *Encyclopaedia*, must be to get this not over-bright pawnbroker out of the way for a number of hours every day. It was a curious way of managing it, but, really, it would be difficult to suggest a better. The method was no doubt suggested to Clay's ingenious mind by the colour of his accomplice's hair. The 4 pounds a week was a lure which must draw him, and what was it to them, who were playing for thousands? They put in the advertisement, one rogue has the temporary office, the other rogue incites the man to apply for it, and together they manage to secure his absence every morning in the week. From the time that I heard of the assistant having come for half wages, it was obvious to me that he had some strong motive for securing the situation."

"But how could you guess what the motive was?"

"Had there been women in the house, I should have suspected a mere vulgar intrigue. That, however, was out of the question. The man's business was a small one, and there was nothing in his house which could account for such elaborate preparations, and such an expenditure as they were at. It must, then, be something out of the house. What could it be? I thought of the assistant's fondness for photography, and his trick of vanishing into the cellar. The cellar! There was the end of this tangled clue. Then I made inquiries as to this mysterious assistant and found that I had to deal with one of the coolest and most daring criminals in London. He was doing something in the cellar—something which took many hours a day for months on end. What could it be, once more? I could think of nothing save that he was running a tunnel to some other building.

"So far I had got when we went to visit the scene of action. I surprised you by beating upon the pavement with my stick. I was ascertaining whether the cellar stretched out in front or behind. It was not in front.

Then I rang the bell, and, as I hoped, the assistant answered it. We have had some skirmishes, but we had never set eyes upon each other before. I hardly looked at his face. His knees were what I wished to see. You must yourself have remarked how worn, wrinkled, and stained they were. They spoke of those hours of burrowing. The only remaining point was what they were burrowing for. I walked round the corner, saw the City and Suburban Bank abutted on our friend's premises, and felt that I had solved my problem. When you drove home after the concert I called upon Scotland Yard and upon the chairman of the bank directors, with the result that you have seen."

"And how could you tell that they would make their attempt tonight?" I asked.

"Well, when they closed their League offices that was a sign that they cared no longer about Mr. Jabez Wilson's presence—in other words, that they had completed their tunnel. But it was essential that they should use it soon, as it might be discovered, or the bullion might be removed. Saturday would suit them better than any other day, as it would give them two days for their escape. For all these reasons I expected them to come tonight."

"You reasoned it out beautifully," I exclaimed in unfeigned admiration. "It is so long a chain, and yet every link rings true."

"It saved me from ennui," he answered, yawning. "Alas! I already feel it closing in upon me. My life is spent in one long effort to escape from the commonplaces of existence. These little problems help me to do so."

"And you are a benefactor of the race," said I.

He shrugged his shoulders. "Well, perhaps, after all, it is of some little use," he remarked. "'*L'homme c'est rien—l'oeuvre c'est tout*,' as Gustave Flaubert wrote to George Sand."

A CASE OF IDENTITY

"My dear fellow," said Sherlock Holmes as we sat on either side of the fire in his lodgings at Baker Street, "life is infinitely stranger than anything which the mind of man could invent. We would not dare to conceive the things which are really mere commonplaces of existence. If we could fly out of that window hand in hand, hover over this great city, gently remove the roofs, and peep in at the queer things which are going on, the strange coincidences, the plannings, the cross-purposes, the wonderful chains of events, working through generations, and leading to the most *outré* results, it would make all fiction with its conventionalities and foreseen conclusions most stale and unprofitable."

"And yet I am not convinced of it," I answered. "The cases which come to light in the papers are, as a rule, bald enough, and vulgar enough. We have in our police reports realism pushed to its extreme limits, and yet the result is, it must be confessed, neither fascinating nor artistic."

"A certain selection and discretion must be used in producing a realistic effect," remarked Holmes. "This is wanting in the police report, where more stress is laid, perhaps, upon the platitudes of the magistrate than upon the details, which to an observer contain the vital essence of the whole matter. Depend upon it, there is nothing so unnatural as the commonplace."

I smiled and shook my head. "I can quite understand your thinking so." I said. "Of course, in your position of unofficial adviser and helper to everybody who is absolutely puzzled, throughout three continents, you are brought in contact with all that is strange and bizarre. But here"—I picked up the morning paper from the ground—"let us put it to a practical test. Here is the first heading upon which I come. 'A husband's cruelty to his wife.' There is half a column of print, but I know without reading it that it is all perfectly familiar to me. There is, of course, the other woman, the drink, the push, the blow, the bruise, the sympathetic sister or landlady. The crudest of writers could invent nothing more crude."

"Indeed, your example is an unfortunate one for your argument," said Holmes, taking the paper and glancing his eye down it. "This is the

Dundas separation case, and, as it happens, I was engaged in clearing up some small points in connection with it. The husband was a teetotaler, there was no other woman, and the conduct complained of was that he had drifted into the habit of winding up every meal by taking out his false teeth and hurling them at his wife, which, you will allow, is not an action likely to occur to the imagination of the average storyteller. Take a pinch of snuff, Doctor, and acknowledge that I have scored over you in your example."

He held out his snuffbox of old gold, with a great amethyst in the centre of the lid. Its splendour was in such contrast to his homely ways and simple life that I could not help commenting upon it.

"Ah," said he, "I forgot that I had not seen you for some weeks. It is a little souvenir from the King of Bohemia in return for my assistance in the case of the Irene Adler papers."

"And the ring?" I asked, glancing at a remarkable brilliant which sparkled upon his finger. "It was from the reigning family of Holland, though the matter in which I served them was of such delicacy that I cannot confide it even to you, who have been good enough to chronicle one or two of my little problems."

"And have you any on hand just now?" I asked with interest.

"Some ten or twelve, but none which present any feature of interest. They are important, you understand, without being interesting. Indeed, I have found that it is usually in unimportant matters that there is a field for the observation, and for the quick analysis of cause and effect which gives the charm to an investigation. The larger crimes are apt to be the simpler, for the bigger the crime the more obvious, as a rule, is the motive. In these cases, save for one rather intricate matter which has been referred to me from Marseilles, there is nothing which presents any features of interest. It is possible, however, that I may have something better before very many minutes are over, for this is one of my clients, or I am much mistaken."

He had risen from his chair and was standing between the parted blinds gazing down into the dull neutral-tinted London street. Looking over his shoulder, I saw that on the pavement opposite there stood a large woman with a heavy fur boa round her neck, and a large curling red feather in a broad-brimmed hat which was tilted in a coquettish Duchess of Devonshire fashion over her ear. From under this great panoply she peeped up in a nervous, hesitating fashion at our windows,

while her body oscillated backward and forward, and her fingers fidgeted with her glove buttons. Suddenly, with a plunge, as of the swimmer who leaves the bank, she hurried across the road, and we heard the sharp clang of the bell.

"I have seen those symptoms before," said Holmes, throwing his cigarette into the fire. "Oscillation upon the pavement always means an *affaire de coeur*. She would like advice, but is not sure that the matter is not too delicate for communication. And yet even here we may discriminate. When a woman has been seriously wronged by a man she no longer oscillates, and the usual symptom is a broken bell wire. Here we may take it that there is a love matter, but that the maiden is not so much angry as perplexed, or grieved. But here she comes in person to resolve our doubts."

As he spoke there was a tap at the door, and the boy in buttons entered to announce Miss Mary Sutherland, while the lady herself loomed behind his small black figure like a full-sailed merchant-man behind a tiny pilot boat. Sherlock Holmes welcomed her with the easy courtesy for which he was remarkable, and, having closed the door and bowed her into an armchair, he looked her over in the minute and yet abstracted fashion which was peculiar to him.

"Do you not find," he said, "that with your short sight it is a little trying to do so much typewriting?"

"I did at first," she answered, "but now I know where the letters are without looking." Then, suddenly realising the full purport of his words, she gave a violent start and looked up, with fear and astonishment upon her broad, good-humoured face. "You've heard about me, Mr. Holmes," she cried, "else how could you know all that?"

"Never mind," said Holmes, laughing; "it is my business to know things. Perhaps I have trained myself to see what others overlook. If not, why should you come to consult me?"

"I came to you, sir, because I heard of you from Mrs. Etherege, whose husband you found so easy when the police and everyone had given him up for dead. Oh, Mr. Holmes, I wish you would do as much for me. I'm not rich, but still I have a hundred a year in my own right, besides the little that I make by the machine, and I would give it all to know what has become of Mr. Hosmer Angel."

"Why did you come away to consult me in such a hurry?" asked Sherlock Holmes, with his finger-tips together and his eyes to the ceiling.

Again a startled look came over the somewhat vacuous face of Miss Mary Sutherland. "Yes, I did bang out of the house," she said, "for it made me angry to see the easy way in which Mr. Windibank—that is, my father—took it all. He would not go to the police, and he would not go to you, and so at last, as he would do nothing and kept on saying that there was no harm done, it made me mad, and I just on with my things and came right away to you."

"Your father," said Holmes, "your stepfather, surely, since the name is different."

"Yes, my stepfather. I call him father, though it sounds funny, too, for he is only five years and two months older than myself."

"And your mother is alive?"

"Oh, yes, mother is alive and well. I wasn't best pleased, Mr. Holmes, when she married again so soon after father's death, and a man who was nearly fifteen years younger than herself. Father was a plumber in the Tottenham Court Road, and he left a tidy business behind him, which mother carried on with Mr. Hardy, the foreman; but when Mr. Windibank came he made her sell the business, for he was very superior, being a traveller in wines. They got 4,700 pounds for the goodwill and interest, which wasn't near as much as father could have got if he had been alive."

I had expected to see Sherlock Holmes impatient under this rambling and inconsequential narrative, but, on the contrary, he had listened with the greatest concentration of attention.

"Your own little income," he asked, "does it come out of the business?"

"Oh, no, sir. It is quite separate and was left me by my uncle Ned in Auckland. It is in New Zealand stock, paying 4½ percent. Two thousand five hundred pounds was the amount, but I can only touch the interest."

"You interest me extremely," said Holmes. "And since you draw so large a sum as a hundred a year, with what you earn into the bargain, you no doubt travel a little and indulge yourself in every way. I believe that a single lady can get on very nicely upon an income of about 60 pounds."

"I could do with much less than that, Mr. Holmes, but you understand that as long as I live at home I don't wish to be a burden to them, and so they have the use of the money just while I am staying with them. Of course, that is only just for the time. Mr. Windibank draws my interest every quarter and pays it over to mother, and I find that I can do pretty

well with what I earn at typewriting. It brings me twopence a sheet, and I can often do from fifteen to twenty sheets in a day."

"You have made your position very clear to me," said Holmes. "This is my friend, Dr. Watson, before whom you can speak as freely as before myself. Kindly tell us now all about your connection with Mr. Hosmer Angel."

A flush stole over Miss Sutherland's face, and she picked nervously at the fringe of her jacket. "I met him first at the gasfitters' ball," she said. "They used to send father tickets when he was alive, and then afterwards they remembered us, and sent them to mother. Mr. Windibank did not wish us to go. He never did wish us to go anywhere. He would get quite mad if I wanted so much as to join a Sunday-school treat. But this time I was set on going, and I would go; for what right had he to prevent? He said the folk were not fit for us to know, when all father's friends were to be there. And he said that I had nothing fit to wear, when I had my purple plush that I had never so much as taken out of the drawer. At last, when nothing else would do, he went off to France upon the business of the firm, but we went, mother and I, with Mr. Hardy, who used to be our foreman, and it was there I met Mr. Hosmer Angel."

"I suppose," said Holmes, "that when Mr. Windibank came back from France he was very annoyed at your having gone to the ball."

"Oh, well, he was very good about it. He laughed, I remember, and shrugged his shoulders, and said there was no use denying anything to a woman, for she would have her way."

"I see. Then at the gasfitters' ball you met, as I understand, a gentleman called Mr. Hosmer Angel."

"Yes, sir. I met him that night, and he called next day to ask if we had got home all safe, and after that we met him—that is to say, Mr. Holmes, I met him twice for walks, but after that father came back again, and Mr. Hosmer Angel could not come to the house any more."

"No?"

"Well, you know father didn't like anything of the sort. He wouldn't have any visitors if he could help it, and he used to say that a woman should be happy in her own family circle. But then, as I used to say to mother, a woman wants her own circle to begin with, and I had not got mine yet."

"But how about Mr. Hosmer Angel? Did he make no attempt to see you?"

"Well, father was going off to France again in a week, and Hosmer wrote and said that it would be safer and better not to see each other until he had gone. We could write in the meantime, and he used to write every day. I took the letters in in the morning, so there was no need for father to know."

"Were you engaged to the gentleman at this time?"

"Oh, yes, Mr. Holmes. We were engaged after the first walk that we took. Hosmer—Mr. Angel—was a cashier in an office in Leadenhall Street—and—"

"What office?"

"That's the worst of it, Mr. Holmes, I don't know."

"Where did he live, then?"

"He slept on the premises."

"And you don't know his address?"

"No—except that it was Leadenhall Street."

"Where did you address your letters, then?"

"To the Leadenhall Street Post Office, to be left till called for. He said that if they were sent to the office he would be chaffed by all the other clerks about having letters from a lady, so I offered to typewrite them, like he did his, but he wouldn't have that, for he said that when I wrote them they seemed to come from me, but when they were typewritten he always felt that the machine had come between us. That will just show you how fond he was of me, Mr. Holmes, and the little things that he would think of."

"It was most suggestive," said Holmes. "It has long been an axiom of mine that the little things are infinitely the most important. Can you remember any other little things about Mr. Hosmer Angel?"

"He was a very shy man, Mr. Holmes. He would rather walk with me in the evening than in the daylight, for he said that he hated to be conspicuous. Very retiring and gentlemanly he was. Even his voice was gentle. He'd had the quinsy and swollen glands when he was young, he told me, and it had left him with a weak throat, and a hesitating, whispering fashion of speech. He was always well dressed, very neat and plain, but his eyes were weak, just as mine are, and he wore tinted glasses against the glare."

"Well, and what happened when Mr. Windibank, your stepfather, returned to France?"

"Mr. Hosmer Angel came to the house again and proposed that

we should marry before father came back. He was in dreadful earnest and made me swear, with my hands on the Testament, that whatever happened I would always be true to him. Mother said he was quite right to make me swear, and that it was a sign of his passion. Mother was all in his favour from the first and was even fonder of him than I was. Then, when they talked of marrying within the week, I began to ask about father; but they both said never to mind about father, but just to tell him afterwards, and mother said she would make it all right with him. I didn't quite like that, Mr. Holmes. It seemed funny that I should ask his leave, as he was only a few years older than me; but I didn't want to do anything on the sly, so I wrote to father at Bordeaux, where the company has its French offices, but the letter came back to me on the very morning of the wedding."

"It missed him, then?"

"Yes, sir; for he had started to England just before it arrived."

"Ha! that was unfortunate. Your wedding was arranged, then, for the Friday. Was it to be in church?"

"Yes, sir, but very quietly. It was to be at St. Saviour's, near King's Cross, and we were to have breakfast afterwards at the St. Pancras Hotel. Hosmer came for us in a hansom, but as there were two of us he put us both into it and stepped himself into a four-wheeler, which happened to be the only other cab in the street. We got to the church first, and when the four-wheeler drove up we waited for him to step out, but he never did, and when the cabman got down from the box and looked there was no one there! The cabman said that he could not imagine what had become of him, for he had seen him get in with his own eyes. That was last Friday, Mr. Holmes, and I have never seen or heard anything since then to throw any light upon what became of him."

"It seems to me that you have been very shamefully treated," said Holmes.

"Oh, no, sir! He was too good and kind to leave me so. Why, all the morning he was saying to me that, whatever happened, I was to be true; and that even if something quite unforeseen occurred to separate us, I was always to remember that I was pledged to him, and that he would claim his pledge sooner or later. It seemed strange talk for a wedding-morning, but what has happened since gives a meaning to it."

"Most certainly it does. Your own opinion is, then, that some unforeseen catastrophe has occurred to him?"

"Yes, sir. I believe that he foresaw some danger, or else he would not have talked so. And then I think that what he foresaw happened."

"But you have no notion as to what it could have been?"

"None."

"One more question. How did your mother take the matter?"

"She was angry, and said that I was never to speak of the matter again."

"And your father? Did you tell him?"

"Yes; and he seemed to think, with me, that something had happened, and that I should hear of Hosmer again. As he said, what interest could anyone have in bringing me to the doors of the church, and then leaving me? Now, if he had borrowed my money, or if he had married me and got my money settled on him, there might be some reason, but Hosmer was very independent about money and never would look at a shilling of mine. And yet, what could have happened? And why could he not write? Oh, it drives me half-mad to think of it, and I can't sleep a wink at night." She pulled a little handkerchief out of her muff and began to sob heavily into it.

"I shall glance into the case for you," said Holmes, rising, "and I have no doubt that we shall reach some definite result. Let the weight of the matter rest upon me now, and do not let your mind dwell upon it further. Above all, try to let Mr. Hosmer Angel vanish from your memory, as he has done from your life."

"Then you don't think I'll see him again?"

"I fear not."

"Then what has happened to him?"

"You will leave that question in my hands. I should like an accurate description of him and any letters of his which you can spare."

"I advertised for him in last Saturday's *Chronicle*," said she. "Here is the slip and here are four letters from him."

"Thank you. And your address?"

"No. 31 Lyon Place, Camberwell."

"Mr. Angel's address you never had, I understand. Where is your father's place of business?"

"He travels for Westhouse & Marbank, the great claret importers of Fenchurch Street."

"Thank you. You have made your statement very clearly. You will leave the papers here, and remember the advice which I have given you.

Let the whole incident be a sealed book, and do not allow it to affect your life."

"You are very kind, Mr. Holmes, but I cannot do that. I shall be true to Hosmer. He shall find me ready when he comes back."

For all the preposterous hat and the vacuous face, there was something noble in the simple faith of our visitor which compelled our respect. She laid her little bundle of papers upon the table and went her way, with a promise to come again whenever she might be summoned.

Sherlock Holmes sat silent for a few minutes with his fingertips still pressed together, his legs stretched out in front of him, and his gaze directed upward to the ceiling. Then he took down from the rack the old and oily clay pipe, which was to him as a counsellor, and, having lit it, he leaned back in his chair, with the thick blue cloud-wreaths spinning up from him, and a look of infinite languor in his face.

"Quite an interesting study, that maiden," he observed. "I found her more interesting than her little problem, which, by the way, is rather a trite one. You will find parallel cases, if you consult my index, in Andover in '77, and there was something of the sort at The Hague last year. Old as is the idea, however, there were one or two details which were new to me. But the maiden herself was most instructive."

"You appeared to read a good deal upon her which was quite invisible to me," I remarked.

"Not invisible but unnoticed, Watson. You did not know where to look, and so you missed all that was important. I can never bring you to realise the importance of sleeves, the suggestiveness of thumb-nails, or the great issues that may hang from a boot-lace. Now, what did you gather from that woman's appearance? Describe it."

"Well, she had a slate-coloured, broad-brimmed straw hat, with a feather of a brickish red. Her jacket was black, with black beads sewn upon it, and a fringe of little black jet ornaments. Her dress was brown, rather darker than coffee colour, with a little purple plush at the neck and sleeves. Her gloves were greyish and were worn through at the right forefinger. Her boots I didn't observe. She had small round, hanging gold earrings, and a general air of being fairly well-to-do in a vulgar, comfortable, easy-going way."

Sherlock Holmes clapped his hands softly together and chuckled.

"'Pon my word, Watson, you are coming along wonderfully. You have really done very well indeed. It is true that you have missed everything of importance, but you have hit upon the method, and you have a quick eye for colour. Never trust to general impressions, my boy, but concentrate yourself upon details. My first glance is always at a woman's sleeve. In a man it is perhaps better first to take the knee of the trouser. As you observe, this woman had plush upon her sleeves, which is a most useful material for showing traces. The double line a little above the wrist, where the typewritist presses against the table, was beautifully defined. The sewing-machine, of the hand type, leaves a similar mark, but only on the left arm, and on the side of it farthest from the thumb, instead of being right across the broadest part, as this was. I then glanced at her face, and, observing the dint of a *pince-nez* at either side of her nose, I ventured a remark upon short sight and typewriting, which seemed to surprise her."

"It surprised me."

"But, surely, it was obvious. I was then much surprised and interested on glancing down to observe that, though the boots which she was wearing were not unlike each other, they were really odd ones; the one having a slightly decorated toe-cap, and the other a plain one. One was buttoned only in the two lower buttons out of five, and the other at the first, third, and fifth. Now, when you see that a young lady, otherwise neatly dressed, has come away from home with odd boots, half-buttoned, it is no great deduction to say that she came away in a hurry."

"And what else?" I asked, keenly interested, as I always was, by my friend's incisive reasoning.

"I noted, in passing, that she had written a note before leaving home but after being fully dressed. You observed that her right glove was torn at the forefinger, but you did not apparently see that both glove and finger were stained with violet ink. She had written in a hurry and dipped her pen too deep. It must have been this morning, or the mark would not remain clear upon the finger. All this is amusing, though rather elementary, but I must go back to business, Watson. Would you mind reading me the advertised description of Mr. Hosmer Angel?"

I held the little printed slip to the light.

"Missing," it said, "on the morning of the fourteenth, a gentleman named Hosmer Angel. About 5 ft. 7 in. in height; strongly built, sallow complexion, black hair, a little bald in the centre, bushy, black side-whiskers and moustache; tinted glasses, slight infirmity of speech. Was dressed, when last seen, in black frock-coat faced with silk, black

waistcoat, gold Albert chain, and grey Harris tweed trousers, with brown gaiters over elastic-sided boots. Known to have been employed in an office in Leadenhall Street. Anybody bringing, etc., etc."

"That will do," said Holmes. "As to the letters," he continued, glancing over them, "they are very commonplace. Absolutely no clue in them to Mr. Angel, save that he quotes Balzac once. There is one remarkable point, however, which will no doubt strike you."

"They are typewritten," I remarked.

"Not only that, but the signature is typewritten. Look at the neat little 'Hosmer Angel' at the bottom. There is a date, you see, but no superscription except Leadenhall Street, which is rather vague. The point about the signature is very suggestive—in fact, we may call it conclusive."

"Of what?"

"My dear fellow, is it possible you do not see how strongly it bears upon the case?"

"I cannot say that I do unless it were that he wished to be able to deny his signature if an action for breach of promise were instituted."

"No, that was not the point. However, I shall write two letters, which should settle the matter. One is to a firm in the City, the other is to the young lady's stepfather, Mr. Windibank, asking him whether he could meet us here at six o'clock tomorrow evening. It is just as well that we should do business with the male relatives. And now, Doctor, we can do nothing until the answers to those letters come, so we may put our little problem upon the shelf for the interim."

I had had so many reasons to believe in my friend's subtle powers of reasoning and extraordinary energy in action that I felt that he must have some solid grounds for the assured and easy demeanour with which he treated the singular mystery which he had been called upon to fathom. Once only had I known him to fail, in the case of the King of Bohemia and of the Irene Adler photograph; but when I looked back to the weird business of the Sign of Four, and the extraordinary circumstances connected with the Study in Scarlet, I felt that it would be a strange tangle indeed which he could not unravel.

I left him then, still puffing at his black clay pipe, with the conviction that when I came again on the next evening I would find that he held in his hands all the clues which would lead up to the identity of the disappearing bridegroom of Miss Mary Sutherland.

A professional case of great gravity was engaging my own attention at the time, and the whole of next day I was busy at the bedside of the sufferer. It was not until close upon six o'clock that I found myself free and was able to spring into a hansom and drive to Baker Street, half afraid that I might be too late to assist at the dénouement of the little mystery. I found Sherlock Holmes alone, however, half asleep, with his long, thin form curled up in the recesses of his armchair. A formidable array of bottles and test-tubes, with the pungent cleanly smell of hydrochloric acid, told me that he had spent his day in the chemical work which was so dear to him.

"Well, have you solved it?" I asked as I entered.

"Yes. It was the bisulphate of baryta."

"No, no, the mystery!" I cried.

"Oh, that! I thought of the salt that I have been working upon. There was never any mystery in the matter, though, as I said yesterday, some of the details are of interest. The only drawback is that there is no law, I fear, that can touch the scoundrel."

"Who was he, then, and what was his object in deserting Miss Sutherland?"

The question was hardly out of my mouth, and Holmes had not yet opened his lips to reply, when we heard a heavy footfall in the passage and a tap at the door.

"This is the girl's stepfather, Mr. James Windibank," said Holmes. "He has written to me to say that he would be here at six. Come in!"

The man who entered was a sturdy, middle-sized fellow, some thirty years of age, clean-shaven, and sallow-skinned, with a bland, insinuating manner, and a pair of wonderfully sharp and penetrating grey eyes. He shot a questioning glance at each of us, placed his shiny top-hat upon the sideboard, and with a slight bow sidled down into the nearest chair.

"Good-evening, Mr. James Windibank," said Holmes. "I think that this typewritten letter is from you, in which you made an appointment with me for six o'clock?"

"Yes, sir. I am afraid that I am a little late, but I am not quite my own master, you know. I am sorry that Miss Sutherland has troubled you about this little matter, for I think it is far better not to wash linen of the sort in public. It was quite against my wishes that she came, but she is a very excitable, impulsive girl, as you may have noticed, and she is not easily controlled when she has made up her mind on a point. Of course, I did not mind you so much, as you are not connected with the official

police, but it is not pleasant to have a family misfortune like this noised abroad. Besides, it is a useless expense, for how could you possibly find this Hosmer Angel?"

"On the contrary," said Holmes quietly; "I have every reason to believe that I will succeed in discovering Mr. Hosmer Angel."

Mr. Windibank gave a violent start and dropped his gloves. "I am delighted to hear it," he said.

"It is a curious thing," remarked Holmes, "that a typewriter has really quite as much individuality as a man's handwriting. Unless they are quite new, no two of them write exactly alike. Some letters get more worn than others, and some wear only on one side. Now, you remark in this note of yours, Mr. Windibank, that in every case there is some little slurring over of the 'e,' and a slight defect in the tail of the 'r.' There are fourteen other characteristics, but those are the more obvious."

"We do all our correspondence with this machine at the office, and no doubt it is a little worn," our visitor answered, glancing keenly at Holmes with his bright little eyes.

"And now I will show you what is really a very interesting study, Mr. Windibank," Holmes continued. "I think of writing another little monograph some of these days on the typewriter and its relation to crime. It is a subject to which I have devoted some little attention. I have here four letters which purport to come from the missing man. They are all typewritten. In each case, not only are the 'e's slurred and the 'r's tailless, but you will observe, if you care to use my magnifying lens, that the fourteen other characteristics to which I have alluded are there as well."

Mr. Windibank sprang out of his chair and picked up his hat. "I cannot waste time over this sort of fantastic talk, Mr. Holmes," he said. "If you can catch the man, catch him, and let me know when you have done it."

"Certainly," said Holmes, stepping over and turning the key in the door. "I let you know, then, that I have caught him!"

"What! Where?" shouted Mr. Windibank, turning white to his lips and glancing about him like a rat in a trap.

"Oh, it won't do—really it won't," said Holmes suavely. "There is no possible getting out of it, Mr. Windibank. It is quite too transparent, and it was a very bad compliment when you said that it was impossible for me to solve so simple a question. That's right! Sit down and let us talk it over."

Our visitor collapsed into a chair, with a ghastly face and a glitter of moisture on his brow. "It—it's not actionable," he stammered.

"I am very much afraid that it is not. But between ourselves, Windibank, it was as cruel and selfish and heartless a trick in a petty way as ever came before me. Now, let me just run over the course of events, and you will contradict me if I go wrong."

The man sat huddled up in his chair, with his head sunk upon his breast, like one who is utterly crushed. Holmes stuck his feet up on the corner of the mantelpiece and, leaning back with his hands in his pockets, began talking, rather to himself, as it seemed, than to us.

"The man married a woman very much older than himself for her money," said he, "and he enjoyed the use of the money of the daughter as long as she lived with them. It was a considerable sum, for people in their position, and the loss of it would have made a serious difference. It was worth an effort to preserve it. The daughter was of a good, amiable disposition, but affectionate and warm-hearted in her ways, so that it was evident that with her fair personal advantages, and her little income, she would not be allowed to remain single long. Now her marriage would mean, of course, the loss of a hundred a year, so what does her stepfather do to prevent it? He takes the obvious course of keeping her at home and forbidding her to seek the company of people of her own age. But soon he found that that would not answer forever. She became restive, insisted upon her rights, and finally announced her positive intention of going to a certain ball. What does her clever stepfather do then? He conceives an idea more creditable to his head than to his heart. With the connivance and assistance of his wife he disguised himself, covered those keen eyes with tinted glasses, masked the face with a moustache and a pair of bushy whiskers, sunk that clear voice into an insinuating whisper, and doubly secure on account of the girl's short sight, he appears as Mr. Hosmer Angel, and keeps off other lovers by making love himself."

"It was only a joke at first," groaned our visitor. "We never thought that she would have been so carried away."

"Very likely not. However that may be, the young lady was very decidedly carried away, and, having quite made up her mind that her stepfather was in France, the suspicion of treachery never for an instant entered her mind. She was flattered by the gentleman's attentions, and the effect was increased by the loudly expressed admiration of

her mother. Then Mr. Angel began to call, for it was obvious that the matter should be pushed as far as it would go if a real effect were to be produced. There were meetings, and an engagement, which would finally secure the girl's affections from turning towards anyone else. But the deception could not be kept up forever. These pretended journeys to France were rather cumbrous. The thing to do was clearly to bring the business to an end in such a dramatic manner that it would leave a permanent impression upon the young lady's mind and prevent her from looking upon any other suitor for some time to come. Hence those vows of fidelity exacted upon a Testament, and hence also the allusions to a possibility of something happening on the very morning of the wedding. James Windibank wished Miss Sutherland to be so bound to Hosmer Angel, and so uncertain as to his fate, that for ten years to come, at any rate, she would not listen to another man. As far as the church door he brought her, and then, as he could go no farther, he conveniently vanished away by the old trick of stepping in at one door of a four-wheeler and out at the other. I think that was the chain of events, Mr. Windibank!"

Our visitor had recovered something of his assurance while Holmes had been talking, and he rose from his chair now with a cold sneer upon his pale face.

"It may be so, or it may not, Mr. Holmes," said he, "but if you are so very sharp you ought to be sharp enough to know that it is you who are breaking the law now, and not me. I have done nothing actionable from the first, but as long as you keep that door locked you lay yourself open to an action for assault and illegal constraint."

"The law cannot, as you say, touch you," said Holmes, unlocking and throwing open the door, "yet there never was a man who deserved punishment more. If the young lady has a brother or a friend, he ought to lay a whip across your shoulders. By Jove!" he continued, flushing up at the sight of the bitter sneer upon the man's face, "it is not part of my duties to my client, but here's a hunting crop handy, and I think I shall just treat myself to—" He took two swift steps to the whip, but before he could grasp it there was a wild clatter of steps upon the stairs, the heavy hall door banged, and from the window we could see Mr. James Windibank running at the top of his speed down the road.

"There's a cold-blooded scoundrel!" said Holmes, laughing, as he threw himself down into his chair once more. "That fellow will rise from crime to crime until he does something very bad, and ends on a gallows. The case has, in some respects, been not entirely devoid of interest."

"I cannot now entirely see all the steps of your reasoning," I remarked.

"Well, of course it was obvious from the first that this Mr. Hosmer Angel must have some strong object for his curious conduct, and it was equally clear that the only man who really profited by the incident, as far as we could see, was the stepfather. Then the fact that the two men were never together, but that the one always appeared when the other was away, was suggestive. So were the tinted spectacles and the curious voice, which both hinted at a disguise, as did the bushy whiskers. My suspicions were all confirmed by his peculiar action in typewriting his signature, which, of course, inferred that his handwriting was so familiar to her that she would recognise even the smallest sample of it. You see all these isolated facts, together with many minor ones, all pointed in the same direction."

"And how did you verify them?"

"Having once spotted my man, it was easy to get corroboration. I knew the firm for which this man worked. Having taken the printed description. I eliminated everything from it which could be the result of a disguise—the whiskers, the glasses, the voice, and I sent it to the firm, with a request that they would inform me whether it answered to the description of any of their travellers. I had already noticed the peculiarities of the typewriter, and I wrote to the man himself at his business address asking him if he would come here. As I expected, his reply was typewritten and revealed the same trivial but characteristic defects. The same post brought me a letter from Westhouse & Marbank, of Fenchurch Street, to say that the description tallied in every respect with that of their employee, James Windibank. *Voilà tout*!"

"And Miss Sutherland?"

"If I tell her she will not believe me. You may remember the old Persian saying, 'There is danger for him who taketh the tiger cub, and danger also for whoso snatches a delusion from a woman.' There is as much sense in Hafiz as in Horace, and as much knowledge of the world."

THE BOSCOMBE VALLEY MYSTERY

We were seated at breakfast one morning, my wife and I, when the maid brought in a telegram. It was from Sherlock Holmes and ran in this way:

> Have you a couple of days to spare? Have just been wired for from the west of England in connection with Boscombe Valley tragedy. Shall be glad if you will come with me. Air and scenery perfect. Leave Paddington by the 11:15.

"What do you say, dear?" said my wife, looking across at me. "Will you go?"

"I really don't know what to say. I have a fairly long list at present."

"Oh, Anstruther would do your work for you. You have been looking a little pale lately. I think that the change would do you good, and you are always so interested in Mr. Sherlock Holmes' cases."

"I should be ungrateful if I were not, seeing what I gained through one of them," I answered. "But if I am to go, I must pack at once, for I have only half an hour."

My experience of camp life in Afghanistan had at least had the effect of making me a prompt and ready traveller. My wants were few and simple, so that in less than the time stated I was in a cab with my valise, rattling away to Paddington Station. Sherlock Holmes was pacing up and down the platform, his tall, gaunt figure made even gaunter and taller by his long grey travelling-cloak and close-fitting cloth cap.

"It is really very good of you to come, Watson," said he. "It makes a considerable difference to me, having someone with me on whom I can thoroughly rely. Local aid is always either worthless or else biassed. If you will keep the two corner seats I shall get the tickets."

We had the carriage to ourselves save for an immense litter of papers which Holmes had brought with him. Among these he rummaged and read, with intervals of note-taking and of meditation, until we were past Reading. Then he suddenly rolled them all into a gigantic ball and tossed them up onto the rack.

"Have you heard anything of the case?" he asked.

"Not a word. I have not seen a paper for some days."

"The London press has not had very full accounts. I have just been looking through all the recent papers in order to master the particulars. It seems, from what I gather, to be one of those simple cases which are so extremely difficult."

"That sounds a little paradoxical."

"But it is profoundly true. Singularity is almost invariably a clue. The more featureless and commonplace a crime is, the more difficult it is to bring it home. In this case, however, they have established a very serious case against the son of the murdered man."

"It is a murder, then?"

"Well, it is conjectured to be so. I shall take nothing for granted until I have the opportunity of looking personally into it. I will explain the state of things to you, as far as I have been able to understand it, in a very few words.

"Boscombe Valley is a country district not very far from Ross, in Herefordshire. The largest landed proprietor in that part is a Mr. John Turner, who made his money in Australia and returned some years ago to the old country. One of the farms which he held, that of Hatherley, was let to Mr. Charles McCarthy, who was also an ex-Australian. The men had known each other in the colonies, so that it was not unnatural that when they came to settle down they should do so as near each other as possible. Turner was apparently the richer man, so McCarthy became his tenant but still remained, it seems, upon terms of perfect equality, as they were frequently together. McCarthy had one son, a lad of eighteen, and Turner had an only daughter of the same age, but neither of them had wives living. They appear to have avoided the society of the neighbouring English families and to have led retired lives, though both the McCarthys were fond of sport and were frequently seen at the race-meetings of the neighbourhood. McCarthy kept two servants—a man and a girl. Turner had a considerable household, some half-dozen at the least. That is as much as I have been able to gather about the families. Now for the facts.

"On June 3rd, that is, on Monday last, McCarthy left his house at Hatherley about three in the afternoon and walked down to the Boscombe Pool, which is a small lake formed by the spreading out of the stream which runs down the Boscombe Valley. He had been out with his serving-man in the morning at Ross, and he had told the man

that he must hurry, as he had an appointment of importance to keep at three. From that appointment he never came back alive.

"From Hatherley Farm-house to the Boscombe Pool is a quarter of a mile, and two people saw him as he passed over this ground. One was an old woman, whose name is not mentioned, and the other was William Crowder, a game-keeper in the employ of Mr. Turner. Both these witnesses depose that Mr. McCarthy was walking alone. The game-keeper adds that within a few minutes of his seeing Mr. McCarthy pass he had seen his son, Mr. James McCarthy, going the same way with a gun under his arm. To the best of his belief, the father was actually in sight at the time, and the son was following him. He thought no more of the matter until he heard in the evening of the tragedy that had occurred.

"The two McCarthys were seen after the time when William Crowder, the game-keeper, lost sight of them. The Boscombe Pool is thickly wooded round, with just a fringe of grass and of reeds round the edge. A girl of fourteen, Patience Moran, who is the daughter of the lodge-keeper of the Boscombe Valley estate, was in one of the woods picking flowers. She states that while she was there she saw, at the border of the wood and close by the lake, Mr. McCarthy and his son, and that they appeared to be having a violent quarrel. She heard Mr. McCarthy the elder using very strong language to his son, and she saw the latter raise up his hand as if to strike his father. She was so frightened by their violence that she ran away and told her mother when she reached home that she had left the two McCarthys quarrelling near Boscombe Pool, and that she was afraid that they were going to fight. She had hardly said the words when young Mr. McCarthy came running up to the lodge to say that he had found his father dead in the wood, and to ask for the help of the lodge-keeper. He was much excited, without either his gun or his hat, and his right hand and sleeve were observed to be stained with fresh blood. On following him they found the dead body stretched out upon the grass beside the pool. The head had been beaten in by repeated blows of some heavy and blunt weapon. The injuries were such as might very well have been inflicted by the butt-end of his son's gun, which was found lying on the grass within a few paces of the body. Under these circumstances the young man was instantly arrested, and a verdict of 'wilful murder' having been returned at the inquest on Tuesday, he was on Wednesday brought before the magistrates at Ross, who have referred the case to the next Assizes. Those are the main facts of the case as they came out before the coroner and the police-court."

"I could hardly imagine a more damning case," I remarked. "If ever circumstantial evidence pointed to a criminal it does so here."

"Circumstantial evidence is a very tricky thing," answered Holmes thoughtfully. "It may seem to point very straight to one thing, but if you shift your own point of view a little, you may find it pointing in an equally uncompromising manner to something entirely different. It must be confessed, however, that the case looks exceedingly grave against the young man, and it is very possible that he is indeed the culprit. There are several people in the neighbourhood, however, and among them Miss Turner, the daughter of the neighbouring landowner, who believe in his innocence, and who have retained Lestrade, whom you may recollect in connection with the Study in Scarlet, to work out the case in his interest. Lestrade, being rather puzzled, has referred the case to me, and hence it is that two middle-aged gentlemen are flying westward at fifty miles an hour instead of quietly digesting their breakfasts at home."

"I am afraid," said I, "that the facts are so obvious that you will find little credit to be gained out of this case."

"There is nothing more deceptive than an obvious fact," he answered, laughing. "Besides, we may chance to hit upon some other obvious facts which may have been by no means obvious to Mr. Lestrade. You know me too well to think that I am boasting when I say that I shall either confirm or destroy his theory by means which he is quite incapable of employing, or even of understanding. To take the first example to hand, I very clearly perceive that in your bedroom the window is upon the right-hand side, and yet I question whether Mr. Lestrade would have noted even so self-evident a thing as that."

"How on earth—"

"My dear fellow, I know you well. I know the military neatness which characterises you. You shave every morning, and in this season you shave by the sunlight; but since your shaving is less and less complete as we get farther back on the left side, until it becomes positively slovenly as we get round the angle of the jaw, it is surely very clear that that side is less illuminated than the other. I could not imagine a man of your habits looking at himself in an equal light and being satisfied with

such a result. I only quote this as a trivial example of observation and inference. Therein lies my *métier*, and it is just possible that it may be of some service in the investigation which lies before us. There are one or two minor points which were brought out in the inquest, and which are worth considering."

"What are they?"

"It appears that his arrest did not take place at once, but after the return to Hatherley Farm. On the inspector of constabulary informing him that he was a prisoner, he remarked that he was not surprised to hear it, and that it was no more than his deserts. This observation of his had the natural effect of removing any traces of doubt which might have remained in the minds of the coroner's jury."

"It was a confession," I ejaculated.

"No, for it was followed by a protestation of innocence."

"Coming on the top of such a damning series of events, it was at least a most suspicious remark."

"On the contrary," said Holmes, "it is the brightest rift which I can at present see in the clouds. However innocent he might be, he could not be such an absolute imbecile as not to see that the circumstances were very black against him. Had he appeared surprised at his own arrest, or feigned indignation at it, I should have looked upon it as highly suspicious, because such surprise or anger would not be natural under the circumstances, and yet might appear to be the best policy to a scheming man. His frank acceptance of the situation marks him as either an innocent man, or else as a man of considerable self-restraint and firmness. As to his remark about his deserts, it was also not unnatural if you consider that he stood beside the dead body of his father, and that there is no doubt that he had that very day so far forgotten his filial duty as to bandy words with him, and even, according to the little girl whose evidence is so important, to raise his hand as if to strike him. The self-reproach and contrition which are displayed in his remark appear to me to be the signs of a healthy mind rather than of a guilty one."

I shook my head. "Many men have been hanged on far slighter evidence," I remarked.

"So they have. And many men have been wrongfully hanged."

"What is the young man's own account of the matter?"

"It is, I am afraid, not very encouraging to his supporters, though there are one or two points in it which are suggestive. You will find it here, and may read it for yourself."

He picked out from his bundle a copy of the local Herefordshire paper, and having turned down the sheet he pointed out the paragraph in which the unfortunate young man had given his own statement of what had occurred. I settled myself down in the corner of the carriage and read it very carefully. It ran in this way:

> "Mr. James McCarthy, the only son of the deceased, was then called and gave evidence as follows: 'I had been away from home for three days at Bristol, and had only just returned upon the morning of last Monday, the 3rd. My father was absent from home at the time of my arrival, and I was informed by the maid that he had driven over to Ross with John Cobb, the groom. Shortly after my return I heard the wheels of his trap in the yard, and, looking out of my window, I saw him get out and walk rapidly out of the yard, though I was not aware in which direction he was going. I then took my gun and strolled out in the direction of the Boscombe Pool, with the intention of visiting the rabbit warren which is upon the other side. On my way I saw William Crowder, the game-keeper, as he had stated in his evidence; but he is mistaken in thinking that I was following my father. I had no idea that he was in front of me. When about a hundred yards from the pool I heard a cry of "Cooee!" which was a usual signal between my father and myself. I then hurried forward, and found him standing by the pool. He appeared to be much surprised at seeing me and asked me rather roughly what I was doing there. A conversation ensued which led to high words and almost to blows, for my father was a man of a very violent temper. Seeing that his passion was becoming ungovernable, I left him and returned towards Hatherley Farm. I had not gone more than 150 yards, however, when I heard a hideous outcry behind me, which caused me to run back again. I found my father expiring upon the ground, with his head terribly injured. I dropped my gun and held him in my arms, but he almost instantly expired. I knelt beside him for some minutes, and then made my way to Mr. Turner's lodge-keeper, his house being the nearest, to ask for assistance. I saw no one near my father when I returned, and I have no

idea how he came by his injuries. He was not a popular man, being somewhat cold and forbidding in his manners, but he had, as far as I know, no active enemies. I know nothing further of the matter."

"The Coroner: Did your father make any statement to you before he died?

"Witness: He mumbled a few words, but I could only catch some allusion to a rat.

"The Coroner: What did you understand by that?

"Witness: It conveyed no meaning to me. I thought that he was delirious.

"The Coroner: What was the point upon which you and your father had this final quarrel?

"Witness: I should prefer not to answer.

"The Coroner: I am afraid that I must press it.

"Witness: It is really impossible for me to tell you. I can assure you that it has nothing to do with the sad tragedy which followed.

"The Coroner: That is for the court to decide. I need not point out to you that your refusal to answer will prejudice your case considerably in any future proceedings which may arise.

"Witness: I must still refuse.

"The Coroner: I understand that the cry of 'Cooee' was a common signal between you and your father?

"Witness: It was.

"The Coroner: How was it, then, that he uttered it before he saw you, and before he even knew that you had returned from Bristol?

"Witness (with considerable confusion): I do not know.

"A Juryman: Did you see nothing which aroused your suspicions when you returned on hearing the cry and found your father fatally injured?

"Witness: Nothing definite.

"The Coroner: What do you mean?

"Witness: I was so disturbed and excited as I rushed out into the open, that I could think of nothing except of my father. Yet I have a vague impression that as I ran forward something lay upon the ground to the left of me. It seemed to me to be something grey in colour, a coat of some sort, or a plaid perhaps. When I rose from my father I looked round for it, but it was gone.

" 'Do you mean that it disappeared before you went for help?'

" 'Yes, it was gone.'

" 'You cannot say what it was?'

" 'No, I had a feeling something was there.'

" 'How far from the body?'

" 'A dozen yards or so.'

" 'And how far from the edge of the wood?'

" 'About the same.'

" 'Then if it was removed it was while you were within a dozen yards of it?'

" 'Yes, but with my back towards it.'

"This concluded the examination of the witness."

"I see," said I as I glanced down the column, "that the coroner in his concluding remarks was rather severe upon young McCarthy. He calls attention, and with reason, to the discrepancy about his father having signalled to him before seeing him, also to his refusal to give details of his conversation with his father, and his singular account of his father's dying words. They are all, as he remarks, very much against the son."

Holmes laughed softly to himself and stretched himself out upon the cushioned seat. "Both you and the coroner have been at some pains," said he, "to single out the very strongest points in the young man's favour. Don't you see that you alternately give him credit for having too much imagination and too little? Too little, if he could not invent a cause of quarrel which would give him the sympathy of the jury; too much, if he evolved from his own inner consciousness anything so outré as a dying reference to a rat, and the incident of the vanishing cloth. No, sir, I shall approach this case from the point of view that what this young man says is true, and we shall see whither that hypothesis will lead us. And now here is my pocket Petrarch, and not another word shall I say of this case until we are on the scene of action. We lunch at Swindon, and I see that we shall be there in twenty minutes."

It was nearly four o'clock when we at last, after passing through the beautiful Stroud Valley, and over the broad gleaming Severn, found ourselves at the pretty little country-town of Ross. A lean, ferret-like man, furtive and sly-looking, was waiting for us upon the platform. In spite of the light brown dustcoat and leather-leggings which he wore in

deference to his rustic surroundings, I had no difficulty in recognising Lestrade, of Scotland Yard. With him we drove to the Hereford Arms where a room had already been engaged for us.

"I have ordered a carriage," said Lestrade as we sat over a cup of tea. "I knew your energetic nature, and that you would not be happy until you had been on the scene of the crime."

"It was very nice and complimentary of you," Holmes answered. "It is entirely a question of barometric pressure."

Lestrade looked startled. "I do not quite follow," he said.

"How is the glass? Twenty-nine, I see. No wind, and not a cloud in the sky. I have a caseful of cigarettes here which need smoking, and the sofa is very much superior to the usual country hotel abomination. I do not think that it is probable that I shall use the carriage tonight."

Lestrade laughed indulgently. "You have, no doubt, already formed your conclusions from the newspapers," he said. "The case is as plain as a pikestaff, and the more one goes into it the plainer it becomes. Still, of course, one can't refuse a lady, and such a very positive one, too. She has heard of you, and would have your opinion, though I repeatedly told her that there was nothing which you could do which I had not already done. Why, bless my soul! here is her carriage at the door."

He had hardly spoken before there rushed into the room one of the most lovely young women that I have ever seen in my life. Her violet eyes shining, her lips parted, a pink flush upon her cheeks, all thought of her natural reserve lost in her overpowering excitement and concern.

"Oh, Mr. Sherlock Holmes!" she cried, glancing from one to the other of us, and finally, with a woman's quick intuition, fastening upon my companion, "I am so glad that you have come. I have driven down to tell you so. I know that James didn't do it. I know it, and I want you to start upon your work knowing it, too. Never let yourself doubt upon that point. We have known each other since we were little children, and I know his faults as no one else does; but he is too tender-hearted to hurt a fly. Such a charge is absurd to anyone who really knows him."

"I hope we may clear him, Miss Turner," said Sherlock Holmes. "You may rely upon my doing all that I can."

"But you have read the evidence. You have formed some conclusion? Do you not see some loophole, some flaw? Do you not yourself think that he is innocent?"

"I think that it is very probable."

"There, now!" she cried, throwing back her head and looking defiantly at Lestrade. "You hear! He gives me hopes."

Lestrade shrugged his shoulders. "I am afraid that my colleague has been a little quick in forming his conclusions," he said.

"But he is right. Oh! I know that he is right. James never did it. And about his quarrel with his father, I am sure that the reason why he would not speak about it to the coroner was because I was concerned in it."

"In what way?" asked Holmes.

"It is no time for me to hide anything. James and his father had many disagreements about me. Mr. McCarthy was very anxious that there should be a marriage between us. James and I have always loved each other as brother and sister; but of course he is young and has seen very little of life yet, and—and—well, he naturally did not wish to do anything like that yet. So there were quarrels, and this, I am sure, was one of them."

"And your father?" asked Holmes. "Was he in favour of such a union?"

"No, he was averse to it also. No one but Mr. McCarthy was in favour of it." A quick blush passed over her fresh young face as Holmes shot one of his keen, questioning glances at her.

"Thank you for this information," said he. "May I see your father if I call tomorrow?"

"I am afraid the doctor won't allow it."

"The doctor?"

"Yes, have you not heard? Poor father has never been strong for years back, but this has broken him down completely. He has taken to his bed, and Dr. Willows says that he is a wreck and that his nervous system is shattered. Mr. McCarthy was the only man alive who had known dad in the old days in Victoria."

"Ha! In Victoria! That is important."

"Yes, at the mines."

"Quite so; at the gold-mines, where, as I understand, Mr. Turner made his money."

"Yes, certainly."

"Thank you, Miss Turner. You have been of material assistance to me."

"You will tell me if you have any news tomorrow. No doubt you will

go to the prison to see James. Oh, if you do, Mr. Holmes, do tell him that I know him to be innocent."

"I will, Miss Turner."

"I must go home now, for dad is very ill, and he misses me so if I leave him. Good-bye, and God help you in your undertaking." She hurried from the room as impulsively as she had entered, and we heard the wheels of her carriage rattle off down the street.

"I am ashamed of you, Holmes," said Lestrade with dignity after a few minutes' silence. "Why should you raise up hopes which you are bound to disappoint? I am not over-tender of heart, but I call it cruel."

"I think that I see my way to clearing James McCarthy," said Holmes. "Have you an order to see him in prison?"

"Yes, but only for you and me."

"Then I shall reconsider my resolution about going out. We have still time to take a train to Hereford and see him tonight?"

"Ample."

"Then let us do so. Watson, I fear that you will find it very slow, but I shall only be away a couple of hours."

I walked down to the station with them, and then wandered through the streets of the little town, finally returning to the hotel, where I lay upon the sofa and tried to interest myself in a yellow-backed novel. The puny plot of the story was so thin, however, when compared to the deep mystery through which we were groping, and I found my attention wander so continually from the action to the fact, that I at last flung it across the room and gave myself up entirely to a consideration of the events of the day. Supposing that this unhappy young man's story were absolutely true, then what hellish thing, what absolutely unforeseen and extraordinary calamity could have occurred between the time when he parted from his father, and the moment when, drawn back by his screams, he rushed into the glade? It was something terrible and deadly. What could it be? Might not the nature of the injuries reveal something to my medical instincts? I rang the bell and called for the weekly county paper, which contained a verbatim account of the inquest. In the surgeon's deposition it was stated that the posterior third of the left parietal bone and the left half of the occipital bone had been shattered by a heavy blow from a blunt weapon. I marked the spot upon my own head. Clearly such a blow must have been struck from behind. That was to some extent in favour of the accused, as when seen quarrelling he was face to face with his father. Still, it did not go for very much, for the older man might have turned his back before the blow fell. Still, it might be worth while to call Holmes' attention to it. Then there was the peculiar dying reference to a rat. What could that mean? It could not be delirium. A man dying from a sudden blow does not commonly become delirious. No, it was more likely to be an attempt to explain how he met his fate. But what could it indicate? I cudgelled my brains to find some possible explanation. And then the incident of the grey cloth seen by young McCarthy. If that were true the murderer must have dropped some part of his dress, presumably his overcoat, in his flight, and must have had the hardihood to return and to carry it away at the instant when the son was kneeling with his back turned not a dozen paces off. What a tissue of mysteries and improbabilities the whole thing was! I did not wonder at Lestrade's opinion, and yet I had so much faith in Sherlock Holmes' insight that I could not lose hope as long as every fresh fact seemed to strengthen his conviction of young McCarthy's innocence.

It was late before Sherlock Holmes returned. He came back alone, for Lestrade was staying in lodgings in the town.

"The glass still keeps very high," he remarked as he sat down. "It is of importance that it should not rain before we are able to go over the ground. On the other hand, a man should be at his very best and keenest for such nice work as that, and I did not wish to do it when fagged by a long journey. I have seen young McCarthy."

"And what did you learn from him?"

"Nothing."

"Could he throw no light?"

"None at all. I was inclined to think at one time that he knew who had done it and was screening him or her, but I am convinced now that he is as puzzled as everyone else. He is not a very quick-witted youth, though comely to look at and, I should think, sound at heart."

"I cannot admire his taste," I remarked, "if it is indeed a fact that he was averse to a marriage with so charming a young lady as this Miss Turner."

"Ah, thereby hangs a rather painful tale. This fellow is madly, insanely, in love with her, but some two years ago, when he was only a lad, and before he really knew her, for she had been away five years at a boarding-school, what does the idiot do but get into the clutches of a

barmaid in Bristol and marry her at a registry office? No one knows a word of the matter, but you can imagine how maddening it must be to him to be upbraided for not doing what he would give his very eyes to do, but what he knows to be absolutely impossible. It was sheer frenzy of this sort which made him throw his hands up into the air when his father, at their last interview, was goading him on to propose to Miss Turner. On the other hand, he had no means of supporting himself, and his father, who was by all accounts a very hard man, would have thrown him over utterly had he known the truth. It was with his barmaid wife that he had spent the last three days in Bristol, and his father did not know where he was. Mark that point. It is of importance. Good has come out of evil, however, for the barmaid, finding from the papers that he is in serious trouble and likely to be hanged, has thrown him over utterly and has written to him to say that she has a husband already in the Bermuda Dockyard, so that there is really no tie between them. I think that that bit of news has consoled young McCarthy for all that he has suffered."

"But if he is innocent, who has done it?"

"Ah! Who? I would call your attention very particularly to two points. One is that the murdered man had an appointment with someone at the pool, and that the someone could not have been his son, for his son was away, and he did not know when he would return. The second is that the murdered man was heard to cry 'Cooee!' before he knew that his son had returned. Those are the crucial points upon which the case depends. And now let us talk about George Meredith, if you please, and we shall leave all minor matters until tomorrow."

There was no rain, as Holmes had foretold, and the morning broke bright and cloudless. At nine o'clock Lestrade called for us with the carriage, and we set off for Hatherley Farm and the Boscombe Pool.

"There is serious news this morning," Lestrade observed. "It is said that Mr. Turner, of the Hall, is so ill that his life is despaired of."

"An elderly man, I presume?" said Holmes.

"About sixty; but his constitution has been shattered by his life abroad, and he has been in failing health for some time. This business has had a very bad effect upon him. He was an old friend of McCarthy's, and, I may add, a great benefactor to him, for I have learned that he gave him Hatherley Farm rent free."

"Indeed! That is interesting," said Holmes.

"Oh, yes! In a hundred other ways he has helped him. Everybody about here speaks of his kindness to him."

"Really! Does it not strike you as a little singular that this McCarthy, who appears to have had little of his own, and to have been under such obligations to Turner, should still talk of marrying his son to Turner's daughter, who is, presumably, heiress to the estate, and that in such a very cocksure manner, as if it were merely a case of a proposal and all else would follow? It is the more strange, since we know that Turner himself was averse to the idea. The daughter told us as much. Do you not deduce something from that?"

"We have got to the deductions and the inferences," said Lestrade, winking at me. "I find it hard enough to tackle facts, Holmes, without flying away after theories and fancies."

"You are right," said Holmes demurely; "you do find it very hard to tackle the facts."

"Anyhow, I have grasped one fact which you seem to find it difficult to get hold of," replied Lestrade with some warmth.

"And that is?

"That McCarthy senior met his death from McCarthy junior and that all theories to the contrary are the merest moonshine."

"Well, moonshine is a brighter thing than fog," said Holmes, laughing. "But I am very much mistaken if this is not Hatherley Farm upon the left."

"Yes, that is it." It was a widespread, comfortable-looking building, two-storied, slate-roofed, with great yellow blotches of lichen upon the grey walls. The drawn blinds and the smokeless chimneys, however, gave it a stricken look, as though the weight of this horror still lay heavy upon it. We called at the door, when the maid, at Holmes' request, showed us the boots which her master wore at the time of his death, and also a pair of the son's, though not the pair which he had then had. Having measured these very carefully from seven or eight different points, Holmes desired to be led to the courtyard, from which we all followed the winding track which led to Boscombe Pool.

Sherlock Holmes was transformed when he was hot upon such a scent as this. Men who had only known the quiet thinker and logician of Baker Street would have failed to recognise him. His face flushed and darkened. His brows were drawn into two hard black lines, while his eyes shone out from beneath them with a steely glitter. His face was

bent downward, his shoulders bowed, his lips compressed, and the veins stood out like whipcord in his long, sinewy neck. His nostrils seemed to dilate with a purely animal lust for the chase, and his mind was so absolutely concentrated upon the matter before him that a question or remark fell unheeded upon his ears, or, at the most, only provoked a quick, impatient snarl in reply. Swiftly and silently he made his way along the track which ran through the meadows, and so by way of the woods to the Boscombe Pool. It was damp, marshy ground, as is all that district, and there were marks of many feet, both upon the path and amid the short grass which bounded it on either side. Sometimes Holmes would hurry on, sometimes stop dead, and once he made quite a little *détour* into the meadow. Lestrade and I walked behind him, the detective indifferent and contemptuous, while I watched my friend with the interest which sprang from the conviction that every one of his actions was directed towards a definite end.

The Boscombe Pool, which is a little reed-girt sheet of water some fifty yards across, is situated at the boundary between the Hatherley Farm and the private park of the wealthy Mr. Turner. Above the woods which lined it upon the farther side we could see the red, jutting pinnacles which marked the site of the rich landowner's dwelling. On the Hatherley side of the pool the woods grew very thick, and there was a narrow belt of sodden grass twenty paces across between the edge of the trees and the reeds which lined the lake. Lestrade showed us the exact spot at which the body had been found, and, indeed, so moist was the ground, that I could plainly see the traces which had been left by the fall of the stricken man. To Holmes, as I could see by his eager face and peering eyes, very many other things were to be read upon the trampled grass. He ran round, like a dog who is picking up a scent, and then turned upon my companion.

"What did you go into the pool for?" he asked.

"I fished about with a rake. I thought there might be some weapon or other trace. But how on earth—"

"Oh, tut, tut! I have no time! That left foot of yours with its inward twist is all over the place. A mole could trace it, and there it vanishes among the reeds. Oh, how simple it would all have been had I been here before they came like a herd of buffalo and wallowed all over it. Here is where the party with the lodge-keeper came, and they have covered all tracks for six or eight feet round the body. But here are three separate tracks of the same feet." He drew out a lens and lay down upon his waterproof to have a better view, talking all the time rather to himself than to us. "These are young McCarthy's feet. Twice he was walking, and once he ran swiftly, so that the soles are deeply marked and the heels hardly visible. That bears out his story. He ran when he saw his father on the ground. Then here are the father's feet as he paced up and down. What is this, then? It is the butt-end of the gun as the son stood listening. And this? Ha, ha! What have we here? Tiptoes! tiptoes! Square, too, quite unusual boots! They come, they go, they come again—of course that was for the cloak. Now where did they come from?" He ran up and down, sometimes losing, sometimes finding the track until we were well within the edge of the wood and under the shadow of a great beech, the largest tree in the neighbourhood. Holmes traced his way to the farther side of this and lay down once more upon his face with a little cry of satisfaction. For a long time he remained there, turning over the leaves and dried sticks, gathering up what seemed to me to be dust into an envelope and examining with his lens not only the ground but even the bark of the tree as far as he could reach. A jagged stone was lying among the moss, and this also he carefully examined and retained. Then he followed a pathway through the wood until he came to the highroad, where all traces were lost.

"It has been a case of considerable interest," he remarked, returning to his natural manner. "I fancy that this grey house on the right must be the lodge. I think that I will go in and have a word with Moran, and perhaps write a little note. Having done that, we may drive back to our luncheon. You may walk to the cab, and I shall be with you presently."

It was about ten minutes before we regained our cab and drove back into Ross, Holmes still carrying with him the stone which he had picked up in the wood.

"This may interest you, Lestrade," he remarked, holding it out. "The murder was done with it."

"I see no marks."

"There are none."

"How do you know, then?"

"The grass was growing under it. It had only lain there a few days. There was no sign of a place whence it had been taken. It corresponds with the injuries. There is no sign of any other weapon."

"And the murderer?"

"Is a tall man, left-handed, limps with the right leg, wears thick-soled shooting-boots and a grey cloak, smokes Indian cigars, uses a cigar-holder, and carries a blunt penknife in his pocket. There are several other indications, but these may be enough to aid us in our search."

Lestrade laughed. "I am afraid that I am still a sceptic," he said. "Theories are all very well, but we have to deal with a hard-headed British jury."

"*Nous verrons*," answered Holmes calmly. "You work your own method, and I shall work mine. I shall be busy this afternoon, and shall probably return to London by the evening train."

"And leave your case unfinished?"

"No, finished."

"But the mystery?"

"It is solved."

"Who was the criminal, then?"

"The gentleman I describe."

"But who is he?"

"Surely it would not be difficult to find out. This is not such a populous neighbourhood."

Lestrade shrugged his shoulders. "I am a practical man," he said, "and I really cannot undertake to go about the country looking for a left-handed gentleman with a game leg. I should become the laughing-stock of Scotland Yard."

"All right," said Holmes quietly. "I have given you the chance. Here are your lodgings. Good-bye. I shall drop you a line before I leave."

Having left Lestrade at his rooms, we drove to our hotel, where we found lunch upon the table. Holmes was silent and buried in thought with a pained expression upon his face, as one who finds himself in a perplexing position.

"Look here, Watson," he said when the cloth was cleared "just sit down in this chair and let me preach to you for a little. I don't know quite what to do, and I should value your advice. Light a cigar and let me expound."

"Pray do so."

"Well, now, in considering this case there are two points about young McCarthy's narrative which struck us both instantly, although they impressed me in his favour and you against him. One was the fact that his father should, according to his account, cry 'Cooee!' before seeing him. The other was his singular dying reference to a rat. He mumbled several words, you understand, but that was all that caught the son's ear. Now from this double point our research must commence, and we will begin it by presuming that what the lad says is absolutely true."

"What of this 'Cooee!' then?"

"Well, obviously it could not have been meant for the son. The son, as far as he knew, was in Bristol. It was mere chance that he was within earshot. The 'Cooee!' was meant to attract the attention of whoever it was that he had the appointment with. But 'Cooee' is a distinctly Australian cry, and one which is used between Australians. There is a strong presumption that the person whom McCarthy expected to meet him at Boscombe Pool was someone who had been in Australia."

"What of the rat, then?"

Sherlock Holmes took a folded paper from his pocket and flattened it out on the table. "This is a map of the Colony of Victoria," he said. "I wired to Bristol for it last night." He put his hand over part of the map. "What do you read?"

"ARAT," I read.

"And now?" He raised his hand.

"BALLARAT."

"Quite so. That was the word the man uttered, and of which his son only caught the last two syllables. He was trying to utter the name of his murderer. So and so, of Ballarat."

"It is wonderful!" I exclaimed.

"It is obvious. And now, you see, I had narrowed the field down considerably. The possession of a grey garment was a third point which, granting the son's statement to be correct, was a certainty. We have come now out of mere vagueness to the definite conception of an Australian from Ballarat with a grey cloak."

"Certainly."

"And one who was at home in the district, for the pool can only be approached by the farm or by the estate, where strangers could hardly wander."

"Quite so."

"Then comes our expedition of today. By an examination of the ground I gained the trifling details which I gave to that imbecile Lestrade, as to the personality of the criminal."

"But how did you gain them?"

"You know my method. It is founded upon the observation of trifles."

"His height I know that you might roughly judge from the length of his stride. His boots, too, might be told from their traces."

"Yes, they were peculiar boots."

"But his lameness?"

"The impression of his right foot was always less distinct than his left. He put less weight upon it. Why? Because he limped—he was lame."

"But his left-handedness."

"You were yourself struck by the nature of the injury as recorded by the surgeon at the inquest. The blow was struck from immediately behind, and yet was upon the left side. Now, how can that be unless it were by a left-handed man? He had stood behind that tree during the interview between the father and son. He had even smoked there. I found the ash of a cigar, which my special knowledge of tobacco ashes enables me to pronounce as an Indian cigar. I have, as you know, devoted some attention to this, and written a little monograph on the ashes of 140 different varieties of pipe, cigar, and cigarette tobacco. Having found the ash, I then looked round and discovered the stump among the moss where he had tossed it. It was an Indian cigar, of the variety which are rolled in Rotterdam."

"And the cigar-holder?"

"I could see that the end had not been in his mouth. Therefore he used a holder. The tip had been cut off, not bitten off, but the cut was not a clean one, so I deduced a blunt pen-knife."

"Holmes," I said, "you have drawn a net round this man from which he cannot escape, and you have saved an innocent human life as truly as if you had cut the cord which was hanging him. I see the direction in which all this points. The culprit is—"

"Mr. John Turner," cried the hotel waiter, opening the door of our sitting-room, and ushering in a visitor.

The man who entered was a strange and impressive figure. His slow, limping step and bowed shoulders gave the appearance of decrepitude, and yet his hard, deep-lined, craggy features, and his enormous limbs showed that he was possessed of unusual strength of body and of character. His tangled beard, grizzled hair, and outstanding, drooping eyebrows combined to give an air of dignity and power to his appearance, but his face was of an ashen white, while his lips and the corners of his nostrils were tinged with a shade of blue. It was clear to me at a glance that he was in the grip of some deadly and chronic disease.

"Pray sit down on the sofa," said Holmes gently. "You had my note?"

"Yes, the lodge-keeper brought it up. You said that you wished to see me here to avoid scandal."

"I thought people would talk if I went to the Hall."

"And why did you wish to see me?" He looked across at my companion with despair in his weary eyes, as though his question was already answered.

"Yes," said Holmes, answering the look rather than the words. "It is so. I know all about McCarthy."

The old man sank his face in his hands. "God help me!" he cried. "But I would not have let the young man come to harm. I give you my word that I would have spoken out if it went against him at the Assizes."

"I am glad to hear you say so," said Holmes gravely.

"I would have spoken now had it not been for my dear girl. It would break her heart—it will break her heart when she hears that I am arrested."

"It may not come to that," said Holmes.

"What?"

"I am no official agent. I understand that it was your daughter who required my presence here, and I am acting in her interests. Young McCarthy must be got off, however."

"I am a dying man," said old Turner. "I have had diabetes for years. My doctor says it is a question whether I shall live a month. Yet I would rather die under my own roof than in a gaol."

Holmes rose and sat down at the table with his pen in his hand and a bundle of paper before him. "Just tell us the truth," he said. "I shall jot down the facts. You will sign it, and Watson here can witness it. Then I could produce your confession at the last extremity to save young McCarthy. I promise you that I shall not use it unless it is absolutely needed."

"It's as well," said the old man; "it's a question whether I shall live to the Assizes, so it matters little to me, but I should wish to spare Alice

the shock. And now I will make the thing clear to you; it has been a long time in the acting, but will not take me long to tell.

"You didn't know this dead man, McCarthy. He was a devil incarnate. I tell you that. God keep you out of the clutches of such a man as he. His grip has been upon me these twenty years, and he has blasted my life. I'll tell you first how I came to be in his power.

"It was in the early '60s at the diggings. I was a young chap then, hot-blooded and reckless, ready to turn my hand at anything; I got among bad companions, took to drink, had no luck with my claim, took to the bush, and in a word became what you would call over here a highway robber. There were six of us, and we had a wild, free life of it, sticking up a station from time to time, or stopping the wagons on the road to the diggings. Black Jack of Ballarat was the name I went under, and our party is still remembered in the colony as the Ballarat Gang.

"One day a gold convoy came down from Ballarat to Melbourne, and we lay in wait for it and attacked it. There were six troopers and six of us, so it was a close thing, but we emptied four of their saddles at the first volley. Three of our boys were killed, however, before we got the swag. I put my pistol to the head of the wagon-driver, who was this very man McCarthy. I wish to the Lord that I had shot him then, but I spared him, though I saw his wicked little eyes fixed on my face, as though to remember every feature. We got away with the gold, became wealthy men, and made our way over to England without being suspected. There I parted from my old pals and determined to settle down to a quiet and respectable life. I bought this estate, which chanced to be in the market, and I set myself to do a little good with my money, to make up for the way in which I had earned it. I married, too, and though my wife died young she left me my dear little Alice. Even when she was just a baby her wee hand seemed to lead me down the right path as nothing else had ever done. In a word, I turned over a new leaf and did my best to make up for the past. All was going well when McCarthy laid his grip upon me.

"I had gone up to town about an investment, and I met him in Regent Street with hardly a coat to his back or a boot to his foot.

"'Here we are, Jack,' says he, touching me on the arm; 'we'll be as good as a family to you. There's two of us, me and my son, and you can have the keeping of us. If you don't—it's a fine, law-abiding country is England, and there's always a policeman within hail.'

"Well, down they came to the west country, there was no shaking them off, and there they have lived rent free on my best land ever since. There was no rest for me, no peace, no forgetfulness; turn where I would, there was his cunning, grinning face at my elbow. It grew worse as Alice grew up, for he soon saw I was more afraid of her knowing my past than of the police. Whatever he wanted he must have, and whatever it was I gave him without question, land, money, houses, until at last he asked a thing which I could not give. He asked for Alice.

"His son, you see, had grown up, and so had my girl, and as I was known to be in weak health, it seemed a fine stroke to him that his lad should step into the whole property. But there I was firm. I would not have his cursed stock mixed with mine; not that I had any dislike to the lad, but his blood was in him, and that was enough. I stood firm. McCarthy threatened. I braved him to do his worst. We were to meet at the pool midway between our houses to talk it over.

"When I went down there I found him talking with his son, so I smoked a cigar and waited behind a tree until he should be alone. But as I listened to his talk all that was black and bitter in me seemed to come uppermost. He was urging his son to marry my daughter with as little regard for what she might think as if she were a slut from off the streets. It drove me mad to think that I and all that I held most dear should be in the power of such a man as this. Could I not snap the bond? I was already a dying and a desperate man. Though clear of mind and fairly strong of limb, I knew that my own fate was sealed. But my memory and my girl! Both could be saved if I could but silence that foul tongue. I did it, Mr. Holmes. I would do it again. Deeply as I have sinned, I have led a life of martyrdom to atone for it. But that my girl should be entangled in the same meshes which held me was more than I could suffer. I struck him down with no more compunction than if he had been some foul and venomous beast. His cry brought back his son; but I had gained the cover of the wood, though I was forced to go back to fetch the cloak which I had dropped in my flight. That is the true story, gentlemen, of all that occurred."

"Well, it is not for me to judge you," said Holmes as the old man signed the statement which had been drawn out. "I pray that we may never be exposed to such a temptation."

"I pray not, sir. And what do you intend to do?"

"In view of your health, nothing. You are yourself aware that

you will soon have to answer for your deed at a higher court than the Assizes. I will keep your confession, and if McCarthy is condemned I shall be forced to use it. If not, it shall never be seen by mortal eye; and your secret, whether you be alive or dead, shall be safe with us."

"Farewell, then," said the old man solemnly. "Your own deathbeds, when they come, will be the easier for the thought of the peace which you have given to mine." Tottering and shaking in all his giant frame, he stumbled slowly from the room.

"God help us!" said Holmes after a long silence. "Why does fate play such tricks with poor, helpless worms? I never hear of such a case as this that I do not think of Baxter's words, and say, 'There, but for the grace of God, goes Sherlock Holmes.' "

James McCarthy was acquitted at the Assizes on the strength of a number of objections which had been drawn out by Holmes and submitted to the defending counsel. Old Turner lived for seven months after our interview, but he is now dead; and there is every prospect that the son and daughter may come to live happily together in ignorance of the black cloud which rests upon their past.

THE FIVE ORANGE PIPS

When I glance over my notes and records of the Sherlock Holmes cases between the years '82 and '90, I am faced by so many which present strange and interesting features that it is no easy matter to know which to choose and which to leave. Some, however, have already gained publicity through the papers, and others have not offered a field for those peculiar qualities which my friend possessed in so high a degree, and which it is the object of these papers to illustrate. Some, too, have baffled his analytical skill, and would be, as narratives, beginnings without an ending, while others have been but partially cleared up, and have their explanations founded rather upon conjecture and surmise than on that absolute logical proof which was so dear to him. There is, however, one of these last which was so remarkable in its details and so startling in its results that I am tempted to give some account of it in spite of the fact that there are points in connection with it which never have been, and probably never will be, entirely cleared up.

The year '87 furnished us with a long series of cases of greater or less interest, of which I retain the records. Among my headings under this one twelve months, I find an account of the adventure of the Paradol Chamber, of the Amateur Mendicant Society, who held a luxurious club in the lower vault of a furniture warehouse, of the facts connected with the loss of the British barque *Sophy Anderson*, of the singular adventures of the Grice Patersons in the island of Uffa, and finally of the Camberwell poisoning case. In the latter, as may be remembered, Sherlock Holmes was able, by winding up the dead man's watch, to prove that it had been wound up two hours before, and that therefore the deceased had gone to bed within that time—a deduction which was of the greatest importance in clearing up the case. All these I may sketch out at some future date, but none of them present such singular features as the strange train of circumstances which I have now taken up my pen to describe.

It was in the latter days of September, and the equinoctial gales had set in with exceptional violence. All day the wind had screamed and the rain had beaten against the windows, so that even here in the heart

of great, hand-made London we were forced to raise our minds for the instant from the routine of life and to recognise the presence of those great elemental forces which shriek at mankind through the bars of his civilisation, like untamed beasts in a cage. As evening drew in, the storm grew higher and louder, and the wind cried and sobbed like a child in the chimney. Sherlock Holmes sat moodily at one side of the fireplace cross-indexing his records of crime, while I at the other was deep in one of Clark Russell's fine sea-stories until the howl of the gale from without seemed to blend with the text, and the splash of the rain to lengthen out into the long swash of the sea waves. My wife was on a visit to her mother's, and for a few days I was a dweller once more in my old quarters at Baker Street.

"Why," said I, glancing up at my companion, "that was surely the bell. Who could come tonight? Some friend of yours, perhaps?"

"Except yourself I have none," he answered. "I do not encourage visitors."

"A client, then?"

"If so, it is a serious case. Nothing less would bring a man out on such a day and at such an hour. But I take it that it is more likely to be some crony of the landlady's."

Sherlock Holmes was wrong in his conjecture, however, for there came a step in the passage and a tapping at the door. He stretched out his long arm to turn the lamp away from himself and towards the vacant chair upon which a newcomer must sit.

"Come in!" said he.

The man who entered was young, some two-and-twenty at the outside, well-groomed and trimly clad, with something of refinement and delicacy in his bearing. The streaming umbrella which he held in his hand, and his long shining waterproof told of the fierce weather through which he had come. He looked about him anxiously in the glare of the lamp, and I could see that his face was pale and his eyes heavy, like those of a man who is weighed down with some great anxiety.

"I owe you an apology," he said, raising his golden *pince-nez* to his eyes. "I trust that I am not intruding. I fear that I have brought some traces of the storm and rain into your snug chamber."

"Give me your coat and umbrella," said Holmes. "They may rest here on the hook and will be dry presently. You have come up from the south-west, I see."

"Yes, from Horsham."

"That clay and chalk mixture which I see upon your toe caps is quite distinctive."

"I have come for advice."

"That is easily got."

"And help."

"That is not always so easy."

"I have heard of you, Mr. Holmes. I heard from Major Prendergast how you saved him in the Tankerville Club scandal."

"Ah, of course. He was wrongfully accused of cheating at cards."

"He said that you could solve anything."

"He said too much."

"That you are never beaten."

"I have been beaten four times—three times by men, and once by a woman."

"But what is that compared with the number of your successes?"

"It is true that I have been generally successful."

"Then you may be so with me."

"I beg that you will draw your chair up to the fire and favour me with some details as to your case."

"It is no ordinary one."

"None of those which come to me are. I am the last court of appeal."

"And yet I question, sir, whether, in all your experience, you have ever listened to a more mysterious and inexplicable chain of events than those which have happened in my own family."

"You fill me with interest," said Holmes. "Pray give us the essential facts from the commencement, and I can afterwards question you as to those details which seem to me to be most important."

The young man pulled his chair up and pushed his wet feet out towards the blaze.

"My name," said he, "is John Openshaw, but my own affairs have, as far as I can understand, little to do with this awful business. It is a hereditary matter; so in order to give you an idea of the facts, I must go back to the commencement of the affair.

"You must know that my grandfather had two sons—my uncle Elias and my father Joseph. My father had a small factory at Coventry, which he enlarged at the time of the invention of bicycling. He was a patentee of the Openshaw unbreakable tire, and his business met with

such success that he was able to sell it and to retire upon a handsome competence.

"My uncle Elias emigrated to America when he was a young man and became a planter in Florida, where he was reported to have done very well. At the time of the war he fought in Jackson's army, and afterwards under Hood, where he rose to be a colonel. When Lee laid down his arms my uncle returned to his plantation, where he remained for three or four years. About 1869 or 1870 he came back to Europe and took a small estate in Sussex, near Horsham. He had made a very considerable fortune in the States, and his reason for leaving them was his aversion to the negroes, and his dislike of the Republican policy in extending the franchise to them. He was a singular man, fierce and quick-tempered, very foul-mouthed when he was angry, and of a most retiring disposition. During all the years that he lived at Horsham, I doubt if ever he set foot in the town. He had a garden and two or three fields round his house, and there he would take his exercise, though very often for weeks on end he would never leave his room. He drank a great deal of brandy and smoked very heavily, but he would see no society and did not want any friends, not even his own brother.

"He didn't mind me; in fact, he took a fancy to me, for at the time when he saw me first I was a youngster of twelve or so. This would be in the year 1878, after he had been eight or nine years in England. He begged my father to let me live with him and he was very kind to me in his way. When he was sober he used to be fond of playing backgammon and draughts with me, and he would make me his representative both with the servants and with the tradespeople, so that by the time that I was sixteen I was quite master of the house. I kept all the keys and could go where I liked and do what I liked, so long as I did not disturb him in his privacy. There was one singular exception, however, for he had a single room, a lumber-room up among the attics, which was invariably locked, and which he would never permit either me or anyone else to enter. With a boy's curiosity I have peeped through the keyhole, but I was never able to see more than such a collection of old trunks and bundles as would be expected in such a room.

"One day—it was in March, 1883—a letter with a foreign stamp lay upon the table in front of the colonel's plate. It was not a common thing for him to receive letters, for his bills were all paid in ready money, and he had no friends of any sort. 'From India!' said he as he took it up,

'Pondicherry postmark! What can this be?' Opening it hurriedly, out there jumped five little dried orange pips, which pattered down upon his plate. I began to laugh at this, but the laugh was struck from my lips at the sight of his face. His lip had fallen, his eyes were protruding, his skin the colour of putty, and he glared at the envelope which he still held in his trembling hand, 'K. K. K.!' he shrieked, and then, 'My God, my God, my sins have overtaken me!'

" 'What is it, uncle?' I cried.

" 'Death,' said he, and rising from the table he retired to his room, leaving me palpitating with horror. I took up the envelope and saw scrawled in red ink upon the inner flap, just above the gum, the letter K three times repeated. There was nothing else save the five dried pips. What could be the reason of his overpowering terror? I left the breakfast-table, and as I ascended the stair I met him coming down with an old rusty key, which must have belonged to the attic, in one hand, and a small brass box, like a cashbox, in the other.

" 'They may do what they like, but I'll checkmate them still,' said he with an oath. 'Tell Mary that I shall want a fire in my room today, and send down to Fordham, the Horsham lawyer.'

"I did as he ordered, and when the lawyer arrived I was asked to step up to the room. The fire was burning brightly, and in the grate there was a mass of black, fluffy ashes, as of burned paper, while the brass box stood open and empty beside it. As I glanced at the box I noticed, with a start, that upon the lid was printed the treble K which I had read in the morning upon the envelope.

" 'I wish you, John,' said my uncle, 'to witness my will. I leave my estate, with all its advantages and all its disadvantages, to my brother, your father, whence it will, no doubt, descend to you. If you can enjoy it in peace, well and good! If you find you cannot, take my advice, my boy, and leave it to your deadliest enemy. I am sorry to give you such a two-edged thing, but I can't say what turn things are going to take. Kindly sign the paper where Mr. Fordham shows you.'

"I signed the paper as directed, and the lawyer took it away with him. The singular incident made, as you may think, the deepest impression upon me, and I pondered over it and turned it every way in my mind without being able to make anything of it. Yet I could not shake off the vague feeling of dread which it left behind, though the sensation grew less keen as the weeks passed and nothing happened to disturb the usual routine of our lives. I could see a change in my uncle, however. He drank more than ever, and he was less inclined for any sort of society. Most of his time he would spend in his room, with the door locked upon the inside, but sometimes he would emerge in a sort of drunken frenzy and would burst out of the house and tear about the garden with a revolver in his hand, screaming out that he was afraid of no man, and that he was not to be cooped up, like a sheep in a pen, by man or devil. When these hot fits were over, however, he would rush tumultuously in at the door and lock and bar it behind him, like a man who can brazen it out no longer against the terror which lies at the roots of his soul. At such times I have seen his face, even on a cold day, glisten with moisture, as though it were new raised from a basin.

"Well, to come to an end of the matter, Mr. Holmes, and not to abuse your patience, there came a night when he made one of those drunken sallies from which he never came back. We found him, when we went to search for him, face downward in a little green-scummed pool, which lay at the foot of the garden. There was no sign of any violence, and the water was but two feet deep, so that the jury, having regard to his known eccentricity, brought in a verdict of 'suicide.' But I, who knew how he winced from the very thought of death, had much ado to persuade myself that he had gone out of his way to meet it. The matter passed, however, and my father entered into possession of the estate, and of some 14,000 pounds, which lay to his credit at the bank."

"One moment," Holmes interposed, "your statement is, I foresee, one of the most remarkable to which I have ever listened. Let me have the date of the reception by your uncle of the letter, and the date of his supposed suicide."

"The letter arrived on March 10, 1883. His death was seven weeks later, upon the night of May 2nd."

"Thank you. Pray proceed."

"When my father took over the Horsham property, he, at my request, made a careful examination of the attic, which had been always locked up. We found the brass box there, although its contents had been destroyed. On the inside of the cover was a paper label, with the initials of K. K. K. repeated upon it, and 'Letters, memoranda, receipts, and a register' written beneath. These, we presume, indicated the nature of the papers which had been destroyed by Colonel Openshaw. For the rest, there was nothing of much importance in the attic save a great many scattered papers and notebooks bearing upon my uncle's life in America. Some of them were of the war time and showed that he had done his duty well and had borne the repute of a brave soldier. Others were of a date during the reconstruction of the Southern states, and were mostly concerned with politics, for he had evidently taken a strong part in opposing the carpet-bag politicians who had been sent down from the North.

"Well, it was the beginning of '84 when my father came to live at Horsham, and all went as well as possible with us until the January of '85. On the fourth day after the new year I heard my father give a sharp cry of surprise as we sat together at the breakfast-table. There he was, sitting with a newly opened envelope in one hand and five dried orange pips in the outstretched palm of the other one. He had always laughed at what he called my cock-and-bull story about the colonel, but he looked very scared and puzzled now that the same thing had come upon himself.

" 'Why, what on earth does this mean, John?' he stammered.

"My heart had turned to lead. 'It is K. K. K.,' said I.

"He looked inside the envelope. 'So it is,' he cried. 'Here are the very letters. But what is this written above them?'

" 'Put the papers on the sundial,' I read, peeping over his shoulder.

" 'What papers? What sundial?' he asked.

" 'The sundial in the garden. There is no other,' said I; 'but the papers must be those that are destroyed.'

" 'Pooh!' said he, gripping hard at his courage. 'We are in a civilised land here, and we can't have tomfoolery of this kind. Where does the thing come from?'

" 'From Dundee,' I answered, glancing at the postmark.

" 'Some preposterous practical joke,' said he. 'What have I to do with sundials and papers? I shall take no notice of such nonsense.'

" 'I should certainly speak to the police,' I said.

" 'And be laughed at for my pains. Nothing of the sort.'

" 'Then let me do so?'

" 'No, I forbid you. I won't have a fuss made about such nonsense.'

"It was in vain to argue with him, for he was a very obstinate man. I went about, however, with a heart which was full of forebodings.

"On the third day after the coming of the letter my father went from home to visit an old friend of his, Major Freebody, who is in command

of one of the forts upon Portsdown Hill. I was glad that he should go, for it seemed to me that he was farther from danger when he was away from home. In that, however, I was in error. Upon the second day of his absence I received a telegram from the major, imploring me to come at once. My father had fallen over one of the deep chalk-pits which abound in the neighbourhood, and was lying senseless, with a shattered skull. I hurried to him, but he passed away without having ever recovered his consciousness. He had, as it appears, been returning from Fareham in the twilight, and as the country was unknown to him, and the chalk-pit unfenced, the jury had no hesitation in bringing in a verdict of 'death from accidental causes.' Carefully as I examined every fact connected with his death, I was unable to find anything which could suggest the idea of murder. There were no signs of violence, no footmarks, no robbery, no record of strangers having been seen upon the roads. And yet I need not tell you that my mind was far from at ease, and that I was well-nigh certain that some foul plot had been woven round him.

"In this sinister way I came into my inheritance. You will ask me why I did not dispose of it? I answer, because I was well convinced that our troubles were in some way dependent upon an incident in my uncle's life, and that the danger would be as pressing in one house as in another.

"It was in January, '85, that my poor father met his end, and two years and eight months have elapsed since then. During that time I have lived happily at Horsham, and I had begun to hope that this curse had passed away from the family, and that it had ended with the last generation. I had begun to take comfort too soon, however; yesterday morning the blow fell in the very shape in which it had come upon my father."

The young man took from his waistcoat a crumpled envelope, and turning to the table he shook out upon it five little dried orange pips.

"This is the envelope," he continued. "The postmark is London—eastern division. Within are the very words which were upon my father's last message: 'K. K. K.'; and then 'Put the papers on the sundial.'"

"What have you done?" asked Holmes.

"Nothing."

"Nothing?"

"To tell the truth"—he sank his face into his thin, white hands—"I have felt helpless. I have felt like one of those poor rabbits when the snake is writhing towards it. I seem to be in the grasp of some resistless, inexorable evil, which no foresight and no precautions can guard against."

"Tut! tut!" cried Sherlock Holmes. "You must act, man, or you are lost. Nothing but energy can save you. This is no time for despair."

"I have seen the police."

"Ah!"

"But they listened to my story with a smile. I am convinced that the inspector has formed the opinion that the letters are all practical jokes, and that the deaths of my relations were really accidents, as the jury stated, and were not to be connected with the warnings."

Holmes shook his clenched hands in the air. "Incredible imbecility!" he cried.

"They have, however, allowed me a policeman, who may remain in the house with me."

"Has he come with you tonight?"

"No. His orders were to stay in the house."

Again Holmes raved in the air.

"Why did you come to me," he cried, "and, above all, why did you not come at once?"

"I did not know. It was only today that I spoke to Major Prendergast about my troubles and was advised by him to come to you."

"It is really two days since you had the letter. We should have acted before this. You have no further evidence, I suppose, than that which you have placed before us—no suggestive detail which might help us?"

"There is one thing," said John Openshaw. He rummaged in his coat pocket, and, drawing out a piece of discoloured, blue-tinted paper, he laid it out upon the table. "I have some remembrance," said he, "that on the day when my uncle burned the papers I observed that the small, unburned margins which lay amid the ashes were of this particular colour. I found this single sheet upon the floor of his room, and I am inclined to think that it may be one of the papers which has, perhaps, fluttered out from among the others, and in that way has escaped destruction. Beyond the mention of pips, I do not see that it helps us much. I think myself that it is a page from some private diary. The writing is undoubtedly my uncle's."

Holmes moved the lamp, and we both bent over the sheet of paper,

which showed by its ragged edge that it had indeed been torn from a book. It was headed, "March, 1869," and beneath were the following enigmatical notices:

"4th. Hudson came. Same old platform.

"7th. Set the pips on McCauley, Paramore, and John Swain, of St. Augustine.

"9th. McCauley cleared.

"10th. John Swain cleared.

"12th. Visited Paramore. All well."

"Thank you!" said Holmes, folding up the paper and returning it to our visitor. "And now you must on no account lose another instant. We cannot spare time even to discuss what you have told me. You must get home instantly and act."

"What shall I do?"

"There is but one thing to do. It must be done at once. You must put this piece of paper which you have shown us into the brass box which you have described. You must also put in a note to say that all the other papers were burned by your uncle, and that this is the only one which remains. You must assert that in such words as will carry conviction with them. Having done this, you must at once put the box out upon the sundial, as directed. Do you understand?"

"Entirely."

"Do not think of revenge, or anything of the sort, at present. I think that we may gain that by means of the law; but we have our web to weave, while theirs is already woven. The first consideration is to remove the pressing danger which threatens you. The second is to clear up the mystery and to punish the guilty parties."

"I thank you," said the young man, rising and pulling on his overcoat. "You have given me fresh life and hope. I shall certainly do as you advise."

"Do not lose an instant. And, above all, take care of yourself in the meanwhile, for I do not think that there can be a doubt that you are threatened by a very real and imminent danger. How do you go back?"

"By train from Waterloo."

"It is not yet nine. The streets will be crowded, so I trust that you may be in safety. And yet you cannot guard yourself too closely."

"I am armed."

"That is well. Tomorrow I shall set to work upon your case."

"I shall see you at Horsham, then?"

"No, your secret lies in London. It is there that I shall seek it."

"Then I shall call upon you in a day, or in two days, with news as to the box and the papers. I shall take your advice in every particular." He shook hands with us and took his leave. Outside the wind still screamed and the rain splashed and pattered against the windows. This strange, wild story seemed to have come to us from amid the mad elements—blown in upon us like a sheet of sea-weed in a gale—and now to have been reabsorbed by them once more.

Sherlock Holmes sat for some time in silence, with his head sunk forward and his eyes bent upon the red glow of the fire. Then he lit his pipe, and leaning back in his chair he watched the blue smoke-rings as they chased each other up to the ceiling.

"I think, Watson," he remarked at last, "that of all our cases we have had none more fantastic than this."

"Save, perhaps, the Sign of Four."

"Well, yes. Save, perhaps, that. And yet this John Openshaw seems to me to be walking amid even greater perils than did the Sholtos."

"But have you," I asked, "formed any definite conception as to what these perils are?"

"There can be no question as to their nature," he answered.

"Then what are they? Who is this K. K. K., and why does he pursue this unhappy family?"

Sherlock Holmes closed his eyes and placed his elbows upon the arms of his chair, with his finger-tips together. "The ideal reasoner," he remarked, "would, when he had once been shown a single fact in all its bearings, deduce from it not only all the chain of events which led up to it but also all the results which would follow from it. As Cuvier could correctly describe a whole animal by the contemplation of a single bone, so the observer who has thoroughly understood one link in a series of incidents should be able to accurately state all the other ones, both before and after. We have not yet grasped the results which the reason alone can attain to. Problems may be solved in the study which have baffled all those who have sought a solution by the aid of their senses. To carry the art, however, to its highest pitch, it is necessary that the reasoner should be able to utilise all the facts which have come to his knowledge; and this in itself implies, as you will readily see, a possession of all knowledge, which, even in these days of free education

and encyclopaedias, is a somewhat rare accomplishment. It is not so impossible, however, that a man should possess all knowledge which is likely to be useful to him in his work, and this I have endeavoured in my case to do. If I remember rightly, you on one occasion, in the early days of our friendship, defined my limits in a very precise fashion."

"Yes," I answered, laughing. "It was a singular document. Philosophy, astronomy, and politics were marked at zero, I remember. Botany variable, geology profound as regards the mud-stains from any region within fifty miles of town, chemistry eccentric, anatomy unsystematic, sensational literature and crime records unique, violin-player, boxer, swordsman, lawyer, and self-poisoner by cocaine and tobacco. Those, I think, were the main points of my analysis."

Holmes grinned at the last item. "Well," he said, "I say now, as I said then, that a man should keep his little brain-attic stocked with all the furniture that he is likely to use, and the rest he can put away in the lumber-room of his library, where he can get it if he wants it. Now, for such a case as the one which has been submitted to us tonight, we need certainly to muster all our resources. Kindly hand me down the letter K of the 'American Encyclopaedia' which stands upon the shelf beside you. Thank you. Now let us consider the situation and see what may be deduced from it. In the first place, we may start with a strong presumption that Colonel Openshaw had some very strong reason for leaving America. Men at his time of life do not change all their habits and exchange willingly the charming climate of Florida for the lonely life of an English provincial town. His extreme love of solitude in England suggests the idea that he was in fear of someone or something, so we may assume as a working hypothesis that it was fear of someone or something which drove him from America. As to what it was he feared, we can only deduce that by considering the formidable letters which were received by himself and his successors. Did you remark the postmarks of those letters?"

"The first was from Pondicherry, the second from Dundee, and the third from London."

"From East London. What do you deduce from that?"

"They are all seaports. That the writer was on board of a ship."

"Excellent. We have already a clue. There can be no doubt that the probability—the strong probability—is that the writer was on board of a ship. And now let us consider another point. In the case of

Pondicherry, seven weeks elapsed between the threat and its fulfilment, in Dundee it was only some three or four days. Does that suggest anything?"

"A greater distance to travel."

"But the letter had also a greater distance to come."

"Then I do not see the point."

"There is at least a presumption that the vessel in which the man or men are is a sailing-ship. It looks as if they always send their singular warning or token before them when starting upon their mission. You see how quickly the deed followed the sign when it came from Dundee. If they had come from Pondicherry in a steamer they would have arrived almost as soon as their letter. But, as a matter of fact, seven weeks elapsed. I think that those seven weeks represented the difference between the mail-boat which brought the letter and the sailing vessel which brought the writer."

"It is possible."

"More than that. It is probable. And now you see the deadly urgency of this new case, and why I urged young Openshaw to caution. The blow has always fallen at the end of the time which it would take the senders to travel the distance. But this one comes from London, and therefore we cannot count upon delay."

"Good God!" I cried. "What can it mean, this relentless persecution?"

"The papers which Openshaw carried are obviously of vital importance to the person or persons in the sailing-ship. I think that it is quite clear that there must be more than one of them. A single man could not have carried out two deaths in such a way as to deceive a coroner's jury. There must have been several in it, and they must have been men of resource and determination. Their papers they mean to have, be the holder of them who it may. In this way you see K. K. K. ceases to be the initials of an individual and becomes the badge of a society."

"But of what society?"

"Have you never—" said Sherlock Holmes, bending forward and sinking his voice—"have you never heard of the Ku Klux Klan?"

"I never have."

Holmes turned over the leaves of the book upon his knee. "Here it is," said he presently:

"'Ku Klux Klan. A name derived from the fanciful resemblance to

the sound produced by cocking a rifle. This terrible secret society was formed by some ex-Confederate soldiers in the Southern states after the Civil War, and it rapidly formed local branches in different parts of the country, notably in Tennessee, Louisiana, the Carolinas, Georgia, and Florida. Its power was used for political purposes, principally for the terrorising of the negro voters and the murdering and driving from the country of those who were opposed to its views. Its outrages were usually preceded by a warning sent to the marked man in some fantastic but generally recognised shape—a sprig of oak-leaves in some parts, melon seeds or orange pips in others. On receiving this the victim might either openly abjure his former ways, or might fly from the country. If he braved the matter out, death would unfailingly come upon him, and usually in some strange and unforeseen manner. So perfect was the organisation of the society, and so systematic its methods, that there is hardly a case upon record where any man succeeded in braving it with impunity, or in which any of its outrages were traced home to the perpetrators. For some years the organisation flourished in spite of the efforts of the United States government and of the better classes of the community in the South. Eventually, in the year 1869, the movement rather suddenly collapsed, although there have been sporadic outbreaks of the same sort since that date.'

"You will observe," said Holmes, laying down the volume, "that the sudden breaking up of the society was coincident with the disappearance of Openshaw from America with their papers. It may well have been cause and effect. It is no wonder that he and his family have some of the more implacable spirits upon their track. You can understand that this register and diary may implicate some of the first men in the South, and that there may be many who will not sleep easy at night until it is recovered."

"Then the page we have seen—"

"Is such as we might expect. It ran, if I remember right, 'sent the pips to A, B, and C'—that is, sent the society's warning to them. Then there are successive entries that A and B cleared, or left the country, and finally that C was visited, with, I fear, a sinister result for C. Well, I think, Doctor, that we may let some light into this dark place, and I believe that the only chance young Openshaw has in the meantime is to do what I have told him. There is nothing more to be said or to be done tonight, so hand me over my violin and let us try to forget for half an hour the miserable weather and the still more miserable ways of our fellow-men."

It had cleared in the morning, and the sun was shining with a subdued brightness through the dim veil which hangs over the great city. Sherlock Holmes was already at breakfast when I came down.

"You will excuse me for not waiting for you," said he; "I have, I foresee, a very busy day before me in looking into this case of young Openshaw's."

"What steps will you take?" I asked.

"It will very much depend upon the results of my first inquiries. I may have to go down to Horsham, after all."

"You will not go there first?"

"No, I shall commence with the City. Just ring the bell and the maid will bring up your coffee."

As I waited, I lifted the unopened newspaper from the table and glanced my eye over it. It rested upon a heading which sent a chill to my heart.

"Holmes," I cried, "you are too late."

"Ah!" said he, laying down his cup, "I feared as much. How was it done?" He spoke calmly, but I could see that he was deeply moved.

"My eye caught the name of Openshaw, and the heading 'Tragedy Near Waterloo Bridge.' Here is the account:

"Between nine and ten last night Police-Constable Cook, of the H Division, on duty near Waterloo Bridge, heard a cry for help and a splash in the water. The night, however, was extremely dark and stormy, so that, in spite of the help of several passers-by, it was quite impossible to effect a rescue. The alarm, however, was given, and, by the aid of the water-police, the body was eventually recovered. It proved to be that of a young gentleman whose name, as it appears from an envelope which was found in his pocket, was John Openshaw, and whose residence is near Horsham. It is conjectured that he may have been hurrying down to catch the last train from Waterloo Station, and that in his haste and the extreme darkness he missed his path and walked over the edge of one of the small landing-places for river steamboats. The body exhibited no traces of violence, and there can be no doubt that the deceased had been the victim of an unfortunate accident, which should have the effect of calling the attention of the authorities to the condition of the riverside landing-stages."

We sat in silence for some minutes, Holmes more depressed and shaken than I had ever seen him.

"That hurts my pride, Watson," he said at last. "It is a petty feeling, no doubt, but it hurts my pride. It becomes a personal matter with me now, and, if God sends me health, I shall set my hand upon this gang. That he should come to me for help, and that I should send him away to his death—!" He sprang from his chair and paced about the room in uncontrollable agitation, with a flush upon his sallow cheeks and a nervous clasping and unclasping of his long thin hands.

"They must be cunning devils," he exclaimed at last. "How could they have decoyed him down there? The Embankment is not on the direct line to the station. The bridge, no doubt, was too crowded, even on such a night, for their purpose. Well, Watson, we shall see who will win in the long run. I am going out now!"

"To the police?"

"No; I shall be my own police. When I have spun the web they may take the flies, but not before."

All day I was engaged in my professional work, and it was late in the evening before I returned to Baker Street. Sherlock Holmes had not come back yet. It was nearly ten o'clock before he entered, looking pale and worn. He walked up to the sideboard, and tearing a piece from the loaf he devoured it voraciously, washing it down with a long draught of water.

"You are hungry," I remarked.

"Starving. It had escaped my memory. I have had nothing since breakfast."

"Nothing?"

"Not a bite. I had no time to think of it."

"And how have you succeeded?"

"Well."

"You have a clue?"

"I have them in the hollow of my hand. Young Openshaw shall not long remain unavenged. Why, Watson, let us put their own devilish trademark upon them. It is well thought of!"

"What do you mean?"

He took an orange from the cupboard, and tearing it to pieces he squeezed out the pips upon the table. Of these he took five and thrust them into an envelope. On the inside of the flap he wrote "S. H. for

J. O." Then he sealed it and addressed it to "Captain James Calhoun, Barque *Lone Star*, Savannah, Georgia."

"That will await him when he enters port," said he, chuckling. "It may give him a sleepless night. He will find it as sure a precursor of his fate as Openshaw did before him."

"And who is this Captain Calhoun?"

"The leader of the gang. I shall have the others, but he first."

"How did you trace it, then?"

He took a large sheet of paper from his pocket, all covered with dates and names.

"I have spent the whole day," said he, "over Lloyd's registers and files of the old papers, following the future career of every vessel which touched at Pondicherry in January and February in '83. There were thirty-six ships of fair tonnage which were reported there during those months. Of these, one, the *Lone Star*, instantly attracted my attention, since, although it was reported as having cleared from London, the name is that which is given to one of the states of the Union."

"Texas, I think."

"I was not and am not sure which; but I knew that the ship must have an American origin."

"What then?"

"I searched the Dundee records, and when I found that the barque *Lone Star* was there in January, '85, my suspicion became a certainty. I then inquired as to the vessels which lay at present in the port of London."

"Yes?"

"The *Lone Star* had arrived here last week. I went down to the Albert Dock and found that she had been taken down the river by the early tide this morning, homeward bound to Savannah. I wired to Gravesend and learned that she had passed some time ago, and as the wind is easterly I have no doubt that she is now past the Goodwins and not very far from the Isle of Wight."

"What will you do, then?"

"Oh, I have my hand upon him. He and the two mates, are as I learn, the only native-born Americans in the ship. The others are Finns and Germans. I know, also, that they were all three away from the ship last night. I had it from the stevedore who has been loading their cargo. By the time that their sailing-ship reaches Savannah the mail-boat will

have carried this letter, and the cable will have informed the police of Savannah that these three gentlemen are badly wanted here upon a charge of murder."

There is ever a flaw, however, in the best laid of human plans, and the murderers of John Openshaw were never to receive the orange pips which would show them that another, as cunning and as resolute as themselves, was upon their track. Very long and very severe were the equinoctial gales that year. We waited long for news of the *Lone Star* of Savannah, but none ever reached us. We did at last hear that somewhere far out in the Atlantic a shattered stern-post of a boat was seen swinging in the trough of a wave, with the letters "L. S." carved upon it, and that is all which we shall ever know of the fate of the *Lone Star*.

THE MAN WITH THE TWISTED LIP

Isa Whitney, brother of the late Elias Whitney, D.D., Principal of the Theological College of St. George's, was much addicted to opium. The habit grew upon him, as I understand, from some foolish freak when he was at college; for having read De Quincey's description of his dreams and sensations, he had drenched his tobacco with laudanum in an attempt to produce the same effects. He found, as so many more have done, that the practice is easier to attain than to get rid of, and for many years he continued to be a slave to the drug, an object of mingled horror and pity to his friends and relatives. I can see him now, with yellow, pasty face, drooping lids, and pin-point pupils, all huddled in a chair, the wreck and ruin of a noble man.

One night—it was in June, '89—there came a ring to my bell, about the hour when a man gives his first yawn and glances at the clock. I sat up in my chair, and my wife laid her needle-work down in her lap and made a little face of disappointment.

"A patient!" said she. "You'll have to go out."

I groaned, for I was newly come back from a weary day.

We heard the door open, a few hurried words, and then quick steps upon the linoleum. Our own door flew open, and a lady, clad in some dark-coloured stuff, with a black veil, entered the room.

"You will excuse my calling so late," she began, and then, suddenly losing her self-control, she ran forward, threw her arms about my wife's neck, and sobbed upon her shoulder. "Oh, I'm in such trouble!" she cried; "I do so want a little help."

"Why," said my wife, pulling up her veil, "it is Kate Whitney. How you startled me, Kate! I had not an idea who you were when you came in."

"I didn't know what to do, so I came straight to you." That was always the way. Folk who were in grief came to my wife like birds to a light-house.

"It was very sweet of you to come. Now, you must have some wine and water, and sit here comfortably and tell us all about it. Or should you rather that I sent James off to bed?"

"Oh, no, no! I want the doctor's advice and help, too. It's about Isa. He has not been home for two days. I am so frightened about him!"

It was not the first time that she had spoken to us of her husband's trouble, to me as a doctor, to my wife as an old friend and school companion. We soothed and comforted her by such words as we could find. Did she know where her husband was? Was it possible that we could bring him back to her?

It seems that it was. She had the surest information that of late he had, when the fit was on him, made use of an opium den in the farthest east of the City. Hitherto his orgies had always been confined to one day, and he had come back, twitching and shattered, in the evening. But now the spell had been upon him eight-and-forty hours, and he lay there, doubtless among the dregs of the docks, breathing in the poison or sleeping off the effects. There he was to be found, she was sure of it, at the Bar of Gold, in Upper Swandam Lane. But what was she to do? How could she, a young and timid woman, make her way into such a place and pluck her husband out from among the ruffians who surrounded him?

There was the case, and of course there was but one way out of it. Might I not escort her to this place? And then, as a second thought, why should she come at all? I was Isa Whitney's medical adviser, and as such I had influence over him. I could manage it better if I were alone. I promised her on my word that I would send him home in a cab within two hours if he were indeed at the address which she had given me. And so in ten minutes I had left my armchair and cheery sitting-room behind me, and was speeding eastward in a hansom on a strange errand, as it seemed to me at the time, though the future only could show how strange it was to be.

But there was no great difficulty in the first stage of my adventure. Upper Swandam Lane is a vile alley lurking behind the high wharves which line the north side of the river to the east of London Bridge. Between a slop-shop and a gin-shop, approached by a steep flight of steps leading down to a black gap like the mouth of a cave, I found the den of which I was in search. Ordering my cab to wait, I passed down the steps, worn hollow in the centre by the ceaseless tread of drunken feet; and by the light of a flickering oil-lamp above the door I found the latch and made my way into a long, low room, thick and heavy with the brown opium smoke, and terraced with wooden berths, like the forecastle of an emigrant ship.

Through the gloom one could dimly catch a glimpse of bodies lying in strange fantastic poses, bowed shoulders, bent knees, heads thrown back, and chins pointing upward, with here and there a dark, lacklustre eye turned upon the newcomer. Out of the black shadows there glimmered little red circles of light, now bright, now faint, as the burning poison waxed or waned in the bowls of the metal pipes. The most lay silent, but some muttered to themselves, and others talked together in a strange, low, monotonous voice, their conversation coming in gushes, and then suddenly tailing off into silence, each mumbling out his own thoughts and paying little heed to the words of his neighbour. At the farther end was a small brazier of burning charcoal, beside which on a three-legged wooden stool there sat a tall, thin old man, with his jaw resting upon his two fists, and his elbows upon his knees, staring into the fire.

As I entered, a sallow Malay attendant had hurried up with a pipe for me and a supply of the drug, beckoning me to an empty berth.

"Thank you. I have not come to stay," said I. "There is a friend of mine here, Mr. Isa Whitney, and I wish to speak with him."

There was a movement and an exclamation from my right, and peering through the gloom, I saw Whitney, pale, haggard, and unkempt, staring out at me.

"My God! It's Watson," said he. He was in a pitiable state of reaction, with every nerve in a twitter. "I say, Watson, what o'clock is it?"

"Nearly eleven."

"Of what day?"

"Of Friday, June 19th."

"Good heavens! I thought it was Wednesday. It is Wednesday. What d'you want to frighten a chap for?" He sank his face onto his arms and began to sob in a high treble key.

"I tell you that it is Friday, man. Your wife has been waiting this two days for you. You should be ashamed of yourself!"

"So I am. But you've got mixed, Watson, for I have only been here a few hours, three pipes, four pipes—I forget how many. But I'll go home with you. I wouldn't frighten Kate—poor little Kate. Give me your hand! Have you a cab?"

"Yes, I have one waiting."

"Then I shall go in it. But I must owe something. Find what I owe, Watson. I am all off colour. I can do nothing for myself."

I walked down the narrow passage between the double row of sleepers, holding my breath to keep out the vile, stupefying fumes of

the drug, and looking about for the manager. As I passed the tall man who sat by the brazier I felt a sudden pluck at my skirt, and a low voice whispered, "Walk past me, and then look back at me." The words fell quite distinctly upon my ear. I glanced down. They could only have come from the old man at my side, and yet he sat now as absorbed as ever, very thin, very wrinkled, bent with age, an opium pipe dangling down from between his knees, as though it had dropped in sheer lassitude from his fingers. I took two steps forward and looked back. It took all my self-control to prevent me from breaking out into a cry of astonishment. He had turned his back so that none could see him but I. His form had filled out, his wrinkles were gone, the dull eyes had regained their fire, and there, sitting by the fire and grinning at my surprise, was none other than Sherlock Holmes. He made a slight motion to me to approach him, and instantly, as he turned his face half round to the company once more, subsided into a doddering, loose-lipped senility.

"Holmes!" I whispered, "what on earth are you doing in this den?"

"As low as you can," he answered; "I have excellent ears. If you would have the great kindness to get rid of that sottish friend of yours I should be exceedingly glad to have a little talk with you."

"I have a cab outside."

"Then pray send him home in it. You may safely trust him, for he appears to be too limp to get into any mischief. I should recommend you also to send a note by the cabman to your wife to say that you have thrown in your lot with me. If you will wait outside, I shall be with you in five minutes."

It was difficult to refuse any of Sherlock Holmes' requests, for they were always so exceedingly definite, and put forward with such a quiet air of mastery. I felt, however, that when Whitney was once confined in the cab my mission was practically accomplished; and for the rest, I could not wish anything better than to be associated with my friend in one of those singular adventures which were the normal condition of his existence. In a few minutes I had written my note, paid Whitney's bill, led him out to the cab, and seen him driven through the darkness. In a very short time a decrepit figure had emerged from the opium den, and I was walking down the street with Sherlock Holmes. For two streets he shuffled along with a bent back and an uncertain foot. Then, glancing quickly round, he straightened himself out and burst into a hearty fit of laughter.

"I suppose, Watson," said he, "that you imagine that I have added opium-smoking to cocaine injections, and all the other little weaknesses on which you have favoured me with your medical views."

"I was certainly surprised to find you there."

"But not more so than I to find you."

"I came to find a friend."

"And I to find an enemy."

"An enemy?"

"Yes; one of my natural enemies, or, shall I say, my natural prey. Briefly, Watson, I am in the midst of a very remarkable inquiry, and I have hoped to find a clue in the incoherent ramblings of these sots, as I have done before now. Had I been recognised in that den my life would not have been worth an hour's purchase; for I have used it before now for my own purposes, and the rascally Lascar who runs it has sworn to have vengeance upon me. There is a trapdoor at the back of that building, near the corner of Paul's Wharf, which could tell some strange tales of what has passed through it upon the moonless nights."

"What! You do not mean bodies?"

"Ay, bodies, Watson. We should be rich men if we had 1,000 pounds for every poor devil who has been done to death in that den. It is the vilest murder-trap on the whole riverside, and I fear that Neville St. Clair has entered it never to leave it more. But our trap should be here." He put his two forefingers between his teeth and whistled shrilly—a signal which was answered by a similar whistle from the distance, followed shortly by the rattle of wheels and the clink of horses' hoofs.

"Now, Watson," said Holmes, as a tall dog-cart dashed up through the gloom, throwing out two golden tunnels of yellow light from its side lanterns. "You'll come with me, won't you?"

"If I can be of use."

"Oh, a trusty comrade is always of use; and a chronicler still more so. My room at The Cedars is a double-bedded one."

"The Cedars?"

"Yes; that is Mr. St. Clair's house. I am staying there while I conduct the inquiry."

"Where is it, then?"

"Near Lee, in Kent. We have a seven-mile drive before us."

"But I am all in the dark."

"Of course you are. You'll know all about it presently. Jump up

here. All right, John; we shall not need you. Here's half a crown. Look out for me tomorrow, about eleven. Give her her head. So long, then!"

He flicked the horse with his whip, and we dashed away through the endless succession of sombre and deserted streets, which widened gradually, until we were flying across a broad balustraded bridge, with the murky river flowing sluggishly beneath us. Beyond lay another dull wilderness of bricks and mortar, its silence broken only by the heavy, regular footfall of the policeman, or the songs and shouts of some belated party of revellers. A dull wrack was drifting slowly across the sky, and a star or two twinkled dimly here and there through the rifts of the clouds. Holmes drove in silence, with his head sunk upon his breast, and the air of a man who is lost in thought, while I sat beside him, curious to learn what this new quest might be which seemed to tax his powers so sorely, and yet afraid to break in upon the current of his thoughts. We had driven several miles, and were beginning to get to the fringe of the belt of suburban villas, when he shook himself, shrugged his shoulders, and lit up his pipe with the air of a man who has satisfied himself that he is acting for the best.

"You have a grand gift of silence, Watson," said he. "It makes you quite invaluable as a companion. 'Pon my word, it is a great thing for me to have someone to talk to, for my own thoughts are not over-pleasant. I was wondering what I should say to this dear little woman tonight when she meets me at the door."

"You forget that I know nothing about it."

"I shall just have time to tell you the facts of the case before we get to Lee. It seems absurdly simple, and yet, somehow I can get nothing to go upon. There's plenty of thread, no doubt, but I can't get the end of it into my hand. Now, I'll state the case clearly and concisely to you, Watson, and maybe you can see a spark where all is dark to me."

"Proceed, then."

"Some years ago—to be definite, in May, 1884—there came to Lee a gentleman, Neville St. Clair by name, who appeared to have plenty of money. He took a large villa, laid out the grounds very nicely, and lived generally in good style. By degrees he made friends in the neighbourhood, and in 1887 he married the daughter of a local brewer, by whom he now has two children. He had no occupation, but was interested in several companies and went into town as a rule in the morning, returning by the 5:14 from Cannon Street every night. Mr.

St. Clair is now thirty-seven years of age, is a man of temperate habits, a good husband, a very affectionate father, and a man who is popular with all who know him. I may add that his whole debts at the present moment, as far as we have been able to ascertain, amount to 88 pounds 10s., while he has 220 pounds standing to his credit in the Capital and Counties Bank. There is no reason, therefore, to think that money troubles have been weighing upon his mind.

"Last Monday Mr. Neville St. Clair went into town rather earlier than usual, remarking before he started that he had two important commissions to perform, and that he would bring his little boy home a box of bricks. Now, by the merest chance, his wife received a telegram upon this same Monday, very shortly after his departure, to the effect that a small parcel of considerable value which she had been expecting was waiting for her at the offices of the Aberdeen Shipping Company. Now, if you are well up in your London, you will know that the office of the company is in Fresno Street, which branches out of Upper Swandam Lane, where you found me tonight. Mrs. St. Clair had her lunch, started for the City, did some shopping, proceeded to the company's office, got her packet, and found herself at exactly 4:35 walking through Swandam Lane on her way back to the station. Have you followed me so far?"

"It is very clear."

"If you remember, Monday was an exceedingly hot day, and Mrs. St. Clair walked slowly, glancing about in the hope of seeing a cab, as she did not like the neighbourhood in which she found herself. While she was walking in this way down Swandam Lane, she suddenly heard an ejaculation or cry, and was struck cold to see her husband looking down at her and, as it seemed to her, beckoning to her from a second-floor window. The window was open, and she distinctly saw his face, which she describes as being terribly agitated. He waved his hands frantically to her, and then vanished from the window so suddenly that it seemed to her that he had been plucked back by some irresistible force from behind. One singular point which struck her quick feminine eye was that although he wore some dark coat, such as he had started to town in, he had on neither collar nor necktie.

"Convinced that something was amiss with him, she rushed down the steps—for the house was none other than the opium den in which you found me tonight—and running through the front room she attempted to ascend the stairs which led to the first floor. At the foot of the stairs, however, she met this Lascar scoundrel of whom I have spoken, who thrust her back and, aided by a Dane, who acts as assistant there, pushed her out into the street. Filled with the most maddening doubts and fears, she rushed down the lane and, by rare good-fortune, met in Fresno Street a number of constables with an inspector, all on their way to their beat. The inspector and two men accompanied her back, and in spite of the continued resistance of the proprietor, they made their way to the room in which Mr. St. Clair had last been seen. There was no sign of him there. In fact, in the whole of that floor there was no one to be found save a crippled wretch of hideous aspect, who, it seems, made his home there. Both he and the Lascar stoutly swore that no one else had been in the front room during the afternoon. So determined was their denial that the inspector was staggered, and had almost come to believe that Mrs. St. Clair had been deluded when, with a cry, she sprang at a small deal box which lay upon the table and tore the lid from it. Out there fell a cascade of children's bricks. It was the toy which he had promised to bring home.

"This discovery, and the evident confusion which the cripple showed, made the inspector realise that the matter was serious. The rooms were carefully examined, and results all pointed to an abominable crime. The front room was plainly furnished as a sitting-room and led into a small bedroom, which looked out upon the back of one of the wharves. Between the wharf and the bedroom window is a narrow strip, which is dry at low tide but is covered at high tide with at least four and a half feet of water. The bedroom window was a broad one and opened from below. On examination traces of blood were to be seen upon the windowsill, and several scattered drops were visible upon the wooden floor of the bedroom. Thrust away behind a curtain in the front room were all the clothes of Mr. Neville St. Clair, with the exception of his coat. His boots, his socks, his hat, and his watch—all were there. There were no signs of violence upon any of these garments, and there were no other traces of Mr. Neville St. Clair. Out of the window he must apparently have gone for no other exit could be discovered, and the ominous bloodstains upon the sill gave little promise that he could save himself by swimming, for the tide was at its very highest at the moment of the tragedy.

"And now as to the villains who seemed to be immediately implicated in the matter. The Lascar was known to be a man of the vilest antecedents, but as, by Mrs. St. Clair's story, he was known to have been at the foot of the stair within a very few seconds of her husband's appearance at the window, he could hardly have been more than an accessory to the crime. His defence was one of absolute ignorance, and he protested that he had no knowledge as to the doings of Hugh Boone, his lodger, and that he could not account in any way for the presence of the missing gentleman's clothes.

"So much for the Lascar manager. Now for the sinister cripple who lives upon the second floor of the opium den, and who was certainly the last human being whose eyes rested upon Neville St. Clair. His name is Hugh Boone, and his hideous face is one which is familiar to every man who goes much to the City. He is a professional beggar, though in order to avoid the police regulations he pretends to a small trade in wax vestas. Some little distance down Threadneedle Street, upon the left-hand side, there is, as you may have remarked, a small angle in the wall. Here it is that this creature takes his daily seat, cross-legged with his tiny stock of matches on his lap, and as he is a piteous spectacle a small rain of charity descends into the greasy leather cap which lies upon the pavement beside him. I have watched the fellow more than once before ever I thought of making his professional acquaintance, and I have been surprised at the harvest which he has reaped in a short time. His appearance, you see, is so remarkable that no one can pass him without observing him. A shock of orange hair, a pale face disfigured by a horrible scar, which, by its contraction, has turned up the outer edge of his upper lip, a bulldog chin, and a pair of very penetrating dark eyes, which present a singular contrast to the colour of his hair, all mark him out from amid the common crowd of mendicants and so, too, does his wit, for he is ever ready with a reply to any piece of chaff which may be thrown at him by the passers-by. This is the man whom we now learn to have been the lodger at the opium den, and to have been the last man to see the gentleman of whom we are in quest."

"But a cripple!" said I. "What could he have done single-handed against a man in the prime of life?"

"He is a cripple in the sense that he walks with a limp; but in other respects he appears to be a powerful and well-nurtured man. Surely your medical experience would tell you, Watson, that weakness in one limb is often compensated for by exceptional strength in the others."

"Pray continue your narrative."

"Mrs. St. Clair had fainted at the sight of the blood upon the window, and she was escorted home in a cab by the police, as her presence could be of no help to them in their investigations. Inspector Barton, who had charge of the case, made a very careful examination of the premises, but without finding anything which threw any light upon the matter. One mistake had been made in not arresting Boone instantly, as he was allowed some few minutes during which he might have communicated with his friend the Lascar, but this fault was soon remedied, and he was seized and searched, without anything being found which could incriminate him. There were, it is true, some blood-stains upon his right shirt-sleeve, but he pointed to his ring-finger, which had been cut near the nail, and explained that the bleeding came from there, adding that he had been to the window not long before, and that the stains which had been observed there came doubtless from the same source. He denied strenuously having ever seen Mr. Neville St. Clair and swore that the presence of the clothes in his room was as much a mystery to him as to the police. As to Mrs. St. Clair's assertion that she had actually seen her husband at the window, he declared that she must have been either mad or dreaming. He was removed, loudly protesting, to the police-station, while the inspector remained upon the premises in the hope that the ebbing tide might afford some fresh clue.

"And it did, though they hardly found upon the mud-bank what they had feared to find. It was Neville St. Clair's coat, and not Neville St. Clair, which lay uncovered as the tide receded. And what do you think they found in the pockets?"

"I cannot imagine."

"No, I don't think you would guess. Every pocket stuffed with pennies and half-pennies—421 pennies and 270 half-pennies. It was no wonder that it had not been swept away by the tide. But a human body is a different matter. There is a fierce eddy between the wharf and the house. It seemed likely enough that the weighted coat had remained when the stripped body had been sucked away into the river."

"But I understand that all the other clothes were found in the room. Would the body be dressed in a coat alone?"

"No, sir, but the facts might be met speciously enough. Suppose that this man Boone had thrust Neville St. Clair through the window, there is no human eye which could have seen the deed. What would he do then? It would of course instantly strike him that he must get rid of the tell-tale garments. He would seize the coat, then, and be in the act of throwing it out, when it would occur to him that it would swim and not sink. He has little time, for he has heard the scuffle downstairs when the wife tried to force her way up, and perhaps he has already heard from his Lascar confederate that the police are hurrying up the street. There is not an instant to be lost. He rushes to some secret hoard, where he has accumulated the fruits of his beggary, and he stuffs all the coins upon which he can lay his hands into the pockets to make sure of the coat's sinking. He throws it out, and would have done the same with the other garments had not he heard the rush of steps below, and only just had time to close the window when the police appeared."

"It certainly sounds feasible."

"Well, we will take it as a working hypothesis for want of a better. Boone, as I have told you, was arrested and taken to the station, but it could not be shown that there had ever before been anything against him. He had for years been known as a professional beggar, but his life appeared to have been a very quiet and innocent one. There the matter stands at present, and the questions which have to be solved—what Neville St. Clair was doing in the opium den, what happened to him when there, where is he now, and what Hugh Boone had to do with his disappearance—are all as far from a solution as ever. I confess that I cannot recall any case within my experience which looked at the first glance so simple and yet which presented such difficulties."

While Sherlock Holmes had been detailing this singular series of events, we had been whirling through the outskirts of the great town until the last straggling houses had been left behind, and we rattled along with a country hedge upon either side of us. Just as he finished, however, we drove through two scattered villages, where a few lights still glimmered in the windows.

"We are on the outskirts of Lee," said my companion. "We have touched on three English counties in our short drive, starting in Middlesex, passing over an angle of Surrey, and ending in Kent. See that light among the trees? That is The Cedars, and beside that lamp sits a woman whose anxious ears have already, I have little doubt, caught the clink of our horse's feet."

"But why are you not conducting the case from Baker Street?" I asked.

"Because there are many inquiries which must be made out here. Mrs. St. Clair has most kindly put two rooms at my disposal, and you may rest assured that she will have nothing but a welcome for my friend and colleague. I hate to meet her, Watson, when I have no news of her husband. Here we are. Whoa, there, whoa!"

We had pulled up in front of a large villa which stood within its own grounds. A stable-boy had run out to the horse's head, and springing down, I followed Holmes up the small, winding gravel-drive which led to the house. As we approached, the door flew open, and a little blonde woman stood in the opening, clad in some sort of light *mousseline de soie*, with a touch of fluffy pink chiffon at her neck and wrists. She stood with her figure outlined against the flood of light, one hand upon the door, one half-raised in her eagerness, her body slightly bent, her head and face protruded, with eager eyes and parted lips, a standing question.

"Well?" she cried, "Well?" And then, seeing that there were two of us, she gave a cry of hope which sank into a groan as she saw that my companion shook his head and shrugged his shoulders.

"No good news?"

"None."

"No bad?"

"No."

"Thank God for that. But come in. You must be weary, for you have had a long day."

"This is my friend, Dr. Watson. He has been of most vital use to me in several of my cases, and a lucky chance has made it possible for me to bring him out and associate him with this investigation."

"I am delighted to see you," said she, pressing my hand warmly. "You will, I am sure, forgive anything that may be wanting in our arrangements, when you consider the blow which has come so suddenly upon us."

"My dear madam," said I, "I am an old campaigner, and if I were not I can very well see that no apology is needed. If I can be of any assistance, either to you or to my friend here, I shall be indeed happy."

"Now, Mr. Sherlock Holmes," said the lady as we entered a well-lit dining-room, upon the table of which a cold supper had been laid out, "I should very much like to ask you one or two plain questions, to which I beg that you will give a plain answer."

"Certainly, madam."

"Do not trouble about my feelings. I am not hysterical, nor given to fainting. I simply wish to hear your real, real opinion."

"Upon what point?"

"In your heart of hearts, do you think that Neville is alive?"

Sherlock Holmes seemed to be embarrassed by the question. "Frankly, now!" she repeated, standing upon the rug and looking keenly down at him as he leaned back in a basket-chair.

"Frankly, then, madam, I do not."

"You think that he is dead?"

"I do."

"Murdered?"

"I don't say that. Perhaps."

"And on what day did he meet his death?"

"On Monday."

"Then perhaps, Mr. Holmes, you will be good enough to explain how it is that I have received a letter from him today."

Sherlock Holmes sprang out of his chair as if he had been galvanised.

"What!" he roared.

"Yes, today." She stood smiling, holding up a little slip of paper in the air.

"May I see it?"

"Certainly."

He snatched it from her in his eagerness, and smoothing it out upon the table he drew over the lamp and examined it intently. I had left my chair and was gazing at it over his shoulder. The envelope was a very coarse one and was stamped with the Gravesend postmark and with the date of that very day, or rather of the day before, for it was considerably after midnight.

"Coarse writing," murmured Holmes. "Surely this is not your husband's writing, madam."

"No, but the enclosure is."

"I perceive also that whoever addressed the envelope had to go and inquire as to the address."

"How can you tell that?"

"The name, you see, is in perfectly black ink, which has dried itself. The rest is of the greyish colour, which shows that blotting-paper has been used. If it had been written straight off, and then blotted, none would be of a deep black shade. This man has written the name, and

there has then been a pause before he wrote the address, which can only mean that he was not familiar with it. It is, of course, a trifle, but there is nothing so important as trifles. Let us now see the letter. Ha! There has been an enclosure here!"

"Yes, there was a ring. His signet-ring."

"And you are sure that this is your husband's hand?"

"One of his hands."

"One?"

"His hand when he wrote hurriedly. It is very unlike his usual writing, and yet I know it well."

" 'Dearest do not be frightened. All will come well. There is a huge error which it may take some little time to rectify. Wait in patience.—Neville.' Written in pencil upon the fly-leaf of a book, octavo size, no water-mark. Hum! Posted today in Gravesend by a man with a dirty thumb. Ha! And the flap has been gummed, if I am not very much in error, by a person who had been chewing tobacco. And you have no doubt that it is your husband's hand, madam?"

"None. Neville wrote those words."

"And they were posted today at Gravesend. Well, Mrs. St. Clair, the clouds lighten, though I should not venture to say that the danger is over."

"But he must be alive, Mr. Holmes."

"Unless this is a clever forgery to put us on the wrong scent. The ring, after all, proves nothing. It may have been taken from him."

"No, no; it is, it is his very own writing!"

"Very well. It may, however, have been written on Monday and only posted today."

"That is possible."

"If so, much may have happened between."

"Oh, you must not discourage me, Mr. Holmes. I know that all is well with him. There is so keen a sympathy between us that I should know if evil came upon him. On the very day that I saw him last he cut himself in the bedroom, and yet I in the dining-room rushed upstairs instantly with the utmost certainty that something had happened. Do you think that I would respond to such a trifle and yet be ignorant of his death?"

"I have seen too much not to know that the impression of a woman may be more valuable than the conclusion of an analytical reasoner. And in this letter you certainly have a very strong piece of evidence to corroborate your view. But if your husband is alive and able to write letters, why should he remain away from you?"

"I cannot imagine. It is unthinkable."

"And on Monday he made no remarks before leaving you?"

"No."

"And you were surprised to see him in Swandam Lane?"

"Very much so."

"Was the window open?"

"Yes."

"Then he might have called to you?"

"He might."

"He only, as I understand, gave an inarticulate cry?"

"Yes."

"A call for help, you thought?"

"Yes. He waved his hands."

"But it might have been a cry of surprise. Astonishment at the unexpected sight of you might cause him to throw up his hands?"

"It is possible."

"And you thought he was pulled back?"

"He disappeared so suddenly."

"He might have leaped back. You did not see anyone else in the room?"

"No, but this horrible man confessed to having been there, and the Lascar was at the foot of the stairs."

"Quite so. Your husband, as far as you could see, had his ordinary clothes on?"

"But without his collar or tie. I distinctly saw his bare throat."

"Had he ever spoken of Swandam Lane?"

"Never."

"Had he ever showed any signs of having taken opium?"

"Never."

"Thank you, Mrs. St. Clair. Those are the principal points about which I wished to be absolutely clear. We shall now have a little supper and then retire, for we may have a very busy day tomorrow."

A large and comfortable double-bedded room had been placed at our disposal, and I was quickly between the sheets, for I was weary after my night of adventure. Sherlock Holmes was a man, however, who, when he had an unsolved problem upon his mind, would go for

days, and even for a week, without rest, turning it over, rearranging his facts, looking at it from every point of view until he had either fathomed it or convinced himself that his data were insufficient. It was soon evident to me that he was now preparing for an all-night sitting. He took off his coat and waistcoat, put on a large blue dressing-gown, and then wandered about the room collecting pillows from his bed and cushions from the sofa and armchairs. With these he constructed a sort of Eastern divan, upon which he perched himself cross-legged, with an ounce of shag tobacco and a box of matches laid out in front of him. In the dim light of the lamp I saw him sitting there, an old briar pipe between his lips, his eyes fixed vacantly upon the corner of the ceiling, the blue smoke curling up from him, silent, motionless, with the light shining upon his strong-set aquiline features. So he sat as I dropped off to sleep, and so he sat when a sudden ejaculation caused me to wake up, and I found the summer sun shining into the apartment. The pipe was still between his lips, the smoke still curled upward, and the room was full of a dense tobacco haze, but nothing remained of the heap of shag which I had seen upon the previous night.

"Awake, Watson?" he asked.

"Yes."

"Game for a morning drive?"

"Certainly."

"Then dress. No one is stirring yet, but I know where the stable-boy sleeps, and we shall soon have the trap out." He chuckled to himself as he spoke, his eyes twinkled, and he seemed a different man to the sombre thinker of the previous night.

As I dressed I glanced at my watch. It was no wonder that no one was stirring. It was twenty-five minutes past four. I had hardly finished when Holmes returned with the news that the boy was putting in the horse.

"I want to test a little theory of mine," said he, pulling on his boots. "I think, Watson, that you are now standing in the presence of one of the most absolute fools in Europe. I deserve to be kicked from here to Charing Cross. But I think I have the key of the affair now."

"And where is it?" I asked, smiling.

"In the bathroom," he answered. "Oh, yes, I am not joking," he continued, seeing my look of incredulity. "I have just been there, and I have taken it out, and I have got it in this Gladstone bag. Come on, my boy, and we shall see whether it will not fit the lock."

We made our way downstairs as quietly as possible, and out into the bright morning sunshine. In the road stood our horse and trap, with the half-clad stable-boy waiting at the head. We both sprang in, and away we dashed down the London Road. A few country carts were stirring, bearing in vegetables to the metropolis, but the lines of villas on either side were as silent and lifeless as some city in a dream.

"It has been in some points a singular case," said Holmes, flicking the horse on into a gallop. "I confess that I have been as blind as a mole, but it is better to learn wisdom late than never to learn it at all."

In town the earliest risers were just beginning to look sleepily from their windows as we drove through the streets of the Surrey side. Passing down the Waterloo Bridge Road we crossed over the river, and dashing up Wellington Street wheeled sharply to the right and found ourselves in Bow Street. Sherlock Holmes was well known to the force, and the two constables at the door saluted him. One of them held the horse's head while the other led us in.

"Who is on duty?" asked Holmes.

"Inspector Bradstreet, sir."

"Ah, Bradstreet, how are you?" A tall, stout official had come down the stone-flagged passage, in a peaked cap and frogged jacket. "I wish to have a quiet word with you, Bradstreet."

"Certainly, Mr. Holmes. Step into my room here." It was a small, office-like room, with a huge ledger upon the table, and a telephone projecting from the wall. The inspector sat down at his desk.

"What can I do for you, Mr. Holmes?"

"I called about that beggarman, Boone—the one who was charged with being concerned in the disappearance of Mr. Neville St. Clair, of Lee."

"Yes. He was brought up and remanded for further inquiries."

"So I heard. You have him here?"

"In the cells."

"Is he quiet?"

"Oh, he gives no trouble. But he is a dirty scoundrel."

"Dirty?"

Yes, it is all we can do to make him wash his hands, and his face is as black as a tinker's. Well, when once his case has been settled, he will have a regular prison bath; and I think, if you saw him, you would agree with me that he needed it."

"I should like to see him very much."

"Would you? That is easily done. Come this way. You can leave your bag."

"No, I think that I'll take it."

"Very good. Come this way, if you please." He led us down a passage, opened a barred door, passed down a winding stair, and brought us to a whitewashed corridor with a line of doors on each side.

"The third on the right is his," said the inspector. "Here it is!" He quietly shot back a panel in the upper part of the door and glanced through.

"He is asleep," said he. "You can see him very well."

We both put our eyes to the grating. The prisoner lay with his face towards us, in a very deep sleep, breathing slowly and heavily. He was a middle-sized man, coarsely clad as became his calling, with a coloured shirt protruding through the rent in his tattered coat. He was, as the inspector had said, extremely dirty, but the grime which covered his face could not conceal its repulsive ugliness. A broad wheal from an old scar ran right across it from eye to chin, and by its contraction had turned up one side of the upper lip, so that three teeth were exposed in a perpetual snarl. A shock of very bright red hair grew low over his eyes and forehead.

"He's a beauty, isn't he?" said the inspector.

"He certainly needs a wash," remarked Holmes. "I had an idea that he might, and I took the liberty of bringing the tools with me." He opened the Gladstone bag as he spoke, and took out, to my astonishment, a very large bath-sponge.

"He! He! You are a funny one," chuckled the inspector.

"Now, if you will have the great goodness to open that door very quietly, we will soon make him cut a much more respectable figure."

"Well, I don't know why not," said the inspector. "He doesn't look a credit to the Bow Street cells, does he?" He slipped his key into the lock, and we all very quietly entered the cell. The sleeper half turned, and then settled down once more into a deep slumber. Holmes stooped to the water-jug, moistened his sponge, and then rubbed it twice vigorously across and down the prisoner's face.

"Let me introduce you," he shouted, "to Mr. Neville St. Clair, of Lee, in the county of Kent."

Never in my life have I seen such a sight. The man's face peeled off under the sponge like the bark from a tree. Gone was the coarse brown tint! Gone, too, was the horrid scar which had seamed it across, and the twisted lip which had given the repulsive sneer to the face! A twitch brought away the tangled red hair, and there, sitting up in his bed, was a pale, sad-faced, refined-looking man, black-haired and smooth-skinned, rubbing his eyes and staring about him with sleepy bewilderment. Then suddenly realising the exposure, he broke into a scream and threw himself down with his face to the pillow.

"Great heavens!" cried the inspector, "It is, indeed, the missing man. I know him from the photograph."

The prisoner turned with the reckless air of a man who abandons himself to his destiny. "Be it so," said he. "And pray what am I charged with?"

"With making away with Mr. Neville St.— Oh, come, you can't be charged with that unless they make a case of attempted suicide of it," said the inspector with a grin. "Well, I have been twenty-seven years in the force, but this really takes the cake."

"If I am Mr. Neville St. Clair, then it is obvious that no crime has been committed, and that, therefore, I am illegally detained."

"No crime, but a very great error has been committed," said Holmes. "You would have done better to have trusted your wife."

"It was not the wife; it was the children," groaned the prisoner. "God help me, I would not have them ashamed of their father. My God! What an exposure! What can I do?"

Sherlock Holmes sat down beside him on the couch and patted him kindly on the shoulder.

"If you leave it to a court of law to clear the matter up," said he, "of course you can hardly avoid publicity. On the other hand, if you convince the police authorities that there is no possible case against you, I do not know that there is any reason that the details should find their way into the papers. Inspector Bradstreet would, I am sure, make notes upon anything which you might tell us and submit it to the proper authorities. The case would then never go into court at all."

"God bless you!" cried the prisoner passionately. "I would have endured imprisonment, ay, even execution, rather than have left my miserable secret as a family blot to my children.

"You are the first who have ever heard my story. My father was a schoolmaster in Chesterfield, where I received an excellent education.

I travelled in my youth, took to the stage, and finally became a reporter on an evening paper in London. One day my editor wished to have a series of articles upon begging in the metropolis, and I volunteered to supply them. There was the point from which all my adventures started. It was only by trying begging as an amateur that I could get the facts upon which to base my articles. When an actor I had, of course, learned all the secrets of making up, and had been famous in the green-room for my skill. I took advantage now of my attainments. I painted my face, and to make myself as pitiable as possible I made a good scar and fixed one side of my lip in a twist by the aid of a small slip of flesh-coloured plaster. Then with a red head of hair, and an appropriate dress, I took my station in the business part of the city, ostensibly as a match-seller but really as a beggar. For seven hours I plied my trade, and when I returned home in the evening I found to my surprise that I had received no less than 26 shillings and 4 pence.

"I wrote my articles and thought little more of the matter until, some time later, I backed a bill for a friend and had a writ served upon me for 25 pounds. I was at my wit's end where to get the money, but a sudden idea came to me. I begged a fortnight's grace from the creditor, asked for a holiday from my employers, and spent the time in begging in the City under my disguise. In ten days I had the money and had paid the debt.

"Well, you can imagine how hard it was to settle down to arduous work at 2 pounds a week when I knew that I could earn as much in a day by smearing my face with a little paint, laying my cap on the ground, and sitting still. It was a long fight between my pride and the money, but the dollars won at last, and I threw up reporting and sat day after day in the corner which I had first chosen, inspiring pity by my ghastly face and filling my pockets with coppers. Only one man knew my secret. He was the keeper of a low den in which I used to lodge in Swandam Lane, where I could every morning emerge as a squalid beggar and in the evenings transform myself into a well-dressed man about town. This fellow, a Lascar, was well paid by me for his rooms, so that I knew that my secret was safe in his possession.

"Well, very soon I found that I was saving considerable sums of money. I do not mean that any beggar in the streets of London could earn 700 pounds a year—which is less than my average takings—but I had exceptional advantages in my power of making up, and also in a facility of repartee, which improved by practice and made me quite a recognised character in the City. All day a stream of pennies, varied by silver, poured in upon me, and it was a very bad day in which I failed to take 2 pounds.

"As I grew richer I grew more ambitious, took a house in the country, and eventually married, without anyone having a suspicion as to my real occupation. My dear wife knew that I had business in the City. She little knew what.

"Last Monday I had finished for the day and was dressing in my room above the opium den when I looked out of my window and saw, to my horror and astonishment, that my wife was standing in the street, with her eyes fixed full upon me. I gave a cry of surprise, threw up my arms to cover my face, and, rushing to my confidant, the Lascar, entreated him to prevent anyone from coming up to me. I heard her voice downstairs, but I knew that she could not ascend. Swiftly I threw off my clothes, pulled on those of a beggar, and put on my pigments and wig. Even a wife's eyes could not pierce so complete a disguise. But then it occurred to me that there might be a search in the room, and that the clothes might betray me. I threw open the window, reopening by my violence a small cut which I had inflicted upon myself in the bedroom that morning. Then I seized my coat, which was weighted by the coppers which I had just transferred to it from the leather bag in which I carried my takings. I hurled it out of the window, and it disappeared into the Thames. The other clothes would have followed, but at that moment there was a rush of constables up the stair, and a few minutes after I found, rather, I confess, to my relief, that instead of being identified as Mr. Neville St. Clair, I was arrested as his murderer.

"I do not know that there is anything else for me to explain. I was determined to preserve my disguise as long as possible, and hence my preference for a dirty face. Knowing that my wife would be terribly anxious, I slipped off my ring and confided it to the Lascar at a moment when no constable was watching me, together with a hurried scrawl, telling her that she had no cause to fear."

"That note only reached her yesterday," said Holmes.

"Good God! What a week she must have spent!"

"The police have watched this Lascar," said Inspector Bradstreet, "and I can quite understand that he might find it difficult to post a letter

unobserved. Probably he handed it to some sailor customer of his, who forgot all about it for some days."

"That was it," said Holmes, nodding approvingly; "I have no doubt of it. But have you never been prosecuted for begging?"

"Many times; but what was a fine to me?"

"It must stop here, however," said Bradstreet. "If the police are to hush this thing up, there must be no more of Hugh Boone."

"I have sworn it by the most solemn oaths which a man can take."

"In that case I think that it is probable that no further steps may be taken. But if you are found again, then all must come out. I am sure, Mr. Holmes, that we are very much indebted to you for having cleared the matter up. I wish I knew how you reach your results."

"I reached this one," said my friend, "by sitting upon five pillows and consuming an ounce of shag. I think, Watson, that if we drive to Baker Street we shall just be in time for breakfast."

THE BLUE CARBUNCLE

I had called upon my friend Sherlock Holmes upon the second morning after Christmas, with the intention of wishing him the compliments of the season. He was lounging upon the sofa in a purple dressing-gown, a pipe-rack within his reach upon the right, and a pile of crumpled morning papers, evidently newly studied, near at hand. Beside the couch was a wooden chair, and on the angle of the back hung a very seedy and disreputable hard-felt hat, much the worse for wear, and cracked in several places. A lens and a forceps lying upon the seat of the chair suggested that the hat had been suspended in this manner for the purpose of examination.

"You are engaged," said I; "perhaps I interrupt you."

"Not at all. I am glad to have a friend with whom I can discuss my results. The matter is a perfectly trivial one" (he jerked his thumb in the direction of the old hat) "but there are points in connection with it which are not entirely devoid of interest and even of instruction."

I seated myself in his armchair and warmed my hands before his crackling fire, for a sharp frost had set in, and the windows were thick with the ice crystals. "I suppose," I remarked, "that, homely as it looks, this thing has some deadly story linked on to it—that it is the clue which will guide you in the solution of some mystery and the punishment of some crime."

"No, no. No crime," said Sherlock Holmes, laughing. "Only one of those whimsical little incidents which will happen when you have four million human beings all jostling each other within the space of a few square miles. Amid the action and reaction of so dense a swarm of humanity, every possible combination of events may be expected to take place, and many a little problem will be presented which may be striking and bizarre without being criminal. We have already had experience of such."

"So much so," I remarked, "that of the last six cases which I have added to my notes, three have been entirely free of any legal crime."

"Precisely. You allude to my attempt to recover the Irene Adler papers, to the singular case of Miss Mary Sutherland, and to the adventure of the man with the twisted lip. Well, I have no doubt that

this small matter will fall into the same innocent category. You know Peterson, the commissionaire?"

"Yes."

"It is to him that this trophy belongs."

"It is his hat."

"No, no, he found it. Its owner is unknown. I beg that you will look upon it not as a battered billycock but as an intellectual problem. And, first, as to how it came here. It arrived upon Christmas morning, in company with a good fat goose, which is, I have no doubt, roasting at this moment in front of Peterson's fire. The facts are these: about four o'clock on Christmas morning, Peterson, who, as you know, is a very honest fellow, was returning from some small jollification and was making his way homeward down Tottenham Court Road. In front of him he saw, in the gaslight, a tallish man, walking with a slight stagger, and carrying a white goose slung over his shoulder. As he reached the corner of Goodge Street, a row broke out between this stranger and a little knot of roughs. One of the latter knocked off the man's hat, on which he raised his stick to defend himself and, swinging it over his head, smashed the shop window behind him. Peterson had rushed forward to protect the stranger from his assailants; but the man, shocked at having broken the window, and seeing an official-looking person in uniform rushing towards him, dropped his goose, took to his heels, and vanished amid the labyrinth of small streets which lie at the back of Tottenham Court Road. The roughs had also fled at the appearance of Peterson, so that he was left in possession of the field of battle, and also of the spoils of victory in the shape of this battered hat and a most unimpeachable Christmas goose."

"Which surely he restored to their owner?"

"My dear fellow, there lies the problem. It is true that 'For Mrs. Henry Baker' was printed upon a small card which was tied to the bird's left leg, and it is also true that the initials 'H. B.' are legible upon the lining of this hat, but as there are some thousands of Bakers, and some hundreds of Henry Bakers in this city of ours, it is not easy to restore lost property to any one of them."

"What, then, did Peterson do?"

"He brought round both hat and goose to me on Christmas morning, knowing that even the smallest problems are of interest to me. The goose we retained until this morning, when there were signs that, in spite of the slight frost, it would be well that it should be eaten without unnecessary delay. Its finder has carried it off, therefore, to fulfil the ultimate destiny of a goose, while I continue to retain the hat of the unknown gentleman who lost his Christmas dinner."

"Did he not advertise?"

"No."

"Then, what clue could you have as to his identity?"

"Only as much as we can deduce."

"From his hat?"

"Precisely."

"But you are joking. What can you gather from this old battered felt?"

"Here is my lens. You know my methods. What can you gather yourself as to the individuality of the man who has worn this article?"

I took the tattered object in my hands and turned it over rather ruefully. It was a very ordinary black hat of the usual round shape, hard and much the worse for wear. The lining had been of red silk, but was a good deal discoloured. There was no maker's name; but, as Holmes had remarked, the initials "H. B." were scrawled upon one side. It was pierced in the brim for a hat-securer, but the elastic was missing. For the rest, it was cracked, exceedingly dusty, and spotted in several places, although there seemed to have been some attempt to hide the discoloured patches by smearing them with ink.

"I can see nothing," said I, handing it back to my friend.

"On the contrary, Watson, you can see everything. You fail, however, to reason from what you see. You are too timid in drawing your inferences."

"Then, pray tell me what it is that you can infer from this hat?"

He picked it up and gazed at it in the peculiar introspective fashion which was characteristic of him. "It is perhaps less suggestive than it might have been," he remarked, "and yet there are a few inferences which are very distinct, and a few others which represent at least a strong balance of probability. That the man was highly intellectual is of course obvious upon the face of it, and also that he was fairly well-to-do within the last three years, although he has now fallen upon evil days. He had foresight, but has less now than formerly, pointing to a moral retrogression, which, when taken with the decline of his fortunes, seems to indicate some evil influence, probably drink, at work

upon him. This may account also for the obvious fact that his wife has ceased to love him."

"My dear Holmes!"

"He has, however, retained some degree of self-respect," he continued, disregarding my remonstrance. "He is a man who leads a sedentary life, goes out little, is out of training entirely, is middle-aged, has grizzled hair which he has had cut within the last few days, and which he anoints with lime-cream. These are the more patent facts which are to be deduced from his hat. Also, by the way, that it is extremely improbable that he has gas laid on in his house."

"You are certainly joking, Holmes."

"Not in the least. Is it possible that even now, when I give you these results, you are unable to see how they are attained?"

"I have no doubt that I am very stupid, but I must confess that I am unable to follow you. For example, how did you deduce that this man was intellectual?"

For answer Holmes clapped the hat upon his head. It came right over the forehead and settled upon the bridge of his nose. "It is a question of cubic capacity," said he; "a man with so large a brain must have something in it."

"The decline of his fortunes, then?"

"This hat is three years old. These flat brims curled at the edge came in then. It is a hat of the very best quality. Look at the band of ribbed silk and the excellent lining. If this man could afford to buy so expensive a hat three years ago, and has had no hat since, then he has assuredly gone down in the world."

"Well, that is clear enough, certainly. But how about the foresight and the moral retrogression?"

Sherlock Holmes laughed. "Here is the foresight," said he putting his finger upon the little disc and loop of the hat-securer. "They are never sold upon hats. If this man ordered one, it is a sign of a certain amount of foresight, since he went out of his way to take this precaution against the wind. But since we see that he has broken the elastic and has not troubled to replace it, it is obvious that he has less foresight now than formerly, which is a distinct proof of a weakening nature. On the other hand, he has endeavoured to conceal some of these stains upon the felt by daubing them with ink, which is a sign that he has not entirely lost his self-respect."

"Your reasoning is certainly plausible."

"The further points, that he is middle-aged, that his hair is grizzled, that it has been recently cut, and that he uses lime-cream, are all to be gathered from a close examination of the lower part of the lining. The lens discloses a large number of hair-ends, clean cut by the scissors of the barber. They all appear to be adhesive, and there is a distinct odour of lime-cream. This dust, you will observe, is not the gritty, grey dust of the street but the fluffy brown dust of the house, showing that it has been hung up indoors most of the time, while the marks of moisture upon the inside are proof positive that the wearer perspired very freely, and could therefore, hardly be in the best of training."

"But his wife—you said that she had ceased to love him."

"This hat has not been brushed for weeks. When I see you, my dear Watson, with a week's accumulation of dust upon your hat, and when your wife allows you to go out in such a state, I shall fear that you also have been unfortunate enough to lose your wife's affection."

"But he might be a bachelor."

"Nay, he was bringing home the goose as a peace-offering to his wife. Remember the card upon the bird's leg."

"You have an answer to everything. But how on earth do you deduce that the gas is not laid on in his house?"

"One tallow stain, or even two, might come by chance; but when I see no less than five, I think that there can be little doubt that the individual must be brought into frequent contact with burning tallow—walks upstairs at night probably with his hat in one hand and a guttering candle in the other. Anyhow, he never got tallow-stains from a gas-jet. Are you satisfied?"

"Well, it is very ingenious," said I, laughing; "but since, as you said just now, there has been no crime committed, and no harm done save the loss of a goose, all this seems to be rather a waste of energy."

Sherlock Holmes had opened his mouth to reply, when the door flew open, and Peterson, the commissionaire, rushed into the apartment with flushed cheeks and the face of a man who is dazed with astonishment.

"The goose, Mr. Holmes! The goose, sir!" he gasped.

"Eh? What of it, then? Has it returned to life and flapped off through the kitchen window?" Holmes twisted himself round upon the sofa to get a fairer view of the man's excited face.

"See here, sir! See what my wife found in its crop!" He held out his

hand and displayed upon the centre of the palm a brilliantly scintillating blue stone, rather smaller than a bean in size, but of such purity and radiance that it twinkled like an electric point in the dark hollow of his hand.

Sherlock Holmes sat up with a whistle. "By Jove, Peterson!" said he, "this is treasure trove indeed. I suppose you know what you have got?"

"A diamond, sir? A precious stone. It cuts into glass as though it were putty."

"It's more than a precious stone. It is the precious stone."

"Not the Countess of Morcar's blue carbuncle!" I ejaculated.

"Precisely so. I ought to know its size and shape, seeing that I have read the advertisement about it in *The Times* every day lately. It is absolutely unique, and its value can only be conjectured, but the reward offered of 1,000 pounds is certainly not within a twentieth part of the market price."

"A thousand pounds! Great Lord of mercy!" The commissionaire plumped down into a chair and stared from one to the other of us.

"That is the reward, and I have reason to know that there are sentimental considerations in the background which would induce the Countess to part with half her fortune if she could but recover the gem."

"It was lost, if I remember aright, at the Hotel Cosmopolitan," I remarked.

"Precisely so, on December 22nd, just five days ago. John Horner, a plumber, was accused of having abstracted it from the lady's jewel-case. The evidence against him was so strong that the case has been referred to the Assizes. I have some account of the matter here, I believe." He rummaged amid his newspapers, glancing over the dates, until at last he smoothed one out, doubled it over, and read the following paragraph:

> Hotel Cosmopolitan Jewel Robbery. John Horner, 26, plumber, was brought up upon the charge of having upon the 22nd inst., abstracted from the jewel-case of the Countess of Morcar the valuable gem known as the blue carbuncle. James Ryder, upper-attendant at the hotel, gave his evidence to the effect that he had shown Horner up to the dressing-room of the Countess of Morcar upon the day of the robbery in order that he might solder the second bar of the grate, which was loose. He had remained with Horner some little time, but had finally been called away. On

> returning, he found that Horner had disappeared, that the bureau had been forced open, and that the small morocco casket in which, as it afterwards transpired, the Countess was accustomed to keep her jewel, was lying empty upon the dressing-table. Ryder instantly gave the alarm, and Horner was arrested the same evening; but the stone could not be found either upon his person or in his rooms. Catherine Cusack, maid to the Countess, deposed to having heard Ryder's cry of dismay on discovering the robbery, and to having rushed into the room, where she found matters as described by the last witness. Inspector Bradstreet, B division, gave evidence as to the arrest of Horner, who struggled frantically, and protested his innocence in the strongest terms. Evidence of a previous conviction for robbery having been given against the prisoner, the magistrate refused to deal summarily with the offence, but referred it to the Assizes. Horner, who had shown signs of intense emotion during the proceedings, fainted away at the conclusion and was carried out of court.

"Hum! So much for the police-court," said Holmes thoughtfully, tossing aside the paper. "The question for us now to solve is the sequence of events leading from a rifled jewel-case at one end to the crop of a goose in Tottenham Court Road at the other. You see, Watson, our little deductions have suddenly assumed a much more important and less innocent aspect. Here is the stone; the stone came from the goose, and the goose came from Mr. Henry Baker, the gentleman with the bad hat and all the other characteristics with which I have bored you. So now we must set ourselves very seriously to finding this gentleman and ascertaining what part he has played in this little mystery. To do this, we must try the simplest means first, and these lie undoubtedly in an advertisement in all the evening papers. If this fail, I shall have recourse to other methods."

"What will you say?"

"Give me a pencil and that slip of paper. Now, then: 'Found at the corner of Goodge Street, a goose and a black felt hat. Mr. Henry Baker can have the same by applying at 6:30 this evening at 221B, Baker Street.' That is clear and concise."

"Very. But will he see it?"

"Well, he is sure to keep an eye on the papers, since, to a poor man,

the loss was a heavy one. He was clearly so scared by his mischance in breaking the window and by the approach of Peterson that he thought of nothing but flight, but since then he must have bitterly regretted the impulse which caused him to drop his bird. Then, again, the introduction of his name will cause him to see it, for everyone who knows him will direct his attention to it. Here you are, Peterson, run down to the advertising agency and have this put in the evening papers."

"In which, sir?"

"Oh, in the *Globe*, *Star*, *Pall Mall*, *St. James's*, *Evening News*, *Standard*, *Echo*, and any others that occur to you."

"Very well, sir. And this stone?"

"Ah, yes, I shall keep the stone. Thank you. And, I say, Peterson, just buy a goose on your way back and leave it here with me, for we must have one to give to this gentleman in place of the one which your family is now devouring."

When the commissionaire had gone, Holmes took up the stone and held it against the light. "It's a bonny thing," said he. "Just see how it glints and sparkles. Of course it is a nucleus and focus of crime. Every good stone is. They are the devil's pet baits. In the larger and older jewels every facet may stand for a bloody deed. This stone is not yet twenty years old. It was found in the banks of the Amoy River in southern China and is remarkable in having every characteristic of the carbuncle, save that it is blue in shade instead of ruby red. In spite of its youth, it has already a sinister history. There have been two murders, a vitriol-throwing, a suicide, and several robberies brought about for the sake of this forty-grain weight of crystallised charcoal. Who would think that so pretty a toy would be a purveyor to the gallows and the prison? I'll lock it up in my strong box now and drop a line to the Countess to say that we have it."

"Do you think that this man Horner is innocent?"

"I cannot tell."

"Well, then, do you imagine that this other one, Henry Baker, had anything to do with the matter?"

"It is, I think, much more likely that Henry Baker is an absolutely innocent man, who had no idea that the bird which he was carrying was of considerably more value than if it were made of solid gold. That, however, I shall determine by a very simple test if we have an answer to our advertisement."

"And you can do nothing until then?"

"Nothing."

"In that case I shall continue my professional round. But I shall come back in the evening at the hour you have mentioned, for I should like to see the solution of so tangled a business."

"Very glad to see you. I dine at seven. There is a woodcock, I believe. By the way, in view of recent occurrences, perhaps I ought to ask Mrs. Hudson to examine its crop."

I had been delayed at a case, and it was a little after half-past six when I found myself in Baker Street once more. As I approached the house I saw a tall man in a Scotch bonnet with a coat which was buttoned up to his chin waiting outside in the bright semicircle which was thrown from the fanlight. Just as I arrived the door was opened, and we were shown up together to Holmes' room.

"Mr. Henry Baker, I believe," said he, rising from his armchair and greeting his visitor with the easy air of geniality which he could so readily assume. "Pray take this chair by the fire, Mr. Baker. It is a cold night, and I observe that your circulation is more adapted for summer than for winter. Ah, Watson, you have just come at the right time. Is that your hat, Mr. Baker?"

"Yes, sir, that is undoubtedly my hat."

He was a large man with rounded shoulders, a massive head, and a broad, intelligent face, sloping down to a pointed beard of grizzled brown. A touch of red in nose and cheeks, with a slight tremor of his extended hand, recalled Holmes' surmise as to his habits. His rusty black frock-coat was buttoned right up in front, with the collar turned up, and his lank wrists protruded from his sleeves without a sign of cuff or shirt. He spoke in a slow staccato fashion, choosing his words with care, and gave the impression generally of a man of learning and letters who had had ill-usage at the hands of fortune.

"We have retained these things for some days," said Holmes, "because we expected to see an advertisement from you giving your address. I am at a loss to know now why you did not advertise."

Our visitor gave a rather shamefaced laugh. "Shillings have not been so plentiful with me as they once were," he remarked. "I had no doubt that the gang of roughs who assaulted me had carried off both my hat and the bird. I did not care to spend more money in a hopeless attempt at recovering them."

"Very naturally. By the way, about the bird, we were compelled to eat it."

"To eat it!" Our visitor half rose from his chair in his excitement.

"Yes, it would have been of no use to anyone had we not done so. But I presume that this other goose upon the sideboard, which is about the same weight and perfectly fresh, will answer your purpose equally well?"

"Oh, certainly, certainly," answered Mr. Baker with a sigh of relief.

"Of course, we still have the feathers, legs, crop, and so on of your own bird, so if you wish—"

The man burst into a hearty laugh. "They might be useful to me as relics of my adventure," said he, "but beyond that I can hardly see what use the disjecta membra of my late acquaintance are going to be to me. No, sir, I think that, with your permission, I will confine my attentions to the excellent bird which I perceive upon the sideboard."

Sherlock Holmes glanced sharply across at me with a slight shrug of his shoulders.

"There is your hat, then, and there your bird," said he. "By the way, would it bore you to tell me where you got the other one from? I am somewhat of a fowl fancier, and I have seldom seen a better grown goose."

"Certainly, sir," said Baker, who had risen and tucked his newly gained property under his arm. "There are a few of us who frequent the Alpha Inn, near the Museum—we are to be found in the Museum itself during the day, you understand. This year our good host, Windigate by name, instituted a goose club, by which, on consideration of some few pence every week, we were each to receive a bird at Christmas. My pence were duly paid, and the rest is familiar to you. I am much indebted to you, sir, for a Scotch bonnet is fitted neither to my years nor my gravity." With a comical pomposity of manner he bowed solemnly to both of us and strode off upon his way.

"So much for Mr. Henry Baker," said Holmes when he had closed the door behind him. "It is quite certain that he knows nothing whatever about the matter. Are you hungry, Watson?"

"Not particularly."

"Then I suggest that we turn our dinner into a supper and follow up this clue while it is still hot."

"By all means."

It was a bitter night, so we drew on our ulsters and wrapped cravats about our throats. Outside, the stars were shining coldly in a cloudless sky, and the breath of the passers-by blew out into smoke like so many pistol shots. Our footfalls rang out crisply and loudly as we swung through the doctors' quarter, Wimpole Street, Harley Street, and so through Wigmore Street into Oxford Street. In a quarter of an hour we were in Bloomsbury at the Alpha Inn, which is a small public-house at the corner of one of the streets which runs down into Holborn. Holmes pushed open the door of the private bar and ordered two glasses of beer from the ruddy-faced, white-aproned landlord.

"Your beer should be excellent if it is as good as your geese," said he.

"My geese!" The man seemed surprised.

"Yes. I was speaking only half an hour ago to Mr. Henry Baker, who was a member of your goose club."

"Ah! Yes, I see. But you see, sir, them's not *our geese*."

"Indeed! Whose, then?"

"Well, I got the two dozen from a salesman in Covent Garden."

"Indeed? I know some of them. Which was it?"

"Breckinridge is his name."

"Ah! I don't know him. Well, here's your good health landlord, and prosperity to your house. Good-night."

"Now for Mr. Breckinridge," he continued, buttoning up his coat as we came out into the frosty air. "Remember, Watson that though we have so homely a thing as a goose at one end of this chain, we have at the other a man who will certainly get seven years' penal servitude unless we can establish his innocence. It is possible that our inquiry may but confirm his guilt; but, in any case, we have a line of investigation which has been missed by the police, and which a singular chance has placed in our hands. Let us follow it out to the bitter end. Faces to the south, then, and quick march!"

We passed across Holborn, down Endell Street, and so through a zigzag of slums to Covent Garden Market. One of the largest stalls bore the name of Breckinridge upon it, and the proprietor a horsey-looking man, with a sharp face and trim side-whiskers was helping a boy to put up the shutters.

"Good-evening. It's a cold night," said Holmes.

The salesman nodded and shot a questioning glance at my companion.

"Sold out of geese, I see," continued Holmes, pointing at the bare slabs of marble.

"Let you have five hundred tomorrow morning."

"That's no good."

"Well, there are some on the stall with the gas-flare."

"Ah, but I was recommended to you."

"Who by?"

"The landlord of the Alpha."

"Oh, yes; I sent him a couple of dozen."

"Fine birds they were, too. Now where did you get them from?"

To my surprise the question provoked a burst of anger from the salesman.

"Now, then, mister," said he, with his head cocked and his arms akimbo, "what are you driving at? Let's have it straight, now."

"It is straight enough. I should like to know who sold you the geese which you supplied to the Alpha."

"Well then, I shan't tell you. So now!"

"Oh, it is a matter of no importance; but I don't know why you should be so warm over such a trifle."

"Warm! You'd be as warm, maybe, if you were as pestered as I am. When I pay good money for a good article there should be an end of the business; but it's 'Where are the geese?' and 'Who did you sell the geese to?' and 'What will you take for the geese?' One would think they were the only geese in the world, to hear the fuss that is made over them."

"Well, I have no connection with any other people who have been making inquiries," said Holmes carelessly. "If you won't tell us the bet is off, that is all. But I'm always ready to back my opinion on a matter of fowls, and I have a fiver on it that the bird I ate is country bred."

"Well, then, you've lost your fiver, for it's town bred," snapped the salesman.

"It's nothing of the kind."

"I say it is."

"I don't believe it."

"D'you think you know more about fowls than I, who have handled them ever since I was a nipper? I tell you, all those birds that went to the Alpha were town bred."

"You'll never persuade me to believe that."

"Will you bet, then?"

"It's merely taking your money, for I know that I am right. But I'll have a sovereign on with you, just to teach you not to be obstinate."

The salesman chuckled grimly. "Bring me the books, Bill," said he.

The small boy brought round a small thin volume and a great greasy-backed one, laying them out together beneath the hanging lamp.

"Now then, Mr. Cocksure," said the salesman, "I thought that I was out of geese, but before I finish you'll find that there is still one left in my shop. You see this little book?"

"Well?"

"That's the list of the folk from whom I buy. D'you see? Well, then, here on this page are the country folk, and the numbers after their names are where their accounts are in the big ledger. Now, then! You see this other page in red ink? Well, that is a list of my town suppliers. Now, look at that third name. Just read it out to me."

"Mrs. Oakshott, 117, Brixton Road—249," read Holmes.

"Quite so. Now turn that up in the ledger."

Holmes turned to the page indicated. "Here you are, 'Mrs. Oakshott, 117, Brixton Road, egg and poultry supplier.' "

"Now, then, what's the last entry?"

" 'December 22nd. Twenty-four geese at 7 shillings and 6 pence.' "

"Quite so. There you are. And underneath?"

" 'Sold to Mr. Windigate of the Alpha, at 12 shillings.' "

"What have you to say now?"

Sherlock Holmes looked deeply chagrined. He drew a sovereign from his pocket and threw it down upon the slab, turning away with the air of a man whose disgust is too deep for words. A few yards off he stopped under a lamp-post and laughed in the hearty, noiseless fashion which was peculiar to him.

"When you see a man with whiskers of that cut and the 'Pink 'un' protruding out of his pocket, you can always draw him by a bet," said he. "I daresay that if I had put 100 pounds down in front of him, that man would not have given me such complete information as was drawn from him by the idea that he was doing me on a wager. Well, Watson, we are, I fancy, nearing the end of our quest, and the only point which remains to be determined is whether we should go on to this Mrs. Oakshott tonight, or whether we should reserve it for tomorrow. It is clear from what that surly fellow said that there are others besides ourselves who are anxious about the matter, and I should—"

His remarks were suddenly cut short by a loud hubbub which broke out from the stall which we had just left. Turning round we saw a little rat-faced fellow standing in the centre of the circle of yellow light which was thrown by the swinging lamp, while Breckinridge, the salesman, framed in the door of his stall, was shaking his fists fiercely at the cringing figure.

"I've had enough of you and your geese," he shouted. "I wish you were all at the devil together. If you come pestering me any more with your silly talk I'll set the dog at you. You bring Mrs. Oakshott here and I'll answer her, but what have you to do with it? Did I buy the geese off you?"

"No; but one of them was mine all the same," whined the little man.

"Well, then, ask Mrs. Oakshott for it."

"She told me to ask you."

"Well, you can ask the King of Proosia, for all I care. I've had enough of it. Get out of this!" He rushed fiercely forward, and the inquirer flitted away into the darkness.

"Ha! This may save us a visit to Brixton Road," whispered Holmes. "Come with me, and we will see what is to be made of this fellow." Striding through the scattered knots of people who lounged round the flaring stalls, my companion speedily overtook the little man and touched him upon the shoulder. He sprang round, and I could see in the gas-light that every vestige of colour had been driven from his face.

"Who are you, then? What do you want?" he asked in a quavering voice.

"You will excuse me," said Holmes blandly, "but I could not help overhearing the questions which you put to the salesman just now. I think that I could be of assistance to you."

"You? Who are you? How could you know anything of the matter?"

"My name is Sherlock Holmes. It is my business to know what other people don't know."

"But you can know nothing of this?"

"Excuse me, I know everything of it. You are endeavouring to trace some geese which were sold by Mrs. Oakshott, of Brixton Road, to a salesman named Breckinridge, by him in turn to Mr. Windigate, of the Alpha, and by him to his club, of which Mr. Henry Baker is a member."

"Oh, sir, you are the very man whom I have longed to meet," cried the little fellow with outstretched hands and quivering fingers. "I can hardly explain to you how interested I am in this matter."

Sherlock Holmes hailed a four-wheeler which was passing. "In that case we had better discuss it in a cosy room rather than in this windswept marketplace," said he. "But pray tell me, before we go farther, who it is that I have the pleasure of assisting."

The man hesitated for an instant. "My name is John Robinson," he answered with a sidelong glance.

"No, no; the real name," said Holmes sweetly. "It is always awkward doing business with an *alias*."

A flush sprang to the white cheeks of the stranger. "Well then," said he, "my real name is James Ryder."

"Precisely so. Head attendant at the Hotel Cosmopolitan. Pray step into the cab, and I shall soon be able to tell you everything which you would wish to know."

The little man stood glancing from one to the other of us with half-frightened, half-hopeful eyes, as one who is not sure whether he is on the verge of a windfall or of a catastrophe. Then he stepped into the cab, and in half an hour we were back in the sitting-room at Baker Street. Nothing had been said during our drive, but the high, thin breathing of our new companion, and the claspings and unclaspings of his hands, spoke of the nervous tension within him.

"Here we are!" said Holmes cheerily as we filed into the room. "The fire looks very seasonable in this weather. You look cold, Mr. Ryder. Pray take the basket-chair. I will just put on my slippers before we settle this little matter of yours. Now, then! You want to know what became of those geese?"

"Yes, sir."

"Or rather, I fancy, of that goose. It was one bird, I imagine in which you were interested—white, with a black bar across the tail."

Ryder quivered with emotion. "Oh, sir," he cried, "can you tell me where it went to?"

"It came here."

"Here?"

"Yes, and a most remarkable bird it proved. I don't wonder that you should take an interest in it. It laid an egg after it was dead—the bonniest, brightest little blue egg that ever was seen. I have it here in my museum."

Our visitor staggered to his feet and clutched the mantelpiece with his right hand. Holmes unlocked his strong-box and held up the blue carbuncle, which shone out like a star, with a cold, brilliant, many-pointed radiance. Ryder stood glaring with a drawn face, uncertain whether to claim or to disown it.

"The game's up, Ryder," said Holmes quietly. "Hold up, man, or you'll be into the fire! Give him an arm back into his chair, Watson. He's not got blood enough to go in for felony with impunity. Give him a dash of brandy. So! Now he looks a little more human. What a shrimp it is, to be sure!"

For a moment he had staggered and nearly fallen, but the brandy brought a tinge of colour into his cheeks, and he sat staring with frightened eyes at his accuser.

"I have almost every link in my hands, and all the proofs which I could possibly need, so there is little which you need tell me. Still, that little may as well be cleared up to make the case complete. You had heard, Ryder, of this blue stone of the Countess of Morcar's?"

"It was Catherine Cusack who told me of it," said he in a crackling voice.

"I see—her ladyship's waiting-maid. Well, the temptation of sudden wealth so easily acquired was too much for you, as it has been for better men before you; but you were not very scrupulous in the means you used. It seems to me, Ryder, that there is the making of a very pretty villain in you. You knew that this man Horner, the plumber, had been concerned in some such matter before, and that suspicion would rest the more readily upon him. What did you do, then? You made some small job in my lady's room—you and your confederate Cusack—and you managed that he should be the man sent for. Then, when he had left, you rifled the jewel-case, raised the alarm, and had this unfortunate man arrested. You then—"

Ryder threw himself down suddenly upon the rug and clutched at my companion's knees. "For God's sake, have mercy!" he shrieked. "Think of my father! Of my mother! It would break their hearts. I never went wrong before! I never will again. I swear it. I'll swear it on a Bible. Oh, don't bring it into court! For Christ's sake, don't!"

"Get back into your chair!" said Holmes sternly. "It is very well to cringe and crawl now, but you thought little enough of this poor Horner in the dock for a crime of which he knew nothing."

"I will fly, Mr. Holmes. I will leave the country, sir. Then the charge against him will break down."

"Hum! We will talk about that. And now let us hear a true account of the next act. How came the stone into the goose, and how came the goose into the open market? Tell us the truth, for there lies your only hope of safety."

Ryder passed his tongue over his parched lips. "I will tell you it just as it happened, sir," said he. "When Horner had been arrested, it seemed to me that it would be best for me to get away with the stone at once, for I did not know at what moment the police might not take it into their heads to search me and my room. There was no place about the hotel where it would be safe. I went out, as if on some commission, and I made for my sister's house. She had married a man named Oakshott, and lived in Brixton Road, where she fattened fowls for the market. All the way there every man I met seemed to me to be a policeman or a detective; and, for all that it was a cold night, the sweat was pouring down my face before I came to the Brixton Road. My sister asked me what was the matter, and why I was so pale; but I told her that I had been upset by the jewel robbery at the hotel. Then I went into the back yard and smoked a pipe and wondered what it would be best to do. "I had a friend once called Maudsley, who went to the bad, and has just been serving his time in Pentonville. One day he had met me, and fell into talk about the ways of thieves, and how they could get rid of what they stole. I knew that he would be true to me, for I knew one or two things about him; so I made up my mind to go right on to Kilburn, where he lived, and take him into my confidence. He would show me how to turn the stone into money. But how to get to him in safety? I thought of the agonies I had gone through in coming from the hotel. I might at any moment be seized and searched, and there would be the stone in my waistcoat pocket. I was leaning against the wall at the time and looking at the geese which were waddling about round my feet, and suddenly an idea came into my head which showed me how I could beat the best detective that ever lived.

"My sister had told me some weeks before that I might have the pick of her geese for a Christmas present, and I knew that she was always as good as her word. I would take my goose now, and in it I would carry my stone to Kilburn. There was a little shed in the yard, and behind this I drove one of the birds—a fine big one, white, with a barred tail.

I caught it, and prying its bill open, I thrust the stone down its throat as far as my finger could reach. The bird gave a gulp, and I felt the stone pass along its gullet and down into its crop. But the creature flapped and struggled, and out came my sister to know what was the matter. As I turned to speak to her the brute broke loose and fluttered off among the others.

" 'Whatever were you doing with that bird, Jem?' says she.

" 'Well,' said I, 'you said you'd give me one for Christmas, and I was feeling which was the fattest.'

" 'Oh,' says she, 'we've set yours aside for you—Jem's bird, we call it. It's the big white one over yonder. There's twenty-six of them, which makes one for you, and one for us, and two dozen for the market.'

" 'Thank you, Maggie,' says I; 'but if it is all the same to you, I'd rather have that one I was handling just now.'

" 'The other is a good three pound heavier,' said she, 'and we fattened it expressly for you.'

" 'Never mind. I'll have the other, and I'll take it now,' said I.

" 'Oh, just as you like,' said she, a little huffed. 'Which is it you want, then?'

" 'That white one with the barred tail, right in the middle of the flock.'

" 'Oh, very well. Kill it and take it with you.'

"Well, I did what she said, Mr. Holmes, and I carried the bird all the way to Kilburn. I told my pal what I had done, for he was a man that it was easy to tell a thing like that to. He laughed until he choked, and we got a knife and opened the goose. My heart turned to water, for there was no sign of the stone, and I knew that some terrible mistake had occurred. I left the bird, rushed back to my sister's, and hurried into the back yard. There was not a bird to be seen there.

" 'Where are they all, Maggie?' I cried.

" 'Gone to the dealer's, Jem.'

" 'Which dealer's?'

" 'Breckinridge, of Covent Garden.'

" 'But was there another with a barred tail?' I asked, 'the same as the one I chose?'

" 'Yes, Jem; there were two barred-tailed ones, and I could never tell them apart.'

"Well, then, of course I saw it all, and I ran off as hard as my feet would carry me to this man Breckinridge; but he had sold the lot at once, and not one word would he tell me as to where they had gone. You heard him yourselves tonight. Well, he has always answered me like that. My sister thinks that I am going mad. Sometimes I think that I am myself. And now—and now I am myself a branded thief, without ever having touched the wealth for which I sold my character. God help me! God help me!" He burst into convulsive sobbing, with his face buried in his hands.

There was a long silence, broken only by his heavy breathing and by the measured tapping of Sherlock Holmes' fingertips upon the edge of the table. Then my friend rose and threw open the door.

"Get out!" said he.

"What, sir! Oh, Heaven bless you!"

"No more words. Get out!"

And no more words were needed. There was a rush, a clatter upon the stairs, the bang of a door, and the crisp rattle of running footfalls from the street.

"After all, Watson," said Holmes, reaching up his hand for his clay pipe, "I am not retained by the police to supply their deficiencies. If Horner were in danger it would be another thing; but this fellow will not appear against him, and the case must collapse. I suppose that I am committing a felony, but it is just possible that I am saving a soul. This fellow will not go wrong again; he is too terribly frightened. Send him to gaol now, and you make him a gaol-bird for life. Besides, it is the season of forgiveness. Chance has put in our way a most singular and whimsical problem, and its solution is its own reward. If you will have the goodness to touch the bell, Doctor, we will begin another investigation, in which, also a bird will be the chief feature."

THE SPECKLED BAND

On glancing over my notes of the seventy odd cases in which I have during the last eight years studied the methods of my friend Sherlock Holmes, I find many tragic, some comic, a large number merely strange, but none commonplace; for, working as he did rather for the love of his art than for the acquirement of wealth, he refused to associate himself with any investigation which did not tend towards the unusual, and even the fantastic. Of all these varied cases, however, I cannot recall any which presented more singular features than that which was associated with the well-known Surrey family of the Roylotts of Stoke Moran. The events in question occurred in the early days of my association with Holmes, when we were sharing rooms as bachelors in Baker Street. It is possible that I might have placed them upon record before, but a promise of secrecy was made at the time, from which I have only been freed during the last month by the untimely death of the lady to whom the pledge was given. It is perhaps as well that the facts should now come to light, for I have reasons to know that there are widespread rumours as to the death of Dr. Grimesby Roylott which tend to make the matter even more terrible than the truth.

It was early in April in the year '83 that I woke one morning to find Sherlock Holmes standing, fully dressed, by the side of my bed. He was a late riser, as a rule, and as the clock on the mantelpiece showed me that it was only a quarter-past seven, I blinked up at him in some surprise, and perhaps just a little resentment, for I was myself regular in my habits.

"Very sorry to knock you up, Watson," said he, "but it's the common lot this morning. Mrs. Hudson has been knocked up, she retorted upon me, and I on you."

"What is it, then—a fire?"

"No; a client. It seems that a young lady has arrived in a considerable state of excitement, who insists upon seeing me. She is waiting now in the sitting-room. Now, when young ladies wander about the metropolis at this hour of the morning, and knock sleepy people up out of their beds, I presume that it is something very pressing which they have to communicate. Should it prove to be an interesting case, you would, I am sure, wish to follow it from the outset. I thought, at any rate, that I should call you and give you the chance."

"My dear fellow, I would not miss it for anything."

I had no keener pleasure than in following Holmes in his professional investigations, and in admiring the rapid deductions, as swift as intuitions, and yet always founded on a logical basis with which he unravelled the problems which were submitted to him. I rapidly threw on my clothes and was ready in a few minutes to accompany my friend down to the sitting-room. A lady dressed in black and heavily veiled, who had been sitting in the window, rose as we entered.

"Good-morning, madam," said Holmes cheerily. "My name is Sherlock Holmes. This is my intimate friend and associate, Dr. Watson, before whom you can speak as freely as before myself. Ha! I am glad to see that Mrs. Hudson has had the good sense to light the fire. Pray draw up to it, and I shall order you a cup of hot coffee, for I observe that you are shivering."

"It is not cold which makes me shiver," said the woman in a low voice, changing her seat as requested.

"What, then?"

"It is fear, Mr. Holmes. It is terror." She raised her veil as she spoke, and we could see that she was indeed in a pitiable state of agitation, her face all drawn and grey, with restless frightened eyes, like those of some hunted animal. Her features and figure were those of a woman of thirty, but her hair was shot with premature grey, and her expression was weary and haggard. Sherlock Holmes ran her over with one of his quick, all-comprehensive glances.

"You must not fear," said he soothingly, bending forward and patting her forearm. "We shall soon set matters right, I have no doubt. You have come in by train this morning, I see."

"You know me, then?"

"No, but I observe the second half of a return ticket in the palm of your left glove. You must have started early, and yet you had a good drive in a dog-cart, along heavy roads, before you reached the station."

The lady gave a violent start and stared in bewilderment at my companion.

"There is no mystery, my dear madam," said he, smiling. "The left arm of your jacket is spattered with mud in no less than seven places. The marks are perfectly fresh. There is no vehicle save a dogcart which

throws up mud in that way, and then only when you sit on the left-hand side of the driver."

"Whatever your reasons may be, you are perfectly correct," said she. "I started from home before six, reached Leatherhead at twenty past, and came in by the first train to Waterloo. Sir, I can stand this strain no longer; I shall go mad if it continues. I have no one to turn to—none, save only one, who cares for me, and he, poor fellow, can be of little aid. I have heard of you, Mr. Holmes; I have heard of you from Mrs. Farintosh, whom you helped in the hour of her sore need. It was from her that I had your address. Oh, sir, do you not think that you could help me, too, and at least throw a little light through the dense darkness which surrounds me? At present it is out of my power to reward you for your services, but in a month or six weeks I shall be married, with the control of my own income, and then at least you shall not find me ungrateful."

Holmes turned to his desk and, unlocking it, drew out a small case-book, which he consulted.

"Farintosh," said he. "Ah yes, I recall the case; it was concerned with an opal tiara. I think it was before your time, Watson. I can only say, madam, that I shall be happy to devote the same care to your case as I did to that of your friend. As to reward, my profession is its own reward; but you are at liberty to defray whatever expenses I may be put to, at the time which suits you best. And now I beg that you will lay before us everything that may help us in forming an opinion upon the matter."

"Alas!" replied our visitor, "The very horror of my situation lies in the fact that my fears are so vague, and my suspicions depend so entirely upon small points, which might seem trivial to another, that even he to whom of all others I have a right to look for help and advice looks upon all that I tell him about it as the fancies of a nervous woman. He does not say so, but I can read it from his soothing answers and averted eyes. But I have heard, Mr. Holmes, that you can see deeply into the manifold wickedness of the human heart. You may advise me how to walk amid the dangers which encompass me."

"I am all attention, madam."

"My name is Helen Stoner, and I am living with my stepfather, who is the last survivor of one of the oldest Saxon families in England, the Roylotts of Stoke Moran, on the western border of Surrey."

Holmes nodded his head. "The name is familiar to me," said he.

"The family was at one time among the richest in England, and the estates extended over the borders into Berkshire in the north, and Hampshire in the west. In the last century, however, four successive heirs were of a dissolute and wasteful disposition, and the family ruin was eventually completed by a gambler in the days of the Regency. Nothing was left save a few acres of ground, and the two-hundred-year-old house, which is itself crushed under a heavy mortgage. The last squire dragged out his existence there, living the horrible life of an aristocratic pauper; but his only son, my stepfather, seeing that he must adapt himself to the new conditions, obtained an advance from a relative, which enabled him to take a medical degree and went out to Calcutta, where, by his professional skill and his force of character, he established a large practice. In a fit of anger, however, caused by some robberies which had been perpetrated in the house, he beat his native butler to death and narrowly escaped a capital sentence. As it was, he suffered a long term of imprisonment and afterwards returned to England a morose and disappointed man.

"When Dr. Roylott was in India he married my mother, Mrs. Stoner, the young widow of Major-General Stoner, of the Bengal Artillery. My sister Julia and I were twins, and we were only two years old at the time of my mother's re-marriage. She had a considerable sum of money—not less than 1,000 pounds a year—and this she bequeathed to Dr. Roylott entirely while we resided with him, with a provision that a certain annual sum should be allowed to each of us in the event of our marriage. Shortly after our return to England my mother died—she was killed eight years ago in a railway accident near Crewe. Dr. Roylott then abandoned his attempts to establish himself in practice in London and took us to live with him in the old ancestral house at Stoke Moran. The money which my mother had left was enough for all our wants, and there seemed to be no obstacle to our happiness.

"But a terrible change came over our stepfather about this time. Instead of making friends and exchanging visits with our neighbours, who had at first been overjoyed to see a Roylott of Stoke Moran back in the old family seat, he shut himself up in his house and seldom came out save to indulge in ferocious quarrels with whoever might cross his path. Violence of temper approaching to mania has been hereditary in the men of the family, and in my stepfather's case it had, I believe, been intensified by his long residence in the tropics. A series of disgraceful

brawls took place, two of which ended in the police-court, until at last he became the terror of the village, and the folks would fly at his approach, for he is a man of immense strength, and absolutely uncontrollable in his anger.

"Last week he hurled the local blacksmith over a parapet into a stream, and it was only by paying over all the money which I could gather together that I was able to avert another public exposure. He had no friends at all save the wandering gipsies, and he would give these vagabonds leave to encamp upon the few acres of bramble-covered land which represent the family estate, and would accept in return the hospitality of their tents, wandering away with them sometimes for weeks on end. He has a passion also for Indian animals, which are sent over to him by a correspondent, and he has at this moment a cheetah and a baboon, which wander freely over his grounds and are feared by the villagers almost as much as their master.

"You can imagine from what I say that my poor sister Julia and I had no great pleasure in our lives. No servant would stay with us, and for a long time we did all the work of the house. She was but thirty at the time of her death, and yet her hair had already begun to whiten, even as mine has."

"Your sister is dead, then?"

"She died just two years ago, and it is of her death that I wish to speak to you. You can understand that, living the life which I have described, we were little likely to see anyone of our own age and position. We had, however, an aunt, my mother's maiden sister, Miss Honoria Westphail, who lives near Harrow, and we were occasionally allowed to pay short visits at this lady's house. Julia went there at Christmas two years ago, and met there a half-pay major of marines, to whom she became engaged. My stepfather learned of the engagement when my sister returned and offered no objection to the marriage; but within a fortnight of the day which had been fixed for the wedding, the terrible event occurred which has deprived me of my only companion."

Sherlock Holmes had been leaning back in his chair with his eyes closed and his head sunk in a cushion, but he half opened his lids now and glanced across at his visitor.

"Pray be precise as to details," said he.

"It is easy for me to be so, for every event of that dreadful time is seared into my memory. The manor-house is, as I have already said, very old, and only one wing is now inhabited. The bedrooms in this wing are on the ground floor, the sitting-rooms being in the central block of the buildings. Of these bedrooms the first is Dr. Roylott's, the second my sister's, and the third my own. There is no communication between them, but they all open out into the same corridor. Do I make myself plain?"

"Perfectly so."

"The windows of the three rooms open out upon the lawn. That fatal night Dr. Roylott had gone to his room early, though we knew that he had not retired to rest, for my sister was troubled by the smell of the strong Indian cigars which it was his custom to smoke. She left her room, therefore, and came into mine, where she sat for some time, chatting about her approaching wedding. At eleven o'clock she rose to leave me, but she paused at the door and looked back.

" 'Tell me, Helen,' said she, 'have you ever heard anyone whistle in the dead of the night?'

" 'Never,' said I.

" 'I suppose that you could not possibly whistle, yourself, in your sleep?'

" 'Certainly not. But why?'

" 'Because during the last few nights I have always, about three in the morning, heard a low, clear whistle. I am a light sleeper, and it has awakened me. I cannot tell where it came from—perhaps from the next room, perhaps from the lawn. I thought that I would just ask you whether you had heard it.'

" 'No, I have not. It must be those wretched gipsies in the plantation.'

" 'Very likely. And yet if it were on the lawn, I wonder that you did not hear it also.'

" 'Ah, but I sleep more heavily than you.'

" 'Well, it is of no great consequence, at any rate.' She smiled back at me, closed my door, and a few moments later I heard her key turn in the lock."

"Indeed," said Holmes. "Was it your custom always to lock yourselves in at night?"

"Always."

"And why?"

"I think that I mentioned to you that the doctor kept a cheetah and a baboon. We had no feeling of security unless our doors were locked."

"Quite so. Pray proceed with your statement."

"I could not sleep that night. A vague feeling of impending misfortune impressed me. My sister and I, you will recollect, were twins, and you know how subtle are the links which bind two souls which are so closely allied. It was a wild night. The wind was howling outside, and the rain was beating and splashing against the windows. Suddenly, amid all the hubbub of the gale, there burst forth the wild scream of a terrified woman. I knew that it was my sister's voice. I sprang from my bed, wrapped a shawl round me, and rushed into the corridor. As I opened my door I seemed to hear a low whistle, such as my sister described, and a few moments later a clanging sound, as if a mass of metal had fallen. As I ran down the passage, my sister's door was unlocked, and revolved slowly upon its hinges. I stared at it horror-stricken, not knowing what was about to issue from it. By the light of the corridor-lamp I saw my sister appear at the opening, her face blanched with terror, her hands groping for help, her whole figure swaying to and fro like that of a drunkard. I ran to her and threw my arms round her, but at that moment her knees seemed to give way and she fell to the ground. She writhed as one who is in terrible pain, and her limbs were dreadfully convulsed. At first I thought that she had not recognised me, but as I bent over her she suddenly shrieked out in a voice which I shall never forget, 'Oh, my God! Helen! It was the band! The speckled band!' There was something else which she would fain have said, and she stabbed with her finger into the air in the direction of the doctor's room, but a fresh convulsion seized her and choked her words. I rushed out, calling loudly for my stepfather, and I met him hastening from his room in his dressing-gown. When he reached my sister's side she was unconscious, and though he poured brandy down her throat and sent for medical aid from the village, all efforts were in vain, for she slowly sank and died without having recovered her consciousness. Such was the dreadful end of my beloved sister."

"One moment," said Holmes, "are you sure about this whistle and metallic sound? Could you swear to it?"

"That was what the county coroner asked me at the inquiry. It is my strong impression that I heard it, and yet, among the crash of the gale and the creaking of an old house, I may possibly have been deceived."

"Was your sister dressed?"

"No, she was in her night-dress. In her right hand was found the charred stump of a match, and in her left a match-box."

"Showing that she had struck a light and looked about her when the alarm took place. That is important. And what conclusions did the coroner come to?"

"He investigated the case with great care, for Dr. Roylott's conduct had long been notorious in the county, but he was unable to find any satisfactory cause of death. My evidence showed that the door had been fastened upon the inner side, and the windows were blocked by old-fashioned shutters with broad iron bars, which were secured every night. The walls were carefully sounded, and were shown to be quite solid all round, and the flooring was also thoroughly examined, with the same result. The chimney is wide, but is barred up by four large staples. It is certain, therefore, that my sister was quite alone when she met her end. Besides, there were no marks of any violence upon her."

"How about poison?"

"The doctors examined her for it, but without success."

"What do you think that this unfortunate lady died of, then?"

"It is my belief that she died of pure fear and nervous shock, though what it was that frightened her I cannot imagine."

"Were there gipsies in the plantation at the time?"

"Yes, there are nearly always some there."

"Ah, and what did you gather from this allusion to a band—a speckled band?"

"Sometimes I have thought that it was merely the wild talk of delirium, sometimes that it may have referred to some band of people, perhaps to these very gipsies in the plantation. I do not know whether the spotted handkerchiefs which so many of them wear over their heads might have suggested the strange adjective which she used."

Holmes shook his head like a man who is far from being satisfied.

"These are very deep waters," said he; "pray go on with your narrative."

"Two years have passed since then, and my life has been until lately lonelier than ever. A month ago, however, a dear friend, whom I have known for many years, has done me the honour to ask my hand in marriage. His name is Armitage—Percy Armitage—the second son of Mr. Armitage, of Crane Water, near Reading. My stepfather has offered no opposition to the match, and we are to be married in the course of the spring. Two days ago some repairs were started in the west wing of the building, and my bedroom wall has been pierced, so that I have had to move into the chamber in which my sister died, and to sleep in the very bed in which she slept. Imagine, then, my thrill of terror when last night, as I lay awake, thinking over her terrible fate, I suddenly heard in the silence of the night the low whistle which had been the herald of her own death. I sprang up and lit the lamp, but nothing was to be seen in the room. I was too shaken to go to bed again, however, so I dressed, and as soon as it was daylight I slipped down, got a dog-cart at the Crown Inn, which is opposite, and drove to Leatherhead, from whence I have come on this morning with the one object of seeing you and asking your advice."

"You have done wisely," said my friend. "But have you told me all?"

"Yes, all."

"Miss Roylott, you have not. You are screening your stepfather."

"Why, what do you mean?"

For answer Holmes pushed back the frill of black lace which fringed the hand that lay upon our visitor's knee. Five little livid spots, the marks of four fingers and a thumb, were printed upon the white wrist.

"You have been cruelly used," said Holmes.

The lady coloured deeply and covered over her injured wrist. "He is a hard man," she said, "and perhaps he hardly knows his own strength."

There was a long silence, during which Holmes leaned his chin upon his hands and stared into the crackling fire.

"This is a very deep business," he said at last. "There are a thousand details which I should desire to know before I decide upon our course of action. Yet we have not a moment to lose. If we were to come to Stoke Moran today, would it be possible for us to see over these rooms without the knowledge of your stepfather?"

"As it happens, he spoke of coming into town today upon some most important business. It is probable that he will be away all day, and that there would be nothing to disturb you. We have a housekeeper now, but she is old and foolish, and I could easily get her out of the way."

"Excellent. You are not averse to this trip, Watson?"

"By no means."

"Then we shall both come. What are you going to do yourself?"

"I have one or two things which I would wish to do now that I am in town. But I shall return by the twelve o'clock train, so as to be there in time for your coming."

"And you may expect us early in the afternoon. I have myself some small business matters to attend to. Will you not wait and breakfast?"

"No, I must go. My heart is lightened already since I have confided my trouble to you. I shall look forward to seeing you again this afternoon." She dropped her thick black veil over her face and glided from the room.

"And what do you think of it all, Watson?" asked Sherlock Holmes, leaning back in his chair.

"It seems to me to be a most dark and sinister business."

"Dark enough and sinister enough."

"Yet if the lady is correct in saying that the flooring and walls are sound, and that the door, window, and chimney are impassable, then her sister must have been undoubtedly alone when she met her mysterious end."

"What becomes, then, of these nocturnal whistles, and what of the very peculiar words of the dying woman?"

"I cannot think."

"When you combine the ideas of whistles at night, the presence of a band of gipsies who are on intimate terms with this old doctor, the fact that we have every reason to believe that the doctor has an interest in preventing his stepdaughter's marriage, the dying allusion to a band, and, finally, the fact that Miss Helen Stoner heard a metallic clang, which might have been caused by one of those metal bars that secured the shutters falling back into its place, I think that there is good ground to think that the mystery may be cleared along those lines."

"But what, then, did the gipsies do?"

"I cannot imagine."

"I see many objections to any such theory."

"And so do I. It is precisely for that reason that we are going to Stoke Moran this day. I want to see whether the objections are fatal, or if they may be explained away. But what in the name of the devil!"

The ejaculation had been drawn from my companion by the fact that our door had been suddenly dashed open, and that a huge man had framed himself in the aperture. His costume was a peculiar mixture of the professional and of the agricultural, having a black top-hat, a long frock-coat, and a pair of high gaiters, with a hunting-crop swinging

in his hand. So tall was he that his hat actually brushed the cross bar of the doorway, and his breadth seemed to span it across from side to side. A large face, seared with a thousand wrinkles, burned yellow with the sun, and marked with every evil passion, was turned from one to the other of us, while his deep-set, bile-shot eyes, and his high, thin, fleshless nose, gave him somewhat the resemblance to a fierce old bird of prey.

"Which of you is Holmes?" asked this apparition.

"My name, sir; but you have the advantage of me," said my companion quietly.

"I am Dr. Grimesby Roylott, of Stoke Moran."

"Indeed, Doctor," said Holmes blandly. "Pray take a seat."

"I will do nothing of the kind. My stepdaughter has been here. I have traced her. What has she been saying to you?"

"It is a little cold for the time of the year," said Holmes.

"What has she been saying to you?" screamed the old man furiously.

"But I have heard that the crocuses promise well," continued my companion imperturbably.

"Ha! You put me off, do you?" said our new visitor, taking a step forward and shaking his hunting-crop. "I know you, you scoundrel! I have heard of you before. You are Holmes, the meddler."

My friend smiled.

"Holmes, the busybody!"

His smile broadened.

"Holmes, the Scotland Yard Jack-in-office!"

Holmes chuckled heartily. "Your conversation is most entertaining," said he. "When you go out close the door, for there is a decided draught."

"I will go when I have said my say. Don't you dare to meddle with my affairs. I know that Miss Stoner has been here. I traced her! I am a dangerous man to fall foul of! See here." He stepped swiftly forward, seized the poker, and bent it into a curve with his huge brown hands.

"See that you keep yourself out of my grip," he snarled, and hurling the twisted poker into the fireplace he strode out of the room.

"He seems a very amiable person," said Holmes, laughing. "I am not quite so bulky, but if he had remained I might have shown him that my grip was not much more feeble than his own." As he spoke he picked up the steel poker and, with a sudden effort, straightened it out again.

"Fancy his having the insolence to confound me with the official detective force! This incident gives zest to our investigation, however, and I only trust that our little friend will not suffer from her imprudence in allowing this brute to trace her. And now, Watson, we shall order breakfast, and afterwards I shall walk down to Doctors' Commons, where I hope to get some data which may help us in this matter."

It was nearly one o'clock when Sherlock Holmes returned from his excursion. He held in his hand a sheet of blue paper, scrawled over with notes and figures.

"I have seen the will of the deceased wife," said he. "To determine its exact meaning I have been obliged to work out the present prices of the investments with which it is concerned. The total income, which at the time of the wife's death was little short of 1,100 pounds, is now, through the fall in agricultural prices, not more than 750 pounds. Each daughter can claim an income of 250 pounds, in case of marriage. It is evident, therefore, that if both girls had married, this beauty would have had a mere pittance, while even one of them would cripple him to a very serious extent. My morning's work has not been wasted, since it has proved that he has the very strongest motives for standing in the way of anything of the sort. And now, Watson, this is too serious for dawdling, especially as the old man is aware that we are interesting ourselves in his affairs; so if you are ready, we shall call a cab and drive to Waterloo. I should be very much obliged if you would slip your revolver into your pocket. An Eley's No. 2 is an excellent argument with gentlemen who can twist steel pokers into knots. That and a toothbrush are, I think, all that we need."

At Waterloo we were fortunate in catching a train for Leatherhead, where we hired a trap at the station inn and drove for four or five miles through the lovely Surrey lanes. It was a perfect day, with a bright sun and a few fleecy clouds in the heavens. The trees and wayside hedges were just throwing out their first green shoots, and the air was full of the pleasant smell of the moist earth. To me at least there was a strange contrast between the sweet promise of the spring and this sinister quest upon which we were engaged. My companion sat in the front of the trap, his arms folded, his hat pulled down over his eyes, and his chin sunk upon his breast, buried in the deepest thought. Suddenly, however, he started, tapped me on the shoulder, and pointed over the meadows.

"Look there!" said he.

A heavily timbered park stretched up in a gentle slope, thickening into a grove at the highest point. From amid the branches there jutted out the grey gables and high roof-tree of a very old mansion.

"Stoke Moran?" said he.

"Yes, sir, that be the house of Dr. Grimesby Roylott," remarked the driver.

"There is some building going on there," said Holmes; "that is where we are going."

"There's the village," said the driver, pointing to a cluster of roofs some distance to the left; "but if you want to get to the house, you'll find it shorter to get over this stile, and so by the foot-path over the fields. There it is, where the lady is walking."

"And the lady, I fancy, is Miss Stoner," observed Holmes, shading his eyes. "Yes, I think we had better do as you suggest."

We got off, paid our fare, and the trap rattled back on its way to Leatherhead.

"I thought it as well," said Holmes as we climbed the stile, "that this fellow should think we had come here as architects, or on some definite business. It may stop his gossip. Good-afternoon, Miss Stoner. You see that we have been as good as our word."

Our client of the morning had hurried forward to meet us with a face which spoke her joy. "I have been waiting so eagerly for you," she cried, shaking hands with us warmly. "All has turned out splendidly. Dr. Roylott has gone to town, and it is unlikely that he will be back before evening."

"We have had the pleasure of making the doctor's acquaintance," said Holmes, and in a few words he sketched out what had occurred. Miss Stoner turned white to the lips as she listened.

"Good heavens!" she cried, "He has followed me, then."

"So it appears."

"He is so cunning that I never know when I am safe from him. What will he say when he returns?"

"He must guard himself, for he may find that there is someone more cunning than himself upon his track. You must lock yourself up from him tonight. If he is violent, we shall take you away to your aunt's at Harrow. Now, we must make the best use of our time, so kindly take us at once to the rooms which we are to examine."

The building was of grey, lichen-blotched stone, with a high central portion and two curving wings, like the claws of a crab, thrown out on each side. In one of these wings the windows were broken and blocked with wooden boards, while the roof was partly caved in, a picture of ruin. The central portion was in little better repair, but the right-hand block was comparatively modern, and the blinds in the windows, with the blue smoke curling up from the chimneys, showed that this was where the family resided. Some scaffolding had been erected against the end wall, and the stone-work had been broken into, but there were no signs of any workmen at the moment of our visit. Holmes walked slowly up and down the ill-trimmed lawn and examined with deep attention the outsides of the windows.

"This, I take it, belongs to the room in which you used to sleep, the centre one to your sister's, and the one next to the main building to Dr. Roylott's chamber?"

"Exactly so. But I am now sleeping in the middle one."

"Pending the alterations, as I understand. By the way, there does not seem to be any very pressing need for repairs at that end wall."

"There were none. I believe that it was an excuse to move me from my room."

"Ah! That is suggestive. Now, on the other side of this narrow wing runs the corridor from which these three rooms open. There are windows in it, of course?"

"Yes, but very small ones. Too narrow for anyone to pass through."

"As you both locked your doors at night, your rooms were unapproachable from that side. Now, would you have the kindness to go into your room and bar your shutters?"

Miss Stoner did so, and Holmes, after a careful examination through the open window, endeavoured in every way to force the shutter open, but without success. There was no slit through which a knife could be passed to raise the bar. Then with his lens he tested the hinges, but they were of solid iron, built firmly into the massive masonry. "Hum!" said he, scratching his chin in some perplexity, "my theory certainly presents some difficulties. No one could pass these shutters if they were bolted. Well, we shall see if the inside throws any light upon the matter."

A small side door led into the whitewashed corridor from which the three bedrooms opened. Holmes refused to examine the third chamber, so we passed at once to the second, that in which Miss Stoner was now sleeping, and in which her sister had met with her fate. It was a homely little room, with a low ceiling and a gaping fireplace, after the fashion of old country-houses. A brown chest of drawers stood in one corner, a narrow white-counterpaned bed in another, and a dressing-table on the left-hand side of the window. These articles, with two small wicker-work chairs, made up all the furniture in the room save for a square of Wilton carpet in the centre. The boards round and the panelling of the walls were of brown, worm-eaten oak, so old and discoloured that it may have dated from the original building of the house. Holmes drew one of the chairs into a corner and sat silent, while his eyes travelled round and round and up and down, taking in every detail of the apartment.

"Where does that bell communicate with?" he asked at last pointing to a thick bell-rope which hung down beside the bed, the tassel actually lying upon the pillow.

"It goes to the housekeeper's room."

"It looks newer than the other things?"

"Yes, it was only put there a couple of years ago."

"Your sister asked for it, I suppose?"

"No, I never heard of her using it. We always used to get what we wanted for ourselves."

"Indeed, it seemed unnecessary to put so nice a bell-pull there. You will excuse me for a few minutes while I satisfy myself as to this floor." He threw himself down upon his face with his lens in his hand and crawled swiftly backward and forward, examining minutely the cracks between the boards. Then he did the same with the woodwork with which the chamber was panelled. Finally he walked over to the bed and spent some time in staring at it and in running his eye up and down the wall. Finally he took the bell-rope in his hand and gave it a brisk tug.

"Why, it's a dummy," said he.

"Won't it ring?"

"No, it is not even attached to a wire. This is very interesting. You can see now that it is fastened to a hook just above where the little opening for the ventilator is."

"How very absurd! I never noticed that before."

"Very strange!" muttered Holmes, pulling at the rope. "There are one or two very singular points about this room. For example, what a fool a builder must be to open a ventilator into another room, when, with the same trouble, he might have communicated with the outside air!"

"That is also quite modern," said the lady.

"Done about the same time as the bell-rope?" remarked Holmes.

"Yes, there were several little changes carried out about that time."

"They seem to have been of a most interesting character—dummy bell-ropes, and ventilators which do not ventilate. With your permission, Miss Stoner, we shall now carry our researches into the inner apartment."

Dr. Grimesby Roylott's chamber was larger than that of his stepdaughter, but was as plainly furnished. A camp-bed, a small wooden shelf full of books, mostly of a technical character, an armchair beside the bed, a plain wooden chair against the wall, a round table, and a large iron safe were the principal things which met the eye. Holmes walked slowly round and examined each and all of them with the keenest interest.

"What's in here?" he asked, tapping the safe.

"My stepfather's business papers."

"Oh! You have seen inside, then?"

"Only once, some years ago. I remember that it was full of papers."

"There isn't a cat in it, for example?"

"No. What a strange idea!"

"Well, look at this!" He took up a small saucer of milk which stood on the top of it.

"No; we don't keep a cat. But there is a cheetah and a baboon."

"Ah, yes, of course! Well, a cheetah is just a big cat, and yet a saucer of milk does not go very far in satisfying its wants, I daresay. There is one point which I should wish to determine." He squatted down in front of the wooden chair and examined the seat of it with the greatest attention.

"Thank you. That is quite settled," said he, rising and putting his lens in his pocket. "Hullo! Here is something interesting!"

The object which had caught his eye was a small dog lash hung on one corner of the bed. The lash, however, was curled upon itself and tied so as to make a loop of whipcord.

"What do you make of that, Watson?"

"It's a common enough lash. But I don't know why it should be tied."

"That is not quite so common, is it? Ah, me! It's a wicked world, and when a clever man turns his brains to crime it is the worst of all. I think that I have seen enough now, Miss Stoner, and with your permission we shall walk out upon the lawn."

I had never seen my friend's face so grim or his brow so dark as it was when we turned from the scene of this investigation. We had walked several times up and down the lawn, neither Miss Stoner nor myself liking to break in upon his thoughts before he roused himself from his reverie.

"It is very essential, Miss Stoner," said he, "that you should absolutely follow my advice in every respect."

"I shall most certainly do so."

"The matter is too serious for any hesitation. Your life may depend upon your compliance."

"I assure you that I am in your hands."

"In the first place, both my friend and I must spend the night in your room."

Both Miss Stoner and I gazed at him in astonishment.

"Yes, it must be so. Let me explain. I believe that that is the village inn over there?"

"Yes, that is the Crown."

"Very good. Your windows would be visible from there?"

"Certainly."

"You must confine yourself to your room, on pretence of a headache, when your stepfather comes back. Then when you hear him retire for the night, you must open the shutters of your window, undo the hasp, put your lamp there as a signal to us, and then withdraw quietly with everything which you are likely to want into the room which you used to occupy. I have no doubt that, in spite of the repairs, you could manage there for one night."

"Oh, yes, easily."

"The rest you will leave in our hands."

"But what will you do?"

"We shall spend the night in your room, and we shall investigate the cause of this noise which has disturbed you."

"I believe, Mr. Holmes, that you have already made up your mind," said Miss Stoner, laying her hand upon my companion's sleeve.

"Perhaps I have."

"Then, for pity's sake, tell me what was the cause of my sister's death."

"I should prefer to have clearer proofs before I speak."

"You can at least tell me whether my own thought is correct, and if she died from some sudden fright."

"No, I do not think so. I think that there was probably some more tangible cause. And now, Miss Stoner, we must leave you for if Dr. Roylott returned and saw us our journey would be in vain. Good-bye, and be brave, for if you will do what I have told you, you may rest assured that we shall soon drive away the dangers that threaten you."

Sherlock Holmes and I had no difficulty in engaging a bedroom and sitting-room at the Crown Inn. They were on the upper floor, and from our window we could command a view of the avenue gate, and of the inhabited wing of Stoke Moran Manor House. At dusk we saw Dr. Grimesby Roylott drive past, his huge form looming up beside the little figure of the lad who drove him. The boy had some slight difficulty in undoing the heavy iron gates, and we heard the hoarse roar of the doctor's voice and saw the fury with which he shook his clinched fists at him. The trap drove on, and a few minutes later we saw a sudden light spring up among the trees as the lamp was lit in one of the sitting-rooms.

"Do you know, Watson," said Holmes as we sat together in the gathering darkness, "I have really some scruples as to taking you tonight. There is a distinct element of danger."

"Can I be of assistance?"

"Your presence might be invaluable."

"Then I shall certainly come."

"It is very kind of you."

"You speak of danger. You have evidently seen more in these rooms than was visible to me."

"No, but I fancy that I may have deduced a little more. I imagine that you saw all that I did."

"I saw nothing remarkable save the bell-rope, and what purpose that could answer I confess is more than I can imagine."

"You saw the ventilator, too?"

"Yes, but I do not think that it is such a very unusual thing to have a small opening between two rooms. It was so small that a rat could hardly pass through."

"I knew that we should find a ventilator before ever we came to Stoke Moran."

"My dear Holmes!"

"Oh, yes, I did. You remember in her statement she said that her sister could smell Dr. Roylott's cigar. Now, of course that suggested at once that there must be a communication between the two rooms. It could only be a small one, or it would have been remarked upon at the coroner's inquiry. I deduced a ventilator."

"But what harm can there be in that?"

"Well, there is at least a curious coincidence of dates. A ventilator is made, a cord is hung, and a lady who sleeps in the bed dies. Does not that strike you?"

"I cannot as yet see any connection."

"Did you observe anything very peculiar about that bed?"

"No."

"It was clamped to the floor. Did you ever see a bed fastened like that before?"

"I cannot say that I have."

"The lady could not move her bed. It must always be in the same relative position to the ventilator and to the rope—or so we may call it, since it was clearly never meant for a bell-pull."

"Holmes," I cried, "I seem to see dimly what you are hinting at. We are only just in time to prevent some subtle and horrible crime."

"Subtle enough and horrible enough. When a doctor does go wrong he is the first of criminals. He has nerve and he has knowledge. Palmer and Pritchard were among the heads of their profession. This man strikes even deeper, but I think, Watson, that we shall be able to strike deeper still. But we shall have horrors enough before the night is over; for goodness' sake let us have a quiet pipe and turn our minds for a few hours to something more cheerful."

About nine o'clock the light among the trees was extinguished, and all was dark in the direction of the Manor House. Two hours passed slowly away, and then, suddenly, just at the stroke of eleven, a single bright light shone out right in front of us.

"That is our signal," said Holmes, springing to his feet; "it comes from the middle window."

As we passed out he exchanged a few words with the landlord, explaining that we were going on a late visit to an acquaintance, and that it was possible that we might spend the night there. A moment later we were out on the dark road, a chill wind blowing in our faces, and one yellow light twinkling in front of us through the gloom to guide us on our sombre errand.

There was little difficulty in entering the grounds, for unrepaired breaches gaped in the old park wall. Making our way among the trees, we reached the lawn, crossed it, and were about to enter through the window when out from a clump of laurel bushes there darted what seemed to be a hideous and distorted child, who threw itself upon the grass with writhing limbs and then ran swiftly across the lawn into the darkness.

"My God!" I whispered; "Did you see it?"

Holmes was for the moment as startled as I. His hand closed like a vice upon my wrist in his agitation. Then he broke into a low laugh and put his lips to my ear.

"It is a nice household," he murmured. "That is the baboon."

I had forgotten the strange pets which the doctor affected. There was a cheetah, too; perhaps we might find it upon our shoulders at any moment. I confess that I felt easier in my mind when, after following Holmes' example and slipping off my shoes, I found myself inside the bedroom. My companion noiselessly closed the shutters, moved the lamp onto the table, and cast his eyes round the room. All was as we had seen it in the daytime. Then creeping up to me and making a trumpet of his hand, he whispered into my ear again so gently that it was all that I could do to distinguish the words:

"The least sound would be fatal to our plans."

I nodded to show that I had heard.

"We must sit without light. He would see it through the ventilator."

I nodded again.

"Do not go asleep; your very life may depend upon it. Have your pistol ready in case we should need it. I will sit on the side of the bed, and you in that chair."

I took out my revolver and laid it on the corner of the table.

Holmes had brought up a long thin cane, and this he placed upon the bed beside him. By it he laid the box of matches and the stump of a candle. Then he turned down the lamp, and we were left in darkness.

How shall I ever forget that dreadful vigil? I could not hear a sound, not even the drawing of a breath, and yet I knew that my companion sat open-eyed, within a few feet of me, in the same state of nervous tension in which I was myself. The shutters cut off the least ray of light, and we waited in absolute darkness.

From outside came the occasional cry of a night-bird, and once at our very window a long drawn catlike whine, which told us that the cheetah was indeed at liberty. Far away we could hear the deep tones of the parish clock, which boomed out every quarter of an hour. How long they seemed, those quarters! Twelve struck, and one and two and three, and still we sat waiting silently for whatever might befall.

Suddenly there was the momentary gleam of a light up in the direction of the ventilator, which vanished immediately, but was succeeded by a strong smell of burning oil and heated metal. Someone in the next room had lit a dark-lantern. I heard a gentle sound of movement, and then all was silent once more, though the smell grew stronger. For half an hour I sat with straining ears. Then suddenly another sound became audible—a very gentle, soothing sound, like that of a small jet of steam escaping continually from a kettle. The instant that we heard it, Holmes sprang from the bed, struck a match, and lashed furiously with his cane at the bell-pull.

"You see it, Watson?" he yelled. "You see it?"

But I saw nothing. At the moment when Holmes struck the light I heard a low, clear whistle, but the sudden glare flashing into my weary eyes made it impossible for me to tell what it was at which my friend lashed so savagely. I could, however, see that his face was deadly pale and filled with horror and loathing. He had ceased to strike and was gazing up at the ventilator when suddenly there broke from the silence of the night the most horrible cry to which I have ever listened. It swelled up louder and louder, a hoarse yell of pain and fear and anger all mingled in the one dreadful shriek. They say that away down in the village, and even in the distant parsonage, that cry raised the sleepers from their beds. It struck cold to our hearts, and I stood gazing at Holmes, and he at me, until the last echoes of it had died away into the silence from which it rose.

"What can it mean?" I gasped.

"It means that it is all over," Holmes answered. "And perhaps, after all, it is for the best. Take your pistol, and we will enter Dr. Roylott's room."

With a grave face he lit the lamp and led the way down the corridor. Twice he struck at the chamber door without any reply from within. Then he turned the handle and entered, I at his heels, with the cocked pistol in my hand.

It was a singular sight which met our eyes. On the table stood a dark-lantern with the shutter half open, throwing a brilliant beam of light upon the iron safe, the door of which was ajar. Beside this table, on the wooden chair, sat Dr. Grimesby Roylott clad in a long grey dressing-gown, his bare ankles protruding beneath, and his feet thrust into red heelless Turkish slippers. Across his lap lay the short stock with the long lash which we had noticed during the day. His chin was cocked upward and his eyes were fixed in a dreadful, rigid stare at the corner of the ceiling. Round his brow he had a peculiar yellow band, with brownish speckles, which seemed to be bound tightly round his head. As we entered he made neither sound nor motion.

"The band! the speckled band!" whispered Holmes.

I took a step forward. In an instant his strange headgear began to move, and there reared itself from among his hair the squat diamond-shaped head and puffed neck of a loathsome serpent.

"It is a swamp adder!" cried Holmes; "The deadliest snake in India. He has died within ten seconds of being bitten. Violence does, in truth, recoil upon the violent, and the schemer falls into the pit which he digs for another. Let us thrust this creature back into its den, and we can then remove Miss Stoner to some place of shelter and let the county police know what has happened."

As he spoke he drew the dog-whip swiftly from the dead man's lap, and throwing the noose round the reptile's neck he drew it from its horrid perch and, carrying it at arm's length, threw it into the iron safe, which he closed upon it.

Such are the true facts of the death of Dr. Grimesby Roylott, of Stoke Moran. It is not necessary that I should prolong a narrative which has already run to too great a length by telling how we broke the sad news to the terrified girl, how we conveyed her by the morning train to the care of her good aunt at Harrow, of how the slow process of official inquiry came to the conclusion that the doctor met his fate while indiscreetly playing with a dangerous pet. The little which I had yet to learn of the case was told me by Sherlock Holmes as we travelled back next day.

"I had," said he, "come to an entirely erroneous conclusion which shows, my dear Watson, how dangerous it always is to reason from insufficient data. The presence of the gipsies, and the use of the word 'band,' which was used by the poor girl, no doubt, to explain the appearance which she had caught a hurried glimpse of by the light of her match, were sufficient to put me upon an entirely wrong scent. I can only claim the merit that I instantly reconsidered my position when, however, it became clear to me that whatever danger threatened an occupant of the room could not come either from the window or the door. My attention was speedily drawn, as I have already remarked to you, to this ventilator, and to the bell-rope which hung down to the bed.

The discovery that this was a dummy, and that the bed was clamped to the floor, instantly gave rise to the suspicion that the rope was there as a bridge for something passing through the hole and coming to the bed. The idea of a snake instantly occurred to me, and when I coupled it with my knowledge that the doctor was furnished with a supply of creatures from India, I felt that I was probably on the right track. The idea of using a form of poison which could not possibly be discovered by any chemical test was just such a one as would occur to a clever and ruthless man who had had an Eastern training. The rapidity with which such a poison would take effect would also, from his point of view, be an advantage. It would be a sharp-eyed coroner, indeed, who could distinguish the two little dark punctures which would show where the poison fangs had done their work. Then I thought of the whistle. Of course he must recall the snake before the morning light revealed it to the victim. He had trained it, probably by the use of the milk which we saw, to return to him when summoned. He would put it through this ventilator at the hour that he thought best, with the certainty that it would crawl down the rope and land on the bed. It might or might not bite the occupant, perhaps she might escape every night for a week, but sooner or later she must fall a victim.

"I had come to these conclusions before ever I had entered his room. An inspection of his chair showed me that he had been in the habit of standing on it, which of course would be necessary in order that he should reach the ventilator. The sight of the safe, the saucer of milk, and the loop of whipcord were enough to finally dispel any doubts which may have remained. The metallic clang heard by Miss Stoner was obviously caused by her stepfather hastily closing the door of his safe upon its terrible occupant. Having once made up my mind, you know the steps which I took in order to put the matter to the proof. I heard the creature hiss as I have no doubt that you did also, and I instantly lit the light and attacked it."

"With the result of driving it through the ventilator."

"And also with the result of causing it to turn upon its master at the other side. Some of the blows of my cane came home and roused its snakish temper, so that it flew upon the first person it saw. In this way I am no doubt indirectly responsible for Dr. Grimesby Roylott's death, and I cannot say that it is likely to weigh very heavily upon my conscience."

THE ENGINEER'S THUMB

Of all the problems which have been submitted to my friend, Mr. Sherlock Holmes, for solution during the years of our intimacy, there were only two which I was the means of introducing to his notice—that of Mr. Hatherley's thumb, and that of Colonel Warburton's madness. Of these the latter may have afforded a finer field for an acute and original observer, but the other was so strange in its inception and so dramatic in its details that it may be the more worthy of being placed upon record, even if it gave my friend fewer openings for those deductive methods of reasoning by which he achieved such remarkable results. The story has, I believe, been told more than once in the newspapers, but, like all such narratives, its effect is much less striking when set forth *en bloc* in a single half-column of print than when the facts slowly evolve before your own eyes, and the mystery clears gradually away as each new discovery furnishes a step which leads on to the complete truth. At the time the circumstances made a deep impression upon me, and the lapse of two years has hardly served to weaken the effect.

It was in the summer of '89, not long after my marriage, that the events occurred which I am now about to summarise. I had returned to civil practice and had finally abandoned Holmes in his Baker Street rooms, although I continually visited him and occasionally even persuaded him to forgo his Bohemian habits so far as to come and visit us. My practice had steadily increased, and as I happened to live at no very great distance from Paddington Station, I got a few patients from among the officials. One of these, whom I had cured of a painful and lingering disease, was never weary of advertising my virtues and of endeavouring to send me on every sufferer over whom he might have any influence.

One morning, at a little before seven o'clock, I was awakened by the maid tapping at the door to announce that two men had come from Paddington and were waiting in the consulting-room. I dressed hurriedly, for I knew by experience that railway cases were seldom trivial, and hastened downstairs. As I descended, my old ally, the guard, came out of the room and closed the door tightly behind him.

"I've got him here," he whispered, jerking his thumb over his shoulder; "He's all right."

"What is it, then?" I asked, for his manner suggested that it was some strange creature which he had caged up in my room.

"It's a new patient," he whispered. "I thought I'd bring him round myself; then he couldn't slip away. There he is, all safe and sound. I must go now, Doctor; I have my dooties, just the same as you." And off he went, this trusty tout, without even giving me time to thank him.

I entered my consulting-room and found a gentleman seated by the table. He was quietly dressed in a suit of heather tweed with a soft cloth cap which he had laid down upon my books. Round one of his hands he had a handkerchief wrapped, which was mottled all over with bloodstains. He was young, not more than five-and-twenty, I should say, with a strong, masculine face; but he was exceedingly pale and gave me the impression of a man who was suffering from some strong agitation, which it took all his strength of mind to control.

"I am sorry to knock you up so early, Doctor," said he, "but I have had a very serious accident during the night. I came in by train this morning, and on inquiring at Paddington as to where I might find a doctor, a worthy fellow very kindly escorted me here. I gave the maid a card, but I see that she has left it upon the side-table."

I took it up and glanced at it. "Mr. Victor Hatherley, hydraulic engineer, 16A, Victoria Street (3rd floor)." That was the name, style, and abode of my morning visitor. "I regret that I have kept you waiting," said I, sitting down in my library-chair. "You are fresh from a night journey, I understand, which is in itself a monotonous occupation."

"Oh, my night could not be called monotonous," said he, and laughed. He laughed very heartily, with a high, ringing note, leaning back in his chair and shaking his sides. All my medical instincts rose up against that laugh.

"Stop it!" I cried; "pull yourself together!" and I poured out some water from a caraffe.

It was useless, however. He was off in one of those hysterical outbursts which come upon a strong nature when some great crisis is over and gone. Presently he came to himself once more, very weary and pale-looking.

"I have been making a fool of myself," he gasped.

"Not at all. Drink this." I dashed some brandy into the water, and the colour began to come back to his bloodless cheeks.

"That's better!" said he. "And now, Doctor, perhaps you would kindly attend to my thumb, or rather to the place where my thumb used to be."

He unwound the handkerchief and held out his hand. It gave even my hardened nerves a shudder to look at it. There were four protruding fingers and a horrid red, spongy surface where the thumb should have been. It had been hacked or torn right out from the roots.

"Good heavens!" I cried, "this is a terrible injury. It must have bled considerably."

"Yes, it did. I fainted when it was done, and I think that I must have been senseless for a long time. When I came to I found that it was still bleeding, so I tied one end of my handkerchief very tightly round the wrist and braced it up with a twig."

"Excellent! You should have been a surgeon."

"It is a question of hydraulics, you see, and came within my own province."

"This has been done," said I, examining the wound, "by a very heavy and sharp instrument."

"A thing like a cleaver," said he.

"An accident, I presume?"

"By no means."

"What! A murderous attack?"

"Very murderous indeed."

"You horrify me."

I sponged the wound, cleaned it, dressed it, and finally covered it over with cotton wadding and carbolised bandages. He lay back without wincing, though he bit his lip from time to time.

"How is that?" I asked when I had finished.

"Capital! Between your brandy and your bandage, I feel a new man. I was very weak, but I have had a good deal to go through."

"Perhaps you had better not speak of the matter. It is evidently trying to your nerves."

"Oh, no, not now. I shall have to tell my tale to the police; but, between ourselves, if it were not for the convincing evidence of this wound of mine, I should be surprised if they believed my statement, for it is a very extraordinary one, and I have not much in the way of

proof with which to back it up; and, even if they believe me, the clues which I can give them are so vague that it is a question whether justice will be done."

"Ha!" cried I, "If it is anything in the nature of a problem which you desire to see solved, I should strongly recommend you to come to my friend, Mr. Sherlock Holmes, before you go to the official police."

"Oh, I have heard of that fellow," answered my visitor, "and I should be very glad if he would take the matter up, though of course I must use the official police as well. Would you give me an introduction to him?"

"I'll do better. I'll take you round to him myself."

"I should be immensely obliged to you."

"We'll call a cab and go together. We shall just be in time to have a little breakfast with him. Do you feel equal to it?"

"Yes; I shall not feel easy until I have told my story."

"Then my servant will call a cab, and I shall be with you in an instant." I rushed upstairs, explained the matter shortly to my wife, and in five minutes was inside a hansom, driving with my new acquaintance to Baker Street.

Sherlock Holmes was, as I expected, lounging about his sitting-room in his dressing-gown, reading the agony column of *The Times* and smoking his before-breakfast pipe, which was composed of all the plugs and dottles left from his smokes of the day before, all carefully dried and collected on the corner of the mantelpiece. He received us in his quietly genial fashion, ordered fresh rashers and eggs, and joined us in a hearty meal. When it was concluded he settled our new acquaintance upon the sofa, placed a pillow beneath his head, and laid a glass of brandy and water within his reach.

"It is easy to see that your experience has been no common one, Mr. Hatherley," said he. "Pray, lie down there and make yourself absolutely at home. Tell us what you can, but stop when you are tired and keep up your strength with a little stimulant."

"Thank you," said my patient. "but I have felt another man since the doctor bandaged me, and I think that your breakfast has completed the cure. I shall take up as little of your valuable time as possible, so I shall start at once upon my peculiar experiences."

Holmes sat in his big armchair with the weary, heavy-lidded expression which veiled his keen and eager nature, while I sat opposite to him, and we listened in silence to the strange story which our visitor detailed to us.

"You must know," said he, "that I am an orphan and a bachelor, residing alone in lodgings in London. By profession I am a hydraulic engineer, and I have had considerable experience of my work during the seven years that I was apprenticed to Venner & Matheson, the well-known firm, of Greenwich. Two years ago, having served my time, and having also come into a fair sum of money through my poor father's death, I determined to start in business for myself and took professional chambers in Victoria Street.

"I suppose that everyone finds his first independent start in business a dreary experience. To me it has been exceptionally so. During two years I have had three consultations and one small job, and that is absolutely all that my profession has brought me. My gross takings amount to 27 pounds 10 shillings. Every day, from nine in the morning until four in the afternoon, I waited in my little den, until at last my heart began to sink, and I came to believe that I should never have any practice at all.

"Yesterday, however, just as I was thinking of leaving the office, my clerk entered to say there was a gentleman waiting who wished to see me upon business. He brought up a card, too, with the name of 'Colonel Lysander Stark' engraved upon it. Close at his heels came the colonel himself, a man rather over the middle size, but of an exceeding thinness. I do not think that I have ever seen so thin a man. His whole face sharpened away into nose and chin, and the skin of his cheeks was drawn quite tense over his outstanding bones. Yet this emaciation seemed to be his natural habit, and due to no disease, for his eye was bright, his step brisk, and his bearing assured. He was plainly but neatly dressed, and his age, I should judge, would be nearer forty than thirty.

" 'Mr. Hatherley?' said he, with something of a German accent. 'You have been recommended to me, Mr. Hatherley, as being a man who is not only proficient in his profession but is also discreet and capable of preserving a secret.'

"I bowed, feeling as flattered as any young man would at such an address. 'May I ask who it was who gave me so good a character?'

" 'Well, perhaps it is better that I should not tell you that just at this moment. I have it from the same source that you are both an orphan and a bachelor and are residing alone in London.'

"'That is quite correct,' I answered; 'but you will excuse me if I say that I cannot see how all this bears upon my professional qualifications. I understand that it was on a professional matter that you wished to speak to me?'

"'Undoubtedly so. But you will find that all I say is really to the point. I have a professional commission for you, but absolute secrecy is quite essential—absolute secrecy, you understand, and of course we may expect that more from a man who is alone than from one who lives in the bosom of his family.'

"'If I promise to keep a secret,' said I, 'you may absolutely depend upon my doing so.'

"He looked very hard at me as I spoke, and it seemed to me that I had never seen so suspicious and questioning an eye.

"'Do you promise, then?' said he at last.

"'Yes, I promise.'

"'Absolute and complete silence before, during, and after? No reference to the matter at all, either in word or writing?'

"'I have already given you my word.'

"'Very good.' He suddenly sprang up, and darting like lightning across the room he flung open the door. The passage outside was empty.

"'That's all right,' said he, coming back. 'I know that clerks are sometimes curious as to their master's affairs. Now we can talk in safety.' He drew up his chair very close to mine and began to stare at me again with the same questioning and thoughtful look.

"A feeling of repulsion, and of something akin to fear had begun to rise within me at the strange antics of this fleshless man. Even my dread of losing a client could not restrain me from showing my impatience.

"'I beg that you will state your business, sir,' said I; 'my time is of value.' Heaven forgive me for that last sentence, but the words came to my lips.

"'How would fifty guineas for a night's work suit you?' he asked.

"'Most admirably.'

"'I say a night's work, but an hour's would be nearer the mark. I simply want your opinion about a hydraulic stamping machine which has got out of gear. If you show us what is wrong we shall soon set it right ourselves. What do you think of such a commission as that?'

"'The work appears to be light and the pay munificent.'

"'Precisely so. We shall want you to come tonight by the last train.'

"'Where to?'

"'To Eyford, in Berkshire. It is a little place near the borders of Oxfordshire, and within seven miles of Reading. There is a train from Paddington which would bring you there at about 11:15.'

"'Very good.'

"'I shall come down in a carriage to meet you.'

"'There is a drive, then?'

"'Yes, our little place is quite out in the country. It is a good seven miles from Eyford Station.'

"'Then we can hardly get there before midnight. I suppose there would be no chance of a train back. I should be compelled to stop the night.'

"'Yes, we could easily give you a shake-down.'

"'That is very awkward. Could I not come at some more convenient hour?'

"'We have judged it best that you should come late. It is to recompense you for any inconvenience that we are paying to you, a young and unknown man, a fee which would buy an opinion from the very heads of your profession. Still, of course, if you would like to draw out of the business, there is plenty of time to do so.'

"I thought of the fifty guineas, and of how very useful they would be to me. 'Not at all,' said I, 'I shall be very happy to accommodate myself to your wishes. I should like, however, to understand a little more clearly what it is that you wish me to do.'

"'Quite so. It is very natural that the pledge of secrecy which we have exacted from you should have aroused your curiosity. I have no wish to commit you to anything without your having it all laid before you. I suppose that we are absolutely safe from eavesdroppers?'

"'Entirely.'

"'Then the matter stands thus. You are probably aware that fuller's-earth is a valuable product, and that it is only found in one or two places in England?'

"'I have heard so.'

"'Some little time ago I bought a small place—a very small place—within ten miles of Reading. I was fortunate enough to discover that there was a deposit of fuller's-earth in one of my fields. On examining it, however, I found that this deposit was a comparatively small one, and

that it formed a link between two very much larger ones upon the right and left—both of them, however, in the grounds of my neighbours. These good people were absolutely ignorant that their land contained that which was quite as valuable as a gold-mine. Naturally, it was to my interest to buy their land before they discovered its true value, but unfortunately I had no capital by which I could do this. I took a few of my friends into the secret, however, and they suggested that we should quietly and secretly work our own little deposit and that in this way we should earn the money which would enable us to buy the neighbouring fields. This we have now been doing for some time, and in order to help us in our operations we erected a hydraulic press. This press, as I have already explained, has got out of order, and we wish your advice upon the subject. We guard our secret very jealously, however, and if it once became known that we had hydraulic engineers coming to our little house, it would soon rouse inquiry, and then, if the facts came out, it would be good-bye to any chance of getting these fields and carrying out our plans. That is why I have made you promise me that you will not tell a human being that you are going to Eyford tonight. I hope that I make it all plain?'

"'I quite follow you,' said I. 'The only point which I could not quite understand was what use you could make of a hydraulic press in excavating fuller's-earth, which, as I understand, is dug out like gravel from a pit.'

"'Ah!' said he carelessly, 'we have our own process. We compress the earth into bricks, so as to remove them without revealing what they are. But that is a mere detail. I have taken you fully into my confidence now, Mr. Hatherley, and I have shown you how I trust you.' He rose as he spoke. 'I shall expect you, then, at Eyford at 11:15.'

"'I shall certainly be there.'

"'And not a word to a soul.' He looked at me with a last long, questioning gaze, and then, pressing my hand in a cold, dank grasp, he hurried from the room.

"Well, when I came to think it all over in cool blood I was very much astonished, as you may both think, at this sudden commission which had been intrusted to me. On the one hand, of course, I was glad, for the fee was at least tenfold what I should have asked had I set a price upon my own services, and it was possible that this order might lead to other ones. On the other hand, the face and manner of my patron had made an unpleasant impression upon me, and I could not think that his explanation of the fuller's-earth was sufficient to explain the necessity for my coming at midnight, and his extreme anxiety lest I should tell anyone of my errand. However, I threw all fears to the winds, ate a hearty supper, drove to Paddington, and started off, having obeyed to the letter the injunction as to holding my tongue.

"At Reading I had to change not only my carriage but my station. However, I was in time for the last train to Eyford, and I reached the little dim-lit station after eleven o'clock. I was the only passenger who got out there, and there was no one upon the platform save a single sleepy porter with a lantern. As I passed out through the wicket gate, however, I found my acquaintance of the morning waiting in the shadow upon the other side. Without a word he grasped my arm and hurried me into a carriage, the door of which was standing open. He drew up the windows on either side, tapped on the woodwork, and away we went as fast as the horse could go."

"One horse?" interjected Holmes.

"Yes, only one."

"Did you observe the colour?"

"Yes, I saw it by the side-lights when I was stepping into the carriage. It was a chestnut."

"Tired-looking or fresh?"

"Oh, fresh and glossy."

"Thank you. I am sorry to have interrupted you. Pray continue your most interesting statement."

"Away we went then, and we drove for at least an hour. Colonel Lysander Stark had said that it was only seven miles, but I should think, from the rate that we seemed to go, and from the time that we took, that it must have been nearer twelve. He sat at my side in silence all the time, and I was aware, more than once when I glanced in his direction, that he was looking at me with great intensity. The country roads seem to be not very good in that part of the world, for we lurched and jolted terribly. I tried to look out of the windows to see something of where we were, but they were made of frosted glass, and I could make out nothing save the occasional bright blur of a passing light. Now and then I hazarded some remark to break the monotony of the journey, but the colonel answered only in monosyllables, and the conversation soon flagged. At last, however, the bumping of the road was exchanged for the crisp smoothness of a gravel-drive, and the carriage came to a stand. Colonel Lysander Stark sprang out, and, as I followed after him, pulled me swiftly into a porch which gaped in front of us. We stepped, as it were, right out of the carriage and into the hall, so that I failed to catch the most fleeting glance of the front of the house. The instant that I had crossed the threshold the door slammed heavily behind us, and I heard faintly the rattle of the wheels as the carriage drove away.

"It was pitch dark inside the house, and the colonel fumbled about looking for matches and muttering under his breath. Suddenly a door opened at the other end of the passage, and a long, golden bar of light shot out in our direction. It grew broader, and a woman appeared with a lamp in her hand, which she held above her head, pushing her face forward and peering at us. I could see that she was pretty, and from the gloss with which the light shone upon her dark dress I knew that it was a rich material. She spoke a few words in a foreign tongue in a tone as though asking a question, and when my companion answered in a gruff monosyllable she gave such a start that the lamp nearly fell from her hand. Colonel Stark went up to her, whispered something in her ear, and then, pushing her back into the room from whence she had come, he walked towards me again with the lamp in his hand.

"'Perhaps you will have the kindness to wait in this room for a few minutes,' said he, throwing open another door. It was a quiet, little, plainly furnished room, with a round table in the centre, on which several German books were scattered. Colonel Stark laid down the lamp on the top of a harmonium beside the door. 'I shall not keep you waiting an instant,' said he, and vanished into the darkness.

"I glanced at the books upon the table, and in spite of my ignorance of German I could see that two of them were treatises on science, the others being volumes of poetry. Then I walked across to the window, hoping that I might catch some glimpse of the countryside, but an oak shutter, heavily barred, was folded across it. It was a wonderfully silent house. There was an old clock ticking loudly somewhere in the passage, but otherwise everything was deadly still. A vague feeling of uneasiness began to steal over me. Who were these German people, and what were they doing living in this strange, out-of-the-way place? And where was the place? I was ten miles or so from Eyford, that was all I knew, but whether north, south, east, or west I had no idea. For that matter, Reading, and possibly other large towns, were within that radius, so the place might not be so secluded, after all. Yet it was quite certain, from the absolute stillness, that we were in the country. I paced up and down the room, humming a tune under my breath to keep up my spirits and feeling that I was thoroughly earning my fifty-guinea fee.

"Suddenly, without any preliminary sound in the midst of the utter stillness, the door of my room swung slowly open. The woman was standing in the aperture, the darkness of the hall behind her, the yellow light from my lamp beating upon her eager and beautiful face. I could see at a glance that she was sick with fear, and the sight sent a chill to my own heart. She held up one shaking finger to warn me to be silent, and she shot a few whispered words of broken English at me, her eyes glancing back, like those of a frightened horse, into the gloom behind her.

" 'I would go,' said she, trying hard, as it seemed to me, to speak calmly; 'I would go. I should not stay here. There is no good for you to do.'

" 'But, madam,' said I, 'I have not yet done what I came for. I cannot possibly leave until I have seen the machine.'

" 'It is not worth your while to wait,' she went on. 'You can pass through the door; no one hinders.' And then, seeing that I smiled and shook my head, she suddenly threw aside her constraint and made a step forward, with her hands wrung together. 'For the love of Heaven!' she whispered, 'get away from here before it is too late!'

"But I am somewhat headstrong by nature, and the more ready to engage in an affair when there is some obstacle in the way. I thought of my fifty-guinea fee, of my wearisome journey, and of the unpleasant night which seemed to be before me. Was it all to go for nothing? Why should I slink away without having carried out my commission, and without the payment which was my due? This woman might, for all I knew, be a monomaniac. With a stout bearing, therefore, though her manner had shaken me more than I cared to confess, I still shook my head and declared my intention of remaining where I was. She was about to renew her entreaties when a door slammed overhead, and the sound of several footsteps was heard upon the stairs. She listened for an instant, threw up her hands with a despairing gesture, and vanished as suddenly and as noiselessly as she had come.

"The newcomers were Colonel Lysander Stark and a short thick

man with a chinchilla beard growing out of the creases of his double chin, who was introduced to me as Mr. Ferguson.

"'This is my secretary and manager,' said the colonel. 'By the way, I was under the impression that I left this door shut just now. I fear that you have felt the draught.'

"'On the contrary,' said I, 'I opened the door myself because I felt the room to be a little close.'

"He shot one of his suspicious looks at me. 'Perhaps we had better proceed to business, then,' said he. 'Mr. Ferguson and I will take you up to see the machine.'

"'I had better put my hat on, I suppose.'

"'Oh, no, it is in the house.'

"'What, you dig fuller's-earth in the house?'

"'No, no. This is only where we compress it. But never mind that. All we wish you to do is to examine the machine and to let us know what is wrong with it.'

"We went upstairs together, the colonel first with the lamp, the fat manager and I behind him. It was a labyrinth of an old house, with corridors, passages, narrow winding staircases, and little low doors, the thresholds of which were hollowed out by the generations who had crossed them. There were no carpets and no signs of any furniture above the ground floor, while the plaster was peeling off the walls, and the damp was breaking through in green, unhealthy blotches. I tried to put on as unconcerned an air as possible, but I had not forgotten the warnings of the lady, even though I disregarded them, and I kept a keen eye upon my two companions. Ferguson appeared to be a morose and silent man, but I could see from the little that he said that he was at least a fellow-countryman.

"Colonel Lysander Stark stopped at last before a low door, which he unlocked. Within was a small, square room, in which the three of us could hardly get at one time. Ferguson remained outside, and the colonel ushered me in.

"'We are now,' said he, 'actually within the hydraulic press, and it would be a particularly unpleasant thing for us if anyone were to turn it on. The ceiling of this small chamber is really the end of the descending piston, and it comes down with the force of many tons upon this metal floor. There are small lateral columns of water outside which receive the force, and which transmit and multiply it in the manner which is familiar to you. The machine goes readily enough, but there is some stiffness in the working of it, and it has lost a little of its force. Perhaps you will have the goodness to look it over and to show us how we can set it right.'

"I took the lamp from him, and I examined the machine very thoroughly. It was indeed a gigantic one, and capable of exercising enormous pressure. When I passed outside, however, and pressed down the levers which controlled it, I knew at once by the whishing sound that there was a slight leakage, which allowed a regurgitation of water through one of the side cylinders. An examination showed that one of the india-rubber bands which was round the head of a driving-rod had shrunk so as not quite to fill the socket along which it worked. This was clearly the cause of the loss of power, and I pointed it out to my companions, who followed my remarks very carefully and asked several practical questions as to how they should proceed to set it right. When I had made it clear to them, I returned to the main chamber of the machine and took a good look at it to satisfy my own curiosity. It was obvious at a glance that the story of the fuller's-earth was the merest fabrication, for it would be absurd to suppose that so powerful an engine could be designed for so inadequate a purpose. The walls were of wood, but the floor consisted of a large iron trough, and when I came to examine it I could see a crust of metallic deposit all over it. I had stooped and was scraping at this to see exactly what it was when I heard a muttered exclamation in German and saw the cadaverous face of the colonel looking down at me.

" 'What are you doing there?' he asked.

"I felt angry at having been tricked by so elaborate a story as that which he had told me. 'I was admiring your fuller's-earth,' said I; 'I think that I should be better able to advise you as to your machine if I knew what the exact purpose was for which it was used.'

"The instant that I uttered the words I regretted the rashness of my speech. His face set hard, and a baleful light sprang up in his grey eyes.

" 'Very well,' said he, 'you shall know all about the machine.' He took a step backward, slammed the little door, and turned the key in the lock. I rushed towards it and pulled at the handle, but it was quite secure, and did not give in the least to my kicks and shoves. 'Hullo!' I yelled. 'Hullo! Colonel! Let me out!'

"And then suddenly in the silence I heard a sound which sent my

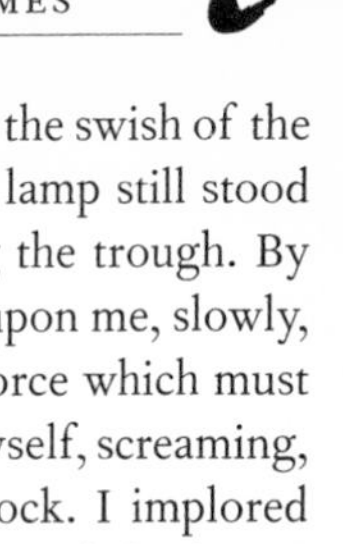

heart into my mouth. It was the clank of the levers and the swish of the leaking cylinder. He had set the engine at work. The lamp still stood upon the floor where I had placed it when examining the trough. By its light I saw that the black ceiling was coming down upon me, slowly, jerkily, but, as none knew better than myself, with a force which must within a minute grind me to a shapeless pulp. I threw myself, screaming, against the door, and dragged with my nails at the lock. I implored the colonel to let me out, but the remorseless clanking of the levers drowned my cries. The ceiling was only a foot or two above my head, and with my hand upraised I could feel its hard, rough surface. Then it flashed through my mind that the pain of my death would depend very much upon the position in which I met it. If I lay on my face the weight would come upon my spine, and I shuddered to think of that dreadful snap. Easier the other way, perhaps; and yet, had I the nerve to lie and look up at that deadly black shadow wavering down upon me? Already I was unable to stand erect, when my eye caught something which brought a gush of hope back to my heart.

"I have said that though the floor and ceiling were of iron, the walls were of wood. As I gave a last hurried glance around, I saw a thin line of yellow light between two of the boards, which broadened and broadened as a small panel was pushed backward. For an instant I could hardly believe that here was indeed a door which led away from death. The next instant I threw myself through, and lay half-fainting upon the other side. The panel had closed again behind me, but the crash of the lamp, and a few moments afterwards the clang of the two slabs of metal, told me how narrow had been my escape.

"I was recalled to myself by a frantic plucking at my wrist, and I found myself lying upon the stone floor of a narrow corridor, while a woman bent over me and tugged at me with her left hand, while she held a candle in her right. It was the same good friend whose warning I had so foolishly rejected.

"'Come! come!' she cried breathlessly. 'They will be here in a moment. They will see that you are not there. Oh, do not waste the so-precious time, but come!'

"This time, at least, I did not scorn her advice. I staggered to my feet and ran with her along the corridor and down a winding stair. The latter led to another broad passage, and just as we reached it we heard the sound of running feet and the shouting of two voices, one answering the other from the floor on which we were and from the one beneath. My guide stopped and looked about her like one who is at her wit's end. Then she threw open a door which led into a bedroom, through the window of which the moon was shining brightly.

"'It is your only chance,' said she. 'It is high, but it may be that you can jump it.'

"As she spoke a light sprang into view at the further end of the passage, and I saw the lean figure of Colonel Lysander Stark rushing forward with a lantern in one hand and a weapon like a butcher's cleaver in the other. I rushed across the bedroom, flung open the window, and looked out. How quiet and sweet and wholesome the garden looked in the moonlight, and it could not be more than thirty feet down. I clambered out upon the sill, but I hesitated to jump until I should have heard what passed between my saviour and the ruffian who pursued me. If she were ill-used, then at any risks I was determined to go back to her assistance. The thought had hardly flashed through my mind before he was at the door, pushing his way past her; but she threw her arms round him and tried to hold him back.

"'Fritz! Fritz!' she cried in English, Remember your promise after the last time. You said it should not be again. He will be silent! Oh, he will be silent!'

"'You are mad, Elise!' he shouted, struggling to break away from her. 'You will be the ruin of us. He has seen too much. Let me pass, I say!' He dashed her to one side, and, rushing to the window, cut at me with his heavy weapon. I had let myself go, and was hanging by the hands to the sill, when his blow fell. I was conscious of a dull pain, my grip loosened, and I fell into the garden below.

"I was shaken but not hurt by the fall; so I picked myself up and rushed off among the bushes as hard as I could run, for I understood that I was far from being out of danger yet. Suddenly, however, as I ran, a deadly dizziness and sickness came over me. I glanced down at my hand, which was throbbing painfully, and then, for the first time, saw that my thumb had been cut off and that the blood was pouring from my wound. I endeavoured to tie my handkerchief round it, but there came a sudden buzzing in my ears, and next moment I fell in a dead faint among the rosebushes.

"How long I remained unconscious I cannot tell. It must have been a very long time, for the moon had sunk, and a bright morning was breaking when I came to myself. My clothes were all sodden with dew, and my coat-sleeve was drenched with blood from my wounded thumb. The smarting of it recalled in an instant all the particulars of my night's adventure, and I sprang to my feet with the feeling that I might hardly yet be safe from my pursuers. But to my astonishment, when I came to look round me, neither house nor garden were to be seen. I had been lying in an angle of the hedge close by the highroad, and just a little lower down was a long building, which proved, upon my approaching it, to be the very station at which I had arrived upon the previous night. Were it not for the ugly wound upon my hand, all that had passed during those dreadful hours might have been an evil dream.

"Half dazed, I went into the station and asked about the morning train. There would be one to Reading in less than an hour. The same porter was on duty, I found, as had been there when I arrived. I inquired of him whether he had ever heard of Colonel Lysander Stark. The name was strange to him. Had he observed a carriage the night before waiting for me? No, he had not. Was there a police-station anywhere near? There was one about three miles off.

"It was too far for me to go, weak and ill as I was. I determined to wait until I got back to town before telling my story to the police. It was a little past six when I arrived, so I went first to have my wound dressed, and then the doctor was kind enough to bring me along here. I put the case into your hands and shall do exactly what you advise."

We both sat in silence for some little time after listening to this extraordinary narrative. Then Sherlock Holmes pulled down from the shelf one of the ponderous commonplace books in which he placed his cuttings.

"Here is an advertisement which will interest you," said he. "It appeared in all the papers about a year ago. Listen to this: 'Lost, on the 9th inst., Mr. Jeremiah Hayling, aged twenty-six, a hydraulic engineer. Left his lodgings at ten o'clock at night, and has not been heard of since. Was dressed in,' etc., etc. Ha! That represents the last time that the colonel needed to have his machine overhauled, I fancy."

"Good heavens!" cried my patient. "Then that explains what the girl said."

"Undoubtedly. It is quite clear that the colonel was a cool and desperate man, who was absolutely determined that nothing should stand in the way of his little game, like those out-and-out pirates who will leave no survivor from a captured ship. Well, every moment now is precious, so if you feel equal to it we shall go down to Scotland Yard at once as a preliminary to starting for Eyford."

Some three hours or so afterwards we were all in the train together, bound from Reading to the little Berkshire village. There were Sherlock Holmes, the hydraulic engineer, Inspector Bradstreet, of Scotland Yard, a plainclothesman, and myself. Bradstreet had spread an ordnance map of the county out upon the seat and was busy with his compasses drawing a circle with Eyford for its centre.

"There you are," said he. "That circle is drawn at a radius of ten miles from the village. The place we want must be somewhere near that line. You said ten miles, I think, sir."

"It was an hour's good drive."

"And you think that they brought you back all that way when you were unconscious?"

"They must have done so. I have a confused memory, too, of having been lifted and conveyed somewhere."

"What I cannot understand," said I, "is why they should have spared you when they found you lying fainting in the garden. Perhaps the villain was softened by the woman's entreaties."

"I hardly think that likely. I never saw a more inexorable face in my life."

"Oh, we shall soon clear up all that," said Bradstreet. "Well, I have drawn my circle, and I only wish I knew at what point upon it the folk that we are in search of are to be found."

"I think I could lay my finger on it," said Holmes quietly.

"Really, now!" cried the inspector, "You have formed your opinion! Come, now, we shall see who agrees with you. I say it is south, for the country is more deserted there."

"And I say east," said my patient.

"I am for west," remarked the plainclothesman. "There are several quiet little villages up there."

"And I am for north," said I, "because there are no hills there, and our friend says that he did not notice the carriage go up any."

"Come," cried the inspector, laughing; "it's a very pretty diversity of opinion. We have boxed the compass among us. Who do you give your casting vote to?"

"You are all wrong."

"But we can't all be."

"Oh, yes, you can. This is my point." He placed his finger in the centre of the circle. "This is where we shall find them."

"But the twelve-mile drive?" gasped Hatherley.

"Six out and six back. Nothing simpler. You say yourself that the horse was fresh and glossy when you got in. How could it be that if it had gone twelve miles over heavy roads?"

"Indeed, it is a likely ruse enough," observed Bradstreet thoughtfully. "Of course there can be no doubt as to the nature of this gang."

"None at all," said Holmes. "They are coiners on a large scale, and have used the machine to form the amalgam which has taken the place of silver."

"We have known for some time that a clever gang was at work," said the inspector. "They have been turning out half-crowns by the thousand. We even traced them as far as Reading, but could get no farther, for they had covered their traces in a way that showed that they were very old hands. But now, thanks to this lucky chance, I think that we have got them right enough."

But the inspector was mistaken, for those criminals were not destined to fall into the hands of justice. As we rolled into Eyford Station we saw a gigantic column of smoke which streamed up from behind a small clump of trees in the neighbourhood and hung like an immense ostrich feather over the landscape.

"A house on fire?" asked Bradstreet as the train steamed off again on its way.

"Yes, sir!" said the station-master.

"When did it break out?"

"I hear that it was during the night, sir, but it has got worse, and the whole place is in a blaze."

"Whose house is it?"

"Dr. Becher's."

"Tell me," broke in the engineer, "is Dr. Becher a German, very thin, with a long, sharp nose?"

The station-master laughed heartily. "No, sir, Dr. Becher is an Englishman, and there isn't a man in the parish who has a better-lined waistcoat. But he has a gentleman staying with him, a patient, as I understand, who is a foreigner, and he looks as if a little good Berkshire beef would do him no harm."

The station-master had not finished his speech before we were all hastening in the direction of the fire. The road topped a low hill, and there was a great widespread whitewashed building in front of us, spouting fire at every chink and window, while in the garden in front three fire-engines were vainly striving to keep the flames under.

"That's it!" cried Hatherley, in intense excitement. "There is the gravel-drive, and there are the rosebushes where I lay. That second window is the one that I jumped from."

"Well, at least," said Holmes, "you have had your revenge upon them. There can be no question that it was your oil-lamp which, when it was crushed in the press, set fire to the wooden walls, though no doubt they were too excited in the chase after you to observe it at the time. Now keep your eyes open in this crowd for your friends of last night, though I very much fear that they are a good hundred miles off by now."

And Holmes' fears came to be realised, for from that day to this no word has ever been heard either of the beautiful woman, the sinister German, or the morose Englishman. Early that morning a peasant had met a cart containing several people and some very bulky boxes driving rapidly in the direction of Reading, but there all traces of the fugitives disappeared, and even Holmes' ingenuity failed ever to discover the least clue as to their whereabouts.

The firemen had been much perturbed at the strange arrangements which they had found within, and still more so by discovering a newly severed human thumb upon a windowsill of the second floor. About sunset, however, their efforts were at last successful, and they subdued the flames, but not before the roof had fallen in, and the whole place been reduced to such absolute ruin that, save some twisted cylinders and iron piping, not a trace remained of the machinery which had cost our unfortunate acquaintance so dearly. Large masses of nickel and of tin were discovered stored in an outhouse, but no coins were to be found, which may have explained the presence of those bulky boxes which have been already referred to.

How our hydraulic engineer had been conveyed from the garden to the spot where he recovered his senses might have remained forever a mystery were it not for the soft mould, which told us a very plain tale. He had evidently been carried down by two persons, one of whom had remarkably small feet and the other unusually large ones. On the

whole, it was most probable that the silent Englishman, being less bold or less murderous than his companion, had assisted the woman to bear the unconscious man out of the way of danger.

"Well," said our engineer ruefully as we took our seats to return once more to London, "it has been a pretty business for me! I have lost my thumb and I have lost a fifty-guinea fee, and what have I gained?"

"Experience," said Holmes, laughing. "Indirectly it may be of value, you know; you have only to put it into words to gain the reputation of being excellent company for the remainder of your existence."

THE NOBLE BACHELOR

The Lord St. Simon marriage, and its curious termination, have long ceased to be a subject of interest in those exalted circles in which the unfortunate bridegroom moves. Fresh scandals have eclipsed it, and their more piquant details have drawn the gossips away from this four-year-old drama. As I have reason to believe, however, that the full facts have never been revealed to the general public, and as my friend Sherlock Holmes had a considerable share in clearing the matter up, I feel that no memoir of him would be complete without some little sketch of this remarkable episode.

It was a few weeks before my own marriage, during the days when I was still sharing rooms with Holmes in Baker Street, that he came home from an afternoon stroll to find a letter on the table waiting for him. I had remained indoors all day, for the weather had taken a sudden turn to rain, with high autumnal winds, and the Jezail bullet which I had brought back in one of my limbs as a relic of my Afghan campaign throbbed with dull persistence. With my body in one easy-chair and my legs upon another, I had surrounded myself with a cloud of newspapers until at last, saturated with the news of the day, I tossed them all aside and lay listless, watching the huge crest and monogram upon the envelope upon the table and wondering lazily who my friend's noble correspondent could be.

"Here is a very fashionable epistle," I remarked as he entered. "Your morning letters, if I remember right, were from a fish-monger and a tide-waiter."

"Yes, my correspondence has certainly the charm of variety," he answered, smiling, "and the humbler are usually the more interesting. This looks like one of those unwelcome social summonses which call upon a man either to be bored or to lie."

He broke the seal and glanced over the contents.

"Oh, come, it may prove to be something of interest, after all."

"Not social, then?"

"No, distinctly professional."

"And from a noble client?"

"One of the highest in England."

"My dear fellow, I congratulate you."

"I assure you, Watson, without affectation, that the status of my client is a matter of less moment to me than the interest of his case. It is just possible, however, that that also may not be wanting in this new investigation. You have been reading the papers diligently of late, have you not?"

"It looks like it," said I ruefully, pointing to a huge bundle in the corner. "I have had nothing else to do."

"It is fortunate, for you will perhaps be able to post me up. I read nothing except the criminal news and the agony column. The latter is always instructive. But if you have followed recent events so closely you must have read about Lord St. Simon and his wedding?"

"Oh, yes, with the deepest interest."

"That is well. The letter which I hold in my hand is from Lord St. Simon. I will read it to you, and in return you must turn over these papers and let me have whatever bears upon the matter. This is what he says:

> 'MY DEAR MR. SHERLOCK HOLMES
>
> Lord Backwater tells me that I may place implicit reliance upon your judgment and discretion. I have determined, therefore, to call upon you and to consult you in reference to the very painful event which has occurred in connection with my wedding. Mr. Lestrade, of Scotland Yard, is acting already in the matter, but he assures me that he sees no objection to your co-operation, and that he even thinks that it might be of some assistance. I will call at four o'clock in the afternoon, and, should you have any other engagement at that time, I hope that you will postpone it, as this matter is of paramount importance.
>
> Yours faithfully,
>
> ROBERT ST. SIMON.'

"It is dated from Grosvenor Mansions, written with a quill pen, and the noble lord has had the misfortune to get a smear of ink upon the outer side of his right little finger," remarked Holmes as he folded up the epistle.

"He says four o'clock. It is three now. He will be here in an hour."

"Then I have just time, with your assistance, to get clear upon the subject. Turn over those papers and arrange the extracts in their order of time, while I take a glance as to who our client is." He picked a red-covered volume from a line of books of reference beside the mantelpiece. "Here he is," said he, sitting down and flattening it out upon his knee. "'Lord Robert Walsingham de Vere St. Simon, second son of the Duke of Balmoral.' Hum! 'Arms: Azure, three caltrops in chief over a fess sable. Born in 1846.' He's forty-one years of age, which is mature for marriage. Was Under-Secretary for the colonies in a late administration. The Duke, his father, was at one time Secretary for Foreign Affairs. They inherit Plantagenet blood by direct descent, and Tudor on the distaff side. Ha! Well, there is nothing very instructive in all this. I think that I must turn to you Watson, for something more solid."

"I have very little difficulty in finding what I want," said I, "for the facts are quite recent, and the matter struck me as remarkable. I feared to refer them to you, however, as I knew that you had an inquiry on hand and that you disliked the intrusion of other matters."

"Oh, you mean the little problem of the Grosvenor Square furniture van. That is quite cleared up now—though, indeed, it was obvious from the first. Pray give me the results of your newspaper selections."

"Here is the first notice which I can find. It is in the personal column of the *Morning Post*, and dates, as you see, some weeks back: 'A marriage has been arranged,' it says, 'and will, if rumour is correct, very shortly take place, between Lord Robert St. Simon, second son of the Duke of Balmoral, and Miss Hatty Doran, the only daughter of Aloysius Doran, Esq., of San Francisco, Cal., U.S.A.' That is all."

"Terse and to the point," remarked Holmes, stretching his long, thin legs towards the fire.

"There was a paragraph amplifying this in one of the society papers of the same week. Ah, here it is.

"'There will soon be a call for protection in the marriage market, for the present free-trade principle appears to tell heavily against our home product. One by one the management of the noble houses of Great Britain is passing into the hands of our fair cousins from across the Atlantic. An important addition has been made during the last week to the list of the prizes which have been borne away by these charming invaders. Lord St. Simon, who has shown himself for over twenty years proof against the little god's arrows, has now definitely announced his approaching marriage with Miss Hatty Doran, the fascinating daughter of a California millionaire. Miss Doran, whose graceful figure and striking face attracted much attention at the Westbury House festivities, is an only child, and it is currently reported that her dowry will run to considerably over the six figures, with expectancies for the future. As it is an open secret that the Duke of Balmoral has been compelled to sell his pictures within the last few years, and as Lord St. Simon has no property of his own save the small estate of Birchmoor, it is obvious that the Californian heiress is not the only gainer by an alliance which will enable her to make the easy and common transition from a Republican lady to a British title.' "

"Anything else?" asked Holmes, yawning.

"Oh, yes; plenty. Then there is another note in the *Morning Post* to say that the marriage would be an absolutely quiet one, that it would be at St. George's, Hanover Square, that only half a dozen intimate friends would be invited, and that the party would return to the furnished house at Lancaster Gate which has been taken by Mr. Aloysius Doran. Two days later—that is, on Wednesday last—there is a curt announcement that the wedding had taken place, and that the honeymoon would be passed at Lord Backwater's place, near Petersfield. Those are all the notices which appeared before the disappearance of the bride."

"Before the what?" asked Holmes with a start.

"The vanishing of the lady."

"When did she vanish, then?"

"At the wedding breakfast."

"Indeed. This is more interesting than it promised to be; quite dramatic, in fact."

"Yes; it struck me as being a little out of the common."

"They often vanish before the ceremony, and occasionally during the honeymoon; but I cannot call to mind anything quite so prompt as this. Pray let me have the details."

"I warn you that they are very incomplete."

"Perhaps we may make them less so."

"Such as they are, they are set forth in a single article of a morning paper of yesterday, which I will read to you. It is headed, 'Singular Occurrence at a Fashionable Wedding':

" 'The family of Lord Robert St. Simon has been thrown into the greatest consternation by the strange and painful episodes which have taken place in connection with his wedding. The ceremony, as shortly announced in the papers of yesterday, occurred on the previous morning; but it is only now that it has been possible to confirm the strange rumours which have been so persistently floating about. In spite of the attempts of the friends to hush the matter up, so much public attention has now been drawn to it that no good purpose can be served by affecting to disregard what is a common subject for conversation.

"'The ceremony, which was performed at St. George's, Hanover Square, was a very quiet one, no one being present save the father of the bride, Mr. Aloysius Doran, the Duchess of Balmoral, Lord Backwater, Lord Eustace and Lady Clara St. Simon (the younger brother and sister of the bridegroom), and Lady Alicia Whittington. The whole party proceeded afterwards to the house of Mr. Aloysius Doran, at Lancaster Gate, where breakfast had been prepared. It appears that some little trouble was caused by a woman, whose name has not been ascertained, who endeavoured to force her way into the house after the bridal party, alleging that she had some claim upon Lord St. Simon. It was only after a painful and prolonged scene that she was ejected by the butler and the footman. The bride, who had fortunately entered the house before this unpleasant interruption, had sat down to breakfast with the rest, when she complained of a sudden indisposition and retired to her room. Her prolonged absence having caused some comment, her father followed her, but learned from her maid that she had only come up to her chamber for an instant, caught up an ulster and bonnet, and hurried down to the passage. One of the footmen declared that he had seen a lady leave the house thus apparelled, but had refused to credit that it was his mistress, believing her to be with the company. On ascertaining that his daughter had disappeared, Mr. Aloysius Doran, in conjunction with the bridegroom, instantly put themselves in communication with the police, and very energetic inquiries are being made, which will probably result in a speedy clearing up of this very singular business. Up to a late hour last night, however, nothing had transpired as to the whereabouts of the missing lady. There are rumours of foul play in the matter, and it is said that the police have caused the arrest of the woman who had caused the original disturbance, in the belief that, from jealousy or some other motive, she may have been concerned in the strange disappearance of the bride.'"

"And is that all?"

"Only one little item in another of the morning papers, but it is a suggestive one."

"And it is?"

"That Miss Flora Millar, the lady who had caused the disturbance, has actually been arrested. It appears that she was formerly a *danseuse* at the Allegro, and that she has known the bridegroom for some years. There are no further particulars, and the whole case is in your hands now—so far as it has been set forth in the public press."

"And an exceedingly interesting case it appears to be. I would not have missed it for worlds. But there is a ring at the bell, Watson, and as the clock makes it a few minutes after four, I have no doubt that this will prove to be our noble client. Do not dream of going, Watson, for I very much prefer having a witness, if only as a check to my own memory."

"Lord Robert St. Simon," announced our page-boy, throwing open the door. A gentleman entered, with a pleasant, cultured face, high-nosed and pale, with something perhaps of petulance about the mouth, and with the steady, well-opened eye of a man whose pleasant lot it had ever been to command and to be obeyed. His manner was brisk, and yet his general appearance gave an undue impression of age, for he had a slight forward stoop and a little bend of the knees as he walked. His hair, too, as he swept off his very curly-brimmed hat, was grizzled round the edges and thin upon the top. As to his dress, it was careful to the verge of foppishness, with high collar, black frock-coat, white waistcoat, yellow gloves, patent-leather shoes, and light-coloured gaiters. He advanced slowly into the room, turning his head from left to right, and swinging in his right hand the cord which held his golden eyeglasses.

"Good-day, Lord St. Simon," said Holmes, rising and bowing. "Pray take the basket-chair. This is my friend and colleague, Dr. Watson. Draw up a little to the fire, and we will talk this matter over."

"A most painful matter to me, as you can most readily imagine, Mr. Holmes. I have been cut to the quick. I understand that you have already managed several delicate cases of this sort, sir, though I presume that they were hardly from the same class of society."

"No, I am descending."

"I beg pardon."

"My last client of the sort was a king."

"Oh, really! I had no idea. And which king?"

"The King of Scandinavia."

"What! Had he lost his wife?"

"You can understand," said Holmes suavely, "that I extend to the affairs of my other clients the same secrecy which I promise to you in yours."

"Of course! Very right! Very right! I'm sure I beg pardon. As to my own case, I am ready to give you any information which may assist you in forming an opinion."

"Thank you. I have already learned all that is in the public prints, nothing more. I presume that I may take it as correct— this article, for example, as to the disappearance of the bride."

Lord St. Simon glanced over it. "Yes, it is correct, as far as it goes."

"But it needs a great deal of supplementing before anyone could offer an opinion. I think that I may arrive at my facts most directly by questioning you."

"Pray do so."

"When did you first meet Miss Hatty Doran?"

"In San Francisco, a year ago."

"You were travelling in the States?"

"Yes."

"Did you become engaged then?"

"No."

"But you were on a friendly footing?"

"I was amused by her society, and she could see that I was amused."

"Her father is very rich?"

"He is said to be the richest man on the Pacific slope."

"And how did he make his money?"

"In mining. He had nothing a few years ago. Then he struck gold, invested it, and came up by leaps and bounds."

"Now, what is your own impression as to the young lady's—your wife's character?"

The nobleman swung his glasses a little faster and stared down into the fire. "You see, Mr. Holmes," said he, "my wife was twenty before her father became a rich man. During that time she ran free in a mining camp and wandered through woods or mountains, so that her education has come from Nature rather than from the schoolmaster. She is what we call in England a tomboy, with a strong nature, wild and free, unfettered by any sort of traditions. She is impetuous—volcanic, I was about to say. She is swift in making up her mind and fearless

in carrying out her resolutions. On the other hand, I would not have given her the name which I have the honour to bear"—he gave a little stately cough—"had not I thought her to be at bottom a noble woman. I believe that she is capable of heroic self-sacrifice and that anything dishonourable would be repugnant to her."

"Have you her photograph?"

"I brought this with me." He opened a locket and showed us the full face of a very lovely woman. It was not a photograph but an ivory miniature, and the artist had brought out the full effect of the lustrous black hair, the large dark eyes, and the exquisite mouth. Holmes gazed long and earnestly at it. Then he closed the locket and handed it back to Lord St. Simon.

"The young lady came to London, then, and you renewed your acquaintance?"

"Yes, her father brought her over for this last London season. I met her several times, became engaged to her, and have now married her."

"She brought, I understand, a considerable dowry?"

"A fair dowry. Not more than is usual in my family."

"And this, of course, remains to you, since the marriage is a fait accompli?"

"I really have made no inquiries on the subject."

"Very naturally not. Did you see Miss Doran on the day before the wedding?"

"Yes."

"Was she in good spirits?"

"Never better. She kept talking of what we should do in our future lives."

"Indeed! That is very interesting. And on the morning of the wedding?"

"She was as bright as possible—at least until after the ceremony."

"And did you observe any change in her then?"

"Well, to tell the truth, I saw then the first signs that I had ever seen that her temper was just a little sharp. The incident however, was too trivial to relate and can have no possible bearing upon the case."

"Pray let us have it, for all that."

"Oh, it is childish. She dropped her bouquet as we went towards the vestry. She was passing the front pew at the time, and it fell over into the pew. There was a moment's delay, but the gentleman in the pew handed it up to her again, and it did not appear to be the worse for the fall. Yet when I spoke to her of the matter, she answered me abruptly; and in the carriage, on our way home, she seemed absurdly agitated over this trifling cause."

"Indeed! You say that there was a gentleman in the pew. Some of the general public were present, then?"

"Oh, yes. It is impossible to exclude them when the church is open."

"This gentleman was not one of your wife's friends?"

"No, no; I call him a gentleman by courtesy, but he was quite a common-looking person. I hardly noticed his appearance. But really I think that we are wandering rather far from the point."

"Lady St. Simon, then, returned from the wedding in a less cheerful frame of mind than she had gone to it. What did she do on re-entering her father's house?"

"I saw her in conversation with her maid."

"And who is her maid?"

"Alice is her name. She is an American and came from California with her."

"A confidential servant?"

"A little too much so. It seemed to me that her mistress allowed her to take great liberties. Still, of course, in America they look upon these things in a different way."

"How long did she speak to this Alice?"

"Oh, a few minutes. I had something else to think of."

"You did not overhear what they said?"

"Lady St. Simon said something about 'jumping a claim.' She was accustomed to use slang of the kind. I have no idea what she meant."

"American slang is very expressive sometimes. And what did your wife do when she finished speaking to her maid?"

"She walked into the breakfast-room."

"On your arm?"

"No, alone. She was very independent in little matters like that. Then, after we had sat down for ten minutes or so, she rose hurriedly, muttered some words of apology, and left the room. She never came back."

"But this maid, Alice, as I understand, deposes that she went to her room, covered her bride's dress with a long ulster, put on a bonnet, and went out."

"Quite so. And she was afterwards seen walking into Hyde Park in

company with Flora Millar, a woman who is now in custody, and who had already made a disturbance at Mr. Doran's house that morning."

"Ah, yes. I should like a few particulars as to this young lady, and your relations to her."

Lord St. Simon shrugged his shoulders and raised his eyebrows. "We have been on a friendly footing for some years—I may say on a very friendly footing. She used to be at the Allegro. I have not treated her ungenerously, and she had no just cause of complaint against me, but you know what women are, Mr. Holmes. Flora was a dear little thing, but exceedingly hotheaded and devotedly attached to me. She wrote me dreadful letters when she heard that I was about to be married, and, to tell the truth, the reason why I had the marriage celebrated so quietly was that I feared lest there might be a scandal in the church. She came to Mr. Doran's door just after we returned, and she endeavoured to push her way in, uttering very abusive expressions towards my wife, and even threatening her, but I had foreseen the possibility of something of the sort, and I had two police fellows there in private clothes, who soon pushed her out again. She was quiet when she saw that there was no good in making a row."

"Did your wife hear all this?"

"No, thank goodness, she did not."

"And she was seen walking with this very woman afterwards?"

"Yes. That is what Mr. Lestrade, of Scotland Yard, looks upon as so serious. It is thought that Flora decoyed my wife out and laid some terrible trap for her."

"Well, it is a possible supposition."

"You think so, too?"

"I did not say a probable one. But you do not yourself look upon this as likely?"

"I do not think Flora would hurt a fly."

"Still, jealousy is a strange transformer of characters. Pray what is your own theory as to what took place?"

"Well, really, I came to seek a theory, not to propound one. I have given you all the facts. Since you ask me, however, I may say that it has occurred to me as possible that the excitement of this affair, the consciousness that she had made so immense a social stride, had the effect of causing some little nervous disturbance in my wife."

"In short, that she had become suddenly deranged?"

"Well, really, when I consider that she has turned her back—I will not say upon me, but upon so much that many have aspired to without success—I can hardly explain it in any other fashion."

"Well, certainly that is also a conceivable hypothesis," said Holmes, smiling. "And now, Lord St. Simon, I think that I have nearly all my data. May I ask whether you were seated at the breakfast-table so that you could see out of the window?"

"We could see the other side of the road and the Park."

"Quite so. Then I do not think that I need to detain you longer. I shall communicate with you."

"Should you be fortunate enough to solve this problem," said our client, rising.

"I have solved it."

"Eh? What was that?"

"I say that I have solved it."

"Where, then, is my wife?"

"That is a detail which I shall speedily supply."

Lord St. Simon shook his head. "I am afraid that it will take wiser heads than yours or mine," he remarked, and bowing in a stately, old-fashioned manner he departed.

"It is very good of Lord St. Simon to honour my head by putting it on a level with his own," said Sherlock Holmes, laughing. "I think that I shall have a whisky and soda and a cigar after all this cross-questioning. I had formed my conclusions as to the case before our client came into the room."

"My dear Holmes!"

"I have notes of several similar cases, though none, as I remarked before, which were quite as prompt. My whole examination served to turn my conjecture into a certainty. Circumstantial evidence is occasionally very convincing, as when you find a trout in the milk, to quote Thoreau's example."

"But I have heard all that you have heard."

"Without, however, the knowledge of pre-existing cases which serves me so well. There was a parallel instance in Aberdeen some years back, and something on very much the same lines at Munich the year after the Franco-Prussian War. It is one of these cases—but, hullo, here is Lestrade! Good-afternoon, Lestrade! You will find an extra tumbler upon the sideboard, and there are cigars in the box."

The official detective was attired in a pea-jacket and cravat, which gave him a decidedly nautical appearance, and he carried a black canvas bag in his hand. With a short greeting he seated himself and lit the cigar which had been offered to him.

"What's up, then?" asked Holmes with a twinkle in his eye. "You look dissatisfied."

"And I feel dissatisfied. It is this infernal St. Simon marriage case. I can make neither head nor tail of the business."

"Really! You surprise me."

"Who ever heard of such a mixed affair? Every clue seems to slip through my fingers. I have been at work upon it all day."

"And very wet it seems to have made you," said Holmes laying his hand upon the arm of the pea-jacket.

"Yes, I have been dragging the Serpentine."

"In heaven's name, what for?"

"In search of the body of Lady St. Simon."

Sherlock Holmes leaned back in his chair and laughed heartily.

"Have you dragged the basin of Trafalgar Square fountain?" he asked.

"Why? What do you mean?"

"Because you have just as good a chance of finding this lady in the one as in the other."

Lestrade shot an angry glance at my companion. "I suppose you know all about it," he snarled.

"Well, I have only just heard the facts, but my mind is made up."

"Oh, indeed! Then you think that the Serpentine plays no part in the matter?"

"I think it very unlikely."

"Then perhaps you will kindly explain how it is that we found this in it?" He opened his bag as he spoke, and tumbled onto the floor a wedding-dress of watered silk, a pair of white satin shoes and a bride's wreath and veil, all discoloured and soaked in water. "There," said he, putting a new wedding-ring upon the top of the pile. "There is a little nut for you to crack, Master Holmes."

"Oh, indeed!" said my friend, blowing blue rings into the air. "You dragged them from the Serpentine?"

"No. They were found floating near the margin by a park-keeper. They have been identified as her clothes, and it seemed to me that if the clothes were there the body would not be far off."

"By the same brilliant reasoning, every man's body is to be found in the neighbourhood of his wardrobe. And pray what did you hope to arrive at through this?"

"At some evidence implicating Flora Millar in the disappearance."

"I am afraid that you will find it difficult."

"Are you, indeed, now?" cried Lestrade with some bitterness. "I am afraid, Holmes, that you are not very practical with your deductions and your inferences. You have made two blunders in as many minutes. This dress does implicate Miss Flora Millar."

"And how?"

"In the dress is a pocket. In the pocket is a card-case. In the card-case is a note. And here is the very note." He slapped it down upon the table in front of him. "Listen to this: 'You will see me when all is ready. Come at once. F.H.M.' Now my theory all along has been that Lady St. Simon was decoyed away by Flora Millar, and that she, with confederates, no doubt, was responsible for her disappearance. Here, signed with her initials, is the very note which was no doubt quietly slipped into her hand at the door and which lured her within their reach."

"Very good, Lestrade," said Holmes, laughing. "You really are very fine indeed. Let me see it." He took up the paper in a listless way, but his attention instantly became riveted, and he gave a little cry of satisfaction. "This is indeed important," said he.

"Ha! You find it so?"

"Extremely so. I congratulate you warmly."

Lestrade rose in his triumph and bent his head to look. "Why," he shrieked, "you're looking at the wrong side!"

"On the contrary, this is the right side."

"The right side? You're mad! Here is the note written in pencil over here."

"And over here is what appears to be the fragment of a hotel bill, which interests me deeply."

"There's nothing in it. I looked at it before," said Lestrade. "'Oct. 4th, rooms *8s.*, breakfast *2s. 6d.*, cocktail *1s.*, lunch *2s. 6d.*, glass sherry, *8d.*' I see nothing in that."

"Very likely not. It is most important, all the same. As to the note, it is important also, or at least the initials are, so I congratulate you again."

"I've wasted time enough," said Lestrade, rising. "I believe in hard

work and not in sitting by the fire spinning fine theories. Good-day, Mr. Holmes, and we shall see which gets to the bottom of the matter first." He gathered up the garments, thrust them into the bag, and made for the door.

"Just one hint to you, Lestrade," drawled Holmes before his rival vanished; "I will tell you the true solution of the matter. Lady St. Simon is a myth. There is not, and there never has been, any such person."

Lestrade looked sadly at my companion. Then he turned to me, tapped his forehead three times, shook his head solemnly, and hurried away.

He had hardly shut the door behind him when Holmes rose to put on his overcoat. "There is something in what the fellow says about outdoor work," he remarked, "so I think, Watson, that I must leave you to your papers for a little."

It was after five o'clock when Sherlock Holmes left me, but I had no time to be lonely, for within an hour there arrived a confectioner's man with a very large flat box. This he unpacked with the help of a youth whom he had brought with him, and presently, to my very great astonishment, a quite epicurean little cold supper began to be laid out upon our humble lodging-house mahogany. There were a couple of brace of cold woodcock, a pheasant, a *pâté de foie gras* pie with a group of ancient and cobwebby bottles. Having laid out all these luxuries, my two visitors vanished away, like the genii of the Arabian Nights, with no explanation save that the things had been paid for and were ordered to this address.

Just before nine o'clock Sherlock Holmes stepped briskly into the room. His features were gravely set, but there was a light in his eye which made me think that he had not been disappointed in his conclusions.

"They have laid the supper, then," he said, rubbing his hands.

"You seem to expect company. They have laid for five."

"Yes, I fancy we may have some company dropping in," said he. "I am surprised that Lord St. Simon has not already arrived. Ha! I fancy that I hear his step now upon the stairs."

It was indeed our visitor of the afternoon who came bustling in, dangling his glasses more vigorously than ever, and with a very perturbed expression upon his aristocratic features.

"My messenger reached you, then?" asked Holmes.

"Yes, and I confess that the contents startled me beyond measure. Have you good authority for what you say?"

"The best possible."

Lord St. Simon sank into a chair and passed his hand over his forehead.

"What will the Duke say," he murmured, "when he hears that one of the family has been subjected to such humiliation?"

"It is the purest accident. I cannot allow that there is any humiliation."

"Ah, you look on these things from another standpoint."

"I fail to see that anyone is to blame. I can hardly see how the lady could have acted otherwise, though her abrupt method of doing it was undoubtedly to be regretted. Having no mother, she had no one to advise her at such a crisis."

"It was a slight, sir, a public slight," said Lord St. Simon, tapping his fingers upon the table.

"You must make allowance for this poor girl, placed in so unprecedented a position."

"I will make no allowance. I am very angry indeed, and I have been shamefully used."

"I think that I heard a ring," said Holmes. "Yes, there are steps on the landing. If I cannot persuade you to take a lenient view of the matter, Lord St. Simon, I have brought an advocate here who may be more successful." He opened the door and ushered in a lady and gentleman. "Lord St. Simon," said he "allow me to introduce you to Mr. and Mrs. Francis Hay Moulton. The lady, I think, you have already met."

At the sight of these newcomers our client had sprung from his seat and stood very erect, with his eyes cast down and his hand thrust into the breast of his frock-coat, a picture of offended dignity. The lady had taken a quick step forward and had held out her hand to him, but he still refused to raise his eyes. It was as well for his resolution, perhaps, for her pleading face was one which it was hard to resist.

"You're angry, Robert," said she. "Well, I guess you have every cause to be."

"Pray make no apology to me," said Lord St. Simon bitterly.

"Oh, yes, I know that I have treated you real bad and that I should have spoken to you before I went; but I was kind of rattled, and from the time when I saw Frank here again I just didn't know what I was doing or saying. I only wonder I didn't fall down and do a faint right there before the altar."

"Perhaps, Mrs. Moulton, you would like my friend and me to leave the room while you explain this matter?"

"If I may give an opinion," remarked the strange gentleman, "we've had just a little too much secrecy over this business already. For my part, I should like all Europe and America to hear the rights of it." He was a small, wiry, sunburnt man, clean-shaven, with a sharp face and alert manner.

"Then I'll tell our story right away," said the lady. "Frank here and I met in '84, in McQuire's camp, near the Rockies, where Pa was working a claim. We were engaged to each other, Frank and I; but then one day father struck a rich pocket and made a pile, while poor Frank here had a claim that petered out and came to nothing. The richer Pa grew the poorer was Frank; so at last Pa wouldn't hear of our engagement lasting any longer, and he took me away to 'Frisco. Frank wouldn't throw up his hand, though; so he followed me there, and he saw me without Pa knowing anything about it. It would only have made him mad to know, so we just fixed it all up for ourselves. Frank said that he would go and make his pile, too, and never come back to claim me until he had as much as Pa. So then I promised to wait for him to the end of time and pledged myself not to marry anyone else while he lived. 'Why shouldn't we be married right away, then,' said he, 'and then I will feel sure of you; and I won't claim to be your husband until I come back?' Well, we talked it over, and he had fixed it all up so nicely, with a clergyman all ready in waiting, that we just did it right there; and then Frank went off to seek his fortune, and I went back to Pa.

"The next I heard of Frank was that he was in Montana, and then he went prospecting in Arizona, and then I heard of him from New Mexico. After that came a long newspaper story about how a miners' camp had been attacked by Apache Indians, and there was my Frank's name among the killed. I fainted dead away, and I was very sick for months after. Pa thought I had a decline and took me to half the doctors in 'Frisco. Not a word of news came for a year and more, so that I never doubted that Frank was really dead. Then Lord St. Simon came to 'Frisco, and we came to London, and a marriage was arranged, and Pa was very pleased, but I felt all the time that no man on this earth would ever take the place in my heart that had been given to my poor Frank.

"Still, if I had married Lord St. Simon, of course I'd have done my duty by him. We can't command our love, but we can our actions. I went to the altar with him with the intention to make him just as good a wife as it was in me to be. But you may imagine what I felt when, just as I came to the altar rails, I glanced back and saw Frank standing and looking at me out of the first pew. I thought it was his ghost at first; but when I looked again there he was still, with a kind of question in his eyes, as if to ask me whether I were glad or sorry to see him. I wonder I didn't drop. I know that everything was turning round, and the words of the clergyman were just like the buzz of a bee in my ear. I didn't know what to do. Should I stop the service and make a scene in the church? I glanced at him again, and he seemed to know what I was thinking, for he raised his finger to his lips to tell me to be still. Then I saw him scribble on a piece of paper, and I knew that he was writing me a note. As I passed his pew on the way out I dropped my bouquet over to him, and he slipped the note into my hand when he returned me the flowers. It was only a line asking me to join him when he made the sign to me to do so. Of course I never doubted for a moment that my first duty was now to him, and I determined to do just whatever he might direct.

"When I got back I told my maid, who had known him in California, and had always been his friend. I ordered her to say nothing, but to get a few things packed and my ulster ready. I know I ought to have spoken to Lord St. Simon, but it was dreadful hard before his mother and all those great people. I just made up my mind to run away and explain afterwards. I hadn't been at the table ten minutes before I saw Frank out of the window at the other side of the road. He beckoned to me and then began walking into the Park. I slipped out, put on my things, and followed him. Some woman came talking something or other about Lord St. Simon to me—seemed to me from the little I heard as if he had a little secret of his own before marriage also—but I managed to get away from her and soon overtook Frank. We got into a cab together, and away we drove to some lodgings he had taken in Gordon Square, and that was my true wedding after all those years of waiting. Frank had been a prisoner among the Apaches, had escaped, came on to 'Frisco, found that I had given him up for dead and had gone to England, followed me there, and had come upon me at last on the very morning of my second wedding."

"I saw it in a paper," explained the American. "It gave the name and the church but not where the lady lived."

"Then we had a talk as to what we should do, and Frank was all for openness, but I was so ashamed of it all that I felt as if I should like to vanish away and never see any of them again—just sending a line to Pa, perhaps, to show him that I was alive. It was awful to me to think of all those lords and ladies sitting round that breakfast-table and waiting for me to come back. So Frank took my wedding-clothes and things and made a bundle of them, so that I should not be traced, and dropped them away somewhere where no one could find them. It is likely that we should have gone on to Paris tomorrow, only that this good gentleman, Mr. Holmes, came round to us this evening, though how he found us is more than I can think, and he showed us very clearly and kindly that I was wrong and that Frank was right, and that we should be putting ourselves in the wrong if we were so secret. Then he offered to give us a chance of talking to Lord St. Simon alone, and so we came right away round to his rooms at once. Now, Robert, you have heard it all, and I am very sorry if I have given you pain, and I hope that you do not think very meanly of me."

Lord St. Simon had by no means relaxed his rigid attitude, but had listened with a frowning brow and a compressed lip to this long narrative.

"Excuse me," he said, "but it is not my custom to discuss my most intimate personal affairs in this public manner."

"Then you won't forgive me? You won't shake hands before I go?"

"Oh, certainly, if it would give you any pleasure." He put out his hand and coldly grasped that which she extended to him.

"I had hoped," suggested Holmes, "that you would have joined us in a friendly supper."

"I think that there you ask a little too much," responded his Lordship. "I may be forced to acquiesce in these recent developments, but I can hardly be expected to make merry over them. I think that with your permission I will now wish you all a very good-night." He included us all in a sweeping bow and stalked out of the room.

"Then I trust that you at least will honour me with your company," said Sherlock Holmes. "It is always a joy to meet an American, Mr. Moulton, for I am one of those who believe that the folly of a monarch and the blundering of a minister in far-gone years will not prevent our children from being some day citizens of the same world-wide country under a flag which shall be a quartering of the Union Jack with the Stars and Stripes."

"The case has been an interesting one," remarked Holmes when our visitors had left us, "because it serves to show very clearly how simple the explanation may be of an affair which at first sight seems to be almost inexplicable. Nothing could be more natural than the sequence of events as narrated by this lady, and nothing stranger than the result when viewed, for instance, by Mr. Lestrade of Scotland Yard."

"You were not yourself at fault at all, then?"

"From the first, two facts were very obvious to me, the one that the lady had been quite willing to undergo the wedding ceremony, the other that she had repented of it within a few minutes of returning home. Obviously something had occurred during the morning, then, to cause her to change her mind. What could that something be? She could not have spoken to anyone when she was out, for she had been in the company of the bridegroom. Had she seen someone, then? If she had, it must be someone from America because she had spent so short a time in this country that she could hardly have allowed anyone to acquire so deep an influence over her that the mere sight of him would induce her to change her plans so completely. You see we have already arrived, by a process of exclusion, at the idea that she might have seen an American. Then who could this American be, and why should he possess so much influence over her? It might be a lover; it might be a husband. Her young womanhood had, I knew, been spent in rough scenes and under strange conditions. So far I had got before I ever heard Lord St. Simon's narrative. When he told us of a man in a pew, of the change in the bride's manner, of so transparent a device for obtaining a note as the dropping of a bouquet, of her resort to her confidential maid, and of her very significant allusion to claim-jumping, which in miners' parlance means taking possession of that which another person has a prior claim to, the whole situation became absolutely clear. She had gone off with a man, and the man was either a lover or was a previous husband—the chances being in favour of the latter."

"And how in the world did you find them?"

"It might have been difficult, but friend Lestrade held information in his hands the value of which he did not himself know. The initials were, of course, of the highest importance, but more valuable still was it to know that within a week he had settled his bill at one of the most select London hotels."

"How did you deduce the select?"

"By the select prices. Eight shillings for a bed and eightpence for a glass of sherry pointed to one of the most expensive hotels. There are not many in London which charge at that rate. In the second one which I visited in Northumberland Avenue, I learned by an inspection of the book that Francis H. Moulton, an American gentleman, had left only the day before, and on looking over the entries against him, I came upon the very items which I had seen in the duplicate bill. His letters were to be forwarded to 226 Gordon Square; so thither I travelled, and being fortunate enough to find the loving couple at home, I ventured to give them some paternal advice and to point out to them that it would be better in every way that they should make their position a little clearer both to the general public and to Lord St. Simon in particular. I invited them to meet him here, and, as you see, I made him keep the appointment."

"But with no very good result," I remarked. "His conduct was certainly not very gracious."

"Ah, Watson," said Holmes, smiling, "perhaps you would not be very gracious either, if, after all the trouble of wooing and wedding, you found yourself deprived in an instant of wife and of fortune. I think that we may judge Lord St. Simon very mercifully and thank our stars that we are never likely to find ourselves in the same position. Draw your chair up and hand me my violin, for the only problem we have still to solve is how to while away these bleak autumnal evenings."

THE BERYL CORONET

"Holmes," said I as I stood one morning in our bow-window looking down the street, "here is a madman coming along. It seems rather sad that his relatives should allow him to come out alone."

My friend rose lazily from his armchair and stood with his hands in the pockets of his dressing-gown, looking over my shoulder. It was a bright, crisp February morning, and the snow of the day before still lay deep upon the ground, shimmering brightly in the wintry sun. Down the centre of Baker Street it had been ploughed into a brown crumbly band by the traffic, but at either side and on the heaped-up edges of the footpaths it still lay as white as when it fell. The grey pavement had been cleaned and scraped, but was still dangerously slippery, so that there were fewer passengers than usual. Indeed, from the direction of the Metropolitan Station no one was coming save the single gentleman whose eccentric conduct had drawn my attention.

He was a man of about fifty, tall, portly, and imposing, with a massive, strongly marked face and a commanding figure. He was dressed in a sombre yet rich style, in black frock-coat, shining hat, neat brown gaiters, and well-cut pearl-grey trousers. Yet his actions were in absurd contrast to the dignity of his dress and features, for he was running hard, with occasional little springs, such as a weary man gives who is little accustomed to set any tax upon his legs. As he ran he jerked his hands up and down, waggled his head, and writhed his face into the most extraordinary contortions.

"What on earth can be the matter with him?" I asked. "He is looking up at the numbers of the houses."

"I believe that he is coming here," said Holmes, rubbing his hands.

"Here?"

"Yes; I rather think he is coming to consult me professionally. I think that I recognise the symptoms. Ha! Did I not tell you?" As he spoke, the man, puffing and blowing, rushed at our door and pulled at our bell until the whole house resounded with the clanging.

A few moments later he was in our room, still puffing, still gesticulating, but with so fixed a look of grief and despair in his eyes that our smiles were turned in an instant to horror and pity. For a while he could not get his words out, but swayed his body and plucked at his hair like one who has been driven to the extreme limits of his reason. Then, suddenly springing to his feet, he beat his head against the wall with such force that we both rushed upon him and tore him away to the centre of the room. Sherlock Holmes pushed him down into the easy-chair and, sitting beside him, patted his hand and chatted with him in the easy, soothing tones which he knew so well how to employ.

"You have come to me to tell your story, have you not?" said he. "You are fatigued with your haste. Pray wait until you have recovered yourself, and then I shall be most happy to look into any little problem which you may submit to me."

The man sat for a minute or more with a heaving chest, fighting against his emotion. Then he passed his handkerchief over his brow, set his lips tight, and turned his face towards us.

"No doubt you think me mad?" said he.

"I see that you have had some great trouble," responded Holmes.

"God knows I have!—A trouble which is enough to unseat my reason, so sudden and so terrible is it. Public disgrace I might have faced, although I am a man whose character has never yet borne a stain. Private affliction also is the lot of every man; but the two coming together, and in so frightful a form, have been enough to shake my very soul. Besides, it is not I alone. The very noblest in the land may suffer unless some way be found out of this horrible affair."

"Pray compose yourself, sir," said Holmes, "and let me have a clear account of who you are and what it is that has befallen you."

"My name," answered our visitor, "is probably familiar to your ears. I am Alexander Holder, of the banking firm of Holder & Stevenson, of Threadneedle Street."

The name was indeed well known to us as belonging to the senior partner in the second largest private banking concern in the City of London. What could have happened, then, to bring one of the foremost citizens of London to this most pitiable pass? We waited, all curiosity, until with another effort he braced himself to tell his story.

"I feel that time is of value," said he; "that is why I hastened here when the police inspector suggested that I should secure your co-operation. I came to Baker Street by the Underground and hurried from there on foot, for the cabs go slowly through this snow. That is why I was so out of breath, for I am a man who takes very little exercise. I feel better now, and I will put the facts before you as shortly and yet as clearly as I can.

"It is, of course, well known to you that in a successful banking business as much depends upon our being able to find remunerative investments for our funds as upon our increasing our connection and the number of our depositors. One of our most lucrative means of laying out money is in the shape of loans, where the security is unimpeachable. We have done a good deal in this direction during the last few years, and there are many noble families to whom we have advanced large sums upon the security of their pictures, libraries, or plate.

"Yesterday morning I was seated in my office at the bank when a card was brought in to me by one of the clerks. I started when I saw the name, for it was that of none other than—well, perhaps even to you I had better say no more than that it was a name which is a household word all over the earth—one of the highest, noblest, most exalted names in England. I was overwhelmed by the honour and attempted, when he entered, to say so, but he plunged at once into business with the air of a man who wishes to hurry quickly through a disagreeable task.

" 'Mr. Holder,' said he, 'I have been informed that you are in the habit of advancing money.'

" 'The firm does so when the security is good.' I answered.

" 'It is absolutely essential to me,' said he, 'that I should have 50,000 pounds at once. I could, of course, borrow so trifling a sum ten times over from my friends, but I much prefer to make it a matter of business and to carry out that business myself. In my position you can readily understand that it is unwise to place one's self under obligations.'

" 'For how long, may I ask, do you want this sum?' I asked.

" 'Next Monday I have a large sum due to me, and I shall then most certainly repay what you advance, with whatever interest you think it right to charge. But it is very essential to me that the money should be paid at once.'

" 'I should be happy to advance it without further parley from my own private purse,' said I, 'were it not that the strain would be rather more than it could bear. If, on the other hand, I am to do it in the name of the firm, then in justice to my partner I must insist that, even in your case, every businesslike precaution should be taken.'

" 'I should much prefer to have it so,' said he, raising up a square,

black morocco case which he had laid beside his chair. 'You have doubtless heard of the Beryl Coronet?'

" 'One of the most precious public possessions of the empire,' said I.

" 'Precisely.' He opened the case, and there, imbedded in soft, flesh-coloured velvet, lay the magnificent piece of jewellery which he had named. 'There are thirty-nine enormous beryls,' said he, 'and the price of the gold chasing is incalculable. The lowest estimate would put the worth of the coronet at double the sum which I have asked. I am prepared to leave it with you as my security.'

"I took the precious case into my hands and looked in some perplexity from it to my illustrious client.

" 'You doubt its value?' he asked.

" 'Not at all. I only doubt—'

" 'The propriety of my leaving it. You may set your mind at rest about that. I should not dream of doing so were it not absolutely certain that I should be able in four days to reclaim it. It is a pure matter of form. Is the security sufficient?'

" 'Ample.'

" 'You understand, Mr. Holder, that I am giving you a strong proof of the confidence which I have in you, founded upon all that I have heard of you. I rely upon you not only to be discreet and to refrain from all gossip upon the matter but, above all, to preserve this coronet with every possible precaution because I need not say that a great public scandal would be caused if any harm were to befall it. Any injury to it would be almost as serious as its complete loss, for there are no beryls in the world to match these, and it would be impossible to replace them. I leave it with you, however, with every confidence, and I shall call for it in person on Monday morning.'

"Seeing that my client was anxious to leave, I said no more but, calling for my cashier, I ordered him to pay over fifty 1,000 pound notes. When I was alone once more, however, with the precious case lying upon the table in front of me, I could not but think with some misgivings of the immense responsibility which it entailed upon me. There could be no doubt that, as it was a national possession, a horrible scandal would ensue if any misfortune should occur to it. I already regretted having ever consented to take charge of it. However, it was too late to alter the matter now, so I locked it up in my private safe and turned once more to my work.

"When evening came I felt that it would be an imprudence to leave so precious a thing in the office behind me. Bankers' safes had been forced before now, and why should not mine be? If so, how terrible would be the position in which I should find myself! I determined, therefore, that for the next few days I would always carry the case backward and forward with me, so that it might never be really out of my reach. With this intention, I called a cab and drove out to my house at Streatham, carrying the jewel with me. I did not breathe freely until I had taken it upstairs and locked it in the bureau of my dressing-room.

"And now a word as to my household, Mr. Holmes, for I wish you to thoroughly understand the situation. My groom and my page sleep out of the house, and may be set aside altogether. I have three maid-servants who have been with me a number of years and whose absolute reliability is quite above suspicion. Another, Lucy Parr, the second waiting-maid, has only been in my service a few months. She came with an excellent character, however, and has always given me satisfaction. She is a very pretty girl and has attracted admirers who have occasionally hung about the place. That is the only drawback which we have found to her, but we believe her to be a thoroughly good girl in every way.

"So much for the servants. My family itself is so small that it will not take me long to describe it. I am a widower and have an only son, Arthur. He has been a disappointment to me, Mr. Holmes—a grievous disappointment. I have no doubt that I am myself to blame. People tell me that I have spoiled him. Very likely I have. When my dear wife died I felt that he was all I had to love. I could not bear to see the smile fade even for a moment from his face. I have never denied him a wish. Perhaps it would have been better for both of us had I been sterner, but I meant it for the best.

"It was naturally my intention that he should succeed me in my business, but he was not of a business turn. He was wild, wayward, and, to speak the truth, I could not trust him in the handling of large sums of money. When he was young he became a member of an aristocratic club, and there, having charming manners, he was soon the intimate of a number of men with long purses and expensive habits. He learned to play heavily at cards and to squander money on the turf, until he had again and again to come to me and implore me to give him an advance upon his allowance, that he might settle his debts of honour. He tried more than once to break away from the dangerous company which

he was keeping, but each time the influence of his friend, Sir George Burnwell, was enough to draw him back again.

"And, indeed, I could not wonder that such a man as Sir George Burnwell should gain an influence over him, for he has frequently brought him to my house, and I have found myself that I could hardly resist the fascination of his manner. He is older than Arthur, a man of the world to his fingertips, one who had been everywhere, seen everything, a brilliant talker, and a man of great personal beauty. Yet when I think of him in cold blood, far away from the glamour of his presence, I am convinced from his cynical speech and the look which I have caught in his eyes that he is one who should be deeply distrusted. So I think, and so, too, thinks my little Mary, who has a woman's quick insight into character.

"And now there is only she to be described. She is my niece; but when my brother died five years ago and left her alone in the world I adopted her, and have looked upon her ever since as my daughter. She is a sunbeam in my house—sweet, loving, beautiful, a wonderful manager and housekeeper, yet as tender and quiet and gentle as a woman could be. She is my right hand. I do not know what I could do without her. In only one matter has she ever gone against my wishes. Twice my boy has asked her to marry him, for he loves her devotedly, but each time she has refused him. I think that if anyone could have drawn him into the right path it would have been she, and that his marriage might have changed his whole life; but now, alas! It is too late—forever too late!

"Now, Mr. Holmes, you know the people who live under my roof, and I shall continue with my miserable story.

"When we were taking coffee in the drawing-room that night after dinner, I told Arthur and Mary my experience, and of the precious treasure which we had under our roof, suppressing only the name of my client. Lucy Parr, who had brought in the coffee, had, I am sure, left the room; but I cannot swear that the door was closed. Mary and Arthur were much interested and wished to see the famous coronet, but I thought it better not to disturb it.

" 'Where have you put it?' asked Arthur.

" 'In my own bureau.'

" 'Well, I hope to goodness the house won't be burgled during the night.' said he.

" 'It is locked up,' I answered.

" 'Oh, any old key will fit that bureau. When I was a youngster I have opened it myself with the key of the box-room cupboard.'

"He often had a wild way of talking, so that I thought little of what he said. He followed me to my room, however, that night with a very grave face.

" 'Look here, dad,' said he with his eyes cast down, 'can you let me have 200 pounds?'

" 'No, I cannot!' I answered sharply. 'I have been far too generous with you in money matters.'

" 'You have been very kind,' said he, 'but I must have this money, or else I can never show my face inside the club again.'

" 'And a very good thing, too!' I cried.

" 'Yes, but you would not have me leave it a dishonoured man,' said he. 'I could not bear the disgrace. I must raise the money in some way, and if you will not let me have it, then I must try other means.'

"I was very angry, for this was the third demand during the month. 'You shall not have a farthing from me,' I cried, on which he bowed and left the room without another word.

"When he was gone I unlocked my bureau, made sure that my treasure was safe, and locked it again. Then I started to go round the house to see that all was secure—a duty which I usually leave to Mary but which I thought it well to perform myself that night. As I came down the stairs I saw Mary herself at the side window of the hall, which she closed and fastened as I approached.

" 'Tell me, dad,' said she, looking, I thought, a little disturbed, 'did you give Lucy, the maid, leave to go out tonight?'

" 'Certainly not.'

" 'She came in just now by the back door. I have no doubt that she has only been to the side gate to see someone, but I think that it is hardly safe and should be stopped.'

" 'You must speak to her in the morning, or I will if you prefer it. Are you sure that everything is fastened?'

" 'Quite sure, dad.'

" 'Then, good-night.' I kissed her and went up to my bedroom again, where I was soon asleep.

"I am endeavouring to tell you everything, Mr. Holmes, which may have any bearing upon the case, but I beg that you will question me upon any point which I do not make clear."

"On the contrary, your statement is singularly lucid."

"I come to a part of my story now in which I should wish to be particularly so. I am not a very heavy sleeper, and the anxiety in my mind tended, no doubt, to make me even less so than usual. About two in the morning, then, I was awakened by some sound in the house. It had ceased ere I was wide awake, but it had left an impression behind it as though a window had gently closed somewhere. I lay listening with all my ears. Suddenly, to my horror, there was a distinct sound of footsteps moving softly in the next room. I slipped out of bed, all palpitating with fear, and peeped round the corner of my dressing-room door.

" 'Arthur!' I screamed, 'You villain! You thief! How dare you touch that coronet?'

"The gas was half up, as I had left it, and my unhappy boy, dressed only in his shirt and trousers, was standing beside the light, holding the coronet in his hands. He appeared to be wrenching at it, or bending it with all his strength. At my cry he dropped it from his grasp and turned as pale as death. I snatched it up and examined it. One of the gold corners, with three of the beryls in it, was missing.

" 'You blackguard!' I shouted, beside myself with rage. 'You have destroyed it! You have dishonoured me forever! Where are the jewels which you have stolen?'

" 'Stolen!' he cried.

" 'Yes, you thief!' I roared, shaking him by the shoulder.

" 'There are none missing. There cannot be any missing,' said he.

" 'There are three missing. And you know where they are. Must I call you a liar as well as a thief? Did I not see you trying to tear off another piece?'

" 'You have called me names enough,' said he, 'I will not stand it any longer. I shall not say another word about this business, since you have chosen to insult me. I will leave your house in the morning and make my own way in the world.'

" 'You shall leave it in the hands of the police!' I cried half-mad with grief and rage. 'I shall have this matter probed to the bottom.'

" 'You shall learn nothing from me,' said he with a passion such as I should not have thought was in his nature. 'If you choose to call the police, let the police find what they can.'

"By this time the whole house was astir, for I had raised my voice in my anger. Mary was the first to rush into my room, and, at the sight of the coronet and of Arthur's face, she read the whole story and, with a scream, fell down senseless on the ground. I sent the house-maid for the police and put the investigation into their hands at once. When the inspector and a constable entered the house, Arthur, who had stood sullenly with his arms folded, asked me whether it was my intention to charge him with theft. I answered that it had ceased to be a private matter, but had become a public one, since the ruined coronet was national property. I was determined that the law should have its way in everything.

" 'At least,' said he, 'you will not have me arrested at once. It would be to your advantage as well as mine if I might leave the house for five minutes.'

" 'That you may get away, or perhaps that you may conceal what you have stolen,' said I. And then, realising the dreadful position in which I was placed, I implored him to remember that not only my honour but that of one who was far greater than I was at stake; and that he threatened to raise a scandal which would convulse the nation. He might avert it all if he would but tell me what he had done with the three missing stones.

" 'You may as well face the matter,' said I; 'you have been caught in the act, and no confession could make your guilt more heinous. If you but make such reparation as is in your power, by telling us where the beryls are, all shall be forgiven and forgotten.'

" 'Keep your forgiveness for those who ask for it,' he answered, turning away from me with a sneer. I saw that he was too hardened for any words of mine to influence him. There was but one way for it. I called in the inspector and gave him into custody. A search was made at once not only of his person but of his room and of every portion of the house where he could possibly have concealed the gems; but no trace of them could be found, nor would the wretched boy open his mouth for all our persuasions and our threats. This morning he was removed to a cell, and I, after going through all the police formalities, have hurried round to you to implore you to use your skill in unravelling the matter. The police have openly confessed that they can at present make nothing of it. You may go to any expense which you think necessary. I have already offered a reward of 1,000 pounds. My God, what shall I do! I have lost my honour, my gems, and my son in one night. Oh, what shall I do!"

He put a hand on either side of his head and rocked himself to and fro, droning to himself like a child whose grief has got beyond words.

Sherlock Holmes sat silent for some few minutes, with his brows knitted and his eyes fixed upon the fire.

"Do you receive much company?" he asked.

"None save my partner with his family and an occasional friend of Arthur's. Sir George Burnwell has been several times lately. No one else, I think."

"Do you go out much in society?"

"Arthur does. Mary and I stay at home. We neither of us care for it."

"That is unusual in a young girl."

"She is of a quiet nature. Besides, she is not so very young. She is four-and-twenty."

"This matter, from what you say, seems to have been a shock to her also."

"Terrible! She is even more affected than I."

"You have neither of you any doubt as to your son's guilt?"

"How can we have when I saw him with my own eyes with the coronet in his hands?"

"I hardly consider that a conclusive proof. Was the remainder of the coronet at all injured?"

"Yes, it was twisted."

"Do you not think, then, that he might have been trying to straighten it?"

"God bless you! You are doing what you can for him and for me. But it is too heavy a task. What was he doing there at all? If his purpose were innocent, why did he not say so?"

"Precisely. And if it were guilty, why did he not invent a lie? His silence appears to me to cut both ways. There are several singular points about the case. What did the police think of the noise which awoke you from your sleep?"

"They considered that it might be caused by Arthur's closing his bedroom door."

"A likely story! As if a man bent on felony would slam his door so as to wake a household. What did they say, then, of the disappearance of these gems?"

"They are still sounding the planking and probing the furniture in the hope of finding them."

"Have they thought of looking outside the house?"

"Yes, they have shown extraordinary energy. The whole garden has already been minutely examined."

"Now, my dear sir," said Holmes, "is it not obvious to you now that this matter really strikes very much deeper than either you or the police were at first inclined to think? It appeared to you to be a simple case; to me it seems exceedingly complex. Consider what is involved by your theory. You suppose that your son came down from his bed, went, at great risk, to your dressing-room, opened your bureau, took out your coronet, broke off by main force a small portion of it, went off to some other place, concealed three gems out of the thirty-nine, with such skill that nobody can find them, and then returned with the other thirty-six into the room in which he exposed himself to the greatest danger of being discovered. I ask you now, is such a theory tenable?"

"But what other is there?" cried the banker with a gesture of despair. "If his motives were innocent, why does he not explain them?"

"It is our task to find that out," replied Holmes; "so now, if you please, Mr. Holder, we will set off for Streatham together, and devote an hour to glancing a little more closely into details."

My friend insisted upon my accompanying them in their expedition, which I was eager enough to do, for my curiosity and sympathy were deeply stirred by the story to which we had listened. I confess that the guilt of the banker's son appeared to me to be as obvious as it did to his unhappy father, but still I had such faith in Holmes' judgment that I felt that there must be some grounds for hope as long as he was dissatisfied with the accepted explanation. He hardly spoke a word the whole way out to the southern suburb, but sat with his chin upon his breast and his hat drawn over his eyes, sunk in the deepest thought. Our client appeared to have taken fresh heart at the little glimpse of hope which had been presented to him, and he even broke into a desultory chat with me over his business affairs. A short railway journey and a shorter walk brought us to Fairbank, the modest residence of the great financier.

Fairbank was a good-sized square house of white stone, standing back a little from the road. A double carriage-sweep, with a snow-clad lawn, stretched down in front to two large iron gates which closed the entrance. On the right side was a small wooden thicket, which led into a narrow path between two neat hedges stretching from the road to the kitchen door, and forming the tradesmen's entrance. On the left ran a

lane which led to the stables, and was not itself within the grounds at all, being a public, though little used, thoroughfare. Holmes left us standing at the door and walked slowly all round the house, across the front, down the tradesmen's path, and so round by the garden behind into the stable lane. So long was he that Mr. Holder and I went into the dining-room and waited by the fire until he should return. We were sitting there in silence when the door opened and a young lady came in. She was rather above the middle height, slim, with dark hair and eyes, which seemed the darker against the absolute pallor of her skin. I do not think that I have ever seen such deadly paleness in a woman's face. Her lips, too, were bloodless, but her eyes were flushed with crying. As she swept silently into the room she impressed me with a greater sense of grief than the banker had done in the morning, and it was the more striking in her as she was evidently a woman of strong character, with immense capacity for self-restraint. Disregarding my presence, she went straight to her uncle and passed her hand over his head with a sweet womanly caress.

"You have given orders that Arthur should be liberated, have you not, dad?" she asked.

"No, no, my girl, the matter must be probed to the bottom."

"But I am so sure that he is innocent. You know what woman's instincts are. I know that he has done no harm and that you will be sorry for having acted so harshly."

"Why is he silent, then, if he is innocent?"

"Who knows? Perhaps because he was so angry that you should suspect him."

"How could I help suspecting him, when I actually saw him with the coronet in his hand?"

"Oh, but he had only picked it up to look at it. Oh, do, do take my word for it that he is innocent. Let the matter drop and say no more. It is so dreadful to think of our dear Arthur in prison!"

"I shall never let it drop until the gems are found—never, Mary! Your affection for Arthur blinds you as to the awful consequences to me. Far from hushing the thing up, I have brought a gentleman down from London to inquire more deeply into it."

"This gentleman?" she asked, facing round to me.

"No, his friend. He wished us to leave him alone. He is round in the stable lane now."

"The stable lane?" She raised her dark eyebrows. "What can he hope to find there? Ah! This, I suppose, is he. I trust, sir, that you will succeed in proving, what I feel sure is the truth, that my cousin Arthur is innocent of this crime."

"I fully share your opinion, and I trust, with you, that we may prove it," returned Holmes, going back to the mat to knock the snow from his shoes. "I believe I have the honour of addressing Miss Mary Holder. Might I ask you a question or two?"

"Pray do, sir, if it may help to clear this horrible affair up."

"You heard nothing yourself last night?"

"Nothing, until my uncle here began to speak loudly. I heard that, and I came down."

"You shut up the windows and doors the night before. Did you fasten all the windows?"

"Yes."

"Were they all fastened this morning?"

"Yes."

"You have a maid who has a sweetheart? I think that you remarked to your uncle last night that she had been out to see him?"

"Yes, and she was the girl who waited in the drawing-room, and who may have heard uncle's remarks about the coronet."

"I see. You infer that she may have gone out to tell her sweetheart, and that the two may have planned the robbery."

"But what is the good of all these vague theories," cried the banker impatiently, "when I have told you that I saw Arthur with the coronet in his hands?"

"Wait a little, Mr. Holder. We must come back to that. About this girl, Miss Holder. You saw her return by the kitchen door, I presume?"

"Yes; when I went to see if the door was fastened for the night I met her slipping in. I saw the man, too, in the gloom."

"Do you know him?"

"Oh, yes! he is the greengrocer who brings our vegetables round. His name is Francis Prosper."

"He stood," said Holmes, "to the left of the door—that is to say, farther up the path than is necessary to reach the door?"

"Yes, he did."

"And he is a man with a wooden leg?"

Something like fear sprang up in the young lady's expressive black eyes. "Why, you are like a magician," said she. "How do you know

that?" She smiled, but there was no answering smile in Holmes' thin, eager face.

"I should be very glad now to go upstairs," said he. "I shall probably wish to go over the outside of the house again. Perhaps I had better take a look at the lower windows before I go up."

He walked swiftly round from one to the other, pausing only at the large one which looked from the hall onto the stable lane. This he opened and made a very careful examination of the sill with his powerful magnifying lens. "Now we shall go upstairs," said he at last.

The banker's dressing-room was a plainly furnished little chamber, with a grey carpet, a large bureau, and a long mirror. Holmes went to the bureau first and looked hard at the lock.

"Which key was used to open it?" he asked.

"That which my son himself indicated—that of the cupboard of the lumber-room."

"Have you it here?"

"That is it on the dressing-table."

Sherlock Holmes took it up and opened the bureau.

"It is a noiseless lock," said he. "It is no wonder that it did not wake you. This case, I presume, contains the coronet. We must have a look at it." He opened the case, and taking out the diadem he laid it upon the table. It was a magnificent specimen of the jeweller's art, and the thirty-six stones were the finest that I have ever seen. At one side of the coronet was a cracked edge, where a corner holding three gems had been torn away.

"Now, Mr. Holder," said Holmes, "here is the corner which corresponds to that which has been so unfortunately lost. Might I beg that you will break it off."

The banker recoiled in horror. "I should not dream of trying," said he.

"Then I will." Holmes suddenly bent his strength upon it, but without result. "I feel it give a little," said he; "but, though I am exceptionally strong in the fingers, it would take me all my time to break it. An ordinary man could not do it. Now, what do you think would happen if I did break it, Mr. Holder? There would be a noise like a pistol shot. Do you tell me that all this happened within a few yards of your bed and that you heard nothing of it?"

"I do not know what to think. It is all dark to me."

"But perhaps it may grow lighter as we go. What do you think, Miss Holder?"

"I confess that I still share my uncle's perplexity."

"Your son had no shoes or slippers on when you saw him?"

"He had nothing on save only his trousers and shirt."

"Thank you. We have certainly been favoured with extraordinary luck during this inquiry, and it will be entirely our own fault if we do not succeed in clearing the matter up. With your permission, Mr. Holder, I shall now continue my investigations outside."

He went alone, at his own request, for he explained that any unnecessary footmarks might make his task more difficult. For an hour or more he was at work, returning at last with his feet heavy with snow and his features as inscrutable as ever.

"I think that I have seen now all that there is to see, Mr. Holder," said he; "I can serve you best by returning to my rooms."

"But the gems, Mr. Holmes. Where are they?"

"I cannot tell."

The banker wrung his hands. "I shall never see them again!" he cried. "And my son? You give me hopes?"

"My opinion is in no way altered."

"Then, for God's sake, what was this dark business which was acted in my house last night?"

"If you can call upon me at my Baker Street rooms tomorrow morning between nine and ten I shall be happy to do what I can to make it clearer. I understand that you give me *carte blanche* to act for you, provided only that I get back the gems, and that you place no limit on the sum I may draw."

"I would give my fortune to have them back."

"Very good. I shall look into the matter between this and then. Good-bye; it is just possible that I may have to come over here again before evening."

It was obvious to me that my companion's mind was now made up about the case, although what his conclusions were was more than I could even dimly imagine. Several times during our homeward journey I endeavoured to sound him upon the point, but he always glided away to some other topic, until at last I gave it over in despair. It was not yet three when we found ourselves in our rooms once more. He hurried to his chamber and was down again in a few minutes dressed as a common

loafer. With his collar turned up, his shiny, seedy coat, his red cravat, and his worn boots, he was a perfect sample of the class.

"I think that this should do," said he, glancing into the glass above the fireplace. "I only wish that you could come with me, Watson, but I fear that it won't do. I may be on the trail in this matter, or I may be following a will-o'-the-wisp, but I shall soon know which it is. I hope that I may be back in a few hours." He cut a slice of beef from the joint upon the sideboard, sandwiched it between two rounds of bread, and thrusting this rude meal into his pocket he started off upon his expedition.

I had just finished my tea when he returned, evidently in excellent spirits, swinging an old elastic-sided boot in his hand. He chucked it down into a corner and helped himself to a cup of tea.

"I only looked in as I passed," said he. "I am going right on."

"Where to?"

"Oh, to the other side of the West End. It may be some time before I get back. Don't wait up for me in case I should be late."

"How are you getting on?"

"Oh, so so. Nothing to complain of. I have been out to Streatham since I saw you last, but I did not call at the house. It is a very sweet little problem, and I would not have missed it for a good deal. However, I must not sit gossiping here, but must get these disreputable clothes off and return to my highly respectable self."

I could see by his manner that he had stronger reasons for satisfaction than his words alone would imply. His eyes twinkled, and there was even a touch of colour upon his sallow cheeks. He hastened upstairs, and a few minutes later I heard the slam of the hall door, which told me that he was off once more upon his congenial hunt.

I waited until midnight, but there was no sign of his return, so I retired to my room. It was no uncommon thing for him to be away for days and nights on end when he was hot upon a scent, so that his lateness caused me no surprise. I do not know at what hour he came in, but when I came down to breakfast in the morning there he was with a cup of coffee in one hand and the paper in the other, as fresh and trim as possible.

"You will excuse my beginning without you, Watson," said he, "but you remember that our client has rather an early appointment this morning."

"Why, it is after nine now," I answered. "I should not be surprised if that were he. I thought I heard a ring."

It was, indeed, our friend the financier. I was shocked by the change which had come over him, for his face which was naturally of a broad and massive mould, was now pinched and fallen in, while his hair seemed to me at least a shade whiter. He entered with a weariness and lethargy which was even more painful than his violence of the morning before, and he dropped heavily into the armchair which I pushed forward for him.

"I do not know what I have done to be so severely tried," said he. "Only two days ago I was a happy and prosperous man, without a care in the world. Now I am left to a lonely and dishonoured age. One sorrow comes close upon the heels of another. My niece, Mary, has deserted me."

"Deserted you?"

"Yes. Her bed this morning had not been slept in, her room was empty, and a note for me lay upon the hall table. I had said to her last night, in sorrow and not in anger, that if she had married my boy all might have been well with him. Perhaps it was thoughtless of me to say so. It is to that remark that she refers in this note:

> My Dearest Uncle—I feel that I have brought trouble upon you, and that if I had acted differently this terrible misfortune might never have occurred. I cannot, with this thought in my mind, ever again be happy under your roof, and I feel that I must leave you forever. Do not worry about my future, for that is provided for; and, above all, do not search for me, for it will be fruitless labour and an ill-service to me. In life or in death, I am ever your loving,
>
> Mary

"What could she mean by that note, Mr. Holmes? Do you think it points to suicide?"

"No, no, nothing of the kind. It is perhaps the best possible solution. I trust, Mr. Holder, that you are nearing the end of your troubles."

"Ha! You say so! You have heard something, Mr. Holmes; you have learned something! Where are the gems?"

"You would not think 1,000 pounds apiece an excessive sum for them?"

"I would pay ten."

"That would be unnecessary. Three thousand will cover the matter. And there is a little reward, I fancy. Have you your checkbook? Here is a pen. Better make it out for 4,000 pounds."

With a dazed face the banker made out the required check. Holmes walked over to his desk, took out a little triangular piece of gold with three gems in it, and threw it down upon the table.

With a shriek of joy our client clutched it up.

"You have it!" he gasped. "I am saved! I am saved!"

The reaction of joy was as passionate as his grief had been, and he hugged his recovered gems to his bosom.

"There is one other thing you owe, Mr. Holder," said Sherlock Holmes rather sternly.

"Owe!" He caught up a pen. "Name the sum, and I will pay it."

"No, the debt is not to me. You owe a very humble apology to that noble lad, your son, who has carried himself in this matter as I should be proud to see my own son do, should I ever chance to have one."

"Then it was not Arthur who took them?"

"I told you yesterday, and I repeat today, that it was not."

"You are sure of it! Then let us hurry to him at once to let him know that the truth is known."

"He knows it already. When I had cleared it all up I had an interview with him, and finding that he would not tell me the story, I told it to him, on which he had to confess that I was right and to add the very few details which were not yet quite clear to me. Your news of this morning, however, may open his lips."

"For heaven's sake, tell me, then, what is this extraordinary mystery!"

"I will do so, and I will show you the steps by which I reached it. And let me say to you, first, that which it is hardest for me to say and for you to hear: there has been an understanding between Sir George Burnwell and your niece Mary. They have now fled together."

"My Mary? Impossible!"

"It is unfortunately more than possible; it is certain. Neither you nor your son knew the true character of this man when you admitted him into your family circle. He is one of the most dangerous men in England—a ruined gambler, an absolutely desperate villain, a man without heart or conscience. Your niece knew nothing of such men. When he breathed his vows to her, as he had done to a hundred before her, she flattered herself that she alone had touched his heart. The devil knows best what he said, but at least she became his tool and was in the habit of seeing him nearly every evening."

"I cannot, and I will not, believe it!" cried the banker with an ashen face.

"I will tell you, then, what occurred in your house last night. Your niece, when you had, as she thought, gone to your room, slipped down and talked to her lover through the window which leads into the stable lane. His footmarks had pressed right through the snow, so long had he stood there. She told him of the coronet. His wicked lust for gold kindled at the news, and he bent her to his will. I have no doubt that she loved you, but there are women in whom the love of a lover extinguishes all other loves, and I think that she must have been one. She had hardly listened to his instructions when she saw you coming downstairs, on which she closed the window rapidly and told you about one of the servants' escapade with her wooden-legged lover, which was all perfectly true.

"Your boy, Arthur, went to bed after his interview with you but he slept badly on account of his uneasiness about his club debts. In the middle of the night he heard a soft tread pass his door, so he rose and, looking out, was surprised to see his cousin walking very stealthily along the passage until she disappeared into your dressing-room. Petrified with astonishment, the lad slipped on some clothes and waited there in the dark to see what would come of this strange affair. Presently she emerged from the room again, and in the light of the passage-lamp your son saw that she carried the precious coronet in her hands. She passed down the stairs, and he, thrilling with horror, ran along and slipped behind the curtain near your door, whence he could see what passed in the hall beneath. He saw her stealthily open the window, hand out the coronet to someone in the gloom, and then closing it once more hurry back to her room, passing quite close to where he stood hid behind the curtain.

"As long as she was on the scene he could not take any action without a horrible exposure of the woman whom he loved. But the instant that she was gone he realised how crushing a misfortune this would be for you, and how all-important it was to set it right. He rushed down, just as he was, in his bare feet, opened the window, sprang out into the snow, and ran down the lane, where he could see a dark figure in the moonlight. Sir George Burnwell tried to get away, but Arthur caught him, and there was a struggle between them, your lad tugging

at one side of the coronet, and his opponent at the other. In the scuffle, your son struck Sir George and cut him over the eye. Then something suddenly snapped, and your son, finding that he had the coronet in his hands, rushed back, closed the window, ascended to your room, and had just observed that the coronet had been twisted in the struggle and was endeavouring to straighten it when you appeared upon the scene."

"Is it possible?" gasped the banker.

"You then roused his anger by calling him names at a moment when he felt that he had deserved your warmest thanks. He could not explain the true state of affairs without betraying one who certainly deserved little enough consideration at his hands. He took the more chivalrous view, however, and preserved her secret."

"And that was why she shrieked and fainted when she saw the coronet," cried Mr. Holder. "Oh, my God! What a blind fool I have been! And his asking to be allowed to go out for five minutes! The dear fellow wanted to see if the missing piece were at the scene of the struggle. How cruelly I have misjudged him!"

"When I arrived at the house," continued Holmes, "I at once went very carefully round it to observe if there were any traces in the snow which might help me. I knew that none had fallen since the evening before, and also that there had been a strong frost to preserve impressions. I passed along the tradesmen's path, but found it all trampled down and indistinguishable. Just beyond it, however, at the far side of the kitchen door, a woman had stood and talked with a man, whose round impressions on one side showed that he had a wooden leg. I could even tell that they had been disturbed, for the woman had run back swiftly to the door, as was shown by the deep toe and light heel marks, while Wooden-leg had waited a little, and then had gone away. I thought at the time that this might be the maid and her sweetheart, of whom you had already spoken to me, and inquiry showed it was so. I passed round the garden without seeing anything more than random tracks, which I took to be the police; but when I got into the stable lane a very long and complex story was written in the snow in front of me.

"There was a double line of tracks of a booted man, and a second double line which I saw with delight belonged to a man with naked feet. I was at once convinced from what you had told me that the latter was your son. The first had walked both ways, but the other had run swiftly, and as his tread was marked in places over the depression of the boot, it was obvious that he had passed after the other. I followed them up and found they led to the hall window, where Boots had worn all the snow away while waiting. Then I walked to the other end, which was a hundred yards or more down the lane. I saw where Boots had faced round, where the snow was cut up as though there had been a struggle, and, finally, where a few drops of blood had fallen, to show me that I was not mistaken. Boots had then run down the lane, and another little smudge of blood showed that it was he who had been hurt. When he came to the highroad at the other end, I found that the pavement had been cleared, so there was an end to that clue.

"On entering the house, however, I examined, as you remember, the sill and framework of the hall window with my lens, and I could at once see that someone had passed out. I could distinguish the outline of an instep where the wet foot had been placed in coming in. I was then beginning to be able to form an opinion as to what had occurred. A man had waited outside the window; someone had brought the gems; the deed had been overseen by your son; he had pursued the thief; had struggled with him; they had each tugged at the coronet, their united strength causing injuries which neither alone could have effected. He had returned with the prize, but had left a fragment in the grasp of his opponent. So far I was clear. The question now was, who was the man and who was it brought him the coronet?

"It is an old maxim of mine that when you have excluded the impossible, whatever remains, however improbable, must be the truth. Now, I knew that it was not you who had brought it down, so there only remained your niece and the maids. But if it were the maids, why should your son allow himself to be accused in their place? There could be no possible reason. As he loved his cousin, however, there was an excellent explanation why he should retain her secret—the more so as the secret was a disgraceful one. When I remembered that you had seen her at that window, and how she had fainted on seeing the coronet again, my conjecture became a certainty.

"And who could it be who was her confederate? A lover evidently, for who else could outweigh the love and gratitude which she must feel to you? I knew that you went out little, and that your circle of friends was a very limited one. But among them was Sir George Burnwell. I had heard of him before as being a man of evil reputation among women. It must have been he who wore those boots and retained the

missing gems. Even though he knew that Arthur had discovered him, he might still flatter himself that he was safe, for the lad could not say a word without compromising his own family.

"Well, your own good sense will suggest what measures I took next. I went in the shape of a loafer to Sir George's house, managed to pick up an acquaintance with his valet, learned that his master had cut his head the night before, and, finally, at the expense of six shillings, made all sure by buying a pair of his cast-off shoes. With these I journeyed down to Streatham and saw that they exactly fitted the tracks."

"I saw an ill-dressed vagabond in the lane yesterday evening," said Mr. Holder.

"Precisely. It was I. I found that I had my man, so I came home and changed my clothes. It was a delicate part which I had to play then, for I saw that a prosecution must be avoided to avert scandal, and I knew that so astute a villain would see that our hands were tied in the matter. I went and saw him. At first, of course, he denied everything. But when I gave him every particular that had occurred, he tried to bluster and took down a life-preserver from the wall. I knew my man, however, and I clapped a pistol to his head before he could strike. Then he became a little more reasonable. I told him that we would give him a price for the stones he held—1,000 pounds apiece. That brought out the first signs of grief that he had shown. 'Why, dash it all!' said he, 'I've let them go at six hundred for the three!' I soon managed to get the address of the receiver who had them, on promising him that there would be no prosecution. Off I set to him, and after much chaffering I got our stones at 1,000 pounds apiece. Then I looked in upon your son, told him that all was right, and eventually got to my bed about two o'clock, after what I may call a really hard day's work."

"A day which has saved England from a great public scandal," said the banker, rising. "Sir, I cannot find words to thank you, but you shall not find me ungrateful for what you have done. Your skill has indeed exceeded all that I have heard of it. And now I must fly to my dear boy to apologise to him for the wrong which I have done him. As to what you tell me of poor Mary, it goes to my very heart. Not even your skill can inform me where she is now."

"I think that we may safely say," returned Holmes, "that she is wherever Sir George Burnwell is. It is equally certain, too, that whatever her sins are, they will soon receive a more than sufficient punishment."

THE COPPER BEECHES

"To the man who loves art for its own sake," remarked Sherlock Holmes, tossing aside the advertisement sheet of the *Daily Telegraph*, "it is frequently in its least important and lowliest manifestations that the keenest pleasure is to be derived. It is pleasant to me to observe, Watson, that you have so far grasped this truth that in these little records of our cases which you have been good enough to draw up, and, I am bound to say, occasionally to embellish, you have given prominence not so much to the many *causes célèbres* and sensational trials in which I have figured but rather to those incidents which may have been trivial in themselves, but which have given room for those faculties of deduction and of logical synthesis which I have made my special province."

"And yet," said I, smiling, "I cannot quite hold myself absolved from the charge of sensationalism which has been urged against my records."

"You have erred, perhaps," he observed, taking up a glowing cinder with the tongs and lighting with it the long cherry-wood pipe which was wont to replace his clay when he was in a disputatious rather than a meditative mood—"you have erred perhaps in attempting to put colour and life into each of your statements instead of confining yourself to the task of placing upon record that severe reasoning from cause to effect which is really the only notable feature about the thing."

"It seems to me that I have done you full justice in the matter," I remarked with some coldness, for I was repelled by the egotism which I had more than once observed to be a strong factor in my friend's singular character.

"No, it is not selfishness or conceit," said he, answering, as was his wont, my thoughts rather than my words. "If I claim full justice for my art, it is because it is an impersonal thing—a thing beyond myself. Crime is common. Logic is rare. Therefore it is upon the logic rather than upon the crime that you should dwell. You have degraded what should have been a course of lectures into a series of tales."

It was a cold morning of the early spring, and we sat after breakfast on either side of a cheery fire in the old room at Baker Street. A thick fog rolled down between the lines of dun-coloured houses, and the

opposing windows loomed like dark, shapeless blurs through the heavy yellow wreaths. Our gas was lit and shone on the white cloth and glimmer of china and metal, for the table had not been cleared yet. Sherlock Holmes had been silent all the morning, dipping continuously into the advertisement columns of a succession of papers until at last, having apparently given up his search, he had emerged in no very sweet temper to lecture me upon my literary shortcomings.

"At the same time," he remarked after a pause, during which he had sat puffing at his long pipe and gazing down into the fire, "you can hardly be open to a charge of sensationalism, for out of these cases which you have been so kind as to interest yourself in, a fair proportion do not treat of crime, in its legal sense, at all. The small matter in which I endeavoured to help the King of Bohemia, the singular experience of Miss Mary Sutherland, the problem connected with the man with the twisted lip, and the incident of the noble bachelor, were all matters which are outside the pale of the law. But in avoiding the sensational, I fear that you may have bordered on the trivial."

"The end may have been so," I answered, "but the methods I hold to have been novel and of interest."

"Pshaw, my dear fellow, what do the public, the great unobservant public, who could hardly tell a weaver by his tooth or a compositor by his left thumb, care about the finer shades of analysis and deduction? But, indeed, if you are trivial, I cannot blame you, for the days of the great cases are past. Man, or at least criminal man, has lost all enterprise and originality. As to my own little practice, it seems to be degenerating into an agency for recovering lost lead pencils and giving advice to young ladies from boarding-schools. I think that I have touched bottom at last, however. This note I had this morning marks my zero-point, I fancy. Read it!" He tossed a crumpled letter across to me.

It was dated from Montague Place upon the preceding evening, and ran thus:

> Dear Mr. Holmes:
>
> I am very anxious to consult you as to whether I should or should not accept a situation which has been offered to me as governess. I shall call at half-past ten tomorrow if I do not inconvenience you.
>
> Yours faithfully,
>
> Violet Hunter

"Do you know the young lady?" I asked.

"Not I."

"It is half-past ten now."

"Yes, and I have no doubt that is her ring."

"It may turn out to be of more interest than you think. You remember that the affair of the blue carbuncle, which appeared to be a mere whim at first, developed into a serious investigation. It may be so in this case, also."

"Well, let us hope so. But our doubts will very soon be solved, for here, unless I am much mistaken, is the person in question."

As he spoke the door opened and a young lady entered the room. She was plainly but neatly dressed, with a bright, quick face, freckled like a plover's egg, and with the brisk manner of a woman who has had her own way to make in the world.

"You will excuse my troubling you, I am sure," said she, as my companion rose to greet her, "but I have had a very strange experience, and as I have no parents or relations of any sort from whom I could ask advice, I thought that perhaps you would be kind enough to tell me what I should do."

"Pray take a seat, Miss Hunter. I shall be happy to do anything that I can to serve you."

I could see that Holmes was favourably impressed by the manner and speech of his new client. He looked her over in his searching fashion, and then composed himself, with his lids drooping and his fingertips together, to listen to her story.

"I have been a governess for five years," said she, "in the family of Colonel Spence Munro, but two months ago the colonel received an appointment at Halifax, in Nova Scotia, and took his children over to America with him, so that I found myself without a situation. I advertised, and I answered advertisements, but without success. At last the little money which I had saved began to run short, and I was at my wit's end as to what I should do.

"There is a well-known agency for governesses in the West End called Westaway's, and there I used to call about once a week in order to see whether anything had turned up which might suit me. Westaway was the name of the founder of the business, but it is really managed by Miss Stoper. She sits in her own little office, and the ladies who are seeking employment wait in an anteroom, and are then shown in one by

one, when she consults her ledgers and sees whether she has anything which would suit them.

"Well, when I called last week I was shown into the little office as usual, but I found that Miss Stoper was not alone. A prodigiously stout man with a very smiling face and a great heavy chin which rolled down in fold upon fold over his throat sat at her elbow with a pair of glasses on his nose, looking very earnestly at the ladies who entered. As I came in he gave quite a jump in his chair and turned quickly to Miss Stoper.

" 'That will do,' said he; 'I could not ask for anything better. Capital! capital!' He seemed quite enthusiastic and rubbed his hands together in the most genial fashion. He was such a comfortable-looking man that it was quite a pleasure to look at him.

" 'You are looking for a situation, miss?' he asked.

" 'Yes, sir.'

" 'As governess?'

" 'Yes, sir.'

" 'And what salary do you ask?'

" 'I had 4 pounds a month in my last place with Colonel Spence Munro.'

" 'Oh, tut, tut! Sweating—rank sweating!' he cried, throwing his fat hands out into the air like a man who is in a boiling passion. 'How could anyone offer so pitiful a sum to a lady with such attractions and accomplishments?'

" 'My accomplishments, sir, may be less than you imagine,' said I. 'A little French, a little German, music, and drawing—'

" 'Tut, tut!' he cried. 'This is all quite beside the question. The point is, have you or have you not the bearing and deportment of a lady? There it is in a nutshell. If you have not, you are not fitted for the rearing of a child who may some day play a considerable part in the history of the country. But if you have why, then, how could any gentleman ask you to condescend to accept anything under the three figures? Your salary with me, madam, would commence at 100 pounds a year.'

"You may imagine, Mr. Holmes, that to me, destitute as I was, such an offer seemed almost too good to be true. The gentleman, however, seeing perhaps the look of incredulity upon my face, opened a pocketbook and took out a note.

" 'It is also my custom,' said he, smiling in the most pleasant fashion until his eyes were just two little shining slits amid the white creases of his face, 'to advance to my young ladies half their salary beforehand, so that they may meet any little expenses of their journey and their wardrobe.'

"It seemed to me that I had never met so fascinating and so thoughtful a man. As I was already in debt to my tradesmen, the advance was a great convenience, and yet there was something unnatural about the whole transaction which made me wish to know a little more before I quite committed myself.

" 'May I ask where you live, sir?' said I.

" 'Hampshire. Charming rural place. The Copper Beeches, five miles on the far side of Winchester. It is the most lovely country, my dear young lady, and the dearest old country-house.'

" 'And my duties, sir? I should be glad to know what they would be.'

" 'One child—one dear little romper just six years old. Oh, if you could see him killing cockroaches with a slipper! Smack! Smack! Smack! Three gone before you could wink!' He leaned back in his chair and laughed his eyes into his head again.

"I was a little startled at the nature of the child's amusement, but the father's laughter made me think that perhaps he was joking.

" 'My sole duties, then,' I asked, 'are to take charge of a single child?'

" 'No, no, not the sole, not the sole, my dear young lady,' he cried. 'Your duty would be, as I am sure your good sense would suggest, to obey any little commands my wife might give, provided always that they were such commands as a lady might with propriety obey. You see no difficulty, heh?'

" 'I should be happy to make myself useful.'

" 'Quite so. In dress now, for example. We are faddy people, you know—faddy but kindhearted. If you were asked to wear any dress which we might give you, you would not object to our little whim. Heh?'

" 'No,' said I, considerably astonished at his words.

" 'Or to sit here, or sit there, that would not be offensive to you?'

" 'Oh, no.'

" 'Or to cut your hair quite short before you come to us?'

"I could hardly believe my ears. As you may observe, Mr. Holmes, my hair is somewhat luxuriant, and of a rather peculiar tint of chestnut.

It has been considered artistic. I could not dream of sacrificing it in this offhand fashion.

"'I am afraid that that is quite impossible,' said I. He had been watching me eagerly out of his small eyes, and I could see a shadow pass over his face as I spoke.

"'I am afraid that it is quite essential,' said he. 'It is a little fancy of my wife's, and ladies' fancies, you know, madam, ladies' fancies must be consulted. And so you won't cut your hair?'

"'No, sir, I really could not,' I answered firmly.

"'Ah, very well; then that quite settles the matter. It is a pity, because in other respects you would really have done very nicely. In that case, Miss Stoper, I had best inspect a few more of your young ladies.'

"The manageress had sat all this while busy with her papers without a word to either of us, but she glanced at me now with so much annoyance upon her face that I could not help suspecting that she had lost a handsome commission through my refusal.

"'Do you desire your name to be kept upon the books?' she asked.

"'If you please, Miss Stoper.'

"'Well, really, it seems rather useless, since you refuse the most excellent offers in this fashion,' said she sharply. 'You can hardly expect us to exert ourselves to find another such opening for you. Good-day to you, Miss Hunter.' She struck a gong upon the table, and I was shown out by the page.

"Well, Mr. Holmes, when I got back to my lodgings and found little enough in the cupboard, and two or three bills upon the table. I began to ask myself whether I had not done a very foolish thing. After all, if these people had strange fads and expected obedience on the most extraordinary matters, they were at least ready to pay for their eccentricity. Very few governesses in England are getting 100 pounds a year. Besides, what use was my hair to me? Many people are improved by wearing it short and perhaps I should be among the number. Next day I was inclined to think that I had made a mistake, and by the day after I was sure of it. I had almost overcome my pride so far as to go back to the agency and inquire whether the place was still open when I received this letter from the gentleman himself. I have it here and I will read it to you:

The Copper Beeches, near Winchester

Dear Miss Hunter

Miss Stoper has very kindly given me your address, and I write from here to ask you whether you have reconsidered your decision. My wife is very anxious that you should come, for she has been much attracted by my description of you. We are willing to give 30 pounds a quarter, or 120 pounds a year, so as to recompense you for any little inconvenience which our fads may cause you. They are not very exacting, after all. My wife is fond of a particular shade of electric blue and would like you to wear such a dress indoors in the morning. You need not, however, go to the expense of purchasing one, as we have one belonging to my dear daughter Alice (now in Philadelphia), which would, I should think, fit you very well. Then, as to sitting here or there, or amusing yourself in any manner indicated, that need cause you no inconvenience. As regards your hair, it is no doubt a pity, especially as I could not help remarking its beauty during our short interview, but I am afraid that I must remain firm upon this point, and I only hope that the increased salary may recompense you for the loss. Your duties, as far as the child is concerned, are very light. Now do try to come, and I shall meet you with the dogcart at Winchester. Let me know your train.

Yours faithfully,

Jephro Rucastle

"That is the letter which I have just received, Mr. Holmes, and my mind is made up that I will accept it. I thought, however, that before taking the final step I should like to submit the whole matter to your consideration."

"Well, Miss Hunter, if your mind is made up, that settles the question," said Holmes, smiling.

"But you would not advise me to refuse?"

"I confess that it is not the situation which I should like to see a sister of mine apply for."

"What is the meaning of it all, Mr. Holmes?"

"Ah, I have no data. I cannot tell. Perhaps you have yourself formed some opinion?"

"Well, there seems to me to be only one possible solution. Mr.

Rucastle seemed to be a very kind, good-natured man. Is it not possible that his wife is a lunatic, that he desires to keep the matter quiet for fear she should be taken to an asylum, and that he humours her fancies in every way in order to prevent an outbreak?"

"That is a possible solution—in fact, as matters stand, it is the most probable one. But in any case it does not seem to be a nice household for a young lady."

"But the money, Mr. Holmes, the money!"

"Well, yes, of course the pay is good—too good. That is what makes me uneasy. Why should they give you 120 pounds a year, when they could have their pick for 40 pounds? There must be some strong reason behind."

"I thought that if I told you the circumstances you would understand afterwards if I wanted your help. I should feel so much stronger if I felt that you were at the back of me."

"Oh, you may carry that feeling away with you. I assure you that your little problem promises to be the most interesting which has come my way for some months. There is something distinctly novel about some of the features. If you should find yourself in doubt or in danger—"

"Danger! What danger do you foresee?"

Holmes shook his head gravely. "It would cease to be a danger if we could define it," said he. "But at any time, day or night, a telegram would bring me down to your help."

"That is enough." She rose briskly from her chair with the anxiety all swept from her face. "I shall go down to Hampshire quite easy in my mind now. I shall write to Mr. Rucastle at once, sacrifice my poor hair tonight, and start for Winchester tomorrow." With a few grateful words to Holmes she bade us both good-night and bustled off upon her way.

"At least," said I as we heard her quick, firm steps descending the stairs, "she seems to be a young lady who is very well able to take care of herself."

"And she would need to be," said Holmes gravely. "I am much mistaken if we do not hear from her before many days are past."

It was not very long before my friend's prediction was fulfilled. A fortnight went by, during which I frequently found my thoughts turning in her direction and wondering what strange side-alley of human experience this lonely woman had strayed into. The unusual salary, the curious conditions, the light duties, all pointed to something abnormal, though whether a fad or a plot, or whether the man were a philanthropist or a villain, it was quite beyond my powers to determine. As to Holmes, I observed that he sat frequently for half an hour on end, with knitted brows and an abstracted air, but he swept the matter away with a wave of his hand when I mentioned it. "Data! Data! Data!" he cried impatiently. "I can't make bricks without clay." And yet he would always wind up by muttering that no sister of his should ever have accepted such a situation.

The telegram which we eventually received came late one night just as I was thinking of turning in and Holmes was settling down to one of those all-night chemical researches which he frequently indulged in, when I would leave him stooping over a retort and a test-tube at night and find him in the same position when I came down to breakfast in the morning. He opened the yellow envelope, and then, glancing at the message, threw it across to me.

"Just look up the trains in Bradshaw," said he, and turned back to his chemical studies.

The summons was a brief and urgent one.

Please be at the Black Swan Hotel at Winchester at
midday tomorrow," it said. "Do come! I am at my wit's end.
HUNTER

"Will you come with me?" asked Holmes, glancing up.

"I should wish to."

"Just look it up, then."

"There is a train at half-past nine," said I, glancing over my Bradshaw. "It is due at Winchester at 11:30."

"That will do very nicely. Then perhaps I had better postpone my analysis of the acetones, as we may need to be at our best in the morning."

By eleven o'clock the next day we were well upon our way to the old English capital. Holmes had been buried in the morning papers all the way down, but after we had passed the Hampshire border he threw them down and began to admire the scenery. It was an ideal spring day, a light blue sky, flecked with little fleecy white clouds drifting across

from west to east. The sun was shining very brightly, and yet there was an exhilarating nip in the air, which set an edge to a man's energy. All over the countryside, away to the rolling hills around Aldershot, the little red and grey roofs of the farm-steadings peeped out from amid the light green of the new foliage.

"Are they not fresh and beautiful?" I cried with all the enthusiasm of a man fresh from the fogs of Baker Street.

But Holmes shook his head gravely.

"Do you know, Watson," said he, "that it is one of the curses of a mind with a turn like mine that I must look at everything with reference to my own special subject. You look at these scattered houses, and you are impressed by their beauty. I look at them, and the only thought which comes to me is a feeling of their isolation and of the impunity with which crime may be committed there."

"Good heavens!" I cried. "Who would associate crime with these dear old homesteads?"

"They always fill me with a certain horror. It is my belief, Watson, founded upon my experience, that the lowest and vilest alleys in London do not present a more dreadful record of sin than does the smiling and beautiful countryside."

"You horrify me!"

"But the reason is very obvious. The pressure of public opinion can do in the town what the law cannot accomplish. There is no lane so vile that the scream of a tortured child, or the thud of a drunkard's blow, does not beget sympathy and indignation among the neighbours, and then the whole machinery of justice is ever so close that a word of complaint can set it going, and there is but a step between the crime and the dock. But look at these lonely houses, each in its own fields, filled for the most part with poor ignorant folk who know little of the law. Think of the deeds of hellish cruelty, the hidden wickedness which may go on, year in, year out, in such places, and none the wiser. Had this lady who appeals to us for help gone to live in Winchester, I should never have had a fear for her. It is the five miles of country which makes the danger. Still, it is clear that she is not personally threatened."

"No. If she can come to Winchester to meet us she can get away."

"Quite so. She has her freedom."

"What *can* be the matter, then? Can you suggest no explanation?"

"I have devised seven separate explanations, each of which would cover the facts as far as we know them. But which of these is correct can only be determined by the fresh information which we shall no doubt find waiting for us. Well, there is the tower of the cathedral, and we shall soon learn all that Miss Hunter has to tell."

The Black Swan is an inn of repute in the High Street, at no distance from the station, and there we found the young lady waiting for us. She had engaged a sitting-room, and our lunch awaited us upon the table.

"I am so delighted that you have come," she said earnestly. "It is so very kind of you both; but indeed I do not know what I should do. Your advice will be altogether invaluable to me."

"Pray tell us what has happened to you."

"I will do so, and I must be quick, for I have promised Mr. Rucastle to be back before three. I got his leave to come into town this morning, though he little knew for what purpose."

"Let us have everything in its due order." Holmes thrust his long thin legs out towards the fire and composed himself to listen.

"In the first place, I may say that I have met, on the whole, with no actual ill-treatment from Mr. and Mrs. Rucastle. It is only fair to them to say that. But I cannot understand them, and I am not easy in my mind about them."

"What can you not understand?"

"Their reasons for their conduct. But you shall have it all just as it occurred. When I came down, Mr. Rucastle met me here and drove me in his dogcart to the Copper Beeches. It is, as he said, beautifully situated, but it is not beautiful in itself, for it is a large square block of a house, whitewashed, but all stained and streaked with damp and bad weather. There are grounds round it, woods on three sides, and on the fourth a field which slopes down to the Southampton highroad, which curves past about a hundred yards from the front door. This ground in front belongs to the house, but the woods all round are part of Lord Southerton's preserves. A clump of copper beeches immediately in front of the hall door has given its name to the place.

"I was driven over by my employer, who was as amiable as ever, and was introduced by him that evening to his wife and the child. There was no truth, Mr. Holmes, in the conjecture which seemed to us to be probable in your rooms at Baker Street. Mrs. Rucastle is not mad. I found her to be a silent, pale-faced woman, much younger than her husband, not more than thirty, I should think, while he can hardly

be less than forty-five. From their conversation I have gathered that they have been married about seven years, that he was a widower, and that his only child by the first wife was the daughter who has gone to Philadelphia. Mr. Rucastle told me in private that the reason why she had left them was that she had an unreasoning aversion to her stepmother. As the daughter could not have been less than twenty, I can quite imagine that her position must have been uncomfortable with her father's young wife.

"Mrs. Rucastle seemed to me to be colourless in mind as well as in feature. She impressed me neither favourably nor the reverse. She was a nonentity. It was easy to see that she was passionately devoted both to her husband and to her little son. Her light grey eyes wandered continually from one to the other, noting every little want and forestalling it if possible. He was kind to her also in his bluff, boisterous fashion, and on the whole they seemed to be a happy couple. And yet she had some secret sorrow, this woman. She would often be lost in deep thought, with the saddest look upon her face. More than once I have surprised her in tears. I have thought sometimes that it was the disposition of her child which weighed upon her mind, for I have never met so utterly spoiled and so ill-natured a little creature. He is small for his age, with a head which is quite disproportionately large. His whole life appears to be spent in an alternation between savage fits of passion and gloomy intervals of sulking. Giving pain to any creature weaker than himself seems to be his one idea of amusement, and he shows quite remarkable talent in planning the capture of mice, little birds, and insects. But I would rather not talk about the creature, Mr. Holmes, and, indeed, he has little to do with my story."

"I am glad of all details," remarked my friend, "whether they seem to you to be relevant or not."

"I shall try not to miss anything of importance. The one unpleasant thing about the house, which struck me at once, was the appearance and conduct of the servants. There are only two, a man and his wife. Toller, for that is his name, is a rough, uncouth man, with grizzled hair and whiskers, and a perpetual smell of drink. Twice since I have been with them he has been quite drunk, and yet Mr. Rucastle seemed to take no notice of it. His wife is a very tall and strong woman with a sour face, as silent as Mrs. Rucastle and much less amiable. They are a most unpleasant couple, but fortunately I spend most of my time in the nursery and my own room, which are next to each other in one corner of the building.

"For two days after my arrival at the Copper Beeches my life was very quiet; on the third, Mrs. Rucastle came down just after breakfast and whispered something to her husband.

"'Oh, yes,' said he, turning to me, 'we are very much obliged to you, Miss Hunter, for falling in with our whims so far as to cut your hair. I assure you that it has not detracted in the tiniest iota from your appearance. We shall now see how the electric-blue dress will become you. You will find it laid out upon the bed in your room, and if you would be so good as to put it on we should both be extremely obliged.'

"The dress which I found waiting for me was of a peculiar shade of blue. It was of excellent material, a sort of beige, but it bore unmistakable signs of having been worn before. It could not have been a better fit if I had been measured for it. Both Mr. and Mrs. Rucastle expressed a delight at the look of it, which seemed quite exaggerated in its vehemence. They were waiting for me in the drawing-room, which is a very large room, stretching along the entire front of the house, with three long windows reaching down to the floor. A chair had been placed close to the central window, with its back turned towards it. In this I was asked to sit, and then Mr. Rucastle, walking up and down on the other side of the room, began to tell me a series of the funniest stories that I have ever listened to. You cannot imagine how comical he was, and I laughed until I was quite weary. Mrs. Rucastle, however, who has evidently no sense of humour, never so much as smiled, but sat with her hands in her lap, and a sad, anxious look upon her face. After an hour or so, Mr. Rucastle suddenly remarked that it was time to commence the duties of the day, and that I might change my dress and go to little Edward in the nursery.

"Two days later this same performance was gone through under exactly similar circumstances. Again I changed my dress, again I sat in the window, and again I laughed very heartily at the funny stories of which my employer had an immense *répertoire*, and which he told inimitably. Then he handed me a yellow-backed novel, and moving my chair a little sideways, that my own shadow might not fall upon the page, he begged me to read aloud to him. I read for about ten minutes, beginning in the heart of a chapter, and then suddenly, in the middle of a sentence, he ordered me to cease and to change my dress.

"You can easily imagine, Mr. Holmes, how curious I became as to what the meaning of this extraordinary performance could possibly be. They were always very careful, I observed, to turn my face away from the window, so that I became consumed with the desire to see what was going on behind my back. At first it seemed to be impossible, but I soon devised a means. My hand-mirror had been broken, so a happy thought seized me, and I concealed a piece of the glass in my handkerchief. On the next occasion, in the midst of my laughter, I put my handkerchief up to my eyes, and was able with a little management to see all that there was behind me. I confess that I was disappointed. There was nothing. At least that was my first impression. At the second glance, however, I perceived that there was a man standing in the Southampton Road, a small bearded man in a grey suit, who seemed to be looking in my direction. The road is an important highway, and there are usually people there. This man, however, was leaning against the railings which bordered our field and was looking earnestly up. I lowered my handkerchief and glanced at Mrs. Rucastle to find her eyes fixed upon me with a most searching gaze. She said nothing, but I am convinced that she had divined that I had a mirror in my hand and had seen what was behind me. She rose at once.

" 'Jephro,' said she, 'there is an impertinent fellow upon the road there who stares up at Miss Hunter.'

" 'No friend of yours, Miss Hunter?' he asked.

" 'No, I know no one in these parts.'

" 'Dear me! How very impertinent! Kindly turn round and motion to him to go away.'

" 'Surely it would be better to take no notice.'

" 'No, no, we should have him loitering here always. Kindly turn round and wave him away like that.'

"I did as I was told, and at the same instant Mrs. Rucastle drew down the blind. That was a week ago, and from that time I have not sat again in the window, nor have I worn the blue dress, nor seen the man in the road."

"Pray continue," said Holmes. "Your narrative promises to be a most interesting one."

"You will find it rather disconnected, I fear, and there may prove to be little relation between the different incidents of which I speak. On the very first day that I was at the Copper Beeches, Mr. Rucastle took me to a small outhouse which stands near the kitchen door. As we approached it I heard the sharp rattling of a chain, and the sound as of a large animal moving about.

"'Look in here!' said Mr. Rucastle, showing me a slit between two planks. 'Is he not a beauty?'

"I looked through and was conscious of two glowing eyes, and of a vague figure huddled up in the darkness.

"'Don't be frightened,' said my employer, laughing at the start which I had given. 'It's only Carlo, my mastiff. I call him mine, but really old Toller, my groom, is the only man who can do anything with him. We feed him once a day, and not too much then, so that he is always as keen as mustard. Toller lets him loose every night, and God help the trespasser whom he lays his fangs upon. For goodness' sake don't you ever on any pretext set your foot over the threshold at night, for it's as much as your life is worth.'

"The warning was no idle one, for two nights later I happened to look out of my bedroom window about two o'clock in the morning. It was a beautiful moonlight night, and the lawn in front of the house was silvered over and almost as bright as day. I was standing, rapt in the peaceful beauty of the scene, when I was aware that something was moving under the shadow of the copper beeches. As it emerged into the moonshine I saw what it was. It was a giant dog, as large as a calf, tawny tinted, with hanging jowl, black muzzle, and huge projecting bones. It walked slowly across the lawn and vanished into the shadow upon the other side. That dreadful sentinel sent a chill to my heart which I do not think that any burglar could have done.

"And now I have a very strange experience to tell you. I had, as you know, cut off my hair in London, and I had placed it in a great coil at the bottom of my trunk. One evening, after the child was in bed, I began to amuse myself by examining the furniture of my room and by rearranging my own little things. There was an old chest of drawers in the room, the two upper ones empty and open, the lower one locked. I had filled the first two with my linen, and as I had still much to pack away I was naturally annoyed at not having the use of the third drawer. It struck me that it might have been fastened by a mere oversight, so I took out my bunch of keys and tried to open it. The very first key fitted to perfection, and I drew the drawer open. There was only one thing in it, but I am sure that you would never guess what it was. It was my coil of hair.

"I took it up and examined it. It was of the same peculiar tint, and the same thickness. But then the impossibility of the thing obtruded itself upon me. How could my hair have been locked in the drawer? With trembling hands I undid my trunk, turned out the contents, and drew from the bottom my own hair. I laid the two tresses together, and I assure you that they were identical. Was it not extraordinary? Puzzle as I would, I could make nothing at all of what it meant. I returned the strange hair to the drawer, and I said nothing of the matter to the Rucastles as I felt that I had put myself in the wrong by opening a drawer which they had locked.

"I am naturally observant, as you may have remarked, Mr. Holmes, and I soon had a pretty good plan of the whole house in my head. There was one wing, however, which appeared not to be inhabited at all. A door which faced that which led into the quarters of the Tollers opened into this suite, but it was invariably locked. One day, however, as I ascended the stair, I met Mr. Rucastle coming out through this door, his keys in his hand, and a look on his face which made him a very different person to the round, jovial man to whom I was accustomed. His cheeks were red, his brow was all crinkled with anger, and the veins stood out at his temples with passion. He locked the door and hurried past me without a word or a look.

"This aroused my curiosity, so when I went out for a walk in the grounds with my charge, I strolled round to the side from which I could see the windows of this part of the house. There were four of them in a row, three of which were simply dirty, while the fourth was shuttered up. They were evidently all deserted. As I strolled up and down, glancing at them occasionally, Mr. Rucastle came out to me, looking as merry and jovial as ever.

"'Ah!' said he, 'You must not think me rude if I passed you without a word, my dear young lady. I was preoccupied with business matters.'

"I assured him that I was not offended. 'By the way,' said I, 'You seem to have quite a suite of spare rooms up there, and one of them has the shutters up.'

"He looked surprised and, as it seemed to me, a little startled at my remark.

"'Photography is one of my hobbies,' said he. 'I have made my dark room up there. But, dear me! What an observant young lady we have come upon. Who would have believed it? Who would have ever believed it?' He spoke in a jesting tone, but there was no jest in his eyes as he looked at me. I read suspicion there and annoyance, but no jest.

"Well, Mr. Holmes, from the moment that I understood that there was something about that suite of rooms which I was not to know, I was all on fire to go over them. It was not mere curiosity, though I have my share of that. It was more a feeling of duty—a feeling that some good might come from my penetrating to this place. They talk of woman's instinct; perhaps it was woman's instinct which gave me that feeling. At any rate, it was there, and I was keenly on the lookout for any chance to pass the forbidden door.

"It was only yesterday that the chance came. I may tell you that, besides Mr. Rucastle, both Toller and his wife find something to do in these deserted rooms, and I once saw him carrying a large black linen bag with him through the door. Recently he has been drinking hard, and yesterday evening he was very drunk; and when I came upstairs there was the key in the door. I have no doubt at all that he had left it there. Mr. and Mrs. Rucastle were both downstairs, and the child was with them, so that I had an admirable opportunity. I turned the key gently in the lock, opened the door, and slipped through.

"There was a little passage in front of me, unpapered and uncarpeted, which turned at a right angle at the farther end. Round this corner were three doors in a line, the first and third of which were open. They each led into an empty room, dusty and cheerless, with two windows in the one and one in the other, so thick with dirt that the evening light glimmered dimly through them. The centre door was closed, and across the outside of it had been fastened one of the broad bars of an iron bed, padlocked at one end to a ring in the wall, and fastened at the other with stout cord. The door itself was locked as well, and the key was not there. This barricaded door corresponded clearly with the shuttered window outside, and yet I could see by the glimmer from beneath it that the room was not in darkness. Evidently there was a skylight which let in light from above. As I stood in the passage gazing at the sinister door and wondering what secret it might veil, I suddenly heard the sound of steps within the room and saw a shadow pass backward and forward against the little slit of dim light which shone out from under the door. A mad, unreasoning terror rose up in me at the sight, Mr. Holmes. My overstrung nerves failed me suddenly, and I turned and ran—ran as though some dreadful hand were behind me clutching at the skirt of my

dress. I rushed down the passage, through the door, and straight into the arms of Mr. Rucastle, who was waiting outside.

"'So,' said he, smiling, 'it was you, then. I thought that it must be when I saw the door open.'

"'Oh, I am so frightened!' I panted.

"'My dear young lady! My dear young lady!'—you cannot think how caressing and soothing his manner was—'and what has frightened you, my dear young lady?'

"But his voice was just a little too coaxing. He overdid it. I was keenly on my guard against him.

"'I was foolish enough to go into the empty wing,' I answered. 'But it is so lonely and eerie in this dim light that I was frightened and ran out again. Oh, it is so dreadfully still in there!'

"'Only that?' said he, looking at me keenly.

"'Why, what did you think?' I asked.

"'Why do you think that I lock this door?'

"'I am sure that I do not know.'

"'It is to keep people out who have no business there. Do you see?' He was still smiling in the most amiable manner.

"'I am sure if I had known—'

"'Well, then, you know now. And if you ever put your foot over that threshold again'—here in an instant the smile hardened into a grin of rage, and he glared down at me with the face of a demon—'I'll throw you to the mastiff.'

"I was so terrified that I do not know what I did. I suppose that I must have rushed past him into my room. I remember nothing until I found myself lying on my bed trembling all over. Then I thought of you, Mr. Holmes. I could not live there longer without some advice. I was frightened of the house, of the man, of the woman, of the servants, even of the child. They were all horrible to me. If I could only bring you down all would be well. Of course I might have fled from the house, but my curiosity was almost as strong as my fears. My mind was soon made up. I would send you a wire. I put on my hat and cloak, went down to the office, which is about half a mile from the house, and then returned, feeling very much easier. A horrible doubt came into my mind as I approached the door lest the dog might be loose, but I remembered that Toller had drunk himself into a state of insensibility that evening, and I knew that he was the only one in the household who had any influence with the savage creature, or who would venture to set him free. I slipped in in safety and lay awake half the night in my joy at the thought of seeing you. I had no difficulty in getting leave to come into Winchester this morning, but I must be back before three o'clock, for Mr. and Mrs. Rucastle are going on a visit, and will be away all the evening, so that I must look after the child. Now I have told you all my adventures, Mr. Holmes, and I should be very glad if you could tell me what it all means, and, above all, what I should do."

Holmes and I had listened spellbound to this extraordinary story. My friend rose now and paced up and down the room, his hands in his pockets, and an expression of the most profound gravity upon his face.

"Is Toller still drunk?" he asked.

"Yes. I heard his wife tell Mrs. Rucastle that she could do nothing with him."

"That is well. And the Rucastles go out tonight?"

"Yes."

"Is there a cellar with a good strong lock?"

"Yes, the wine-cellar."

"You seem to me to have acted all through this matter like a very brave and sensible girl, Miss Hunter. Do you think that you could perform one more feat? I should not ask it of you if I did not think you a quite exceptional woman."

"I will try. What is it?"

"We shall be at the Copper Beeches by seven o'clock, my friend and I. The Rucastles will be gone by that time, and Toller will, we hope, be incapable. There only remains Mrs. Toller, who might give the alarm. If you could send her into the cellar on some errand, and then turn the key upon her, you would facilitate matters immensely."

"I will do it."

"Excellent! We shall then look thoroughly into the affair. Of course there is only one feasible explanation. You have been brought there to personate someone, and the real person is imprisoned in this chamber. That is obvious. As to who this prisoner is, I have no doubt that it is the daughter, Miss Alice Rucastle, if I remember right, who was said to have gone to America. You were chosen, doubtless, as resembling her in height, figure, and the colour of your hair. Hers had been cut off, very possibly in some illness through which she has passed, and so, of course, yours had to be sacrificed also. By a curious chance you came upon her tresses. The man in the road was undoubtedly some friend of hers—possibly her *fiancé*—and no doubt, as you wore the girl's dress and were so like her, he was convinced from your laughter, whenever he saw you, and afterwards from your gesture, that Miss Rucastle was perfectly happy, and that she no longer desired his attentions. The dog is let loose at night to prevent him from endeavouring to communicate with her. So much is fairly clear. The most serious point in the case is the disposition of the child."

"What on earth has that to do with it?" I ejaculated.

"My dear Watson, you as a medical man are continually gaining light as to the tendencies of a child by the study of the parents. Don't you see that the converse is equally valid. I have frequently gained my first real insight into the character of parents by studying their children. This child's disposition is abnormally cruel, merely for cruelty's sake, and whether he derives this from his smiling father, as I should suspect, or from his mother, it bodes evil for the poor girl who is in their power."

"I am sure that you are right, Mr. Holmes," cried our client. "A thousand things come back to me which make me certain that you have hit it. Oh, let us lose not an instant in bringing help to this poor creature."

"We must be circumspect, for we are dealing with a very cunning man. We can do nothing until seven o'clock. At that hour we shall be with you, and it will not be long before we solve the mystery."

We were as good as our word, for it was just seven when we reached the Copper Beeches, having put up our trap at a wayside public-house. The group of trees, with their dark leaves shining like burnished metal in the light of the setting sun, were sufficient to mark the house even had Miss Hunter not been standing smiling on the doorstep.

"Have you managed it?" asked Holmes.

A loud thudding noise came from somewhere downstairs. "That is Mrs. Toller in the cellar," said she. "Her husband lies snoring on the kitchen rug. Here are his keys, which are the duplicates of Mr. Rucastle's."

"You have done well indeed!" cried Holmes with enthusiasm. "Now lead the way, and we shall soon see the end of this black business."

We passed up the stair, unlocked the door, followed on down a passage, and found ourselves in front of the barricade which Miss

Hunter had described. Holmes cut the cord and removed the transverse bar. Then he tried the various keys in the lock, but without success. No sound came from within, and at the silence Holmes' face clouded over.

"I trust that we are not too late," said he. "I think, Miss Hunter, that we had better go in without you. Now, Watson, put your shoulder to it, and we shall see whether we cannot make our way in."

It was an old rickety door and gave at once before our united strength. Together we rushed into the room. It was empty. There was no furniture save a little pallet bed, a small table, and a basketful of linen. The skylight above was open, and the prisoner gone.

"There has been some villainy here," said Holmes; "this beauty has guessed Miss Hunter's intentions and has carried his victim off."

"But how?"

"Through the skylight. We shall soon see how he managed it." He swung himself up onto the roof. "Ah, yes," he cried, "here's the end of a long light ladder against the eaves. That is how he did it."

"But it is impossible," said Miss Hunter; "the ladder was not there when the Rucastles went away."

"He has come back and done it. I tell you that he is a clever and dangerous man. I should not be very much surprised if this were he whose step I hear now upon the stair. I think, Watson, that it would be as well for you to have your pistol ready."

The words were hardly out of his mouth before a man appeared at the door of the room, a very fat and burly man, with a heavy stick in his hand. Miss Hunter screamed and shrunk against the wall at the sight of him, but Sherlock Holmes sprang forward and confronted him.

"You villain!" said he, "where's your daughter?"

The fat man cast his eyes round, and then up at the open skylight.

"It is for me to ask you that," he shrieked, "you thieves! Spies and thieves! I have caught you, have I? You are in my power. I'll serve you!" He turned and clattered down the stairs as hard as he could go.

"He's gone for the dog!" cried Miss Hunter.

"I have my revolver," said I.

"Better close the front door," cried Holmes, and we all rushed down the stairs together. We had hardly reached the hall when we heard the baying of a hound, and then a scream of agony, with a horrible worrying sound which it was dreadful to listen to. An elderly man with a red face and shaking limbs came staggering out at a side door.

"My God!" he cried. "Someone has loosed the dog. It's not been fed for two days. Quick, quick, or it'll be too late!"

Holmes and I rushed out and round the angle of the house, with Toller hurrying behind us. There was the huge famished brute, its black muzzle buried in Rucastle's throat, while he writhed and screamed upon the ground. Running up, I blew its brains out, and it fell over with its keen white teeth still meeting in the great creases of his neck. With much labour we separated them and carried him, living but horribly mangled, into the house. We laid him upon the drawing-room sofa, and having dispatched the sobered Toller to bear the news to his wife, I did what I could to relieve his pain. We were all assembled round him when the door opened, and a tall, gaunt woman entered the room.

"Mrs. Toller!" cried Miss Hunter.

"Yes, miss. Mr. Rucastle let me out when he came back before he went up to you. Ah, miss, it is a pity you didn't let me know what you were planning, for I would have told you that your pains were wasted."

"Ha!" said Holmes, looking keenly at her. "It is clear that Mrs. Toller knows more about this matter than anyone else."

"Yes, sir, I do, and I am ready enough to tell what I know."

"Then, pray, sit down, and let us hear it for there are several points on which I must confess that I am still in the dark."

"I will soon make it clear to you," said she; "and I'd have done so before now if I could ha' got out from the cellar. If there's police-court business over this, you'll remember that I was the one that stood your friend, and that I was Miss Alice's friend too.

"She was never happy at home, Miss Alice wasn't, from the time that her father married again. She was slighted like and had no say in anything, but it never really became bad for her until after she met Mr. Fowler at a friend's house. As well as I could learn, Miss Alice had rights of her own by will, but she was so quiet and patient, she was, that she never said a word about them but just left everything in Mr. Rucastle's hands. He knew he was safe with her; but when there was a chance of a husband coming forward, who would ask for all that the law would give him, then her father thought it time to put a stop on it. He wanted her to sign a paper, so that whether she married or not, he could use her money. When she wouldn't do it, he kept on worrying her until she got brain-fever, and for six weeks was at death's door. Then she got better at last, all worn to a shadow, and with her beautiful hair